W9-CVA-548

Mephisto Waltz

by

Gisela Zebroski

Jones Harvest
PUBLISHING

Jones Harvest Publishing
5400 East State Road 45
Bloomington, Indiana 47408

Visit our Web site at www.jonesharvest.com.

Printed in the United States of America

First Printing

ISBN-13: 978-1-60388-304-7
ISBN-10: 1-60388-304-5

This book is dedicated to my father, Dr. Woldermar Rudolph, who fell at the Battle of Berlin and my courageous mother, Lucie Bernsdorff-Rudolph, whose daring decisions saved our lives. Her love for America brought us here so that her children could pursue their life in liberty.

Chapter 1

Poland, 1943

The din at the Café Esplanade had subsided, though the place was packed with soldiers heading for the Russian front. Olga von Schenck kept on playing a popular march on the piano, but the voices of the singers faded. She shivered. A sudden chill had descended, despite the heat and thick cigarette smoke. The Evil One was on the prowl. She played faster, pounding the tempo of the march into the keyboard. *Why don't you sing louder*, she wanted to shout, *pretend all will be well!*

A male voice at her back said, "Pigs squealing in the slaughterhouse."

Trembling, Olga did not dare turn around, though the piece had come to an end. She was not ready to deal with this desperate soul pleading for salvation. During her séance with Father this morning, she had been told that she would meet a man who needed her. But she had nothing left to give.

"I'm done dealing with cannon fodder," the voice said with an articulate Saxon accent. He did not seem to care that his defeatist comment would cause her trouble. Of course he knew of the consequences. This part of Poland had been annexed to the Reich and fell under its jurisdiction. Hitler did not tolerate any talk of defeat; his spokesman, Dr. Goebbels, proclaimed that a miracle weapon was at hand and would bring final victory. Had some phantom come to warn her?

Olga played *I Know Some Day A Miracle Will Happen*, ever conscious of the ominous presence of the desperate man behind her. He was doomed. The war against Poland had escalated to include the whole world. Better not to think about it and just enjoy the music.

The man behind her did not budge. His aftershave had the clean scent of 4711. What did he want? Her heart throbbed. Cold sweat seeped from her pores.

1

"Play the *Mephisto Waltz*," he demanded. "That's the music we are dancing to." She wanted to snap back, but the words stuck in her mouth. Something was wrong. As medium, she knew the dangers of the Evil One. Father had warned her. All of Germany had fallen under its spell.

One of the soldiers shouted, "play *Lily Marlene*." He'd rather not think of the slaughterhouse, and would sing while he could.

Troubled, Olga played the request. The men sang along.

"Why do you play such trash?" the man said. "I know you're a pianist. Don't insult us; we aren't brain dead, you know. Even mice can think, and we've become a nation of mice who attacked the cat."

What was he getting at, Olga wondered, though she knew. The man rubbed her nose into the disaster the Reich was facing, except that her confrontation was not as imminent as his. The front was deep in the heart of Russia, a thousand kilometers away. If it ever reached Poland it would not be any time soon. In the meantime, she would go on entertaining the men who fought the Red Army and kept them at bay.

Olga flushed, and wished she could take off her black sweater. It wasn't much to look at anyway. Clothes were of no interest to her. Between practicing the piano, her séances, and looking after her child, there was no time to think of her looks. Since Stalingrad, people had been forced to face reality. In a state of shock, they worried about their men fighting at the front. The enthusiasm of the Blitz had turned to fear.

"The *Mephisto Waltz*!" the man insisted, as if he had not mentioned it before. "Can't you at least say something? Acknowledge my request!" Rather than be offended by his anger, Olga pitied his despair.

"Sorry," she said, facing the upright and the notes on its stand. Not that she needed them—the simple tunes played themselves. She embellished them for her own amusement. "I can't play it. I fooled around with it some years ago at the conservatory, but never studied it. Besides, Mephisto doesn't need a waltz. He's content having angry people come to him. Desperate souls make easy picking." She played another march. The men marked time on the dance floor and sang with raspy voices. Female voices joined in—local women, whose husbands served somewhere in German-occupied Europe or Africa.

"Don't give me that. I know you can do it. Try. For my sake. Show me that you honor my request." Was he pleading?

"Another round of beer," shouted a soldier from one of the tables. The café, once Polish, was now run by Frau Metzger, the new German proprietor. "And one for the piano player before Katyusha serenades us with her lethal tunes."

"That chap has a sense of humor," the man behind her said. "But I am still waiting for *Mephisto Waltz*."

The light bulb above the upright focused on her notes rather than her face.

Yadwiga, the Polish waitress, placed a glass of foaming beer on top of the piano. She was obliged to work here.

"Thanks," Olga said, and concluded the piece with diminishing chords. Picking up the sweating glass, she turned to the bothersome guest. He was no phantom but an angry young officer with shifting blue eyes. A vicious red scar snaked across his cheek, another over his shaven head. He must have seen hell. Had he gone mad trying to come to terms with it, or did he cling to a last shred of hope?

The audience grew restless and called out their requests. "*Caprifischer!*" "*Unter den Dachern!*" "*Wolgastrand!*"

"*Mephisto Waltz*," demanded the lieutenant again, his eyes boring into hers.

Just don't get involved, she told herself.

"Shocked?" he said, a sarcastic twist on his bloodless lips. "On the front I jump to Mephisto's whim. I must hear his waltz so that I can deal with him."

Olga returned to the keyboard and played the foxtrot a soldier had requested.

"Do you have any idea what is going on out there?" the man implored.

Olga smiled patiently, like a nurse telling a dying man he would soon get better. She had her own problems.

"Why do you insist on pretending that you're not a pianist? Don't lie to me."

Olga tensed as his arm brushed her shoulder. He did not need her pity. He wanted her to listen to him. She too longed to share her lonely life with someone. "I appreciate your confidence," she said, while playing the tune her fingers knew so well. "I studied to be a pianist. But the

3

Mephisto Waltz? Liszt wrote it for himself. It is a great piece for a master at the keyboard, unlike me."

"But you could try. Perhaps Mephisto would help you."

"That's what I'm afraid off," Olga said, turning toward him. His hollow cheek twitched. Pain overwhelmed him. His eyes pleaded for relief.

The dancers shouted more requests. A whiff of French perfume drifted by. Lotte's husband served in France and sent her perfume and silk stockings. Olga's husband Lothar did not even send her letters. His messages came through his mother, a countess, who took pleasure in censoring them before sharing them with Olga.

"David defeated Goliath with his sling shot," the officer said. He was talking to himself. "We're stuck with frozen guns and orders from hell."

People talked, guffawed, and giggled.

"The *Mephisto Waltz*," he repeated. "You please everybody else."

Olga shrugged. This was what she got for getting involved with the audience.

"God ignored our prayers," he murmured. "Let the Devil feast on our blood."

"We must make the best of life," she said, hoping he would leave.

"What life?"

"The life of your soul."

He cried out. "What do you take me for? A whimpering idiot? Not yet!" His strident voice offended her. What right did he have to pick on her, wounded or not? "You are not alone," she blurted out, her eyes wild with anger. She brushed the curls from her hot forehead and clenched her fists. She had heard all the reproaches she could handle from Lothar. She didn't need this man to come up with more. "I am hired to entertain!"

"I know," he said indifferently. "So why don't you do that?" He pulled up a chair and settled down. "We don't need miracles for that. Just go on playing whatever you like. I'll stay here until you play the *Mephisto Waltz*." He rose and leaned against the upright. "Go ahead. I'm listening."

Tipsy giggles jingled from the front tables. Nobody paid attention to the officer talking to the piano player. The smell of fried potatoes and sauerkraut reminded Olga that she had missed her supper. "You don't even know me, yet you blame me for all the ills of this world."

He listened to her music for a while, then said, "People shun the truth. They deny we are suffering from a terminal illness. Men die by the millions so that you can play silly love songs in a cafe."

He was right. But what choice did she have? Besides, she liked entertaining.

"The Allies demand unconditional surrender," he went on. "It's victory or death." Then he leaned over her shoulder, whispering, "It'll be death."

Olga evaded him with her silence.

"The *Mephisto Waltz*!" he cried out. "That's the music we're dancing to. Stalingrad cost us the war. Mephisto watched us slaughter each other. Never had a better laugh than when we stepped into his trap." He tapped his fingers against the wood.

Shell-shocked. Poor fellow. "I told you, I can't play the *Mephisto Waltz*," Olga said patiently, turning toward him. Why could he not pretend the Third Reich would win the war, that the miracle weapon would restore peace and glory, and they would live happily ever after? But he had to put his life on the line and suffer the lethal Russian winter. Coming from Latvia she knew about that. She wouldn't be here if her family hadn't been obliged to flee the Soviets when they invaded her country.

She extended her hand. "Olga von Schenck."

He took it and held it in a warm grip, his eyes locking with hers. "Ingo Kroll. Can you understand why I must hear the *Mephisto Waltz*?"

She shrugged, tired of arguing with him, and played *Auf der Heide*, an all time favorite. The men sang along, "*Und das heisst: Erika.*" Their hob-nailed boots marked time as if they were back in Russia marching toward the Volga River. "*Marsch, zwo, drei...*"

"We gave it our all," Kroll recalled. "Dying men shot with frozen hands. My buddies...God, how could You be so cruel? Lutz, Feldmann, Herzog, Steiner. Even the boy, Egon Hinzel. Cried out for *Mutti* when the bomb tore him apart." A muffled sob overcame him. Olga played louder, hitting heavy chords. "*...und das heisst: E-r-i-k-a.*"

"Day and night," he mumbled in a thick voice. "Pounded us with *our* supplies, mind you. Yes! Slaughtered us with weapons the guerillas had stolen from us. Vicious ghosts."

"*Marsch, zwo, drei...*"

"The Russians kept on coming like ducks in a shooting gallery. Then fever got me. Typhoid. A bomb exploded. It spared me, but got Lutz. *Herr Reichspropagandaminister* Dr. Goebbels never talks about things like that, does he?" His harsh laughter gave her the chills. "Don't talk to me about miracles! Hah. Who needs miracles?"

Olga hit the last chord. People clapped. For her music or their survival?

Olga fingered the opening passage of the *Mephisto Waltz*. She had not touched it in years. After she married Lothar, also a pianist, she rarely had an opportunity to practice. The piano was his, and he insisted on having it to himself. He was gone now, and she didn't miss him. Actually, she felt relieved.

Kroll caught on. "That's it. Please go on."

"I can't remember the rest. People want to dance."

Tired of waiting, the couples on the floor returned to their seats.

"You can do it."

Olga fingered the notes, encouraged by his enthusiasm. Nobody had ever supported her playing, certainly not Lothar. The *Mephisto Waltz* tempted. If she could play it, then she could play all the pieces she worked on day after day.

"You see," Kroll said, electrified, "It's coming."

Frau Metzger watched Olga from behind the counter, a deep frown between her thinly plucked brows. The audience fell silent, waiting curiously.

Kroll's warm grip on Olga's shoulders fired her on. "That's it," he cried out, fostering the agitated, throbbing music that pulled them into the netherworld. The wild beat of thundering chords echoed the heaving, panting heartbeat of Faust's lust for Gretchen. Her innocence would restore his youth. Olga understood that part, remembering the shame she had gone through when Lothar forced himself upon her. Cloven hoofs drummed from the keyboard. The proximity of the tormented young man opened her own hell and drew her to his.

The second movement aroused a brutal thrust of sadistic pleasure. The old upright creaked under her pounding out the chords. Then the wistful song of a nightingale transcended the fury—Gretchen's frightened soul cried out for salvation. Olga's repressed desire shot forth with intense sensuality. She quickly built the tempo up into a frenzy, rocking against the keyboard, cheeks burning, a seductive smile on her shining lips. Why not tempt that frustrated officer, bring him back to life? Real life.

The audience stared transfixed by the spectacle. Waitresses and kitchen help watched. They'd never heard of Faust, but knew of Mephisto's power over young virgins. The lieutenant cast a spell on Olga. How shamelessly she tempted him, the tip of her tongue gliding between half-open lips. The music pounded through the room and reminded the soldiers of their impending martyrdom.

Olga hammered out the final chords of Mephisto's triumph. Holding on to the last note, she wished she could vanish from view. She had allowed it to happen, and would now pay for it. Hunched forward, her eyes closed, she whispered, "Father, protect me."

As if he had heard her prayer, Father guided her hands to the keyboard and had her play Liszt's *Liebestraum*, followed by his *Consolation*. The men reached for the hands of the women at their side, smiling. They saw hope. They would see their loved ones again.

Kroll clapped. "Thank you, Frau von Schenck."

The audience rose to a standing ovation, shouting, "Bravo! Bravo."

Kroll's hollow cheeks blushed. "Your music ..." he said. "Divine. I needed that."

She apologized. "It wasn't *my* music."

He took her hands and kissed them. "So it was Franz Liszt who wrote it. Olga, you're wonderful. I hope you don't mind my calling you Olga. You're an enigma I'd love to decipher."

She shrugged. "There isn't much to know."

Kroll sat down facing her. "Let me be the judge. Your mysterious blue eyes hide some secret. What is it?"

"You wouldn't understand."

He rubbed her shoulders. "How do you know? I am listening. I have all night."

A sweet tingling rushed through her heart. His eyes had an adoring glow. He ordered more beer. "I just spent two weeks at home in Dresden," he said. "Slept in my bed, had three meals in the dining room. My mother and my fiancée, Johanna, looked after me, unless they were tending to the wounded. They believe in Hitler's mission as if he were God." His voice grew agitated. "We got into arguments. How can they blame the world for everything we got ourselves into? To them Dr. Goebbels' speeches are the Gospel. Educated women, running around with blinders." The corners of his mouth dropped in disgust. She enjoyed his passion now, and his thoughtful gestures. What had he gone through to earn an iron cross and those rows of medals on his new uniform?

Yadwiga brought open faced sandwiches and beer. "Frau Metzger says for hero."

He raised his glass toward Frau Metzger, smiling. "Thanks to the generous donor." His blue eyes shone with youthful vigor. The sarcastic twist to his mouth was gone, and a natural color had returned to his lips. Now that he was halfway normal, he had a masculine appeal. His shaven head and the red scars no longer bothered her. At least his teeth had not been knocked out, and the straight nose escaped the explosion. "My mother is the epitome of a German Hausfrau," he told her. "Her home is her shrine to perfection."

Olga chuckled. "She wouldn't approve of my topsy-turvy apartment. What's your father like?"

"He's a physician. Fights bacilli as the ultimate enemy. A wonderful man—German to the core. A humanist and healer. I wished I could be like him."

The people on the dance floor awaited the next number. Olga played *The Merry Widow Waltz*, wondering whether she should invite him home so they could talk.

Kroll blotted his lips.

One of the soldiers asked for *Some Day a Miracle Will Happen*.

"I used to hate that syrupy song," he said.

"So I noticed."

"Now I can see why people like it."

"The heart has reasons the mind cannot know," Olga said.

"Heart?" he said. The corners of his mouth dropped. "I forgot I have one."

"Perhaps you should discover it. I devote my life to matters of the soul and communicate with the spirits. My guardian angel appears whenever he can get through."

"Get through? What?"

"The barrier that separates living souls from departed ones." She could tell that he had never been in touch with the other world. Some people thought she was crazy. But so was he, in his own way. She smiled. Not a bad combination.

Chapter 2

Over the past two hours Olga had come to like Kroll, a witty, well-educated man from Dresden. Between pieces he had talked about his experiences at the front that had sent him home on recovery leave. "Too bad I didn't meet you earlier," he said. "Then I wouldn't have gone home at all, but stayed right here in Litzmannstadt."

"There isn't much to see here," she said.

"You are here. That's all I'd need."

Olga enjoyed his acceptance of her. She too would have been happy to have him here as a friend, or more. She sensed that the potential was there. Two lonely souls needed company. Obviously his relationship with Johanna did not mean that much. She found it reassuring, and the prospect of continuing their friendship delightful. Yes, he was the kind of man she could relate to. Since Lothar didn't care for her letters, she could write to Ingo about all the happenings in her life. As the hours passed he became more attractive.

By quitting time, they were as comfortable with each other as if they'd shared their lives from the beginning. The apartment to which she had been assigned had been taken from a Polish or Jewish family. She hated to live there, but had no choice. He would bring it to life. Her daughter, Anyna, would like him too.

Kroll's eyes kept in constant contact with Olga, as if he hoped to hypnotize her into inviting him. He even held her coat for her when she concluded the evening.

"I don't know how much time you have," she said, slipping her hands into the sleeves. "But if you don't mind spending it with a not too well-behaved six-year old, I'd enjoy having you join us for a simple supper."

His broad smile required no words. Now she could see the full extent of his appeal, the warmth of his smile and polite gestures of his fine hands. "I can't think of anything I'd rather do," he said and picked up her notes.

She waved them away. "I don't need those. At home I play the kind of music you like. Though I doubt I'll be playing much tonight. My neighbors don't appreciate it."

"Encore! Encore!" shouted the men, hoping this evening would go on forever. Some lit a fresh cigarette, others ordered more beer. Frau Metzger nodded an encouragement, but Olga shook her head. Kroll smoothed out the shoulders of her coat. They were ready to spend the rest of the evening with each other.

"What I really need is food for the soul," he said. "Surely you can see how much influence you have on me. I'm as tame as a lamb and as sane as a kitten. That's your doing. I can feel my soul and my heart. They're warm and human again. The *Mephisto Waltz* threw the devil out. You're the best medicine I could ask for; now my recuperation can start. Thank you, Olga. But come. We mustn't keep your little girl waiting. Children expect us to live up to our promises. What's her name?" he asked, following her to the back door.

Sidling between the crowded tables, Olga smiled at the men she passed. "Anyna,"

"Unusual name."

"A Latvian diminutive of Anna."

"I am looking forward to meeting her. Your eyes are so lovely. Let me discover their mystery. I'm sorry I acted like a mad man. Usually I'm a pretty decent fellow. Your music lifted the spell. I can't thank you enough."

He opened the back door for her. It squeaked on its rusty hinges. Freezing air gushed at them as they stepped outside into the darkness. The temperature had dropped and the packed snow on the street distinguished the sidewalk from the black buildings on both sides. The door clicked shut.

He took her arm, and let Olga guide him like a blind man. It felt so good being with him. "It isn't very far," she said. "We can walk. Let the gossips wag their tongues. I can tell that you're an honorable man."

He squeezed her waist and chuckled. "An officer and a gentleman."

To her surprise Olga did not care whether he was or not. There was no turning back now, not that she wanted to.

"There is no point depriving ourselves of what little pleasure life still has to offer," Kroll said. "Our nation is doomed."

"Doomed?" she retorted. "What makes you say that? The miracle weapon..." She felt his hard squeeze. He did not believe in it or any other miracle.

They walked in silence. "Yes, yes of course," he said, regret in his voice.

"So you see. We are not doomed," she argued, for no particular reason.

The impenetrable darkness had no bright side. The blackout was strictly enforced. Not a star in the sky. Another cloudy winter night, except that her heart felt warm and filled with life. Ingo's presence put a spring in her step.

"Does Anyna look like you?" he asked. "Blonde curly hair, blue eyes, and your talent for music that draws people into its spell?"

"No curls," Olga said, holding on to his arm to keep from slipping on the ice. "Her hair is dark and straight."

"I bet she is thoughtful and kind, like you," he said, guiding her.

"Anyna is quite stubborn." She slipped on the ice and landed in his arms, in no hurry to get back on her feet.

"Are you all right?" he asked, holding her. She could not see his lips but felt them near hers. He did not take advantage of it.

"Quite so, thank you." The icy breeze blew coal smoke from nearby chimneys. An old truck rattled by. The barely visible slits reminded her of tired eyes bouncing in the darkness. Belching exhaust fumes wafted toward them. It shifted gears, then drove on.

Ingo's warm breath brushed her cold cheek. Would he kiss her? Had she obliged him to behave like a gentleman? "You challenged me into attempting the impossible," she said. "I never play anything in public unless I know it by heart. The *Mephisto Waltz* yet. You dared me as if your life depended on it. Why?"

"Things got to me. We, and millions of others, are victims of this war. But you can do something about it. I am bound by my oath. I wanted to challenge you to act on something you were not comfortable with. When you attempted the waltz, I felt that I had accomplished something. Made it happen. You proved me right—played the waltz as I'd never heard it before."

She stopped and held him back.

"But you are wrong, Ingo. I was NOT myself," Olga cried out. "An entity took charge of my body and played the piece. No. Don't say anything," she interrupted even before he could contradict her. "I know what I am talking about. Don't take the power of evil lightly. They tempt us and then ask their due. They turn us into monsters. They use men to destroy each other."

He pondered her statement while they walked. "You could be right."

The uninitiated could not understand, and were not meant to. The spirit world was dangerous territory for those who didn't have a guardian angel for their protection. They soon reached the weathered gate of her building. Pulling the heavy key from her purse she said, "My dear Ingo. I'm so glad you came."

She traced her gloved finger over the healthy cheek she could barely see. "Let's get out of the cold."

The vapor of their breaths merged. "I'm so grateful for your gift of letting me spend my last evening at liberty with you. Tomorrow I'll be off to Mephisto's favorite playground." He put his arm around her shoulder and gave her a warm hug, then pushed the heavy door open. Ignoring the dim stairwell and its musty smell of the ages, they raced each other upstairs over the old creaking steps.

Olga lived on the third floor. She unlocked the door to her apartment and let him pass. "Please, come right in."

Little footsteps pattered through the living room. Anyna threw herself at Olga. "Mami, Mami. You're home!"

Olga scooped up her child, returned the stormy embrace, and kissed Anyna's hot cheeks. The child in her arms, she said, "This is Leutnant Kroll."

Anyna eyed the uniformed stranger suspiciously, then extended her little hand. "I am pleased to meet you, Herr Leutnant. I am Anna Magdalena von Schenck and I am a baroness."

"My pleasure, baroness," he said, and gallantly kissed her hand. "You can call me Uncle Ingo."

"How do you do, Uncle Ingo," she said, holding on to her mother's neck. "But you're not my uncle."

Stasya, the maid who looked after Anyna while Olga was at work, had braided red ribbons into her hair that matched her hand-knit sweater.

"From now on I will be," Ingo said, smiling. He looked so formal in his cap and greatcoat. "Your mother must have named you after the second wife of our great composer, Johann Sebastian Bach. Her name was Anna Magdalena. He composed many wonderful pieces for her."

"Anyna knows some of them," Olga said. "I play them for her at bedtime."

He took her coat and searched for a place among the crowded pegs along the wall, finally draping it over a jacket.

"Now look, Anyna," Olga said. "A true baroness does not brag about her title."

"But Grandmaman said …"

"Grandmaman does not tell people she's a countess, does she?"

Anyna blushed all the way up to the hairline, "Because everybody knows it."

In the living room Olga cleared the toys from the table and gathered up her music and the cards she had used earlier for a reading. The low hanging lamp with its round lampshade concentrated its pool of light on the table, leaving the heavy china cabinet, bookcase, and sofa in the dark. The cold air added to the hostile atmosphere of this alien place, with its foreign odor of people who had lived here before. Coal, like everything else, was rationed. Stasya only heated the kitchen where they ate their meals and Anyna spent her time.

Now Ingo's presence filled the room with warmth and life. It was as if he belonged here, had always lived here.

Anyna planted her feet in a broad stance. "How did you know where my name comes from?" she demanded, her wide-set eyes fixed on his face. She was small and delicate for her age, and had her father's large mouth and brown eyes, and his pride.

"It's quite obvious. Your mother loves music and probably likes to play Bach. While she carried you she hoped you would become a musician like she is."

Anyna nodded. "I suppose you're right. What happened to your face?"

"Anyna, it's impolite …" Olga interrupted.

"Let her speak," Ingo said. "I'm glad she asked. Sometimes people are too polite. I was wounded," he explained. "That happens to many soldiers who are out fighting the war. But it's the wounds you can't see that hurt."

Anyna pondered this. "How can they hurt when you can't see them?"

"If you could see them, they could be cured."

She sat down on the straight-back sofa. "Mami plays the piano, but Daddy is a pianist. When he's home he plays all the time and composes, like Bach. We have lots of music that he wrote, right Mami? Now he is in Africa." She grew excited, jumped up and pulled Kroll over to the old sofa. "I know where Africa is! Do you want me to show you on the globe?"

"By all means, Baroness," Kroll said. "You are a smart little girl. I can't think of anybody your age who knows where Africa is."

"You see, Mami? Grandmaman also teaches me how to be a baroness."

"That must be difficult," he said.

Stasya came in wearing a gray cardigan over a brown dress. She had taken off her apron so that Ingo could see that she was not a regular maid, but a handsome young woman who carried her pride on her sleeve. Her hair had been set in crisp waves, and she even wore lipstick that she must have put on when she heard Ingo's voice.

"*Essen fertig*, Pani Olga," she announced with a sidelong glance at him.

"We'll eat here, Stasya. Please make a fire and set the table for three. It's freezing."

"You say we must save coal."

"Not tonight. We have a visitor."

Stasya bent down in front of the stove so that her tight skirt would outline her shapely buttocks. Where did she get those silk stockings from? Poles were supposed to be in short supply of everything, but in reality they provided whatever Germans could not get. The goods probably came from a supply train the partisans had robbed. Stasya struck a match and held it under the paper and kindling until flames flared up.

"Where is your globe, Baroness?" Kroll asked. "After you show me Africa, I'll show you where Dresden is. That's where my home is."

"Do you know where Riga is?" Anyna asked. "That's where I was born."

15

Hauling the globe from a small table by the massive bookcase, she put it down on the dining table right under the light. Olga watched Ingo join Anyna, waiting until she found Africa.

"That's where Daddy fights against the British," she said, pointing her little finger at Tunisia, then turning the globe. "Look here. Can you see that? It says Riga, right? I can't read yet, but I can draw. Do you want to see my drawing?"

He took her hand and looked into her eyes. "I would like that very much. You are a lovely little baroness."

She frowned, her eyes focused on his. "You may call me Anyna, Uncle Ingo. I only said that about being a baroness because people think I don't know anything. But when I tell them I'm a baroness they're impressed."

"I believe every child deserves respect, whether she's a baroness or not. Only babies like 'cootchy, cootchy coo, you're my little goodie poo.'" He nuzzled her neck. Anyna squealed.

Olga watched them in amazement. Ingo's kindness toward Anyna took Olga's heart by storm.

"You're so funny, Uncle Ingo. Daddy says, I'm an ugly mutt. I wouldn't mind being an ugly duckling and growing into a beautiful swan, right Mami? Do you know the story of the Ugly Duckling?" She knit her brows. "You know what he does?"

Kroll shook his head. "No idea."

Stasya spread a white tablecloth over the large table and took out the gold and blue-rimmed dishes from the buffet.

"He makes me stand in a corner until I ask him for forgiveness, even when I did nothing wrong. 'Just so you don't get big ideas,' he says." Anyna imitated her father's haughty voice. "He also hits me with knitting needles and laughs. He says I must get tough. Only tough people make it in this world. And you know what?" She slipped her hand into Kroll's.

He shook his head.

"Look, darling," Olga said. "I don't think Daddy meant any harm."

"You don't know, Mami, because you're not at home when he does that. When he goes away, he locks me into the closet. Once I came out before he came back. He got so mad." She ignored her mother's disapproving glances. "It's true, Mami. Uncle Ingo is my friend. He knows that eating dead flies is sick, right Uncle Ingo? I didn't tell Mami, so he wouldn't get mad at her."

Olga was at a loss. Anyna had never mentioned any of this to her, and now Kroll had her confidence. Why did Lothar mistreat his daughter? Did he blame the child for her existence? He had a sadistic streak and enjoyed tormenting Olga, but Anyna had nothing to do with this. Lothar and his perverse notions of righteousness. "We must not tell our problems to…" She stopped herself. Ingo was their friend now. Anyna had accepted him.

Anyna blushed. Her lower lip quivered. Tears formed in her eyes. She felt guilty for tattling. "You don't know, Mami."

Ingo picked her up and put her on his lap. Rocking her in his arms he said, "It's all right, Anyna. Of course we believe you. It isn't easy being a child. Some fathers don't understand that."

She put her arms around his neck, and pressed her face against his. "You are so nice, Uncle Ingo. Sometimes Daddy brings me candy."

"You see," Ingo said. "He loves you in his own fashion."

He held her and rocked.

"Lothar isn't used to children," Olga said, wondering why she apologized for him. "He longs for recognition with his music, but refuses to compose pieces that glorify the Reich. Having a family was not in his plans."

"I understand," Ingo said.

Anyna ran her tiny finger gingerly across his scar. "Does it hurt?"

"Not now, when you touch it. You are a very special child."

"I love you too, Uncle Ingo. You are the best uncle I ever had." She fingered Ingo's medals. "Did you get them for shooting Russians?"

"Not intentionally." His face twitched. The scar reddened.

Anyna slipped from his lap. "Grandmaman said Daddy is missing in action. She said he is probably a prisoner of war. In Africa many men surrendered."

Olga stared dumbfounded at Anyna. "When did she say that?"

"This afternoon, when I visited her. She said the Americans are decent people and will not harm him. She said, Daddy is lucky to be taken by the Americans."

Ingo nodded. "The Allies will release him after the war is over. It'll take some time. We're in it over our ears."

That meant Lothar would not be back for a long time, Olga thought, and felt great relief. Perhaps he would never come back, and she would finally be free.

Stasya brought in a platter with steaming potatoes, carrots, and ground beef patties and set it on the table.

Ingo talked about his childhood in Dresden and the pranks he played with his sister Ingrid. Olga could not get enough of him, delighted by his refined manners, his easy banter, the casual yet respectful conversation with Anyna.

"You must come to Dresden and see the Semper Opera," he said, taking a second helping. Stasya had prepared extra food for tomorrow's lunch. They would manage. Olga was surprised that Stasya had set the table with crisp napkins and shining silver. She had her good moments.

Ingo unbuttoned his coat. The iron cross was fastened to his tie. "Dresden is the most beautiful city in Germany," he said. "August the Strong was a powerful king who loved art and architecture. Until 1866, Saxony was as powerful as Prussia. That's when they formed the North German Confederation known as the Second Reich."

"I like your stories," Anyna said, her cheeks warm and fresh. "I am so glad you came. Nobody ever visits us except Aunt Lucie and Aunt Ottie who always complain about something. Now we have you. You will come again, won't you?" she implored, placing her hand on his. He cradled it like a little bird.

"I would like to very much, Anyna. Only for the moment I am very busy," he said. "Thanks for the invitation. We can exchange letters. Words can be so dear."

"I'll always think of you, Uncle Ingo."

After Stasya had cleared the table, Olga rose. "Bedtime."

Anyna glanced at Ingo for support. "You're a good little girl who obeys Mami."

"When I'm in bed, will you come and tell me a story, Uncle Ingo?"

"If you hurry up. No skipping on your washing routine or brushing your teeth," he warned.

Anyna gave her mother a quick kiss, "Thank you for supper, Mami," and dashed off. "You'll see, Uncle Ingo, how fast I can do it."

Ten minutes later, she awaited Uncle Ingo and her mother in bed, propped up against her pillow. "You may sit here, Uncle Ingo," she said, pointing at the edge the way she had watched her grandmother direct her visitors. "After you tell me a story Mami will play a lullaby. I love *Cradlesong* best of all. I know the words too."

Ingo punched down the bulging eiderdown and stretched out over it. The green lamp shade on the nightstand cast its mellow light over Anyna's face. Her dark hair fell over her shoulders. If only he would not have to leave again, Olga thought. But nothing could stop the morning light from rising.

"Once upon a time," she heard him say in his gentle Saxon accent, "in the city of Bremen, lived an old rheumatic dog…"

While cleaning up the washstand, Olga dabbed a drop of perfume behind her ear. How long could she keep him here? If this was Mephisto's temptation, so be it.

"The bandits fled when the animals barged into the house and finished the dinner."

Anyna asked, "Do you think that is what happened to the people who used to live here? Did soldiers scare them away? That's what Stasya says."

"Could be."

"Omi and Grandmaman fled from Latvia when the Bolsheviks came. That's why they came here. We left Berlin because bombs exploded on our house. You came here because you must go and fight the Russians."

"True," he said. "Just remember, when disaster strikes, it's never the end of the world."

"You *can* believe in miracles, Ingo," Olga teased.

He rose. "I'd say that my being here tonight is a miracle." After pulling the comforter under Anyna's chin, he bent down and kissed her forehead. "Good night, my little baroness. And remember, you don't ever have to be afraid."

"That's easy for you to say. You're big and strong and an officer. You can shoot people. I'm only a child."

"Ah! But a baroness is never afraid."

Anyna sat up again. "You're right. I don't have to be afraid. Only of Daddy, because he's a baron."

Ingo laughed out loud, showing white pearly teeth. "I guess you have a point."

Anyna clung to his neck. "Promise you will come back tomorrow, Uncle Ingo. I'll be waiting for you. I'll draw you a special picture."

He held her. "In the Army we must obey orders."

"But you're an officer."

"Everybody must obey."

She tilted her head, and watched him head for the door. "I don't like the army."

"Neither do I. Goodnight, sweet Anyna."

She waved. "Do come back soon. I'll pray for you, Uncle Ingo."

"I'll need it." He blew a kiss, then left the room.

Olga held her daughter, feeling the warm clean skin on her lips. "Good night, sweetie."

Chapter 3

"What a precocious little girl," Ingo said when Olga joined him in the living room.

"She's an only child. And I'm working. You see…" How could she explain the ugly story? Mendelssohn's song without words was her answer.

"Every life has its secrets," he said, standing behind her, his warm hands resting on her shoulders.

After Anyna's revelation, Olga could no longer pretend she was the lonesome wife of a man at war. As a friend, he deserved to know the truth. She turned toward him. He took her hand and kissed it. "Music touches the heart like nothing else," he said in a soothing voice. "You relate through it. I feel your pain. Perhaps you are still sorting things out. Anyna is a sweet and bright little girl with a mind of her own."

"I had no idea that her father…"

"Children have their secrets too."

"I suppose." Olga was hurt and confused. "Why would she tell you rather than me?"

"I feel honored that she did, Olga. I'm an outsider she can talk to freely."

Playing a Chopin nocturne, she swallowed the lump in her throat. Ingo touched all the sensitive places in her heart. Praise confused her. Insults had been the regular fare when Lothar had been around.

Liszt's tender *Souffle* sounded like a prayer. With Ingo's warm hands on her shoulders she abandoned herself to him. Only hours ago she had resented him; now they belonged together. *Oh, God in Heaven, don't let anything happen to him.*

Chopin's jubilant *Andante Appassionata* burst forth in triumph over envy and slander. Never before had she been so happy, so fulfilled, so in tune with a friend who happened to be a man. The last chords diminished in the dim room. His gentle hug sent waves of joy through her heart. She placed her hands on his and leaned back against his chest. His arms folded around her. They remained in silence.

"Can you play Beethoven's *Moonlight Sonata?*" he whispered, as if his voice could break the magic between them.

"One of my favorites," she said, and recreated the image of a balmy summer night, a world at peace, lovers embracing under a full moon. The driving crescendo in the second movement took Beethoven's lovers closer to each other in a surge of sounds until, satiated, they returned to the stillness of the night, gazing at the stars.

Ingo's presence, his breath on her head, the caressing touch of his hands allowed Olga to live out the fantasy of her music. She longed for his kiss, to hold him and treat his wounds, not just the physical ones. She could make him feel whole again. But a woman must wait to be invited and then act coy, even if she desperately longed to be with the man. He had come to her as if in answer to a prayer she had dared not pray. His uniform smelled of smoke from the café, hours on an overcrowded train, and traces of his 4711 aftershave. The old fashioned print above the piano, showing a girl praying to the moon, no longer felt foreign. The man she had hoped to find some day had come to her. He was here now, his hands on her shoulders, in tune with the music she played.

Breaking the spell that could only lead to one thing she said, "Let me get some wine."

"Wine? Don't tell me. Where did you get it? From France of course."

Olga nodded. "He was stationed in France before he was sent to Africa. Loved Paris, as you can imagine. Everybody loves Paris. When he came home on leave, he brought me some wine. He spent most of his time with his mother, except when he wanted to play the piano. Anyna was with them. I am no baroness, you see. I would not want to be one. Not like them."

Ingo settled down at the table, and watched her pull a bottle from the buffet, then uncork it. He had become part of the home. She would imagine him there for years to come. "Let me get some cheese." She folded her arms around his neck and playfully kissed the tender skin of his shaven head.

He held her back when she attempted to leave, and embraced her. "Thanks for letting me come. I never knew a woman like you. From now on you will be with me wherever I go. I shall see you in the darkness of winter and the sweltering heat of summer. Out in the vastness of Russia, I'll imagine being here with you. Having somebody to share my affection with will make time pass quickly. Out there, in Russia, I listen to music that plays in my mind or recite poetry—unless I'm in combat, of course."

She tore herself away and hastened to the kitchen, then returned with a plate filled with sliced Swiss cheese. His eyes had lost their restless, angry squint. He watched her place the plate on the table, and filled the glasses.

"Let's drink to this special moment."

"To each other," she said.

He sipped the wine as if it were a magic potion. The radio played the *Front Request Program*. The sensual tango stirred her passion for this man. She longed to fall into his arms and dance with him around the table. Instead, they clinked glasses and spoke with their eyes.

"Chateau Neuf du Pape," she said, a beguiling smile on her moist lips. "Something you don't get every day."

"Or ever," he teased, swirling the wine around, then sniffed. "Excellent bouquet. That is all I know about wines. I never got to be stationed in France. For me it was Russia. To you, Olga."

"To you, Ingo. I never thought I'd get to like you so much."

He winked. "Let's drink to our friendship."

The word "our" sent her heart flying. Father had picked Ingo for her. Their union was predestined. They held hands. Soothing music underscored the magic of this moment. There would be a long afterwards. His wounds would heal and his hair grow back. He had shed his jacket and now relaxed in his khaki shirt, tie and collar open. There was no engagement band on his left hand. Had he broken off with Johanna? He mentioned his younger sister, Ingrid. "We are true friends. She isn't like our mother, more like the aunts we adore." Talking about his family transformed his face to youthful exuberance. He had a mischievous twinkle in his eyes and a quick smile. She imagined his hair thick and brown, and his cheeks would fill out as soon as he had some rest. She appreciated that he didn't smoke nor did he gulp down the wine for the alcohol, but appreciated the delicate flavor. With his anger gone, he was an educated young man from a good family.

"Don't you get terribly lonely here?" he wondered.

"No. Actually I am very happy to have a place of my own. You can't imagine what life was like before, when I shared a room with Lothar and Anyna in Berlin. I don't even want to think about it. I was actually glad when the bomb struck the building and I was evacuated to this place. My mother lives upstairs, and my sister Ottie not too far from here. I also have close friends from my youth. I spend most of my time at the piano, in meditation, or at occasional séances. Father, my guardian angel, visits me at times and guides me through difficult moments. He saved Anyna, and even told me that I would meet somebody today who needs my help. Is there something to that?" she asked impishly.

"I'd say. You saved my sanity. That's almost as good as saving my life," he said in earnest, and kissed her hand. "I can't get over how lovely you are, so gentle and kind. A delectable and wise young woman. I consider myself extremely fortunate to have found you, and thank Father for guiding me to you."

A rush of heat colored her cheeks. She withdrew her hands. "You're teasing."

"On the contrary. I'm drawn to you and can't imagine leaving you behind."

They sat at the table while he poured more wine. Olga drank quickly, but could not calm her agitation. *Leaving you behind?* Did that mean he wanted to stay with her, that something terrible would happen in his absence? She did not want to get into it, just to stay in the moment. His eyes had the depth of a clear midnight sky, open and vulnerable. They were so close now that she could see the tiny specks of his whiskers and the inflamed skin around his scar. Her heart throbbed with desire. Yes, desire. He shared her feelings. "Here, have some more cheese," she said quickly. "I have plenty. Frau Metzger lets me eat at the café."

Visibly disappointed by her changing the subject, he picked up a slice of cheese and ate it. "I should probably leave. I have no pass."

"But nobody would find you here."

"That makes it even worse. But let's not think about it. This evening with you is too precious to break up now. I'll risk it and take the consequences."

"For me?"

"Of course, for you," he said and took her hand again, evidently the only contact he dared make. She appreciated his consideration. Had he obliged her to go to bed with him, she would not have fought him off, but would have lost the admiration she had now. Sex would ruin everything. Though she longed for it, and would have enjoyed the intimacy of being in his arms, and most of all his kisses, it never stopped there. Not that she had any experiences other than the cruel ordeals with Lothar.

She tilted her glass back and forth, watching the red wine catch the light from the lamp. "Are you a professional soldier?"

"Do I look like one?"

"I wouldn't know, since I don't know any."

"I trained to become a teacher. I studied philosophy and German literature."

She leaned into the circle of light so that he could see her small face, the inviting smile and the dimple on her left cheek. Her hair curled into her face.

He took her hand and pressed it against his cheek. "You are so beautiful, Olga. What did you mean when you talked about the spirit world that guides your life? Tell me about your guardian angel who supposedly sent me to you. How do you know? I am quite inclined to believe you." He looked deep into her eyes, searching for the answer to the mystery of love. "I never felt so close to anybody. It seems as if I have known you all my life. Amazing, isn't it? You are my gift from heaven."

"And you mine," she said quickly and handed him the bottle. "We might as well finish it."

He refilled their glasses. "Am I forgiven?"

"Forgiven for what? Your heart cried out and I heard it." He was coming to terms with his doomed life. "I'm so glad you came."

"Likewise. My father wanted me to become a physician like he. I didn't feel the calling. How can I consult people begging for my help when I know there is none? At the front, I know I made the right decision. But I admire the men and women who devote their lives to helping others, like my parents. They believe in Germany's mission. So does Johanna. Our relationship is like a frozen lake in the arctic that will never thaw out."

Olga was glad that he was free, and wished she could say the same for herself. Her head felt so light. She giggled. The radio announcer read off messages from families to their loved ones at the front. "I love the request program," she said. "From now on I'll think of you whenever it comes on. That'll be our date, yes? I'll think of you at other times too, of course. But Monday night will be our special night."

He caressed her fingers. "Yes. I'll visit you here, in this room."

"By candlelight," she added, went to the credenza to pull out a candle which she lit. Then switched off the light.

"I guess you were in hell when you played *The Mephisto Waltz*," he said. "You acted out the part. People at the café saw it too. It was like an act of exorcism. It certainly worked on me."

Olga tensed. "I had no idea. You challenged me and then that entity took over. A very scary and dangerous thing. Often you can't escape them once they take hold of you. Everything has a price. This one may be back to demand his due. Still, it was an exhilarating experience. I would like to become a pianist. The entity knows that of course, and saw his opportunity. He showed me what it feels like to be a virtuoso."

"You were that, and a lot more. Beguiling and mysterious and, I hope you won't mind my saying so, sensual." The look in his eyes now questioned her reaction.

"Since we're friends and I'm kind of tipsy, why not tell you the truth. Yes, it was a sensual experience. Not by volition, mind you. The entity aroused me, obliged me to tempt you. Entities can take over your body and your life, if you let them. By fulfilling your wish they take you—body and soul. There is no escape. I'm sure that's what happened to our men who evicted the Poles and Jews in this city. They took pleasure in passing out the pain and power under which they had suffered as children. Petty people who had been restrained, beaten and punished. Cruelty breeds cruelty. But let's not talk about it."

He shrugged. "We can't close our eyes to it. I see it out in Russia all the time. Not that I can do anything about it unless I want to go on an *ascension mission*—be sent on an assignment I couldn't possibly survive. Now the Russians are paying us back. God help those who fall into their hands. It's bad out there. Can you see why I had to hear *The Mephisto Waltz*? Your rendition allowed me to snap out of it. Art can do that. Goethe does it with his poetry. It can humanize a world that forgot what that's like."

The Front Request Program played a slow waltz.

"I know what demons are all about," he reflected. "Under fire, people promise anything to be saved. Since God does not help, they try the Devil. It's all the same, really." His hand trembled. A deep frown furrowed his forehead. His eyes filled with pain. "We all want to live. Have a right to live. But our leaders play with our lives as if we're pawns in a game. Casualties are numbers, not suffering, screaming men. Don't let me go on." His scars reddened.

"It's all right, Ingo," she said, running her hand over his arm. "You'll make it."

"Hm. You think so?" He thought for a moment. "Strangely enough, I believe you." He cradled her face in his warm hands. "You've become my life." The tenderness in his voice invited her kiss.

Olga lowered her lids and waited.

Instead of kissing her he said, "I see a deck of cards. Would you give me a reading? I'd be curious to know what you come up with. I'm ready to accept anything." He gazed at the dark ceiling. "Thank you, Father, whoever you are. I care for your daughter."

"I care for you too, Ingo," she said, picked up the deck and handed it to him. "Shuffle carefully, and concentrate on a question while I stoke the fire. But don't tell it to me."

He shuffled nervously, his lips tight. "So far I've been lucky. The grenade that caused this injury saved me from dying in Stalingrad. Hitler abandoned the men who fought, froze, and starved for him. He ignored General Paulus's pleas for support. That was the straw that broke our faith in him and his mission. The man is mad. He's the death of Germany with his 'to the last man' doctrine. Don't we have a right to live?" His lips trembled while he held back the scream. He clutched the cards as if they held the key to his destiny.

Olga poked the glowing coals before shoveling fresh clumps on top. A dark cloud of smoke formed, curling through the coal dust. Flames shot through the ashes. She closed the iron gate. Click. Rising she said, "You will live, Ingo."

"You are my saving grace," he said in a low voice, watching her come toward him.

She sat down. "Now, with your left hand, drop the deck into three stacks. What I'm going to tell you comes from my inner voice. We all have one." She picked up the stacks in reverse order, closed her eyes, and fell into a trance. "God, in Your love and mercy, protect us. Beloved Father, speak to me."

Spreading out the cards one by one, she said, "In the past year your life was in great turmoil. You were hurt, distressed, in physical and emotional pain. Swimming against the stream is perilous. Follow the flow until you find a life boat. It will come. Trust your inner voice rather than your logic."

He was all ears now, listening to her as if she uttered divine revelations.

Olga continued her interpretations, pointing at the key cards as they came up.

"A woman close to you exerts her influence. Trust her counsel. Do not dwell on your disappointments—bless them and let them go so that you can free your heart for the beauty of the world. When you think you can't cope, rise above it and go on. Every step takes a different turn. Don't be afraid to go on, no matter what.

"Going into the future, I see confidence and determination. Always trust your guidance. It will help you overcome the difficulties you face. Do not carry the burden of others. We each have our own destiny.

"I am to tell you that your guardians will see you through this war. You are in God's hands, created in His image. Your life has infinite possibilities. Intuitively, you will make the right decision. Go forward, and accept the love and support coming toward you."

Olga opened her eyes and saw Ingo's bewildered gaze. The ticking clock punctuated the silence. Her longing for him had deepened. Leaning toward her he awaited further disclosures.

"Can you relate to what I said?" she asked.

"Yes," he mumbled in a thick voice. What did he see? The trenches? Bombs exploding around him? Dying men? Russia's merciless cold? Lost battles? Immense suffering?

Olga waited. The spirit world could shock the uninitiated.

"How do you know all that?" he asked, fidgeting with his empty glass, now smudged with traces of red wine. The cheese was gone. "Forgiveness and love. I have found love," he whispered, reaching for her hands and pulling her up. "Let's sit together on the sofa. I sense there is some tragedy connected with Anyna. Would you tell me about it?"

"Anyna?" Anxiety contracted her stomach. "I'd rather not."

"Why? You said we are friends." He held her in a warm embrace. "Perhaps you must get things off your chest. It still hurts, doesn't it?"

How did he know, Olga wondered, enjoying his protective arm around her. True friends did not keep secrets from each other, nor did they feel ashamed for something they had not done.

Ingo stretched his legs across the old rug, and leaned against the stiff backrest of the sofa with its foreign smell and broken springs. It had served a family she would never know.

"What happened in Riga?" he asked, holding her hand.

"That city belongs to another lifetime," she reminisced, visualizing the three-story family home where she had spent her youth. Their apartment had been on the second floor. Widowhood was too hard on her mother. So when a scrawny bachelor proposed, she accepted.

"All he had going for himself was that he was a male and my mother's husband. She too was a pianist, and accompanied silent movies. Herr Fricke never bothered to get dressed." Olga chuckled. "Naturally, we wouldn't listen to him. He always followed us around like a dachshund with a high-pitched bark, 'Just wait until your mother comes home.' That threat didn't work, because mother wouldn't say anything."

Ingo laughed. "A dachshund yet."

Olga snuggled up to him. "Herr Fricke admired Lothar von Schenck, a talented musician and good chess player. Lothar visited us often. He liked friends his mother would not approve of. She wanted an aristocrat for her son, since she called herself a countess. But after the Latvian land reform, the aristocracy had to give up most of their land and barely made ends meet. My mother had an apartment building. Not very glamorous but she made a living.

"When Lothar and Herr Fricke played chess they tore the world apart. Lothar hated his stepfather, the count, who had squandered whatever land and money his mother had left. There is nothing more pathetic than an impoverished nobleman," Olga said. "Especially one who would not take a job. He probably had no skills other than playing the noble suitor to the countess, which cost her dearly."

He hugged her. "So where does Anyna come in?"

Olga slipped aside, wishing she had not told Ingo. Now everything would be wrong again. "You don't really want to hear this," she said.

"On the contrary. True friends share their secrets. They trust each other."

This man had almost too many virtues. What would she do when his dark side arose again? "It happened on a Sunday afternoon," she said. Why not tell him the story and see how he would react? What did she have to lose? "Lothar and I were going to play duets, but I refused to play his compositions. They chilled my blood."

"The music got him excited," Ingo said sarcastically. "It gets everybody excited. You should've been honored that he played with you."

"I was, of course. He was the master," Olga remembered that dark winter day in her mother's home. "But he couldn't understand why I didn't like his music. He'd grabbed me and kissed me. I was in shock. Not that I didn't like him, but not in that way. He shoved me over to the sofa, pushed up my skirt and pulled down my panties.

"You should've heard him bellow like a bull mounting a cow. I was scared of him, and didn't dare move while he unbuttoned his fly." She shuddered and sunk into herself. "I don't have to tell you the rest," she whispered, overcome by the memory of his forcing himself into her when she had never experienced sex before. They were alone in the house. Nobody heard her screams. Worst of all had been his tongue, filling her mouth with slimy spit. She had convulsed, which only incited him to pump harder until a warm liquid ran over her inner thighs.

"In the end he said, 'There. Was that good?'"

Ingo cradled her head against his chest and stroked her hair. "You are wonderful, my sweet Olychka. I guess, Anyna is the result of that attack."

"I don't know what I'd do without her. She is my life. A blessing.

"Imagine, after that he sat down and played his unbearable composition," Olga remembered. "*Life in the Catacombs*. I pretended nothing had happened. Later we had tea. I returned to the conservatory in Jelgava. The rest is pretty obvious."

He kissed her eyes. "Thank you, Olga, for confiding in me. From now on you can tell me everything. I would like to be a friend you can love and trust."

"Love and trust," she repeated in a whisper. Was that possible between a man and a woman? His ingratiating smile said that he meant it.

"I was so embarrassed," she recalled. "I figured he got carried away. He's so sensitive about his music. You know how artists are."

"Geniuses yet," Ingo said.

Shame reddened her face. Her lips trembled. Lothar had ruined her life, not she his, as he always claimed.

"In a way he is," Olga said. "People hated Stravinsky when his *Firebird* was first performed."

Ingo held her in a tender hug. "You are such a dear for defending him."

Tears filled her eyes. The lump in her throat thickened. His gentle strokes reassured her that she had found somebody who cared for her. "Cry, my love," he whispered. "Let the tears wash the pain from your soul. I am here to love and protect you."

She wept over her past and the future, when Ingo would be gone and they would long for each other. "I never told anybody."

"As you said before, because nobody would believe you. Women carry the burden."

"How do you know?" she asked, sniffling. "How come you are so wise?" He handed her his handkerchief. She blew her nose and wiped her tears.

"Happens all the time."

"Months later, when I told Lothar that I was pregnant, he insisted I get an abortion. The shame made me sick. Kill my baby even though I hated its father? The scandal! A Baron von Schenck didn't do things like that. I was so naive. I prayed." She clung to Ingo. His warm grip encouraged her to go on.

"Where could I go? How could I raise my baby alone? It kept on growing inside of me. Lothar insisted on an abortion. I finally saw no choice, and went, weeping all the way. The woman at the door looked like an executioner, blood all over her smock. A girl stumbled out, clutching her belly, sobbing.

"The woman demanded the money Lothar had borrowed. I paid, and followed her into a dark, stinking room. In my soul I could hear the cries of the women who had been obliged to murder their babies; I could smell their dead bodies as if I had landed in hell. Yes, I know, I have a vivid imagination. But now my baby would be killed and dumped into the garbage. I had no idea how it was done, and got scared when I

31

climbed on the table. The baby moved. It begged me for its life." Olga's voice broke off.

"How did you save your baby, Olga?" Ingo asked, rubbing her shoulder.

She wiped her eyes. "When the woman left the room, the table lamp shone on my belly. It had grown big. I didn't know anything about giving birth or anything else.

Suddenly my head was jerked to the door. A brilliant light flickered against the ceiling.

Father had come. 'You must not let them kill your baby,' he said. 'She is a soul that chose you as her mother.' I was responsible for a soul seeking reentry into the world.

"The woman returned. She couldn't see the light. 'Get those legs apart,' she said, holding some instrument. Her big, ugly face had small, evil eyes. The light flickered and vanished. I screamed, 'Don't touch me.'

"'You should've thought of that before getting involved with boys.'

"I jumped from the table. She did not hold me back. I had already paid her."

Ingo nuzzled Olga's neck. The love she had felt earlier was gone. Ingo was a man who could get her into trouble again.

"Now you think…" Olga said, biting her lips.

"That you're a brave and wonderful woman. Forgive me, Olga, for my snotty remarks."

She held his hand and kissed it. "Thank you for listening to me." She wanted him to know the whole story. "Lothar was furious. He blamed me for ruining his life and his career, as if he had one. When he could not talk me out of keeping my baby, he played the chivalrous gentleman to avoid a scandal. We got married so that the poor thing would have a proper name. We planned to get a divorce; we had no idea the marriage banns would be posted."

Ingo chuckled. "The Countess found out."

Olga nodded, torn between desire and the consequences. She rose and stoked the fire. "She stormed into my mother's home, dressed in black, a veil over her face as if she was coming to a funeral. My mother was wonderful. When I mentioned divorce, the countess screamed, 'A von Schenck does not divorce. You should have thought about that before.'

"From then on his whole family despised me. Of course it was all my fault."

Ingo rose to help Olga shovel more coal into the stove.

"The baby was born. The Countess introduced me as her daughter-in-law, and calls Anyna 'little baroness.' She was a year old when Lothar received a small legacy from his aunt and went to Berlin, where he studied at the conservatory. We intended to leave Anyna behind in a home for children. She did not cry, but the sadness in her beautiful eyes broke my heart. I could not leave without her.

"In Berlin we lived in a small room. I sold cigarettes at the movies and gave piano lessons while Lothar attended classes. Then the war broke out. Lothar was drafted. Our building was bombed. That's how I got here."

He held her in his arms. "You're here for the time being. But thank you for sharing your secret."

"Don't think I'm unhappy," she said. "One of these days Lothar's compositions will be published. I like my job at the Esplanade. The men appreciate my music."

Their hands clasped, Olga admired his groomed fingernails. Everything about him was so appealing, even the cuts on his head and face.

"You are a mysterious young woman," he said, and looked deep into her eyes.

"I'm no fortune teller, but I can tell you there'll be no victory. Just unconditional surrender which will not be kind to the German people. You will never return to Riga." His eyes filled with tears.

Olga held him and rocked him. "You and I will survive. Father will see to it. In spirit, we shall always be together. I'll be with you and will guide you. Trust me."

She led him to the kitchen, where he rekindled the fire in the hearth. Soon tiny flames licked through the rings under the tea kettle. Once the water boiled, she poured it over dried apple peels and handed him a cup. "To our future."

He sipped the tea as if it were a holy sacrament.

Olga pulled up the black-out shades and watched dawn rise over the ancient roofs of the city. Smoke curled from the chimneys. Venus held onto her place in the sky until daylight faded her. Holding each other, they watched the new day come up that would take him away.

He recited a poem in his warm Saxon accent.

Oh happy the man who hopefully aspires
Out of this sea of error to arise!
What man knows not, is just what he requires;
What man knows, he cannot use in any wise.
But let us not by gloomy spirits mar
This hour radiantly serene!

His embrace tightened. She folded herself into it.

"Goethe was a mystic," he said. "He knew the world beyond, its glory and its abyss. He created Mephistopheles' tale. When things get rough, I hum Beethoven's Ninth and remember that he saw life in all its beauty despite his suffering."

"The *Ode to Joy*?" she wondered.

Ingo nodded. "He saw a world of brotherhood. You are my life, my sweet little Olychka."

The light in his eyes dazzled her with his love and desire. With a quick resolve, he covered her face with wild, random, artless kisses. Fired by their passion, their mouths pressed against each other. They kissed with carnal greed, making up for years of loneliness. Every cell in her body longed to be with him, to experience the climax only he could bring.

The bedroom door beckoned. Sweet temptation was but a few steps away.

His hands cupped her breasts, gently caressing her hard nipples. Panting, he promised, "I'll come back. This afternoon. As soon as ..."

The door opened and Anyna appeared in her flannel nightgown, rubbing her eyes. "Uncle Ingo? You're still here?" She ran toward him.

Ingo scooped her up, and carried her toward the window. "Good morning, little baroness." He kissed the rosy cheek and brushed the tousled strands from her face. "I hope you had happy dreams. We are watching the sunrise."

"Sunrise?" Anyna wondered, taking a closer look. "That's no sunrise. Only clouds. Dark, ugly clouds."

"Ah. That does not mean the sun is not there. It is always there, waiting for the clouds to go away so that it can shine for us. The world is as beautiful as you make it."

Anyna stared at the gray sky, a puzzled look in her eyes. "You're right, Uncle Ingo. I can see the sun and smell the flowers. Look, Mami. It's so bright, I need sunglasses."

Anyna clung to Ingo's neck, her head pressed against his. "Will you tell me another fairy tale?"

He put her down. "I'm afraid I must go. My carriage turned into a pumpkin. Just remember that the sun is always here for us."

In his greatcoat, his cap cocked, Ingo was no longer the officer Olga had met yesterday, but the man she had fallen in love with. His kiss would linger. In spirit they would be together.

He hugged Anyna.

"We'll miss you very much, Uncle Ingo," she said.

He opened the door to the cold, dark hall, blew a quick kiss, and ran off like a thief, skipping every other step.

At the bottom of the stairwell he waved back, then opened the heavy gate and was gone.

Olga and Anyna ran to the living room window, where they watched him run down the empty, snow-covered street.

Holding her daughter in her arms Olga whispered, "May God have mercy on you."

Chapter 4

By suppertime, Olga was pacing around the table in her cold living room like a donkey turning a wheel. Ingo would not come back. He couldn't if he tried, but her heart refused to accept it. Her soul longed stubbornly for another chance, a few more minutes together so that she could tell him about the pain he would be going through—the flames, the blood she had read in his cards. He had no choice. Only ignorant men and egomaniacs believed in their power. Ingo was neither. He knew what awaited him without her saying it, and struggled with that knowledge.

Olga massaged her cold arms and hands. The room with its large table and heavy chairs was again a foreign place, and reminded her of a morgue with her corpse waiting to be removed. The books on the shelves had Polish titles and smelled of mildew and dust. Exhausted, she dropped onto the worn sofa, where hours ago she had fallen in love with Ingo. The broken springs squeaked. The lamp on the piano cast its light on the black and white keyboard. Music was all she had left of him, the tunes they had enjoyed when she hardly knew his name. How could all that have happened in such a short while?

Ingo! With her eyes closed she imagined him in a crowded train heading toward the battlefield. One of the millions of men defending the Russian front. Ahead of him lay lethal cold, an unflinching enemy, and orders that made no sense.

A tremor shook her body. A golden light appeared at the dark ceiling, and spiraled toward her. "Father!" she whispered, feeling his spirit fill the room. Olga could not see him, but he was here. *I know how difficult it is for you to break the barrier that separates our worlds*, she said without uttering a sound. *Thank you for sending me Ingo. I miss him so.*

Waiting for his message, she poised her pencil over her notebook, then closed her eyes and fell into a trance.

It was not until her hand was done writing that she could read what she had scrawled across the page.

Dear child. I hurt when you suffer. God is good and just, but His plans are mysterious and unshakable. Bow your head to His omnipotence, and worship His all-encompassing love. Trust His wisdom and praise Him with devotion.

Ingo's love will help you through the war. The Evil One has set the world on fire. It will burn until it has destroyed all the world you know. Many will perish. Heed my warnings and thank God for His mercy and His protection. Desperate souls are easy prey.

If you do not hear from me, it is because I am not free to come to you. Still, I am always with you.

She whispered, "Thank you, Father," then sat down on the piano stool and played Mozart's *Agnus Dei.*

Anyna slipped in, wrapped her arms around her mother's neck, and leaned her head against her back. "You played that for Uncle Ingo, didn't you? He can't come tonight."

Olga picked up her little girl and carried her to the warm kitchen. How did she know?

Stasya stood at the iron stove and fried chopped onions in bacon. Olga had taken the evening off in case Ingo came.

"Did you see the Iron Cross, Stasya?" Anyna asked. "Uncle Ingo is a real hero."

Stasya shrugged. German heroes were her enemies.

Anyna held up her braids. "Look, Mami, Omi gave me new bows. I wanted to look pretty when Uncle Ingo came."

Olga gasped. Of course Anyna had told her grandmother about Ingo. The Countess would pry, but Olga had to get over being so sensitive, like a guilty youngster. She was a mother now, an adult, and had the right to live her own life. Didn't she?

She pulled out the chair where Ingo had sat a few hours ago. Her heart refused to accept that the doorbell would not ring. What good was her cherished independence now? Nothing but yawning emptiness, a cold bed, and an aching heart.

Ingo! You loved and accepted me. You did not blame me for what happened, but reassured me that I had been wronged. How I hate pious people who take pleasure in blaming others, rather than soothing their pain with a kind word.

Stasya poured boiling water from the teakettle over a pot of dried herbs. The steam rose into the diffuse light of the kitchen. Big drops ran along the sweating window pane. Olga stirred her tea. This morning Ingo had held her hand. He had kissed her and she had kissed him back in a way she had never kissed anyone before.

Anyna tugged at Olga's sleeve. "Omi said the Fuhrer will speak tonight."

"Really? Then we better listen to him. Perhaps he has some good news." Olga ignored the sneer in Stasya's dark eyes. If the roles were reversed, Olga would be serving Stasya. Her mother had scrubbed floors after the Bolsheviks conquered Latvia. The winner set the rules.

"Do you have a boyfriend, Stasya?" she asked, regretting the question. Her maid's private life was none of her business.

"My fiancé in England," she said defiantly.

"Oh? What's there for him?"

"England is free country."

"Free from whom? They're at war like us." Olga felt her resentment grow, not toward Stasya, but at the world that put them into such ridiculous circumstances. "What did you do before the war?"

"I was teacher. Germans not want teacher. No school for Polish children. Say we stupid Slavs." Their conversation helped take Olga's mind off waiting. She should have gone to work.

"You know, Stasya, if you don't want to work here, I'd be glad to get you a job somewhere else. Makes no difference to me. I'd rather be alone than look at your angry face all the time."

Stasya raised her hands in protest. "No, no. Is good here. Many Germans no good, but you good."

"Whatever that means," Olga said, and drank her bittersweet tea.

Stasya's frown mellowed. A smile would transform her face to beauty, but that eternal frown spoiled everything. She was an attractive young woman. Her thick dark hair had sharp, stylish waves that framed her oval face. The white collar of her silk blouse was fresh, and her dark cardigan of soft wool. She always wore silk stockings. Olga did not deal with the Polish black market. Not because it was dangerous, but because it undermined the war effort. In broad daylight, Polish boys jumped on the slow moving horse-drawn wagons and pushed cargo into the street, where their friends would pick it up and vanish before anybody could stop them. With the front in constant need of cannon fodder, the German police force dwindled away, giving the Poles more freedom.

The radio announced, "The Allied leaders, Churchill, Roosevelt, and Stalin are meeting in Casablanca. They demand unconditional surrender. After the news we shall broadcast a speech from our Fuhrer, live from the *Reichskanzlei* in Berlin."

Olga's mother, Mathilde, came in. Anyna jumped up and embraced her grandmother. "Come, come, Omi. The Fuhrer will speak in a few minutes."

"Easy, child, I'm not as young as your mother." She glanced at Olga, a stern look in her eyes. That was for "Uncle Ingo." She was quick to criticize, and never got around to praising anybody.

Olga pulled out a chair for her mother while the radio played the bombastic music that always introduced their Fuhrer.

After his traditional address of *Volksgenossen und Genossinnen*, Hitler talked about the Casablanca Conference. "Unconditional surrender? Never. Deliver every man, woman and child to their mercy? Not as long as there is a German Reich. Rest assured, we hold the winning trump in our hands. Our enemies are making their plans without us. We shall NEVER," he cried out, pausing for emphasis, "NEVER give in to their demands. Whoever toyed with the thought of our suing for peace, will know that our enemies leave us no options. They want our blood. Our miracle weapon is at hand. We shall fight for the glory of our *Vaterland*, the Third Reich. I ask you again, do you want butter or cannons?"

A roar of applause opted for cannons. "The Reich will show the world that we are a powerhouse fighting for our freedom. No Henry Morgenthau will reduce us to a nation of cavemen." The mesmerizing cadences that had conquered a nation and sent men off to fight for the Reich's noble mission was doing it again. He condemned communism and the world Jewry who manipulated the allies into fighting against Germany. After elaborating on the "shameful dictate of Versailles" he called on his people to "fight until final victory is ours. German men and women dedicate their lives to our noble cause. They deserve our highest praise.

"Fur Fuhrer, Volk und Vaterland, Sieg Heil"

Hundreds of enthusiastic voices thundered from the radio. *"Sieg Heil"* One again, Hitler's explosive speech had overwhelmed all rational thought and fired the people to more sacrifices—not that they had any choice. Win or die. The men in the trenches would pay for these words with their blood.

Ingo! My beloved Ingo. You will be saved.

Stasya dished out the soup, the corners of her mouth drawn. She knew the truth—Germany's defeat meant her liberation. Poles risked their lives when they listened to BBC on short wave radios. Those caught were executed, which didn't keep them from doing it.

A commentator said, "*Reichsfeldmarschal* Erwin Rommel relinquished his command of the Afrika Korps and is on his way home."

Relinquished, Olga wondered. More likely dismissed because he could not defeat the Allies, but was obliged to surrender like General Paulus. The Desert Fox had been caught in a trap set by his enemies and could not deliver the victory Hitler demanded – but he saved hundreds of thousands of lives.

Was that how Lothar was taken prisoner? He was no hero and was fond of America. He admired Adolf Hitler and believed in Aryan supremacy, yet knew how to stay away from the front lines. At a prison camp, he would profit from his command of English.

"The Red Army launched an offensive against the city of Kharkov," the announcer said. "The city is now declared a fortress."

Was Ingo heading for that inferno? Olga ate the bean and potato soup without tasting it. Would Kharkov be another Stalingrad? Had Hitler gone mad? Brute force could not win this war. Not against those cunning Russians and their guerillas. Women soldiers were known to be cruel beasts who tortured the men before killing them. Their thirst for blood and revenge had no limits.

Stasya ladled hot water from the well into metal containers that served as bed-warmers.

Anyna licked the last drop of soup from her spoon. "Thank you, Mami, for supper. I'll draw a picture for Uncle Ingo." She dabbed the corners of her mouth with her napkin.

"Honestly, Anyna," Mathilde said. "Is that what the Countess teaches you? Just wipe your mouth like everybody else. The Countess has a lot of fleas on her head." She took her napkin and wiped her wilted lips, then rolled it up and stuck it into the napkin ring. "God only knows what will become of you after the Countess is done teaching you to be a princess.

Where do you think you'll find a prince? You'd better become a regular girl who can attract a regular fellow. Somebody who can take care of you."

"I will marry an officer," Anyna said. "Like Uncle Ingo."

"Really? That is, should there be any left by the time you grow up." Mathilde heaved herself out of the chair. Though she was thin and only fifty-two, she looked and acted like an old woman. Her shapeless, colorless dresses and the old shawls she wrapped over her thin shoulders emphasized her indifference toward life.

"I better get back to the piano," Olga said, slipping into her coat. Ingo would not come, but she would play for him.

The fresh hyacinth she had bought for Ingo awaited her on the clean dining table. Stasya had cleared and waxed it. *Ingo! How can I bemoan my petty hardships while you, who respect the Russians, must bear the pain of sending your men to their deaths?* Olga leafed through the music of *Mephisto Waltz* and its dizzying array of notes. Had she actually played this? No wonder the people at the Esplanade forgot to breathe. Perhaps after working on it for a couple of years she might master it, but she could never come up with the grand performance Ingo had inspired. Better to stay away from Liszt entirely. The Evil One had brought Ingo. He would return and demand his due.

"Dear God, have mercy on us," she whispered, and played *Meditation*.

Four days later she found Ingo's postcard in the mailbox, and pressed it to her lips, then admired the handwriting and finally the picture of a statue of Chopin. She took it to her bedroom, looking into the mirror to see herself as if Ingo stood behind her. Her face had never been so alive and charming. Then she read.

Sweet Olga, Forgive me for not showing up. I know you waited. My men had searched for me. Nobody knew where I was. Your spirits protected me from being found out. You showed me life and love! Thank you for your patience and trust. You shall always be in my heart. Gratefully yours, Ingo.

Olga read it over and over again standing in the swath of light filtering through the lacy curtains. "Ingo!" she whispered, watching the wet snow drip from the eaves across the street. Spring was on its way.

The front door opened.

Olga slipped her treasure under the pillow before meeting her mother in the hallway.

"I got some potatoes and carrots for you," Mathilde said, panting. "Special allotment."

Olga took the shopping net, put it down among the shoes and boots, and helped her mother take off her padded coat. "Why do you always wear that silly looking hat? It's so old-fashioned."

"Because I like it," Mathilde said, going straight into the living room. "Do I criticize you for running around in your robe all day?"

Olga kissed her mother's wrinkled cheek. Since she'd left their home in Riga and been resettled in Poland, she acted as if her life no longer mattered. Her thinning gray hair, tucked into a bun, looked as unkempt as the tired features of her face. Her skin had lost its color. Shaggy brows, drooping lids, and that mournful expression in her eyes always expressed a state of grief. Olga and her sister Ottie could not cheer their mother up. Mathilde was homesick, and they had no remedy for that.

"Altmann got a shipment of children's shoes," she said on her way to the kitchen. "Didn't you get a coupon for Anyna? Her shoes are getting too tight."

Still in her coat, Mathilde settled down at the table, rubbing her cold hands. "What's all this about an Uncle Ingo? Was this so-called 'uncle' here? Overnight?"

Blood surged to Olga's face. "What if he was?" she snapped. "He's a young officer I met at the Esplanade. Don't you think I'm old enough to run my own life?"

"You should be. Still, age doesn't keep us from making blunders. People talk. Think of Herr Hauser. As block warden he must keep track of everybody in the building."

Olga shrugged. "Hauser? What does he have to do with anything?" She could barely keep her temper in check, and hated herself for reacting like that. Why couldn't people leave her alone? She was so sick of all this.

"For Heaven's sake, Olga, what's gotten into you? Had you told me about the mishap with Lothar in time, we could've..."

"What?" Olga winced. "Got rid of Anyna?"

Mathilde jerked back. "Of course not. It's just that we don't want any more mishaps."

"You are insulting me, *Mutter.*"

"Do we have to be enemies?"

Olga leaned across the table and stared into her mother's tired eyes.

"I knew you would pay for your mistake, Olga."

"So I did. I made my bed and I sleep in it. Are you happy now?"

"Why are you so jumpy today? I'm just trying to be helpful."

Olga drummed her fingers on the worn oilcloth. "I can do without that."

Mathilde slumped forward, and buried her head in her cracked hands. Olga leaned over her mother's shoulder. "I'm sorry, Mutter. I'm tired too. I can assure you, no more strangers in my apartment. So relax."

Mathilde sighed. "If the Countess finds out."

"She will. Anyna likes Ingo. He is so good with children. Unlike her father."

Mathilde dropped her thickly veined hands on the table. "I see. And you want me to believe you only talked to him?"

Olga seethed. "One more word and I'll scream!"

"I worry about you, Olga, and those spirits you deal with. Your Aunt Agnes went mad, remember? Let me warn you."

Olga fished for the coupon among the papers in the drawer of the cupboard. "Good for one pair of children's shoes. I'll send Anyna up as soon as she comes home."

The Esplanade was once again filled to capacity, mostly with soldiers who paid for their beer and schnapps with the extra coupons they received when on furlough. Young and not so young men sang along to their requests. By now most men were in uniform.

Lily Marlene brought out the dancers, their jack boots scraping against the floor. Giggles and guffaws. Loud toasts. The soldiers talked about Russian POW's who volunteered to fight with them against communism under a General Vlasov. Their arms locked, they swayed to the lilt of Olga's waltz. Everybody had a good time, or pretended to, ordered beer for Olga, and carried on as usual.

Frau Metzger came over to the piano. "What a night, Frau von Schenck. You got the boys swinging. Show them what they are fighting for. Any news from that lieutenant?"

Olga shook her head.

"Did you hear Dr. Goebbels's speech last night? Isn't he an inspiration? People applauded like mad. So did I." Frau Metzger wiped the sweat from her large round face. The food she received for many of those extra coupons ended up in her stomach. Her huge bosom strained against her white coat. "The miracle weapon is ready to go into action. Final victory is at hand. They'll chase those Russians back to where they belong." She blinked the smoke from her eyes. "My Wilhelm wants to move to Russia once we get rid of the Soviets," she said. "He likes it there. We'll clean up the country and make it a model place. Did it before. The Germans who emigrated to Russia and America a hundred years ago all got rich. That tells you something, doesn't it?" Her pungent body odor fouled the already stuffy air.

Frau Metzger's dream was to settle in Russia and work the virgin soil. Would Ingo move with her to Latvia? Johanna did not mean anything to him. Olga played a slow waltz. What was she thinking? Even if Lothar would grant her a divorced—which he probably would not, just to spite her—who would take a divorced woman in, with child yet? Not Ingo's narrow-minded mother. Olga might as well get that out of her mind right now. She played, *In der Heimat da gibt's ein Wiedersehn*—we shall meet again in our homeland. Only hers was gone.

Chapter 5

The following morning, Olga found Anyna in the kitchen. "Grandmaman will come for a visit," she said, and bit off a piece of rye bread with margarine and jam, washing it down with sips of warm milk from her enameled tin mug.

Olga swallowed. "How nice," she lied, sitting down at the table. "When? I'm very busy, you know." She checked Anyna's corduroy jumper. "It's getting too tight, my sweet. Perhaps Omi can widen it for you. I like the way she threaded that red ribbon through the loops. Very pretty. Matches your bows." The maroon jumper and her own salmon silk robe came from her friend, Lucie, whose discards were Olga's treasures. A matching pink sash cinched her waist. Would Ingo ever get to see Olga wear it, open the sash and explore what awaited him underneath? Crazy thought.

Indifferent toward Olga's uneasiness, Stasya set down a mug of steaming ersatz coffee, made of roasted grains and chicory. What did she think of Ingo's visit? She pretended that it did not take place.

"Grandmaman says you never visit her," Anyna said, shaking her little head. Her warm cheeks resembled apple blossoms.

"Did you tell her about Uncle Ingo?" Olga asked.

Anyna blushed, lowered her head, and licked the jam from her small fingertips. "All I said was..." her eyes met Olga's, open and filled with pride, "that he is from Dresden and a real hero. And that we saw the sun rise even when it was cloudy."

Olga nodded. The damage was done. "That's all right, my sweet. You told the truth. Only sometimes ..." How could she explain that the Countess fished for morsels of gossip to use as reproaches?

"I like Uncle Ingo," Anyna said. "He is the best uncle I ever knew. Even better than Uncle Gottfried."

Olga chuckled. "I don't know about that. But he is very nice."

"He is a hero, right Mami?"

"That he is. Saw many a bloody battle." Olga remembered him saying, "I must shoot people I do not know or hate." From the time Hitler and Stalin had taken charge of their countries, they had locked horns, determined to wipe out the other. Sitting in their palatial offices, they sacrificed millions of men for their mad ambitions. Ingo was one of them, fighting a war Germany could not win.

Anyna wiggled her front tooth. "Look, Mami, it's loose. Will the tooth fairy come?"

Olga loved that sweet mouth and the complete trust in her daughter's adorable brown eyes. She tested the tooth. "You are right. It'll come out in a couple of days. You'll get new teeth. Larger ones that'll fit into your growing head."

"As big as yours?" Anyna asked, folding her napkin, then placing it beside her empty plate. "I want to look like you, Mami."

"You are lovely the way you are."

Disappointed, Anyna lowered her head. "Do you think I'll look like Grandmaman? In that beautiful portrait of her when she was young?"

"You carry her blood."

"That's what she says. She says if I act right, everybody will know I'm a baroness." Anyna rose from the table and kissed Olga's cheek, leaving a wet spot. "Thank you for breakfast, Mami. Did you see my new shoes?" She lifted her little foot and showed her ankle-high boots. "Aren't they pretty? Omi said she will wrap my braids around my head like a Bavarian girl. Where is Bavaria?"

"In Germany."

"Grandmaman says in summer she will move to Bavaria. It's much nicer there than here in Poland. There are lakes and high mountains with snow that never melts. The Alps. Did you know that, Mami? Can we move there too?"

Not if she could help it, Olga thought, hugging her little girl. With the Countess and Lothar out of her life she would be free at last. "For that we need special permission. This is our assigned place."

At the sink, Anyna stretched toward the faucet and wet the little sponge she would clean her slate board with after the teacher had checked the homework. Paper was rationed; only the older students had copybooks.

After seeing Anyna off, Olga went to the living room and pulled Gershwin's *Rhapsody in Blue* from the stack of notes on the dining table. The piece, with its novel rhythm and jazzy approach, fascinated her. Music of the new world was just what she needed. A new world. Why should she care that it was written by a Jew? There might even be a day when she could play it in Germany. In a new Germany!

Lothar had bought the sheet music in Berlin before the Third Reich began censoring everything that had been composed by Jews. Lothar had played jazz, and once enjoyed showing off his knowledge on the subject. He and his mother had created their own world they considered superior to the rest. Lothar was her darling son, whom she preferred to her children from her second marriage. They barely tolerated Olga as the mother of Lothar's child, a child he tended to deny.

Olga pounced on the keyboard but could not release her frustration over the trap she found herself in. Flipping through the notes, she remembered Berlin—the overcrowded room where Lothar always occupied the piano so that she could not play, though he knew how much she longed to work on her music. Every time the baby cried, he would take it out on her. "Can't you get that brat to shut up? How do you expect me to work?"

Sharing the small kitchen and bathroom with the eternally grumpy landlady had always been an ordeal. No matter what Olga did, how carefully and quietly she prepared their meals, the landlady would exclaim, "How can anybody be so clumsy?" Olga still felt the intimidation. How glad she was when a bomb destroyed the damn building. Justice was served. What difference did it make that her meager possessions were consumed? That detestable part of her life went up in the sacrificial flames. Even her music. Her favorite note books were saved in her emergency suitcase. Lothar had already been drafted and did not miss anything, least of all her. She had felt great relief when he had been called up. For the first time in her life, Olga was on her own.

Now she had her own place. So it was a Polish or Jewish home—it was hers now, and had a piano she could play on as much as she pleased. What a blessing. Then Father had come to her again. Now that Ingo had come into her life, she couldn't ask for more.

In celebration, she played Chopin's *Grand Polonaise*. In her mind's eye she saw Ingo riding in an armored vehicle. Snow flurries whirled and hid him from Russian tanks that lurked in the distance.

"Watch out, Ingo. They are setting a trap."

Olga practiced *Rhapsody*, determined to master it and feel Gershwin's liberated world of movement, pulsating with a kind of life she had never known. Some day she would be there. How could Lothar compare his macabre, dissonant sounds—the outbursts of a sick mind—to genius? Once she mastered *Rhapsody*, she would enter a new world. Germany might win the war, but then Lothar would come home. If Germany lost, the Russians would come. *Rhapsody* would be the key to her life, not the *Mephisto Waltz*.

Her fingers grew stiff from cold. Rubbing her hands, she went to the kitchen wondering when the Countess would show up.

Lucie came for a visit, dressed, as usual, in a fur coat and cap. She landed in Olga's embrace. "Did you hear that Hitler declared total war?" she asked in an agitated voice. "Fight to the last man. Do you know what that means? They'll take Gottfried. I'm out of my mind while he pretends everything is fine." She went to the living room and sat down at the table. "Reads those stupid newspapers from cover to cover and tells me, 'Nothing but lies.' So much for male logic. We should make the most of our time together." Her voice broke up. Sobbing, she dropped her head on her arm.

Olga, still in her flannel house coat, her curls tied into a red scarf, stroked the fur on Lucie's shoulder. Stasya had lit a fire in the living room, but the musty chill lingered on.

"There's nothing we can do," Olga said softly.

Lucie perked up. "What do you mean, there's nothing we can do? Olga, only you can say things like that. We can't just let those men sitting in their fine homes in Berlin tell us to sacrifice our men." She fished a hanky from her muff and blew her nose. "I must calm down. Gottfried hates hysterical women."

"But he loves you," Olga said, lighting a candle stump. The smell of sulfur rose in the air. The Evil One was around.

"So he does. He's probably as concerned as I am. But why can't we talk about it?"

Because you always get carried away and make a scene, Olga thought, lighting a candle.

"I bet he discusses everything with those women he deals with. Flirts with them as if he were single. You get to accompany his voice. He adores you. What do I have? A man who won't talk to me. Either adds stupid numbers, sings, or reads the paper. And at night I can't get close to him for fear I'll get pregnant again. What an awful life."

Olga wished she had that kind of a problem, or should she count her blessings? "Let's see what the cards have to say."

"Great idea." Lucie picked up the deck from the table, shuffled, then cut it into three stacks.

They sat in silence. The candle flickered. Somebody was here. Not Father. His light appeared on the ceiling. Who was it?

Olga turned inward. "I see great tension around you, and some unresolved questions concerning a man. I am to tell you not to worry about him. It will be resolved to your satisfaction. In the near future you will take a long trip and derive great benefits from it. You will also experience some unpleasant events. But don't worry, everything will work out. You will find new opportunities. Your guardians are here. Trust them.

"There is a pain in your heart that need not be there. But the pain in your belly is real. Consult a good physician. Do it soon. He will prescribe a cure. Follow his advice conscientiously.

"There is a woman in your life who pesters you with falsehood and jealousy. That problem is hers, not yours. Evil minds disrupt our lives like dark storm clouds. Bless her and let her go.

Going into the future I see a happy summer. The storm clouds gathering will not reach you for some time. Make good use of your life. Prepare yourself for change.

This is a good time for major decisions. Always trust your intuition; it has served you well in the past, and will serve you in the future. Do not let other people influence you. Remember, God is with you. He loves you and will protect you."

Olga returned from her trance and looked up.

Lucie smiled. Her forget-me-not eyes looked bright again. She blushed, not from embarrassment but from the warmth of emotions. Her

49

smile was different, pensive and thoughtful, traits Olga had never seen in her boisterous friend.

"Thank you, my dear." she said cheerfully. "You are right about the pain in my belly. I keep ignoring the cramps. Dr. Landmann can't find anything. Which doesn't mean a thing. All he can see is a pregnancy in its sixth month, or an acute case of measles. I will consult the famous Dr. Sauerbruch in Berlin. He will know what is wrong and find a cure. And then I will see my brother, Sigurd. Maybe he can get Gottfried's deferment extended before it comes up, keep Gottfried's file hidden—he's on the draft board."

Lucie jumped up and hugged Olga. "Olinka, you saved my life. Remember when you told me that my little Hans had to see a doctor for a pain in his arm and you insisted I go straight to the hospital? Thank God you did. He would've died of a ruptured appendix." Chuckling she raised her artfully drawn eyebrows. "The things one gets to experience when you have four children. Walter is a real handful. At twelve he thinks he's an adult and wants to volunteer for the Army. Am I ever glad he isn't older."

The candle no longer flickered. "Thank you, Father," Olga whispered.

Lucie picked up the cards again and sat down. "Let me do the yes-or-no spread," she said, and shuffled, then placed the cards in two vertical rows. They had played this game in their childhood, asking whether a certain boy had some interest, would go to the beach during their summer vacation, or get a new dress for their birthday.

When the last pair came up Olga said, "The answer is, 'yes'."

"I don't believe it," Lucie cried out, and swept the cards from the table. Her fur toque landed on the floor. "It can't be."

"What can't be?" Olga asked, holding Lucie's hand to keep her from wiping the sheet music off the table as well. "It's just a game."

Lucie covered her face with her hands. "I asked whether Gottfried will be drafted."

Olga felt a jolt. Gottfried. Yes, his time would come, but not now. "But you just said that your brother will help. Didn't the cards say you will spend a beautiful summer? That didn't mean alone. Perhaps you can get a significant appointment for Gottfried that will get him a dispensation."

"Like what? You have to be a big shot in the party. Or a scientist."

"You can do it, Lucie. You always get what you want." Including Gottfried, Olga thought.

Lucie twisted her leather glove, then straightened her back and raised her chin in the pose of a queen. "You're right," she said defiantly, her eyes gleaming.

Olga shook her head, amazed by the sudden transformation. "You missed your calling. Play the Queen of Sheba in Berlin."

"Thank you, Olinka." She raised her hands as to a crowd. Perfume wafted into the room. "You are right. I'll prove to those empty-headed party bigwigs that they will not get my husband. There is at least one Baltic German woman they cannot push around." She lifted herself into a stance of conquest and flaunted her famous smile. "Men are so vulnerable to flattery. I tell you, Olga, dropping a handkerchief is more effective than wiggling your fanny. That's a fact. Even the high and mighty jump when you give them a sidelong glance. It's an old, old trick, Olinka."

Olga laughed so hard that she had tears in her eyes. Would Ingo fall for Lucie too?

"I should've been an actress," Lucie said, as if Olga didn't know that from the time she had met her years ago in Riga. "And you a concert pianist. Anything but fall for that worthless Lothar." She rose and watched the snowflakes fall against the window pane. "How could you let him get you pregnant? All he wanted was your inheritance. The Countess, that old whore..."

"Lucie!" Olga protested, and then wondered why. "You can't say that!"

"It's true and you know it. Now there's an actress for you. She plays her game to perfection. Knows how to make people feel inferior. Clever woman. We should take lessons. You must stand up to her, Olga, and tell her to go to hell." Lucie stood at the window silhouetted against the gray sky. Her vitality had returned. "Olinka, this was fun. I came here worried to death." She picked up her toque and cocked it, then slipped into her gloves. "You are lucky Gottfried didn't fall for you. He would've wrung you dry. He needs a wall of resistance and a strong hand, else he's like a bee that flies from flower to flower. With women throwing themselves at his feet, all he has to do is pick them up and give them what they're begging for." She crossed her arms. "You would've kissed his feet and waited for his kick. Some people beg for abuse."

No doubt Lucie had noticed Olga's adoring eyes toward Gottfried. Now, with Ingo in her life, Lucie had nothing to worry about. She probably never did—Olga was no threat to Gottfried's passionate love for her.

"From now on practice saying no!" Lucie ordered. "But I must go. See you after my trip to Berlin. Ingo sounds like a great man. Keep me posted. Let him be chivalrous. Don't give anything away. Men don't appreciate hand-outs. They're hunters and warriors. Let him earn it."

Ingo's letter arrived the following Friday. Olga dropped her groceries on the kitchen table, kissed Anyna, and took her treasure to the bedroom where she threw herself on her bed and pressed the field post envelope to her face.

March 12, 1943

My darling Olychka!

Sorry for taking so long in writing to you. I know you are waiting for news. Yes, I arrived at my new quarters in Russia in one piece—the usual skirmishes, train wrecks and whatnot. Throughout the long trip I only thought of you. You are always with me. A new experience I cherish. I never expected it. I can see now why people enjoy writing letters. That too is a new experience. Out here, in the Russian winter, writing can be difficult as a warm room, privacy, and a table are not always available.

Amazing how destiny joined us. Considering the circumstances, my meeting you and my transformation are a miracle. I was so disgusted that I couldn't keep my mouth shut. I just had to scream. I'll never know why I picked on you. You endured it all with the consideration of a saint. When you played The Mephisto Waltz *we both experienced something miraculous. I sensed a transfiguration. Did you feel that too? From then on our destiny was linked. I am still thinking about all you said, especially your card reading. You have the true gift of clairvoyance. I keep hearing your voice. It's true. It comes whenever we find ourselves in a difficult situation. Demons took over our world. They are not earthbound and are beyond our reach.*

The best things in life come so unexpectedly. Now that I've found you, I know what I missed. Please accept me as your friend and soul mate, if that is not too presumptuous to ask.

In Warsaw I found a park that had the Chopin's statue— you saw on the postcard I sent you. Sitting on a bench I imagined your playing his immortal music. Your soul was with me. I imagined your dimpled smile and kissed your lips.

Anyna is a lucky girl. She gets to hear your wonderful music. Thank you for that unforgettable evening we shared. It brought me salvation and healed my bleeding heart.

Please write soon, and forgive my rudeness.

A special kiss for my little baroness. I wished I could come over and play with her. Unfortunately I don't expect any leave for a long time.

Affectionately yours, Ingo.

Olga folded the letter, slipped it under her pillow, and danced into the kitchen.

Anyna looked up from her slate board where she practiced M's. The chalk squeaked. "Did you get a letter from Uncle Ingo?"

"Yes, yes, my sweet. He sends you greetings."

Chapter 6

The shrill sound of the doorbell cut rudely into Olga's piano practice. Her heart thumped. The Countess. That was all she needed. What a pest.

The bell rang out again, a long demanding shriek. She had heard Olga playing the piano.

Olga rose reluctantly, and headed for the door like a victim awaiting punishment. Where was Stasya? Not that it mattered.

The bell rang out again. When would the Countess understand that Olga had no intention of catering to her mother-in-law? The bell rang in quick successions demanding to be answered.

Olga clenched her teeth, tied up her robe and yanked the door open. "Lucie? Gottfried?" she mumbled, her cheeks flushed. "I thought..."

Lucie hugged Olga. Things always turned out differently than she thought. "We just got back from Berlin," Lucie said. "Thought we'd stop by on our way home. We knew you'd eventually open the door." Her fur coat smelled of perfume, soot and cigarette smoke from the train.

Gottfried embraced Olga like a sister.

"How did it go?" Olga asked. "Did you get a deferment?"

"Yes," Lucie said, releasing Olga's embrace. "We're so lucky. Not officially, mind you. But Sigurd assured us that he can swing it. Hitler is serious about using every able-bodied man for the war effort. Why not take some of those big-bellied party studs? Dodging bullets would do them a world of good. You wouldn't even want to know what is going on behind the scenes. They plunder and kill, right Gottfried?"

Gottfried pulled out a chair.

Olga cleared away her books and papers.

"Air raids every night, and still life goes on."

Olga visualized the ruined buildings. People staring at what used to be their home, then taking their children and the emergency suitcase and reporting to the transit station to find temporary beds. Olga remembered coming out of the air raid shelter. The building she had lived in was gutted, a blessing in disguise. She had been evacuated to Litzmannstadt and assigned an apartment in the same building as her mother.

Lucie talked about the parties that resumed as soon as the all clear sounded. Since the district about to be bombed was announced, those living in a different part of the city went on celebrating.

"You'd be amazed how Berliners adapt to the raids. When you meet them in the morning they act as if nothing happened and go to work."

Olga cleared the ashes in the stove while Gottfried crumpled up a newspaper and lit it with a match. "That's about all this paper is good for," he said, watching the fire rise into lively flames.

"Things don't look good, do they?" she whispered.

"We went to five o'clock tea dances," Lucie said. She sat at the table and watched Olga and Gottfried build a fire. "The cabarets are funnier than ever. Furtwangler conducted Brahms. World-class performance. It's good to be in the real world."

Olga listened to her friend rave about the big city, glad that she had this apartment. "I'm running out of coal. We don't usually heat this room."

"I'll send you some over," Gottfried said. "I never thought I'd be dealing in the black market. But then, why not? Our sacrifices cannot save us…"

Olga looked at the door. "You can talk, Gottfried. There's nobody here." He looked pale and tired. The furrow between his thick brows had deepened. Though they always traveled first class, wagon lits were no longer available. Luckily, the trains still ran on schedule and on time.

"If only this war would stop," Lucie said, casting a plaintive glance at Gottfried. Olga would miss him too. Not as much as Ingo. Would anybody notify her should he be killed?

"Everybody talks about the miracle weapon," Olga said, rubbing her cold hands. The room was still freezing cold.

"People believe in it as if it were the second coming," Lucie said. "Final victory! Glory to the Reich. Our Fuhrer, our savior. Don't get me started." She picked up Anyna's sketch pad and tore out a page. "Back in '38 I thought the world of Hitler. Gottfried did not agree."

"All this *Heil Hitler* was ridiculous," he said. "Now we're so used to it that we do it automatically, like saying good-morning."

"The whole problem started when the Poles refused that Corridor," Lucie said, getting up and going to the tile-covered stove. "Hitler's a charmer and a flirt; he hypnotizes you like a snake. You should have seen him. Thousands of people screaming. Hundreds of red flags in the air like sails. SS goose-stepping with the precision of the corps de ballet. What a show."

She caught Gottfried's eye.

He shrugged and leaned against the straight back chair, dwelling on his own thoughts while Lucie dramatized her experiences. She loved being on stage. "Now we're cornered. Berliners act like the people during the last days of Rome. Parties and fun is all they can think of. Sigurd threw one in our honor, right Gottfried? I love Berlin. Litzmannstadt is such a dump." She dropped the corners of her lovely mouth.

The fire slowly took the chill out of the room. Rain had set in, and splashed against the window pane.

"How I miss my friends and relatives," Lucie said. "We should have moved to Posen. But you know Gottfried. He believes in following orders. *'Fuhrer befiel, wir folgen Dir.'*"

He ignored her comments.

"The 'Eden' is as elegant as ever," she raved. "Most of the men are in uniform. Gottfried looked out of place in his suit and tie. You never know what people think. Of course, there are men working on important defense contracts. The V-1 or V-2 didn't change a thing. Churchill is not about to throw in the towel."

"We need a defense against those Katyushas," Gottfried said.

Olga remembered the soldier's joke about Katyusha's serenading Ferdinand, the German super tank. Where was Ingo now? Dodging bombs? "Let me make some tea," she said.

"Don't bother," Lucie said. "We can't stay. Gottfried's mother is staying with the children, spoiling them rotten."

"Why didn't Stasya open the door?" Lucie asked. "You can't let her do whatever she wants. She is your maid, remember?"

"I'd rather not fuss at her," Olga said, wishing Lucie would not meddle in her affairs. She was right, only Olga had no way of making Stasya do anything.

"Then, for heaven's sake, get rid of her. I bet she's part of the underground. She makes no bones about how she feels about us. You better watch out, Olga. Don't think she appreciates your generosity. She's the enemy."

"Did you see Dr. Sauerbruch, Lucie?" Olga asked to change the subject. She hated all this talk about the war.

"I did. He diagnosed gallstones. I must have surgery before they rupture. It scares me to death. But I can't ignore it. Dr. Sauerbruch said that I'm risking my life by not taking care of it." She clutched her belly and moaned. "Why is all this happening to me?"

Olga hugged Lucie's trembling shoulders. "Let's play a song before you leave," she said, sitting down at the keyboard. After playing the opening measure of Gottfried's favorite piece he joined her and sang.

Alle Tage ist kein Sonntag,
Alle Tage gibt's keinen Wein,
Aber Du sollst alle Tage recht lieb zu mir sein.
Und wenn ich einmal tod bin, sollst Du denken an mich,
Auch am abend, eh Du einschlafst,
Aber weinen darfst Du nicht.

Olga heard the sadness in his voice and swallowed her tears. He knew that he would not survive the war. The lump in her throat cut off her voice.

Every Day is not a Sunday. Every day we can't drink wine.
But, every day you will be mine.
When I am gone, do think of me.
Close your eyes, but do not cry.

That night, Olga held Anyna as if she could protect her from the tragedy that would strike them.

"Are you all right, Mami? Did something bad happen?" She wiggled out of the embrace.

"No, my sweet. I just want you to know how much I love you." Olga tucked the comforter around Anyna's shoulders. "Everything is fine, my sweet. Good night."

Anyna blew a kiss before Olga switched off the light.

Back in the living room she played *Liebestraum*. The music transported her to Ingo. The tremor in her hand announced Father. Olga lit a candle and poised her pencil over the notebook. "Father, please protect us. We need you. Don't let Satan take over our lives."

A bright light appeared. Golden circles spiraled against the dark ceiling. Her hand wrote faster and faster as the candle flickered. The grandfather clock ticked, loud and ominous and then darkness returned.

"Thank you, Father, for your love and your blessing."

The message was written in a meticulous script, not her usual scribbles.

Dear child! God is merciful and wise. His light shines upon you. Some day you will join us, but first you must fulfill the life destined for you. You were chosen to experience the magnificence of God's light few living people get to see. God rewards the innocent. Martyrs and war heroes have a sanctified place. Their sins are forgiven. God loves every soul. Trust His wisdom and remember that suffering on earth leads to eternal light and God's grace.

You are in God's hands, made in His image. I cannot prevent the pain you will experience. Keep your heart pure and your mind clear so that God can dwell in your soul. Whenever you leave your body, make sure that Satan cannot enter it. He is sly and takes advantage of vulnerable people. As his power grows so does his appetite. Desperate souls believe his false promises.

Farewell, my child. Your loving Father.

"Father!" she cried out. No answer. Satan's gruesome head appeared. His claws reached for her. "Ingo is with me," he taunted.

"You are lying. That is not Ingo."

"Then where is he?"

"Leave him alone. You have no power over him."

A stranglehold crushed her chest. "Father!" she screamed. "Father, help!" Darkness. Silence. "Almighty God, do not forsake us. We are at Your mercy. Please protect Ingo."

Olga barely noticed the spring sun shining through the open window of the living room. Time had ceased to exist. Lost in her séances and music, she barely made it to the Esplanade. Stasya took care of Anyna, dressed and fed her, and made sure the child got to school on time. She even taught Anyna Polish songs and nursery rhymes. On Tuesdays, Anyna visited the Countess where she learned proper manners.

Sitting by the open window, Olga inhaled the fragrant air from the linden tree.

The doorbell rang.

"Gottfried! What a surprise." They embraced. With his office only a few blocks away, he came over whenever he felt like having a cup of tea and a chat. In his light summer suit and felt hat he still looked so debonair.

"Any liqueur left?"

Curious, she smoothed her floral dress. "I still have the bottle you gave me. And thanks for the potatoes."

"Life is so precious when you know that your time is running out," he said, opening the bottle and then pouring the thick berry liqueur into crystal cordials glasses. "To you." It did not sound cheerful, nor did he take the usual small sips, but emptied the glass into his mouth, then filled it again. "The Allies signed a treaty in Casablanca," he said after he had swallowed. "They demand unconditional surrender." He put the glass down. "Hitler will fight to the last man."

Olga stared at him, unable to comprehend the meaning of it all. "The miracle weapon..." was all she could say. It sounded downright stupid.

He tipped the bottle back and forth, his mind far away. Did he see himself among those millions of soldiers fighting for their lives? Of course Hitler was not about to surrender to the Allies, who probably wanted him along with the Reich.

Gottfried gazed into her eyes. He did not need to say anything. The way he kissed her hand spoke for him. "Our souls are immortal," she said, "and so is music. It motivated me to do my best when I accompanied your wonderful voice."

"The only consolation left," he said, and pulled the chair back for her to sit down next to him. "Yes, our music will be a cherished memory when they call me up and I'll be doing push-ups and all the other exercises that are supposed to make me a good soldier." His chuckle hurt, yet there was nothing she could say that would ease the inevitable.

"Back in Riga you meant the world to me. Music allowed me to talk to you about my feelings."

He patted her hot cheek. "I was not deaf, and appreciated the wonderful accompaniment. Had I said anything, I would've either given you false hope or hurt your feelings. Yes, our music was divine, but I was not in love with you."

Did he say 'in love?' Olga had never heard him talk about such intimate matters. Gottfried was undergoing the kind of change that came with great emotional upheaval, with pain and loss.

"Can you understand," he said, and placed his groomed hand on hers, "that touching you would have ruined our friendship?"

Deeply embarrassed, Olga stacked up the sheet music she had scattered all over the table. Used to his aloofness, his sudden intimacy left her at a loss. "I'm ashamed," she said. "I really didn't mean to…"

"It's all right. We don't have to hide our thoughts and feelings anymore. Not only are we old enough to talk openly, we may not have much time left to see each other."

The gravity of his statement hit hard. He knew that he would not survive the war and so did she. "You are right, of course. I appreciate your bringing it up. With Ingo in my heart now, I have learned to talk about my feelings. And you, Gottfried, will always be my closest friend, the love of my youth, and my most treasured partner in music."

He pulled her over to him. Pain, fear and doubt were gone. "Without love there is no life, there is only living," he said. "Insight comes somewhat later, but not too late. We lived and enjoyed what life had to offer. Lucie expects another baby. It'll be hard on her."

Olga nodded. "She is strong. By the way, it'll be a boy."

"Really? How do you know?" He chuckled. "Silly question. I should know better by now. My Olinka is a clairvoyant. What's in the cards for me?"

She shrugged. "I only know that your son will be blond and tall."

"Have you ever been wrong?" he wondered. "I mean, dead wrong?"

"Not to my knowledge."

Stasya knocked and entered. "A letter for you."

After Stasya left Olga asked, "Do you believe the Poles might attack us?"

"No chance. The Gestapo is alive and well."

"What about the Jews?" she asked, seeing him to the door.

"That's a matter we'd better not talk about."

As soon as he left, Olga went to the kitchen, picked up the mail, and took it to the window sill where she had once waved goodbye to Ingo. The sun warmed her back. Birds chirped in the linden tree. A coachman clucked his tongue.

My beloved Olychka, she read.

Your letters are my sanctuary. At times your closeness overwhelms me. Your clairvoyance is miraculous. I see you at home, kissing Anyna good night, or entertaining frightened soldiers on their way to a very difficult task. Katyusha is on a rampage these days and fires off with fury. We are preparing for an offensive. Shells or no shells, we follow orders.

I am dreaming of a time when love will replace death. These innocent little wildflowers remind me how beautiful life could be if we were not set on destroying each other. Since I cannot think of new words to describe my love for you, I'll repeat the ones I wrote before. I love you with all my heart. I've loved you from the moment we sat down on that old sofa with the broken spring. You have no idea how hard it was for me not to take you into my arms and keep you there forever. That would have ruined my chances of ever seeing you again. Now I look back on the most memorable night of my life. Your love keeps the humanity in my heart.

Olga choked back her tears.

Should anything happen to me, I will always be with you. Our souls are one. Yes, I once mocked that song. Now I know what it is all about. A beautiful line indeed.

Your sweet face surrounds me with its gentle beauty. How I wish I could run my hands through your thick curls, look into those mysterious eyes that can see beyond, and kiss your lips. I imagine the softness of your body and dwell in its warmth. Do you realize how much I depend on you? Your faith gives me the power of a Hercules and Samson combined. I never thought I would confide in a woman, but you opened my heart so that my love can pour out to you, without shame or embarrassment.

If you search your heart, dear Olychka, you will find that we love each other. You are that special woman for me. Your music sings in my heart together with the love call of the birds. Sounds banal, I know. But can you deny it?

She looked at the blue sky and lazy white clouds hanging suspended above the old roofs across the street. *I love you, Ingo. More than anything in the world.*

She kissed the paper then clutched it to her heart. Ingo. My beloved Ingo.

Should I be spared and get home leave, as unlikely as it seems, would you accept my love? I know you are not free. Still, it would mean so much, knowing that you await me at the other end of the world. Remember, I love you. Ingo.

With the sun on her face, Olga closed her eyes. *Dear God, let us be together. Just once.*

On the 5th of July, the news announced that Army Groups Center and South had launched an offensive against the Red Army that would push the Soviets back and assure the Reich a decisive advantage.

Four months too late, Olga thought. The Russian summer was short and half of it already gone. The Devil played his tricks again. This battle would be bountiful for him.

She closed the shutters and stretched out on her bed.

Focusing on her heartbeat and breathing, she saw a blue light rise from the darkness. Ingo emerged. He wore a dusty uniform, helmet in hand, and lead his men through a wheat field. Bullets exploded around them. Dark clouds gathered. Did he see the Russian tank rolling toward him? A German Stuka spotted it. The pilot fired. Ingo dropped to the ground. The tank fired at the plane as Ingo scuttled away. Flames flared up. Ingo and his men reached the forest. Father had protected him.

Ingo. I feel you. Some day we'll be together. Our souls are one.

A light spread through the room. The pink hue transformed to a deep blue, covered the whole ceiling, flickered, and vanished. What did it mean? Father?

Chapter 7

February 1944.

The radio above the kitchen table blasted out Franz Liszt's bombastic *Les Preludes*. Finally a successful military strike, Olga hoped, and exchanged curious glances with her mother. They sat at the kitchen table watching Stasya put down plates and cutlery. Anyna drew a snowman. During the Blitz, special announcements had been broadcast daily, sometimes several times a day, whenever the Wehrmacht took another Polish, and later Russian, town. Big strikes at sea were announced with the name of the enemy ship sunk, and her gross registered tonnage. After the Bismarck met her fate, the announcements diminished. During the battle of Stalingrad, people sat on pins and needles worrying about their loved ones. When the city fell, a heavy black silence crushed the land. Sparse victory headlines could no longer rouse their spirits, nor could Hitler's raging speeches rekindle the fire that had once driven them to heroic deeds. Unlike Ingo, who had thrown a fit at the Esplanade, people sat in darkness and waited for the miracle weapon.

Ingo was out there on the freezing steppes of Russia, while Lothar enjoyed the comforts of an American POW camp. Was that justice?

No matter how the media presented the news, it did not look good. The *Volkischer Beobachter* could stretch the gains and minimize the losses only so far. The war had turned from offensive to defensive. Allied air strikes leveled German cities. Civilian casualties mounted at an alarming rate.

Was the miracle weapon finally launched, Olga wondered? Had somebody invented a snowsuit to kept the men in Russia from freezing to death? Mathilde knitted socks for Ingo. Over the past two years, the Wehrmacht had lost almost as many men to the cold as they did on the battlefield. The soldiers stuffed whatever they could under their inadequate uniforms while the Russians enjoyed the warmth and comfort of their quilted jackets and felt boots. Mathilde's knitting needles clicked to the crescendo of Liszt's stirring music.

Stasya stood at the stove and checked the vegetables. Onions sizzled in a pan and gave off an appetizing aroma.

Olga threaded her needle. Anyna's green velveteen jumper was getting too short. In her mind's eye, she saw Ingo crouched in a dugout awaiting an attack.

Watch out. They're coming. Run to the left.

Lucie's pregnancy had given Gottfried another deferment. In her dream last night, Olga saw Germany sink into a sea of flames. Would it swallow her too?

The music drummed out a grand finale.

Lucie no longer complained about being bored in this city. The Poles sold the goods they stole from the Germans back to them on the black market and made the most of life.

"Enjoy the war," had become a popular slogan as supplies were running out. Olga lived in her own world. The future had no meaning for her.

Anyna drew a picture of the coal thief carrying a black sack. The poster hung on every street corner and kiosk. Olga admired the sly expression that warned people of spies and thieves.

"Mami, please write, '*Psst! Der Kohlenklau geht um!*'" She pushed her pad across the table. "Claudia's daddy was arrested. He came home on leave from Russia. She is not allowed to talk to anybody about it. But I'm her best friend." Anyna frowned. "He's in the SS and has an iron cross like Uncle Ingo."

Mathilde looked up, but did not say anything.

"Claudia's father is Baltic German, like us."

Olga watched Stasya's reaction. Had the man been caught supporting the Polish underground, protecting a Jew, or listening to BBC? Perhaps he had bought things on the black market. Lately everybody was suspect. All kinds of people disappeared. She poured boiling water over the dried linden blossoms they had gathered last summer.

A crisp voice on the radio announced, "*Das Oberkommando der Wehrmacht gibt bekannt*, the Russian winter offensive was launched. The enemy was caught by total surprise. The Wehrmacht broke through the

Russian lines and are now on their way to Kirovograd. Kiev will be retaken shortly." A zesty march celebrated the victory.

As expected, *Reichspropagandaminister* Dr. Goebbels assured the German people that, "this is the moment we were waiting for. Once again the Reich will prove our supremacy. We strike hard and pitiless. Fight with dedication and commitment and send our enemies packing. The miracle weapon is at hand and show the likes of Henry Morgenthau and his gang of war mongers that his plan to reduce our nation to cavemen will make him look like the fool he is. All those who harbor thoughts of defeat listen to me. We shall never concede to unconditional surrender. Never!" His proclamation thundered over the airwaves like the cloven hooves in the *Mephisto Waltz*.

"We shall cleanse the world of Jews and communist. We shall eliminate their dirty work." He paused allowing the applause to ebb. "We herewith declare total war. The men at Casablanca who signed that infamous treaty made their account without us. Our forces are on the road to final victory. Never again shall this nation bow its heads to shameful dictates.

"We appeal to every German to dedicate his life to this sacred and noble mission. *Fur Fuhrer, Volk und Vaterland, Sieg Heil.*"

Olga imagined the short man standing on a podium in his brown uniform, his hand raised in the German salute.

Thousands of voices cried, "*Sieg Heil. Sieg Heil.*" The wooden box on the kitchen shelf vibrated. A brass band played *Deutschland, Deutschland uber alles* followed by Die *Fahne hoch, die Reihen fest geschlossen.*

Stasya stabbed the boiling potatoes on the stove, then draped a towel over the lid before she drained the steaming water into the cast iron sink. Her housekeeping skills had improved.

"Let's hope they can pull it off," Mathilde said, pulling a length of yarn from the ball. Anyna caught it before it rolled over the edge of the table. She had helped unravel one of Lothar's hand-knit sweaters and rolled up the yarn.

Total war, Olga thought. As if that could stop those flying fortresses from coming into German airspace by the thousands. "Every man, woman and child" included her and her family. Ingo, and Gottfried, Lucie, and their children, and millions of other people were obliged to fight to the bitter end. Enjoy the war. Two years ago everything had looked so good. Latvia had been liberated from the Soviets, so was most of Russia. Olga had counted on returning to her homeland. Now that was out of the question. There was no life for Baltic Germans under Soviets, only imprisonment or execution.

Lately there had been no transports coming through town. Olga played for her lonely friends, who stopped by for tea just to get out of the house. Her music sounded wistful and lifeless. The women danced with each other. Frau Metzger's irascible mood was as dark as the cloudy days. Business without the soldiers and their special rations was hardly worth pursuing. In desperation, she nibbled whatever she could find.

Anyna looked up. "May I listen to the Front Request Program with you, Mami, please?" Her eyes pleaded. Uncle Ingo, whom she had met only once, was still the most important man in her life, so important that she never complained about her homework and went to bed without fussing. In his letters he always attached a note for her and praised the drawings she sent him.

"All right," Olga reluctantly agreed. She had looked forward to wallowing in her fantasy. Ingo had become part of her. She could no longer appease her burning desire by caressing herself.

"Mami can talk to Uncle Ingo," Anyna told Mathilde. "So can I."

"That's enough, Anyna," Mathilde said, pounding on the table. "I told you that we can't talk to people who are not here. No, don't argue." She turned to Olga, "See what you are doing? Remember Aunt Tilly? She saw faces that frightened her to death and drove her to commit suicide. So please…" Olga knew the story of Aunt Tilly who had heard a voice instructing her to kill herself in order to save her lover. Why did her mother bring this up now?

"What is suicide?" Anyna asked, balancing her cup.

"Not a subject for little girls," Mathilde chided.

"We are Uncle Ingo's family," Anyna said. "That's what he said, right Mami?"

Mathilde jammed her needle into the sock. "Your daddy is a prisoner of war in America." Her lips pinched shut with anger rather than scold her daughter. "When the war is over, he will come home. You are his family."

"But I want Uncle Ingo to be my daddy."

Mathilde sighed. "I'm getting too old for this. You asked for it, Olga. What will you tell Lothar when he comes home?"

Olga bit off her thread. Her teeth clenched.

"I know life isn't easy for you," Mathilde said. "But you made your bed ..."

Olga drummed her fingers on the table and counted to ten. "So I did! Don't you think I am old enough to live my own life?"

"Evidently not," her mother said, counting stitches.

Olga ignored the reproach. Why did people pick on her?

Stasya placed the bowl with steaming potatoes on the table along with braised turnips. Anyna received a bowl of farina for supper.

Seething, Olga reached for a potato and mashed it with her fork.

"Your father was murdered by the Bolsheviks," Mathilde said. "I had two children to feed and a four-unit building to look after with tenants who could not pay their rent. Food was so scarce that finding some was all we could think of. The Bolsheviks confiscated property and stripped us of our possessions, including food."

Olga knew that of course. She had heard it a hundred times, but made no comment—she preferred it to those eternal reproaches. "I was a young woman like you and missed my husband. Don't look at me like that. I was not born old. Widowhood is a sad lot. Herr Rank was not the kind of husband I had in mind, but he married me. That gained me some respect and allowed me to return to society. Yes, Olga, that is the lot of a widow, particularly a young widow. Women hate you and men think you are desperate for them." The resignation in her eyes hurt. Olga had never thought of her mother as a woman, nor of Herr Rank as a husband. Did she actually sleep with that caricature of a man? She thought of the widows coming to the Esplanade longing for their husbands, while she hoped that hers would not return.

After Herr Rank passed away, Mathilde deteriorated, though fifty-four was not that old. She let her eyebrows go natural and pulled her pepper-gray hair into a bun. Her wilted skin had the color of skim milk. The nondescript, shapeless dress did nothing for her flat bosom. She always wore old felt slippers and did not care that her stockings sagged. Mathilde had given up on being a woman. What had happened to the pretty girl in the photo she kept in her bedroom? All smiles, thick curls bobbed, her eyes shining with life. All that was gone, faded into indifference, or was she suffering from homesickness for Riga and her friends and relatives? Perhaps she longed for affection from her daughters. Somehow they had lost the habit from the time they were children. Already by adolescence they were indifferent toward their mother. Perhaps they could not forgive her for marrying somebody like Herr Rank.

What if someday Anyna turned away from her mother? Fortunately, she loved Ingo and would be glad to have him around, should he ever come.

Anyna watched them, taking in every word.

Mathilde and Olga exchanged glances.

The radio played a waltz. Stasya, in her usual gray sweater and charcoal skirt, fed fresh coal into the stove, then ladled hot water from the well into the bed warmers she had lined up on the sink. Who was this young woman? What went on in that pretty, angry head of hers? What did the BBC tell her? No doubt, they agitated the Poles into rising against the Germans. Why hadn't they supported the Polish war back in 1939? Couldn't they see that the Poles were unreasonable in not granting Hitler the corridor?

Ingo was out their fighting, while Lothar, the rapist, waited out the war in Nebraska!

As soon as the Front Request Program came on, Mathilde and Stasya left. Olga switched off the light. Anyna brought her pillow and put it on her chair so she could watch the flames lick through the rings on the stovetop.

The sweet melody of *Do You Hear my Secret Call* put Olga in the romantic spell she always felt at this hour. She lit a candle and imagined Ingo sitting at the table.

"Ingo, is something wrong?" she whispered. "Please talk to me. I've been waiting for you. I long for you. I'm dying without you."

"Everything is wrong," he said, and was gone.

Olga stared at the empty chair.

"I saw Uncle Ingo. Did you see him too, Mami?" Anyna said later, on her way to the bedroom.

Olga gasped. "How could you see him? He is at the front."

"I know. But you always say that souls can meet even when people are far away. His soul came. I know he was here."

Olga thought of her mother's warning.

"I know you saw him too. Did he say something about me?"

"He was not here, Anyna. It's wishful thinking."

Anyna slipped into her warm bed. Olga tucked the featherbed around Anyna's neck and kissed her. "Goodnight, sweetie."

"I see Uncle Ingo. He is right here, with us."

"Please, Anyna. Don't say things like that. Omi will be very upset when she hears you talk about Uncle Ingo as if he is here. Now go to sleep." She turned off the light and left.

While she played *Liebestraum* Ingo caressed her shoulders. He was here.

On Tuesday, Anyna, her cheeks flushed from the frost, returned from her weekly visit to the countess, and fell into her mother's embrace. "Grandmaman is not feeling well. She asked for you. Nobody comes to visit her other than me. Her friends were killed in Russia and Riga. Can we go tomorrow?"

Tomorrow? Olga searched for an excuse. Nothing came to mind, nothing Anyna would believe. How could she lie to her little girl? No, this time there was no escape. Despite the Countess's denying Lothar's paternity, she cherished her only granddaughter. No point in putting off the inevitable and suffer the anticipation. She might as well go and get it over with.

After lunch, Olga put on the blue coat Mathilde had tailored from a wool blanket. It had a white rabbit fur collar and a matching muff. She pulled a beret over her curls, then took Anyna's hand.

Once they crossed Adolf Hitler Street—every main street was named after the Fuhrer —she turned into Hermann Goering Street. During the first years of the German annexation, many of the old buildings had been repaired and a sewer system installed. The textile industry ran at full speed, manufacturing synthetic silk used for underwear and stockings as well as for parachutes. Smoke stacks rose from the gray buildings like huge columns.

The fog cloaked the street scene in its haze, softening the stucco facades and dull windows. Only the gold cross on the steeple of the Catholic Church gleamed, reminding the people of their souls.

Two boys in short pants and old caps skidded over the frozen sidewalk. "Stop that!" shouted their mother. "You'll ruin your soles. Do you want to walk around with holes and wet feet?"

Olga smiled, thankful for the felt boots Lucie had given her. Gottfried's friend ran a shoe factory. The leather soles crunched against the frozen snow.

Anyna pulled Olga's hand. "Come on, Mami, *Grandmaman* is waiting. She says you don't like her." She ran up the squeaking stairs filled with the damp smell of winter.

Olga stopped at the landing. "Let's just say we have different opinions." This too would pass. As long as she kept her mouth shut, the Countess would not get anywhere with her reproaches.

An elderly Polish maid in a black dress and white apron opened the door. "Madame la Comtesse in boudoir," she said.

Anyna led the way across a drawing room, where Olga recognized the family treasures the Countess had saved from being auctioned off.

"That is grandmaman when she was young," Anyna said, pointing to an almost life-size portrait of the Baroness Frederika von Schenck, painted with her whippets, her lavish villa in the background. Olga admired the ravishing beauty and noticed Anyna's striking resemblance— the same wide cheekbones and fine nose, those large dark eyes and thick straight hair. The Countess could not really deny Lothar's paternity, but her pride would not let her give in. The artist portrayed her as a haughty beauty, but caught the sensuous expression on her mouth that men had adored. No smile. With her brimmed hat, parasol, and a white gown that showed off her slender hips, she was posed like the ladies in Gainsborough's portraits. The painter must have exaggerated her waist and stretched the swan-like neck. Though Olga despised the woman, she had to admit that the Countess was still an eye-catcher. No wonder she considered Olga's homemade clothes provincial. Olga had never had the opportunity to enjoy the finer things in life, and did not care that much about them.

The damask upholstery in the drawing room had faded, the gilded wood worn down, but the fine craftsmanship of an elegant manor was all there.

"You may come in," the Countess said from the next room.

Anyna opened the door, entered the sacred chamber, and bowed her head to the Countess. The old lady sat propped up against brocade-covered pillows like an aging diva, a blanket of flame-red fox pelts spread over her legs, a gift from some Russian prince who had courted her before the Baron had won her hand.

"Do close the door, Anna Magdalena. We are not in Riga. Oh, those wonderful days of my youth. The chivalry. The elegance and savoir faire before that fool started a war. Prince Anatole Nikolaievich told me years ago, 'when you cannot live in style, why live at all?' The Bolsheviks killed him before he could become a taxi driver in Paris. *Degoutant, ne c'est pas, ma cherie?*" she said, holding out her white hand. Anyna kissed it with reverence.

Olga closed the door. "How are you, Countess?"

"Still alive for reasons I fail to see. Hitler asked us to come here, but he didn't mention that he expected us to get along without coal or decent food. My son is a prisoner of war. At least he is in America and not at the mercy of those Soviet barbarians. If I could correspond with my friend, Arthur Jonathan McCormick, Lothar would be released into his custody." She sighed, touching her forehead with the back of her dainty hand.

"Come closer, Anna Magdalena, so that I can see you better. Have you done your homework? Yes? I am glad you came and brought your mother. We do not see much of each other, which is as it should be, considering the circumstances of our relationship. But, never mind. I must bear my cross." She leaned her head into the pillow, enduring the painful visit.

Anyna adjusted the angora shawl over her grandmother's shoulders. "Mami is very busy," she said, sitting down on the footstool next to the Countess's chaise.

Same old game, Olga thought. With Lothar gone, the charade no longer worked. Vindictive people took pleasure in torturing others. The Reich not only provided this apartment, they gave her a maid and a pension, something she could not afford in Riga. The Latvians had expropriated most of her land, leaving her with a manor she could not keep up. She finally sold it to pay off her debts. From then on, she could barely make ends meet, but pretended she still had plenty. That must have fooled Herr Rank into plotting Lothar's interest in Olga. He probably figured that he was a good catch. Little did he know.

The Countess's once black hair had a classic part in the center and was gathered into a twist. White streaks at the temples and crow's-feet around her eyes were the only signs of her age. No blemishes marred her marble-like features. While touring the United States with her husband, she found out she was pregnant. Doctors advised the couple against a hazardous sea voyage. Thus Lothar was born in New York. During that time she met a Mr. McCormick, who had offered her his heart and fortune. He even wanted the baby she carried. She declined and returned to Riga. Lothar still blamed her for not staying in America. Then the war broke out, and Lothar's father was killed. The Countess had married a charming young aristocrat and had two children, but now he too was gone.

"I am glad you came, Olga," she said. "As you can see, I am still here. But no sympathy, please." She raised her dainty hands in mock protest. "I cope with this country ruled by crude men who hide their ignorance behind fancy uniforms and flap around like crows. Now young hoodlums bully their elders. Chivalry and respect died in the trenches of the Great War."

Olga observed the familiar show, amused by the Countess's eloquence. Once she got going nobody could stop her, or wanted to. Olga was obliged to stay for a while, and did not mind listening rather than say something and then be reproached for her inappropriate comment. "We are at the mercy of this upstart," the Countess said in her articulate voice. "He used to be a tolerable actor, but the stage is getting too big for him and he forgets his lines. For that they cheer him on like the rats following the Pied Piper into the sea. Those who call others *Untermenschen* should take a look at themselves." She raised her voice for emphasis. "Aryan supremacy, whatever that means. The man should have been a fiction writer. But he has no plot. Fortunately there are still some educated men left." She dabbed her forehead with a lace-trimmed handkerchief soaked in perfume, exhausted by her speech.

Olga bit her tongue. No comment. Like Lothar, once the old lady got going she fell into an orgy of her own rhetoric.

"I miss my son. Missed him long before he was drafted. How could I know that some scheming woman would trap him? You wanted him and you got him. I am only glad he did not forget his old mother altogether. His first letter from America came to me. I am truly grateful for that. As for the rest…" She folded her thin white hands and pinned Olga down with her eyes. "This is my sanctuary, away from the uncouth people of this city." She gestured to the photos in silver frames. "They keep me company here, at this outpost of civilization. My granddaughter will never know that world, but at least I can teach her manners so that some day, when she escapes this ugly hole, she will appeal to the kind of society she belongs to and perhaps even remember me." She closed her eyes. The blood-red lips against the Countess's white face reminded Olga of a vampire.

Anyna's eyes shone as she listened to her grandmother's speech. The little Baroness had a rough road ahead of her. Even if she found a blue-blooded partner, Olga doubted he would be worth it. Perhaps the Countess wanted to lure Anyna away from her mother, to strike that final blow. Or was she grooming the child to be her servant, a puppet like Lothar?

"I know how difficult life can be," the Countess said. "After all, I was not born old. I lost my father at sixteen and became a widow at twenty-eight. My beloved husband left me with a small child and the care of our properties without ever explaining anything."

She dabbed her nose. "There I was. Armin Count von Eberswalde was the perfect husband. He came from one of the best families. He had class and savoir faire. He did everything for me. A perfect gentleman. Loved company and the hunt. You come from a fine family, Anna Magdalena." The Countess stroked the fox blanket. "Why don't you pull up that pillow for me, dear," she said in a mellifluous voice.

Anyna puffed up the pillow with great care, making sure that the Countess was comfortable, then obediently returned to her stool.

"Thank you, dear. You cheer my life. You lift me from the darkness of vulgarity."

The maid brought tea, which she served in English bone china cups.

"Thank you, Elsbeta, that will be all." The maid bowed the way the Countess had taught her. Olga imagined the curses festering behind the elderly woman's round face.

73

"I shall move to Bavaria this summer," the Countess said. "I will not be here when the Russian hordes descend on this place. I saw all I'll ever care to see of them in 1918."

Now that was more than she could have hoped for, Olga thought, but left it at that. With the front hundreds of kilometers away, she had nothing to fear.

"Don't think the Russians will stay behind their borders," the Countess said as if reading Olga's thoughts. "I never did expect much sense out of you. It does not take a soothsayer to know that they will go as far as they can until somebody stops them. Only I cannot see who will. They will come, plunder, and do all the things they are famous for. The Poles will join them and do their part to finish us off."

"Finish us off?" Olga wondered aloud. "No chance."

"Oh, dear. What did I just say? Intelligence is not your strong suit, young lady. Nor is the word lady appropriate." She leaned back into her pillows, projecting an air of infinite patience toward a hopeless imbecile. "What do you think? We reduced them to a nation of slaves. The proud Poles? They've fought the Russians for centuries. They'll slaughter us as soon as they get a chance."

What was she saying? The Poles slaughter Germans? "I will help you move," Olga said, trying to look concerned.

"Thanks. I bet you can't wait to get rid of me." She pulled an envelope from under Lothar's portrait on the mahogany table on her left. The photographer had masterfully caught Lothar's aristocratic face, well suited for the black uniform of the SS. How she hated that cold superiority he felt toward everyone but his mother. To her, he was the obedient son.

"The letter is addressed to me," she said, holding it up with pride.

Olga did not care what he wrote or to whom he addressed his letters as long as he left her alone.

"The Americans treat him adequately. They respect his background. He speaks good English and was appointed as interpreter for the camp." She raised one of her thinly plucked brows. "Of course, his fellow officers envy him. He is used to that. People of our station…" She petted Anyna's head. "Daddy sends you his regards. His next letter will come to you."

"How thoughtful of him," Olga said, ignoring the icy look in the Countess's squinting eyes. "When you reply, please tell him that we are fine and glad he is well."

"May I see Daddy's letter?" Anyna asked, reaching for it.

"Asking for a letter addressed to another person is rude, Anna Magdalena. Remember that."

"I am sorry, Grandmaman."

"That is better. You may pull up my fox blanket and take your leave. It is time for my nap. Thank you for your visit."

Olga took her mother-in-law's cold, limp hand as if it were a snake. In a moment she would leave. At home she could wash off the nauseating perfume.

"Adieu, Anna Magdalena," the Countess said, stretching her lips into a smile.

Anyna kissed her grandmother's hand.

Back on the street the sun came out. The frost sparkled on the snow. Olga skidded on the slippery sidewalk with her arms stretched out. Free! Soon she would be free for good.

Anyna skidded along. "You haven't laughed like that for a long time, Mami. What did Daddy say in his letter?"

"I did not read it. Don't you love those glitters. Uncle Ingo will visit us soon."

"He will?" Anyna asked incredulously. "How do you always know these things?"

Chapter 8

Ingo leaned against the icy wind, blinking in the whirling snowflakes. His eyes watered from the sub-zero cold. The Blitzkrieg was in its fifth year, with no end in sight. Adolf Hitler was determined to fight to the last man; he now recruited soldiers from POW camps. Many Russians, particularly Cossacks who had been devastated by Stalin's purges, opted to join the Wehrmacht to fight their mutual enemy. But America's unlimited support, Russia's deadly winter, and her vast territory made Stalin an unbeatable adversary. Stalin had even sacrificed the people of Stalingrad as a defense against the Germans rather than evacuating them. Amazing that the Wehrmacht—mired in endless snowfields with frozen vehicles, on the verge of freezing to death in their inadequate clothes—still had some fighting spirit left.

He shivered. His army coat offered little protection against the cutting wind. The cold penetrated the layers of clothes as if he did not have them on. His hands and feet ached so bad that he could not wait to get back to the hut. Still, being out here in the silence of the wintry day helped him cope with the pain in his soul. His cracked lips were swollen. Tears froze on his cheeks. The shawl around his face felt cold and stiff. Wading through the white powder, he stepped around the remnants of the broken equipment, a leftover of yesterday's assault. Why had the Russians ceased fire and retreated when they could have wiped the Germans out? Did they believe they needed more force to deliver the final blow, or were they preparing an encirclement? They had the Germans in a bind. As soon as the sky cleared up they would return.

Had Hitler considered Russia's vastness when he launched his attack? He had been so convinced of his might that he did not even deem the Soviets a serious enemy. The Russian people had prayed for a liberator from Stalin's purges, but with the Germans treating their prisoners worse than animals, they would rather die under Stalin than under some crazed SS.

Panting through the moist woolen shawl his mother had sent him, he smelled the stench of his own breath. His stomach contracted from hunger. Pulling one leg after another from the soft, deep snow stimulated his circulation. He was getting warm again. The pain in his feet began to vanish. Hitler should have retreated from Stalingrad instead of insisting fanatically that General Paulus had to defend it to the last man.

Ingo ground his teeth. Hitler's blunders cost millions of lives. He flaunted his now dwindling force. By announcing his offensives in advance, he gave the Russians ample time to prepare their defense. Their remarkable network conducted by the partisans gave the Russians every advantage. They were everywhere, like Olga's spirits, whereas German intelligence was spotty and unreliable.

A gentle snow blanket covered the body of a frozen horse. Some birthday, he thought. Perhaps his gift was being alive. His pulse had a regular beat despite the churning anger in his guts. Damn those tears; the frost was getting to him. Olga probably knew this was his birthday. She was here with him now. He heard her voice, which had guided him. How he wished he could see her, hold her in his arms, tell her how much he loved her and depended on her. How much longer would he have to trudge through this fathomless land, prey to the Big Bear hunting him with his giant claws and insatiable appetite for blood?

Ingo pulled the wet shawl from his mouth and inhaled the fresh icy air. It congested his lungs. Skeleton trees stood against the hazy winter sky. If he could only hibernate like them and wake up when the war was over. He slapped his arms against his back.

Did his mother feel the first signs of spring when she gave birth to him? Germany had been at war then too. Father had patched up the wounded while Mother took care of her baby. Now, two decades later, Father repaired the damages of war again. The Black Reaper was on the loose, swinging his scythe. Where would his end come from? One of those snow mounds where snipers hid under burnt-out tanks, trucks, and carts waiting for an opportunity to return to their lines? Snipers knew their craft and delivered quick, merciful deaths that took him to that other world Olga communicated with.

"I know you are here!" he called out, his teeth chattering. In a minute he would have to address his men at the command post and smile while telling them they were trapped in an encirclement, lie they would get troop support and their orders to break out any moment now. They knew their supply of weapons and ammunition was running out and that they were surrounded by countless fresh and well-equipped Russian troops, T-34 tanks, Katyushas and flame throwers. Stormoviks would descend like vultures, coming for the kill.

Give them hope. He must give them hope when none was to be found. Tell them that they had a way out. An order to retreat would allow him to slip away. But that order was not about to come. Hitler would sacrifice his men, punish them for losing the battle. Surrender was unthinkable. The Russians would haul them off without food or shelter. They were at the end of their strength.

He waded faster. Would she come when he delivered his devastating message? The men waited for him at the only hut that had survived the battle. They had patched up the windows and roof and repaired the stove. Wooden parts of broken vehicles fed the fire.

Smoke curled from the chimney into the milky sky. Should he mention faith? Eternal life? Not when they fought to live.

The ache in his hands and feet was gone. The whistling wind softened to a gentle breeze, still cold, but no longer lethal. "Olga!" he whispered through his cracked lips. The lump in his throat persisted. "Let me live."

The broken turret of a burnt-out tank faced him from the whiteness. Soon others would arrive and open fire. He climbed over the remains of a horse cart, then entered the smoke-filled hut. His vision blurred. Officers and non-coms talked in loud voices. The iron plate of the stove was red hot. Water boiled in an old kettle.

Staff Sergeant Kunz had lost so much weight that his worn and faded uniform coat hung on him like a hand-me-down. He had a tin mug with hot tea for his superior. Last year, he and the men had surprised their CO with a cake they had baked and a bottle of vodka, which they shared. This morning, those still alive lit a candle stump and stuck it into their last piece of dry bread and wished him many happy returns. No glee flickered in their exhausted faces. Front rats cherished the momentary quiet and replenished their energy.

"Dear God, why do you hate us so?" Ingo mumbled into the thick smoke hanging like a dark cloud over the heads of the men. Through the ice-encrusted window he saw others crawling from their dugouts. The snow glittered in the light of a passing sunray.

"Eh, Gustav," Halder, one of his men, said, "Better get ready for another dance with Katyusha."

"Only if she dances to my tune," quipped Engel. "We'll be out of here in no time, right, *Herr Hauptmann*?"

"You know we will, Engel," Ingo said lightly. "Ivan can't scare us."

"Once we repair the carts we could get the trucks to pull them."

"Good idea," Ingo said. "Let's hope we'll get a day or two of rest. But I wouldn't count on it. So get your men hustling."

"*Zu Befehl*, Herr Hauptmann."

Ingo returned the smile. Over the years he and his men had become family.

He left the hut and walked over packed snow that crunched under his boots. Somewhere behind the shrubs a tank revved. The clearing sky would invite Russian planes. "I am ready, Olychka," he said into the vapor of his breath, and hastened back to the heat of the hut. The weather-beaten door squeaked. How many generations of people had called this home? Had they escaped or had they been killed? He would live.

Later that day, the orders came through that his unit was to join the main body under the command of General Stemmermann. Stuck. The men had repaired enough vehicles to move their equipment. Clouds had gathered, keeping them hidden from Russian planes, but the temperature was rising. Russia's weather was as unpredictable as its people.

"From ice to mud in one quick step, Herr Hauptmann," Leutnant Schafer said. A tall and haggard young man drafted straight from the school bench, he was still wet behind the ears.

"No more frostbite and amputations," Ingo said.

Schafer did not get it. "I hear the mud is worse than ice."

"Could be," Ingo said. "We have no choice." Another obstacle, he thought. The thick and tenacious goo made all movement a struggle.

"We're ready for Kvitki," Kunz reported, not bothering with a salute.

Kvitki would be their next target. "Strike the enemy and beat him back," Ingo said, rehashing the nonsense the command post handed out whenever they faced impossible odds. In his pack were a couple of ribbons he had received for surviving the enemy. He would prefer a furlough to surprise Olga at the Esplanade. After putting on whatever would fit under his greatcoat he picked up his helmet.

Outside, the mild air thawed the snow. The men tested motors, hitched up equipment and shouted orders. Low flying Junkers droned overhead. If the Ninth Panzer Division could stop the Russians from closing the small gap of the encirclement, they had a chance.

The *rasputitsa*, or thaw, could stop the whole operation dead in its tracks and make the Germans easy targets for the Soviets. The Russians knew they had the Germans in their pincers and would finish them off in a wall of fire. They would wipe out the 88th Infantry Division the way they had liquidated the Sixth Army at Stalingrad.

Ingo dragged his mud-caked boots, watching the exhausted men push the wheels of their vehicles through the melting snow. A snow storm would answer their prayers.

At the command post, Ingo found his fellow officers. Their smoke diffused the dim light coming through the dirty window. Loud voices, nervous laughter. Two men from the Signal Corps worked the field transmitter.

General von Stemmermann sat at the wooden table reading his messages. He came from the old school of Prussian officers whose unbending discipline served as model for the younger officers. He removed his horn-rimmed glasses and looked up. Satisfied that he had everybody's attention, he put his papers aside and rose tall and erect. His intelligent blue eyes demanded respect. Over the last few years, deep lines had formed on his gaunt face. He was a man's man who did not expect from others what he was not willing to do himself.

The silence in the room magnified the roaring planes, tanks and tractors. Every officer knew what was at stake.

"The *rasputitsa* is not part of our plan," Stemmermann announced in his crisp, articulate voice. "It will hamper all movement. Within hours we may find ourselves stuck. Nonetheless, we shall get our men out of this trap. First, we must keep the Russians from closing in on us until our relief arrive to help us break out. Our main target is Hill 239." The general pointed his swagger stick at a red circle on the map. "The only possible breakout point for us. The forest on both sides is infested with Russian tanks. Cerberus guards the gates of Hades." A black line indicated the peanut-shaped encirclement around the villages Khilki and Komarovka. As a final test of endurance the men would have to cross the meandering Gniloy Tikich River. "It has two bridges, both of which will be blown up by the time we get there. The bank will be guarded; pontoons would be suicide."

The men stared at their commander, their faces tense, eyes locked not to reveal their inner turmoil. Ingo knew their thoughts. They had no illusions about their task. All that mattered now was that they got out. Nobody must be left behind. They could make it, had to believe in it. It was their only chance, their only hope. Every one of them wanted to live.

"We are 56,000 men. The Panzer Corps coming to our aid is under attack. They may not get here in time. The landing strips for our aircraft are softening under the thaw. Pioneers are rebuilding them on drier ground, but I doubt they will get done in time. Preserve your ammunition whenever possible."

General Stemmermann took off his glasses and made eye contact with every one of his officers, unable to conceal the severity of their mission. Even if they succeeded, there would be few survivors.

"*Generalfeldmarschall* von Manstein is doing all he can to get us the permission to break out. General Seidemann's VIII Air Corps with its 1,550 aircraft will keep us supplied from Uman. Our lives and those of 56,000 men depend on our capturing Hill 239."

The General nodded with a warm smile. The fear vanished from the eyes of his junior officers. They were in this together and would get out together, fight another battle, another encounter with death. Ingo felt the power of that moment, the bond he had with his comrades and the affection they shared.

"Panic, gentlemen, is our worst enemy. Tell every *Landser* that the East Prussian Division is on its way and so are the 1st, 14th, 16th, and 24th Panzers. Once we get the order to retreat, we'll be on our way. Now go and tell your men the good news."

The officers cheered. The general smiled. Ingo thanked God and his guardian angel. This would not be another Stalingrad. Stemmermann would break out even if Hitler refused to give the order. In leaving he turned to his friend, Erich Haberle, "We'll do it again." They had attended university in Tubingen together and served in the same division.

"That's what it takes to make general," Haberle said, a gleam of hope in his tired eyes. "He'll get us out even if he must risk his own life. A true Prussian."

Ingo picked his way between the puddles that formed in the wet snow. "What do you hear from your family?"

"So far Stuttgart has not been hit. Rations are being cut. My mother and her brother inherited the family farm. My father was drafted. He is— let me think—fifty-one. Things are getting bad, Ingo. Really bad," he whispered, though nobody was within earshot. "Let's pray we'll meet again on the other side of the Gniloy Tikich, or whatever that silly river is called."

The droning of Junker-52's and Henkel-111's vibrated in the air. They brought supplies and picked up wounded. Russian anti-aircraft fired. Bombs exploded.

"Nasty muck," Ingo remarked to the men pushing an anti-tank gun. His boots sunk in with every step. The wet dirt released them with a sucking sound. Coats, hands and faces were smeared with mud.

"At least we're not freezing, Herr Hauptmann," one of the men said, straining against a wheel.

"Relief is on the way. We should be out of here in no time."

"That's just what I said, Herr Hauptmann. Our Fuhrer wouldn't abandon us. He needs us. We've been damn good soldiers. We'll lick Ivan, right, Herr Hauptmann?"

"Goes without saying. Carry on," he added in a fatherly tone. The men at the front lived from moment to moment. As soon as a battle was over, they settled back into their customary way of front life. Did they really believe the war could be won? That some miracle weapon would bring final victory? Or did they just count their blessings for another day of life in freedom? Even that was relative.

Ingo returned to the hut and sat down in the crowded room. This would be his last opportunity to write Olga and his parents. They deserved a kind word. Even if support troops arrived, and the permission to break out came through, fighting their way out and crossing the river were nearly insurmountable obstacles.

The Komarovka encirclement was not the only hot spot on Hitler's map of emergencies. The Nikopol bridge on the lower Dnepr was severely threatened. The Crimea isolated the Seventeenth Army from the main front. Those men needed support as much as the men here.

"Olga," he whispered, "I need Father's protection. Please stay by and keep watch."

Chapter 9

Two days later, Hitler's order to break out and retreat still had not come. Ingo and his men fought off Russian attacks. Every passing minute gave the Soviets an irretrievable advantage, time to bring in more forces and crush the trapped Germans.

In his Fieseler Storch aircraft, General von Vormann reconnoitered the route over which his "sledgehammer," the 24th Panzer Division, should come. "Finally," he mumbled, watching the indefatigable column of tanks, vehicles and grenadiers drag their heavy guns through the mud, like a dark stream cutting through the countryside.

"They're on their way!" he told his command post.

Ingo waded through the ankle-deep morass that pulled the boots off his men's feet and ripped the tracks off armored carriers. The unrelenting soil stopped tractors and trapped horses. At times, not a single wheel turned. Only the tanks and assault guns of the 5th SS "Viking" Panzer Grenadier Division crawled along, wasting an intolerable amount of fuel.

The overnight frost brought no relief. Worse, it hardened the mud on the tank treads and had to be thawed with blowtorches. Stemmermann kept regrouping, shortening fronts and switching free forces to critical points. He abandoned the Dnepr River and pulled in the XLII Corps's feelers in the north. He rescued a battalion at one point, and reinforced a threatened sector at another. The battle over Korsun and its airfields had raged for twelve days now. Over the past four days, Bavarians, Hessians, Franconians, Austrians, Saxons, men from the Saar-Palatinate, Belgians, Dutchmen, and Scandinavians from the Waffen SS volunteer regiments defended their positions against the steady assaults of half a dozen Russian Armies.

Every day cost thousands of lives. The Russians broke through at Nikopol and threatened General Schorner's entire Army detachment which sorely missed his 24th Panzers—Hitler had ordered them back to Apostolovo.

Ingo clenched his fists and slapped his thigh. He fumbled with the pistol in its holster. "*Verfluchte Scheisse!* Olga, where are you now that I need you?" Shivering, his coat and boots caked with mud, he watched his men dodge explosions in their bare feet. The mud had swallowed their boots. The sunny skies of the past days had illuminated the German positions like search lights and the Soviets had not wasted time. They would open fire any minute now.

A dozen mud-splashed officers stood around the dirty hood of an armored truck and studied the billowing map on its hood. Their teeth chattered under white lips. Grenades exploded everywhere, throwing up clumps of mud. The Soviets pounded the German defense and tightened the circle like a pack of wolves closing in on their prey.

General Stemmermann pointed at the map bending in the wind. "General Breit's attack cut through the enemy positions in the north here," he explained. "Bake and his phalanx of thirty-four Tigers and forty-seven Panther tanks is on the way. Breit ordered the bulk of the experienced SS *Leibstandarte*, the shock troops, and spearheads of the 1st Panzer Division into action. Once we retreat, they'll await us at the Gniloy Tikich River."

Retreat? Ingo wondered. Who would be left?

The general looked up, holding down the map with his swagger stick.

"We are ordered to shorten our front lines and move the pocket toward Shenderovka," he said, drawing an oval circle around the Korsun airfield. "By shifting our divisions we'll get this peanut to face north and confuse the Soviets. Our exit is Komarovka. Hill 239 is our next target. Unless we control that hill, they'll pick us off like lice on a shorn head. With that behind us, we can face the last hurdle—the Gniloy Tikich River. Not wide, but deep and freezing cold, as you can imagine. We can't swim across." He showed no signs of frustration or despair, or even the biting cold. Only the gray of his face showed that he was freezing like everybody else.

The plan made sense, Ingo thought. But executing it was another matter. His nerves had settled down. The twinge in his stomach was gone.

Shrouded in snow flurries, Ingo returned to his men. Medics carried the wounded to dressing stations. Moans, torn flesh, and trails of blood were part of his life. The explosions had moved further away, where they threw up fountains of dirt leaving giant craters. Two assault guns fired. Their shafts jerked back. German and Soviet planes passed overhead. Some dropped their cargo. Others bombed or engaged in dog-fights. The howl of Soviet rockets blasted into the cacophony.

"Have mercy. Shoot me," whimpered a body beyond repair, his face a bloody pulp. He could not see Ingo's sympathetic nod. How could humans shoot each other so freely but refuse to deliver a *coup de grace* to a dying man as they would to a horse?

Two days later the pocket had shrunk so much that every Soviet bomb was a hit. The airlift of wounded was an act of heroism for the pilot and his crew.

Ingo entered the bunker where Gefreiter Decker operated his wireless. "There they are again, Herr Hauptmann," he said. "Those traitors. Listen to this. General von Seydlitz wants us to capitulate. How can a German officer stoop so low! Wants to save his hide by supporting the Soviets. How can he believe their promises? Some men are slow learners." He scratched his head. Fleas and lice were part of their torments. Decker was worse off than the rest; the bites had inflamed his skin and left festering scabs all over. Ingo controlled the urge to scratch and only did so when the itch became unbearable.

"Good food and accommodation," Decker mocked. "Complete safety. Employment for everybody. The men will remain in their units and work under their commanding officer. Sure, with a Russian boot up your ass and the friendly surroundings of a Siberian labor camp, set in the unspoiled nature of the Taiga, where summer comes and goes before you know it happened." He stretched his lips in disgust exposing his plaque-stained teeth.

A heavy kaboom shook the earth around them. Dirt rained into the bunker. "Worker's paradise. We know all about that, don't we, Herr Hauptmann? Father Stalin is a real pal when it comes to spoiling his people. What will he do to his enemies? The only way I'll join him is as a dead man." He removed his headset. "The last bullet is for me."

Ingo chuckled. "Don't get melodramatic, Decker. Better concentrate on how we can get out of here." The struggling men reminded him of flies trying to escape the fly paper. "Have you seen that man before?" He pointed at a short and stocky officer wearing a clean uniform.

"His name is Alders," Decker said. "Belongs to the 72nd. Why?"

"What is he doing here?" Ingo asked.

"No idea. Let me check?"

"Do that," Ingo said, and left the bunker. "What brings you to us, Lieutenant?"

The man's dark eyes shifted. "I'm comparing our marching orders, Herr Hauptmann. How long will you stay here?"

"Long enough to find out where you came from. Who's your commanding officer?"

The man hesitated. "General Breit," he said jovially, squirming under Ingo's intense gaze. "I must be on my way. I'm expected…"

Decker called out from the hut, "The 72nd has no record of a Lt. Alders."

Ingo pulled out his revolver. "You're under arrest."

Kunz and Decker grabbed the man before he could run. A grenade exploded twenty meters away. "You can't hold me. Here's my ID." Cold hatred and fear flashed in his eyes. His lips tightened to a thin line.

"Show that to the *Abwehr*. We are defending our country."

"But look…"

Kunz twisted the man's arm and marched him off. "Traitor. Coward."

"I had no choice. They made me do it," Alders pleaded.

"Tell that to the *Abwehr* too. They'll enjoy your story." Trembling with disgust, Ingo restrained himself from slapping the frightened man's pale face.

Schafer spat out. "The nerve of them. Can't wait until they finished us off. What do they pay a man like that? A loaf of bread and a night with a Russian woman? The swine. Execution is too merciful for the likes of him."

"We can't be careful enough about spies, Decker." Ingo scanned the faces of the men around him. "We'll attack Novaya-Buda at 2030 hours and capture Hill 200. The open slope has no cover. The dark and our white cover-ups should keep us hidden. Once we hit Sukhiny-

Shenderovka we'll hold it until reinforcements arrive. I know it's easier said than done. But we can do it. Did it in the past. We wouldn't want it any other way."

The men nodded. Their gaunt and tired faces showed warmth and respect. Once they broke out, they would survive.

"Remember, 2030 hours. We're heading west, to liberty!"

"To liberty," echoed the men, waving their arms, a transfigured gleam in their eyes.

That afternoon clouds gathered. A dark night was their only chance of catching the Russians by surprise.

At 2030 hours Schafer reported, "The men are ready."

Ingo met them in the darkness. Their white camouflage tunics blended with the snow. Explosions flared. The frosty air hampered their breathing. After repeating his instructions, he led the way into the dark, followed by hundreds of faintly crunching steps on the ghostlike march.

Half an hour later, they reached a grove. "Here's the slope," Ingo whispered. They were in enemy territory. "From now on every man for himself and God with us all."

The men collapsed to the ground and crawled toward the Soviet positions. Ingo felt bits of dry grass, rocks, and clumps of dirt under the frozen snow. The thin ice crust crunched under his elbows. His lungs strained. Was this a mine field? An explosion would rip him up and betray the position of his men. But Olga had promised he would survive. He believed her. He had to believe her. She was here, with him. *Thank you, dear love.*

"*Stoy! Parole!*" demanded a Russian voice from the darkness.

Ingo could not see the man. "*Los!*" he ordered, cocking his pistol and running toward the Russian trenches. Surprised, the Russians reacted too slowly. The men struck left and right, crushed heads and stabbed chests. As soon as they controlled the Soviet position, their horse-drawn units followed. By midnight, they had captured the ground around Hill 200 and reached the Sukhiny-Shenderovka road where an unsuspecting column of Russian tanks and multiple mortars passed.

"*Flak! Los!*" Ingo shouted in a dither of battle fever. At a range of 200 meters, the convoy came under fire. Russian trucks carrying gasoline burst into flames, lighting up the landscape and the softly-falling snowflakes.

At 0100 hours they attacked Novaya-Buda.

By 0230, the village was in German hands. Soviet transport and cavalry units, snatched from their sleep, fled, leaving 252 prisoners behind.

The Hamburg SS "Germania" Panzer Grenadier Regiment fought in hand-to-hand combat. Belgian volunteers of the "Wallonie" Assault Brigade repulsed the massive Soviet attacks. One of the two hundred casualties was their commander, Colonel Lucien Lippert. Leutnant Leon Degrelle assumed command and held Novaya-Buda against enemy attacks.

Ingo met the young man, whose unquestioning ideology softened his own cynicism.

"Mon ami," the Belgian said. He sported a big smile and a thin blonde mustache. "Don't be disappointed. Who expects perfection? Not in peace. Not in war. We're fighting the grand enemy, like Napoleon. In the end it will all be for the best, *vraiment. Tiens,* have a *coupe de rouge.* My men always carry some wine. Makes fighting easier, *ne c'est pas*? Now we hold Novaya-Buda. A big name for a village. In ten years we meet again, drink wine and remember our fight out here in Russia."

Ingo enjoyed Degrelle's straightforward outlook. The wine warmed and relaxed him. It would be good to meet this young man ten years from now, but not likely.

The village huts were still warm from the men who had recently slept here. They had windows, tables and chairs. The pungent smell of homegrown Russian tobacco and male body odors were typical for Russian country life. The men found potatoes and fried them with bacon in a huge iron pan. Thick slices of country bread and fresh pickles made a feast. Passing bottles of vodka, the men relaxed as if they would stay for weeks on end.

Ingo settled down in an old, rough-hewn chair, stretching his legs and watching his men carry on like children. He felt warm affection for the fellow front rats under his command. Would Hitler let them break out and retreat? "What are our casualties, Kunz?" he asked. "I think we were extremely lucky."

Decker set up his wireless.

"You said it, Herr Hauptmann," the burly man agreed, and lit his pipe.

"Any news from General Stemmermann?" Ingo asked. As soon as the Russians got wind of what had happened, they would be back with a vengeance. A moment later he was asleep.

Somebody shook him. "It's *Oberst* Winkler."

Ingo took the field receiver. "*Zu Befehl.*"

"State your position."

"We are holding Novaya-Buda," Ingo reported. "Constant enemy attack. Lt. Degrelle is a capable man. We had heavy losses—six tanks and four anti-tank guns. We have no heavy armor. The Russians pound us from close range. The falling snow is our only camouflage."

"Keep your position, Kroll, until we get our orders to break out. I doubt that the III Panzer Corps will get here in time. They're locked in battle."

"Those unnecessary losses," Ingo said. They understood each other. The orders to break out should have come days ago.

Winkler said no more. "Be prepared for an all-out thrust to Dzhurzhentsy."

Ingo acknowledged with a snappy, "*Jawohl*, Herr *Oberst*," and hung up. "Still no word from the Supreme Command," he told Decker, who scratched his arm pits.

"These lice sit everywhere. They like my smell."

"Even the pests are after us."

Decker licked his fingertip and moistened an infected blotch on his neck. "I feel like pouring gasoline over my body for a good hurt rather than this itch."

"I wouldn't do that," Ingo said. "Things are bad enough already. As soon as we get out of here you better get yourself treated before your infections take over." Buttoning his coat, he headed for the door. "Watch that radio and send a messenger as soon as the orders come through. In the meantime, I'll make my rounds and see who's left."

His men had set up defense posts in the trenches. Hartmann offered him the vodka bottle he had liberated. "It's good to be warm for a change," he said, ignoring the grenades exploding around them. The Soviets knew the location of their trenches in Novaya-Buda. A nearby horse and his cart blew up. Men dropped to the ground.

"Everybody out!" Ingo shouted, running along the trenches. Not that he needed to—his seasoned soldiers knew what to do. "To the end of the road. They won't suspect we're there. We'll push toward Komarovka."

Ingo found Degrelle surrounded by his tank commanders. "We must get out."

Ingo shouted against the earsplitting noise. "I need your support. The III Panzers are still trying to take Hill 239. I'll notify headquarters. We'll regroup to the north."

"We could've done without this," Degrelle shouted, his face crimson with fury. Blood dripped from his forehead. "I'll wait for your men, Kroll."

"Thanks." Ingo ran toward his hut. Decker must send the message before the wireless unit was broken. Men, vehicles, and sleds carrying the wounded hastened away from the exploding rockets. "To the north! North!" he shouted.

Decker packed up his unit when Ingo arrived. "Signal Stemmermann that we can't hold our position. We're pushing toward Komarovka. The Soviets will fire until we're wiped out. You get out of here, *now*. I don't want you here when they blow up this hut." Ingo ran off. His lungs pumped to capacity. Zigzagging like a rabbit he dodged the explosions. An armored *Kubelwagen* blew up and burst into flames. Men screamed. If General Manstein didn't get the order to break out now, they were lost. Degrelle and his tanks were his only defense. What if the cloud blanket cleared?

Ingo waved.

"We are ready," Degrelle said, ignoring the cut on his face.

"Let's wait ten more minutes," Ingo said. "I don't want to leave anybody behind. The Soviets think we're finished and expect us to come out with our hands up. Keep waiting, Ivan." His hoarse voice held no humor.

The thickly falling snow camouflaged their escape and hid the heavy armor and motorized vehicles from view. Degrelle leaned over the map.

Ingo studied it. "This wooded area should give us cover, even if we run into a camouflaged T-34 or two. I believe in destiny and mine is guided by a knowing hand."

Degrelle stared at his new friend.

"That's right, *mon ami*," Ingo said. "We'll talk about it some other day. Now, the Russians expect us to use that road or return to the pocket. Can you see any alternative?"

Degrelle shook his head. The snow settled on his cap, coat, and thin face where it melted into his wound. "*D'accord.*"

"Then let's go."

Orders were relayed. The Tigers roared up and rolled off with clinking chains like clumsy monsters laboring in the falling snow.

Ingo mounted one of the horses. A cart approached. "Decker?"

"Mission accomplished, Herr Hauptmann. General Stemmermann received the orders to break out. Password: Freedom. Objective: Lysyanka. Time: 2300 hours. We'll meet the others at Komarovka. They know we are coming. Support is on the way."

"Finally!" Ingo cried out and waved to his men. "Onward!"

Dusk settled in. Darkness was their only friend.

Olga, you did it again. But there will be a price. Mephisto wants our souls.

The disappointed Russians pounded the German position with every available gun, firing into the churned-up field where trees were stumps and the wounded covered the bare ground. Now that an escape was in sight, the Germans defended themselves with equal vigor, fighting for their lives. At what was left of Komarovka, the severely wounded were bedded down on stretchers exposed to the cold and the falling snow. They would soon die. The air lift had stopped. The remaining 4,000 men sat wedged in among the command posts of battalions, regiments, and divisions. Despite the shelling, they repaired stranded guns, tanks, armored vehicles, and horse-drawn wagons using parts from those beyond saving. The field kitchens worked around the clock using their remaining stock. Documents, war diaries, and letters fed the open fires. Only weapons, fighting vehicles, and field kitchens would be evacuated.

The women of the signal auxiliaries were divided among the various units and placed under the protection of experienced commanders. Everybody knew what awaited them should they fall into Russian hands.

Ingo and his exhausted grenadiers, and Degrelle with his battered Walloons, waited until everybody was accommodated before picking their way to the Chief of Operations for a briefing.

The meeting was already in session when they squeezed into the room where the commanders crowded around a table. A kerosene lamp illuminated the map and the handsome face of Major Hermani. Ingo thawed out in the thick, hot air and relaxed in the company of his fellow officers. The grueling march and the battle for Hill 200 still gripped his bones.

"Here is Khilki-Komarovka," the Major said, pointing at the map. "We will set out in three ramming wedges against the enemy without artillery preparation. We must dislodge them at bayonet point, then break through to Dzhurzhentsy and Hill 239 in one decisive movement. There we will join the III Panzer Korps."

"Decisive movement? How?"

"Corps Detachment B is to the right," explained the Major. "The Division in the middle. The SS Viking Panzer Grenadiers on the left here. That makes roughly 40,000 men under the command of General Lieb. General Stemmermann will remain with the rearguard."

Ingo followed the positions of the various divisions with interest. Only when the Major mentioned that the non-transportable wounded would be left behind with their doctors and nursing staff to be handed over to the Soviets, only then did his heart sink.

"That's impossible," he moaned.

"I know," the major continued. "It's the most painful aspect of the plan. We have no choice. It's our only chance of getting out alive."

What if he were wounded, Ingo wondered. The Russians had no use for healthy men, and would not care for the wounded. They even dug up German graves and scattered corpses.

"Everybody should write a few lines to their families and exchange their letters with somebody else. You do want a last greeting to reach home."

Hermani talked about fellowship that would undergo its supreme test during the next hours. Everybody knew what to expect.

Should he write Olga, Ingo wondered, or his parents? He should say something to Johanna and tell her that even if he survived, he would not return to her. He had no personal belongings to dispose of except for Olga's letters, which he kept in his breast pocket. Should he destroy them in case he was captured or killed? Why would anybody take an interest in them?

As soon as the meeting adjourned, he pulled them from his pocket and threw them into the fire except for the one where Olga declared her love for him. Then he went back to the command post and wrote to her.

Russia, February 16, 1944

My beloved Olga,

These words flow so easily, as if I had called you that all my life. It's dark here, and quiet, a perfect place for devoting my heart to you. I missed the last Request Program, but I thought of you and felt your presence. How I wish I could hold your hands and kiss your lips, abandon myself to our love. Some day the most precious part of you, that sacred door to your being will open up to me. I live in your love. Can it be true?

We are heading for another storm. It's part of our lives out here, like the passage of time that occurs without our noticing it. We fulfill our duties, plod through our tasks, eat, drink, and sleep when we can. These tasks demand all our attention and ingenuity. The lucky ones succeed. Thanks to you, I am one of them. You've touched my heart—it's yours forever.

From the time I met you, I have been alive and real. I even feel compassion again. My existence is blessed with an acute awareness and sensitivity. You gave me the most precious thing life has to offer—your love and affection. I shall love you for all time to come in this and any other world.

Ingo.

Reading the letter tears welled up. Had he actually written that? He, the angry, sarcastic man of a year ago when he first approached Olga? Could his love for a woman he only knew through letters have such an impact?

He looked at Degrelle, compelled to speak, to share his surging emotions with a friend. But the young man was in his own private world. Instead of interrupting, Ingo pulled another sheet of field post stationery from his pocket and wrote to his father.

They had not seen each other since his father had volunteered to patch up the severely wounded at the Vienna Army Hospital three years ago. They had never exchanged many words, and did not need to. He had always admired his father, who treated his wife with tenderness and respect. Since he could not change tradition and a woman's role in the family, he supported his wife's zeal to support the German Reich and appreciated her efforts to be the perfect mother and housewife.

Ingo smiled. He would certainly support Olga's love for music and her professional career as pianist and teacher, should she chose one.

Lieber Vater!

This is such an extraordinary moment in my life that I need to share it with you, the cause of my existence. You were always close to me, always understood me. You made no demands, you allowed me to develop on my own. Though you never mentioned it, I can now see things your way. We never spoke of love or showed affection, but I want you to know how much you mean to me. It does not come easy.

Ingo paused, and blinked the tears from his eyes, then went on to say how much he appreciated the honorable life his father had lived and felt a deep warmth well up. He licked the flap and turned to Degrelle, whose heart had not yet been poisoned by anger and hatred. The German uniform seemed out of place on this man. In speech and manners, Degrelle was so different from his German colleagues, but he had chosen to join the ranks of those who had set out to fight Communism. This was an ugly war, but so were all holy wars.

"We'll make it, Degrelle." He whispered, so as not to disturb the others. "Do you want to trade letters with me? I've survived so many close calls that I'm not worried. After the inferno at Stalingrad I feel immune to death."

"*Bien sur.* That's not it. I'm not afraid. My men and I can fight. You saw how they handle Russian tanks. Like acrobats, *non*? Takes a *Panzerfaust*, runs up to the tank, and kaboom!" Degrelle leaned his fresh young face into his hands. He wore a signet ring. Ingo noticed his slender fingers and graceful motions. Women probably adored him.

"Then what bothers you? You don't have to tell me, of course. I don't mean to pry."

"You are a friend, Kroll. It's when I write to *Maman* that I get sad. She's so good. I'm her only child. She didn't want me to go to war. Not with the Germans. But I wanted to fight communists. To wipe them out before they wipe us out. I must fight."

Ignoring the clinking chains of the passing tanks and the voices shouting commands, they traded letters and parted with a warm handshake.

Ingo joined his men. Trucks, *Kubelwagen*, and motorcycles skidded in the mud. What used to be a dirt road had been churned up. Low flying He 111's dropped boxes of ammunition and shells. The men scuttled off before the crates hit them. Shouts and screams pierced through the explosions and the blue and yellow flares.

General Lieb and his staff rode in on horseback. In his fur cap, he looked like a Russian.

A signal officer stepped up and saluted. "We lost contact with General Stemmermann. Hill 239 is still in Russian hands."

"Damn," said the General. "By now that hill must be covered with German bodies and littered with burnt-out tanks. We must warn Stemmermann that he is marching straight into a trap. He believes the hill was taken. He must retreat, if he can."

"I can't see how, Herr General."

Lieb checked his watch under a flashlight. "2300 hours. *Vorwarts! Marsch!*"

Ingo took his orders and rode back to his men, picking his way through the maelstrom of troops and vehicles desperately trying to escape death. Ninety-two of his men awaited him in the dark. A biting wind whirled snow — ideal weather for their clandestine march toward Dzhurzhentsy.

Within an hour they reached the road where a column of Soviet tanks approached. Ingo heard them before he made out their hulks in the dark. This was not part of their plan. All he could think of was bluff. In their white tunics they all looked alike. They had no way of knowing that the Germans had escaped.

He stopped, waved and shouted, "*Stoi!*" one of the few Russian words he knew. To his surprise the giant monsters respected his command. They stopped. They could not catch his face or insignias. Unsuspecting, they assumed Ingo was one of them. He waved a greeting and then signaled his men to follow him across the road, expecting to be cut down by a bullet. Should the Russians discover his identity, he and his men were mincemeat. The tanks rolled off.

At the forest, Ingo trembled. They had to keep moving and vanish before daybreak.

"God, what luck," Decker whispered as if the Russians could hear him. He was so nervous that he had stopped scratching.

A fire erupted in the distance. "The next brigade was not as lucky," Ingo remarked. "But they are better equipped to fight."

"*Jawohl*, Herr Hauptmann," Decker said and blew his nose. "There's one good thing about this."

"What's that?"

"No mines."

By daybreak the Soviets had discovered Ingo and his men, firing on them with tanks, guns and mortars. The open field gave no cover and without armor-piercing weapons, Ingo had no defense. Russian T-34's awaited him on the slope, pumping shells into the valley he had to pass. Ingo lowered his binoculars. "*Verfluchte Scheisse!*"

Sergeant Erhart, the wizard of anti-tank tactics, took his sidekick, Corporal Schatz, to a handcart and picked out three anti-tank grenades. "I'll take care of Ivan, Herr Hauptmann," he said, his face as white as his tunic. Once they came within view of the tanks, the two men slithered across the lip of the ravine toward them, jumped up, and fired. Crump! Crump! Crump! The first T-34 went up in smoke, providing cover for the men. The crew perished. Schatz knocked out two more and Erhart got the last.

The remaining hulks set in motion. But instead of charging at the invisible enemy, they turned around and disappeared. The road was clear. The men cheered, pressed forward, and soon joined Colonel Muller and the remainder of the 72nd Infantry Division awaiting them in the woods.

Ingo stood on a tank at the edge of the forest, and watched a single rider come galloping up the slope. To his left a column of peasant carts loaded with wounded men drove up bearing a Red Cross flag. A dozen T-34's rattled toward them and opened fire. Their machine guns mowed down the horses, then crushed the wagons and with them the wounded.

Ingo wretched. "The swine! Retaliation for our escape."

Muller nodded, his face a white mask of despair.

The horseman galloped into a gap of 50 yards between a Stalin-II and a T-34 tank, spurring the steaming animal through the driving snow. He crossed the open field toward the woods. A shell struck the horse's head. It collapsed on the frozen ground. The rider struggled out of his stirrups and snatched his rifle. Ingo ran out to his rescue, caught the exhausted man in his arms and pulled him into the woods.

"Close call. Thanks, buddy."

Ingo and Decker wrapped him in a blanket.

"Colonel Franz. You saw that, didn't you? The wounded of the 'Viking' Division." His voice broke.

Muller pulled a flask of schnapps from his greatcoat and poured it into Franz's mouth. "I thought I'd seen my share of atrocities. But that was deliberate murder. We know what we're up against."

Ingo remembered Olga's words. "The Devil's helpers feed on human blood." Who was she? Where did he fit in? "We must move on."

The men struggled to their feet.

"General Gille could not leave the wounded behind," Franz said, struggling back to his feet. "Didn't have the heart. Who does? Then that! Dr. Isselstein was among them. One of our best surgeons. God only knows how many lives he saved. May the Lord have mercy on their souls." He crossed himself and stood in silent prayer. Every head bowed. Shots cracked, and two Walloons appeared. "*Merde*. Machine guns block us."

Franz picked up his rifle. "I have a scope." He jogged off, followed by Ingo and Muller. Ingo stopped at the clearing, and fell to the ground, then crawled under the cover of pine branches, following footprints and wheel tracks.

Franz scanned the terrain. "There they are. A machine gun nest." He aimed and fired. The men fell. "They will not bother us again."

When nothing stirred, they crawled toward the shallow dip, threw a stone at it, and waited. Nothing. Rifles cocked, Ingo and Franz peeked in. "Dead!"

They collected the Maxims and ammunition and returned to the column.

Ingo found some crackers in his pocket. His bottle still had some schnapps. Life felt good again.

Major Hermani joined him. "You are the most successful column in the operation. The XLII Corps took a terrible beating. Still no news from General Stemmermann. Hill 239 cost more lives than I care to mention. I pray he is not one of the casualties. A fine officer and a gentleman."

Ingo remembered the disciplined Prussian. Whatever had happened, he took it like the man he was.

A column of Russian tanks awaited the Germans at Hill 222, east of Lysyanka, a stone's throw from salvation.

Guns fired. Those not killed dropped into the snow for cover. Others ran off and set up a defense against the now charging Russian infantry. Ingo, Muller and Hermani fired the sub-machine guns they had snatched from their fallen men.

"Keep running," Ingo shouted to his men, retreating behind the shrubs along the banks of the Gniloys Tikich River. The men panicked and fled toward the bank. It was just what the Russians had intended.

The dark, gurgling river was no more than thirty yards wide, but treacherous. Ice bobbed in the fast-flowing current. More and more men crowded the bank, the ominous roar of T-34's and Stalin II's behind them.

The men jumped into the gurgling river while tanks fired mercilessly into the crowd on the banks. Death cries, screams, and commands blended into the noise of the high-explosive shells. Stampeding men shoved each other into the stream and struggled in the icy water. Once caught in the rapid current, they began to drown. From shore, thirty yards of river looked like an easy crossing, but the freezing stream required strength and a clear head.

"Damn that panic," Ingo screamed, fighting off the onslaught. "Spread out! Spread out! Listen, men. Spread out!"

Some stopped and stared at the tanks in their back, pushed forward by those behind them. Ingo fired his gun to get their attention, but it was as effective as an exploding balloon amid fireworks.

Colonel Franz screamed, "Stop, men, stop!"

Some cool-headed men shed their greatcoats and jumped into the water. Within minutes they reached the other bank and clapped their arms like giant birds, then helped others.

Franz chose a clear spot and jumped. In a few forceful strokes he reached the other bank, grabbed the branches of a willow and held on. They caught his coat. Ingo watched him struggle. His motions grew feeble. Leutnant Guldenpfennig ran to the rescue and pulled Franz from the river.

Ingo supervised his men during the crossing. Major Hermani got through. General Gille organized the crossing of his "Vikings" personally. Wearing his fur cap, he directed the operation with his knobby stick. So far some 4,500 men had made it; he was not about to lose any now. The tractor he had driven into the river as an emergency footbridge was carried off by the stream.

Ingo and eight men formed a human chain between swimmers and non-swimmers, then stepped into the icy water gurgling around them. Drowning men screamed for help. The icy water became unbearable. His legs went numb. Despite his efforts, he could no longer bear the torment and crossed the river. His men pulled him up on the slippery bank. Ignoring his violently shivering body, he helped others reaching the bank.

Wagons, horses and human bodies came bobbing down the turbulent river. More and more men grabbed Ingo's stiff and freezing hands. He slipped twice and almost fell back into the stream.

The Walloons marched up carrying their wounded on peasant carts along with their fallen commander, Colonel Lippert. Four men wrapped his body in a sheet of canvas and piloted it across the river, rather than leave him to the Russians.

General Lieb rode across on his swimming horse, though the gelding was swept from under him and drowned.

Division after division arrived and tested their final endurance. The Russian tanks kept firing into the fleeing crowd. The ground was now littered with bodies, obliging others to step over them.

The Thuringian Panzer engineers under Major Braun built a number of emergency footbridges, enabling the rear guards to cross the river without leaping into the icy water.

Ingo succumbed to the agony of cold. His frozen hands could no longer hold others. Flapping his arms, he ran to the outpost before he too turned into a casualty. His wet uniform was frozen stiff. Water sloshed in his boots. His teeth chattered as if he had been shocked. In the overcrowded and overheated hut, thick with the stench of wet clothes and unwashed men, he fought his way through the mass of shivering bodies toward the hot pot-bellied stove. The men had stripped to their shorts and rubbed life into the numbed muscles of their white scrawny bodies. They were safe.

Soldiers from the outpost brought cauldrons of hot soup. "Where's your bowl?" a large man asked, ladle in hand.

Ingo stood in his underwear like everybody else. "What do you mean my bowl?" he bellowed. "Do you think I had nothing better to do than worry about my goddamn mess kit? Get us some bowls. Now!"

"Shell-shocked," the men whispered.

One of them, as skinny as an Indian cow, picked up the fight. "We're through being treated like cannon fodder."

"Hell!" bellowed a tall, haggard man, who grimaced with pain. "What's all this anyway? Taking one's hide to market and what do you get? Who wants soup anyway. Where's the schnapps!"

"Look, man, we're doing all we can," the man with the ladle said. The soldiers ignored him and shoved toward the stove. Those nearby were deep red and sweaty but refused to step back. More men stumbled into the hut. Their angry grumbling grew louder.

Aware that he had caused the unrest, Ingo said in a soothing voice, "Look, men. There are other izbas around. Not so crowded. They have schnapps."

"How do you know?"

"Because I saw it," Ingo lied, rubbing his arms. "I'm going there myself. I'm starved."

The newcomers went on. Others, warm now, got dressed and left. Ingo picked up his coat and noticed Degrelle's soaked letter. Had his survived? No matter. He could write new ones.

The heat of the room slowly penetrated his body, but the shivers ravaged on. Stacks of blankets arrived. He grabbed one, and wrapped it around himself rather than sit in his wet clothes. Slowly, he warmed up.

On his way to the command post he rejoiced. *Olga! I made it!*

Over the following days, the commanders counted their losses and organized the survivors. The men took turns staying in the huts. They repaired their uniforms, ate and slept. Tanks, anti-tank guns and a column of trucks stood in formation awaiting further orders.

At the command post, the officers chatted until General Lieb called them to order. His eyes bright, a congenial smile on his face, he stood tall in his new, crisp uniform, the thinning hair combed back. "What I have to tell you requires no explanation or plan," he said. "*Generalfeldmarschal* von Manstein has granted all survivors of the Korsun pocket a two-week recuperation leave in Poland."

Nobody moved.

"What's the matter. Don't you believe me? We will start deployment right away. The men need rest, and so do you."

"Are you sure?" Ingo wondered.

"Did our Supreme Commander agree to that?" Franz asked.

General Lieb nodded. "Probably under pressure, but he did."

The news traveled. The whole camp of 35,000 men turned into a festival. Fatigue, aches, and even the cold were briefly forgotten.

"I'll believe it when I board a train going west," said the stoic ones.

Ingo visited Degrelle and his Walloons. The young commander had been promoted to captain and would probably receive a medal of valor. He and three thousand men and civilians had survived the ordeal.

"Hey, Degrelle," Ingo shouted, waving to his friend. "Sure glad you made it. Did you hear our orders? Recuperation leave. What do you say to that? In Poland."

"You are joking, *mon ami*!

"I must tell my men right away." He had tears in his eyes.

"I'm afraid your letter got soaked," Ingo confessed.

"Good. Now Maman will get good news. I sent your letters off." Degrelle turned to his men. "Good news. Two weeks furlough."

The men threw their caps into the air as Ingo headed for the staff office. "Olychka, my love," he sang, "I'll see you at the Esplanade and celebrate our miracle."

Chapter 10

On her way to the Esplanade, Olga skidded over the frozen sidewalk like a happy child. Over the past three weeks she had been so worried about Ingo, often questioning Father's promise. She had sensed the danger he was in, saw the enemy everywhere, and shared his frustration and despair. Two days ago, the darkness had lifted. Father's message said that Ingo was safe and would come to her. Of course that was impossible. Still, stranger things had happened. There was hope.

This morning Father had come to her. His message had been dubious, *Ingo is on his way.* Physically? Spiritually? A letter? What difference did it make so long as he was safe and with her in spirit. During her meditation she felt a surge of contentment. Olga watched a bright orange sun rise. Ingo. Her love for him thrived on expectation.

Stasya was gone. Gottfried had arranged a job for her in his friend's shoe factory. In gratitude, Stasya had offered her help when Olga would need it. Help? What could a Pole do for her anyway?

Olga skidded across a frozen puddle like an ice-skater. Who said a grown woman had to be serious? Let the passers-by frown and the old street sweeper think she had lost her mind. The flock of little gray sparrows pecking at fresh horse dung took off.

The Esplanade was packed with soldiers. In the thick smoke Olga could barely discern their faces. Their loud chatter and the giggling women reminded her of old times. The men were back and called out for *Noch ein Bier.*

"What's going on?" she asked Frau Metzger. "Where did these men come from?"

"The Russian front," Frau Metzger said, her big face all smiles as she drew beer from the spigot.

"What? The Russian front? Are you serious? Going west?" Olga looked around. The soldiers' thin, pale faces grinned. Could the one she was waiting for be among them? That would be asking too much. But then, she had that feeling. Running her fingers through her curls, she scanned the faces. If Ingo were among them, he would make himself known. She sat down at the keyboard and opened the lid. Who cared about her mended stockings and scuffed shoes as long as they could admire her slender legs. Her bulky sweater, the only one she had, hid her breasts.

Applause.

"Thank you and welcome. It's been a while since we had so many of you here. The transports heading east stopped coming."

The men chuckled. Some flocked to the dance floor, and soon marked time to her slow waltz, *Love, You Heaven on Earth*. Hobnailed boots scraped against the wood. The women sang along.

"Any requests?" Olga asked.

A voice with a Saxon accent called out, "*I Know Some Day a Miracle Will Happen.*" It rang out like church bells. Olga's heart raced. Her face flushed. Silence set in; all eyes were on her.

"Ingo?" she cried out, jumping up. "Ingo!"

The dancers stepped aside.

He rose, all smiles. It was him, not a fantasy or a dream. He was actually here in the flesh. All of him, whole.

Olga ran toward him, bumping into the men until she landed in his arms. He swung her around like a child. They kissed and laughed.

"Ingo! Is it really you? My darling, you are here. Look, Frau Metzger, it's Ingo. Remember him? Our hero. Imagine." She presented him to the crowd.

He took little notice of their applause. Turned toward her, he put his arm around her shoulders, and held her in a gesture of belonging. Olga squeezed his hand. Frau Metzger handed him the beer she had just drawn. "Here, have this," she said. "If only my Otto would come home. I haven't heard from him for some time."

Ingo took the glass, saluted Frau Metzger, then followed Olga to the piano. The crowd sat down and watched them.

"I promised I'd come back, didn't I?" he said. "Sorry it took so long."

She held his hand and closed her eyes. "Ingo, is it really you?"

"It's as close as it gets."

"You can't imagine how happy I am. Out of my mind." Her hot face beamed. This was too good to be true. The smoke and stuffy air was forgotten. Ingo had come back.

"I know how you feel, my Olychka." They embraced. Olga felt the stiff cloth of his new uniform. He lifted her off the ground. "Olga," he whispered. "My darling."

A delicious sensation surged up. This was not an out-of-body experience, nor a trance. They were together.

Their arms wrapped around each other, they turned to the audience. "We have been waiting for each other for a long time," she said with a dimpled smile. "Probably every one of you is waiting for somebody. Our wish came true. Perhaps, yours will too. Let me play his request for all of you."

The men clapped and stomped.

"I love you so, Olychka," he said softly into her ear while she played. Not a trace of anger or cynicism marred his voice. He had found love, its healing power and whole wonderful magnificence.

"How long can you stay?" she asked, getting to the refrain.

"How long can you put up with me?"

"Forever and ever! And beyond."

He grinned. "How about two weeks?"

"Two weeks?" Olga lost her beat. "Two weeks? Ingo! Two whole weeks. That's too good to be true."

Leaning against the upright, he watched her embellish each tune into a concert piece. Trills and arpeggios lifted the melody like her throbbing and swooning heart. Inspired by her artistry, the dancers performed intricate figures, whirling their partners around and catching them again. The soldiers at the tables tapped their feet.

Frau Metzger filled glass after glass. Hilde served schnapps from Frau Metzger's special reserve.

During intermission Olga drank from Ingo's glass, her eyes on his. The gaunt face had become familiar again, and his happy smile contagious. His amusing chatter had an intimate familiarity. She could not wait to run her fingers through the thick short waves of his hair. Nobody had shaved them down to stubble. A deep line cut between his brows and three furrows ran across his forehead. The pain and hardship of the front had left their marks on his oval face.

He turned the page for her. "You are everything I dreamed of, only a thousand times better. A million times more beautiful than I remember. And your music! It flows straight into my soul, whips up my blood, and some other places I dare not mention. Your love, my darling, makes you divine. You radiate. Your fire ignites every man's heart. Mine in particular. Do you realize what it means to be so close and not touch you? Good thing you can't read my mind. I'll suffer in silence and be as good as a choir boy. Honestly, unless..."

"Unless?" she teased, without interrupting her play.

"Unless you allow me to stay on that old sofa of yours. Unless, well, unless you let me hold your hand. Unless, you care enough. Trust me enough. What can I say?"

She winked impishly. "Unless I would die if you didn't." She could barely concentrate on her music. Let the patrons protest and Frau Metzger throw a fit. This was her night, and Ingo was a war hero.

Hilde brought fresh beer. "On the house. With Frau Metzger's compliments."

Ingo raised his glass to the plump woman behind the counter.

"I'll pretend it's true," he said. "It's been so long. A year is an eternity. Your eyes enchant me. Can it be love? Keep playing. If I didn't have two weeks, I would do things Frau Metzger would not approve of. But what right do I have to deprive Schafer there and Kunz of your artistry." He waved to them. "They earned it. You have no idea what we went through." He took a long swallow of beer, then downed a jigger of schnapps. "I love your mysterious eyes. No, don't say anything. Let me guess what they divine."

She played a tango. The catchy rhythm fired up the dancers. Their steps, tender voices, and soft laughter echoed through the room like gentle waves. Cigarette smoke, perfumes, beer, and floor wax added to the homey atmosphere. It was all so wonderful.

"The men devour you with their eyes," he said. "But I'm not jealous. You are mine. You chose me, didn't you? To have and to keep, forever and ever?"

Her heart pounded so hard that she skipped some of the accompaniment. Sweat pearled on her forehead. "Yes, for ever and ever."

The applause began before she finished the piece. The audience watched Olga and Ingo. Hilde wiped her tears. The men pressed the hands of the women they danced with. Even Frau Metzger had warmed up. The kitchen help came and watched. Everybody had loved ones they pined for or mourned.

Ingo reached for her hand and kissed it. "I love you so, Olga. What will it be like holding you in my arms and…"

"Wait and see. Your letters were so touching. When it comes to writing, I have no talent at all. I speak through my music."

Her waltz invited him to her home, her heart—all of her.

At quitting time, Ingo whisked her to the back door, waving a quick good-bye to Frau Metzger. The moment the door closed, he pulled Olga into his arms and kissed her hungrily, passionately. He was so aroused now that he would have taken her right there, in the cold street. She barely noticed the bright moon and did not feel the cold at all, though her breath formed vapor. Ingo had come. He was here. Would stay with her in her bed. Anyna was not at home. They could dwell in the fire of their passion. For the first time she would experience the power of sex. She pulled him along. "Let's go! Let's go. Come quick. We have no time to lose."

"Do you mean it? My Olychka?"

Their steps crunched on the frozen snow, faster and faster.

"We'll be all alone. Anyna is at my mother's."

"Olychka, you miracle of miracles," he said panting. "How I longed for you." At the door he kissed her again, looking up at the sky. "I want the moon and stars to hear me, Olga. They are my witnesses. Everything within me loves everything about you. Olga, you are my life."

She closed her eyes and abandoned herself to his kiss. Their lips lingered, exalting in the happiness they brought each other. "My love is as deep as the night, as bright as the moon, and as eternal as the stars above. I cannot be whole without you. Just as life needs water, and roses need sun, I can only live with your love." She kissed his eyes, warm cheeks and lips. Neither the frosty air nor the dark street interfered with their rising desire.

Running up the stairs, every fiber in her body yearned for him. The old steps squeaked. Olga giggled. On the next landing he caught her hand, stopped, and kissed her. At her door he took the heavy key and unlocked it. "And here comes paradise," he said as he lifted her up and carried her over the threshold. "From now on we belong together."

As soon as he put her down, he almost ripped off her coat and folded his arms around her. "This calls for music." They danced to the tango on the radio, their bodies molding toward each other. The bulge in his trousers aroused her even more.

He tousled her curls. The strip of light coming from the open door pointed at the bed. "There is magic in your hair," he whispered, and took off her sweater. While he unzipped her skirt she loosened his tie, unbuttoned his shirt and then his trousers. "Are you sure?" he wondered, quite ready to go ahead. "I was not prepared for such a welcome. You are divine." He unfastened her garters and unhooked her bra, then cradled her small breasts. "Will you really share all that wonder with me?"

"Share?" she mused. "Unless you take it, what good is it?"

Now it was her turn to discover his body. She held his powerful erection and kissed him. How sweet it was, so warm and alive. "Ooh. Your body gives me such a thrill. You are wonderful, my love. I've been longing for this, imagining…"

In a swift motion he pulled her toward him and rolled into bed. She pulled the covers over them, then offered her body to him for his gentle fingers to caress. He knew just where. Her pelvis rose, eager to received him. "Yes, yes." Within moments she was all his, abandoning herself to the ecstatic rising of her sensuality. She was ready to come, but wanted him to be with her at that moment—it would be the first time with a man, her man.

He eased off, leaving her craving him until he slipped into her. It was all so natural, so simple, so unbelievable. Love joined couples. Clinging to him, she pulled him tighter and closer, so that he could penetrate deeper and deeper. To her surprise, it did not hurt at all. She wanted more, to have him thrust harder, faster. "Yes, yes, yes. Now."

But he would not oblige, prolonging their first union to its ultimate conclusion. No pain, just pleasure, that oceanic feeling she had heard of but never felt. The sweetness of his warm, caring hands lifted her into the heavens. The explosive climax pulled her into total surrender. Her body convulsed with delight. From now on she was all his. A joyous cry escaped her chest. Their passionate kisses surged until the climax ebbed. His gentle strokes allowed her to linger just a little bit longer, while she gratefully held his moist organ like a little bird resting in her warm hands, sweet and lovable.

Her touch aroused the sleepy little thing. It stretched and tightened until it rose again in all its glory, boasting its prowess.

The second climax erupted quickly. "I could go on and on," she whispered.

He nuzzled her. "We don't have to do it all in one night. Remember there are thirteen more to come. This little fellow needs some rest. The big fellow too. I've been on the go for weeks. I'll wake up in your arms. A living dream."

Olga had no idea what time it was when the doorbell rang; the black-out blinds kept the apartment dark.

"I'll get rid of whoever it is," she said, slipping into her silk robe. The brush smoothed her unruly curls. Her face was still red and her lips burnt.

A second, then a third ring.

Now what? The Gestapo? "All right! I'm coming!" she shouted, and unlocked the door. Like an apparition, the veiled face of her mother-in-law confronted her.

"Don't tell me you are still in bed?"

"Good morning, Countess," Olga said, surprised at her cool voice. "If you give me a minute, I'll get dressed. I did not expect a visitor at this hour."

"Obviously. The artist's life. Aren't you going to ask me in?" She did not wait for an invitation, and marched straight into the living room, her fox boa draped around her neck.

"Anyna is at school," Olga said.

"I would hope so. May I remind you that her name is Anna Magdalena, and that I did not expect to find her here. Sorry to impose on your precious time."

That did not keep her from taking possession of the living room.

"Since Muhammad will not come to the mountain," the Countess continued, "I had no choice but make the arduous trip myself. Not an easy task, considering my age and the weather. You certainly don't care whether I'm on the verge of death." She gestured with her gloved hand. "Let's not talk about me. If it were not for Lothar asking me to see you, I would not bother. I'll never know what he sees in you. But that's neither here nor there. My poor son is under the impression that you suffer great hardships."

"I would write, but you insist..."

"There's no point in bothering him with your domestic trivia. He has enough problems."

Olga pulled out a chair, and helped her mother-in-law sit down. She still had the slender body and classic features that turned people's heads. The uninitiated admired her. Olga knew better, and once again saw the ugly and dark side of this chiseled face with its porcelain-smooth skin and large brown eyes, as devious as that of a vampire. The fashionable hat suited her well. She had style.

"You can write to Lothar not to worry about me."

"That's what I keep telling him. But he is so concerned. As if he does not have enough to cope with at the POW camp, far away from home. He cannot reach my friend, Mr. McCormick. Another burden I have to bear. Frederick could get Lothar more liberty. But we are at war, and enemies of the Americans. A hopelessly stupid predicament." She lifted the veil from her white face. The Countess's eyes chastised Olga for spoiling Lothar's career. As if he ever had one.

Ingo was waiting.

The Countess raised her chin, and presented her famous profile. "Nobody cares how difficult it is for me to keep house, considering my heart condition and migraine headaches. But my so-called daughter-in-law cannot be bothered. Not that I expect charity."

"Your 'so-called daughter-in-law,'" Olga said, retying the sash of her robe, "is busy raising a child and making a living, And now, please excuse me, but I must practice for my performance tonight."

The Countess dropped the corners of her painted mouth in a gesture of disgust. "Some performance. As if the trash you play can be considered music?" She shrugged. "I once had a staff of eleven taking care of my house, and now must fend for myself while my so-called daughter-in-law has the audacity to tell me that she is busy sleeping in and is not interested in my visit. By now you should be able to play those trashy tunes in your sleep. Not that I ever saw any talent in your tinkering. Poor Lothar." She dabbed her nose with her cologne-drenched handkerchief. Lothar had probably sent it to his mother while he was stationed in France. "Well, I will not intrude any longer."

Olga pulled up the blackout shades. Daylight caught the empty glasses on the table. "With Stasya gone ..."

"You never knew how to treat a servant. Stasya came with the spoils of victory."

Olga let it pass. "How are Nicky and Lara?" she asked, referring to Lothar's half-brother and sister.

"Fine, thank you. They are wonderful children who appreciate their mother, something Anna Magdalena has yet to learn. From the time Lothar left, she lost her manners and respect. Poor Lothar has no idea what is happening to his daughter."

"His daughter? But I thought..."

"A technicality. There are certain similarities."

"I'm tired of those old accusations. If you don't consider Anyna your grand-daughter, why don't you just leave her alone. We can manage without your help." She faced the Countess, wishing she could hide Ingo's coat lying on the floor. "If you have a letter from Lothar ..."

"What letter? I merely wanted to see what I can report to him about Anna Magdalena. Father or not, he did and does look after her."

"To tell you the truth, I would prefer he would consider us non-existent!" Olga wished she had not said that.

"Look, Olga. I know how you feel about us. I know you can't live up to our standards, but at least you could appreciate what I do for your child. Some day she will be grateful, believe me. People judge you by your manners and your speech. Training starts in the cradle. How can you let Anna Magdalena refuse to kiss my hand? This may be a minor matter to you. But where do you draw the line? Pretty soon she will eat with her fingers and leave the house without gloves." The Countess wrapped the boa around her neck. She was getting cold but would not admit it.

Olga was freezing too, but made no attempt at starting a fire. "I'll mention it to her."

The Countess pursed her lips. "She had the audacity to say that other children don't kiss their grandmother's hand. How can she compare herself to street urchins? Polacks? If this absurd war had not come about, I would have sent her to a Swiss boarding school. Now the borders are closed. God only knows what will become of her. Lothar is so naïve. He has no idea who he is dealing with." She sighed, pressing the back of her hand against her forehead. "Pearls to the swine."

"The world changed..."

"What did I just say?" The Countess moaned in utter despair. "Pearls to the swine. You did not hear a thing I said, did you? The Reich will collapse, but life goes on. Manners will make a difference, not money. Noblesse oblige. She is a baroness. Dear Lord, why do You punish me so?"

"God has nothing..."

"Not another word, please. I must leave before my heart breaks. Lothar asked me to look after you. Dear God, why don't You take me now. This world is getting too much for me." She closed her eyes, waiting for Olga's apology.

"Let me open the door for you."

The Countess fumed. "I never saw a more heartless person. Here I am, on the verge of death, and you throw me out. But I must bear my cross. My poor son..."

Olga knew the trap. "You can write to him that we are fine."

"I can see when I am not wanted," the Countess whined. "There is no gratitude in this vulgar world. I managed to climb all those stairs, despite my poor health, mind you. Don't bother telling Anna Magdalena about my visit. The poor child is a victim. She has some talent. Nothing spectacular. With proper upbringing she might make a mark. But that is not about to happen." She paused at the hallway. Hanging on top of Olga's and Anyna's coats were Ingo's officer's cap and coat.

"Oh!" she said, as if she had found Olga in a brothel. "I see. Well, that explains everything. Sorry I disturbed your tête-à-tête. Give your friend my regards. Poor Lothar. He deserves better." With a jerk of her chin, she stomped out.

Olga watched her step over the threshold, knowing that this would start a new and vicious chapter in her relationship with her mother-in-law. What was there to say? And why bother? It could hardly get any worse. The Countess headed for the stairs like a wounded queen, or a victorious one? Now she had some real gossip to feed to Lothar.

Olga closed the door, and ran through the cold living room back to Ingo.

"There you have it," she muttered, cuddling into his arms. The warmth of his body reassured her. "She does it every time. The bitch has a sixth sense. Knows how vulnerable I am. But she can't touch me now. You are my shield, Ingo. I belong to you."

They held each other. "Don't take it to heart, *mein Liebling*," he said. "She needs you and Anyna. A lonely old woman who clings to you because you are all she has."

Olga warmed up in Ingo's embrace. Her face rested against his chest. She played with his hairs and nipples. "Thank you for saying that, Ingo. Anyna is my life and my joy." The scent of their love-making stimulated their need.

He nuzzled into her neck. "You are the loveliest woman on earth. That old woman is jealous because you have what she craves. Youth and beauty. If she destroys Lothar's wife, she can have him to herself. Perfectly logical."

Olga sunk her lips into his. As long as he was here, nobody could touch her.

Ingo helped Olga make a fire in the stove while she rummaged through the larder. All she found was ersatz coffee and some bread. Then she scraped some jam from a glass jar and found just enough milk for coffee.

After breakfast, they built a fire under the hot water boiler in the bathroom.

"I live the life of a nun," she said. "Take care of my child, look after my mother—still, I can't win." Tears filled her eyes. "All these years. You can't imagine, Ingo. The Countess is a curse I must endure. Can you see it?" She sobbed into his chest.

He held her. "Better than you think. We all have emotional ties that burden and haunt us. Didn't you say, bless it and let it go? That's what it takes. I know it isn't easy. But we must try, rather than be victims of other people's schemes. We have each other."

Where did Ingo's insight come from, Olga wondered. Had years at the front developed his philosophy and deep understanding?

He dabbed the tears from her eyes. His warm, soothing voice unraveled the thick knot in her soul.

He had put on his moss-green uniform shirt and trousers, but stayed in his stocking feet. The stiff new boots stood in the hallway.

"Your clothes look so new," she remarked.

"Men coming from the front are supposed to look decent, not to frighten people at home. That's why we must stay in Poland." He winked. "Suits me fine. My buddies long for their wives or mothers. Perhaps they can come here to Poland."

"And you?" Olga asked, putting a fresh towel next to the tub, then returning to the kitchen.

"You are my home," he said. "This is where I belong." He kissed her hand. A broad smile crossed his lean face.

"Is it that bad?" she asked.

He nodded. "Remember my advice. Get out of here before the Russians come. They will, believe me. We can't stop them, only slow them down."

Olga gasped. "Where do you want me to go?"

"West."

She held his hand against her cheek.

"I can't believe I am here, in this kitchen," he said. "Every time a tank explodes or an enemy falls, I think: one less trying to kill me. Then it occurs to me that the man I killed is a man like myself. A reasonable fellow. The tank has six nice fellows inside burning to death. We could be friends. But we can't think about that. We are enemies. The numbers are stacked against us." A deep frown furrowed his forehead. His cheek twitched. "We and the Russians want to control Europe. The Russians will succeed."

Ingo buried his face in his hands. His shoulders trembled.

Olga held him. Stroking his head, she saw burning tanks and men crying for help.

He chewed on his bread and sipped ersatz. "The Countess was a good antidote," he said. "Absurd, but real. I used to mock my mother for fussing over every speck of dust. Now I know that she craved recognition and praise. The only way she could excel was cooking and keeping house. This intelligent and capable woman could not pursue a career or do some other meaningful task except community work. The Movement allowed her to do that. With the National Socialist Women she could do real work, organize projects for women and children, educate and indoctrinate. My father did not want her to work in the Party, but he could not stop her. He never understood what makes women so effective in their work, except his nurses. It only came to me now. I understand why you enjoy entertaining at the Esplanade when you should be playing in a concert hall."

"Yes, yes," Olga agreed. "Now you can see why I was so frustrated when Lothar would not let me use the piano. That's almost as bad as going hungry while there is plenty of food on the table. The piano is my life."

"As it should be." Ingo pulled her on his lap.

She leaned her head against his. "I'm no good at housework. Nor do I make it my business what other people wear. I run around in anything I like, or nothing." She chuckled. "As you can see, I don't fuss about my clothes. My friend Lucie scolds me for it. You did not care what I wore when you talked to me, did you?"

He rocked her. "All I knew was that you were the most fascinating, attractive, adorable, and beautiful woman I'd met."

"I wish my mother could hear that."

"I will tell her."

"She will not believe you. But why don't you tell your mother that you appreciate all the work she does?"

He shook his head. "That would be all wrong. Perfection must go unnoticed, else it looks as if she takes pride in it. Remember, her being a wife and mother is her duty, as is helping others. If I detect she resents doing it, she's flunked."

Olga poured the last of the milk into their ersatz. She should go grocery shopping, only this was the end of the month and she had almost no coupons left. "You are right. We keep pretending. Perhaps Lothar never knew how I longed to play the piano."

"Because he is an artist and a genius," Ingo said and winked.

"So you remember?"

"I had plenty of time to think about it. I also found out who the artist and genius around here is. I can't wait to get a taste of Gershwin's music. *Rhapsody in Blue*. What a strange name. Why blue? Let's hope it's the music of the future rather than the *balalaika*. When I am your husband, Olga …"

Olga looked up. "Did you say, husband?"

"That's right, husband. Some day we shall get married. That's what you predicted. I will insist that you play in public. Share your God-given talents with the world."

Had she heard right? Was he proposing?

Olga led him to the bathroom. "The water should be hot by now."

The warmth of the small room felt like summer. "Just right," she said. Soon steaming hot water splashed into the tub. "A good soak will do you good. Wash off all the grime of the past year. I'll come and scrub your back. Start a new life with a clean body and clear mind. Here, look, real French soap. While you soak I'll play the first part of *Rhapsody in Blue* for you. It's a very complex piece you may not like right away. Just listen to that jazzy beat, the fine phrasing, and original harmony this George Gershwin came up with."

Ingo shook his head in disbelief. "Is all this happening to me? Am I still on this earth?"

Olga laughed. "Of course. Step into the warm water and find out how good it feels. This huge old tub has room for two. How do you like that?" She helped undress him and admired her beloved man in his natural state. His treasure was slightly inflated but not to the point where he would want to satisfy it right away. Just feeling good.

Noticing her admiration for him he opened her robe, admired her well-formed body, and said, "You're so enticing."

"First the bath." He stepped into the tub, and slowly slipped into the water until it covered his scrawny and white body.

"God, does that feel good."

Olga left and played *Rhapsody in Blue*. The music of her future.

"Fascinating!" he called out from the bathroom.

"Isn't it? Cars, skyscrapers, factories, shops, trams. What energy and yet, can you hear the swooning lovers, the longing melody, the colors of Broadway with its tap-dancing girls? After practicing it for awhile I got to see that world."

"The water is cooling off," he reminded her.

She found him luxuriating in the large tub, his body red from the hot water, his hair wet. Drops of water ran over his face. He slipped aside. "Come, my love, and be mine."

"Yours," she said. "Yours forever." She dropped her robe and slipped into the tub. The water received her with its warmth. Two weeks, she thought, running her lips over his moist skin.

Chapter 11

The next morning Anyna stormed into the apartment. Olga could barely restrain her from racing into her bedroom. "We have a visitor."

"I know. Uncle Ingo came. I told Omi all along, but she wouldn't believe me. Can I greet him, Mami?"

"Not now. You must get ready for school. Uncle Ingo came from the war and is very tired. He needs lots of rest. Now, let's have breakfast."

Anyna was already in her coat, her satchel strapped to her back, when Ingo came out. "There's my little baroness," he greeted her.

"Uncle Ingo!" she cried out, and flung herself into his arms. He lifted her up and carried her. "I'm so glad you came," she said in a rush of words. "We've been thinking about you all the time. And we always listen to the *Front Request Program*. Mami lights a candle. I can hear the music from my room. Omi knits socks for you. When I'm older I'll knit you a sweater. Mami says it's terribly cold in Russia. It's pretty cold here too. But we always have a warm kitchen. I tried to draw your medals. Can I draw them after I come home from school? My teacher says the Iron Cross is a medal of valor. And that you are a great hero."

He kissed Anyna's forehead, then put her down. "You're the sweetest young lady I know. I'll be here for two weeks. Plenty of time for you to copy the medals."

"Two weeks!" she said, throwing her arms around him. "That's wonderful. You belong to us. Why can't you stay with us?"

He held her. "Because I must fulfill my duty. Fight the war, so that you will be protected from the bombs."

"Oh, I know. That's why Grandmaman is leaving for Bavaria. Mami, can I stay home. Just this once? Please?"

Olga shook her head, resisting Anyna's persuasion. "You'd better go now. Else you'll be late. We'll be here when you come back."

"Yes, sweet baroness," Ingo said sternly when she appealed to him, and turned her toward the door.

"You can call me Anyna. You're our family." Before she could say more she was pushed out the door.

"See you later," Ingo said.

"Unbelievable what children will come up with when they want something," Olga said, closing the door.

Now in broad daylight, the world had changed. Olga wished she could talk as freely as Anyna without worrying about what he would think. Yesterday was so unrestrained that she now felt embarrassed. Despite all the letters they had exchanged, they were virtual strangers. Yet, he took her into his arms and showed no signs of being shocked by her behavior. His cheekbones protruded and his eyes sat deep in their sockets. What had earned him and his men the furlough she wondered, setting two clean plates on the kitchen table. His mud colored sweater, the unbuttoned khaki shirt and clean trousers were new.

"We should go shopping for food," she said.

"I've got plenty of ration coupons. The Wehrmacht wants us to come back well fed so that we can do more fighting." Olga did not respond to the bitterness in his voice. Instead, she took the coupons and let him help her put on her coat.

"You should make evacuation plans, my love. I would feel much better if I knew you were safe in Germany. The Allies are not our friends, but they are not barbarians either. The Poles could stage an uprising if they find out that we can no longer keep them under control. Go to Dresden. My parents will take you in. My aunts will love you as much as I do."

"Love you as much as I do," resonated in Olga's mind like a song, though she doubted it. His mother had picked a girl from the neighborhood who fit into the family. Olga was not only married, she had a child.

"We'll see how things work out," she said evasively. "For the moment there's nothing to worry about. I'm not naïve, and will not take unnecessary chances. So rest assured that we'll be fine."

They had reached the street when a cold wind chased dark clouds above the rooftops of the three-story buildings, mostly tenements. They enjoyed shopping for bread, meat, margarine, potatoes. "Will there ever be a time again when we can buy what we need?"

"Not any time soon," Ingo said, helping her carry the groceries.

By the time Anyna returned from school they had prepared a good lunch. Anyna talked about her day and then mentioned that Stasya had come by last week. "She said not to worry, that she'll protect us."

"Protect us?" Olga wondered. "From what?"

"Partisans," Ingo said. "They have an underground network that wreaks havoc. They come out at night, and pilfer and destroy whatever they can get their hands on. They're smart and well organized. Stasya probably belongs to them. So, please listen to me, Olga. This is a very serious matter.

"Once our defenses weaken, anything can happen. This is enemy territory, though it has been annexed to Germany. Just because our government calls it so doesn't meant the Poles will let us get away with it. They'll kill you at the first opportunity."

Olga stared. Where did he get that idea? No point in arguing about it, certainly not in Anyna's presence. She could talk about it at school. He had already said too much. She blinked at him and jerked her head toward Anyna who was talking about how Grandmaman would leave as soon as it got warmer.

He got the message. "I'm just kidding," he said. "Of course the Poles will not do anything. They're our friends."

Dusk had set in when the three of them left for the Esplanade. The gray stucco buildings looked even grimier now. The city hibernated and waited for the thaw, Olga thought, remembering what Ingo had told her. What was going on behind those dark and sleepy facades? If he was right—and why shouldn't he be—she should consider some escape plan. She would talk to Gottfried about it. He certainly wouldn't want anything to happen to Lucie and his children.

The Esplanade teemed with soldiers and the women they had met last night. Their loud voices resounded through the thick smoke. Ingo set up two chairs next to the piano. Frau Metzger did not mind Anyna's presence. Business was booming. Her voluminous body was squeezed into a brown suit, sweat pearling on her red face, as she ordered the waitresses around like a drill sergeant.

A purple shawl draped over her black sweater, two combs holding back the mass of her curls, Olga and "her family" headed for the piano. The women cast curious glances at her. Of course they knew she was married and that Lothar served in the SS.

"It's so good to see you all here," she said to her audience. "By popular demand I'll play *I Know Some Day a Miracle Will Happen* for you."

The crowd responded with rousing applause. Cigarette smoke already filled the air, along with the intense smell of beer and sauerkraut. The kitchen help cooked up a storm for the hungry men who had plenty of coupons.

Ingo smiled. The pallor and the dark rings under his eyes reflected his lack of sleep, but his eyes glowed with love. Olga played for him.

Hilde brought beer and soda. She had put on lipstick and eyebrow pencil. Amazing what men could do in a woman's life, Olga mused.

"Don't you look pretty," she told Anyna.

"My name is Anna Magdalena, Baroness von Schenck. "

"Yes, I know. But for me you are still Anyna. A pretty name."

Ingo bowed with panache. "Noblesse oblige, you know."

At closing time, Anyna yawned. "Mami, you played all my favorite songs."

"Mine too," Ingo agreed.

Anyna did not fuss over bed time so long as Ingo told her a story— the shortest Olga had ever heard.

Ingo was still asleep when Olga saw Anyna off to school. "Be sure you go straight to Omi's when you come home. She will have lunch ready for you and will bring you down on her way to the Esplanade.

"But Mami…"

"No buts. We'll spend the evening together, I promise."

After a lavish breakfast of boiled eggs and fresh rolls, Ingo insisted that they go to the railway station to pick up his luggage. Their hands were always in contact with each other. They kissed and laughed all the way to the tram.

The large station hall was crowded with refugees hovering over their luggage like hens brooding over their eggs. The women wore black cloaks over quilted coats like Russians. "Volga Germans," Ingo explained. "They fled from the Soviets. The Russians are on a killing spree. Please, Olychka, leave Poland."

"Yes, yes," Olga said, watching a young mother rock her baby, her eyes lost in space. What did she see? What had happened to her?

A group of seventeen-year-old soldiers marched in, pumped up with a patriotism that would vanish as soon as the first bullets zipped past their heads. Basic training could not prepare them for the horrors of the battlefield.

"Cannon fodder," Ingo whispered at the baggage claim counter, then handed his claim check to a bulky woman in a navy blue uniform. She glanced at his medals, blushed and left. Moments later she returned with a beaten up suitcase. "I'm sure it's all there, Herr Major. How are things at the front? My husband and my two brothers are out there. Hans is with the 76th Infantry. I haven't heard from him for some time. I supposed you don't have time to write. He isn't much of a letter-writer to begin with."

Ingo lifted the suitcase. "Feels all right." Then turned to her, "The mail is slow and often gets lost. But keep on writing. We love letters from home."

The woman nodded. "I write every week. There isn't much to say, you know, other than that we're waiting for the final victory."

"The 76th is not a front line division."

She clutched his hands. "Thank you for saying that. I was so worried. Had he fallen, I would have been notified, right?" Her eyes searched his for reassurance.

"Absolutely. Our system is air-tight. Have faith."

"I do," the young woman said. "It's waiting that..."

Ingo took his suitcase. "Fighting is worse."

Leaving the terminal Olga asked, "Why would somebody steal your suitcase?"

"Because war is about destruction. The more the better."

The bitterness in his voice hurt. Olga knew so little about the war.

He waved down a *droshke*. The old carriage squeaked and bounced over the cobble stones. They passed Richard Wagner Strasse and headed for Adolf Hitler Strasse.

"What is in this treasure chest?" she asked, holding his gloved hand under the leather cover.

He laughed. "Food. The ultimate treasure these days."

At the apartment, Ingo unpacked his treasures.

"Real coffee!" Olga cried out, holding up the can. "Flour, sugar. What's in this box?"

"Chocolate bars for good girls," he said, lifting her up and whirling her around.

"Anyna will be out of her mind when she tastes it. I don't think she's ever had chocolate."

What had been a wonderful day left Olga thoughtful. They had visited Gottfried and Lucie, who confirmed Ingo's concern regarding their future. Neither Anyna's chatter nor Chopin's nocturne could ease the foreboding. She tried not to think about it—to enjoy Ingo's presence, his tenderness, his gallantry—but that heavy uneasiness in the pit of her stomach would not leave.

In bed, Olga nuzzled against his warm skin, her legs wrapped around his.

He stroked her hair. "Are you all right, Olychka?"

"No, not really. I feel like I'm walking to my execution."

"If you take my warnings to heart, you will be fine. I doubt the Brits or Americans will hurt you. Just stay away from the Russians."

"The Brits and Americans! You mean they will come to Germany?" Olga could not imagine such a picture. They would come and take Germany? But she did not say a thing. This was a night for love, not a night to talk about war and its consequences.

"Probably. All I'm asking is that you don't believe Hitler's promises of any miracles. God is not on his side, or anybody's. Never was." His fingers caressed her belly. The big black unknown vanished as soon as he discovered her pleasure spot.

"It is all about trust," she whispered, heaving her pelvis toward him.

His lips sucked at her neck while she held his big and full-blown erection. How hot and exciting it was. His body responded to her manipulations. Her own desire grew impatient, awaiting him moist and plump. He fondled it as she squealed with delight. Just another minute, a little more before she could no longer bear to wait. It came quickly, and would come again, exploding into an orgasm that overwhelmed all thought. Now that they were familiar with each other, they could prolong their excitement until they fell into total rapture.

Under the warmth of the comforter they held each other. This was true love, Olga thought. Sex without love was torture. For years, Lothar's sadistic demands had kept her in fear, anticipating pain and humiliation. Ingo fulfilled her so completely.

Johanna obviously did not believe in sex before marriage, did not know what she missed. No wonder she had not been eager to be with him during his visit, when he desperately needed her love. How could she be so naïve, and believing her work to save the hopelessly ruined Reich was more important than saving a man dying of despair?

"My marriage to Johanna would have been like that of my parents," he said, as if he read her thoughts. "A comfortable habit. You and I, my sweet Olychka, will be passionate lovers for the rest of our lives."

She purred into his chest, "The rest of our lives."

"I love you so, Olychka. You mysterious Sphinx. My gate to Heaven. My paradise." He kissed her in places nobody had ever touched before, and aroused her to titillating heights.

That night she awoke from a dream, choked with tears. She had seen Ingo ride on a donkey naked. Snow everywhere. Foreign soldiers prodded the donkey with bayonets. She tried to chase them away, but could not move. Two women screamed. "You can't have him. He belongs to us. To us."

Ingo wiped the tears from her cheeks. "Please, Ingo, don't ever leave me," she wailed, clinging to him.

"My heart will always be with you. Our souls are one, remember?" he reassured her.

She laced her fingers into his, resting her head against his shoulder. "To have and to hold."

A long kiss united their bodies. Soon his powerful organ pulsated in her hands, ready to enter her again. But instead of reacting she cried out like a wanton child. Then, beside herself, she demanded ever new highs and refused to surrender. Not now, not yet. There must be more, much more. An insatiable lust assailed her body. She clawed, sucked and bit like an angry cat. What she had detested in Lothar now became the source of her own passion. Unashamed and unconcerned, she abused him with her excess and would not let go even when he withdrew. That only fired her need to conquer him, to subdue him to her wiles. He writhed and moaned but she carried on, sucking, squeezing, pulling. She had to hurt him.

Intoxicated by ecstasy she could not see the tears in his eyes or the awesome lust in his tormented young body. He worked her over until she cried out and begged, "Stop! Please stop!"

Wet, exhausted, and limp he let go. Dazed, Olga pulled the crumpled sheet over their naked bodies. He grabbed her head and drew it back, sucking at her lips like a drowning man seeking air, then buried his head in her hard, moist breasts. "Olga." He sighed. "How did you know that I needed that? You freed and strengthened me. We'll get through this war. I know we shall."

"Father will protect us and bring you back to me."

He leaned into the crook of her arm. "I love you, *Liebling*. You returned me to life."

The clock struck six times. Olga stumbled out of the bed and ran to the cold living as she had done before and slipped between the icy sheets on the sofa. So far Anyna had not discovered her mother in his bed.

Staring at the ceiling, she waited for the light. "I'm ashamed, Father. The Evil Spirit overcame me. You are a healer. Protect us from the Evil One. Was it his brutality that shocked Ingo's broken heart back into life? Please, Father, stay with us."

A faint blue light appeared and grew into golden rays. Her hand vibrated. Trembling, Olga went to the table and picked up her pencil.

There is much suffering in store for all of you. But be strong; you will get through. Trust your inner voice. God is with you. Love gives you wings and strength. It will help you endure the tests that God has in mind for you. We must not question His wisdom or will. Farewell, my child.

The writing stopped. The light vanished. Olga ran back to the sofa, closed her eyes, and listened to her heartbeat until she drifted off.

Anyna appeared. "Good morning, Mami."

"We must not disturb Uncle Ingo," Olga whispered and got up. Her body ached from lack of sleep.

"If I'm so quiet that he can't hear me, may I kiss Uncle Ingo good-bye?"

Olga nodded, and opened the bedroom door. Ingo was sound asleep, breathing in a strong, even rhythm.

Anyna bent down and kissed his cheek, then pulled up the featherbed like a little mother and whispered, "I love you, Uncle Ingo."

After seeing Anyna off, Olga returned to Ingo's bed.

He rubbed her shoulder. "You are cold, my love. Come, let me warm you up."

She nestled into his embrace. "I hope you don't mind that my mother and sister are coming over for lunch. With that out of the way we'll have no other disturbances. Just each other and Anyna."

"Your family is my family," he said sleepily. "We don't pick our families."

Olga kissed him, hoping her bossy sister would be civil.

Anyna brought her grandmother. She threw herself at Ingo's neck. "Look, I got an A. See?" She pulled her slateboard from her satchel.

"Well, Anyna," Mathilde said, "don't you think you should introduce me to your guest?"

"But Omi, you know Uncle Ingo."

"Now I do," Mathilde said, following Ingo and Anyna to the kitchen. Anyna pointed at her board. "See what the teacher wrote. 'Very good,' right?"

"That's what it says," Ingo agreed. "A perfect score. You did beautiful work. Neat and precise." He tousled Anyna's hair. "Well done, little one."

Olga saw her mother's grim smile. Why couldn't she admit that something nice had finally happened? If she would only take care of herself—rather than wear that shapeless frock, the ancient gray sweater, and those sagging stockings.

Ingo took out dishes, carried them to the dining table, and checked the fire.

"I never saw a man help out in the kitchen," Mathilde said, watching him from the kitchen chair.

"Olga is busy preparing the meal," he said. Despite the tumultuous night, he looked fresh and rested. He had put on his uniform, as if he was about to see his commanding officer. The ladies deserved respect.

Ottie stumbled in, wheezing and puffing. "Those God-awful stairs will kill me," she announced before she saw Ingo. Except for her blue eyes, she had nothing in common with Olga. Heavy-boned and well-padded, her large bosom strained against the buttons of her suit and her swollen feet were too big for her delicate French pumps—a gift from her husband, Gerd.

Ingo took her hand, and kissed it. "So glad to meet Olga's charming sister, Ottilie." He took her coat, and hung it up on top of all the others in the cluttered entry hall.

Ottie blushed all over her puffy cheeks. "I'm glad somebody appreciates my virtues, Major Ingo, also known as Uncle Ingo. Anyna has been raving about you from the time you came here. What was it? About a year ago? Now I see why."

Anyna curtsied. "He is the nicest uncle in the world."

"You see, Ottie," he said. "I hope you don't mind my calling you that, since we are almost family."

Her penciled-in brows shot up. "You don't say. Well, that's fine with me. What mysterious wind blew you into this dungeon?" She stood behind a dining chair examining the table, set today with the fine dinnerware the former owners of the apartment had left behind. "I never saw this place so tidy. Nothing like having a man in the house. No matter what we tell her, Olga is always too busy with her music, telling fortunes, consulting spirits…" She sighed, "You know what I mean. Anything that keeps her from doing housework." Ottie blotted her big face. "Things were worse when that aristocratic husband of hers was around. Anyna takes care of herself." Ottie stretched her painted lips in disgust.

"I'm fine, Aunt Ottie. Really."

"Has it ever occurred to you," Ottie asked, "that children do not voice their opinion?"

Anyna shrugged, picked up her slate board, and showed it to her aunt. "Look, I got an A."

"So you did. Probably because Uncle Ingo helped you."

Anyna shook her head. "Not at all, right Uncle Ingo? I did it all by myself."

"Have it your way," Ottie said, watching Ingo pull out the chair for her and then plunking herself down. "I didn't come here to argue with a six-year-old. Where is our baroness anyway?"

"Olga is in the kitchen," Mathilde said, distributing the napkins on the table.

Ingo put down the silver. "We'll have roast beef and stewed cabbage."

"Not bad. I didn't think she had it in her to prepare a decent meal. Without Stasya she probably lives on bread and jam. Stasya was no gem, did whatever she pleased. Still, she kept the house more or less clean. Too bad you can't meet my husband, Gerd. He's stationed in France, right outside Paris. Sends us food, clothes, and wine. I brought a bottle to celebrate the occasion. Would you uncork it, Ingo? It must breathe. Vintage wines require proper treatment."

Ingo ignored the request and tended to the fire.

Ottie watched him, "Never thought my sister would attract a man like you. But you never know. She has her good moments, I guess."

He ignored Ottie's sly look, and shoveled coal into the stove. The dust flare up.

"First time this table was ever set," Ottie said. "A tablecloth yet. You might even find some wine glasses." She pulled a cigarette from her silver case, tapped it against the hard surface, then placed it between her thick lips.

"Allow me," Ingo said, struck a match, and lit it. Ottie puffed, then exhaled the smoke through her wide nostrils.

"A Gauloise from France," she said. "Quite strong, like their coffee. Leave it to the French. Here, try one."

"No, thanks, I don't smoke."

"Where are the wine glasses?" she asked, but made no attempt to get up. "I'll never know what Olga saw in Lothar. Never did a useful thing in his life. Composing weird pieces is not going to make any money for him, ever. Olga slaved away for him. She shouldn't have married him. I'll never know what got into her—seducing him when he really meant to date me. Well, that's what she got." She saw Anyna eyes watching her and said no more.

"Where can I find a corkscrew?" Ingo asked. So she didn't know the truth. Ottie probably believed that a Baron von Schenck would not rape a friend. How he hated those sadists hiding behind the shining armor of righteous chivalry and dutiful dedication to the cause. The man had almost destroyed Olga. How many other people had he tormented in the name of justice? Serving in the SS gave him plenty of opportunities.

Ingo joined Olga in the kitchen where she stirred the gravy.

"I'm sorry, *Liebling*," she said. "This is one of Ottie's bad days. She isn't usually that aggressive. But please, for my sake, don't get into an argument. Just let it go. We both know that she doesn't mean it. She's desperate. I have you, my music, and Father. She has nothing. Pretends that Gerd loves her. You are the kind of man we all dream of."

He chuckled, lifting the lid off one of the pots. "I better stir that pudding."

"It's true, darling," she said. "You are an honest and decent man, fighting at the front while men like Gerd get stationed in France. God knows what he does there. He married Ottie because of her inheritance. When we were resettled to Poland and assigned an apartment similar to the one we had left behind in Latvia, he claimed they had lived in my mother's house and was assigned to a place three times the size of the one they had in Latvia. Gerd serves in the Gestapo. He hasn't been home for a long time. For good reason, I guess. He probably has a mistress in France and doesn't even think of Ottie and his son, Berthold. Sends gifts to keep Ottie pacified. I suspect she knows." Olga punctured the potatoes with a fork. "Almost done. So is the meat. Doesn't it smell heavenly? This will be an unforgettable lunch." She wiped her hands on her apron. "Just tell Ottie that she's wonderful." Olga hugged him. "It's so good to have you here. You brought me life."

The gravy thickened. For once everybody could eat their fill. Ingo fished a pickle from a jar on the table and munched it; he needed all the food he could get to replenish his energy. Olga felt guilty for their nightly pleasures, hoping lots of butter and meat would make up for his lack of sleep.

Anyna came in. "It smells so good in here." She lifted one of the lids. "Pudding!" she cried. "Chocolate pudding!"

Olga smiled. "For good and obedient girls. Now go and sit down. Everything is ready. We'll come in a minute." She winked at Ingo.

"In my thoughts I will always be here, with you and Anyna," he said, and arranged the carrots around the sizzling roast before he carried the platter to the dining room.

As soon as everybody was seated, Ottie raised her glass with a big smile for Ingo. "So glad you came to visit us. Let's hope the war will be won soon so that all our men can come home." They clinked glasses smiling. "I hope you like it," she said, beaming with pride. "A fine vintage. Gerd wouldn't send me anything cheap. He knows his wines."

"Thanks for sharing it with us, Ottie," Ingo said, and kissed her hand.

She blushed. "Well, it's good to get some appreciation. Here's to you. It really is good, don't you think?" She had emptied half her glass, and passed it back to him. He could tell that she was trying to upstage Olga.

He poured. "I can't remember ever drinking anything so superb. Thanks again, Ottie. You look so charming. So glad I have the privilege of meeting you and Frau Bergman."

After the dishes were cleared away, Anyna watched Olga dish out the chocolate pudding. It wobbled in the glass dish. With Uncle Ingo here, every day was like Christmas.

He distributed the last drops of wine.

"Life can be so good," Ottie said. "Good food and a glass of wine make the world a better place, don't you think, Ingo? I do hope you'll stick around. You are a ray of sunshine in this dreary place."

Olga giggled. She was not used to wine. Or was it Ingo's presence that made her so happy? A perfect combination.

The following morning a blanket of low-hanging clouds promised more snow. The dim light held no shadows. Ingo produced all the light Olga needed. Their life had almost settled into a routine. He was in charge of the fire while she took care of the food. Sitting at the table in the sweater Mathilde had knitted for him, he spread butter on his rye. His face had filled out and had a healthy complexion. Even the dark rings under his eyes had disappeared. Unfortunately, that also meant his time was almost up.

He took Olga's cards from the shelf and unwrapped the silk scarf, then shuffled them carefully as if a wrong card could change his life forever.

Olga, still in her silk robe, watched his slender, graceful hands slip the stacks into each other. Every morning they took a bath together, rubbed each other's back and laughed, then watched the water gurgle down the drain. The radio announcer read the news. Ingo shook his head in disbelief. "I wonder who writes it. If only half of it were true, we would be making great strides. But no such luck. No wonder you feel so safe here in Poland. But please, Olga, don't let them fool you. We can't stop the Russians from advancing. With American support they can go on forever, which is a lot more than we can say for ourselves. We are running out of everything. And declaring total war won't turn the tide." When he saw her defiant eyes he said. "You're right. Enough of that. Let's see what the cards have to tell us."

Ceremoniously, Olga took the deck from his hand, closed her eyes, and whispered, "Divine spirits, please share your wisdom with us so that we can see your light."

Ingo cut the deck. She picked up the stacks and started a spread, studied the pattern, then closed her eyes, awaiting divine revelations.

"Going back you passed through a long period of pain," she said as the words came to her. "A loving God protected you. Let me tell you that those experiences will help you cope with what is yet to come. Through hardships you gather strength and confidence. Always remember that as long as you follow our guidance, you will pull through. Evil spirits are always around you but we'll shelter you from them."

Olga put down more cards, shocked by the apparent danger she saw. She put down another row. "Here we go. The aura of love carries you on its wings. This love will stay with you forever. Your inner voice will guide you through the darkness until you'll reunite with the woman of your heart. She will be with you at all times and guide you.

"Going into the future, a woman who has been close to you will cause you grief with her jealousy. She disapproves of your choice. That is her problem, not yours. Bless it and let it go.

"I see death. But that does not surprise you. Do not grieve. Remember, they come to a better world that awaits all living souls. Trust your guardian angel."

Olga gathered the cards. "That's it for now," she said. No need to reveal the pain she saw, the fire, the crosses.

He gazed at her for some time. "Can you tell me whether I'll marry the woman I love?"

She closed her eyes and searched her heart. Then she let him pick out five cards. After studying the pattern she felt her heart pounding. "She is right here," Olga said, pointing at the queen of hearts, at one end, "and you at the other. There's an ocean between you. Unless you can cross it, you will be obliged to live in different worlds." His puzzled look did not oblige her to reveal anymore—the obstacles, the trials, and the pain he would endure before he could come to a peaceful world. "So the answer is yes." Did he hear the quaver in her voice? Of course he did not know the meaning of the ace of spades.

He awaited further disclosures. When she said no more, he took her hands and gazed into her eyes. "I want to marry you, Olga," he said. "I can provide for you and Anyna. I would like to be her father. She loves me and I love her. Honestly, Olga. Will you divorce Lothar and marry me?" He kissed her hands. "I wish I could marry you right now and make you mine." His eyes were filled with a love that brought tears to hers. He obviously had no idea what was in store for them, did not know Lothar's hate for her. He would deny her a divorce just because she wanted it so much.

Returning his squeeze, she smiled ruefully. "You are my life. No matter where you are, we are always together."

He rose, scooped her up in his arms, and swung her around. "We shall prove to the world," he said, "that love can carry us through Hell so that it can take us to Heaven."

But how?

Chapter 14

Time rolled faster and faster toward the dreaded day. Then it came. That afternoon, Ingo and Olga took Anyna to the zoo. They watched the lion pacing restlessly in his cage.

"That's how I felt before you came and set me free," Ingo said.

She took his hand and pressed it to her cheek.

The afternoon dragged on. Her giggles sounded weak, his jests brittle. No matter what they did—throwing snowballs in the park, running along the swept paths, stopping for tea at Café Sonne on Adolf Hitler Strasse—the pain of his departure hovered over their lives like a storm cloud ready to break. Nothing could stop time.

Anyna drew out her bedtime story, asking more and more questions. She clung to Uncle Ingo for her goodnight kiss and would not let go. Standing by the small iron bed, Olga remembered how she had torn herself away from her baby to follow Lothar's dictate. Anyna had been no more than a year old then, yet she already sensed that she was about to be abandoned by her parents, left in a hostile world. She did not cry; she did not need to. The helplessness and despair in her large, mournful eyes wrenched Olga's heart. After having fought for her child's existence, Olga had taken on the impossible task of raising her baby despite the objections of her husband, who saw Anyna as nothing but an inconvenience, and had never changed his mind. But Olga could not keep Uncle Ingo to be the loving father Anyna longed for. He had to leave. Once again they would be alone, waiting.

Olga played *Liebestraum*. The once passionate piece had no life. It sounded like a lament. Even Mozart could not touch a vital chord in her. The tempo was too slow and then too fast, her touch heavy and ponderous. Every piece was a requiem.

Stretched out on the sofa, his eyes closed, Ingo listened to the music. Could he hear her pathetic attempts or was he lost in his own dread?

What were her troubles compared to his? She needed faith in Father's promise. If she and Ingo could not believe in a future together, there would not be one.

Mendelssohn's spirited *Rondo Capriccioso* kindled a fresh verve and brought the youthful exuberance of the young composer into the dark room. The melody ran this way and that, up and down, like children at play.

An angry knock interrupted Olga's emphatic flourish. Her heart thumped furiously. She kept on playing. Damn them all, she fumed. After the second round of knocking, she played even louder and finished with angry final chords. "Why do these people insult me?" she cried out. "What is an extra five minutes to them? So it is past ten. I would not say anything if I were practicing scales, or stumbling over some dumb passage over and over again, but here I am, pouring my soul into this music and all those idiots can hear is noise!" She rose and paced around the table, muttering into the darkness. "They're jealous, that's what. Can't stand to see somebody happy. Some people are such ugly, vicious creatures. They have to hurt others. Why can't they appreciate this heavenly music? Morons." The words tumbled out, releasing a fury and pain she could no longer suppress. How would she survive the long days and nights of loneliness in this cold and dark home?

Ingo caught her arm, and pulled her onto his lap. "The neighbors did not complain before when you played into the night."

Olga shrugged, her hands clenched into fists. "Why should they?"

He bounced her on his knee. "Now, be a good girl, Olychka."

She leaned against him and tousled his hair. "You're right. I'm sorry."

He rose, turned on the radio, and bowed. "Will you grant me this dance?"

"With great pleasure."

When the waltz was over, Ingo left the room. Olga picked up the hyacinth on the table and inhaled its sweet scent. In the past she would have given anything to have a moment with Ingo. Now that he had come, was with her, her prayers had been answered. She should be grateful. Had she not found the deepest love a human could experience? She must not spoil what little time they had left.

He returned with his hands behind his back. "I have a surprise. You must guess what it is."

She shrugged, too upset to care. "You know I'm no good at this."

"If you can't guess, you know what will happen. Your prince will turn into a frog." The twinkle in his eye coaxed her into playing along. Olga chuckled, peeking behind his back.

He wheeled away before she could catch him. "No cheating. I am offering you the kingdom of my love, my hand and my heart, and a tropical island on the continent of our fantasy. Isn't that worth something?" Warm, throaty laughter rose from his chest.

She smiled, not to let him down. "A grand gift indeed. Not that I have a clue what you're hiding. Honestly, Ingo, don't do this to me."

He would not give in. Judging from his grin, he could not wait to show her.

"Could you at least give me a hint?" she prodded. "Is it a book?"

"No, not even close. Try again. It's something you'll enjoy. We'll both enjoy."

She pointed at the bedroom door.

He shook his head. "That comes later, and cannot be wrapped in a package."

"Tell me if I'm hot or cold," she bargained. "Is it something to eat?"

Ingo nodded. "Lukewarm."

She danced toward him to the beat of the music. "Something to drink?"

"Warm."

"A bottle of wine!"

"Getting hot."

She threw up her arms. "I've got it, Ingo. If it isn't wine, it's got to be champagne!"

"Right!" He held up the bottle like a trophy. "This is your prize. Your prince can stay in human form to love and serve his queen for the rest of his life. May I ask for two glasses so that we can share the magic potion that will shield us from evil entities?"

"And take us away on a magic carpet to the land of dreams."

"Where love reigns and beauty is queen," he said, wrenching the cork from the bottle. "While King Music keeps us dancing cheek-to-cheek."

The cork popped. The bubbles gurgled into her glass and foamed over the rim. She caught them with the tip of her tongue. "No need to waste it."

Raising his glass he gazed into her eyes. "To everlasting love."

"And to roses that bloom in winter, light that breaks the darkness, and heat that melts the snow."

Sipping the fizzing champagne, they danced in close embrace to waltzes, tangos, and foxtrots, falling deeper and deeper in love with every step.

At midnight the music program signed off. The bottle was empty, their sadness gone. On the way to their bedroom, Olga leaned into his arms and giggled.

"Nobody can take that away from us," he said, pulling off her sweater. Ingo helped her step out of her skirt; Olga pulled the sleeves of his jacket from his shoulders. She kicked off her pumps. He pulled the stockings from her legs. Moments later they faced each other, illuminated by the strip of light coming from the living room.

He took her hands and held them, his eyes on her face and nude body. "I ask you, Olga Bergmann, to be my wife. To have and to hold until death do us part."

A warm shiver ran through her, sweet with longing for this wonderful man she had come to love like no one else in this world. With a warm squeeze, her eyes trained on his, she saw herself reflected in his pupil. She had never looked or felt more beautiful, more desirable, more perfect than now. She offered it all to him when she said, "Yes, Ingo, I do. I love you more than life."

His sinewy body, long legs, and broad chest awaited her with all the incredible marvels their love had to give. His mouth, his tongue, the tender touch of his hands joined hers. In spirit they would be together. The whole of this man standing in front of her asked her to be his until death would take them to the other world. Father had promised he would spare them the dark menace, promised that some day they would share this love day in and day out as husband and wife. Ingo's powerful erection offered the glorious gift their union would produce on this, their wedding night. With his warm hands on her small body, he kissed her nipples and caressed her hips.

"And you, Ingo, will you be my husband? To have and to hold?"

"I will. I shall always love you."

With their hands clasped, the ceremonial kiss became a ritual. They pledged their lives to each other in front of the altar of the universe, sanctifying their union.

"And thus God declares us husband and wife," he said solemnly. "Ingo and Olga Kroll."

Humming, *Here Comes the Bride*, he picked her up and carried her to bed. In an onrush of desire, she inhaled the scent of his body, sucked at his warm and tender skin, and pulled him toward her. He returned her embrace. "Olychka, my beloved Olychka," he whispered. "You make me the happiest man on earth."

In an ancient ritual he kissed her eyes, forehead, and cheeks. "I shall always be yours."

The last hours of their togetherness surpassed all others. He would be back. Someday, he would be back.

In the morning Ingo and Olga prepared breakfast as usual.

"I'm looking forward to your drawings, Anyna, my sweet little friend" Ingo said. "I'll write to you. And don't worry if you don't hear from me for some time. I shall never forget you. Remember that. Your letters mean the world to me." He took her little hand and kissed it. "You have a big task ahead, Anyna, reminding Mami that Uncle Ingo is always with you and loves you both very much. I rely on you, Anyna. You are like a daughter to me. Someday, the three of us will be together, you'll see."

"Will you come back on leave soon?" she asked.

Ingo shook his head. "Not very likely. We have a lot of fighting to do."

"We'll miss you, Uncle Ingo. Miss you a lot. Life has never been so nice. I love you so much." She put her arms around his neck, and leaned her face against his. "You're the best, most wonderful hero in all of Germany."

He held her. "Just remember, we are family. Be sure you tell that to my parents when you go to Dresden. My sister, Ingrid, will love you. She'll be your big sister."

"When you marry Mami, I'll be your step-daughter, right?" She drained the warm milk from her tin mug. "I'm so glad you'll be with us, not Daddy. I don't love Daddy the way I love you, Uncle Ingo."

Olga fussed with the dishes, hiding her tears.

They accompanied Anyna downstairs and watched her walk away to school. Before turning the corner she blew them a kiss. Thick snow flurries danced over the dirty snow and shrouded the gray old buildings. Hand in hand Ingo and Olga climbed upstairs. Back in the kitchen time dragged on. What could she say that would make their parting easier? If she believed Father, they were both heading for an inferno, only his was closer at hand.

The cold and cloudy day sent its milky light through the steamed-up kitchen window.

"I'll divorce Lothar," Olga said. "Let the Countess find an aristocratic wife for him. I've done their bidding long enough."

With his fingertips, Ingo picked up crumbs from the table and licked them off. "He is not bothering you. But come and sit on my lap. Here are the addresses of my family in Dresden and my aunt in Berlin. Johanna and I were never in love with each other, only did not know it. Before I met you I had no idea what I was missing. Now love is all I can think of. The tenderness of your touch, that warm body, your thirsty kisses and, well…" He purred. Was there time?

Rocking on his lap, she caressed his cheek and felt his whiskers. "Our Fuhrer will take care of us."

He jumped up, throwing her to the floor. "How can you say that now?" he shouted. "Can't you see what he is doing to us? Wake up, Olga. He is killing the people he is supposed to protect. You have no idea what you're saying."

Olga struggled to get up. She stared at him, the white lips, the fury in his eyes—the face of a frustrated and angry young man who could no longer suppress his fury. The face of their first meeting. She flushed with shame. How could she say something so insensitive? This was no consolation; it was an insult. "I'm so sorry, Ingo. I didn't mean it. You must believe me. It's the way we talk, darling. Pointless, stupid talk." She pressed his trembling hand. "I'll do as you said. I'll leave as soon as the Russians reach Poland. Honestly."

His face relaxed. His hand returned her squeeze. "I am sorry for getting carried away." He held her. "Now remember what you said. Ingrid will write to you. You might as well get acquainted with her. We are very close. She is a kind person. You will like her."

"I know I will, Ingo." She glanced at the clock. "We still have time. The bed is warm. Why not spend the last minutes together."

He followed her, still concerned for her safety. "There is no way out, you know. The Reich is running out of fuel. Our allies will side with the winner. We've made no friends, just forced nations into submission. You can't expect loyalty from them. The Allies want unconditional surrender. Our Fuhrer is not about to grant it to them. Only his death can save us, and he is not about to sacrifice himself for the nation he blames for his downfall. He wants us go down with him."

"But we can't let that happen," she insisted, lying down.

"Of course, we can't," he said in a tired, resigned voice. "We still have a lot of blood to spill on the muddy roads of Europe."

She pressed her face against his chest. "Why do you say things like that?"

He held her. "Because I'm a man of reason, or at least try to be. *Fuhrer, Volk und Vaterland* made sense to a student of history, literature and philosophy. Germany had to be rescued from slow annihilation. I'm also a humanist, not a demagogue. My battered, misguided and doomed *Vaterland* needs me."

She had no idea what he was talking about, only felt the pain and sadness in his heart. Her flimsy shield of courage dropped.

His kiss had no warmth. It was all her fault. She did not stop him when he got up and packed while she put fresh coals on the glowing embers. The fire flared like a last breath of life. The crumpled sheets, pillows and blankets were relics of an unforgettable night. She would be alone again.

Ingo knelt on the suitcase to press it shut. Gottfried's warm underwear, socks and sweaters would protect him against the cold.

"We still have a little time, *Liebling*," she said, pressing her thumb on the knot he was about to tie.

"I'll always remember this room," he whispered, as if his voice could disturb the ghosts. "Our pink room. Every time you look into the mirror, imagine that I am looking at you."

The grandfather clock struck the noon. Olga counted the sonorous bong, bong, bong while they faced the mirror. "Herr and Frau Kroll live here," he said wistfully, and kissed her.

At the station, they joined the soldiers awaiting their trains.

Lucie and Mathilde peeled away from the crowd of gray-green and black uniforms. "We thought we could make your parting easier," Lucie said.

"Why? I am fine." She resented the intrusion, wanted to be alone with Ingo and then hide her tears in a dark corner somewhere, rather than entertain meaningless chatter.

"On such occasions," Lucie said, "people like you tend to get carried away. The train to Warsaw is on time and should be here any minute. I'll go to Posen next week and visit my brother Max. He flirts with the Nazis so that he can help his Polish friends. He's out of his mind. If the Gestapo finds out, he's a dead man. But you can't tell him anything. During the Revolution he played a similar game. Well, each to his own. At least he knows what's really going on. Perhaps I am better off not knowing."

Olga was too busy watching Ingo greet his men. Others milled around. Ingo was no longer part of her.

"I'll get Janek to build us a chicken coop to keep some hens and a rooster," Lucie said to distract Olga as if she cared about fresh eggs and rabbit meat. The baby was due in July. At least Gottfried was still around. Olga only saw Ingo in his greatcoat, the officer's cap cocked. From time to time he look at her, smiled and then returned his attention to his men.

"I can't see why anybody would bomb Litzmannstadt," Lucie said. Only Mathilde listened. Some of the women the men had met at the Esplanade had come to see them off.

"I'm glad you and Ingo found each other," Lucie said. "He's a nice chap. Though I wonder why he doesn't believe in the miracle weapon. When it's our only hope."

The train pulled in. Ingo picked up his suitcase. He would ride in the first class compartment reserved for officers. As soon as he had deposited his luggage, he returned to the platform and took Mathilde's hands. "Please give us your blessings, *Mutter*. Olga and I were married last night. Not formally of course. Not yet. But as soon as it's possible, she will be my wife. Thank you for bringing this wonderful woman into the world." He kissed Mathilde's cheek.

Mathilde's tired eyes lit up. Were those tears? Neither one of her two sons-in-law had ever shown respect, much less affection toward her. Lothar dished out his merciless sarcasm. Gerd treated her as a failure for not amassing the inheritance he had counted on. Now that she had nothing to give, he ignored her.

She embraced Ingo. "Be well and come back. We'll pray for you."

The soldiers adjusted their packs and got ready to board the train.

"When do you expect to reach the front?" Lucie asked.

"Sooner than I care to," Ingo said. "Two days, unless we encounter broken tracks or partisan attacks. Transports to the front are unbelievably swift. A one-way trip."

Olga watched the mouth she had kissed, listened to the sound of his voice and admired his loving eyes. Over the past two weeks he had become a regular young man again, enjoying a family life others took for granted.

The locomotive hooted and let off jets of white steam. It was ready to take off.

Lucie and Mathilde hugged Ingo then stepped back. Olga held him for the last time. A tender kiss was all they could share in public. Olga felt his pain. "You will come back, Ingo. We will always be together. I'll think of you day and night. I love you so."

The soldiers boarded the troop train. The doors slammed shut like prison gates. Ingo let go of Olga and boarded, then pulled down his windows and leaned out, smiling. "Keep well and go to Dresden," he shouted.

The train set in motion. Olga ran alongside. "Ingo! Ingo!"

"Olga!" The grating and squeaking wheels took him and his men back to the battlefield. Moments later the tracks were empty. A freight train loaded with guns and armored *Kubelwagen* waited to be pulled to the Russian front.

Mathilde and Lucie took Olga's arms and took her away. Why couldn't they leave her alone? Let her run home, hide in the bed still warm from his body, and lick her wounds like an injured animal.

"We know how you feel, Olinka," Mathilde said. "We must bear our pain. Life goes on."

"Let's have lunch at the *Bayrische Stuben*," Lucie suggested. "I'm starved."

What did Lucie know about pain, Olga wondered, tears running down her cheeks unchecked. Let them see how she felt. She was no stoic

German woman who kept her feelings under control. Why pretend? She had not asked them to come. *Father! I need you.*

"Things will settle down," Mathilde said, genuine empathy in her voice.

"Never." Olga bawled. "Never."

They crossed the station square. Tears blinded her. She let them pull her along like a prisoner. With Ingo gone, her life was meaningless, unbearable, pitiful. "Ingo."

By the time Olga arrived at the Esplanade she moved with ease. "Life goes on," she told Frau Metzger.

"We have some new customers. They're on their way back as well."

"Poor chaps," Olga said. "Let's make their last day a pleasant one." She opened the piano, imagining Ingo sitting beside her. From now on she would always play for him. Some day he would be back. She had to believe that, or go mad.

That night Anyna said, "You must not cry, Mami. Uncle Ingo will come back and we'll be together again. You know we will." She pulled Olga down to the pillow. "I love you, Mami. And I love Uncle Ingo."

After playing a lullaby, Olga sat down on the sofa and gazed into the darkness. *Thank you, Father, for helping us through this day.*

A faint blue light flitted across the ceiling. It was not Father's golden rays and circles. The eerie color formed spikes pointing east. Sardonic laughter cut into the silence. "He's gone, gone, gone."

I know that, Father, but he will come back.

Ugly cackles echoed through the dark room. "Back? Why would he?"

"What do you mean? Who are you? What do you want? Father, protect me from this entity!" Olga buried her head in her hands and prayed, "Dear God in Heaven, have mercy on us."

The blue light flickered and was gone. A violent shiver raked her trembling body. "Dear God, protect us from evil. Father, where are you? What happened?" Helpless and abandoned, Olga broke out into violent sobs.

Chapter 15

"I don't suppose you heard that the Allies not only landed in Normandy but advanced into France," the Countess said huffily, passing Olga. She waltzed into the living room as if she owned the place, meticulously dressed in a white linen suit and wide-brimmed hat, a veil over her eyes. "Do you at least appreciate that Count Claus von Stauffenberg sacrificed his life in an attempt to kill that monster? How could he fail? The bomb exploded as planned, right next to Hitler. It barely touched him. He must have the Devil's protection. With that we lost everything." A menacing glance from her accused Olga as if this was her fault. "You converse with the Underworld, no doubt plotting my downfall." The artificiality in her articulate speech had been trained to suit her make-believe image.

Olga pulled out a chair for her mother-in-law, unable to resist the dictates of her upbringing. "I heard it on the morning news," she said, watching the Countess lean her parasol against the empty seat, then gracefully lower herself, as if acting in a period drama. She was not sure whether she should sound disappointed or act as if…what? Hitler's life and madness really mattered? "He was caught and executed."

"How could he fail?" the Countess said, pushing Olga's music books aside.

Olga did not trust her mother-in-law. A cold chill crept over her spine despite the hot and humid day. The demons must have come in. The Countess was one of them.

"Hitler will kill every member of the von Stauffenberg clan and those who were part of the conspiracy. How could those generals fail?"

Olga shrugged. No matter what she said, the Countess would ridicule her. Too bad Anyna was at school. Summer vacation would start next week.

"I suppose you heard that the Poles staged an uprising in Warsaw. Those fools figured the Soviets would support them. They are certainly close enough to break through. But the Russians are no friends of the Poles. Lucky for us."

Olga was aware that the Russian front had moved west almost as far as Warsaw, no more than 200 kilometers from Litzmannstadt. The Poles were rebelling. So far the German defense had held them back. What would happen when the Poles took over? It could happen.

"At least it will keep the Poles down," the Countess observed. So far Litzmannstadt showed no signs of unrest. The city was as peaceful as if there was no war going on. Whatever brewed underground was not evident. If only she could get a sign from Ingo.

"What I am trying to say," the Countess went on, "is that the enemy is too close for my comfort. I am not about to greet the Russians when they come. I shall leave for Bavaria. I had my share of the Bolsheviks during the revolution." She lifted her chiseled chin. "I am packing."

Finally, Olga thought. "I'd be glad to help."

"No doubt. You cannot wait to get rid of me so that you can devote yourself to your ghosts and your lovers." The Countess lifted the veil from her milky white face and daintily dabbed her forehead with a monogrammed handkerchief. Not a breath of air disturbed the sweltering heat. "Jadwiga will take care of it. That is her job. What will she do when I am not around to guide her? She is helpless."

The Countess obviously had no idea that her Polish maid was probably as glad to see the Countess leave as everybody else. How could anyone be so conceited?

"The war is not over yet. It may not be over for some time, unless we surrender. That is obviously not in our Fuhrer's plan. The lives of those fighting for him are of no concern. The Allies will conquer a graveyard. If you had any brains at all, you would take Anna Magdalena and move west."

Olga nodded. "I am considering it," she lied. No point in talking about her plans. With the Countess gone, Litzmannstadt would be wonderful. Should she offer tea? The breakfast dishes were still on the table. In summer, the living room was cooler than the kitchen. What if the Russians broke through at Warsaw and advanced to Litzmannstadt? If there were any danger, Hitler would surely evacuate the German

144

families living here. Dresden gave her an uneasy feeling. It would be the last resort. Perhaps she could volunteer for something and be sent to Germany.

Olga took the dishes into the kitchen. Leftover food scraps no longer existed. They ate every crumb. She wished she could come up with a halfway reasonable argument, but even mentioning the miracle weapon would bring her under the Countess's well-aimed fire. She was right about the danger of staying here in Poland. Ingo had warned her. Now air raids had hit the city. Nothing big, not compared to the carpet bombs that wiped out the cities in Germany. The Russians were not interested in destroying the cities they would conquer. Their proximity was quite obvious.

If only Ingo would send her a message. Why did Father ignore her pleas?

"Let's not talk about that, Olga," the Countess said.

About what? Olga wondered.

"Stalin will take Poland as he took the Baltic States and reestablish the Russian Empire of 1914. The Poles have no defense. First, he will kill as many of them as possible while liberating Poland, and then annex it to the Soviet Union. He does it every time." She pulled her shoulders back and raised her head for Olga to admire her posture and profile. "I have no delusions about men and the evil that lurks in their hearts."

And in yours, Olga thought, wiping her sweaty forehead with the back of her hand. A crude gesture and gross faux pas. The Countess' thin brows sprung up. Olga went to the window and inhaled the hot dusty air but could not get rid of the sulfur. The old buildings baked in the blistering sun. The humidity begged for rain. School children ran noisily along the sidewalk. Anyna should be among them unless she dawdled with friends.

"How do you know all that?" Olga asked.

"Because I happen to know history, and the ways of the world have not changed. Power-hungry men wage wars to build empires. Their methods are always the same. Besides, even censored news contains some facts. I don't need spirits to tell me that the Allies are moving in for the kill. The Reich is a giant *Kessel*. Are you listening, Olga? The Russians are at Warsaw! The Poles are rioting. We live in Poland, in case you forgot. I bet the Poles have a lively underground right under our noses, ready to kill every German in town with that Stasya of yours at their head."

Stasya would protect her, Olga remembered, but said, *"Gauleiter* Greiser will evacuate us. Our Fuhrer will not let us down."

The Countess shook her head in disbelief. "I can't believe what I just heard. Did I not just tell you that Hitler only thinks of himself? Why should he care about useless families that will clutter the roads? Let them die." Her blood red lips stretched and emphasized her disgust. "I came because Lothar asked me to look after you, a most unpleasant task. You never did make sense; why should I expect it now?"

The white curtains billowed into the room like dancing ghosts, stirring up the smell of sulfur that was everywhere now. The merciless sun was hotter than hell. During the past few days new transports of soldiers had come by, heading west. The men coming to the Esplanade celebrated their good fortune. Though the Americans were known to be fierce fighters, they adhered to the Geneva Convention and did not slaughter their prisoners or sent them on death marches. What if everybody surrendered to them? Who would keep the Russians at bay? *Ingo, where are you?*

The old clock struck the quarter hour. Of what? Did it matter?

"Don't count on your lover," the Countess sneered. "He licked his cream. You are no different from any other woman. Men are like bees sucking their nectar wherever they can find it. And for that you committed adultery? Yes, adultery! What will you tell your daughter when she grows up? That you betrayed her father while he suffered in a prisoner of war camp?" Evil glee flashed in her dark eyes.

Olga looked at the dusty table. Ingo. What did the Countess know about him? "Anyna loves Ingo," she said, and regretted it.

"Does she really? What do you know about children? They're pets who will do anything for a treat. I raised three."

All of whom hated their mother, Olga thought, except Lothar and she was not so sure about him. Her heart pounded. Why was she wasting her time with this when she could be trying to find Ingo in her séance? He had to be alive, else he would come to her. "Please excuse me. I am very busy. Playing at…"

"I know, I know. Entertaining soldiers is more important than talking with your mother-in-law. I never expected gratitude. Anna Magdalena pretends to be fond of that soldier. I also know how much she adores her daddy. Don't think she doesn't know how much he suffers knowing that his wife, her mother, does bad things with strange men."

Olga wiped her clammy face on a handkerchief. Through the window she saw a flock of swallows cruise in formation. How could she get rid of the Countess?

The ghostlike curtains swept toward Olga, reaching for her, beckoning. They pointed toward the bedroom and the mirror. The Countess rose—torso erect, head raised—and adjusted her veil. Swinging her parasol like a cane, she waltzed toward the door. Before the war she had cheered Hitler and flaunted her Aryan heritage.

Olga opened the front door. "Good bye, Countess."

"Nobody can accuse me of not warning you, Olga," she said with the dignity of a wounded queen. "I fulfilled my son's wishes." She pulled on her gloves, adjusting each finger. Stopping at the threshold, she turned around. "You are a foolish and ungrateful woman. Nobody can save you from the mess you've made of your life. For every moment of happiness you will pay with years of pain. I know what I am talking about. I was in love when I married the Count. He adored me. We were happy. Little did I know that he was addicted to gambling and would take everything I offered for granted. Nicky and Lara are wonderful children. The war spoiled our beautiful life.

"Just tell me," the Countess said, "what makes you think your passing soldier will return? Was it worth breaking your vows?"

"Vows?" Olga muttered. Her marriage had been an obligation.

"Indeed. That's what marriage is all about. It would be worth your while to remember that. Lothar pays for your life. Your soldier boy is gone. The Russian Front fells them like tin soldiers." With a savage smile she watched Olga squirm. "None of your great leaders has ever set foot in America. Or in Russia for that matter. They look at the map, draw lines on the paper, and imagine that they will replace the hammer and sickle with a swastika. Simple. Only Moscow has its own plans and is not about to surrender. The Russians have their famous winter as a solid ally, not to mention the Americans." She leaned against her parasol. "I'll never know why God took Stalin's side. Not that Hitler deserves His support." She lifted her chin and walked out. "Adieu, Olga. Anna Magdalena deserves a proper upbringing. I know how difficult it is for you, since you are ill-equipped to pass on what you never learned. Still, I would appreciate it if you'd respect what I taught her. She understands what's at stake. She wants to be lady and is willing to work at it."

"Of course," Olga said, stepping aside.

"Love is an illusion, Olga. I could have accepted Mr. McCormick's generous offer when he asked me to marry him. He even wanted my unborn child. His Texas ranch is probably as big as all of Latvia. But it was not right. How was I to know that Lothar's father would pass away so suddenly? Why is it so hard for you to accept the wisdom of an experienced woman? I just want what is best for you and Anna Magdalena." She paused. Olga remained silent. "I might as well save my breath."

"I will divorce Lothar."

The Countess stopped just as Olga was about to close the door. "Divorce him?" she said, as if the miracle weapon had become a reality.

"A very foolish move, Olga. My son has the generosity to forgive your indiscretion and respect his obligation to his daughter."

Olga's cheeks burnt as if she had been slapped. Her fingers tightened around the door handle. *Just don't say anything.* She waited for the Countess to march out victoriously in her dainty white pumps.

"I'll never know what a man sees in you, Olga. It must be the music. Lonely men are vulnerable. Why did you pick on Lothar and deprived him of a suitable match? How you seduced him. It's still not clear that he is the father. But as long as he acknowledges it, who am I to judge. Men have their needs, but women don't have to accommodate them. For heaven's sake, Olga, don't look so shocked."

"Good-bye, Countess," Olga said, and shut the door, then ran to the bedroom and gazed into the mirror hardly recognizing the face staring back at her. Those large and frightened eyes were not hers. There was Ingo standing beside her. "Ingo, my darling. You heard what she said. But don't worry; we are a married couple."

Anyna hop-skipped into the room. "I saw grandmaman on the stairs. She is going to Bavaria. Who will look after her? Jadwiga can't wait for Grandmaman to leave. Uncle Nicky and Aunt Lara don't like her either. Nicky deals with the Poles on the black market and listens to BBC. I saw him. He said I must not tell anybody." She followed Olga into the kitchen. "She only has me. I am a baroness, you see. That makes me special. I must always act like one." She climbed onto Olga's lap and cuddled against her. A distant thunderclap echoed. The wind blew in. "Come, Anyna. After lunch we can go to the swimming pool. It's so hot."

A dark foreboding had settled in Olga's chest. This time there would be no escape.

Two weeks later, the radio announced that the Red Army had reached the outskirts of Warsaw. The Polish insurrection was crushed.

"Warsaw?" Lucie said, pressing her tanned hands against her temples. "Do you realize what this means, Olga? Warsaw is practically in our back yard. That old witch was right. My sister-in-law, Herta, lives in Saxony and has asked us to come. She rented an apartment for me. Marisha and Janek are crating some of our furniture. I'll take some linens, dishes, and furniture for two rooms. Gottfried is setting up a warehouse there. It'll be our escape. Nobody will look for us there."

Olga sat on a garden chair and rocked the chubby new baby. He smelled clean and fresh, his skin ever so soft. The blood pulsated behind the yet unformed skull. There was something so wholesome and natural about a baby. He smiled with his toothless mouth and drooled. Would he survive? Would any of them survive?

Anyna played in the sandbox with the other children.

"Remember the Jewish uprising in Warsaw last year?" Lucie asked. "Do you suppose there were signs of a rebellion in our ghetto here? The Jews are all gone. It seems strange not having anybody looking at you from behind barbed wire." She rested on a chaise lounge to keep her swollen legs elevated. The birth had been hard on her. She had delivered at the nearby Army hospital during an air raid.

"Who is to know what will happen next?" Olga wondered, rocking the baby. He was already four weeks old. Lucie sported a healthy tan. She spent most of her days with the baby here in the garden, enjoying the fragrance of the flowers, trees, and the meadow. They used the grass to feed the rabbits and chickens that augmented their rations. The flower beds now grew vegetables. Soon the first tomatoes would be ripe. A swarm of bees buzzed around the hollyhocks along the fence. A hen cackled in the chicken coop announcing that she had laid an egg.

"Do you hear from Ingo?" Lucie asked.

Olga shook her head. The baby grew restless and cried.

"Feeding time," Lucie said, baring her breast. "I love the feeling of his little mouth on my nipples. Such peace."

The following week, Lucie and her children left for Saxony. Olga saw her off at the station. More and more refugees showed up and moved on. Nobody wanted to stay in Poland. People reported Russian atrocities. "They come like wild dogs, rape and kill whoever they can find," a young woman said, carrying her little girl on her lap. "We barely got away. Nobody told us they were coming. Evacuation? Come on! We were left to die."

On her way home, Olga remembered the Countess saying that families had become baggage the Reich had no use for. Hitler no longer planned for the future, knew that he would not be around when the children grew into cannon fodder.

At home the radio talked about final victory and the miracle weapon as if this was news. Hitler asked his people to endure. "The Red Horde will never reach Germany." He did not explain why he had left his famous *Wolfsschanze* and returned to Berlin, nor how the Allies happened to get to the heart of Italy, France, the Balkans, and now Warsaw. Where was Ingo? She had not heard from him for some time, nor could she reach Father. Had they abandoned her?

Anyna came home and pressed her sweaty face to Olga's. How long could Germany hold out? Should she leave for Dresden now? How would Frau Kroll receive her? What about Johanna? Just because Ingo thought they were no more than friends did not mean Johanna shared his opinion. To her Olga was an intruder—what if she loved Ingo and intended to marry him? The Krolls must have agreed to take Olga in to accommodate Ingo's wishes.

"Mami, why don't you say something? Fraulein Arnold told us about the Ice Age. Did you know that it covered most of Europe all the way to the Alps? All the people who once lived here died. For many years it was so cold that nothing grew. Do you think we will have another Ice Age?"

"Not any time soon, my sweet. For the moment it is very hot outside."

Spreading some jam on a slice of bread, Olga sensed a tremor in her hand. Father had finally come. With a deep sense of relief she told

Anyna, "Eat your bread and drink your milk. I'll be back shortly. And please, do not disturb me, yes?"

"Yes, Mami."

At the dressing table in her bedroom, Olga closed her eyes. Sweat poured from her face. The stench of sulfur rose.

Why do you ignore Ingo's pain? He is suffering. He cannot come because you do not love him.

The writing stopped. When Olga read it she broke into tears. Why didn't Father send her a greeting, a message of love, some encouragement? Was he angry at her? What had she done to upset him? Ingo was suffering? Where? How? *Please, Father, talk to me. Help me. You brought us together, don't abandon us now.*

All day the memory of the strange encounter haunted her. After tucking Anyna into bed, she played Schumann's *Traumerei. Endstation*, the book Lucie had given her, did not keep her attention. Her heart sought Ingo, a sign, a message. Why didn't he respond? Anxious, she picked up her cards, worn and limp from frequent use, and remembered Ingo sitting in the chair facing her. Where was he now?

The first card was the jack of hearts. Ingo's card. The ten of spades dampened her joy. A harbinger of sorrow. A warning? She quickly completed the spread, ignoring a horrific whisper. She wanted to stop the reading, leave well enough alone, but her fingers would not move. Had the entity that had brought Ingo to her returned? Was another *Mephisto Waltz* coming up?

"Father! Father! Where are you? Help me. Please, protect me!"

The ceiling remained dark. Instead of the joy that always accompanied Father's visits, she was frightened and helpless. The queen of hearts was followed by the seven of clubs, and the seven of spades meant caution. But the ace of spades! The death card. It couldn't be. Her blood throbbed in her ears. Abruptly she mixed up all the cards on the table. Gone. Finished. It was all stupid anyway, everybody knew that. No more readings. She must stay away unless Father was protecting her. But he refused to come. The ugly old furniture grew bigger and bigger. She was going mad.

With trembling fingers, she picked up the book again and saw men running along trenches. Ingo called out, "Can't you see? There are no miracles. They don't happen. Not on demand."

"But they do happen," she insisted, gasping for air. The unbearable, stifling heat bathed her in sweat, drenching her clothes. There it was again, that stench of sulfur. After turning off the light, she tore the window open, ripped off her clothes, and fell into bed. With her eyes closed, she saw a blue square appear on the ceiling. Somebody slipped into her bed. Paralyzed with fear she saw Ingo. "I don't need you, Olga," he said in an angry voice.

"Ingo, Ingo, I love you," she whispered.

"Love. Don't be silly. I brought a whore. Only she can make me happy."

A lanky woman in a black bra and tiny panties slipped into bed. "He's mine. All mine."

"Please, Ingo, don't do this to me. I'll do whatever you want, but don't torture me like this."

"You're such a prude. A prude, you hear? I hate prudes."

Olga cried.

The woman disappeared. Ingo buried his head in Olga's lap. "I'm sorry, Olga. I'm no good for you. Forgive me."

"I love you so much, Ingo. Please, don't play tricks like that."

He would not lift his head, and vanished.

With tears streaming down her face, Olga prayed, but nobody came. She was lost.

Staring at the rain pelting her window, Olga felt lost. After a sleepless night, she felt sick, frustrated, and ever so tired. What did she really know about Ingo? First he had insulted her, then obliged her to play the *Mephisto Waltz*. He had inspired the Evil One to enter her. Her desperate need for love had made her vulnerable. Had she become the victim of an ugly game? Father had warned her often enough. The Countess had warned her. Every moment of bliss was followed by unhappiness and disappointment. And here she was with all her clever superiority, nothing but a lost soul. Without Ingo there was no life for her. How could she protect herself?

That night she played Massenet's *Meditation*. Suddenly her fingers banged the keys in a brutal rendition of the *Mephisto Waltz*. playing like a bird colliding with the bars of its cage. Her lap burnt as if hot coals had been dropped on it. Olga jumped up and threw a wet towel on her thighs, but the fire kept burning.

"Help me, Olga, help me!" she heard Ingo cry.

"What do you want me to do?"

His cries persisted through the night. He moaned like a man on the rack. By morning she had enough. "If you don't quit, I'll sleep in Anyna's room."

The voice stopped, and she fell asleep.

After Anyna left for school, Olga returned to her bed and gazed at Ingo's photo on her nightstand. Was he looking at her? His eyes were alive, the smile real. She pulled the blanket over her head and saw a pink light. It turned blood red with Ingo's face at the center.

He had committed suicide. His soul was no longer with her. Why did he do it? Didn't he know that taking his own life led to damnation? Now he would roam with other evil spirits and haunt her.

Olga jumped out of bed and ran to the living room. Her cards tempted. When she reached for them her fingers turned to claws and refused to pick them up. She sank into a chair. Circles spun in front of her eyes. Her head droned. She fell deeper and deeper into an abyss of horror, harrying lights, and jeering shapes.

"Ingo," she cried. "Ingo! Don't leave me."

A flash of lighting struck—then an earth-shattering thunderbolt. Voices cried out in the street. Thousands of them. The ebb and flow of a chant. A funeral procession. Two black horses pulled a hearse with Ingo's body. Six soldiers dressed in black followed.

Olga ran downstairs. All she found was a horse pulling a decrepit wagon filled with crates. Two women stopped and stared at her unkempt appearance. She buttoned her duster. Then, in a sudden impulse, she threw herself at the horse. The animal bucked. Olga slipped and fell, struggled back to her feet, and ran home.

In her apartment she saw blood everywhere. "Ingo, why do you torture me so?"

Anyna found Olga in a catatonic stupor. "Mami, what happened? Talk to me."

Olga could not move, not even when she saw Anyna run off to fetch Mathilde.

"I knew this would happen sooner or later," her mother said. "You wouldn't listen to me. All that fortune telling. Now we're lost."

Olga sobbed, her head buried in her arms. "He is dead."

"Who is dead?"

"Ingo. I saw him."

"Now, that's enough. Stop that nonsense. You know what happens to people who lose their mind? They're taken to an asylum. They get killed like unwanted pets. Do you want that to happen? Pull yourself together. We could be evacuated any day now. I can't take you with us like this. Snap out of it."

"The Jews," Olga whispered, her eyes wide in horror. "Don't you see their blood? I took their bed. You see their blood? It's everywhere." Her teeth chattered despite the heat.

"Enough, Olga," Mathilde ordered, her arm over Olga's shoulder. "Nobody is here, Olinka. There is no blood. This is your apartment. The heat got to you. Let me close the curtains."

"But the blood," Olga shrieked. "It's all over."

Anyna cried out. "Mami, Mami, there is no blood. Nobody is here." She held Olga's hand. "Uncle Ingo is not dead. He will come soon."

Mathilde stood up. "Let me get you some belladonna drops. That will calm you down."

Olga clung to Mathilde's arm. "Don't leave me, Mama."

During the night Ingo appeared again, but did not torment her. The deep sadness in his eyes hurt Olga more than the ugly games he had played earlier.

No matter how desperately she begged Father to come to her, he did not. Mama was right, she could not go on like this.

The last drops of rain dripped from the wet trees. Heavy black clouds rolled across the sky. The buildings smelled of stucco. A burst of sunlight turned the moisture into steam that rose from cracked walls and broken flagstones. Olga jumped over the puddles. What would Ilona Huzak say when she heard of Olga's bizarre experiences? Olga thought the world of her friend, a mystic and fortune teller she could trust. Two years ago they had met at the Esplanade and built an instant rapport. If Ilona could not help, nobody could. Olga knew that Ingo was not dead, else...What? How could she be sure there was no purgatory? The apparitions had been as real as the children playing hopscotch across the street. The stench and the pain were real and were the price she paid for dealing with the underworld. Ilona did it, but never mentioned anything about inconveniences, much less torment. Had she ever annoyed the spirits who provided for her? How did she deal with their tricks? What if Ingo was one of Satan's helpers?

Ilona opened the door in a golden turban and shimmering damask caftan. Her golden slippers had pointed toes. Rows and rows of charms tinkled on her chest; she always wore dozens of bangles. Gold was her favorite color. Olga saw her reflection in Ilona's large black eyes. Her chalk white face reminded Olga of a Geisha, except that Ilona was anything but. A clever Gypsy, she played the role of an exotic bird to lure powerful men into her nest. Her fantastic predictions of mysterious fortunes earned her handsome sums of money, food and jewelry from greedy men. She had told Olga about the bigwigs who believed every word she muttered and protected her from the zealots herding Gypsies into concentration camps. Now that the war had turned, the powerful Nazi leaders were jumpy. They wanted her reassurance that the miracle weapon would work, or that some other miracle would protect them from defeat.

Ilona reached for Olga's hand with a genuine smile, exposing gold teeth. "My dear, I am so glad to see you, but not the Evil One hovering over you. Did he get hold of you again? You look ghastly." She bolted the door, then fastened the chain.

"What happened? Is Mephisto coming for his due? You must be careful."

Olga followed Ilona into her inner sanctum decorated like a Turkish tent with gold and red silk panels. Incense and sandalwood rendered the exotic atmosphere Ilona had created for her gullible clients.

"I am devastated, Ilona," Olga whispered, as if one of the entities could hear her and punish her for tattling.

"So I see. Sit down. I am somewhat rushed—an important client insisted that I see him right away." She took a seat on the magnificent purple and gold maharajah chair. "What happened? Any news from Ingo? He is obviously fine, else my beloved Wilhelm would inform me."

Ilona understood the spirit world like no one else. Even Adolf Hitler had sought her advice. "I had to be careful," she had confided. "He is a very dangerous and powerful man. I had no intention of having him dispose of me. He feeds on flattery and the lies he insists people tell him. Trusts no one, and makes spur of the moment decisions that he often contradicts. It drives his staff and generals crazy. Instead of telling him to sue for peace and go into exile or some such thing, I assured him that the miracle weapon will bring victory. One of the men on his staff recommended that I leave for Poland and arranged for me to get this apartment. Should he ask for me again, he'd tell Hitler that I defected. Clever. Nobody would look for me here."

Sitting on a Moroccan leather stool, Olga admired her friend's sangfroid in dealing with the powerful. Ilona picked up her cards from the polished copper table and shuffled them quickly with her spider-like fingers. The blood red polish on her long fingernails matched her lipstick. Olga would love to live in a place like this, wearing glamorous clothes and giving readings for money, but she felt that would betray Father's trust. Instead she melted into the crowd in her simple white blouses and patterned skirts. Only the large and restless eyes in her tanned face startled. She never wore lipstick or even plucked her brows. Her petite body and tiny waist often led people to think she was much younger than her twenty-seven years.

"Well, Olga dear," Ilona said, passing the deck to Olga. "You look as if the Gestapo is after you, or the demons of Hell. I guess it's all the same." She sat in the lotus position and pulled a cigarette from a silver case and inserted it into a long, ebony holder.

Olga shook her head. "It's about Ingo. He haunts me."

"Ingo? Why would he do that? I told you he's fine."

Olga kept shaking her head. "Not so at all. I know this sounds crazy, but it's driving me out of my mind. I'm in deep trouble, Ilona. I need your help," she pleaded, knowing that her story sounded ludicrous. Why should Ilona believe that Ingo came to her bed, talked to her from the mirror, and even brought a whore with him? She would laugh when she heard that Olga felt haunted by the blood of the Jews in the Ghetto. What if Ilona agreed with Mathilde that Olga had lost her mind in her passion for Ingo? An insane asylum would be as bad as a concentration camp. The Reich eliminated useless people rather than waste food and facilities on them. They needed every bed, nurse and doctor for the wounded.

Olga gazed at the lantern above her head, which reminded her of Aladdin's lamp. On the rosewood table stood a statue of Vishnu, and pictures of Yogananda Swami and Ilona's fallen husband, Wilhelm, in his SS uniform. He was always with her now. If Ingo were dead, he would come to her too. The Evil One had nothing to do with Ingo.

"I know all this sounds ridiculous," Olga said in a timid, apologetic voice. "Yesterday I got so upset that I ran into the street. A voice told me that Ingo's body was in a hearse. I jumped at a horse pulling a wagon. He bucked and almost killed me with his hoofs. What about the smell of sulfur everywhere? Doesn't that mean I've landed in Hell? It's everywhere—the house, the street, even the Esplanade. "She clutched her hot face. "Nobody else smells it."

"Do you smell it now?" Ilona asked in her raspy Hungarian accent.

Olga shook her head. "No. Only your perfume. It's divine—my apartment is a nightmare. I see grotesque faces sneering at me. Ingo's grin is mean and ugly. I can't talk to anybody about it. My mother will take me to an asylum unless I snap out of it. I wish I could; I can't eat or sleep. I need your help, Ilona. I'm desperate. There must be something you can do. Find Ingo for me. Please?"

Olga talked quickly, eager to get it off her chest. "When I hear his voice and see his face, I want to be with him so much that I don't care whether it looks like him or not. All I can think is that he is with me and needs my help. How can I refuse? He is suffering. You should hear him moan. But then he mocks me. What shall I do? I feel like a trapped animal. I miss him so much. If only Father would come and console me, but he stays away. You can't imagine how desperate I am." Olga broke into sobs, too tired to care that she was making a fool of herself.

"So I see, my dear," Ilona said.

"Do you suppose I am being punished for loving him? Is that it? Am I committing adultery? You know that Lothar never wanted me or the baby. We were never married in church. So it can't really be a sin," she whispered between sobs. "Ingo loves me, Ilona. I know he does. Please, Ilona, tell me the truth. Did I land in Hell?" Olga's voice broke. "Who will care for Anyna? She is terribly upset. I am tormenting my child"

Ilona drew on her cigarette. The aroma of Turkish tobacco was part of Ilona's world. Blowing out the smoke she said, "You are too vulnerable. Why do you insist on pleasing everybody? No doubt, Ingo loves you. That's why he would not make you suffer and mock you; he is no sadist. Just because you want him so badly, you feel you must do something to earn it. It's a silly notion. Lonely women get carried away by their fantasies. Most suicides are unhappy lovers. Don't fall into that trap. Reward his love by returning it. That's all there is to it. Too bad you can't talk to him. Letters often get lost, you start brooding, and before you know it, you think he doesn't love you."

Ilona tapped the ashes into a silver dish. "You want my advice? Trust your destiny. Didn't Father assure you that you would survive the war and be together someday? What more do you need? Ignore those visions and return to your music and meditation. I'm sure Ingo is fine and that you will soon get a letter from him."

Olga nodded reluctantly. If it were only that simple. But she did not argue. "Of course you are right. When I met Ingo he was possessed. Now the Evil One has gotten to me. If I could only divorce Lothar and be free. I belong to Ingo." She shuffled, then returned the cards to Ilona.

"My dear Olga," Ilona said with exaggerated patience. "You don't belong to anybody. Why would you want to? Be your own person and get rid of those demons before something terrible happens to you."

Like a sorceress, Ilona murmured her incantations with her eyes closed, summoning her guardian angel. Her face assumed the expression of a Buddha. "Wilhelm. Come to me. What can you tell us about Ingo?" With swift motions she lined up the cards in a vertical spread. Her bangles clanked. "Father is here. He's been trying to contact you, but could not reach you. Some powerful entity blocks his path. Pray to God and ask Him to break the spell."

"Do you see Ingo?" Olga asked, staring at Ilona. The cigarette burnt in the ashtray like a soul on a pyre.

"Father says that Ingo is all right, and not very far from here. He is surrounded by Russian tanks. He needs your prayer and guidance."

"Can you see him, Ilona?" Olga implored.

Ilona's brows shot up. "No. But I feel powerful guidance right now."

Olga knew the glorious feeling when Father came to her, and closed her eyes to listen to Ilona's murmuring.

"Your troubles are very real. Your soul is in jeopardy unless you free yourself from the clutches of those who pretend to be Ingo. Father wants me to tell you that he is watching over you. He will come to you as soon as the path is clear. You must resist temptation. Those entities are playing tricks on you, teasing you. Ignore them."

Elated, Olga watched Ilona turn one card after another. Her bejeweled fingers worked with the grace of a magician. After studying the layout she said, "I see a man who is madly in love with you. He is a good and caring man who misses you as much as you miss him. He too suffers from the separation and needs your messages. You must not doubt his feelings for you. Don't think his love is too good to be true. I am to tell you that love is God's gift. You will see him soon."

Here or in the other world, Olga wondered.

"Going into the future, I see many hardships for you. You must leave the city. Danger lurks everywhere. I see a monumental tragedy coming, like lava flowing from a volcano. Make sure it does not catch you. The spirits will try to protect you if you follow their guidance.

"I see two women who will help you. Decent women who care for Ingo. There is another who will reject you. Pay no heed to her. Ingo will always be there for you, but there is little he can do for you—you will have to find your own path and pursue it. Pick flowers from among the weeds."

Ilona gathered the cards and laid out another spread. "Remarkable. Look for yourself. Ingo's card is right here almost touching yours. You know what is best for you and your family. People can set traps. Be your own master and trust your inner voice.

"I see riches for you, a new life where your music will reach many hearts. Just keep going and you will do well. You will need much courage to liberate yourself from all those who impose on you."

She replaced the spread. Olga was surprised at Ilona's interpretation. Every soothsayer had her own source. The king of spades came up surrounded by minor cards. "That is a man who will influence your life," Ilona said. "He isn't a bad man, just selfish. You will need him, but don't allow him to dominate your life. Always remember, you are nobody's property. In the end, you will be with the man you love."

She pointed to the cards. "See for yourself, Olga. Here is the king of spades, looming larger than life. Below is the queen of spades, a powerful figure. Don't be afraid of them, just make sure you don't join their act. They operate on their own stage. Though you are obliged to be in their proximity, you are not part of their world. And here is the Evil one. Get rid of him. We are heading for trouble. Can you see this? The ace of hearts will get you through. An unusually revealing spread. Be very, very careful, my dear Olga. In this war life has lost its meaning. I wonder who will be left when this war is over. Judging from this spread, you will."

From the sadness in her friend's voice, Olga gathered that Ilona knew she would not be among the lucky ones. She would join Wilhelm.

Impulsively, Olga hugged Ilona. "My dear friend, you've saved my life. Unfortunately, all I can give you is my undying gratitude."

Ilona stroked Olga's cheek with the back of her slender fingers. Her dilated pupils had a distant look. What did she really see? "I have plenty of generous clients. I don't need a thing. Ever since Wilhelm left me I have been waiting to join him. Now run along, my child, and count your blessings."

Olga skipped every other step and ran into the street like a kitten let out of a cage. The air was still hot and humid, and the sun stung on her back. The street and the buildings had dried.

At the grocery store she bought farina, sugar, butter, milk and bread. A stand offered fresh cucumbers, tomatoes and even lettuce. Over the past week she had lost what little flesh she still had. She could not wait to get something to eat and hug Anyna, telling her that all would be well. On her way to the tram, Olga sang with the bird chirping in the dense foliage of the chestnut tree. Ingo was close by. Perhaps he could get leave. Her streetcar approached. She slung the shopping net over her shoulder, and passed the crowd of people waiting at the stop, mainly Poles who would cram into the second car. Once on board, Olga remembered Ilona's prediction. Find immense riches? How did she get that idea? Would Ingo be with her then? Perhaps Germany would win the war after all and she could return to Latvia. Who was to know?

Entering the stuffy apartment building, she saw Ingo in his uniform standing at the stairs waving at her. No, it was not him. Could not be him. Still her heart pounded. Not with fear, but with anticipation. He followed her into the apartment and came in.

"Go away," she said feebly, glad that Anyna was at Mathilde's. She must not give in to temptation. After putting the groceries away, she made herself a sandwich and drank some tea. Suddenly she gagged. The tea cup slipped from her hand and broke on the stone floor. Bending down to pick up the pieces, blackness returned. She was lost.

That night Ingo came to her bed, kissed her hands, arms, and face. Was this an out-of-body visit?

"Ingo, my darling, is it you?"

"What do you think?" he said in a soothing voice, then disappeared.

The silence magnified her heartbeat pounding in her chest. A mosquito buzzed, circling her face in search of blood. Then she saw "END" written in big block letters.

Ilona did not understand that Ingo was in trouble. She was wrong when she said it was a trick. "Ingo," Olga pleaded. "Please come back to me. I need you so."

Later that night Ingo's face appeared in the mirror again, sad and reproachful.

"Where are you?" she asked. "Tell me how I can help you. I'll do anything."

"I can't talk about it," he said, and disappeared.

Olga had no idea why she had gone to the Catholic church when she was not even Catholic. The heavy oak door squeaked on its rusty hinges. Three candles burned in front of the crucified Christ. The faces of St. Peter, St. George fighting the dragon, and St. Francis tending to his birds stared at her from their chapels. A powerful force pushed her toward the main altar. Facing the giant crucifix, her head jerked away. Terrified, she crawled into a dark niche, pressing her hands against her face. "Please, dear Lord, save me. Have mercy on Ingo and me." Eerie whispers reverberated through the empty church, ghosts of those who had been consecrated here. Tiny blue-white lights flickered everywhere.

"Father, help me. I meant no harm when I allowed Ingo to come to my bed. I love him, Father. You brought him to me. You blessed us. Why do you punish me now?"

With her eyes closed, she waited for his answer. Nothing stirred. A fly buzzed frantically, trying to free itself from fly paper. It grew large and awesome. Black eyes stared at her. Olga fell to her knees. "Dear Lord, You are the power and the glory. I'm nothing but a tiny pebble in your universe. Hear my prayer. Save Ingo."

A deep peace filled her soul. The church brightened. The smell of decay vanished and incense filled the air. She opened her eyes. The saints had their usual benevolent expressions.

"Thank you, oh Lord."

The following days plunged Olga into a nightmare.

"Don't bother me now," she scoffed when Anyna clung to her hips. "I must save Uncle Ingo. Go and talk to Omi." Anyna would not let go, and had to be shoved aside. Olga ignored her pleading and tears. Ingo lived in the mirror now and showed up whenever she talked to him. But the face staring at her now was her own. Large ominous eyes dominated a pale mask she could barely recognize. Her mouth gaped as if it searched for words that would not come.

"Ingo," she whispered.

He appeared. "Take that Easter card I sent you and cleanse the room of your transgression. Can't you see that I'm suffering hellish torments for my sin?" The voice had a foreign sound, but it was his face in the mirror.

"What sin?"

"Don't ask stupid questions, you nasty little cunt. God demands penance. Prove that you love me."

"What do you want me to do?" Olga pleaded. No matter what she did, he always criticized her. She got nowhere.

"I told you, take the card and cleanse the room. Go over every spot we touched." He watched her from the mirror, making sure she did not miss a spot where she had experienced happiness. Was it her excess that brought this on? Did he forget that she had cured him?

Following his instructions, she marked figured eights over the pillows on which they had slept, the sheets that had covered them, and the floor they had walked on. Even the window from which they had admired the sky.

"That won't do at all," he said. "Find eight Catholic priests, split their tongues, and nail them to the crosses of four Catholic churches in Russia, where I took my life."

Horrified she cried, "No, you didn't take your life."

"I counted on you. You're a mean cunt."

"There are no Catholic churches in Russia and you didn't take your life."

"Good-bye, Olga. You've sent me back to Hell."

"Don't say that, Ingo. I'm here. I'll do anything, I promise."

He was gone. The mirror reflected the uncovered bed, flowery wallpaper, and nineteenth century picture of a young woman admiring the full moon. Olga threw herself on the bed and cried into her pillow.

The next morning, Olga locked herself into her room and ignored her mother's summons.

That night Ingo's voice returned. "If you had an inkling of the suffering I endure, you would help me."

"What do you want me to do? Tell, me, darling."

"Don't call me darling. Call me angel. And erase all the stupid thoughts from your mind." He had the clipped, sharp language of Herr Hensel, her fifth grade teacher. Images from her childhood popped up in her mind. Scenes of her home in Riga, her school chums, and Lucie coming to her birthday party. She left with Gottfried. Her friends in obscene acts. Ottie grinning. Her huge thighs spread apart, a lusty grin on her fat lips. Lothar reached under her skirt. "Don't be a prude, a prude…" echoed.

"No thoughts, I said. How do you expect to save me when all you can think of is fucking? Get down on your hands and knees and mark figure eights. I'm in Hell because of you."

The ritual went on and on. Cursed and humiliated, Olga followed his instructions, nauseated by the stench of sulfur rising from the old wooden floor and shabby rug.

Whenever Olga left her room, Anyna came running and clung to her mother crying, "Mami, Mami, I'm here. Mami. What's wrong?"

"Don't bother me now. Uncle Ingo needs my help. He's in Purgatory suffering horrible pain."

"But Uncle Ingo…"

"I said, don't bother me. Do you want to kill him?"

Mathilde brought a glass of tea. "Take a sip, Olga. You must be dying of thirst. You have no right to break Anyna's heart with your madness. If Ingo finds out what you have been up to, pretending he made you do it yet, he will be shocked. You are under a spell and must get out before it is too late. Now drink this."

"You don't understand, Mama."

"I understand better than you think. You're obsessed with love. Lothar's coldness, your own hypersensitivity, dealing with the forbidden world of the spirits did you in. If you don't care what happens to you or to Anyna, at least think of Ingo, who is fighting for us at the front. Don't destroy his love for you. Who wants a hysterical woman?"

"Ingo is suffering."

"True. But not the way you think. I wrote to him. If anything had happened to him you would have heard about it. Now take a sip and be a good girl." Mathilde's calm voice soothed Olga's frazzled nerves. As soon as she took a sip, she pushed the glass away and screamed. "Don't you dare touch me. You stink. I must not drink. It will kill him."

"Just take another sip, my child," Mathilde pleaded, holding the glass up to Olga's lips.

"You're a bitch, Olga," Ingo reproached her. "A cruel, selfish bitch. Now get rid of that junk in your stomach. You must be pure."

"For what?"

"For death."

She ran into the kitchen, pulled off he gas hose, and pushed it into her throat, then vomited.

Mathilde wrestled the dirty hose from Olga.

Enraged, Olga hit her mother and knocked her down. "I told you to leave me alone." Then she pushed the dirty rubber hose back into her throat. "Just let me die."

Mathilde tore the hose from Olga's hand, took her arm and pulled her to bed. Olga obliged, too tired to resist. All she could think of was sleep. Or death. As soon as she laid her head on the pillow he sneered, "How dare you lie down? Is that all you can do? Now we must start all over again..."

Chapter 17

Hauptmann Ingo Kroll pulled the sun-baked helmet from his head and wiped the sweat from his face and neck. The gritty handkerchief scraped against his week-old beard. His steps crunched on the sandy road. Lulled into oblivion by the scraping feet of his men, he wondered whether Olga played *Liebestraum* or did she practice *Mephisto Waltz?*

From time to time, he blinked at the endless steppe. When would strafing Russian fighter planes show up and give the long German column the final blow? So far they had not noticed the German stragglers who had escaped the encirclement. The golden rye, heavy with grain, covered the land as far as his eyes could see, all the way to the blue horizon. Floating white clouds offered no shade. His swollen feet strained against his worn boots. Three years ago he had come to Russia as part of a victorious army, convinced the people would receive them with open arms and the war would soon be over. Instead, they had landed in a hornet nest of determined people who had no intention of letting others run their country, no matter how bad things were under Stalin. They understood that an Adolf Hitler was no savior. Who could blame them? Not he. Ingo Kroll had witnessed enough atrocities committed against the Russian people.

Instead of claiming victory, the German Wehrmacht limped home licking their wounds. They still had a long ways to go. God only knew what the Russians would do once the Reich surrendered. Like Olga, he wished for an acceptable outcome, but he could not see one.

Escaping their last encirclement had been more than a stroke of luck. More than a blessing from God. All he could think was that Olga's powers had guided him. Had she not predicted that he would survive the war? Why question it? Count his blessings and march on—west, toward Poland, still hundreds of kilometers away. What would Olga say when he showed up at her doorstep again, though there was nothing he could do for her? He missed her guidance now. How had he lost it? Had she given up on him? How else could he explain the sudden silence? He felt like a spectator in a theater after the curtain had fallen, but the lights weren't coming back on. She had to know his predicament.

Once a young Ingo Kroll had cheered for his Fuhrer, proud to endure the rigorous officer's training. Now he wished he had never been born. The thought jolted him back to reality. Self-pity was destructive and meaningless. He was no coward crying for Mami. Not his mother anyway. She would not allow it, raising him to master self-discipline. His body could enter a robot state, forgetting exhaustion, hunger, and thirst. He would live so that he, Olga, and Anyna could be a family. Instead of moping around, he'd better watch for Russian Stormoviks or bombers, which they couldn't escape without a grove or knoll for cover. Sooner or later the Russians would show up, and notice the long columns of men and equipment, the escapees of their encirclement at Bobruysk. Then all the Russian pilots had to do was dive down and settle their account with some well-aimed bombs. Those fellows were well-trained and dedicated to their cause. Victory meant the end of the war, nothing less would do.

Ingo's boot caught a rut. He stumbled, steadied himself, and marched on. Even a sprained ankle could be fatal. The severely wounded filled the wagons to capacity. Those with minor injuries endured their pain and kept walking. Nobody wanted to be left behind. Twenty days of fierce fighting and their miraculous escape had taken their toll. Hungry and thirsty men pushed on, counting their blessing.

Blisters, sunburn, and mosquito bites were a common nuisance. That itch, his own stench, and his sweat-drenched uniform were a way of life. Ingo shook his canteen. The last bit of water sloshed inside. He took a short sip, swished the tepid water around in his dry mouth, then swallowed it. The gritty taste between his teeth vanished. His mouth felt almost clean, but the thirst remained. Who was to know when they would come across a creek not guarded by Russians, so that they might replenish their water supply. 376 men, squeaking wagons, and the clinking chains of armored vehicles made an easy target for tanks.

Olga, can you hear me? Don't desert me. You feed my soul. You are my daily bread and water.

The sensation that he had landed in Hell twisted his gut. What made human beings fight wars, kill each other in the name of winning?

Sensitivity numbed, love betrayed, dignity mocked, men turned into vengeful monsters trained to kill. A soldier fought because he was ordered to do so.

Ingo waved his grimy handkerchief at the swarm of mosquitoes feasting on his face, then rubbed his burning eyes and closed them again. Dozing, he imagined Olga at the piano playing *Rhapsody in Blue*—the music of her future. He could not see a future, even if he survived the war. What would the Allies do to Germany? Enjoy the war, peace will be Hell to pay. His parched lips stretched into a bitter grin.

Olga, I love you so, my sweet, enchanting wizard. An intense passion filled his groin. Now? Here? Was he losing his mind?.

The men sang *At Home We Shall See Each Other Again*. They too dreamed of home and peace.

The wagon at his side hit a pot hole. The wounded cried out. They had been placed side by side like logs. The lucky ones were unconscious, the others bore their pain with muffled moans. Everybody clung to whatever shreds of life were left in him, praying for God's mercy and an injection of morphine. Every breath, no matter how painful, was precious.

Neumann's chalk-white face had feverish eyes and ashen lips. Blood seeped through the army blanket. Despite years of seeing men die, writhe in pain and plead for help, Ingo's compassion had not diminished. He pitied Neumann, ravaged with pain. His bloodless lips quivered. He was too proud to scream. "Water," he begged through chattering teeth.

Ingo hesitated. Should he waste his precious water on a man who would die within the hour?

Neumann was a friend. They had fought together, laughed together. How could he ignore those desperately pleading eyes? He unscrewed the cap of his canteen and poured some drops into the dying man's quivering mouth. The wagon rattled and shook. Neumann licked the water from his lips. His tormented body had ceased to function, but his will to live persisted. "Thank you, Herr Hauptmann." He remained silent for a moment, then asked, "Do you believe in God?"

Ingo stroked Neumann's clammy forehead. "Yes," he said, hoping it would give the man peace. "Do you?"

"No. I believe in our Fuhrer and our mission."

Ingo had heard that before, had believed in it himself until he saw Hitler's meaningless actions and hateful indifference toward the conquered, his people, and the men who sacrificed their lives for him. "God will receive you when the time comes," he said.

Neumann's wan face relaxed. "But the time has not come, has it?" he gasped. "Will He fix my body? That shrapnel is lodged in my intestines, I think. Not good."

"No, not good. Only God can heal that wound. You might try prayer." Was Olga here?

"We are all in God's hands," the wounded man next to Neumann said. He was not as bad off as Neumann. "Just accept Him and watch the change in you. It's powerful."

Ingo jumped down, and resumed his march alongside the wagon. A hot breeze fanned his sweaty head, but could not dry his sticky hair. Had Olga come to him again? A tenderness overcame him as dust particles crunched between his teeth. The wobbly wheels on the cart squeaked. The driver was one of the wagon men, requisitioned from the occupied population, obliged to serve the German Wehrmacht with their horses and wagons. Ingo could not imagine getting along without these burly fellows who wore their shabby coats through both winter and summer. Their odor, the stench of axle grease and sweating horses, had a comforting familiarity. He was still at liberty rather than a prisoner of war, still alive and walking.

The young men at the head of the column sang, *Auf der Heide* over and over again as if they had forgotten the end. The beat propelled them forward, step by step. The melody reminded Ingo of the Esplanade and his transformation. He scanned the sunny sky for approaching planes. Now that the Americans supported the Russians, the Luftwaffe could not keep up with them. Henry Ford must have retooled his factories and churned out military equipment at the rate he had manufactured his cars. The Russian T-34 tanks swarmed like bloody mosquitoes.

With the Allies fighting in Sicily and gaining ground, they could be attacking anywhere along the French coast. That meant…no, he'd better not think about it. On the other hand, if Hitler needed more fighting men in the West, he might be transferred. He should be so lucky. Speculations got him nowhere.

Ingo hummed along with the men and marched to their beat, wide awake now. The red poppies and blue cornflowers dotting the golden rye reminded him of Sunday outings with his family. Ingrid used to pick them and weave them into a wreath for her blonde hair. She was a lovely girl, always cheerful and full of ideas. They had enjoyed their Hitler Youth training and often talked about those days.

Neumann moaned.

"It won't be long," Ingo assured him. They had taken the poor wretches along because nobody had the heart to leave them behind. Jakob Neumann was from Dresden. Ingo had pulled him from an explosion only to extend his agony.

A flock of birds burst from the rye. The men quickened their pace. A hidden enemy? Nothing stirred in the softly swaying field. The battle between Communism and National Socialism was running its course. The ideologies had not changed, but their blood was running out as it had in the Great War. Stalin, the cunning fox, would win this war and take over Hitler's place as master of Europe. Nobody could resist his slick strategies and maneuvers.

Ingo kicked a pebble, watching it fly into the weedy ditch. Politics! The Versailles Treaty had changed the face of Europe in an attempt to wipe out Germany. After this war the winners would do it again. Sweat poured from his face and ran into his eyes. He needed water—clear, cool water—and some consolation.

Neumann moaned. *God have mercy and release this man from his misery.*

Olga believed that suffering people did penance for some wrong in their past lives. Without confession there could be no redemption. Neumann did not believe in God.

A horse neighed and pulled at his bit, shook his mane and paused until the slap of the reins got him going. He probably wished he could graze in the rye and fill his empty stomach. But they were in a hurry. At any moment all hell could break loose. Hooves clicked in a syncopated beat to the scraping steps of the men. The wagon hit another rut. Neumann cried out. "Can't you watch out?" Silence. Then, "Mutter! Have mercy. The pain! Water!"

Ingo leaned over the rough-hewn edge of the wagon. The foul smell of decaying flesh, urine, and imminent death rose from the dirty blankets. "We're almost there," he lied.

Neumann wailed. "Where? Just shoot me. There's no life for me." His bloody hands released his torn belly. Why didn't he lose consciousness?

"We're almost at Stolptsy. There's a field hospital and morphine."

The dying man nodded and closed his eyes. He clung to life because he was afraid to die.

Ingo heard the *Mephisto Waltz* and remembered Olga pounding out the wild and throbbing chords. Her passion had disarmed him, liberated him from his anxiety and anger. He needed her now.

His diarrhea acted up, rumbling through his intestines. After relieving himself in the ditch, he marched on. When would the partisans show up? The cruelty of those notorious rifle women in civilian clothes put any man to shame. Unlike the wiles of a Lorelei, luring men to their deaths on the cliffs of the Rhine, the rifle women enjoyed the screams of each German they cut up and left bleeding to death, his penis stuck in his mouth like a pacifier.

"I have a girl at home," Neumann said. "I never told you about Traude, did I? If I die, would you tell her that I only thought of her? Her address is in my wallet. Would you tell her that?" He gasped. "I should've told her. She's waiting for me. Now it's too late."

"Of course I will," Ingo said, glad that Olga knew how much he loved her.

"Traude is young," Neumann whispered through quivering lips. His breath slowed down. The wagons rattled along. Would he be next, Ingo wondered, closing the man's eyes as he had done so often over the past four years, fighting a war they could not win. He reached under the blood-soaked tunic and found the wet photo of a pretty girl with braids wrapped around her head. The ink on the back had bled out. "To Jakob, from Traude." He took it and jumped down from the wagon, stumbling against a rock. "Damn. *Verfluchte Scheisse. Verdammte Schweinerei.* Why? Why? Why all this shit?"

The passing men nodded.. "You're right, Herr Hauptmann," Kunz agreed. He too had survived the battles. "We should all scream to the Heavens."

Ingo felt the blood rush into his face. How could he, an officer, lose his temper? "Carry on, men," he said in a loud voice. "Neumann has died. He was a good man. Loyal to his *Vaterland*. May he rest in peace."

The men bowed their heads and sang *Ich hatt einen Kameraden*, as if at a military funeral. The lump in Ingo's throat choked him. Tears welled up and blurred his vision. He stared at the sand under his feet so that the men could not see his face. What was he doing here in Russia anyway? Why struggle when all was lost? He should close his eyes and be done with.

The men started another song. "Long is the road back to our homeland, so long, so long." Their steps picked up speed. Every minute counted. Ingo sang along, glad that death had delivered Neumann from his suffering. His mother and Traude would cry for him. Ingo lashed out at pesky mosquitoes. They should bury Neumann and let one of the limping men ride, but they could not spare the time. He scanned the horizon. Was that dark line in the distance a grove? The edge of a forest where they could find shelter? Or was it a mirage, tempting them like a thirsty man with the promise of water?

The droning of planes interrupted the song. The men scuttled into the rye and burrowed into the ground like scared mice. The wounded were left at the mercy of the bombs. The earth trembled under the ear-splitting explosions, tearing up hapless men, horses and vehicles. The Stormoviks circled around and returned for a second attack. A third destroyed what was left.

The stench of burning wood, fuel, and flesh, the moans of the wounded, and cries of the dying animals were part of every battle.

Ingo was not hardened enough to ignore his own helplessness. Brushing off the dust, he said to Kunz, "Let's see what can be salvaged. They'll be back. So let's get on with it. Repair minor damage and burn the rest. No need to leave our supplies for the Partisans."

"*Jawohl*, Herr Hauptmann," Kunz replied dutifully, as if he needed instructions. A true NCO knew what had to be done, and did it.

"Those who can walk should be on their way," Ingo said. "We must reach that forest before the Reds return."

"Yes, sir," Kunz said. "The wounded are dead. Twenty-two new casualties. One of the armored trucks is on fire. We still have two machine gun units, two repairable trucks, four wagons and three horses." Insect bites had left red blotches on his swarthy, unshaven face, streaked with sweat and dust.

"A mess," Ingo acknowledged. "Send a vanguard to the grove. We don't want any more surprises. The Partisans know that this is the only road through the Pripyat Marshes. They're as bloodthirsty as these goddamned gadflies and mosquitoes." He slapped his cheek and caught a persistent insect.

Kunz formed a column and set the men in motion. Ingo noticed a young soldier with tears in his eyes, lips quivering. "What's your name, soldier?"

The boy jumped to attention and saluted. "Schutze Olsen. *Zu Befehl*, Herr Hauptmann."

"At ease. Stay close to Kellermann. He will teach you how to survive a war. Right Kellermann?"

"*Jawohl*, Herr Hauptmann," Kellermann said. He was no more than nineteen, but had seen enough action and looked confident. "I shot down three tanks and took eleven prisoners, sir."

"Well done, Kellermann. You see, Olsen, it isn't that hard. Stay with our men and you'll be in good hands."

"I'll catch me a few tanks in no time," the boy said. His dusty, sunburnt skin darkened.

"I know you will, Olsen," Ingo said. "You'll get your chance soon, believe me. We're not running out of enemies. And fear is one of them. Sits in your guts. You wouldn't be human if you were not afraid. Right, Kellermann?"

The soldier nodded. "Just ignore it, Olsen," Kellermann said. "Else you'll be running around with shitty pants."

Ingo smiled. "I bet you always dreamed of fighting Russians. Show them what a real German is. Told your friends that you would chase them back single-handedly. We all did. But you can't do it alone. Together we are a strong force. We'll get to them sooner or later. Just remember, when you see somebody who doesn't look German, shoot. These fellows don't believe in warning you before they fire."

The boy's face beamed with pride. "*Jawohl*, Herr Hauptmann."

"Then let's march on to victory."

Only half the column had reached the forest when the Stormoviks returned. The rest fanned out, crawling into the green corn, a better cover than the rye.

"We must scout out a different route," Ingo told Kunz as planes dove at them. Random bombs hit the grove, but missed the men and vehicles.

"There are other stragglers here," Kunz said after the planes swung off and their roaring faded away.

"Great. Let's get everybody assembled. Check their materiel and see whether there are any officers among them. We must set up a defense. Get transportation for the wounded. After a short rest we are off to Stolbtsy. We must move as fast as we can." He noticed the desperate look in the eyes of the exhausted men slumped on the churned up moss and trampled-down bracken. Black smoke billowed from the burning vehicles, but nobody paid attention. A week of uninterrupted marching and fighting, with little food and water, had taken its toll. Ingo ordered the troops to rest, except for the cook, who summoned his creativity to stretch his skimpy supplies into a meal for the starved men. The march through the swamp, plagued by more blood-thirsty insects, would require whatever strength and skill the men could muster.

Olsen leaned against a crusty oak. Kellermann stretched out beside him.

Both of them were asleep when Ingo closed his eyes. He saw Olga running through flames. "Don't torture me, Ingo. Let me go. I'm finished." She fell to the ground and sobbed.

"I'm coming, my love." He could not move. The field between them grew wider and wider. Huge blackbirds dropped from the sky and hacked at her face and heart. She fought them off, but they came back.

"Olga! Olga! I'm coming." She stood alone, her arms stretched out. "God is in me now," she said, floating away in a white gown. A bright light trailed behind her.

Kunz shook his shoulder. "It's time, Herr Hauptmann."

Where was he? Ingo wondered. What happened to Olga? The dream had shaken him to the core. She was in trouble. Something terrible had happened to her. Was she hurt? Had she been caught in an air raid? Those vultures could be enemy planes.

He rose wearily, massaged his face, and smoothed out his hair. The smell and humidity of the forest meant marshland was close.

He summoned the rising men. "The faster we walk, the quicker we'll get to safety. The cook has some food for you. Eat on the run. We must get out of here before the Russians return. It should be dark in an hour or so. Great camouflage but dangerous. Be sure to stay on the path in single file. We've studied the map and have a flashlight. By now the Partisans know of our presence. They'll set a trap. Keep your rifles and bayonets handy, but save your bullets. We don't have any to spare."

Leaving the grove, Ingo remembered Degrelle and his enthusiasm. He wished he had some wine for his men, or schnapps. Should they be surrounded in the marshes, they would starve to death unless they surrendered. Those loyal Walloons had carried their slain commander out of the chaos of Cherkassy. Degrelle's courage had saved thousands of soldiers and Russian civilians. Ingo would do the same. They would get to safety.

During the long march through the sultry night a faint smell of sulfur rose from the wet, soggy soil. Ingo remembered his dream. What could have happened to Olga? As soon as he reached Stolbtsy he would send her a letter.

Chapter 18

Olga buried her head in her arms and withdrew into herself. "Oh, Ingo, if I only did not love you so much. First Lothar, now you. Why do you torture me? What more do you want? I'm exhausted, starved, and sick of it all."

"So you don't love me anymore," said the voice in the darkness.

"You know I don't mean it that way," she whimpered. "It's just, can't you see, we're getting nowhere. I love you so. More than my life. Else I would not do any of this."

"Then prove it. I'm suffering. And you talk of love…"

Her body was on fire. Helplessly, she watched him lie on his stomach, his legs tied. She heaved herself up and licked figure eights over his image on the floor.

"That's better. Look, I'm dancing. Will you grant me the next waltz?"

She got up, and raised her arms to him. "With great pleasure, Ingo."

"Oh, you stupid bitch. How can you believe everything people say? Don't you get it? The pain is killing me. Help!"

Olga felt her body torn apart, as if she were on the rack while he roasted over an open fire. Swarms of demons poked at him with pitchforks.

"Don't watch me," he shouted. "I can't stand it."

Touched by his consideration, even while suffering such agony, she resumed licking figure eights. If she could only pray. Every time she saw a cross a knife stabbed her heart. Without God they were doomed. Tears streamed from her burning eyes, but when she raised her hand to wipe them off, her cheeks were dry.

In the morning, Ingo had disappeared. She dressed quickly in a gray blouse and buckled a belt to keep her brown skirt in place. Over the past days, she had lost even more weight. When would all this come to an end? Would she survive the ordeal?

Sitting down at the piano, she heard the door open. Mathilde and Gottfried came in without ringing the bell. In his uniform, Gottfried looked like a stranger.

Why had they come? Something was amiss. "I really can't talk to you now," she said, troubled by the concerned looks on their faces. "I am terribly busy."

"Not too busy to greet a friend, Olga," Gottfried said, and kissed her cheek. "How are you? I have not seen you for weeks. What's going on? Your mother tells me that you suffer from delusions."

His jovial tone upset her. "Delusions? Not at all. I must save Ingo. Please excuse me." She ran into her room and locked the door. "Dear Lord. You are the power and the glory..." The nauseating smell of sulfur reminded her that she was still in the clutches of demons. Invisible claws ripped at her flesh. Ugly mouths blew stinking breath. She sank to her knees and passed out.

As they tried to open the door, Mathilde said. "This has been going on for days. Olga thinks Ingo is dead and she must do penance for him to relieve his suffering in purgatory. If she keeps this up, she'll die. You talked to the doctor, Gottfried, didn't you?"

He nodded. "Dr. Gruber is an old friend of mine. The mentally disturbed are not treated kindly," he said. "As far as I know, they are euthanized. Dr. Gruber assured me that he'll look after Olga."

"Thank you," Mathilde said. "If we don't do something, she'll kill herself. It's all so horrible."

Gottfried put his weight against the door and broke the lock. They found Olga on the floor, unconscious. He patted her face, which resembled a death mask. "I don't understand any of this. I didn't think spirits existed. Now I have proof. I never thought she would go to such extremes for anybody. What makes her think Ingo is dead in the first place?"

Mathilde brought a wet washcloth and placed it on Olga's forehead.

"She is such a sweet young woman," Gottfried said. "I enjoy her music. She has a special knack for accompanying my voice. We made a great duo." He slipped his arm under her neck and knees, and carried her to her bed. How light she was—nothing but skin and bones. Her head lolled against his shoulder like that of a sleeping child. Putting her down, he told Mathilde, "Lucie and the children are in Saxony. I got two weeks off to get my business in order before I'll get my assignment." He helped Mathilde spread a light blanket over Olga's limp body. "I wasn't cut out for military service, that's for sure. The young drill sergeant takes pleasure in watching me struggle along. His voice shatters glass. I'm glad Lucie will be in Saxony when the front collapses."

Olga moaned. "It's all right, dear," Mathilde said, rubbing Olga's temples. When Olga remained unconscious, Mathilde turned to Gottfried, "Are you saying the front will collapse?"

The doorbell rang. Two burly men in white coats entered. "We'll take it from here," the heavier one said. He had the bulbous red nose of a drinker and smelled of liquor. His short gray hair was cut like a brush.

"Come, Olinka dear," Mathilde said, "these men will take you to the hospital. You need help. The doctor will give you a tranquilizer."

Olga opened her eyes and stared at the men in disbelief. "Mama? What do they want?"

"They will take you to the hospital, dear."

"Hospital? But I can't leave now. If I quit, all is lost. Forever. Can't you see?"

Mathilde ignored Olga's pleading, torn between wanting to save her daughter and giving in to her. "Nothing is lost, dear. You'll be back in no time."

Olga's eyes widened in horror when the big man reached for her. "Please, Mami. Not now. I can't go now."

One man grabbed her arms, the other took her legs, and they carried her off.

Olga reached for Mathilde. "Please, Mami, I beg you. Ingo depends on me."

The men hauled Olga out the door like a piece of baggage.

"For heaven's sake," Mathilde cried, following them. "Don't be so rough." She watched them jerk Olga's writhing body down the stairs. In the street, they dumped her into their van like an animal, and slammed the doors shut.

"I will go with you," Mathilde said, and climbed into the cab.

"I'll visit you at the hospital, Olga," Gottfried shouted.

Why the hospital? Olga thought, rubbing her back. She was not ill. Nobody understood. Who was to know what they would do to her there? "I can't help you now, Ingo. Sorry. I tried. If I resist, they will keep me locked up forever. Or kill me. I must do what they say. Please forgive me, darling." The van bumped over the cobblestones on tubeless tires and ran on wood gas—petrol for civilian use was no longer available.

At the hospital, Olga watched her mother fill out the admission form. The hard, bony features of the nurse frightened her. In a timid voice she asked, "Can I see the doctor now?"

"In due time, Frau von Schenck. Now follow me."

Olga embraced her mother. "How can you do this to me, Mami?"

"It will save your life."

With tears streaming down her cheeks, Olga followed the nurse down a hall that smelled of formaldehyde and other disgusting hospital odors. A chunky male nurse pushed a gurney. The patient had been strapped down, his eyes dull from pain. What would they do to her? Her knees weakened. Her hands trembled. Fear overwhelmed her. There would be no way out. She would die here.

The ward she was assigned to had two rows of beds, ten on each side. A tinted window dimmed the light and obscured the dismal appearance of the patients. It had iron bars. There would be no escape.

The nurse pointed to the back. "The last bed on the right is yours. Take your clothes off and put these pajamas on."

Olga stared at the crude clothes. The patients watched her pick up the sack-like top and hold it against her thin body. Were they creatures from Hell? "You mean, you want me to stay *here*? With these people? And wear that? I'm not crazy." She avoided the eyes of the grotesque beings under their shabby army blankets. One of the women sighed. She was younger than the rest, with bright eyes and a large face. What was she doing here?

The nurse snapped. "That's what they all say." She wore a stiff white nurse's cap and a gray uniform.

"But you can see for yourself," Olga insisted and pulled away. The nurse grabbed Olga's wrist and yanked her back. "I don't think you want to find out how we keep our patients in line. You were brought here for a reason. We have no time for hypochondriacs when thousands of wounded need our help. I'll never know why we bother with all you deadwood. If it were up to me...Now get those on and get into bed before I lose my temper."

"I can't stay here."

"I guess you didn't hear me. Or can't you understand German? Now, for the last time, do as you are told, or else..." The nurse pointed at a creature standing on one leg, her face twisted into a mask of insanity like one of Goya's drawings. "You don't want to find out the other option. Now get into those clothes and give me yours."

"Yes, nurse," Olga said, unbuttoning her blouse in front of all the watching women. The doctor would come soon and release her. Actually, she was so exhausted that she wouldn't mind sleeping for a while. Gottfried would look after her. He knew the doctor. Was his name Gruber?

The shapeless shirt hung on her shoulders like a crude sheet. A drawstring held up the giant trousers. Prison garb. Would they chop off her hair as they'd done to the other patients? What would they say when she returned to the Esplanade?

The nurse rolled up Olga's clothes and marched out. Her shoes clicked against the polished linoleum.

Slipping between the rough, clean sheets, Olga hoped she would get used to the smell of disinfectant. Hunger contracted her stomach. Her throat hurt from the gas hose. What if she had caused an injury that got infected? It was stupid to have done that. The whole matter was ridiculous. She closed her eyes. Her body relaxed. The grunts, whimpers, moans, and babbling faded. Somebody cried out, "No, no shocks," and sobbed.

Olga searched for music in her mind. Nothing came up. Dozing off, she felt Ingo slip into her bed.

"You found me. I'm so glad you came, but there's nothing I can do for you, darling. I'll make up for it as soon as I get out of here. I promise. Don't be angry. Please forgive me."

By evening she still had not seen a doctor. The watery vegetable soup had not filled her stomach, or even eased her hunger. A blood-red emergency lamp came on above the door, reminding her of a watchful eye that never closed. "Dear God, why have you forsaken me? If you're omnipotent and merciful..." Olga did not dare go on. Tears stung her eyes. Wet tears. She was not lost after all.

Dr. Gruber took off his thick, metal-framed spectacles and looked up at Olga, then rose and shook her cold, clammy hand. Last year they had called him out of retirement and he returned to his former post, replacing a psychiatrist who had been drafted to serve shell-shocked men coming from the front. So much for his golden years. He should leave for Germany before the war reached him here in Poland. But he must wait for official evacuation orders. Considering the hardships other people endured, his was but a minor sacrifice.

"Please sit down, Frau von Schenck. I hear you're an old friend of Gottfried's. I've had the pleasure of attending his recitals, here and back in Latvia. Yes, a great voice. He can move you to tears."

She smiled, producing the sweetest dimples. Despite her crude institution garb, Dr. Gruber found her a lovely young woman. No wonder Gottfried was so fond of her. Her wan complexion worried him, as did the restless glimmer in her eyes. Some mysterious disorder troubled her soul. Delusions, it said on the admission form. Imagining her lover suffering in purgatory. It was far-fetched, but over the years he had heard so much that this did not surprise him. Now he was supposed to help her snap out of it, as if it was as easy as getting a trained dog to behave.

Like so many young women, her problem was loneliness and love. That in itself was a state which could drive sensitive women to attempt suicide. An artist and musician yet. He had dealt with women like her who believed death would reunite them with a fallen lover. Gruber marveled at such passion. Even before he had married Martha, he had never felt that he would lose his mind if anything happened to her. He would miss her, of course. Miss the comfort of a well-organized home and the warm body that shared his bed.

Returning the spectacles to his nose, he picked up her file. She was apprehensive, of course, like all his patients when they first arrived. Later they trusted him, believing he would not adhere to the cruel logic that disturbed people were of no use to the world and might as well be gone. He saw no benefit in the painful treatments he was obliged to administer. Who had time for psychotherapy? And he was not sure that it returned a deranged mind to a normal life.

Gruber leaned back into his chair and folded his wrinkled hands over his belly.

"Well, Frau von Schenck, what's the problem?" he asked in the warm, fatherly tone that usually instilled confidence in his patients. She could be a beauty, he decided, if it not for those sunken cheeks and the frightened stare in her large blue eyes. Something moved him to get up and put his arm around her, but he resisted the temptation.

Olga talked in a low, childlike voice, her eyes focused on his. "It's all a mistake, *Herr Doktor.* Neither Gottfried nor my mother listened to me." Her voice grew louder and insisted, "I should *not* be here." Leaning across the desk she reminded him of a kitten begging to be petted. "As you can see, I'm not crazy, not like those people in the ward. The nurse is a monster, but she can't intimidate me. Do you know what she said?"

He shook his head, though he knew. His once thick brown hair had thinned to sparse strands that no longer covered his pate.

"If I don't do as I'm told, she will show me." Olga folded her hands, imploring. "She can't torment me, can she? It's horrible to be among them. All those disgusting sounds. They scare me to death."

"Is that so?" he said, feasting on her sweet mouth. She dramatized her statements with hand gestures. He knew it all only too well. The nurse could torment her, even give her a lethal injection instead of a tranquilizer. Nobody would question her. Only Sister Waltraut was not the type, just tired and irascible. He nodded thoughtfully. "Well, as far as I'm concerned, you do look quite normal and intelligent. An outburst of indignation is a positive trait. Let's assume there's nothing wrong with you. Now, why don't you eat, drink, or sleep? You talk to somebody called Ingo, who is at the front, and spend hours licking the ground. Must be hard on your tongue. No wonder your mother is concerned about you. Wouldn't you be? You are a mother."

Gruber opened the folder, giving her time to think and prepare her argument, or agree. The charges were incriminating. He could only release her to her mother if Olga cooperated.

"My mother is overprotective," she said quickly. "She and I have nothing in common. Besides, she can't stand my husband and now thinks that having a, well, friend, would only cause us more problems. But she's all wrong. Ingo is a wonderful man, not like my in-laws—mean, egotistical people." Her eyes sparked, as if it was his fault that she had married the wrong man.

"So, what makes you think that Ingo is in Purgatory?" he asked. The frightened twitch of her lower lip made him feel sorry for her. He rubbed the waddle under his chin. "Let me read what I wrote down during my interview with your mother. I have no reason to question her statement. She told me that you are talking to yourself. That you refuse food and drink. You insist on standing for hours in a stupor and smell peculiar odors nobody else can detect. You lick the floor." He looked up and saw her blush.

"It may seem strange to you, *Herr Doktor*, but I can explain it all." Her voice had quieted.

"She also says that you talk to the mirror," Gruber went on. "It seems you see Ingo there, who asks you to perform these rather uncalled for acts. You ignore your child, your job and yourself. Yet you have no proof that Ingo is dead. And even if that were true, what makes you think that your depriving yourself of the necessities of life could help him in any way whatsoever? Purgatory yet. There is no such thing. Can you see that?"

Olga agreed, and felt ashamed for acting the way she had. Cradling her face in her hands, she wondered how she could convince the doctor that she was sane. Of course he was right. She had questioned her own sanity. That was past now. At least Mama had not reported being attacked, nor that Olga had attempted suicide with the gas hose.

She sensed that the old doctor wanted to help her. He was not cold and cruel like the nurses. "I only pretended that Ingo was in the mirror. I miss him so. He is in great danger. I see things other people don't, but that doesn't mean I'm crazy. I communicate with my deceased father. He is my guardian angel."

"Fine," Dr. Gruber said. "We all need one."

Olga grew confident. "So you see, Ingo and I are so close I can communicate with him through ESP. Father takes my messages to him. He warns Ingo of traps and protects him from danger." She paused, wondering whether any of this made sense to the doctor. Why had this happened to her? Perhaps she really was crazy. Normal people did not communicate with departed souls.

"Your explanation is quite plausible," he said, watching her eager expression—that of a child talking herself out of a bad situation. What did he know about schizophrenic minds, haunted people suffering from paranoia? To her, all this was real, only he could not stand-by and let her destroy herself and endanger her family. He really could not help her. The electric shocks they applied to hallucinating patients only intensified their anxiety. He hated to see this lovely young woman be destroyed by them. But if he could not get her to snap out of her derangement on her own, he had no choice. Sooner or later, he would be obliged to transfer her to the asylum for the incurably insane, where she would be euthanized.

"So you see, doctor," she said quickly, gleaning hope from his concern.

"It's your behavior that poses a threat to your health and well-being," he said. "I'll keep you under observation. If you can convince me that you will not jeopardize your health, neglect your child, and can live a more or less normal life, I will release you. You are as thin as a ghost. Your complexion reminds me of sour milk. You must be starved." He smiled.

"But I can't stay here," Olga protested, afraid she would lose Ingo, and added quickly, "I have work to do. I perform at the Esplanade. We have daily transports coming in from the front. The men enjoy my music. You should come and hear me. My daughter needs me. What if I promise not to do anything abnormal, will you let me go?"

He shook his head. He had worked with hundreds of disturbed people, but doubted that he had cured any of them.

"Our evacuation orders may come any day now. The Poles could stage an uprising here, as they did in Warsaw. No, my dear Frau von Schenck, I cannot just let you go. First you must convince me that you not only understand the severity of our situation here in Poland, but that you are able to act in a reasonable fashion should we get our evacuation orders.

"There is absolutely nothing you can do for your friend Ingo. Nothing. Your starving, or whatever else you do, is of no benefit to him. Worse, if you arouse suspicion, you could be arrested and be a lot worse off than you are here, in this hospital. The assassination attempt on our Fuhrer has the Reich in uproar. If our top generals believed that Germany would be better off without our Fuhrer, and risked their lives to remove him, they must have had good reasons. Things are coming to a head. You will need all your physical strength and a rational mind to cope."

"Like what?" she asked impatiently. He could not keep her here. What good would that do? Ingo needed her.

"The obvious," Gruber said in a slow, tired voice. "A clash between us and the underground would be a bloodbath. You should plan to leave Poland. The people staying behind will not be treated kindly by either Poles or Russians."

She stared at him in disbelief. How could he say things like that? If anybody heard him, he could be arrested and executed. On second thought, he was right. She had to come to her senses, Ingo or not. She must save Anyna, her mother, and Ottie. The Countess knew what would happen and had left. She did not need a sixth sense. Lothar knew it too, long before anybody else. Though he was proud to be an Aryan, he was no fool to believe in a thousand-year Reich. He always said that the Americans had money, power, and common sense. Ingo was stuck at the Russian front, fighting a battle he could not win—provided he was still alive. In either case, there was nothing she could do for him.

"You are right, Dr. Gruber," Olga said sweetly, and smiled with the innocence of a child. "Totally and completely right. I am sorry for causing so much trouble. I am fine and ready to do what I can."

"Glad to hear that. Let me run some tests while I keep you under observation for a couple of days."

Olga jumped up. "A couple of days?"

"That's how long it will take. I will get you a more comfortable room. I owe that to Gottfried."

"Days?" Olga implored. "My daughter is only eight. She misses me."

"No doubt. But I want to be sure that you will not relapse and try to save Ingo again from some imaginary purgatory."

All she could think was that she would be locked up while Ingo suffered.

Back in the ward, Olga coughed from the sickening smell of urine, fear, and disinfectant. The cacophony of suffering, the stifling heat, and lack of ventilation made her ill. Sweat beaded on her face and dripped down her back. Would Gruber get her out of here? Better yet, release her? How could she convince him that she was all right?

Stretched out on top of her sheets, she heard the troubled souls crying for help. Who was the evil spirit pursuing her? Gruber was part of the plot. At night, all the horror would return. On and on, until she was sedated into a catatonic stupor devoid of all will, and then eliminated to save food for people fighting the war. How could she love a man so much that she caused her own destruction? She must give him up. *Father, please come to me. I need your help and your protection. Please, Father. Come and save me.*

With darkness, her longing for Ingo became unbearable. *I am sorry, Ingo. I did all I could. But they will not let me go home. What can I do?*

"Nothing," Ingo said. "I'm condemned to eternal suffering for as long as you're on earth."

What do you mean?. That I should kill myself? The windows are locked. They watch me. I must convince Dr. Gruber I'm well.

"Dr. Gruber, Dr. Gruber. Who cares about Dr. Gruber? What's my suffering to him? It's useless, Olga. Good-bye."

He was gone.

Father, please come to me. Deliver Ingo from his torment. She raised her head only to be painfully pulled back by an invisible power. The stench of sulfur permeated the stuffy air. She was damned, abandoned to the Devil. Frightened, she spent the night motionless on her back. With her eyes shut, she watched grotesque images flash by.

The following day, Olga only ate a few spoonfuls of soup to not upset the nurse. Ingo wanted her to die.

That night, he appeared again.

Tell me, Ingo, she begged, *What can I do for you?*

"Nothing. You let me down. So don't bother."

I'll do anything. I'll even die for you. I am wasted.

"Then do it before eight o'clock." He was gone.

At what she guessed to be eight, Olga went to the toilet. Unlike the other people on her ward, she could still walk. After passing six stalls, she reached the window and took the cord attached to the blackout blind. She stepped on the bench underneath, wrapped the loose end around her neck, and jumped to the floor. "Ingo, I am coming."

The cord cut into her neck, then tore apart.

She remained on the floor rubbing her aching neck, surprised at the sudden joy she felt. God had saved her. He didn't want her to die. "Thank you, oh Lord."

Moments later the hellish stench rose again.

"Forgive me, Ingo. I'm coming, I swear." Looking around, she noticed the window sill. Surely, if she tied the rope short enough it and jumped it would strangle her. What if somebody came in and stopped her? What difference would it make? Once she was dead nobody could touch her. She would be together with Ingo.

After testing the rope, making sure it would hold, she jumped. "I'm coming, Ingo."

Instead of dangling, the rod broke. She crashed to the floor.

Alarmed by the noise, the nurse came running in. "You idiot. What do you think you are doing? Making a fool of me, are you?" She slapped Olga hard, then dragged her to the dispensary where she forced some bitter tasting drops into Olga's mouth.

Olga spat them out. She was not allowed to drink.

The nurse slapped her again, but did not insist that she swallow the drops. "Have it your way, you fool. Get back to your room. Anymore nonsense and I'll give you an injection that will take you to the hereafter in a hurry."

As if Olga cared. One way or other she had to fulfill her promise tonight.

As soon as the nurse left, Olga snuck into the locker room where she found a box that had a rope wrapped around it. She ignored the voice saying, "don't do it." Instead, she tied it to the curtain rod and then around her neck. Once again she jumped from the window sill. The weight of her body again broke the rod. She fell against a bench and cried out in pain. Death would not come.

Instead, the nurse rushed in. "Not this one again. You idiot! What's wrong with you? Most people would thank God to be alive and well." She unwrapped the cord from Olga's neck and kicked her in the side. "Why should I care about people like you? Let them die, if that's what they want. Saves us work. Dr. Gruber, that old fool, insists we must treat you gently. Been sleeping with him, have you? Can't imagine it's much of a treat. We should send you away rather than waste our time."

Olga stumbled back to her ward, aching all over. She rubbed her neck, crushed by her disappointment. She had failed. Ingo would never return.

"I'm not crazy!" mocked the nurse. "Then what do you call this? Ever heard that wrecking blackout blinds is a capital offense? I should report you to the authorities. Let them deal with you. Saboteur. You're asking for it, young lady."

She put Olga in a straitjacket, and threw her on the bed like a bundle. A painful stab cut into her back. The pain shot up her neck. Her throat, her stomach, everything hurt. The worst of it was the turmoil in her heart. What should she do now? Dr. Gruber would not believe her. Perhaps he and the nurse were right. She was crazy.

"I'm sorry," Olga mumbled.

"You better be," the nurse said. "Why do you want to kill yourself? Don't tell me it's some lover? How can women be so stupid. Love isn't everything. Don't you have a child, parents, friends? No lover is worth taking your life for. Think about it. Love comes and goes."

"Not this one," Olga said. Her voice was dull. It was not her voice at all.

"They're all the same, believe me." The nurse had calmed down. "Just don't let me catch you again, else it's my turn to take action. And it won't be funny!"

After she left, Olga felt the intense curiosity of the other women in the room. They knew better than to make a sound. They had been beaten, humiliated, and ridiculed. The red light above the door stared at her, growing larger and larger until the whole room was soaked in its monstrous light. Yes, she was crazy, and deserved to be punished. It was all her own fault.

The silence in the room, interrupted by heavy breathing and an occasional sigh, added to Olga's remorse. She had choices these women did not have. They were like the Jews in the Ghetto. The men killing each other at the front. These women mourned their own loved ones. Ingo's was not the only lost soul. She had made such a mess of her life. Love was driving her crazy.

She searched for music, for the melodies she loved and had played so many times. Nothing came. Silence, pain, and that red light at the door had become her world. *Some Day a Miracle Will Happen* had lost its meaning. Miracles did not happen, only disasters. She had never felt so alone, so abandoned, so stupid!

The young woman from the opposite bed appeared in the dark with a glass of water. "Here. Have some. It'll help. What happened?"

"I fell," Olga lied. "It's a long story. This straitjacket is killing me. I'm lying on my wound."

"I know about falling. I'm epileptic. I've fallen many times. Hurts like hell."

"You're an angel. I really need one now. I feel so lost. How can you stand this place?"

"I can't," she whispered softly. Olga had not paid any attention to this young woman before, other than noticing she didn't look crazy. "You're ill, not insane."

"We all have problems we cannot deal with. We need help. But nobody cares. My name is Beate. I'll get a compress for your back."

Olga felt ashamed. Ingo was her illness. Ingo!

Beate returned with a wet washcloth, untied the straitjacket, and cooled Olga's wound.

The night nurse came in and cast her flashlight over the beds. It caught Beate dropping to the floor.

"What do you think you're doing?" she cried out. "As if I don't have enough problems. Accomplices, are you? Don't tell me you're trying to escape. That's all I need. Damn you all." She hit Beate, chased her back to bed, and tied up Olga's straitjacket. "No more nonsense out of you."

At least the nurse had not found the compress, Olga thought, and dozed off despite the pain.

As dawn crept through the tinted windows, Olga could see that she was a victim of forces Father had warned her of. Why had she not seen this before? Everybody was right. She was a fool.

That afternoon, Beate came over. She had a narrow forehead, flat nose and thick lips. Her brown hair had been snipped off and the hospital garb fell loosely over her thin body. The meager meals could not sustain life, and were not meant to. Beate was a rose among weeds. Perhaps the other women had been roses once, before some disorder destroyed them.

The following night, Beate refreshed the compress and stroked Olga's face She massaged her shoulders and arms to stimulate the circulation. "When I was little my mother took me to the movies. You remind me of Sleeping Beauty. Remember when the prince came to awaken her? Such lovely curls! Like gold. People like you get to go home. Then I'll be alone again. Frau Hirsch and Frau Fischer will not be here much longer. They will be taken away and put to sleep. They'll never be all right."

Olga embraced Beate and kissed her cheek. "You're the sweetest girl I ever met. And the loveliest. I 'm so sorry I caused so much trouble."

"Don't worry. It didn't hurt. But you're in pain; I see it in your eyes. I know about that. Tomorrow they'll shock me. That's how I know it's Wednesday. It hasn't cured anybody, but they keep doing it. I dread it all week, hoping it will stop, or that I will die from it. Perhaps they want to kill me. There must be easier ways, less painful. When your mother comes, make sure you tell her not to let them give you shocks."

Beate left the straitjacket untied until morning, then returned and tied it up loosely so that Olga could still move. "Sorry, Olga. Perhaps your mother can get you out of this."

"I love you, Beate. You've saved my life."

"Since my mother was killed by the bombs and my father at the front, I'm alone. Nobody wants me. I haven't had a seizure in years, but they keep me here just in case." She kissed Olga and ran back to her bed.

At daybreak, Olga noticed that she had not slept all night. Had Father sent Beate to her? "Thank you, Father."

Mathilde came during afternoon visiting hours. Olga had witnessed Beate's convulsions, her pleading when they pushed a piece of wood into her mouth, and the moans that followed the voltage charging into her body, and was traumatized as if she had suffered it herself.

Mathilde untied the straitjacket. "What is that for? Why are you still in this ward? Look what I brought you. A letter from Ingo."

"Ingo?" Olga repeated, as if she was hearing the name for the first time, and checked the handwriting. It was his. Mailed nine days ago. She tore it open.

"He must be well," Mathilde said.

Olga read. *My darling Olga, my sweet love.* The words threw her into a dither. Her heart pounded. If she were alone, she would sing and dance or cry for joy.

I haven't had a chance to write to you for some time. Has it been days, weeks? We were so busy that I lost track of time. You did not write either. Are you all right? I know the mail gets lost. But write anyway. Most letters do get through.

The Russians are all stirred up this summer. The heat fosters their frustration. So much for the Russian hospitality you told me about. They desperately want to get rid of us, while we are determined to stay here. That's a clear conflict. But don't worry, darling. I'm a seasoned veteran and know how to stay out of trouble.

Summer is a special season when the crops we need for winter ripen. I don't know how much of it will be left for us to harvest. Still, nature keeps on producing no matter what we do. The golden fields of rye feed my imagination with hopes for peace and prosperity. Some day it will return to us. I pick cornflowers and pretend they are for you. They would look so lovely in your golden hair. On our wedding day you must wear a wreath of blue flowers. Then we'll spend our honeymoon dancing through the meadows.

Thinking of our future helps me overlook the inconveniences of the present. Your sweet face is always with me. Your music sings in my heart. We are one in spirit and love. I can hear your voice telling me that I have a guardian angel who protects me. You live in me, as I hope I live in you.

I kiss and embrace you with all my heart. I love you, forever.

Ingo.

"Ingo," she whispered, her lips quivering, then looked at her mother.

"Well? Is everything all right? A long letter."

"Ingo is fine," Olga said.

"You see. There was no need for your escapades. What made you think he was dead? Never mind. You do things nobody can understand. You should go out and meet people. I'll tell Dr. Gruber that you are well if you promise to ignore whatever voices you hear. Life is so short, why waste it on wild fantasies? In any case, you will get a better room. Just stop acting up." Her pinched face and tired eyes added to Olga's guilt for leaving Anyna in her mother's care.

"What about Beate?" she asked, pointing across the room. "She is the nicest person I've ever met. Can she come with me? There must be some way for her to get out of here. I'll talk to Dr. Gruber."

"So will I," Mathilde promised. She wore the same faded floral dress that fell over her shapeless body with the indifference of a curtain. With her hair tied into a bun she looked older than Olga remembered.

That afternoon, Olga and Beate were taken to a new room in a wing for minor cases. It had four beds, a table, chairs, and Gottfried's radio. Now Olga could listen to the *Front Request Program.*

Gottfried's visits became special events. Olga anticipated them eagerly.

"Tell me, Olga," he said, taking her arm for a stroll through the park, "why would a beautiful and talented young woman like you try to kill herself? You have a husband you don't care for, but he is not around. Ingo loves you, Anyna is a sweet child. You have friends, and the people at Esplanade who adore you. Why would you want to take your life? What are you escaping? What is bothering you? You aren't pregnant, are you?" He stopped, and gazed into her eyes.

Olga's blood rushed into her face. "Of course not." She laughed. "I would love having Ingo's baby. No. I was trying to save him."

"Save him? From what? Getting killed? That, my dear, is not in your power."

"He is already..."

"What? Dead? How do you know?"

Olga caught herself. Here she was, saying the same old nonsense. No, Ingo was not dead. "I was under the impression that Ingo had committed suicide and was being punished in purgatory for committing adultery."

"Honestly, Olga." He took her by the shoulders, and shook her hard. "That's ridiculous. So all that I heard is true?"

She felt rotten—at the verge of tears.

He took her into his arms and held her, then fished for a handkerchief in his coat pocket. "There, there. Blow your nose and then let's talk about it. Perhaps I can help. I am your friend, Olga. I hope you're aware of that."

His consideration set off another flood of tears. On the bench, with her back to the sinister gray walls, she leaned her head against his shoulder and felt the rough cloth of his uniform. He had become a soldier, property of the crumbling Reich.

A bumblebee buzzed over a daisy, then flew on to the blue bells, red clover buttons, and yarrow dotting the meadow. Soon the grass would be cut and used for animal feed. Accompanied by the song of the birds, Olga told him of Ingo's suffering. "I must follow the instructions or be punished as well."

She paused. He waited.

"Who are *they*?" he asked, holding her.

"I wish I knew. Evil, unformed entities of the underworld."

"Lucie says you are a medium who sees beyond." He cradled her face in his hands, and held it up to his. "The world around us is in flames. For the moment, we are sitting on an island that will soon be swept away. So, don't rush to your death for nothing. I would miss you very much. I know that you cared for me more than I could reciprocate."

How she had longed for this moment, waited for years for words like the ones he had just spoken. Now it no longer mattered. They both belonged to others. She felt fulfillment.

"I loved you, Gottfried."

"I heard it in your music, Olga. You always talk of destiny. There it is. We gave each other much more than love."

She could not believe he was saying that. What did she know about Gottfried, other than that he was the best-looking man she had ever met, and had a voice that melted hearts? Now he showed the tender side of a loving friend.

"You were so young, Olga, and infatuated."

They held each other for a long time, letting the breeze fan their faces. A deep contentment settled in their hearts, satisfying a desire they had held years ago. She would cherish this moment for the rest of her life.

"Next week," he said, "I must report to my unit in Posen and take my place in the war machinery. Many will not see the end. I may be among them." He placed his warm hands on her shoulders. "Just promise me that you will keep an eye on Lucie, if you can. With the new baby she will have a hard time getting by. Why don't you join her in Saxony? Isn't Ingo from Dresden?"

She nodded, scraping her wooden sandal against the sandy gravel under the bench. "I cannot leave Litzmannstadt now. Perhaps things will turn around. The miracle weapon…"

He shook his head. "Don't make me laugh. Nothing can save us."

Nothing, Olga thought. And he would be among the casualties. But they would be together, always.

At the door, he kissed her lips in a tender farewell. "Our music is locked in my heart" he said, "and will remind me of you whenever I sing."

She waved good bye, and watched him walk away.

That evening Olga and Beate listened to the *Front Request Program* play *Every Day Is Not A Sunday*. It was Gottfried's favorite. She thought of their friendship, the torch she had carried for him. Love had many faces.

Ingo leaned against the piano and smiled. He raised a bottle of champagne. "For you, darling." Anyna embraced him. Hand in hand, they danced to the music coming from the radio.

"Ingo!" she whispered, and knew that he was alive.

The following day, Mathilde brought a telegram from Ingo.

Olga's heart dropped. "A telegram?" She tore it open, then read, "I am waiting for news. Reply by wire."

"Well?" Mathilde said, sitting down on a chair in the visiting room. Olga did not mind seeing the same old dress and straw hat.

"He is waiting for news, Mama. Imagine. *He* is awaiting news. Thinks I'm not writing."

"Did you?"

Olga shook her head. "No. I thought…" A dizzy spell overcame her. Her senses waned. She sank to the floor.

When she awoke, Dr. Gruber stood at her bedside giving her an injection. "She will be all right," he said. "You can take her home, Frau Bergmann. She will be better off in your care. I will sign her release."

"Do you mean that, doctor?" Olga whispered.

"We need the space. I'll miss your company. You were a most unusual case." He chuckled and winked behind his thick spectacles. "Perhaps we can continue our conversation at the Esplanade. I would enjoy hearing you play."

Olga embraced the doctor and kissed his wrinkled cheek. "Thank you, Dr. Gruber. When you come, I'll play the *Spring Sonata*." She laughed. "I am also a very good fortuneteller."

"You better stay away from that. You saw what happened. Next time it might be fatal."

Chapter 19

Another year had passed. 1945 looked even more dismal than 1944, Ingo thought, wading through the deep snow. The hem of his greatcoat swept the powder from the crust which crunched with every step. Just like this war. The snow looked smooth, the countryside flat, ready for the taking. Then the enemy crawled from the ground, like moles, and cut the Germans to pieces. By now the Wehrmacht had landed in a fathomless abyss. After years of fighting, Ingo had come to admire the enemy for being as determined to defend their homeland as Hitler was to take it. Since Russia covered a third of the globe, and had the support of most of the world, the Reich had run itself into a corner and could only hope for unconditional surrender. Only Hitler was not about to deliver himself to his enemies. He traded his life for the blood of his people. The one thing German and Russian soldiers had in common was that both faced a homegrown enemy at their back—Germany had the Gestapo and Russia the NKVD, ruthless men who betrayed their own men in order to escape combat.

Last night's snowfall covered bunkers and dugouts. Hitler's highly visible winter offense was already two weeks behind schedule, giving the Russians plenty of time to dig in and set traps. Once again, Hitler had undermined the only advantage the soldiers had against their ever more powerful enemy. After all their early blunders, the Soviet generals understood that Hitler's irrational moves threw his capable generals into despair. Those who objected were replaced or eliminated. The attempted coup on his life had left Hitler more paranoid. He trusted no one.

"Damn, damn, damn," Ingo shouted into the night. A thick cloud blanket kept the Stormoviks away. Once daylight returned and the clouds broke, they would come for the kill. Army Group A held the banks of the Vistula River in the heart of Poland. His men sat in their dug-outs, shivering. He would soon join them.

Glad that his body was still intact Ingo was convinced that Olga's magic really worked. He could still walk, fight, and love—should that become available. How long? No doubt the Russians sat right behind those trees waiting for the weather to clear up. They were in no hurry. Victory would be theirs. He could sense them like an old man feeling a change in the weather. Hitler's meaningless offensive in the Ardenne had only proven that his orders made no sense at all. He had squandered his last elite troops and crucial weapons needed at the Eastern Front. Sheer madness. Ingo ground his teeth. His eyes watered from the cold. The young recruits would be sacrificed for the new suicide mission they were on.

"Can you hear me, Olga?" Ingo called out into the icy wind. "You must leave." A branch load of snow fell from a nearby tree and dusted his cold face. He imagined her at the piano playing Chopin for Anyna. How could she ignore the flames devouring the Reich? Had Father warned her of the looming disaster? Her last letter spoke of love and hope for the future. Without her there was no life for him. She was at liberty to act, while he was bound to his oath and would fight to the bitter end—waiting for disaster to strike again. Once the Russians broke through the front nobody could stop them from advancing to Litzmannstadt. Hitler would not evacuate the people. The *Gauleiters* had orders not to stir up panic. So why tell people they were about to be sacrificed for the convenience of their Fuhrer? Women, children, and the elderly could not escape on a moment's notice. The thought of seeing Olga at the mercy of the Soviets made him sick.

He licked snowflakes from his cold lips. The tears froze on his cheeks. Wading through the soft snow kept him warm. He would survive. Winter would pass. It always did. Three stars appeared in the black sky—a good omen. At dawn, the Russians Katyushas would fire. By now they knew exactly where the German units were located.

"Olga, go west," he screamed, his breath steaming. "Go! Before it's too late. Can you hear me, darling? The Russians want blood. God help the German women."

The command post had been set up in an old farmhouse. Officers crowded around the crude table by the hearth. Many of them no more than eighteen. They played cards under the light of a kerosene lamp.

Their fresh young faces showed the first growth. Nobody smiled, or pretended to jest. They were scared.

"It's too quiet," Kunz said, pouring a shot of schnapps for Ingo. "Not a good sign."

The warmth eased Ingo's apprehension. Still, he could not shake off that ominous feeling. "The weather is clearing up," he announced.

Kunz nodded. Over the years he had come to look after his commanding officer like a valet. "We knew it would." He refilled the glass, then took the enameled teapot from the hearth, poured some tea into a tin mug and handed it to Ingo. The young men envied the warm relationship Kunz and Ingo shared.

Ingo rubbed his frozen hands over the hot iron plate, then took the mug.

"What's wrong with some visibility," said Schmidt, a handsome youth of twenty from Danzig.

"We need all the camouflage we can get," Kunz said.

Schmidt blushed. "Yes, of course. Just an observation."

"When things look too good, they are," Ingo said, watching the men at the card table, pretending to be interested in their game of blackjack. Their voices rose and fell. Most of them would be among the casualties. Ingo would reproduce dozens of letters of condolence, adding a personal line about the man who had fallen. It would mean a lot to the recipient— mother, wife, fiancée. *Your son gave his life in a heroic battle for Führer, Volk und Vaterland.*

This was no time for small talk, not with death at the doorstep. He put the mug down and shed his coat, then pulled a copy of Goethe's *Faust* from his pack. The third his father had sent him. The two previous were destroyed during a battle. He let it fall open and read.

> *Mephisto, do you see... there—,*
> *Far off stands a child alone, so pale and sweet!*
> *She drags herself slowly from the place,*
> *As if—as if she walked with fettered feet.*
> *I must confess I seem to see*
> *A likeness to my little Gretchen's face.*

Closing his eyes, he envisioned Olga in her apartment wrapped in blankets. "Listen to me, Olga. Go west to Dresden. You will be safe there. Don't wait for me."

A blast jolted him out of his reverie. He jumped up, slipped into his coat, and dropped the helmet on his head. The young officers fumbled with their battle gear, shaken by the unexpected barrage.

Kunz showed up, his helmet tight, rifle in hand. "The Russians attack. We must hold our position."

"Of course," Ingo said sarcastically. "Everybody out. Into the trenches."

Flares illuminated the farmhouse. A steady succession of explosions left no doubt that this was a big one. The windows shattered. Ingo ran to the command bunker, dodging a Russian grenade blast. Katyusha missiles whooshed overhead and detonated amid the German positions.

The young officers raced after him, some cut down by bombs. German artillery were smashed before they could fire. Ingo heard the sound of ammunition exploding in a chain reaction, tearing men from their stands. The fuel depot had been hit by a hailstorm of well-aimed rockets. The thunderous sound drowned out the screams. Flames rose throughout the village, swallowing the farmhouse where Ingo's officers had played cards minutes earlier. He jumped into a dugout and found Kellermann on the field telephone. Olsen took down the messages.

"Major Becker ordered that we must hold the position at any cost," Kellermann reported. A nearby hit shook the ground and threw Ingo against the wall. Clumps of dirt fell back into the dugout.

"*Verfluchte Scheisse.*" What did Becker think Ingo should use as defense against a force he could not see? They'd be lucky if anybody was left after the Russians got through. "Wire back. 'Overwhelming attack. Need air support.'"

The artillery fired blindly at the Russian rocket launchers and were soon knocked out. The trees that had been camouflaging the dugouts fell. The fires swelled with each explosion. Ingo ran short laps between mounds of dirt and debris. "Get out of the firing line," he shouted. All attempts to regroup and defend got nowhere. Snow and dirt in his mouth, he gagged on the smoke of burning fuel. The intense heat had melted the snow and struggling men slipped on the wet ground.

Grenades felled the dark figures scuttling to safety. How long could this inferno last?

Another torrent of rockets. Ingo threw himself into a nearby dugout filled with corpses and a moaning body.

Then all was quiet. The planes left. He crawled out to see a mortally wounded man drag his bleeding body over the muddy snow. "Help. Help me."

The deep rumbling of tanks grew louder, their treads clinking in the hush. Ingo crawled into a dugout and watched the behemoths drive up out of the mist. The eerie scene helped calm him. He grabbed a broken pine branch and placed it over his head, then dropped to the ground pretending to be dead. The tank's giant gun sniffed around the territory like the trunk of a steel elephant.

"Olga, leave!" Ingo whispered, waiting to be crushed under the treads of an approaching T-34.

Olga relaxed in a bathtub stuffed with her pillows and featherbed. Yesterday an air raid had knocked out all the windows in her apartment, except those in the bathroom, which faced the courtyard. The hot water heater that had supplied the baths she and Ingo had shared gave plenty of heat. Perhaps she and Anyna could take a bath later that evening. Anyna had coped with the air raid rather well. They had been in the shelter while the bombs fell, glad that the building was not destroyed when they returned. With her eyes closed, she felt Ingo's presence. Why did he want her to leave? He was in danger, not she, and Father would protect him. Where would she go? Dresden would be her last resort. Something told her that she would not be welcome there. Besides, only yesterday Hitler had reassured the German people that the miracle weapon was within their grasp. The Russians would be stopped, and the Allies driven back.

Anyna was so engrossed in her drawing that she paid no attention to Olga. Though it was the depths of winter, she drew a meadow with multicolored flowers. With electricity restored, life went on more or less as usual. Olga had not called on Father since the incident with the Evil One. After she returned from the asylum, she had found her Bible open and read, "For a small moment have I forsaken thee; but with great mercies will I gather thee. In a little wrath I hid my face from thee for a moment; but with everlasting kindness will I have mercy on thee, saith the Lord thy Redeemer." From then on she felt cured, and swore never to deal with the spirits again. It had been her own fault. Father had warned her not to expose herself to the spirits and rely on their support. Only he could be trusted.

Despite the overheated bathroom her teeth chattered. Ingo was desperate. He insisted she leave right now. *But it's past eleven. Where do you want me to go? I can manage in the bathroom. The train station? How will I get there? The tram doesn't run at night. You know that. I'll freeze to death. Father will protect us.*

Still, Olga could not ignore her growing apprehension and climbed out of the tub, slipped into her coat and went to the bedroom. Frosty air streamed through the broken window of the dark room. Loud voices rose from the street. Who was out there at this time of night?

A woman in the street shouted. "Nobody can stop me. Not you, or you, or anybody. Come Karlchen."

Olga rushed to the window. Black figures swarmed through the snow-covered street, pulling sleds and pushing prams loaded with suitcases and children. Her pulse quickened. The radio in the bathroom played, *Wine, Women and Song*. Anyna pulled at Olga's arm. "What are you doing here, Mami? Come back where it's warm. You'll catch a cold. Who are those people?"

"I think they're fleeing," Olga said. "Wait here. I'll be right back." Anyna ran after her mother, down the stairs and into the street.

"Where are you going?" Olga asked one of the passing woman.

"Where do you think? The Russians are coming!"

"The Russians? How do you know? The radio..."

"You can't believe the radio. The front collapsed. You'd better get out of here." She kept pushing her handcart over the frozen street. More people came streaming out of the buildings, heading for the station. The darkness did not slow them down, hauling their emergency suitcases on prams and sleds down the street. Sleepy children whined, others went along in silence through the freezing night. The German border was hundreds of kilometers away.

Olga and Anyna ran back to the house. "They've abandoned us," a woman said, bundled up beyond recognition. "I heard it from others coming from East Prussia. There is no miracle weapon. Lies, nothing but lies. I lost my husband and a son. I've got one left. No Russian will shoot him and rape me. Savages…"

Running upstairs, Olga noticed that the other tenants did not seem to care. Certainly not Hauser, the block warden. He would follow whatever orders were issued. If none came, he'd stay here until the Russians…The Russians. Ingo had warned her. He still did. Ottie met Olga in the stairwell. "We must flee, Olga. The Russians could be here any moment. My neighbor said the air raids softened up the city for the invaders. They're on their way. We should've left when the Countess said…" She followed Olga into the dark apartment, a woolen shawl wrapped around her head. Layers of clothes had doubled the size of her body. Bertie had been dressed for a long walk as well.

"Go and get Mama," Olga said. "I must get dressed and pack a few things. We'll need food. Who knows when we'll find some. Think of the children. We must get a train. Get Mama and lets get to the station. We'll have to walk and will be lucky if the SS doesn't stop us. Bertie can stay here in the bathroom. It's warm and has light."

Both children reluctantly went to the bathroom, nervous and confused.

Ottie took off. "If Mama doesn't leave…" she said gruffly.

"Then you make her," Olga said. "She must come right away. We can't wait another minute. Once word gets around, people will stampede to the train."

With Ottie gone, Olga used a candle. With the windows broken the blackout blinds no longer covered them properly. She didn't need the Gestapo on her back. In her bedroom, she stuffed Ingo's letters into her rucksack and some warm underwear, shoes, socks and then packed some clothes for Anyna. Finally she went to the kitchen and took whatever staples she had—bread, margarine, sugar, boiled potatoes, and cottage cheese. She packed a knife and a spoon as well as a bowl. If they didn't get a train…Better not to think about that. There had to be trains. Getting to the station would be the problem. With her mother and the children in tow they would move slowly.

Anyna's tin mug and plate landed in her suitcase. Olga had to kneel against the snaps to close.

The candle flickered. A light appeared above the armoire. "Father!"

At the table Olga picked up her pencil and pad. A sense of peace and love filled her heart. Father had come to save her. He would protect Ingo. Her hand wrote quickly. When it stopped Olga closed her eyes. "Thank you, Father, for coming to me in my moment of need. You give me strength and hope."

In the bathroom, she ignored the children's questions and read.

My beloved daughter,

With lies and deceit the Evil One had lured you into his power. We tried, but could not rescue you. We sent our messages to you. Now that we have reestablished contact we shall do our best to guide and protect you. Leave this city immediately. Great pain awaits you, but you are strong and will survive. We cannot save Gottfried. He is so dear to us. We shall call him home. He will not suffer. Remember that our power only works for those who believe in us. Ingo does. So does Lucie. Farewell, my daughter. Trust our guidance.

Father.

Olga reread the text, hoping to find a clue, some encouragement or guidance. Nothing.

Anyna put her head against Olga's shoulder. "We'll go to Dresden, Mami. Uncle Ingo will come to us there. He said so."

"Yes, he did," Olga said absentmindedly. "Now both of you listen to me," she told the children. "We are going on a long walk. I expect you to be strong and courageous. Help Omi when you can. We must leave the city before the Russians get here. The two of you stay together at all times. Do you hear?" She made eye contact with each child. "No matter what. Now I'll dress Anyna and then we'll be off."

By the time Ottie and Mathilde arrived, both Olga and Anyna had put on all they could possibly wear and were getting too warm. "We must stay together at all times," Olga said, then cast a last glance into the bedroom she had once shared with Ingo. "When will we see each other again?"

Shouldering her rucksack she said, "I'm ready to go," and left the apartment. "I'm getting Anyna's sled from the basement. I'll catch up with you in the street."

"I never thought it would come to this," Mathilde said, "So much for *Fuhrer, Volk und Vaterland.* Why was I cursed to live through two wars and a revolution? Those confounded communists. Lenin was a curse on mankind. He started it all."

Hauser came out as Olga passed his door. "Where do you think you're going, Frau von Schenck? I have strict orders."

Olga kept running down. "You go right ahead and welcome the Russians."

Ottie pushed him aside, and followed Olga. "We're not about to become victims of your great Fuhrer and the Russian savages."

"I'll report you," he shouted.

The street teemed with people when Olga stepped out with the sled. The children sat down one behind the other. Olga put Mathilde's suitcase in front of Bertie. "You hold on to this." Then she picked up the rope and pulled the sled down the icy street. The runners crunched. Bent down as if under a heavy burden, Mathilde held on to Ottie's arm to not slip on the ice. The temperature kept dropping. How far could they walk? Would they find a train and get on along with all those people heading toward the station? Nobody wanted to be left behind. It was about time that German women took matters into their own hands. Why had they waited so long? Hitler's passionate but meaningless promises had mesmerized them. Like Olga they'd believed him for convenience sake. Now they would pay for it.

Struggling along with her load, Olga kept her eyes on the street. It was so dark that she could not discern whether the buildings had been hit or not. The total blackout worked.

The roar of heavy bombers approached.

"No alarm?" Ottie asked, a frightened quiver in her voice.

"Could be our planes," Olga said, not about to stop for anything. Some people hesitated. It was too dark to discern the signs indicating the shelter. "Keep going," she shouted and accelerated. "We must get to the station before they blow it up." Her rucksack weighed a ton. Did she really need all that stuff? But how you could she leave Ingo's letters behind?

Flares lit up the city and hung suspended over the silent buildings. Most people ran toward the shelters. The Poles awaited the Russians— their liberators. The Jewish Ghetto had been evacuated during the Polish uprising in Warsaw.

Planes circled overhead.

"They'll kill us," Ottie shouted. "We must get to a shelter."

"No," Olga screamed. "The station. Hurry, Mama. We must get there before they drop their bombs."

Ottie held her sister back. "Stop! You're crazy."

Olga shoved her sister aside and ran on over the slippery surface, now clearly visible. Her lungs pumped, sucking in the freezing air. She wheezed, sweat dripping from her face.

On the sled, Anyna consoled the crying Bertie. "We'll be all right. Mami knows the way."

"Don't tell me," Ottie screamed. "There must be hundreds of them. Let's get to the shelter."

"You run along, girls," Mathilde pleaded. "I can't go so fast. I'm exhausted."

A succession of explosions erupted further down the street. The children screamed. Mathilde cried. Ottie sobbed hysterically and ran off with surprising speed. Olga pulled the sled like a draught horse. Dust and debris blew toward them and searchlights crisscrossed the black sky. Flak artillery fired at the planes.

"We must get into a shelter," Ottie shouted.

Olga ignored the demand. "The station. Quick." Her scarf had slipped from her face. Her lungs ached. Panting, she blinked the smoke from her eyes.

Mathilde held back. "Leave me. The Russians have no use for old women."

"Keep going," Olga demanded. "We must catch a train."

At the station, a stampede of people ignored the attack and stormed the train, ready to kill for a place. The stationmaster whistled and shouted, "No trains for civilians. Only wounded."

SS guards pointed their rifles at the onslaught of women, ready to shoot. The boys were raised to obedience. "Go home," one of them shouted, the helmet drawn down on his face. "Wait for your evacuation orders. There'll be proper transportation for everybody. Civilians must not leave the city."

"Really?" Ottie cried out from the crowd. "So that our goddamn party studs can leave in comfort. I'm not gonna wait for the Reds to give me the honor of their fuck."

"Ottie!" Mathilde protested.

"Now we have children giving us orders," Ottie said.

The boy cocked his gun.

Olga pulled her sister back. "Let's get out of here."

A train set in motion. People clung to doors, roofs and bumpers. They would freeze to death. The planes circled the city like birds of prey. Firefighters worked the pumps, shooting water into the flames. Boys and elderly men from the *Volkssturm* marched through the street carrying their anti-tank *Panzerfaust*. The Reich's last defense. Searchlights caught a plane; flak fired and hit. The plane came down, flames trailing behind.

People cheered as they scuttled off seeking safety.

"Keep moving," Olga shouted into the pandemonium.

"You don't say," Ottie said panting, her face as red as the swastika on the station.

"Run!" Olga shouted at the top of her lungs, pulling the sled and hauling her luggage. Something warned her of acute danger. "Quick, Ottie, quick. Run!"

Mathilde found new strength, and kept up the pace, puffing. A cluster of bombs dropped on the station and killed the people storming the train. The boys and the wounded they protected found their deaths.

The scare charged the survivors with new energy. Everybody ran, heading west. Bombs exploded around them. Olga charged ahead, pulling the sled over the slippery ground. The fires melted the snow. Puddles formed. She had to find snow covered areas for the sled. Turning around, she saw the station in a sea of flames. Many of the bombs seemed to drop at random, allowing her to escape.

The explosions finally stopped. The bombers had accomplished their mission and returned to wherever they had come from. Fires burned everywhere. When would the Russian tanks show up? They traveled at forty kilometers an hour, unless somebody fought them off. Who? Ingo?

The church had not been hit. The golden cross gleamed in the eerie light of the flames and flares. *Never again will I fall for the temptations of malevolent entities*, Olga prayed. *Please forgive me, Father. If it is Your will, I'll go to Dresden.*

Chapter 20

The intense heat of the fires melted the snow. Olga trudged over the wet street scraping the heavy sled over the bare cobblestones. Anyna and Bertie huddled in shock. Mathilde followed in silence. How long could she keep up? Olga wished she had a second sled for her mother and their suitcase.

Flames rose from broken windows, doors, and roofs illuminating the night. A wall had collapsed and the debris fed the flames. More and more women and their families streamed into the streets and joined the exodus.

Olga pulled off her damp shawl and unbuttoned her coat. Teenage and elderly firefighters pumped water into the flames, or carried injured people from the burning buildings. Many suffered from smoke inhalation. Others appeared in their nightclothes, a fur coat thrown over them. Ottie's face glistened with sweat.

A sobbing woman grabbed Olga's arm and pointed at a burning building. "Help me. Somebody, help me. My mother is in there. We must get her out."

Olga wriggled free. "Let go of me. The Russians are coming."

The woman's wet eyes widened in horror. "The Russians? I can't leave my mother here."

Olga walked on. "How do I get to Pabianice?" she asked a soot-covered firefighter.

He wiped the sweat from his face and pointed ahead.

"Just keep on going. Adolf Hitler Strasse will get you out of town." He looked her up and down. "It's quite a ways."

"I guess. We have no choice. The station was wiped out."

"Sierdze has a station."

"Let's hope so," she said, glad that the bombing had stopped. "Are you staying?"

He nodded. "This is my home."

Once they left the burning buildings behind, darkness returned. Olga wrapped her shawl around face to protect it from the biting wind and quickened her pace. The packed snow aided the sled runners. Silhouettes of other fleeing Germans hastened with them over the snow. Anyna and Bertie had fallen asleep. Walking alongside, Ottie braced them from dropping off.

Olga imagined Sodom and Gomorrah. Hitler had exalted himself as God. His followers had saluted and worshipped him. Was this their punishment? Had pride led to their downfall?

The straps of her rucksack cut into her shoulders. Ingo's letters. Was he also marching somewhere through the night, snow squeaking under his steps, or was he riding in a vehicle?

Around her, sled runners swished and carts rattled. A stinking truck labored by. A whip cracked. Only the stars blinked, indifferent to the fate of the fleeing people, distant and mysterious. Stasya would soon be liberated. She had not shown up as promised. Perhaps she had been taken by surprise as well. She was part of the resistance that would see to it that the German people who had invaded her country would be punished.

"Did you get your evacuation orders?" asked a woman at Olga's side.

"No." Olga said curtly. She hated when people interrupted her thoughts.

"My cousin escaped from the Russians in East Prussia. She told me to leave right away. Of course, I didn't believe her. The Reich is always looking after women and children. Now this. They must have been caught by surprise and couldn't get things done fast enough. If our Fuhrer only knew all the things people do behind his back. He wouldn't stand for any of this."

Another truck passed, forcing them off the road. "I bet it's filled with loot," she said. "Gauleiter Greiser took off instead of taking care of us. If our Fuhrer only knew."

Olga pushed on. Every minute was precious, a matter of life and death.

A convoy of army trucks headed east, taking young men to their deaths. Like thieves, others sped west, escaping the war zone, blowing their stench at the people they were supposed to help. Two uniformed men drove up on a motorcycle. The one riding in the side-car shouted, "Keep to the side. You're blocking the road!" The people moved aside, and walked in single-file rather than wind up in the deep snow.

"*Verflucht nochmal!*" shouted a man in a black uniform at an elderly couple who could not get out of his way fasts enough. "Can't you hear? Bunch of idiots!"

It was too dark to see his face. His voice sounded young and aggressive.

"How dare you call me an idiot!" Ottie shouted, trembling with rage.

"God save us from hysterical woman," he snapped. "We're building a defense …"

"About time," Ottie said. "How come we didn't get evacuated?"

"I had nothing to do with that."

"Instead of helping us, you want to push us into the snow. How about lending a hand before the Russians catch up with us?" Ottie was all fired up now. "Get us on one of those trucks and take us to safety."

"We are at war."

"So I noticed—else I wouldn't be here!"

Others nodded in silence.

"We need our trucks for the wounded."

"Sure," Olga said. "What about those trucks carrying documents, of all things?"

"We're sick of getting pushed around," one of the women said.

People had gathered around Ottie, blocking the road. Horns blew. Motors revved.

"Damn it, get off the road," the soldier screamed, then drove off on his motorcycle.

"He's just following orders," a female figure said into the darkness. She picked up her luggage and stepped aside. Others followed her example. Traffic lurched forward.

Ottie stood her ground. "I'm exhausted. And that kid has the nerve to push us off the road." Her voice dropped. "I can't go on." She stumbled, and fell into the soft snow weeping.

Mathilde sank down beside her. "I'll stay here with Ottie."

Olga blinked the tears from her eyes. She dropped her rucksack and sat down on her suitcase. The dozing children leaned against each other on the sled. Heavily loaded farm wagons passed, carrying the family essentials and feed for the horse.

"I'm freezing, Mami," Anyna whimpered.

Olga wrapped a blanket around Anyna's back, then rubbed the shivering little body. The children should be walking, but they were too tired to stand up. Their hands and feet had to be frozen. How much longer could they endure this cold?

Wind whistled across the snowy fields beyond the tree line marking the road. Olga massaged her aching fingertips and stomped to bring circulation back to her feet. Two women dropped their baggage. More and more bags, valises, and bundles littered the roadside. So far there were no casualties. Everybody pushed on as best they could.

Ottie heaved herself back to her feet patting the powdery snow from her coat. "We must get a ride before the Poles come and strip us. We should've left yesterday."

Yesterday, Olga thought. Had there ever been a yesterday?

By day-break, Olga was too exhausted to take another step. The convoys carrying wounded soldiers rolled by. Nobody knew what was going on. The walkers slowed to a shuffle. Staying behind meant death. Olga led Mathilde with one arm, and dragged Anyna with the other. She had tied the rope pulling the sled across her chest.

"At Sierdze we'll catch a train and be off to Dresden," she kept saying like a mantra.

Ottie whined in a little girl's voice. "I can't go on."

A truck, caught in the clot of slow moving vehicles, stopped. Olga dropped her charge and grabbed the door handle. Standing on the running board she cried, "Please, please, give us a lift. Just a little ways. Save my old mother, my sister, our children."

"We got orders," the driver said curtly. "We carry important documents."

"Documents?" Olga shouted. "Who needs documents? We are German mothers and their children. We need help. At least let us sit on those precious documents."

"Can't do it. We got orders." The driver found a gap in the traffic and pulled away, tossing Olga in front of a horse. Its hooves slipped as it tried to escape her. Olga closed her eyes. Let him trample her to death.

Helpful arms pulled her up.

"Documents," said one of the women who helped Olga up. "We're just trash."

Olga nodded, too tired and cold to care. "We should get to Sierdze soon," she whispered.

Bertie whimpered. Anyna trembled, but suffered in silence.

What if the Russians beat her to Sierdze?

Ingo pushed the snow-laden pine branch aside and crawled from his hole. His body ached from the cold and resisted his efforts to stimulate circulation. The pain in his hands and feet drew tears to his eyes.

The Russian tanks had disappeared. Their infantry would move in any moment now. A handful of German survivors was an easy catch. The Soviets were on a roll, pushing toward Berlin. No doubt they considered the territory theirs to keep.

Snow covered the frozen pools of blood, dead soldiers, and horses like a blanket. White powder dusted the burnt-out tanks, twisted guns, and splintered wagons. Nothing stirred, not even the air. The total stillness reminded him of death. It would be like this—unimaginable nothingness.

Ingo flapped his arms and pounded his toes against a tank, whose hull echoed into the stillness. Once again the Russians had attacked with uncanny precision. They knew every German move. The Polish underground had people everywhere, probably even in German headquarters. They observed every movement, listened in on conversations, tapped the wireless, and divined Hitler's erratic orders. They supported the Soviets, despite their defeat of the desperate uprising in Warsaw, when Stalin's expected support did not materialize. They had to welcome the Russians as friends, or be slaughtered by them.

Stalin would not let a little country like Poland stop his conquest, Ingo thought. He had big plans.

For Germany the war was lost. Ingo swallowed the bile rising from his empty stomach. Even their close allies, the Italians, had surrendered. The Austrians would do likewise and claim they had been coerced into joining Hitler. Mussolini hung on because his fate depended on Hitler's support.

Ingo scanned the windswept countryside with its wrecked trees and noticed Kunz dig out. He was not alone. His faithful NCO would share whatever was in store for them.

"How happy I am to see you, Kunz," Ingo said, truly relieved and delighted. He would have grieved for the man who had accompanied him for the past two years. Kellermann and Olsen appeared. Others joined, greeting their buddies with muffled shouts of recognition. The wounded had frozen to death.

"Let's see what we have left," Ingo said, as if the men did not know what to do. He had to say something, hear his voice, know he was still in command. "We must get out of here before the Partisans show up." That too was a given.

Litzmannstadt was no more than seventy kilometers away. Had Olga left, or was she waiting for him? Her remarkable gift must have told her how close he was.

A count revealed 37 survivors, eight sleds, two wagons, and two starved and frightened horses. Kunz discovered three machine guns and an anti-tank gun. They also had eleven Panzerfausts and enough rifles to fend off Partisans.

After a long march through a forest, they found an isolated farmhouse. The bodies of a man, three women, and a girl where sprawled out in the yard. The man had been shot in the head and chest. His blood on the sheepskin was frozen. The women and girl had succumbed in the snow with their faces down, as if ashamed to be without their underwear. Pools of frozen blood had formed beneath their thighs. They wore hand-knit stockings on their thin legs and crude, homemade felt boots.

"May God have mercy on your souls," Ingo said. The man must have tried to keep the Russians from raping his family and had been shot after witnessing the disgrace. A common tactic.

The men filed quietly into the farmhouse. The brutality and savagery of war reminded them of their own families, whom they could not protect. Once inside, they made a fire, found food, blankets, and feed for the horses. Two soldiers slaughtered the hungry cow. Others caught the hens and cut off their heads. Soon everybody was busy helping the cook cut up vegetables, peel potatoes, pluck the hens and quarter the cow. Working in their shirtsleeves, they poured water into the huge cauldron the farmer had used for cooking hog feed, and stoked the fire in the brick stove.

One of the men brought an armful of vodka bottles.

"Now this is what I call living!" cheered one of his buddies, relieving him of his load. The stoppers on the hand-blown bottles were quickly removed and the bottles passed around. Soon the smell of frying meat, and wood and cigarette smoke had everybody forgetting the ordeal they had just been through.

Ingo enjoyed the buzz in his head and the warmth in his body. It was all so simple. *Thank you, Olga, for keeping an eye on me.*

"A couple of hours ago I thought I'd never warm up again," his buddy Erich Haberle said. "When you're in dire straits you appreciate the simple pleasures in life." Haberle was from Stuttgart, and often talked about his family and the farm that supplied their clan with food.

"We were lucky, Erich," Ingo said. Drinking on an empty stomach had his mind fuzzy and his body slack. Turning to the cook, he asked, "Can't you fix us something that'll tide us over?"

"Turnips and carrots are very good raw and have lots of vitamins."

The men washed the vegetable in a bucket of water and munched away. How long had it been since they had sat in a warm room? Though it was packed, nobody complained. Every man counted his blessings and soaked up the heat.

Chewing on a carrot, Ingo found a cold bedroom and crawled into the first bed, ignoring its odor and the rough sheets. He fell asleep the moment he put his head down.

Olga was running through a burning town. Giant flames licked at her. "Olga, Olga, get away," he cried, but the words stuck in his mouth, his body paralyzed. She didn't even see him, just stared at a church steeple. The cross. What about it? Explosions erupted. Olga raised her arms, "I'm coming, Ingo."

Kunz woke Ingo with a gentle shove. "Soup's ready. The men are eating. We must move on."

Ingo opened his eyes. Where was he? Olga? What did all that mean? Was she having another spell? Deeply troubled, he joined his men in the kitchen. They sat on the benches or the floor, slurping hot chicken stew from their mess kits. The aroma of freshly baked bread and roasting meat made Ingo's mouth water. The heat drew sweat from his pores. The men made room for him on the bench by the table. Kunz, whose short hair and whiskers had grown over the past weeks, brought him a bowl of stew. Ingo chewed on the tender meat and vegetable. The thick broth tasted heavenly. "Schultz, you outdid yourself," he told the cook. "Food for the gods."

"The kitchen's well stocked—the Russians didn't take a thing. Must have been in a hurry. But couldn't pass up the chance to screw the women."

Ingo let it pass. "I suggest that each of you take as much food as you can carry. Who knows when we'll find more. Pack some feed for the horses. We should catch up with our lines soon." They were in enemy territory. Once the Partisans caught wind of it, they would corner them at night. They had the support of the people.

Erich poured vodka into Ingo's cup. "It's amazingly good. Not the usual home-distilled stuff that burns like acid. We found this five-liter baby." He pointed at a huge round glass container sitting in a basketweave holder. He beamed as if he had come across a priceless treasure. The men grinned. Some had fallen asleep. Others ate as if to make up for the past and store up for the future. Their cheeks flushed under dark whiskers. They celebrated life. "Amazing what food and schnapps can do for a *Frontschwein,*" Kellermann said. He toasted young Olson who could barely hold his head up, but was not about to show it. Leaning against the wall, he sang along with the harmonica one of the men always carried in his pocket.

Ingo felt so good that he sang along, thinking of Olga playing for his men at the Esplanade. *Auf der Heide.* Overwhelmed with love for her, he let himself float on the familiar tune and the alcohol, grateful for a moment's peace. I love you so much. His tension was gone. His stomach strained against his trousers, but he would not let that keep him from eating more. "This is so good," he told the cook.

"Cooking is fun when you have something to cook with!"

Everybody laughed. The scene reminded Ingo of the tale he had told Anyna about the abandoned animals of Bremen who had scared the bandits away and then feasted on the food they'd left behind.

Over the following two days other stragglers joined them. Nobody knew where the Russians or the front were. The farmers they encountered showed no hostility, and even asked to come along. They had no use for the Soviets, and no inclination to have their farms taken under the communist system. Ingo had to decline. Though many civilians had fled with the retreating German Army in the past, he was not about to risk moving with people who could not defend themselves when discovered. Still, the farmers gave them food and feed. "We don't want the Russians to take it."

Though they traveled by night, spending days in barns, Ingo never knew whether they would be trapped. Who was to know what really went on in the minds of the people? A handful of stragglers made an easy target for Partisans.

To cope with the freezing cold, the men cut out holes in old potato sacks and pulled them over their heads. Ingo laughed. "You'll scare the hell out of the Partisans."

Before they reached Litzmannstadt, Ingo and his men rejoined Army Group North. Once again, they were part of a well-organized, disciplined army now under the command of General Hossbach. He told Ingo that the Russians had broken through the 500-kilometer front and that the Germans had to regroup. Posen was declared a fortress, but Litzmannstadt would be passed up. "I'm so glad you came," he said. "All I have now are injured and barely recovered men."

Ingo shrugged. He was exhausted, and wished that he could sleep for the rest of his life. Two years ago he had limped out of Stalingrad. Then Olga came into his life and gave it meaning again. Now, even that wondrous feeling that had allowed him to thrive in this bloody war was diminishing.

As they approached Litzmannstadt it returned. "Sweet, beloved Olga," he sang into the frozen night. "I'm coming."

Snowflakes fell like cotton balls against the windshield and clogged up the wipers, further diminishing visibility. In the darkness it was nearly zero degrees. The drivers followed each other in a convoy by guessing the proximity of the vehicle ahead of them. Day travel was suicidal—Russian Stormoviks controlled the air and could pick them off whenever they showed up. Ingo felt safe under the capable command of General Hossbach.

Gisela Zebroski

On the outskirts of Litzmannstadt, he saw flames rising from the city against the black sky. The Russians had softened up the territory and would take it, if they hadn't done so already. Since General Hossbach had no orders to defend the city, they would bypass it. Was Olga still there, Ingo wondered, or had the civilian population been evacuated?

"Let's drive into the city," he ordered the driver. "I have some business to take care of." Ingo didn't care that the man cast a quizzical glance. The soldier knew better than to question the orders of his superior. Kunz would come along to Olga's apartment.

Driving into the city, Ingo noticed lights in some of the windows. That meant the German command had surrendered to the Poles and left the city. But in that case, what were all those people doing in the street? Wagons, women with buggies, sleds, handcarts. Whole buildings were in flames. There must have been an air raid.

"Hurry," he told the driver. With the lights coming from the buildings and the fires, there was plenty of visibility. The truck rattled along, obliging people to step aside.

Ingo prayed that Olga had left, and at the same time hoped he might see her, even if only for a minute or two. Once they reached Adolf Hitler Strasse, Ingo knew his way. "At the second street here you turn right. We're almost there," he told the driver. His heartbeat quickened in anticipation.

"I won't be long," he told Kunz when they stopped in front of Olga's building. "You wait in the truck."

Running up the stairs, he bumped into Polish women hauling clothes and bedding from Olga's apartment. So she was gone. A deep sadness overcame him. He would not see her now, perhaps never again. Still, he must find out what happened. He checked his Mauser before he entered the apartment, in case he ran into Polish resistance fighters. The door stood open and the lights were on. Icy air wafted in from the broken windows. Two women ransacked Olga's china cabinet, packing their treasure into a large travel basket. They didn't even notice him.

Hauser, dressed in a hat and coat, had followed Ingo. "Herr Hauptmann," he said, a quizzical look in his dull eyes. "I'm so glad you came. I need help. Would you look at this?" Suddenly he shouted in his thin, nasal voice, "You must stop those Poles! Shoot them. You have a gun. They won't listen to me. Frau von Schenck left. I told her that she

214

must wait for evacuation orders, but she and her sister paid no attention to me. They insulted me." He protested. "Took their mother and the children and left as if I didn't exist."

Ingo ignored Hauser, shocked by the clothes and bedding strewn over the floor. Nothing here reminded him of the happy days he had spent with Olga. Just another war-torn home with broken windows. Without her, the world was an empty place.

Hauser kept on talking until Ingo blurted out, "I didn't come here to listen to you. So get lost. Everybody, out!" he shouted, waving at the startled women. "Out, I said. *Now*. Everybody out."

Stunned at the order, Hauser stared at Ingo. "But you're supposed to…"

"*Raus*! I said. Don't you understand German?"

Hauser grumbled, then stepped back.

The women rummaging through the bedroom looked up, like pigs interrupted in their feeding, then shrugged, and went on opening drawers. They knew he wouldn't do anything. The Germans had given up the city. What was he doing here anyway?

"Get out! Now!" he thundered at them.

The older of the two, a thick black cloak wrapped around her broad shoulders, dropped the corners of her mouth and shrugged as if to say, have it your way. You can't stay here. She knew he was the young woman's lover. Everybody knew.

Ready to use physical force, Ingo stepped toward them. How dare they desecrate this place, where he had experienced the most delicious hours in his life.

Rather than succumb to his threat, the women took pity and wandered out.

He felt helpless and betrayed, though he did not know why. Everything had become so pathetic. His life was crumbling along with the once Great German Reich. Devastated, he sat down on the bed and stared at the broken mirror. A pair of panties had fallen to the floor. He picked them up and held them to his face. Who was that strange-looking fellow staring back at him? His cap was cocked over a cold face he barely recognized. The dark-rimmed eyes, the tight lips, the woolen shawl wrapped over his ears. A year had passed since they had faced each other in the nude and declared their love.

Now she was gone, and he would be alone.

Kunz came in and touched Ingo's arm. "We must get back, Herr Hauptmann. We left without orders."

"Yes, I know. She's gone."

"Good thing," Kunz said.

Ingo could not surrender to defeat, not after five years of fighting. Still, Kunz was right. There was nothing he could do for her now. It was getting cold.

In the kitchen he found a plump woman taking down Anyna's tin cup. "Herr Hauptmann, no be mad," she said like a mother, lifting the shawl from her face. She had kind eyes. "Frau Olga good woman. Go to Germany."

He felt moved. This woman had known Olga. Had even cared for her.

"Thank you," he said and left.

In the living room, they ran into a handsome young woman wearing a black coat. Her face looked familiar, despite the red shawl she had wrapped around her head. It was Olga's former maid, Stasya.

The voices outside got louder.

Her cold eyes flashed.

"Let's go, Herr Hauptmann," Kunz said. "It's their place now."

Stasya, a Partisan. A cold-blooded killer. But she had not harmed Olga, and had been good to Anyna. This was her victory. Her moment of triumph. Her dream was coming true. Poland would be free again. Or would it?

"We must go," Kunz urged. "We still have a lot of fighting to do."

Stasya watched Kunz like a cat stalking her victim. The intense look in her dark eyes testified to her immunity to pain. She had fought underground, fought in the dark, had shot people in the back. But she had no reason to harm him.

"When did Frau von Schenck leave?" Kunz asked in a casual, conversational tone.

Stasya relaxed. "Last night. I see her walk with family. Little Anyna. Nice girl."

"Thank you for telling me," Ingo said. What Stasya had done was no longer his business.

She raised her chin. "We free people now."

"So you are," he said, and glanced at the piano as if Olga's beautiful music would issue forth. They had promised their lives to each other. Now it seemed more unlikely than ever that they would ever come together. Not for some time, was that not what she had foretold? "I shall always love you, Ingo," he heard her say. "Always, always."

On their way down the stairs, he told Kunz, "She's a great pianist."

The women in the stairwell swarmed back. Stasya was not among them.

Climbing into the truck, Ingo hummed *I Know Some Day a Miracle Will Happen*. He had to believe in it or succumb to despair.

Chapter 21

Olga practiced *Rhapsody in Blue* in her mind. She could not wait to get to a keyboard and try out her new interpretation. The piece had so many unique passages, new and different like Stravinski's *Firebird*. Gershwin was every bit as innovative, without coming up with unbearable twelve-tone scales. Would she ever hear an orchestra perform *Rhapsody*? Not while Hitler was in power, obsessed with his anti-Semitism.

Dusk fell. Or had the clouds thickened, protecting them from strafing Russian planes? The small lanterns swaying under the wagons reminded her of ghosts. Olga's hands and back ached from the load. Attaching the rope of her sled to one of the wagons she could walk without pulling it. Oh, sweet freedom. The children dozed, but Mathilde and Ottie could not keep up with the pace of the horse. Skidding over the frozen ground, Olga untied the rope again. How she hated all that baggage. Her whole life had become nothing but cumbersome baggage. Oh, to be free again, sitting in her warm kitchen, listening to the *Front Request Program*. How much longer would there be a *Front Request Program*?

Her shoulders ached from the weight of Ingo's letters. Her love for him had become a burden. It had robbed her of common sense. She should have prepared for this long journey to Dresden with warm clothes and food rather than waiting to the last minute.

"You should have seen those Russian tanks drive into our village," the woman next to her said. Had she been talking all along behind the black shawl? She also had her child sitting on a sled she pulled. "If they break through, they'll bulldoze us like saplings. You never saw anything like it. I was hiding in our cellar and watched them drive into the square, killing whoever stood in their way. The soldiers stormed into the Post and demanded vodka. Frau Treff didn't have any." The woman pulled the shawl from her mouth and focused her tired eyes on Olga. She was about Olga's age.

"Short and shaggy fellows in padded jackets," she said. "Funny fur caps with ear flaps. Kind of makes sense in this cold. I bet they could pull those visors down too. I pity our soldiers now that I know how cold it gets. People said the Russian men are Mongols who come and kill and rape because that's what they do to their enemies in Mongolia. Just hope we get away. I'm so scared." She panted.

Olga did not care to hear anymore, and glanced back. Ottie and Mathilde were keeping up. Every step brought them closer to safety, wherever that was. Sooner or later, there had to be a railroad station with trains for mothers and children. The Reich always looked after families.

"The Russians never found me," the woman added triumphantly. "Guess what I did?" She did not wait for Olga's answer. "I remembered that in winter soldiers wear white tunics. So I pulled out some bed sheets and wrapped them around me and my son. Wasn't that clever? Once it got dark I took my emergency luggage, packed my little boy on this sled, and took off through the backyards like a thief. The soldiers were busy celebrating their victory. Must have found some schnapps at one of the farms. We got away."

Olga trudged on, half asleep. Anyna and Bertie dozed on the sled.

"Some Russians not only raped the women, they nailed them to walls and then shot them," the woman said. She obviously had to get it off her chest. "Eventually they shot everybody—men, women, children. God help us all. If we only had that miracle weapon. It's bound to come any day now, don't you think so?"

Olga nodded.

"I came to a village where the Russians had killed 72 people and ran over the rest with their tanks. Refugees, like us." She spat at the snow, then wiped the tears from her eyes. "*Schweine.* No, why insult innocent pigs? No animal would do that. I'm so glad I'm with this trek. Then again, we make a perfect target for Russian planes. Sooner or later they'll show up."

Olga wished she had taken sheets instead of Ingo's letters.

"Guess what they did to some French POW's working at the manor?" the woman said, glad she could share her harrowing experiences. "The fools thought the Russians would liberate them. As if a Russian knows the difference between a Frenchman and whoever, or cares. They cut off the Frenchmen's fingers to get their wedding bands. I swear! I'm sure they would have given their rings. They screamed and protested. The Russians didn't care." The woman's voice fell into a confidential whisper. "After all that, those sons of bitches lined them up and shot them. Just like that. Their Allies. So help me God, I just keep on going. Don't know when I slept last and don't care. My legs move on their own. A couple of times a wagon gave us a ride. We've been walking all the way from East Prussia."

One of the women screamed out and collapsed. "I'm going to deliver a baby," she cried. "Help me. Somebody help. It's coming."

The women gathered round. One of the wagons stopped. "You can load her up in the back," the woman who owned it said. "My mother is a midwife. She'll help." With the help of two soldiers, they heaved the pregnant woman and her child up on the wagon, and then her bags. The pram stayed behind. One of the refugees grabbed it and redistributed her bundles. The wagon pulled away, crunching against the packed snow with the screaming woman inside. How could the mother and newborn survive this merciless cold?

Another mother, who had carried her dead baby for some time, placed the bundle in the snow and walked away, tears running into her shawl.

The elderly couple that had been walking in front of her stepped aside. They would not struggle any further. Their bodies were so cold; death would come quickly. And the temperature kept dropping.

More and more bundles and bags landed in the snow. Olga's rucksack was getting heavier and her steps more cumbersome. Anyna was walking through the biting frost to keep from freezing to death. Mathilde had taken her place, unable to make another step. Olga and Ottie had wrapped their mother and Bertie in blankets, but they needed a source of warmth to thaw them out.

Olga gazed at the stars blinking down at her from the black sky. As soon as dawn broke through, they would become easy targets for Russian planes. But no need to worry about that. She doubted they would survive the night.

Ottie rubbed Bertie's back. "I'm so cold, Mami," he said plaintively. "Why can't we stop?"

"Because the Russians will kill us when they come," Anyna said. "We must find Uncle Ingo."

"Uncle Ingo, Uncle Ingo," he mocked. "What if he isn't coming? What will we do then? I'm freezing, and so are you. You're just pretending to be so noble."

"Because I am," Anyna insisted, and stomped her foot. "And I know that Uncle Ingo will come. So stop complaining, Bertie. Sometimes you're a real baby."

"And you're a show-off."

"That's better than being a baby," Anyna said behind her shawl.

Olga smiled.

At dawn the intense cold peaked. Olga saw no point in guessing the temperature. Her hands and feet ached so badly that she wanted to cry. No matter how hard she stomped on the frozen road, or rubbed her hands, or slipped them under her armpits, or slapped them against her chest, her body would not warm up. When would hypothermia set in? How much longer could she bear this? Why not step aside like the old couple and let nature take its course?

The rosy strip on the horizon widened, casting its hue against the dark sky and the flat, snow-swept landscape. The fleeing people and their wagons, the military trucks and armored vehicles passing them on their way to the front, made perfect targets for strafing Russian planes. How would they defend themselves?

Rather than imagine the bloodshed and horror, she thought of the first night she had spent with Ingo—their first kiss and Anyna's unexpected interruption. They had pretended to watch the sunrise. Father had bestowed a special gift on Anyna when he saved her. Olga felt deep gratitude and found new strength.

One of the horses slipped and barely missed the sled with his hooves. The children cried out. Two soldiers helped the horse back on his feet while others steadied the wagon. The neighing, squeaking wheels, and swishing sled runners resumed their pace. Nobody wanted to be left behind.

Ilona had seen this coming. "We shall not see each other again in this world. There will be many boulders in your path. Be strong, you can overcome them. Only the chosen will survive this war." Olga hoped she would be one of them. Her life had only begun now that Ingo was part of it.

Mathilde sank from the sled and moaned. "I can't go on, girls."

Olga helped her mother back up, and noticed German tanks in the distance. The front was closing in. What if they were caught in the crossfire? *Father, do not forsake us.*

Pale winter sun spread pink sparkles on the snow. The world kept turning, indifferent to the plight of these desperate people. Ingo was nearby; Olga sensed his presence. The battlefield would close in on them. How she wished she could load her family onto a flying carpet and sail away. Instead, the sound of approaching planes had her heart pounding.

"Stormoviks," she heard somebody say. The military convoy stopped—they had no anti-aircraft guns. The men jumped from their trucks and scuttled into the snow.

"Drop everything and run," Olga shouted, fighting off panic. "Quick! Into the snow like the men. Hurry!" She yanked Anyna off the sled, and immediately sank into the deep snow, which absorbed their steps as if they were wading through water. "Quick, quick," she urged.

Anyna screamed out.

Blinded by the snow, and petrified by the roar of the descending bombers, Olga stumbled and fell just as the first circling planes cast their shadows across the field. Their motors howled as they descended for the attack. Olga felt the roar of their propellers like a sudden gust of wind. Screaming people scattered or crawled under the wagons. The wounded, if they had survived the freezing cold, were left to die. A machine gun fired, then stopped. Germany's defenses had been spent.

Olga pinned Anyna down with her body. A spray of bullets exploded nearby, leaving holes in the snow. Cold sweat broke out all over her body. She trembled, overwhelmed by fear, certain that the guns fired at her.

"Please, Father, protect us. Don't forsake us. Dear God have mercy," she murmured, amid the hysterical cries of injured and frightened. Sheltering Anyna's little body under hers, Olga would at least save her child.

Anyna was silent, in shock.

Salvo after salvo of bombs rained down on the people and their horses. The Russian gunners enjoyed the hunt. *Father! Father! Please protect us. Protect Ingo. I'm sorry I ignored your warnings. Please forgive me one more time.*

Finally, the planes took off. The sound of their motors diminished. Olga raised her head, but would not let go of Anyna.

"They're gone, Mami."

"Yes," Olga whispered, embracing her child. Overwhelmed with gratitude, she kissed the cold face, readjusted her shawl, and brushed off the snow. They had survived. "Yes, my sweet," she said. "They're gone. We're saved."

Hand in hand, they waded back to the road, where people threw blankets over burning wagons. Bleeding horses whinnied in agony and torn bodies writhed. Ottie struggled back, and shook her gloved fist at the sky. "*Verfluchte Schweine*," she shouted, as if the departed pilots could hear her, or cared.

"Watch your tongue, Ottie," Mathilde scolded. "The children can hear you."

"Tell that to the Russians." Ottie fumed, yanking up her luggage and returning it to the sled, then wrapping Bertie into his blanket. In a state of shock, he stared motionless at the pale blue sky, waiting for the planes to return.

Soldiers shot the injured horses. The burning trucks and dead men stayed behind.

"Get back into the snow," one of them yelled, his helmet drawn over his forehead, battle-gear in hand. "They'll be back. They always strike twice."

"Strike twice?" Olga repeated, shaking in apprehension.

"Get away from the road unless you want to stay here permanently."

The roar of the approaching planes left no time for discussion. Olga grabbed Anyna's hand and waded back into the snow. Children screamed. Adults shouted warnings to each other. The motors droned like angels from hell, about to descend.

"Here they come," Ottie shrieked, collapsing in the deep snow.

Anyna curled under her mother's chest, a chick under the wings of a hen. The hungry whine closed in. *Father, please, protect us.*

Olga's senses waned. Eyes closed, she withdrew into herself. Father was taking her away from this island of destruction. The bombs whistling through the air and howling engines were just a distant noise that belonged to another world. "Thank you, my beloved, faithful guardian," she whispered, feeling Anyna's breath against her face.

The planes finally left. Olga could not bring herself to open her eyes. Her world was so peaceful, without hunger or cold. She had been saved and would be protected during this arduous trip.

Still trembling, Anyna tugged at her mother's arm. "Come, Mami, we must go. The planes are gone. They won't be back. That was the second time."

By evening they had reached Lask, a small town built around a church square. Refugee wagons camped everywhere, lanterns hung from driver's benches like tired eyes. Trucks drove by with emergency lights, two slits against a bulky hood. Black figures plodded in silent procession, as if following a hearse to their own funeral. How many would survive this war?

Mathilde found a snow-covered bench in front of a dark farmhouse and dropped down. Sighing she said, "You go on, girls. I lived my life..."

Ottie let go of her luggage. It landed in the snow. "Mother!" she ordered. "We're not going to stay here. We've gotten this far, and we'll keep on going."

Olga dumped her rucksack. Enjoying the momentary relief, she stretched her aching back. "I'll try to get something to eat," she said, and knocked at the weathered door of a dark home.

A stout woman came out, looked Olga up and down and slammed the door shut. Stunned Olga stared at the black door as if it would open again. No stranger had ever treated her with such unconcealed hostility, shutting her out when she hadn't even said anything. Good thing she had not asked for food.

"So much for local hospitality," Ottie sneered.

The hungry and exhausted children whimpered.

"I'll try the church," Olga said, not about to let Ottie win.

"Go right ahead. The priest was probably drafted. But don't let me discourage you."

Ignoring her sister's sarcasm, Olga knocked at the door of what looked like the parish. When nothing stirred, she knocked again, louder and louder, gathering courage and determination. This time she would succeed. Somebody had to be here.

The door opened to a hand's breath. A toothless old man, a worn cap drawn over his wrinkled face stared at her. The dim light coming from the hall showed his patched jacket—a servant.

"Is the pastor home?" she asked quickly, pushing her foot into the crack before he could close the door.

"*Nie*," he said.

"I need help," she implored. "My mother, two children. We walked from Lodz." She used the Polish name of the city. "We're cold and starved. The children need a toilet. *Prosze bardzo,* I'll pay you."

"Money no good."

"I have no gold."

He hesitated, scratched his head under the cap, then let go of the door. "*Prosze, pani,*" he said reluctantly, and held up his kerosene lamp to show her the way inside.

The cold, dark hallway smelled of homegrown tobacco. "*Dziekuje bardzo,*" she said, bowing her head. "We're desperate. Please let us warm up and rest. We must get away from the Russians."

"Very dangerous," he said.

"I understand. God will reward you."

He shrugged, then watched her open the door again and wave to Ottie.

"Only short time," he said, obviously regretting letting her in.

"I promise," Olga agreed as her family filed into the large hall, hauling their luggage. Though it was not heated, the home felt warm and safe.

He escorted them to the kitchen, where he had a fire going in the large iron hearth. The sudden warmth, the scrubbed kitchen table, and smell of baked bread brought tears to Olga's eyes. Father had saved her.

They shed their wet clothes, then sat down at the table which had once fed a large family. He picked up the kettle from the cooktop, poured boiling water into an ancient pot, and added a handful of dried tea leaves. Soon the aromatic scent of mint bloomed.

Olga saw mugs lined up on a shelf, and put them on the table. He brought a pitcher of milk and a chipped sugar bowl. "You not tell nobody," he whispered as if somebody could hear him, shaking his wizened head. Evidently, helping Germans invited the wrath of the Polish community.

"I understand. Thank you from the bottom of my heart. You're a good man."

"Vladek," he introduced himself shyly.

"I'm Olga," she said, shaking his bony hand. The skin was dry and cracked from a lifetime of menial work. "We're so grateful. We can't thank you enough. You've saved our lives, Vladek."

Anyna curtsied, which inspired Bertie to click his heels and bow his head. "We've been walking a long time," she told Vladek in the Polish Stasya had taught her. "And we're terribly hungry."

Sipping their tea, they watched Vladek cut off thick slices from the huge loaf of freshly baked farm bread and then spread butter and jam on them.

"*Pan* Vladek," Anyna said. "You're better than Santa Claus. Much better."

He grinned, showing his toothless gums.

Anyna ate her bread. With a grateful smile she rubbed her belly. In her red sweater, she was her charming self. The wet coats and blankets had been spread out over the chairs to dry. "So good, Pan Vladek. The best." He fried sausages and potatoes in a big, wrought iron pan. Olga took off the children's boots and rubbed Anyna's cold feet. "If you hadn't opened the door..." she said. "We must never give up. There are kind people everywhere in the world."

Olga noticed the fear and reluctance in his eyes. His hands trembled. Did he suspect that somebody had seen him take in a German family?

After dishing out the food, he pulled a bottle of schnapps from the cupboard and poured it into four shot glasses.

Olga raised hers. "To Polish hospitality," she said. Her body had warmed up, though sporadic shivers still crept up her back.

Ottie's large face turned red and shining. "Anyna is right. This is like Christmas."

Vladek refilled their glasses and cut up the remaining bread.

Mathilde's tired eyes still had that forlorn look, but she no longer seemed desperate. Food and rests would give her the strength to struggle through another day on the road. Cradling her warm mug she leaned against the table and said in a thick voice, "Thank you, Pan Vladek," and reached for his hand. A few days ago such intimacy between a Pole and a German would have been unthinkable. He withdrew his hand and slipped it under the sleeve of his patched jacket while he watched the door as if he expected somebody to come who would disapprove of his having Germans in the kitchen.

Ottie gobbled up the food like a hungry puppy, making sure nobody would take it away before she was done. "Eat your potatoes, Bertie," she said. "We don't know when we'll find some food again. I know you're tired. But first, you eat." Turning to Olga she said, "The Countess, that old shrew, knew what we would be up against."

"She's my grandmaman," Anyna said.

"So she is," Ottie said, draining her mug.

"*Dziekuje bardzo*, Pan Vladek," Anyna said, touching his hand. "Very good."

Vladek petted Anyna's head. "*Kochanie*, you sweet girl."

"I'm sweet too," Bertie said.

"Why do you always have to budge in," Anyna said, then gave Vladek her most endearing smile. "Boys can't be sweet, right? That's only for girls."

Bertie planted his little fists against his hips. He wore a thick sweater and training pants. "Well, I wouldn't want to be sweet anyway. I'm tough and I got courage."

"All right," Anyna said and turned to Vladek. "You *kochanie*, Pan Vladek."

His toothless smile amused the children. "German soldiers come and take food. Pastor go away. He German."

Olga nodded. No doubt he was drafted. "And you wait for the Russians."

He shook his head. "*Nie*. No Russian. No German. We not want anybody."

"I understand. We would rather go home to Latvia too. But the Russians took it."

He nodded. "You can sleep here—little. Is very dangerous."

Olga was too tired to care. She and the family followed him and his kerosene lamp to the bedrooms. The ancient, four-poster beds had neat featherbeds and large pillows that had not been used for some time. The musty smell lingered in the icy rooms.

"God bless you, Vladek," she said. "*Dziekuje bardzo*," and hugged him. "God will reward you." As soon as she crawled under the featherbed with Anyna, she was asleep.

Olga had no idea where she was when Vladek shone his lantern into her eyes. She gave him a blank stare as he told her, "You must go, right away. Quick. *Predko, predko*!" he urged, shaking his light impatiently over her face.

"Uuh," she wondered as her memory returned. The parish. The Poles. "*Russky*?" she asked, jumping out of bed while he explained something in Polish.

"You go *predko*."

"*Dobze. Dobze*," she mumbled, shaking Anyna awake. "Wake up. Wake up. Quick. We must go."

Anyna rubbed her eyes, looking from one to the other. "Pan Vladek," she said recognizing the old man, then translated while Olga helped her dress. "People from the town will come. If they find us here, we'll all be in trouble. Him too."

Oh you kind old man, Olga thought. "Thank him for us, Anyna, while I get Omi and Ottie up." Vladek had risked his life for them. How could she ever thank him for that?

As soon as the groggy children were dressed, they found Vladek in the kitchen. He had hot milk, fried potatoes, and thick slices of buttered bread waiting for them. They gulped it down while slipping into their coats and picking up their luggage. At the door, he handed Olga a small bag with sandwiches. "For children."

Olga swallowed her tears when she kissed his scratchy cheek, and hugged him. "God bless you, Vladek. I shall never forget this. You saved our lives"

Anyna offered her little hand and curtsied. "*Kochanie*, Pan Vladek. *Bardzo* d*ziekuje*."

Back in the dark street, Olga struggled with the cold, and the unknown dangers awaiting them. "We must find a second sled," she said to be doing something.

"Sure," Ottie said, as if Olga would call for a limousine to take them to the station.

"Good luck. Just don't do anything heroic. The old man gave me the creeps."

After agreeing that Ottie would wait for Olga at the village well, Olga took off and crept along a fence. Frozen snow squeaked under her feet. Distant artillery fire flashed in the black sky—the front was closing in. A second sled would let them pull the children and their luggage. They could move faster and escape the tanks at their back.

At what looked like a barn, she heard animals rustling in the straw. The gate wasn't locked, and Olga slipped inside, wondering why nobody had taken the cows. That could only mean that the retreat had happened so fast that the military didn't have time to confiscate food. The peaceful cows and the pungent smell of their dung belonged to an undisturbed world that would soon be annihilated.

Groping along the wall, her hands touched the runners of an old farming sleigh among the tools and ropes. She pulled it down, and set it on the straw. Under her breath, she apologized to the farmer for stealing his sled. From the looks of things, he may not need it much longer. This would soon become a war zone that would destroy everything. The animals would be taken by whichever army arrived first, and slaughtered. Now at least the sled would save her family.

Through the open gate, she noticed the dimmed lights of an approaching car and waited. It stopped at the corner blocking the road, then cut the motor. The darkness hid her from view. Against the snow, she could distinguish three men climbing out of the cab. They carried guns and spoke in Polish while they positioned themselves in a roadblock.

Wondering how she could escape with her sled unnoticed, she saw a truck drive up slowly. The roadblock forced it to stop. A window opened. "What's going on?" the driver demanded in German.

The Poles jumped at the door and pulled the driver out. He clung to the steering wheel, shouting, and kicking at his assailants. "What do you think you're doing?"

Olga heard the crack of a punch, and then, with a deep moan, he let go of the wheel. The men pulled him out like a sack threw him to the ground, and surrounded the defenseless driver. One of the men held him, another twisted his arm.

The driver winced in pain, swearing, "You goddamn Polacks."

A woman appeared at the window, while a husky, teenage boy slipped out from behind the wheel and threw himself at the men. A single blow knocked him down.

"What do you want from us?" the woman demanded icily in German.

"Revenge. You killed my family." The man pulled her from the cab.

She challenged him, positioning herself in front of him, like a guard. "We killed nobody, you insolent barbarian. Leave us alone."

The man slapped her face. She stumbled and screamed, "How dare you."

He hit her again. This time she fell to the ground.

"Don't you touch my mother," the boy bellowed, struggling back to his feet. A kick threw him down again. He moaned, rubbing his chest.

Olga was terrified. If they found her, what would they do? She clutched the sleigh handles and slowly backed up while the men tormented the people.

"You'll hang for this," the driver on the ground threatened. "All of you."

One of the Poles kicked him again. "Now is my turn." He swung his foot at the man again, hitting harder.

"I killed no one," the man shouted defiantly. "They'll catch you…"

"Oh no. Not again, Ingelheim. Remember Abrahim Davidson?"

Ingelheim? Who was he? What did he do?

The Pole pressed his foot against the man's chest.

He winced. "You're crazy. My name is Alfons Muller."

"Sure. Ingelheim. And my name is Adolf Hitler."

"You brute," the boy cried out, and struggled up again. A fist in his face stopped him in his tracks. He did not cry. "That's all you're good for," he sneered, "you Polish shitheads."

The Pole faced the boy. Perhaps he admired his courage.

"Leave my family alone," the woman screeched. "We haven't done anything to you. They should've gassed you all."

"Be quiet, Gudrun," Ingelheim ordered, exasperated.

The Poles grabbed her legs and threw her against the ice. Olga was sure the woman's back was broken. The other Pole opened his fly and pissed on her face.

Ingelheim groaned. "You goddamn swine."

While the Poles finished the Ingelheims off, Olga escaped into the darkness. Haunted by the screams of the tortured people, she pushed the sled into an alley.

That day, the biting wind developed into a snowstorm. Mathilde and the children walked to stay alive. Olga fought against the wind, wrapped in a whirling mass of thick, dense snowflakes that hid them from Russian planes. She had not mentioned last night's scene to Ottie or her mother, though it haunted her. Ingo had to cope with such things day in and day out. No wonder he had found himself on the verge of losing his mind.

Mathilde stopped and stomped into the thick snow by the roadside to relieve herself. People paid no attention, fighting the snowstorm. When she returned she groaned. "Why don't you girls just leave me here. I've lived my life."

"Don't you start that again, Mama," Ottie said. Her reproach had lost its bite. "We're doing all we can. What more do you want?"

"Nothing."

The finality struck Olga with its pain. "I'll wave down a truck," she said.

"Good luck," Ottie said contemptuously. "Pull up your pants and let's see whether your cute legs still get men worked up. Soldiers are desperate." She pulled a sled against the ferociously blowing wind. "Have you looked at yourself lately?" she said, panting. "Sex-starved boys will do anything. Honestly, Olga. Whatever beauty you might have had, is gone. You resemble a scarecrow at the end of summer, a walking ghost."

"Now look, girls," Mathilde said in a meek voice. "Stop that bickering and act like adults." She wheezed, then coughed into her shawl.

Olga left her sled and stepped into the roadway, ignoring the truck coming toward her. The driver slammed on the brakes and blew his horn. The truck skidded on the ice, almost hitting two people who had seen it coming and jumped out of its path. The convoy stopped. The driver shouted, "Can't you watch out? I almost killed you."

"It'd be a quick death rather than a slow one," she said unperturbed, her teeth chattering, and pointed at Mathilde and the two children. "We need help. We're exhausted. Frozen," she shouted, over the sounds of the laboring motors.

Soldiers jumped from the truck, stretched, and swung their arms and legs. They welcomed the chance to move.

"Please," Olga pleaded, "take my mother with you. We've been on the road for days. Just a little ways."

"You're asking an awful lot from a common soldier" one of the men said.

"I'm desperate. The two children will freeze to death unless we get help. We walked all the way from Litzmannstadt. I can't believe we're still alive. A Pole had more heart than our own Germans. He took chances and gave us food and let us warm up. Please, give us a lift. I know your rules. But we're people, German people." She rubbed her freezing arms.

"All right, all right," the man said jovially. "Let's help her. Come boys, let's squeeze *Oma* in." He and another soldier took Mathilde's arms and pulled her up, while a third pushed her from behind. "Come right up, *Muttchen*. We have no idea where we're going, but come along. The children too? I'm afraid, we can't take all of you. If our CO finds out..."

Olga caught the young man's eyes—they understood each other. Their lives were at the mercy of fate, whoever controlled it. "I can't thank you enough. Please drop them off at the next town."

"Mami!" Anyna cried when the soldiers lifted her to the truck, reaching for Olga. "Mami. Mami!"

"Anyna, you'll be fine, I swear. We'll meet at the church. You know we will."

Anyna's desperate cries were the greatest torment Olga had ever suffered. What if they didn't find each other again?

"We'll take care of you, little one," the soldiers assured Anyna. She did not hear them and kept on screaming, "Mami! Mami!"

The column set in motion, and Anyna's cries faded away.

"We'll meet at the church," Olga shouted over the roar of the motors. More and more trucks passed—clumsy, dark green hulks bearing an iron cross on their hoods. Their stench took her back to hell, the hell she had been in before. Once she gave in, there would be no escape. Soon the trucks were gone, and only the farm carts remained, slowly pulling back onto the snow-covered road. Ghost-like trees ran along the ditch.

Olga sobbed. "Anyna. My treasure. My love."

Ottie took her arm, but Olga could not stop. She collapsed on the sled where Mathilde had been earlier and bawled. "Father, don't forsake us now."

Passers-by, trudging over the packed snow, reassured Olga. Others gave her a sympathetic nod. Then music formed in her mind. *Liebestraum.* It was as if she were carried off, back to her beloved piano, playing for Ingo.

"We must go," Ottie urged. "The artillery fire is coming closer."

"Yes, of course. I'm sorry," she said in a thick voice, then blew her nose and took the handles of the sled. "We must walk faster."

Ottie picked up her pace. Olga felt ashamed for breaking down when her sister had gone through the same tragedy. Her child was on that truck as well. "I'm sorry, Ottie."

The snowfall lightened; it had to be late afternoon. Darkness would set in soon. How long ago had the children left? How would they find each other in a blacked-out village? The clinking of tank treads rattled against the up- and down-shifting motors. Explosions disrupted the steady roar. Olga drew deeper into her coat, her neck contracted behind her collar like a turtle, only there was no hiding from the fighting that could break out any moment now, no shelter. The occasional barns and knolls sprinkled across the snow- covered fields would be targets. They had to get away from the front before combat started.

"Hurry, Ottie," she said, as if her sister were the obstacle. They were both exhausted and had a load to pull. Running familiar melodies through her head took her mind off the encroaching danger and her fear for the children.

The wheel of a farm wagon rammed against a rock and broke. Olga heard the cracking wood. The horse skidded as the wagon fell to the side, but did not capsize.

"Why did you pack so much stuff?" said a man in passing. He was too much in a hurry to help. So was everybody else. The woman climbed from her bench, indifferent toward the shouts of the drivers whose path her wagon blocked.

"Do you know how far we've traveled?" she defended herself. "Why don't you help me fix it instead of complaining? I don't want to fall into the hands of the Russians. Not now."

The convoy had stopped. Soldiers were ordered to move the wagon off the road, rather than help the woman fix the wheel. She protested, "You just want me to die! My life and that of my family is expendable, isn't it!"

Olga found herself behind a truck filled with soldiers. Those sitting on the siding looked down at her. She raised her hands in supplication, "Please, please, take us along. Save us. We must get away. Our children are in the next village."

"You know they can't take us," Ottie said.

Olga kept pleading, "Please. Please. Just take us a little ways."

"What do you say, boys," one of the soldiers said from behind his shawl. "Do we have room for two pretty ladies? I'll stand for a while. How about you, Manfred?"

Suddenly, the whole crew wanted to stand. Two men pulled Ottie up, loaded the sleds and luggage, and brought Olga on board. "Welcome, girls."

"I don't suppose you know where you're going?" Olga asked, warmed by the closeness of the men and the tarp that sheltered them from the wind. It flapped like a tent.

"What difference does it make? The enemy is everywhere."

Olga gasped. Sitting down, Ottie kept her thoughts to herself.

"The Russians should be beyond those trees," the soldier said. "When the weather clears up, you'll see their tanks. Hear those explosions? That's them fighting the *Grossdeutschland* Panzers."

The truck jolted over a bump.

Olga thought of Ingo. "You wouldn't happen to know a Hauptmann Kroll?" she asked.

The man shook his head. In the dim light, she saw his tired eyes. "Things didn't go according to plan. The Russians knew about our offensive and beat the hell out of us."

Olga was too shocked to speak.

"That doesn't mean anything happened to your Hauptmann. Our units got mixed up and regrouped. He's probably all right. Perhaps he was lucky enough not to be caught in it, though pretty much all our divisions on the Eastern Front were engaged."

"Engaged?" Olga repeated, as if an all-out offensive could be described in such simple terms.

"What's going to happen now?" Ottie asked. She had either overcome her fear, or was certain that they would find the children in the next village, wherever that was.

"Who knows," the soldiers said, holding on to the frame that supported the tarp. "The generals plan and we fight."

Ottie pressed him. "What about the front? Where is the front?"

The soldiers exchanged glances. Some nodded, others shrugged.

"You ask a lot of questions, lady, that we can't, and aren't allowed, to answer. As long as we fight, we can defend ourselves. Who wants to be taken by some Russkies and shot or taken prisoner, which is worse?"

"We're fighting to the last man, you know," the soldier standing in front of Olga said. He seemed to be an educated man, who spoke clearly and articulately. He knew he would not survive the war.

Ingo would. She sensed his presence now, and closed her eyes. The truck bumped over the frozen ruts in the road, the motors laboring and spewing out fumes. Ingo.

The man adjusted his stance. "If we fight long enough," he said, "we should run into the Americans."

"Don't pay any mind to him," his buddies teased. "Gets carried away with his fantasies. It's a game we play when the going gets too rough. Figuring out different scenarios—you know, what we'll do when the war is over."

"You mean won," Ottie said.

"We haven't played that one for a while. We'd consider ourselves lucky to be taken prisoner by the Americans."

Olga joined in. "Only how will you get to the Americans? They're in France and you're in Poland. And besides, they won't take Germany. My husband is a POW in America. He's not suffering, not really." How was it that she thought of Lothar now?

"I wouldn't think so," the man in front of her said. He stood so close that his knees touched hers. Amazing that the men had been willing to take all of Olga's luggage and even the sleds.

"The Italians surrendered," he said. "They knew we can't win the war. But you can't just give up. We should negotiate. But our Fuhrer is not about to abdicate."

Olga knew that Hitler would never surrender, not as long as there was one man left to fight. The whole conversation made no sense, and

235

she found herself drifting off toward Ingo, seeking him out. He had to be here. Why didn't he respond? He must be very busy.

The man whose knees touched hers, pulled down his shawl. He was probably twenty or so, but looked older. Thin, pale, a week's growth on his tender skin. The scar across his cheek reminded her of Ingo. His teeth chattered. Those heavy greatcoats and jackboots didn't keep the men warm. Didn't Ingo say that they lost almost as many men to frostbite as they did in battle?

The truck jerked. The standing men bounced against each other, and struggle to retain their balance. "Hitler is the enemy," one of them said.

Olga felt too tired, too cold, and too frightened to speculate, surprised that the men didn't stand behind their leader. They even talked about the failed assassination attempt by Graf von Stauffenberg as a misfortune. Nobody she knew of would dare say that in public. But these men trusted each other.

Now they talked about making peace with the Allies, and joining them to force the Soviet Union to capitulate. Only Stalin was like Hitler, treasuring his life so much that he didn't care how many men were sacrificed to protect him and his position. "Once we are rid of Stalin, we can return to a normal life."

All Olga could think of was that she was part of the Wehrmacht now, and that Russian fighter planes would have a lot of fun attacking a German column. Would the truck stop so that she and Ottie could get off with all their baggage? What if they didn't go the same way as the truck with the children and Mathilde? On the verge of panic, she hummed *I Know Some Day A Miracle Will Happen.*

"What about the miracle weapon?" Ottie asked.

"A fairy tale for children and gullible adults," the soldier said, twisting his lips into a pitiful smile.

"So there's no hope," Olga said, as if she hadn't known that all along and added quickly, "What do you normally do for a living?"

He reached under his helmet and scratched. "Living?" he said in a distant tone. "Seems silly to even think about work. Even surviving will take some doing. I was a student of law in Berlin when I got drafted. That's where I'm from."

"I know Berlin well," Olga said, rubbing her stiff, frozen hands. If they just wouldn't hurt so. Her gloves, her pockets, not even sticking them under her arms, did do a thing to protect them from the cold. Massaging them between her legs had no impact. Her whole body was frozen and had no warmth to give. In a moment her heart would freeze too, and she would just turn to a block of ice and crack. Berlin. Had she actually lived there once and sold cigarettes and chocolates from a box in the theater?

And then there was Dresden, somewhere on another planet. Ingo wanted her to go there. Meet his family. Nothing, absolutely nothing, felt right about that. The city, his family, the world he came from would not want her. She had no business heading there, but where else could she go? Berlin? That was insane. She must head for Dresden.

Chapter 22

Olga and Ottie found Mathilde and the children in the village of Zloczew. The mayor had opened the movie theater for refugees. The women of the National Socialist Welfare had a soup kitchen going, and fed warm milk and bread to the children. People traveling with their horses received feed and water. Boys ran around the dark square in happy abandon.

Berthie asked, "Will we get to see a movie? Omi got seats in the second row."

"I doubt it," Olga said, patting Anyna's warm cheek. She too would enjoy a movie. Something romantic to take her mind away from all this. Why not an operetta? She craved music, and would give anything to pour her uprooted emotions into the piano.

The heated hall had become a transit camp. Bundled-up figures peeled off their wrappings and massaged their aching limbs. Others waited in line at the toilets. The local official assured everybody that the Grossdeutschland Panzers would beat the Russians back in no time.

Olga kept her doubts to herself, ignoring the mayor's tale of the Battle in the Ardennes, "Once again the Reich is victorious. No enemy will set foot on German soil." The pot-bellied man strutted around in his brown SA uniform as if he had the power to make it happen. Like a schoolmaster, he pointed his swagger stick at Olga.

She shrugged, remembering the soldiers in the truck who were fighting for buffoons like this fellow. In a day or two, he would hide behind a civilian coat and hat like the people he now treated with exaggerated benevolence, and run for his life.

"We'd better leave as soon as we've had something to eat and a short rest," Olga said, relaxing into a folding chair. She stretched her tired legs, and noticed the wet areas on her pants where the snow had melted. Her feet and hands had warmed up in the heated hall, but shivers still rushed through her like after-shocks. No point in longing for a bed and a moment's peace and quiet from all the jabber around her. The children had recovered from the strain and cold, and now chased each other down the aisles, stumbling over luggage and the legs of their elders. The smell of wet clothes, cigarettes, and dirty diapers fouled the air.

Pulling off her boots Olga was grateful that she had escaped serious injuries and frostbite. Her nose ran from the sudden warmth. How long could she afford to stay here? The mayor obviously had no idea how close the Russians were, else he would not be so relaxed. Perhaps he had not even heard that the winter offensive had been a flop and that the Wehrmacht was in retreat.

Mathilde's cheeks looked flushed, her eyes feverish. Olga put her arm around her mother's shivering shoulders. How frail she was under the old gray sweater. How long could she survive this? If she came down with a fever, they would have to leave her behind, or risk their lives to stay with her. Olga dropped the thought. "We'll stay for the night," she said. That much she could risk. "By morning, you'll feel better. Perhaps we'll get some transportation to take us west. By now, the civil defense has got to be organized. As soon as we get a train, we'll head for Dresden." She spread the blankets she had taken from a stack out on the floor for Mathilde and the children. Two women from the Social Services brought a bucket of hot soup and refugee women held out their bowls.

Looking at Mathilde's wan face, the young women dishing out the soup said, "I'll bring you some aspirin. You'll feel better in the morning. We're setting up quarters for those of you who need care." Her cheerful smile showed no anxiety. She obviously had no idea that Armageddon was about to descend upon her as well. In her impeccably starched uniform and crisp white cap, she talked as if troubles only happened to others.

"Thanks," Olga said, wondering whether she should enlighten the young women. Not that she would believe her. She savored the hot bean, carrot, and potato stew and chewed on the chunks of meat. The noise had died down while the hungry crowd devoured the food. Some people packed away hunks of the freshly baked bread the young women passed out. They knew that this was no safe haven.

Dresden flashed in Olga's mind like a distant vision. Ingo's world was as unreachable as he was. She didn't belong there, and must keep going west. From now on, Olga was a refugee.

Ottie had gobbled down her soup. "This is quite good," she said, licking her lips, then lit a cigarette, inhaled, and leaned back. Her warm face relaxed. She helped Bertie finish his soup. "Now children, go to sleep. We'll need all the energy we can get. Who knows when we'll get a ride. We might as well be prepared for the worst."

"The worst?" Anyna asked, licking her spoon clean. "You mean airplanes will come again and drop bombs on us?"

"Could be," Ottie said, taking a long drag on her cigarette.

"In any case, we'll know what to do," Olga said. "We'll get through this. If we're lucky, we'll get on a truck." She winked at Ottie, hoping she would get the message that there was no need to frighten the children. They looked and acted normal, but who knew what was going on inside of them.

As soon as the women bedded their children down, the noise subsided. Anyna and Bertie fell asleep immediately. Mathilde rested with her eyes closed. Ottie sat quietly in the chair next to Olga. This was no time for small talk and meaningless speculations.

Olga dozed off. She saw Ingo coming toward her. He ran and ran, but could not reach her. No matter how hard she tried, she could not move and cried out.

Somebody shook her. "Mami! Mami! Wake up! People are leaving! Omi and Aunt Ottie say they're too sick to go on. People say the Russians are coming—they'll be here soon."

Rubbing her eyes, Olga looked at Anyna's concerned face. She was dressed in her cap and coat, ready to leave. The hall was almost empty except for a few women collecting luggage and children. Only Mathilde and Ottie luxuriated in their blankets.

"Why aren't you dressed?" Olga asked.

"I could ask the same of you," Ottie retorted. "Mother and I've decided to stay. We've had enough." She rested her head on a rolled blanket. Her eyes and red cheeks looked feverish. This was all wrong. They couldn't give up now. A distant rumble came from the front.

"I see," Olga said, slipping into her boots. She had to push hard to get her swollen feet in them. Women urged their children to hurry up.

She had to get her mother and Ottie up and moving. An idea came to her. "I can't make you come along," she said. "If you want to stay, that's your choice. But I'll take the children with me. They deserve to live. Come, Bertie. I'll help you get dressed."

Ottie sat up. "You can't do that. Bertie is *my* son. Don't you dare take him," she cried out, ready to fight.

"So he is. Then, let me suggest that you act like a responsible mother."

Ottie struggled to her knees. "You know, Olga, you're a pain in the neck."

"I know what you think of me, Ottie, and I don't care." She was so sick of all this.

"You're an adult and can decided for yourself. Act as you please. But the children depend on us, and I must look after them. They will come with me."

She took Mathilde's hand. "If I were you, *Mutter*, I'd get up and come along," she said in a warm, caring voice. "Every bit of life is precious, and you're not that sick. So let's go."

"Damn it," Ottie cried out, grabbing Bertie's coat, then reached for Mathilde's hand. "Come, *Mutter*. Olga is right. We must go."

Ten minutes later, Olga faced darkness, the biting frost, and crackling snow again. Most of the people were gone. Some armored vehicles rolled toward the front. She could barely see them, or the old buildings. Olga and Ottie jerked the sled forward.

"You can lean on me, *Mutter*," Ottie said. "I know this is hard on you. It isn't easy on us either. Sometimes I feel old too. But we must go on and live."

Daylight broke through the densely falling snow. Anyna and Bertie played guessing games. Mathilde's hacking cough would not stop. She was ill.

"We must get *Mutter* on a truck," Olga said, watching a military convoy pass.

"I can't say you weren't successful before."

Ten minutes later, Olga had a driver agree to take Mathilde and Anyna to the next town. "Be sure you stay at the church or nearby so that I can find you again," Olga admonished. "If we lose each other, try to get to Dresden. You have Frau Kroll's address. We'll meet there."

Gisela Zebroski

Ottie and Berthie also got a ride. Olga watched them vanish into the falling snow. Suddenly alone, she felt an immense emptiness. Though her load had lightened and the sled glided with ease over the packed snow, a deep sadness overcame her. What if... She had better not think that way. Father was with her, and would see to it that they survived.

Tying her sled to a slow-moving wagon, she let the horse pull her along as well. The runners swished effortlessly over the packed snow. If Ingo were with her, this would be real fun. She held on to the luggage while the runners jumped over the ruts left by the armored vehicles. Humming her favorite songs helped her forget the circumstances and the cold.

Images of her past ran through her mind like a silent movie. Her room at home in Latvia. Recitals and applause. Her accompanying Gottfried in Lucie's elegant home. Lothar popped up for a moment, and vanished. The Berlin Opera where she sold cigarettes and sweets. The Esplanade in Litzmannstadt. Ingo, his head shaved, fresh scars on his face. The *Mephisto Waltz*. "That's the music we are dancing to," he insisted. Instead she hummed *Liebestraum* into the falling snow.

The rope pulling her sled broke, and left the sled behind. The horse following her stumbled. Helping hands pull her aside.

"I wished I had a sled like yours," the woman helping her said. They walked together. "Did you lose your family too? My Gretchen is dead."

"My family went ahead on a truck," Olga said.

"The Russians killed my parents," the woman continued. "My baby froze to death. But life goes on. I promised God I'll accept His will. He gives and He takes. I never thought I'd feel that way, but here I am. If you let me put my bundle on your sled, I'll help you push."

Waltraut was good company. Her easy banter distracted them from the approaching artillery fire. Olga could not see her face, but judging from her lively voice she was young. She came from a small town in East Prussia. "I'd rather land in Hell than in the hands of the Russians," she kept saying.

At Lututow, the sky cleared up. The snow-covered wagons and people blended into the landscape. The golden cross on the church steeple gleamed in the eerie light of the cloudy day. The old village was still intact.

242

"I must go to the church and find my family," Olga told Waltraut as they parted.

The fresh snow had no wheel marks or footprints. Where was everybody? Evacuated? Had Mathilde and Anyna had been forced to leave? Where would Olga find them? Dresden? How would they get there? How would she?

The weathered church door was locked. Nobody answered at the parish either. The homes, with their drooping eaves and stacks of firewood, showed no signs of life. Mathilde and Anyna had to be here. Olga sensed it strongly.

Two soldiers drove up on a motorcycle with a sidecar. Skidding over the fresh snow, one of them shouted, "You must leave immediately. This town will be defended. All civilians must vacate."

"My mother," Olga said. "My mother is here, and my little girl."

"Didn't you hear me? What are you doing here anyway? Spying? Your papers." The man, his battle-gear strung over a white tunic, talked through a shawl covering his mouth.

"I'm looking for my mother," Olga insisted. "We walked all the way from Litzmannstadt. They got a ride on a truck. We're supposed to meet here. I must find them." Nobody would push her around. "Does a spy come in with a sled?" Russian rockets exploded in the distance.

"See?" the soldier said indifferently. "That's what you'll get, if you stay here. In an hour this place will be gone. I bet your mother left. I saw trucks and a train taking refugees. You'll find your mother at the station. Go before it's too late."

Helpless and frightened, Olga scanned the empty square. "Thank you for warning me, but I can't leave. Just forget you saw me."

"Suit yourself," the soldier said, accelerated, and rode off.

Why didn't Mathilde come out? She had to be in one of those buildings. Three men hauled a machine gun unit toward the square. Tank treads clinked. Something told her that Ingo was here. She must find him.

One of the soldiers said, "Unless you want to see what hell is all about, you'd better get out of here and count your blessings." Olga knew he'd be glad to trade places with her. She had seen Hell, and did not want to see it again.

Swallowing the lump in her throat, Olga let two soldiers lift her and her luggage on to a truck. They closed the sideboard, and waved to the driver. An irresistible urge to stay overcame her. At a sharp turn Olga threw her luggage down and jumped off before the truck picked up speed. Her legs absorbed the fall. Nothing was broken. With her luggage back on the sled she returned to the church. The shawl soaked up her hot breath. Her hands and feet felt warm again. The explosions no longer frightened her. She knew she would find her mother and Anyna at the church.

Her pace quickened as she returned to the square. Darkness had fallen. A German officer approached her.

"Ingo! Ingo!" she cried out, and ran toward him though she could not see his face.

"Olga?"

They collided in a passionate embrace. He was here; he had come to her. Heaven. Overcome by passion, they clung to each other as if their love could shield them from the deadly rockets all around them.

"I love you so, Ingo," she whispered. His kisses, his desire, his tight embrace answered her questions. They would love each other forever. The densely falling snow sheltered them like a curtain.

"*Liebling*. My Olychka. Where did you come from?"

"Father brought me to you so that I can tell you how much I love you before I see your mother in Dresden."

Their lips found each other again and again. They could not let go. The shining cross on the church steeple overruled Stalin's warning.

"I prayed for this miracle," he said. "Dear God, thank you." He kissed the snowflakes from her eyes and lips. "I shall love you forever. Olychka, don't ever forget me. You are my wife until death takes us away. But you must leave. Right now!"

"I must find Mama and Anyna. Did you know I would come? I knew you were here, I just knew. When they put me on a truck I jumped down."

He held her. "I feel you all the time. Yes, I sensed that you might come. I went to your place in Litzmannstadt hoping to find you there, but I was glad that you were gone. Stasya was there." He kissed her again, then tore himself away, panting. "You must leave. *Now*. I cannot bear to watch you die."

Her head jerked aside. Look!" she cried out. "What did I tell you? Mama and Anyna. Now, do you believe in miracles?"

Anyna came running toward them, her arms outstretched. "Mami! Mami! Uncle Ingo. We thought we were lost. Everybody left."

Laughing, Olga picked up her little girl and reached for her mother's hand. Ingo followed. His arms around his family, he took charge of the sled. "Let's go. You must get out of here," he ordered

"Come Olga," Mathilde urged. Grenades exploded here and there, as they hastened toward the highway.

"Where is Ottie?" Olga asked.

"She didn't show up," Mathilde said. "Her truck must have taken a different direction."

At the road, Ingo stopped a civilian truck.

"If you must leave Dresden, go to my aunt's in Wunsdorf. She will take care of you. We are very close. She will be our anchor-point in case..."

The driver stuck his head out. "At your order, Herr Hauptmann."

"All vehicles must surrender to the Wehrmacht. Your papers!"

The driver handed Ingo a document he read with the help of a flashlight. "What's in that truck?"

"Documents for *Gauleiter* Greiser."

"I see. Let me take a look."

"Herr Hauptmann," the driver said nervously, "I can assure you everything is in order. We went through four road blocks already. I must hurry."

"I want to see those documents," Ingo insisted. "Else you'll take this women and the child to the next station."

"But I can't. I have strict orders. Nobody must touch the truck."

"Is that so! I order you to open it."

A bomb exploded nearby, throwing off a blast of air. The driver squirmed. A beautiful, fur-clad woman leaned out. "The truck is completely full. I barely got on. I work for *Gauleiter* Greiser."

"Now, for the last time, you either take these people on or my men will confiscate the truck. We don't need those documents." Ingo pointed his gun at the driver.

Gisela Zebroski

"For heaven's sake, Herr Hauptmann," the woman implored. "We'll take them, all right? The old woman can sit in front and the younger one and the child can go in back. There's a sofa they can sit on."

Ingo kept his Mauser at the ready.

Another heavy shell hit the roadside. Other vehicles passed. Would Ingo survive this battle? Would she, Olga wondered.

Indifferent to the dangers and explosions, he helped Mathilde into the cab. "Do I have your word of honor," he asked the driver, "that you will take these people to a station where they can catch a train going west?"

Visibly relieved, the man promised, "Absolutely."

Ingo lifted Anyna up to the bed, then embraced Olga with a long kiss before she climbed in.

The village was in flames now. The golden cross gleamed in their light.

"Good bye, my sweet little baroness. Don't forget your Uncle Ingo."

"Never. I'll never forget you."

"Let's go," the driver shouted.

The truck set in motion. "I'll wait for you," Olga cried. "Forever."

Ingo ran off into the inferno. How long could he survive the battlefield? *Father, my Father, please, don't abandon us.*

The truck sped away, leaving the burning village for others to defend.

Chapter 23

The train steamed toward Dresden. Its familiar rhythm soothed Olga's nerves. Sitting on her suitcase, she gazed sleepily through the narrow slit between two standing women. The children on the train perched on luggage, or dozed on their mothers' laps. Anyna leaned against Olga. Mathilde had sunken into herself, her eyes closed. She wheezed. The wrinkles had deepened and her cheeks sunken. Even if they found a hospital or doctor, they had no time to stop. Olga felt sorry for her mother, but was not about to risk their lives. They had to move on.

The sun came out, turning the pristine snow into a glittering blanket. An occasional grove, a line of trees, a farm, a village, passed in quick succession. Children walked to school. Two-story homes had shining windows and wrought-iron balconies. The people living in them were oblivious to the dangers about to descend upon them. The wheels jumped over switches throwing the passengers off balance. Eager faces craned toward the windows. A sign passed.

"Dresden," a woman said. "We've made it to Germany."

The truck driver had kept his promise, and delivered Olga to the next station. For two long days she had been detained in Benschen, while trains brought more and more refugees. The platforms were overcrowded. People took turns warming up in the building. Two women delivered their babies on a table with the help of a midwife. Nature would not wait. How could the newly borns survive the cold?

Finally the stationmaster announced that an incoming train would take the refugees west. People stampeded, fighting to get inside with their bundles. Nobody wanted to be left behind. Olga, Mathilde, and Anyna were among the first to climb into the car. Mathilde even secured a window seat, which she held through the long trip. At times Anyna would sit on her grandmother's lap. Some women deposited their children on the luggage rack, others sat on their luggage. Those who could not get on clung to the closed doors, stood on running boards, or climbed up on roofs. They soon vanished, driven off by the cold.

Half-timbered buildings and ornate stucco facades fit Ingo's description of his home town. Olga felt the urge to keep going. She did not belong here. But everybody had to disembark. Once she found her bearings, she would join Lucie in Bautzen. Together they would figure out what to do.

The train shook and rattled as it switched tracks. Iron screeched against iron. Olga could not wait to be free of the thick air and the bodies pressing against her. What would Frau Kroll say when Olga appeared at her threshold as Ingo's…what? Girlfriend? Fiancée when Olga was still married? What had he told his mother? Up to this point, he had been a good son. He did well in school, followed his Fuhrer's call to arms, and proved his heroism. Had she spent sleepless nights worrying about him? Had she been embarrassed over his breakdown? That he had shown his humanity? From his description his mother did not believe in showing affection. Neither did Johanna, else they would have spent his time at home in each other's arms.

The women on the train talked about Dresden. "They have facilities for refugees. We'll get a bed and a warm meal. That's all I need," said the woman next to Olga, collecting her luggage. The train slowed down. More and more tracks appeared. Freight trains loaded with war machinery waited for a locomotive to take them to the front.

Another sign for Dresden passed. She had arrived. As soon as they stopped, a voice on the platform announced, "Everybody out. The train will return east."

Except for Olga, nobody had to be told twice. The refugees could not wait to get out and get some fresh air after the long ride. In her mind's eye, Olga saw the buildings in flames, the glass roof collapsing, and the people, now streaming toward the exit, dead.

"Is this where Uncle Ingo lives," Anyna asked.

A train marked with Red Cross signs stood on the next track. The suffering men aboard it would give anything to cope with Olga's problems rather than their pain. All they had to look forward to was more pain. Or death.

Olga took her mother's arm, and ushered her to a nearby bench. "Stay close," she told Anyna.

A little boy twisted and turned. "I got to go, Mami, else I'll pee in my pants."

"We're in Dresden!" cheered a young woman. "Safe! *Sieg Heil.*"

The others were too exhausted to speak. Enthusiasm no longer filled the sails of the *Grossdeutsche Reich.* Anyna tugged at Olga's hand. "Come, Mama. Let's go to Uncle Ingo's house. Ingrid will be there."

"I know, darling, I know." Olga picked up Anyna, and held her. Yes, they had arrived safely. Ingrid would help.

Mathilde waved at one of the volunteer women who had come to help refugees. In her tattered coat and scarf she was almost unrecognizable. "We need help," she implored, her bloodless lips quivering.

"That's what we're here for," the pretty girl said cheerfully. "My name is Rosalie. We've got places set up for you. Milk and cookies for the children. Tea and sandwiches for adults. Cots, blankets, washrooms. Everything is toasty. Let me call one of the Hitler Youth boys. They'll help with your luggage."

The young woman ushered them out of the station, where bundled refugees huddled in clusters with their luggage. "They're waiting for a train going west rather than coming in and warming up," Rosalie explained. "Stubborn people. They insist the Russians will come, and you can't convince them that they won't. We don't have any air raids to worry about. The Allies promised not to bomb Dresden if we don't touch Oxford or Cambridge. As you can see, they're keeping their promise."

They crossed a wide street where streetcars passed and stopped. Well-dressed people went about their business or took one of the horse-drawn cabs. Ingo had not exaggerated—Dresden was a sight. Once Ottie showed up, they could explore the famous buildings, visit the museum, and perhaps even attend the opera. If it were not for the covered wagons of refugees in the square, nobody would believe there was a war going on, and that the front was only some hundred kilometers away.

"As soon as we can implement the miracle weapon we'll beat the Russians back. Dresden is perfectly safe."

A group of men, three abreast and in unfamiliar uniforms, sauntered past.

"British prisoners of war," Rosalie explained. "I've seen Americans too." She smiled a greeting, but they paid no attention to her.

They would know *Rhapsody in Blue*, Olga thought. In their country, people could play Gershwin or whatever they liked. Perhaps, some day— who was to know?

"Once you are registered," Rosalie said, "the housing authorities will assign you to a room. But here we are." She opened the door to the Refugee Shelter, where an elderly woman in a fur jacket received them. "Welcome to Dresden," she said, shaking hands. The large hall had rows of clean cots with pillows and army blankets. Olga appreciated the warmth, and the smell of food. While she took Anyna to the washroom, Rosalie helped Mathilde settle down on a cot. Some of the women dressed or undressed their children. Young mothers had a station to change diapers.

After relieving themselves and cleaning up, Olga and Anyna returned to Mathilde. "It's good to be in Germany," she said. "Everything is clean and orderly. We'll get some food shortly."

Others filed into the facility. Young volunteers helped them settle down, or showed them to the dining hall, where long tables with benches had been set up.

Mathilde waddled along, too hungry to pass up the food. "It feels so good to have a place to rest. I never thought we'd make it this far. If Frau Kroll has no space for us, we'll be taken care of by the authorities." Throughout the trip, Olga had mentioned her apprehension over seeing Frau Kroll. If she hadn't promised Ingo, she would not bother now.

The volunteers brought soup as soon as Olga and her family sat down. Vegetables and bits of beef, along with slices of rye bread, made a good meal.

Warm and sated, Anyna teased the little boy next to her. "We walked all the way from Litzmannstsadt," she boasted.

"And we came from Posen. That's a lot farther. They didn't want to let us go." He was no more than seven, with red cheeks and lively blue eyes.

"That's nothing, because I know where Posen is. I bet you have no idea where Litzmannstadt is."

They bickered while his mother told Olga how they had slipped through the barrier the Army had set up. "Imagine. While they fight to the last man? It didn't take much imagination to figure out what would become of us."

"Are you going to stay in Dresden?" Olga asked, passing her plate for a refill.

The woman shrugged. "I'm too tired to think about that. For the time being I'll stay here. Wait and see, so they say."

Again Olga had a premonition that something was not right. She must move on. Why not head for Berlin? She had the address of Ingo's aunt in Wunsdorf. Forget about Frau Kroll, and save herself an unpleasant encounter. The Reich was obviously well equipped to take care of refugees, and would look after Olga and her family until Ottie showed up.

It was still afternoon when they settled down on their cots. Mathilde fell asleep immediately, and snored. Olga was too nervous and apprehensive to sleep. Rather than forgetting about Frau Kroll, she might as well get it over with. If Ingo had written her, she knew about the situation.

Anyna leafed through a picture book provided by the shelter. They also had toys, and a playroom for children.

"I'm going to visit Frau Kroll," Olga said, rising.

Anyna jumped up, and put the book aside. "Let me come with you, Mami."

Olga glanced at her mother and decided to let her sleep, then asked one of the helpers for directions. Gutenberg Street was on the other side of the Elbe River, in Neustadt.

At the station, Olga found a horse-drawn cab. Together with Anyna, she enjoyed the ride through the postcard-pretty city. The buildings did not have a scratch on their half-timbered facades, ornate carvings, and decorations. Storefronts, hotels, and statues caught their attention. The horse cantered over the swept streets. Crossing the long bridge, Olga shivered. Icy, moist air rose from the frozen river, while a cold chill ran over her spine—that foreboding again. Neither Anyna's happy chatter, marveling at the children skating, nor Olga's admiration of the beauty of Ingo's city could distract her.

"Do you suppose Ingrid will be at home?" Anyna asked. Her white rabbit cap and collar were torn, and so was her coat. What would Frau Kroll think of her Olga's soiled clothes under the woolen coat?

Gisela Zebroski

Anyna bubbled with excitement. "Look, Mami, look," she called out every time they passed a camp of refugees, a shop window, or a child pulling another on a sled. They had left theirs in Benschen. It was good to be in Germany again, where people lived according to familiar traditions and in relative peace.

Gutenberg Street was lined with two-story homes belonging to complacent middle-class families. The snow had been swept from the sidewalks, and the shining windows reflected the dark sky. It might well snow again, Olga thought.

The driver let them out. Olga recognized the balcony and front yard Ingo had described. A polished brass plate read, "Dr. med. Wilhelm Kroll."

"Uncle Ingo's father!" Anyna cried, and rang the bell.

"Be sure to curtsy and say 'I am glad to make your acquaintance, Frau Kroll.'"

"I know what to say, Mami."

Quick, self-assured footsteps approached. Olga's heart sank. The door opened. A stern, handsome woman in her fifties appeared, and scrutinized Olga. The disdain in her cold blue eyes was palpable. Even an unwanted solicitor would have fared better. Frau Kroll knew who was calling on her. Her finely plucked brows knitted to a frown. "You must be Olga von Schenck," she said curtly, as if she had hoped Olga had perished.

"Yes. Pleased to meet you, Frau Kroll. And this is my daughter, Anna Magdalena."

Anyna curtsied. "I am glad to make your acquaintance, Frau Kroll."

Visibly embarrassed, Frau Kroll nodded. "How do you do." They faced each other in the freezing air. The tall and slender woman stood erect, like a school mistress facing a tardy student. The striking resemblance between mother and son eased Olga's apprehension. She was his mother; she had carried him in her womb.

"I don't know what came over him when he asked you to come here," Frau Kroll said. "He knows how busy I am. The war changed him. We became strangers." Her stare kept Olga at bay, making sure that she would not invade the family home.

"He went through a lot of pain," Olga said. "War can devastate the soul. I'm sorry we dropped in unannounced. Ingo insisted. We saw each

252

other three days ago. He was defending the village we fled from. He sends you his love."

Frau Kroll cringed as Olga called her son by his first name and crossed her arms defiantly. Her hand-knit sweater did not protect her from the icy wind. Disdainfully, she raised her chin. Now that Olga was here, she was not about to be pushed aside. There was nothing vicious in Frau Kroll. She was rigid, and embarrassed by a situation that did not suit her.

"Thank you for the message," she said, stepping back into the house, ready to close the door. "Mothers are the last to know what is going on in their sons' lives. He forgets that I am managing this household without help, not to mention my duties at the hospital."

"Please forgive me, Frau Kroll," Olga said. "I did not mean to intrude, and will not take up any more of your time. We'll be on our way. In case Ingo inquires, please tell him that we are fine, staying at the Refugee Shelter. And give our regards to your husband and to Ingrid."

"I'd better close the door now," she said. "We are wasting heat."

The door closed. Olga stared at it in disbelief, then took Anyna's hand and walked away. The air felt warmer now. She would send Ingrid a note, and leave it up to her to come or not. Perhaps she worked at the Refugee Shelter.

"I don't like Frau Kroll," Anyna said. "She doesn't like us, but Uncle Ingo does. Right Mami?"

"She is Uncle Ingo's mother, and we must respect her." Walking down the street, Olga remembered Ingo's words. "My mother treats the war like a disease."

Looking back, Olga envisioned bombs. Fires. Mayhem. She must leave Dresden as soon as she contacted Ingo. There would be no final victory, only disaster.

"I *must* go to the bathroom," Anyna said. "It's urgent. I thought I would go at Frau Kroll's." She slipped her hand between her legs and jumped around.

Olga looked at the fenced-in yards, glad that Anyna did not insist.

"And I can't go behind a bush," Anyna said. "There isn't one with leaves on it."

Olga laughed. "So my little baroness needs a proper WC, I suppose."

"Ingo's mother doesn't know that, does she? That I'm a baroness? When Uncle Ingo tells her, she'd want us to stay with her."

Olga took Anyna into her arms. "Anyna, I can't believe what I'm hearing. Now let's see where we can find a toilet for you."

"We could ask somebody."

"Like that woman?" Olga wondered, watching a young woman in a beret that matched her navy blue coat approach them. She walked briskly, swinging her arms. "Excuse me," Olga said. "My daughter desperately needs a bathroom. Could you help us out?"

"I'd be glad to. I live a block away from here."

"This is my daughter, Anyna. She's desperate."

"Anyna? Then you must be Olga! I am Ingrid Kroll, Ingo's sister. Welcome to Dresden." She embraced Olga. "I'm so glad you made it. That you came. Anyna, Ingo wrote me how much he loves you, sweetheart. But why am I standing here talking? A friend of mine lives across the street. Come quick."

She pulled Anyna along. "I bet you saw my mother. She has her heart set on Johanna. A nice girl, but Ingo loves you. Johanna doesn't even care. It's a suitable arrangement."

Ingrid rang the doorbell of a handsome villa, more elaborate than the Kroll home. A woman answered, and greeted Ingrid.

"Frau Ehrhardt, may we use your bathroom?" Ingrid asked. "It's urgent. I'll introduce my friends in a minute."

"Come, sit down, Olga," Ingrid said, as if it were her home. "Take off your coat and stay awhile. Astrid will make us some tea. She's such a dear. We've been friends for years." Ingrid's charm and unassuming manner reminded Olga of Ingo. She longed to talk about him and get to know her.

The home, furnished with heavy turn-of-the-century drapes, dark wallpaper. and upholstery, was warm and comfortable. Ingrid pulled down the black-out blinds, then switched on the light. Olga relaxed in one of the armchairs, amused by the hand-crocheted doilies that protected the armrests. Ingrid was not exactly a beauty, but her friendly and outgoing personality animated the plain features of her long face and pronounced nose. She wore her brown hair pinned back, allowing it to fall to her shoulders. The collar of her blouse was folded over her blue blazer. Her pleated plaid skirt matched the color.

In her soiled brown cardigan, unwashed curls, and felt boots, Olga probably looked like a peasant visiting the manor house.

Ingrid did not seem to mind. "Do you have some schnapps around, Astrid?" she asked when her friend returned from the bathroom where she had left Anyna. "I think Olga needs a pick-me-up. Things must have been hair-raising. My poor dear. Ingo is so fond of you and little Anyna. I can't imagine being a refugee. Can you, Astrid? Imagine walking away from our beautiful Dresden and not knowing where you'd wind up!"

"You'd be amazed," Olga said. "Once you have bombs exploding all around you…" She told them some of the happenings on the road, and how she had lost Anyna and her mother and found Ingo.

Astrid, a woman in her late thirties dressed in a tailored suit, said. "So we're being lied to. The front collapsed. Nothing is fine. And the miracle weapon an illusion." Her voice grew agitated. "The refugees coming in droves don't want to stay here. They know that we can't stop the Russians at Gorlitz. It's a stone's throw from Dresden. Once they break through, they'll be here in no time."

Ingrid leaned forward as if she would argue, but remained silent, her face tense.

Anyna returned. "Mami, you must see the bathroom and the beautiful pictures." When nobody responded, she sat down on a chair and waited.

"It's all right, Ingrid," Olga went on. "You don't have to go anywhere right now. Let's see how things develop. For the moment, we're glad to be here. You can't imagine how much we appreciated the hot soup and the bread at the shelter."

"Ah yes, I forgot all about the schnapps. Please forgive me. Your tale, Frau von Schenck, had me forget my duties. I'll be right back."

"Astrid is my very good friend," Ingrid said. "As soon as I talk to Tante Lore, you can move to her place. She's expecting you. She's my father's sister. We're very close."

"You really don't have to put yourself out," Olga said quickly.

Astrid brought glasses of schnapps, and a tray with cheese and sardine sandwiches. She even had a glass of milk for Anyna, and a piece of streusel cake.

"I know what you're thinking," Ingrid said. "I'm sorry about Mother. She didn't mean it that way. Ingo should've known better. Mother is used to being in charge. Discipline and obedience, you know. But he's been away from home for years, and used to giving the orders. Why should he obey his mother? Perhaps he isn't even aware that she still looks at him as her son who should do as he's told. So you see, Olga, it has nothing to do with you."

Olga downed the schnapps. Yes, she understood, only that didn't help. Perhaps Olga should have taken her leave right away, should have gotten the hint from those cold eyes, which told her she was not welcome. Now she felt embarrassed.

"I'm so glad you came, and that Ingo's found a woman he can truly love," Ingrid said. "Mother picked out Walter Braun for me. I can tell you right now, I'll never marry him. I can't stand the man. She can invite him all she wants. He's a big deal in the Party, else he would be at the front. Pretty soon, that won't mean much. Mother doesn't know that I have somebody very special in mind. His name is Thomas, and he's the most wonderful man in the world. He's fighting the war, like Ingo." She blushed and smiled.

Olga felt drawn to her potential sister-in-law. Listening to the two friends banter, she forgot her rags and shared their concerns as if she had lived here all her life.

"Tante Lore is expecting you," Ingrid said, holding up her glass for another shot of schnapps. "She knew how Mother would react. Let's not think about it. I'm so glad you're here." She hugged Olga, smelling fresh and appealing with clean white teeth and gentle eyes under arching brows.

"Thank you, Ingrid. So am I. We'll stay for a couple of days and then move on."

"Where to?" Astrid asked, crossing her legs. After days on the road, being here in this warm home, among people who didn't have a care in the world, seemed unreal.

Olga shrugged. "West."

Both women insisted the Russians would not reach Dresden. Olga had heard all the arguments before. Let them live in their illusion. Ingrid talked about the Semper Opera, the Zwinger and museums. They urged Olga to tell them how she'd met Ingo.

"The *Mephisto Waltz* brought us together," Olga said, but did not mention the Evil One who had used her.

"I heard you are quite a pianist," Ingrid said.

"I studied at the conservatory. The piano is my voice. Music is my life." She put down her glass. If Tante Lore was anything like Ingrid, Olga would consider herself lucky.

"Do come and see us again," Astrid said. "We need to hear more about what is really going on. Even if it's so frightening."

Ingrid took Olga to the streetcar. "I'll pick you up tomorrow and take you to Tante Lore's. She'll be delighted to have you."

"I'm so glad you're Uncle Ingo's sister," Anyna said when the tram arrived. "I don't have a sister, or a brother. Uncle Ingo knows wonderful stories. Do you know stories too?"

"I do, Anyna. But not like his. Ingo is a great story-teller and a writer. I'll let you read some of his stories, Olga. You'll be amazed."

A writer? No wonder he wrote such beautiful letters, Olga thought.

Lore Hoffmann lived on the second floor of an old, well-kept building. Her elegant home had three bedrooms, a salon, dining room, kitchen, bathroom, and separate toilet. She greeted Olga, Mathilde, and Anyna with the warm hug Olga had hoped to find on Gutenberg Street. "Consider this your home," she said, her jovial smile an open invitation. Her tailored suit, accented by a filigree brooch, hid her middle-age spread. She had the healthy, cheerful attitude of a woman of means. Her gray hair was wrapped in a twist, softened by stray ringlets. "I'm so glad I can share my home with you. Ever since my dear husband passed away, it's been too quiet. I can't thank Ingo enough for sending you to me." She shook Anyna's hand. "So you're the little baroness."

"How do you do, Tante Lore," Anyna said respectfully. "My Grandmaman is a countess. She went to Bavaria. Some day we'll go to Bavaria too."

They settled down in a living room furnished with antiques. Anyna sat on a dainty armchair, her hands folded in her lap. "She taught me how to be a proper baroness. Can you imagine, she was upset when I told her said I would not kiss her hand anymore." She knit her brows. "Do you want me to kiss your hand, Tante Lore? I don't mind. People kiss each other on the cheek."

Lore Hoffman pretended to think. "Kissing the cheek is indeed more common, though here in Dresden we don't kiss each other in public."

"Oh," Anyna said. "I saw Uncle Ingo kiss Mami's lips. That's because he loves her."

"Is that so," Tante Lore said. "Our little baroness keeps a watchful eye on you, Olga. I hope you don't mind my calling you Olga. I'm Ingo's aunt, and you are part of his family now. I know we'll all get along famously. Ingrid will bring some clothes for you; they may not be quite your size, but we can have them altered."

"Mama is an excellent seamstress," Olga said.

"That's true," Mathilde agreed. She had settled down on the sofa. "If you have clothes to alter or repair, I'd be more than happy to do that for you, Frau Hoffmann."

"In that case, you could pick out something from my wardrobe, Frau Bergmann."

Ingrid talked about her work as volunteer. "More and more refugees are arriving. Most of them want to stay in their wagons and move on. Did you notice that Dresden has turned into a giant Gypsy camp, Tante Lore? They have fires going everywhere. Some of them come from East Prussia, others from Silesia and Thuringia. The Russians are closing in. I didn't want to say that in front of Frau Ehrhardt. One never knows. Even your best friends can turn you in."

"Everybody should be prepared to leave," Olga said. "When Gorlitz falls …"

"Gorlitz falls? But that's impossible. We can't leave Dresden." She touched her head, as if the prospect was not only unthinkable, but a disaster she could not handle.

"Ingo wants us all to leave," Olga said, restraining her voice from sounding desperate.

Tante Lore and Ingrid shook their heads. "Let's not paint the devil on the wall," Tante Lore said. "Let's wait and see. Ingo doesn't know that we are well taken care of." She rose slowly. Despite the shortages, she had maintained her weight. "I'd better check the stew." She hugged Olga. "I'm so glad you came."

The soft light of the table lamp caught Ingo's photo. She imagined him relaxing on the sofa where Mathilde sat. He belonged in Tante Lore's sophisticated home, with its antique furnishings and collection of Meissen figurines. Leather-bound classics filled the book cases. A fringed shawl covered the baby grand. Olga leaned over Tante Lore's cuddly shoulders. "It's so good of you to let us stay here. This feels like coming home after a very long journey, right Mama? We had a home like this in Riga. This calls for a celebration." Olga opened the piano lid. "What would you like to hear?"

"Your choice." She pulled Anyna onto her lap. "I'm so glad I'll have a little granddaughter now." Then glanced at Mathilde. "I hope, you don't mind sharing her, Frau Bergmann."

"Not at all."

"I like you a lot, Tante Lore," Anyna said, and kissed her new aunt's cheek.

Olga tested the ivory keys. The rich sounds invited her to play *Liebestraum* for Ingo. It was a message to him, and soon erupted into passion lovers felt for each other. He was always part of her music. Nobody could take that away from her.

Chapter 24

Ingrid stood in the hall of the military hospital, waving a fieldpost envelope. She and Olga volunteered to care for the wounded coming in from the front. "Guess where I found it?" she asked.

Olga ripped it from Ingrid's hand. "From Ingo!" Pulling the scissors she used to cut off blood-encrusted bandages from the pocket of her uniform, she saw that it was addressed to Gutenberg Strasse, rather than Tante Lore's address, and postmarked February 2, 1945. Ten days ago. Had her letters explaining the incident with his mother been lost?

"Don't you care where I found it?" Ingrid asked.

Olga forgot her friend. He was alive! It was all she could think of.

"At home," Ingrid said. "I happened to be there when the mail arrived. *Mutter* tried to snatch it away from me. You should've seen her. She demanded I give it back. I refused. It's addressed to you. She has no right to keep your mail. For once I disobeyed. How can she intercede, and hide your letters from you? She was furious. I've never seen her like that. Her face was beet-red. I don't know what's gotten into her. Usually she'll do anything for people who need her help."

My beloved Wife,

I received your letters, but no answer to mine. Perhaps they are lost. Things are chaotic. Please listen to me, my love. Take Anyna and go west. The farther the better. Tante Lore is a wonderful woman and I would never ask you to do this, if I could see an alternative. Dresden will not be spared in the destruction of Germany. The inner city is always the target area. I wrote to Tante Gertie in Wunsdorf. She awaits you. I doubt the Russians will get there. The Allies are gaining ground. Let's hope they'll capture Germany before the Russians do. But please, leave right away. Convince Ingrid that she must come with you. I know Mutter will not move. She'd rather die than take anybody's advice. Explain the situation to Tante Lore.

If Mutter *would get to know you, she would take you in with open arms. But there is no time for that now. Trust your guidance. Father watches over me, but we must act. He cannot make us go.*

I love you, my darling. Will love you forever. Knowing you're in harm's way drives me to distraction. Dresden will be next.

I thrive under your guiding light. I would give anything to be with you now. Ingo.

Ingrid rolled up a bandage. "What's he saying? Please, tell me."

Olga pressed the letter to her heart. They were together again.

"For heaven's sake, Olga, what did he write? We must get back to work."

"Yes, I know," Olga mumbled, dwelling in the sweetness of her love.

"Water, water," pleaded the wounded man lying on a stretcher beside her. His head was completely bandaged. His bloodless lips quivered. Days ago, he had been a strong and healthy young man. Now the fate of the Reich was written on his trembling body.

Olga poured drops of water into his parched mouth. "Ingo wants us to go west," she told Ingrid, stepping aside so that a nurse could pass with her gurney. The patient, or what was left of him, was unconscious.

"Water."

Olga poured more water into the open mouth which reminded her of a little bird waiting for feed. He needed morphine. Wounded men arrived by the truck- and trainload. The Labor Service Girls could not keep up.

"Dresden is the safest place in Germany," Ingrid said. "But you go ahead, Olga. You're a refugee."

Olga gazed into Ingrid's innocent eyes. She had no idea what lay ahead for her if she didn't leave. "If you stay you'll be at the mercy of the enemy."

Ingrid pressed her palms against her temples. She obviously had no idea what would happen when the Russians came. The man, or was he a boy, on the stretcher wanted more water. His hand groped for hers. She took it, and held it for a moment to reassure him that he was not alone. Blood seeped from his chest. "The doctor will take care of you shortly," she lied. "He'll relieve your pain."

"Thank you, nurse," he whispered. "You are so kind. Like my Margit. I couldn't tell her how much I care for her. Now it's too late."

"I'm sure you'll get recuperation leave."

A faint smile slipped over his white lips. "You think so? Then I could tell her."

"And get a sweet kiss from her." Olga did not bother to write down the girl's name.

More and more Red Cross trucks arrived in the courtyard. Nurses and girls from the Labor Service ran through the snow, unloading the wounded and bringing them inside.

"We must leave tonight," Olga told Ingrid on their way to the dressing station. "Get to Tante Gertie's. Ingo sees no alternative. Dresden will be next!"

Ingrid followed Olga along the long hallway lined with stretchers. "*Mutti* will be shocked. She's convinced we'll win the war. It'll break her heart."

Olga did not care what Frau Kroll thought. "In our nurse's uniforms they won't stop us when we get on a train for wounded. There are no trains for civilians. I know what that means. After supper we'll take Anyna and go to the station."

"But we promised her that we'd go to the circus," Ingrid said. "I got tickets. Why don't we leave after the show?"

Olga picked up her pace. Their shoes clicked against the stone floor. The stench of unwashed bodies, blood, urine, and formaldehyde and the moans of suffering men had become Olga's world. They should probably skip the circus, she thought, but did not want to disappoint Anyna. She never complained. If only that anxiety would settle down.

The head nurse, a tall and haggard woman with drooping lids over tired eyes, stopped them. "Don't you girls have anything to do?" she asked irritably.

"We're on our way to the dressing station," Olga said.

In the courtyard, voices shouted orders. Engines revved. "I'm taking off," Olga said. "I must visit Lucie before she leaves Dresden—she's not about to wait for the Russians to come. Gottfried may have arrived. I'd love to see him before we leave. Who knows what will happen next."

On February 13, Air Chief Marshal Sir Arthur Harris called his early morning meeting to order. His well groomed hands rested on the polished table. He was tired and didn't mind showing it. His arguments for bombing German cities to wear down their resistance had worn him out. He'd won every one, but never without long, tedious deliberations. A war was about killing. But every time he mentioned his theory that terror tactics would bring the German people to their knees, and the war to an end, he was confronted with new arguments. The British sense of fair play was all wrong when it came to tyrants like Hitler, or Stalin for that matter, both of whom didn't give a damn about other people's lives.

He stroked his thick, graying mustache. Though his hairline had receded, his jowls drooped, and he had developed a paunch, he considered himself a good looking officer. As Air Chief Marshal, he expected proper respect. The carefully tailored uniform fit his broad shoulders. He carried himself with dignity. Anyna the faces of his wing commanders, he felt more powerful than George VII. Once again his strength and authority would triumph over the meek, and win him a place in history as the man who defeated Hitler's Reich. Many of his leading officers owed their promotions to his strategies, and they knew it.

"Gentlemen," Harris said, "With this mission, our victory over Germany is at hand. Carpet bombing demonstrates our strength. One would think the firestorm in Hamburg would have taught them a lesson." He paused, expecting applause. It would come as soon as they heard of his plan. "But they are not getting it," he hammered out, tapping his swagger stick against the table. "Hitler keeps promising them some miracle weapon, and they believe him." He raised his stick like a baton. "If the Germans had such a weapon, our massive raids would have wiped it out."

Cigarette and pipe smoke shrouded the tense faces of his pilots. No comments? What was wrong with them? Why couldn't they see that their mission was to wipe out the enemy? Over the past weeks he had juggled the PM, the Allied Strategic Air Forces, and the British Ministry to get the full strength of the Bomber Command behind his area offensive. General area bombing was the key to Germany's collapse. All that consideration for the German people was ludicrous. Precision targets! As if that were possible. How was he supposed to hit a target in a blacked-out city? Even if they bombed at lower altitude, exposing themselves to the German anti-aircraft guns, they could only guess at their targets. Daytime raids were risky. The bombardiers would get the railroad station, and some tracks, which the Germans repaired in no time.

"If you say so, Sir Harris," one of the American officers said. "It doesn't seem right."

Harris could not remember his name. "Isn't that what the Germans did to us?" he said, on the verge of losing his temper. "Or would, if given an opportunity. We have more bombs than we'll ever need. What are we saving them for? The planes are available. The German air defense is running out of fuel."

He smirked. The men grunted.

"The Reich is finished. Let's give them the coup de grace and declare final victory."

No cheers. The Americans shrugged. This wasn't their war. Theirs was in the Pacific. They would not hesitate if it came to carpet bombing Tokyo.

"Well, gentlemen." It would be wrong to show the joy he felt at seeing a German city go up in flames. "We are ready for Dresden. According to the meteorological reports, we have a thin cloud layer at 20,000 feet. The Bomber Command's airfields will be fit for landing when you return from your nine-hour flight. It should be nothing more than a routine mission."

He took off his metal-rimmed spectacles, and glanced at the officers watching him. They still did not share the excitement he felt over the attack on Dresden. Victory was at hand. "So far we destroyed forty-five of Germany's sixty leading cities," he proclaimed. "But our task is far from done. Germany is still functioning. We have Magdeburg, Halle, Leipzig, Dresden, Chemnitz, Breslau, Nuremberg, Munich, Koblenz and Karlsruhe awaiting us. The Soviets have asked for our support. They're pushing toward Berlin. Stalin has offered a prize for the general who gets there first. He wants to beat us to it. But that's another story."

The uniformed men studied the map of Dresden, talking to each other in low voices. "The marshalling yards are an important junction for all traffic moving east," Harris informed them, pointing at the black lines crossing the city. "Dresden is crammed with refugees and wounded. An ideal psychological blow for the German people, I dare say. Those Teutonic monsters are a tough breed. They don't take hints." He cleared his throat as he marked the inner city for destruction. "Sir Portal believes we must strike while the Russians are less than a hundred miles away. They've reached the Oder River. Air Marshal Osland, the Bomber

Command's Liaison Officer at Supreme Headquarters, has given us the clearance and executive order to attack."

"I can't help my misgivings," said Sir Saundby, senior member and Harris's right hand man. "Unfortunately, I see no alternative and concur. But mind you," he added in a low voice, "only because the order was issued."

Harris shrugged, ignored the comment, and pointed out their targets. "Well, gentlemen, here is our plan." His voice vibrated with excitement, though ordering area bombing rather than aim at selective targets was risky. Had Stalin not asked for maximum assistance at the Yalta Conference and the Allies granted that wish? The Russians were determined to win this war and collect their spoils. Wiping out German cities would certainly help their advance. The Reich was in its death throes anyway.

"We'll launch the attack in three stages," he lectured in his nasal voice. "Our first strike, led by Maurice Smith here, our highly skilled Wing Commander, will deceive the German fighter squadron into believing that this is our main thrust. Three hours later, when they return to their base to refuel, we'll arrive with our second bomber stream and drop the incendiaries. By then, fire services and other civil defense will be fighting the conflagrations of the first attack. That means there will be no defense when we deliver our second blow with the rats in our trap. A can't miss strategy."

The American commanders slouched as usual. No discipline. "Just so you don't think we intend to do this alone," he told them sharply, "you will deliver the third strike."

The Americans nodded indifferently, almost bored. They did not appreciate mop-up work.

"Within three hours, the fires in the inner city should be wild, burning down the buildings. A strong ground wind will fan the incendiary loads concentrated on the boundaries of the target sector— our ground zero.

"After Operation Thunderclap, the Germans will know what they are up against and throw in the towel." Harris paused. Several men lit fresh cigarettes, others puffed nervously. The message was clear. A sardonic smile stole over his thin lips. The strike on Dresden would give those Nazi bastards what they deserved. "To prove the efficacy of this plan," he added with unconcealed pride, "after our first strike the fire brigades from the surrounding areas will come to aid Dresden. At that point No. 5 Group Sector will drop the bombs required to start a fire storm like we saw in Hamburg." He wrote down the schedule on the blackboard.

"At 22:03 hours, 243 Lancasters will drop 1,477 tons of explosives and phosphorous. Then, at 1:23 hours, 529 Lancasters will unload 1,181 tons. The Americans will take 311 of their B-17's and drop 771 tons." He made eye contact with them. "Mark my word, Operation Thunderclap will be a historical event!" he announced triumphantly.

The men copied the figures from the blackboard. Dresden would be erased from the map. Victory was at hand, and Harris would get the credit for it.

Olga took a tram to the ancient *Frauenkirche*. Lucie and her children were staying at Hotel St. Petersburg, which belonged to Gottfried's uncle Ulrich. She had arrived four days ago, packed and ready to leave for Austria as soon as Gottfried arrived. Convinced that the Russians were at her heels, she could not wait to get away. Last night Olga had found Lucie in a state of hysteria. "We must leave Dresden," she'd insisted. "We'll either get bombed or the Russians will break through. I'm no soothsayer, but I know the signs and can hear my inner voice shouting to leave." For once, Olga shared Lucie's outburst. How they would get a train was another matter. Austria would be a good place to hide out until the war was over.

The tram trudged along at a snail's pace. If Lucie could manage with her five children, the youngest still a baby, Olga could certainly manage with a competent nine-year-old. Leaving the tram, she watched children wander through the snow-covered streets in their Carnival costumes, singing *Laterne, laterne, Sonne Mond und Sterne*. Shrove Tuesday. Anyna wore a Little Red Riding Hood outfit Tante Lore had made.

Olga rushed into the dim, 18th century inn, with its smell of the ages, and slammed the door shut. At the bar stood elderly men, drinking beer and smoking homegrown tobacco. They watched her curiously. To them nothing had changed. They had adapted to the shortages—beer was still available, restaurants served food for coupons, and the opera had regular performances. Schools and universities educated the young and fed them lunch. If it were not for the refugees camped out in the streets, squares, and the railway stations, this would be a day like all the others. But Olga's apprehension would not subside.

Gottfried's uncle, an elderly man with thin white hair and a fleshy nose, received her at the counter where he carefully poured beer from the tap.

"Is Lucie in her room?" Olga asked.

He shook his grizzly head, and twisted his waxed Kaiser Wilhelm mustache. "She left. You should've seen her. Acted like a madwoman." He leveled the foam from the glass, checked the height, then poured some more. "She woke me up in the middle of the night and insisted I must get her a cab. Just like that." He snapped his fingers. "Wanted to go to the station that very minute. The children were dressed and the luggage ready to go. Getting five children into the train would be an ordeal not to mention all that luggage. Said she'd a bad dream. Saw Dresden in flames. Would you run off every time you have a bad dream?"

Dresden in flames! She was not alone in her vision, Olga thought.

"I found her a cab and was glad to see her leave. She would not even wait for Gottfried, who's supposed to come today. Completely lost her mind."

Olga took her leave. "Should he come, be sure to tell him that I'll get in touch when he's back in Berlin."

Outside in the dark and freezing street, she glanced at the silhouette of the round cathedral with its giant cupola. Suddenly flames broke out. They looked like the ones she had seen in Poland, winding into the black sky. Gigantic flames that engulfed the town and her. The apparition chilled her blood, and sent goosebumps down her back. Then it was gone and all was dark again. Olga rushed away, passing wagons parked around the square. Their small lanterns showed women preparing meals while children stood around. Cold damp air wafted from the nearby Elbe River.

Father, Olga prayed, *what are you trying to tell me? I'll leave tonight. Show me the way.*

Nothing stirred. *Dear God, don't let the Evil One attack me again. Father, protect me. You sent me Ingo's warning. I will talk to Frau Kroll, though I know her answer.*

On the tram to Neustadt, she heard the lively chatter of Labor Service girls who had come to help refugees and wounded soldiers. "Many of the refugees stay in the same freight cars they arrived in, waiting to move on. They'd rather freeze than come to our shelter," a rosy-cheeked girl told her friends.

Was that another message, Olga wondered. The tram rattled across the Elbe River, huge blocks of ice crashing against each other in the turbulent waters.

Gutenberg Street stood in deep silence. She had visited Astrid Ehrhardt a number of times, and knew the way well. If Ingo had not asked her to warn his mother she would not be here now, but it was her duty. Anticipating a rebuff, she rang. The door opened. Frau Kroll's icy glare required no words. The corners of her otherwise pretty mouth dropped. "You?" she said. "I thought I made it clear that we have nothing to say to each other."

Olga swallowed the insult and pulled her shoulders back. She was well dressed in her nurse's uniform and had nothing to hide. "I came because Ingo asked me to urge you..."

"I don't need a messenger. He writes to me directly."

"Then you must know that the Russians..."

"The Russians are my business. And let me tell you once and for all that I do not want you to meddle in my affairs." She was about to close the door, then added, "What makes you think you have the answers?"

"Experience," Olga said quickly, to start a conversation. "May I suggest..."

Frau Kroll stood beside the half open door. "Now look, young woman. I'm not interested in your experiences, affairs, or your life."

"In that case, I am sorry I disturbed you. Goodbye, Frau Kroll."

"Ingo is a fool if he thinks of marrying you, a married woman with child, yet."

Olga heard the disdain in Frau Kroll's voice, and wished she could explain. Instead, she turned around and left, hearing the *Mephisto Waltz* play in her mind. That's the music we are dancing to. Frau Kroll was not dancing. She stewed over things she could not change, and would rather die than admit it.

"I'm sorry, Frau Kroll, that you hate me so much," Olga shouted back.

The door slammed shut.
"Goodbye, Mother."

Chapter 25

Oberst Muller entered the divisional headquarters of the 1st Fighter Division at Doeberitz, in the outskirts of Berlin. The airmen called it the battle opera house because of its amphitheater-like structure. The nervous activity, foul air, hum of ventilators, and ticking of teleprinters combined with the low buzz of the telephone operators aggravated his headache. It had been throbbing since yesterday, when he saw the latest map on Soviet advances. His beloved homeland was doomed, despite all the sacrifices the people had made, and would make. Hitler was not about to surrender, nor was there any hope for that miracle weapon—a manned rocket that would repel the bombers invading Germany. Before impact, the pilot would bail out. A tricky maneuver, but it worked and would keep the bombers at bay, at least for a day or two. The Allies would quickly find out that the Reich had only a hundred of them. Still, it would boost morale and slow down the destruction, so that the refugees from the East could escape the Soviets. They should have been put into operation three months ago. For some unexplainable reason, Hitler refused to deploy them, or the squadrons of fighter planes and spare fuel he kept for emergencies. What was he waiting for? Was he so entrenched in his own make-believe world that he did not realize the true state of the Vaterland? It was diminishing at an alarming rate. How could he sit in his comfortable bunker, knowing that thousands of his men were being slaughtered? Was he waiting for the Allies to smoke him out? If Stauffenberg's assassination had succeeded, Germany could've sued for peace, like Italy. Muller had grappled with the thought from the time he had learned of the heroic act. As an officer of the Luftwaffe, rather than a member of the Party, he was proud of his profession.

Hitler had become paranoid, and suspected every general. Even Rommel, German's national hero, had been obliged to commit suicide so that he could be promoted and given a heroes burial.

Rubbing his skull, Muller wished he could rearrange the illuminated writing that projected position, altitude, strength and course of enemy formations, as well as his own. The dots changed according to reports and observations from radar sets, aircraft spotters, listening posts, reconnaissance planes, and units in action. There would be no action on his part today. His orders read: "Top priority is the operation of fast bomber formations at the front line area by day, and strafer-aircraft against the same targets by night. The loss of the synthetic oil production demands that the operation of all fighter defense be curtailed." No fuel for his fighter squadrons! The cities would be undefended. He unbuttoned his coat, "So, what's going on?"

Leutnant Kraft, in charge of operations, pointed to the dots. "Some 244 bombers are heading toward Berlin." The loss of his leg had grounded him from active duty. "The question is, what will old Harris do with his other 750 serviceable bombers tonight? And where will the 244 drop their cargo? Leipzig?"

Muller shrugged. "Could be. Let's keep an eye on them!" He was upset, and did not care if his younger assistant noticed it. As officer in the German Luftwaffe, he considered every enemy bomber entering German air space unhampered a personal defeat. He ached to fight them, but his men were grounded like naughty children, while the enemy came and went as he goddamn pleased. How could it have come to this?

His orderly filled his tea cup. The cigarette tasted like hay, and smelled like burning straw.

Why did the bombers change course, rather than head toward Berlin? The third formation of red arrows on the screen showed that this would not be the usual nuisance raid on Berlin.

"I think they're heading for Leipzig," Kraft said.

Muller studied the arrows. "I believe they're heading for Dresden!"

"Dresden, Herr *Oberst*? They wouldn't—not Dresden!"

"And why not?" Muller said sarcastically, ready to smash the screen.

Half an hour later, there was no doubt. "Alarm Dresden *Klotsche* to scramble the V/NJG 5 night-fighter squadron off the field. That blood-thirsty son-of-a-bitch Harris is after Dresden. God help Dresden!"

Anyna jumped up and down in her seat, laughing at the three clowns mounting an obstinate donkey. They looked for his head under his tail, checked his hooves for fleas, and coaxed the balking animal to kneel. Sarrasani was Germany's second ranking circus, and had a theater-like winter home in Dresden with the necessary stables and facilities for its famous lions, elephants, Arabian horses, and polar bears. Olga, Ingrid, and Anyna enjoyed the Flying Aces' incredible trapeze stunts. Scantily dressed girls rode bareback horses standing up. Elephants sat on small stools, while trained monkeys in bell-hop uniforms performed tricks.

The *Rakotzy March* accompanied six black stallions in a dance number. How gracefully they placed their front hooves. Many of the children in the audience had come in their Mardi Gras costumes. Anyna would not part with her red cap and cape. Then three gymnast's performed to *I Know Some Day A Miracle Will Happen.*

"Ingo loves the circus," Ingrid said. "We had a trapeze in our yard. You should have seen him, as agile as a monkey. Did you hear him play the piano?"

"No," Olga whispered, to not disturb the people around them.

The sirens blared. Struck by panic, Olga clawed the armrests of her seat, suppressing the urge to jump up and run. Had she missed the boat again?

Two clowns announced, "The hundred forty ninth false alarm. Everybody knows that Tommy will not hit us. Still, we must obey and go to the shelter."

"Obedience is a virtue," teased his counterpart with panache, strutting around the arena like an arrogant rooster. "In case you don't know where to go, the shelter is right underneath this building. Follow the signs. There you'll be as safe as a baby in his mother's womb. After the all clear we'll resume the show." He rocked an imaginary baby in his arms, fumbled with a pacifier, and cooed, "rock-a-bye baby."

The chuckling audience filed toward the exit.

Olga stopped Ingrid. "Let's not go down."

"What? Of course we must. They'll arrest us."

"I know. Still, come with me, Ingrid. This shelter is not safe."

Ingrid jerked free from Olga's hold. "Don't be silly."

"Ingrid, please..." Olga pleaded.

"Now look, Olga," Ingrid demanded, "we must do as we're told. I will not turn you in, though I should. For your own good." Her eyes darkened like her mother's. The mouth tightened. Fighting off the stream of people running toward the shelter, Olga begged, "Please, Ingrid, listen to me," and tugged at her arm.

"Keep going," grumbled one of the women. "You're blocking the way. The toilet is to the right."

Ingrid followed Olga to the wall, away from the crowd. "You listen to me, Olga," she said irritably. "I'm going down and you'd better do the same."

"I guess we must part company," Olga said. They exchanged a polite hug. "Goodbye, Ingrid."

The loudspeaker announced: "*Achtung! Achtung!* A large formation of enemy bombers is approaching the city. Acute danger of attack. Proceed to the shelter immediately. Anyone caught in the open will be arrested."

"You see, Olga!" Ingrid said. "You'd better come down."

Olga pulled Anyna away from the crowd. This time, she would listen to her inner voice. Near the toilet, she found an emergency exit and left the building. Out in the street the sirens wailed, urging people to seek shelter. The ominous droning of heavily loaded bomber squadrons announced their presence and the purpose of their visit. Dresden would come under fire. Panting into the frosty air, she pulled Anyna along a wall.

Anyna screamed out as bright red and green lights lit up the city. Every building became visible, marking the target area for destruction. She was right in it. Anyna tugged at Olga's arm. "Let's go to the shelter. Come Mami." Her frightened eyes wide, she stared at the silent city awaiting its execution. She knew that planes dropped bombs.

Olga wished she could fly away before the bombs fell. Small planes cruised overhead. Did they aim for her and Anyna? Above them flew big planes in perfect formation. The ground trembled under their heavy loads of explosives.

Wing Commander Maurice Smith, Master Bomber for the first attack, called out, "Controller to Marker Leader, can you hear me? Over!" He watched the Mosquito marker struggle with the Loran beams at 20,000 feet altitude. He hated this assignment. Last November he had been excused from acting as Master Bomber during the disastrous attack on Freiburg im Breisgau. Air Marshal Saundby had accepted Smith's objection when he explained that he had studied there, and had many friends living in the target area.

Though he had never visited Dresden, he saw no reason why they should destroy its irreplaceable, centuries-old art. His orders read that he must lead 244 Lancasters to drop their bombs on Dresden and create a sea of flames that would devour the city. Saundby had voiced his doubts. So had the American general, Spaatz, who'd told Sir Harris that the United States did not believe in terror bombing. But Churchill and Sir Harris were adamant about destroying Germany's morale. The bombs were available, why not use them since the war was coming to an end anyway? To Smith, that was the worst reason of all. How could they kill tens of thousands of civilians in order to get rid of their explosives? He'd rather see the bombs defused and scrapped. His stomach tensed. Where was the German anti-aircraft fire? Were they really running out of fuel? Then why this punishment?

He knew the German people, and had enjoyed their friendship. They had not asked for this war anymore than he had. Hitler had sucked them into his spell. Aryan superiority! How many Germans were blonde and blue-eyed anyway? A few in the north. Central and southern Germans were of medium height, had brown hair and brown eyes, including Hitler! They'd had no business imposing reparations the German people could never pay. Hitler refused; no wonder he became the man of the hour.

"I hear you loud and clear at strength five," reported the Marker Leader.

"Do you see the Primary Green dropped by 83 Squadron?"

"I do. The cloud isn't very thick."

"What do you make the base of it?"

"About 2,500 feet."

The flares burnt brilliantly over the city now. The town looked serene and peaceful, an enchanted princess unaware of the Evil breathing down on her. The Marker Leader radioed from his Mosquito. "Those black-and-white half-timbered buildings remind me of Hereford."

Smith ignored the comment. "I'm over the railway tracks, coming from the Central Station. I see the right-hand turn of the river and some bridges. We're on the right track. Going down to 2,000 feet. Releasing the 1,000 pound target indicator bomb. I'm at the hospital ground now. Some complex. Marked with a Red Cross." The Mosquito swooped over the stadium toward the river, at 300 miles an hour. The camera flashed over the hospital's railway siding. He could see people unloading wounded soldiers from a train. The bombs blasted the sidings off the map.

"Controller to Marker Leader. Back up. Back up."

"Controller to Plate-rack Force," repeated Smith into his VHF transmitter, flying in his Mosquito 3,000 feet above the silent city. "Come in and bomb glow of red T.I.'s as planned." It was 22:10—zero hour. He wanted to witness the commencement of the attack and make sure all went well, then get out. His tanks were getting light.

Not a single gun defended Dresden. Not even a muzzle flash. The heavy, four-engine Lancasters could bomb from lower altitudes for a more even distribution of bombs. A vivid blue flash split the darkness, as a stick of bombs fell wide of the target sector and exploded. It must have hit an electric power installation.

"The 4,000 and 8,000 pounders are smashing windows and ripping off roofs," announced the Marker Leader. "They are falling okay now. Over."

"Yes, Marker Leader. They look pretty good."

"Hallo, Plate-rack Force," said Master Bomber. "That's good bombing. Come in and aim for the red T.I.'s as planned. Careful, don't overshoot, somebody! Controller to Marker Leader. Go home now, if you like. Thank you."

"Hallo, Controller! Thank you. Going home."

By 22:18 hours, the bombing covered the whole sector. One or two tell-tale splashes of light appeared in the dark. Some of the bomb loads went down wide.

"Hallo, Plate-rack Force. Try to pick out the red glow. The bombing is getting wild now." Smith had three minutes to go. At 22:21, he called up Link 1 Lancaster aircraft for the last time, turned his Mosquito onto the new bearing, and headed home.

"Controller to Link 1. Send home!"

Panic driven, Olga ran aimlessly through the empty streets. The familiar buildings marked for demolition stood in passive silence. Where could she go? The shrieking sirens stopped their infernal howling. Cluster lights from the flare markers floated above her head, like giant balloons in a fantasy play. The bombers dropped their cargo. Shrill whistling pierced the heavy droning of their motors. The city quivered in anticipation of its death blow, like a condemned man awaiting his execution.

Olga clutched Anyna in her arms, as if she could protect her child. Anyna screamed, as bombs exploded in quick succession, creating a cauldron of Hell. Wave after wave of them, some close, others farther away, dropped as in a deadly hailstorm. The buildings around her collapsed. The air displacement blasts tore at her. Anyna stopped screaming, paralyzed by fear. Olga saw a sign marked for an air raid shelter, and picked Anyna up, carrying her to the shelter, ignoring the refugee wagon going up in flames. Horses neighed, reared, and dropped to the ground. Flames shot into the air, like fountains of light. "Open your mouth!" she shouted. Shock waves could burst their lungs. Glass shards rained from broken windows. Bile rose from the pit of her stomach and filled her mouth. "We're almost there."

Anyna did not hear her, nor did she care when a roof flew off, sending a cascade of sparks into the street, followed by a cloud of ancient dust. Olga coughed and jumped aside. The hull of a building burst into fresh flames. Dropping bombs whistled, crashed, and exploded. The heat melted the snow. Olga slipped in a hot puddle in front of the building that held the shelter. Anyna fell down, but did not cry. Together they stumbled inside, and ran down the narrow steps. The walls creaked. Gasping for air, she pounded on the door. "Open up. Quick." The beams shifted. The door opened. Helping arms pulled her and Anyna inside.

Frightened people asked questions. Olga had no answers, too shocked and exhausted to speak. The women comforted Anyna. The emergency bulb swayed. Cracks zigzagged across the stucco walls. Panic stricken faces, trembling lips, and whimpering children stared at the beams. Would they hold?

The walls heaved, but held.

Olga pressed Anyna to her bosom, her face a death mask. Should they survive this, would she ever overcome the shock? The thick air smelled of smoke, cold sweat, and fear. The densely packed people sat in silence. Cold sweat dripped from Olga's forehead and armpits. Anyna did not respond to Olga's cooing or her caresses. *Please, Father, protect us. I know, it's my fault.*

"Hell. This is Hell," a woman cried out. "I hate the men who do this to us."

Disapproving eyebrows shot up. A German woman was not supposed to complain.

"Think what the men are going through at the front," said an elderly woman in a fashionable hat.

Women endured, Olga thought, and obeyed. First their parents, then their teachers, husbands, and bosses. How could Ottie always assert herself? Where was she? What had happened to her? She was on her own, not obliged to sit like a martyr in a shelter that might or might not withstand the attack. Olga missed her feisty sister.

A massive explosion rocked the ground. Muffled screams, whimpers, then silence. The red emergency bulb swayed back and forth. Mothers clutched their children. The wall next to the door cracked and plaster drizzled from the tear. Ashen faces stared at each other. Cold sweat pearled on their foreheads. Trembling hands held each other. They were trapped.

A woman, her head covered with a scarf, sobbed into a handkerchief she pressed against her mouth. Suddenly she jumped up, clutching her baby, and forced her way between the people toward the door. "I can't stand this anymore. I must get out of here!"

"Panic means death," said a man in the mustard colored uniform of the S.A. as if this were an everyday occurrence.

"This is the best place you can hope to be right now," Olga said softly, remembering what it was like outside. "I've been through this before, in Berlin and Litzmannstadt. This is a solid shelter. We're lucky."

"We didn't need them," the woman justified the lack of shelters. "Nobody expected an attack on Dresden." The conversation distracted people from their fear.

"Our Fuhrer promised total war. Here it is," the lady in the hat said.

Fight to the last man and woman, Olga thought.

A heavy bomb hit the ground. The earth shook. Frightened eyes stared at each other, and the walls. "A blockbuster," the SA man said. "The shelter was built with foresight."

The women nodded gratefully. The second blockbuster threw them against each other, as if they sailed on a stormy sea. "Dear God, have mercy." The walls swayed. Children whimpered. People clenched their teeth. Nobody wanted to be blamed for weakness and panic, or worse, hysteria. The red bulb flickered. The door cracked at the frame. Powdered plaster seeped in, followed by a stream of black smoke.

"We must get out of here," Olga cried out. "Else we'll be buried alive."

The member of the S.A., a scrawny man in his late fifties, unbolted the door. Smoke gushed in. He slammed it shut with the help of two other men. People coughed and wretched. "Dip your scarves into the water buckets and follow me through the emergency exit to the shelter on Liliengasse."

Wet scarves wrapped over faces, people climbed gingerly over the debris blocking the steep narrow stairs. The front door had been blown off and hung on its hinges. Olga pushed it aside and crawled through, pulling Anyna behind her. Flames licked at them.

"Everybody back!" ordered the SA man. "The emergency exit. Quick. The walls are collapsing."

More bombs exploded.

"That fire will kill us."

"Keep going," Olga told Anyna, facing the flames engulfing the city. Some people caught phosphorous on their coats and threw themselves into hot puddles, then ran off screaming as living torches.

The bombing stopped. The planes departed into the night. Their job was done. The flames crackled noisily, feeding on wooden beams, household goods, and equipment. They swooshed about in sheets.

"They always bomb twice," Olga mumbled. "We must get back to the circus," she told Anyna. They walked quickly despite the wild conflagrations raging everywhere. The bombers had done a thorough job. Hot gusts of wind blew into the fire.

Two boys in soiled Hitler Youth uniforms operated a fire hose. All the water of Dresden could not touch the work of the incendiaries and time-delayed explosives. Many of the water pipes were broken, and flooded the cobble stones. If it were not for Ingrid and Mathilde, Olga would leave Dresden on foot.

Coughing people streamed from the shelters and searched for a way home. Others dug for family members in the hot debris. Wrecked wagons, charred horses, and burning trucks blocked the streets. The smoke and ashes irritated Olga's throat and eyes. The ocean of flames would burn the letters she had hauled all the way from Litzmannstadt. She touched the one she always carried with her in her bra. It would stay with her as long as she lived, or until they were together again.

Blockbusters had formed craters big enough for a bus. Buildings collapsed as soon as the their beams caved in. Flames licked through window openings like billowing curtains. Brigades of workers arrived, among them POW's and foreign laborers. Injured people were placed on stretchers and carried off. Fire engines passed, noisily picking their way around the obstacles. Olga pulled Anyna aside, not to be run over.

The Sarrasani complex burnt like a giant torch. Five dappled horses in their show finery huddled frightened in the street. A llama ran aimlessly from side to side, looking for an escape. Soldiers cleared the emergency entrance, their coats dripping wet.

"What about the people in the shelter?" Olga asked, wiping the sweat from her face.

The man looked up, his face glistening. "Full hit. The shelter wasn't reinforced. It couldn't withstand the blockbuster."

"What about the people?" Olga asked, though she knew the answer.

He shrugged. "See for yourself. Do you have somebody in there?"

Swallowing the lump in her throat, her eyes blinded with tears, she could see that nobody could survive the flames rising from the open hole. Ingrid would not listen. For once, Olga had done the right thing. From now on she would always follow her inner voice, and ignore the people who tried to stop her.

Anyna pulled Olga's hand. "Come on, Mami. It's too hot. And I'm tired."

"A quick death," the man said, running the back of his sleeve over his smudged face. "God knows what happened to all those refugees at the station. The wounded. That's what they mean by total war."

The wounded, Olga thought. They were not meant to live after all.

"We must find Omi," Olga said, wishing she had a hand cart for Anyna. The child was too heavy for her to carry, and too tired to walk on her own.

At 1:30, three hours after the first attack on Dresden, Squadron Leader C.P.C. de Wesselow, the appointed Master Bomber of the second attack, headed toward the target with his incendiaries. The 529 Lancasters under his command carried enough high explosives to spread the fires and keep the heads of the fire fighters down. He was glad to be in the air, rather than in that city whose fate he was about to deliver. The first wave of the No. 3 Bomber Group was 4,000-pound high explosive blockbusters and 750-pound clusters of incendiaries. The second wave included a 500-pound general purpose high-explosive bomb and the 750-pound clusters. Another group would drop small bomb containers and metal trunks from their bomb bays, creating showers of small bombs. These scattered incendiaries had a useful random effect, and 650,000 of them were on their way to finish off Dresden.

At 1:23, the Blind Illuminator Lancasters would release their flares. At 1:28, the Master Bomber arrived. The whole center of the city was already swept by a violent fire-storm, making it impossible to identify the target point. A strong south-westerly wind and the pall of smoke from the burning city obscured the whole eastern section.

`"Deputy Master Bomber to Master Bomber."

"Come in, Le Good."

"Do you want us to concentrate our bombing on the burning area, or what?"

De Wesselow thought for a moment. Why waste more bombs on what looked like a hundred percent hit by the previous attack? Besides, the smoke was so thick that the markers could not be distinguished.

"Can't see the railway yards either," the Deputy said. "Concentrate the main force on areas not affected by the previous attack. First to the left, then to the right, and finally over the existing fire and flare areas."

Both the Master Bomber and his Deputy stayed over the target area throughout the twenty-minute attack to observe the effects of the raid. Despite their careful monitoring, the marshalling yards to the south-west, their original target, had escaped major damage.

Perhaps the Americans would have better luck. By the time they arrived, the smoke should have dissipated, giving them good visibility. The bomb blankets of their 1,350 Flying Fortresses and Liberators could hardly miss the yards. The Reds were pushing westward. If they kept up their momentum, they could hit Dresden within a week. In that case, the marshalling yards might come in handy.

"To all bombers! Well done. Let's go home!" de Wesselow ordered. Smith was right, he thought. There was no flak, nor a single fighter around. After that flak barrage over the Ruhr, this run was a piece of cake.

Chapter 26

Olga reached a wide, four-lane boulevard with a median of what had been a row of trees. Bombs had snapped off their crowns, leaving decapitated stumps backlit by the eerie light of the fire. Dazed residents wandered past, scattering this way and that to escape the spreading flames. The fire was everywhere.

"Looks bad," a wounded airman said in passing, then stopped.

Olga choked back her tears. "My mother…"

"The shelters are reliable. They have underground connections like the tunnels of moles. I wouldn't worry too much. Once the fire dies down…" His voice was hoarse. "Go to Terrassen-Ufer by the river. The fire can't hurt you there."

She noticed his pinned sleeve. As a nurse, she had grown accustomed to amputations and missing limbs. Did Ingo still have all of his?

Anyna clung to her arm. "Let's go, Mami."

The airman lingered on, the strain of the past hour engraved on his sweaty face. "I've been through two years of war," he said, as if to himself. "The savagery of it all." He swallowed his curses. "The emergency crews will get the people out from their shelters and extinguish the fire," he assured Olga. "Your mother will be all right. But you'd better get out of here. Incendiaries are nasty business. That's their purpose. Tommy did quite a job. Go to the river." He walked away, and joined a crew of firefighters shooting water at a burning wall.

Trucks blew their horns and rang their bells. A wall collapsed, and two people screamed. Olga searched for a shelter where they could sit down and rest. *The enemy always bombs twice* drummed through her skull like a splitting headache.

Anyna trudged along, ignoring the charred remains of corpses, sprawled horse carcasses, and burning wagons. She sloshed through puddles and stumbled over debris, her eyes and nose running, irritated by the thick smoke that curled from the smoldering buildings. Olga did not dare stop. Every time she cleared her parched throat it only grew more raw. The wet blanket on her shoulders had dried. Their shoes were soaked and wrecked. A firefighter leaned against his pump.

"Would you please hose us down?" Olga asked.

The cold water perked her up. Anyna shook herself like a dog, then trudged on. Ingo would be crushed when he learned that his beloved Dresden had turned to a pile of rubble. But his home in Neustadt should be all right. The target had been Old Town.

Her inner voice grew louder. She must leave the city. The Red Army would arrive soon. From Altmarkt to the Elbe River was at least a half-hour's walk. Ingrid's wet shoes pinched. A sobbing woman crouched by the bleeding remnants of her horse. "I should've known better than stay in this city," she told Olga. "We needed rest. Dresden was supposed to be safe. Nicky pulled us all the way from East Prussia. He needed some rest." A boy Anyna's age tugged at his mother's her sleeve. *"Komm Mutter. Wir mussen gehn."*

Olga patted the woman's shoulder. "I'm a refugee too."

A brigade of POW's dug for trapped people in the rubble of a building. Olga passed an emergency stations where young women dressed wounds and set up soup kitchens. But she must not stop. Her inner voice urged her on.

The cupola of the Frauenkirche cathedral stood in a wreath of flames just as she had envisioned it that afternoon. The solid stone walls did not burn. Had Gottfried arrived? Should she look for him at his uncle's shelter? It would be so good to see him, to have a friend, somebody to lean on.

Anyna dropped to the ground. "I can't go on, Mami. I can't. And I won't." Her Little Red Riding Hood outfit was in shreds, the cap askew. Dark smudges streaked her face. "I don't care if I burn up. I'm tired, Mami."

"Just a little ways longer, darling. We're almost there."

"Where's *there*?" she demanded stubbornly. "I'm tired. I want to go to bed."

In a flash of anger, Olga grabbed Anyna's shoulders and shook her. Anyna's spiritless head wobbled back and forth. "Now stop this! Pull yourself together and act like the baroness you claim to be. I have no bed, not even a room. Nothing. We can't stay here. See that?" She pointed at the burning buildings. "We must get out of here. The fire is spreading. See that cupola? That's where Tante Lucie stayed. We'll go there and rest."

"But I can't go on, Mami," Anyna insisted, tears running down her hot cheeks.

Olga jerked Anyna to her feet. "Stop saying that. Get up and walk. Remember, *the enemy always strikes twice.*"

Anyna balked like the donkey they had seen at the circus.

Exasperated, Olga plopped down beside her child and buried her head in her arms. Anyna was right—what difference did it make whether they died now or later? The bombers would return and finish them off. Father awaited her in Heaven. Ingo would soon join them, if he wasn't awaiting them already.

A middle-aged man in a stained SA uniform reached for Olga's hands. "You'd better keep going," he urged. "The fire will build up to a storm, like a hurricane. There will be no escape. I saw it happen in Hamburg."

"A firestorm?" Olga asked, incredulous. "My daughter is exhausted."

"Is that so?" The man spoke like a schoolmaster. "Surely a big girl like you can walk two more blocks." He winked at Olga. The cut across his big face reminded her of Ingo, only this man was much older, had a clean-shaven face, and spoke in a Bavarian dialect. He pulled Anyna up.

"I'm a baroness," she said, and stomped her little foot on the wet flagstones. "And I am tired, can't you see?"

"That's pretty obvious. Still, take my advice and get to Augustus Bridge before it is blown up. Neustadt was barely hit. Once you get across the river, you'll find help. I know it's quite a ways, but you can do it. Perhaps you can find a ride. Whatever you do, you must not stay here." He touched his lips with his forefinger and whispered confidentially, "Don't tell anybody that I told you. So you see, little baroness, or should I call you Little Red Riding Hood? You'd better get going before the big bad wolf gets you."

"I'm not afraid of the wolf," Anyna said, in her haughty baroness voice.

"Good. Then get to the river."

Anyna took Olga's hand. "That's as far as I'll go. Not a step farther. Then I'll sit down and wait for Uncle Ingo."

"Why don't you do that. I supposed Uncle Ingo is a very important person."

"Oh yes. He's an officer and has an iron cross."

"Then you would want to look your best for him, not burnt to a crisp."

A strong, hot wind stoked fresh flames.

Minutes later she heard the drone of approaching bombers. Firefighters exchanged quizzical glances. People stopped digging. Others dropped the furniture they had rescued from their damaged homes, and ran. A siren wailed out. Fear struck Olga. The deep roar in the sky announced another armada. The air vibrating, Olga and Anyna ran after the people hurrying across the square. Firefighters left their stations, and hurried toward the shelter as flares cast their brilliant light over the already stricken city. They hung suspended over the Frauenkirche. Old Town would get a second going over. This time there would be nothing left. The deep, steady roar of the heavily loaded bombers became louder and louder. There had to be hundreds of them. What more did they want?

Anyna stepped into puddles. The water splashed into her shoes. "Run faster, Mami."

The man had mentioned Hamburg. That firestorm had been the worst in history because of the phosphorous the Allies had dropped. Thousands had burned to death.

Anyna stumbled and fell. Olga picked her up, and dragged her to the shelter where firefighters, soldiers, women in singed coats, and their shrieking children funneled into the narrow entrance. Inside, Olga squeezed through the tightly packed people who would not budge. The stuffy cellar quickly filled up to capacity. People sat on crude benches or their emergency suitcases, or stood in the packed space, their eyes frozen with fear. They knew what was coming, and wondered whether the shelter could withstand the unimaginable impact of the explosives about to be dropped on them.

Olga squeezed herself and Anyna toward the emergency exit, in case the entrance broke through. She could not imagine being buried alive. Anyna sank to the floor and clung to Olga's legs. More and more desperate people rushed into the shelter: soldiers, nurses, girls from the Labor Service, boys in their Hitler Youth uniforms, elderly men with Home Front armbands, injured women, mothers and their children, and older couples who comforted each other. All listened to the merciless droning overhead.

The whistling sent cold chills down Olga's spine. Her heart beat against her chest as if it needed more space. The bombs exploded in quick succession, shaking the earth. Pallid, quivering lips mumbled prayers. Eyes squeezed shut. Fingers pressed into waiting ears. Children, paralyzed with fear, clung to their mothers. A man cleaned his fingernails with stoic indifference. His wife stared at the concrete floor, as if she wished she could clean it instead of waiting to be blown up. Or was she hiding her fear from him, intimidated by his sneers? Olga sympathized with her, glad that Lothar was gone from her life. Lothar. Why did he come to mind now? Because he was part of the evil world?

Her arms around Anyna, she felt the trembling little body and smelled the smoke on her torn outfit. "Think of a song. *Schlafe mein Prinzchen schlaf ein.*"

"I told you I could walk to the bridge," Anyna said. A queen did not wail, she fought. Her little girl fought.

A young mother rocked her baby, crooning a lullaby. She repeated the same line over and over again like the patients at the asylum in Litzmannstadt. Was Beate still alive?

A tall soldier rushed in, then helped with the heavy plank that sealed the door and bolted it shut like the hatch of a submarine. The depth charges kept dropping. Their explosions reverberated through the shelter. Her heartbeat doubled. Olga felt drained from the strain of fearing for her and Anyna's life. There was no hope for Mutter and Tante Lore now.

The tall soldier turned around. Their eyes met.

"Gottfried!" she cried out. For a moment, she forgot the trembling earth and the explosions causing it. Even her fear. Father had not abandoned her.

"Olga!" His greeting sounded like deliverance.

People let Gottfried squeeze past to Olga while blockbusters ripped the world apart. He was thinner, his features more pronounced, but still exuded the debonair confidence she had fallen in love with so long ago. The crude uniform did not belong to him, but it fit into this place. The days when they wore fine clothes were gone. She pressed into his embrace. With Anyna between them, they felt protected against the devastation, resting in the warmth of kindred spirits. The earthquakes, thunderclaps, and fires outside were no longer part of their lives. People watched them, and drew courage from the chance union. They envied the child for her place in his arms. Perhaps their own loved one would show up unexpectedly.

"Olga," he whispered, kissing her sweaty cheek. His tender touch and familiar scent spelled home.

"Lucie left yesterday," she told him, resting against his shoulder. "I had hoped I might run into you. We were on our way to Uncle Hermann's." The emergency bulb swayed. The reinforcement beams quivered under the impact of the explosions.

Gottfried nodded. "I talked to him, then left hoping to find you."

"And here we are. Guided toward each other."

A bomb hit the building above. People cried out. Anyna clung to Gottfried, as if he could protect her. "I'm so scared!"

"We're in a good shelter. See? It can't get any worse than a direct hit." His voice sounded compassionate and reassuring.

Olga believed him. Should they be killed, they would die together. "Our music," she said, clasping his hands and swallowing. But fear kept raking her body. *Music. I must think of music.* Nothing came. Blank. Gershwin. Where was the *Mephisto Waltz?* She must take control of the violence in her heart. Stay collect and in control. Gottfried could not see her eyes. He leaned his cheek against her head.

Plaster and dust trickled through jagged cracks in the door. The ground shook. How much longer would the ceiling hold up? Where was that music? *Yours Is My Heart Alone.* That melody was part of her life. Where was it now? Gottfried picked up Anyna. She put her arms around his neck and clung to him. They were together. *I must not faint. Breathe. Think of music. Ingo. Our wedding night.*

"We'll be all right," Gottfried assured her, but his voice betrayed him. He was just as afraid as she. How much longer would it take for those Flying Fortresses to drop their bombs? How many more did they have? A personal message from Mr. Morgenthau. "*Yours Is My Heart Alone.* Can you think of the melody, Gottfried? We played it so often."

The walls and floor shook, as if they were on a boat at the mercy of a stormy sea. The beams shifted. Olga closed her eyes and moaned. The melody. Where was that melody? She had always known it. Would the beams hold? Panicked eyes in waxen faces stared at the ceiling. Mothers rocked their whimpering children, "Don't be afraid. We'll be all right."

Olga hummed *Some Day a Miracle Will Happen.* Gottfried joined her, rocking Anyna to the beat. She did not move. Had she fallen asleep? How good it was to have Gottfried here. Their love was different than what she felt for Ingo. A bond they had shared for so long.

"Olinka! I never realized how much you mean to me," he whispered. His hot breath caught her ear. In that uniform he smelled of smoke and trains and sweat.

The light went out. Olga clung to Anyna. Gottfried held them. A moment later the emergency bulb came on again, swaying back and forth, mesmerizing the people watching it and the quivering walls.

In soft whispers, Olga told him how she had fled from Litzmannstadt, described the village where she had run into Ingo and found her mother, and the reluctant old Pole who had saved them.

"I believe in your magic, Olinka." His strained chuckle was no more than a feeble attempt at easing the tension. The thick and stuffy air lacked oxygen. "Father is with us."

Anyna's white face looked like a mask.

Olga felt nauseated and gasped for air. The densely packed people whispered, sighed, and said woeful prayers.

Another blast assaulted the already strained reinforcements. She gazed at Gottfried. "The people who built this shelter," he said, "had no idea they would be dealing with blockbusters. Weaponry decides the outcome of a war." Then whispered, "Ours is depleted. That's why you don't hear our defense." He did not even bother mention the miracle weapon. Gottfried probably considered it a laughable fantasy of a desperate Goebbels, as if the German people had it in them to protest. After learning that the generals who had plotted the assassination attempt on Hitler had been hung on butcher's hooks, all further attempts had stopped.

Gottfried hummed into the noise of the detonations, *Yours Is My Heart Alone.*

Olga's eyes lit up. "You got it. I just couldn't think of it."

The ceiling was cracking and crumbling now. The beams shifted. Children cried out. Hail Marys and Lord's Prayers were murmured in the din. Part of a wall collapsed and falling bricks injured two boys. Smoke seeped through the cracks. People coughed.

"We must get out through the emergency exit," Gottfried shouted against what sounded like a waterfall—the firestorm! Wax-like faces stared at him in awe.

"Get out! The fire!" Olga cried. Action distracted her from her fear. Gottfried and two other men unbolted the warped door. Debris spilled toward them. A thick cloud of smoke welled through the opening.

"Close it!"

The soldiers pressed their weight against the door, and pushed it shut. Gottfried clamped the plank down.

"Knock out the breakthrough," an officer ordered. A soldier grabbed the pickaxe and hammered against the bricks. Once the hole was big enough, Olga pushed Anyna through, then crawled out, followed by Gottfried.

The tunnel led to the adjacent shelter. It was not damaged, but the people inside looked as if they were sleeping.

"They're asphyxiated. Carbon monoxide poisoning," Gottfried said, pulling Olga and Anyna to the next emergency exit. "Quick, Olga. Hurry!" he shouted. "There's no oxygen."

The people following them turned around.

Olga stopped in front of a large gray cylinder, taller than she, blocking the way. It ticked.

"A time bomb," Gottfried said, pulling Olga away. In passing he picked up one of the buckets and splashed the water over their heads. Leaving the shelter he shouted, "Stay close. Watch the suction."

Outside, they were surrounded by sheets of fire. Their faces wrapped in wet shawls, they dodged toppling trees and avoided the now burning stacks of furniture people had rescued from the previous attack.

"We're lost," Olga cried, frying in the unbearable heat. Smoke rose from the back of her coat. The planes overhead still had more bombs to drop, feeding an insatiable demon.

Carrying Anyna, Gottfried shouted, "We must run to Neumarkt." Olga stayed at his heels. Billowing flames flooded the entire avenue and engulfed a woman pushing a pram. She was sucked into the inferno. Her screams echoed through the roar. Gottfried ran on. As long as they stayed in the middle of the street, they would get past the flames. Burning objects crashed down from collapsing buildings.

At the square, melting snow had filled the holes left by the bombs. They soaked their singed and smoking coats in the puddles.

Burning people, contaminated with phosphorous, jumped into a tall water tank. Their screams of pain quickly turned to shouts for help. When Gottfried and Olga reached for them, they could not catch the hands reaching up the iron wall. Swimmers grappled with each other to stay afloat. Olga bent down as far as she could. Gottfried caught her just before she would have been pulled in.

"We can't help them," he said and left. Their cries diminished. The fire roared.

"Never panic," advised an elderly man, whose coat had burned to tatters, his hair singed.

More and more living torches staggered to the square screaming. Olga and Gottfried pulled off their coats and helped extinguish the flames.

"We must get out of here!" Gottfried shouted. "To the river! I'll carry Anyna. You follow me. Remember, I will not stop for anything. This is our only chance of getting out alive. I know this city well. The river isn't far." He jogged off with Anyna on his shoulders. Olga cursed Ingrid's shoes. The distance between them grew. Olga slipped on the wet and broken cobble stones. Charred bodies littered the street amidst bits of timber, and blocked her path. Olga tripped on a brick and fell, burning her palms on the hot cobble stones. Sheets of flames closed in on her. Gasping for air, she searched for Gottfried. He was gone and so was Anyna. She would live.

Exhausted Olga could not force her body to hurry. "Father! Help!" Tears streamed from her burning eyes and dried instantly. A fiery roof came crushing down and blocked the street. Fresh flames shot up. "I must go on," Olga kept telling herself. "I must. I must. God help me." Hot suction pulled at her like tentacles from Hell. "Panic means death. Father!"

As soon as Gottfried reached the Elbe River, he put Anyna down and sucked in the cool air, pulling it deep into his hungry lungs. Floating shards of ice crashed against each other, driven by the force of the swelling stream. He sat down on a bench, and put Anyna on his lap. As a farmer, he had witnessed hailstorms destroy a crop, a late frost kill the blossoms that carried the promise of a plentiful harvest, and had seen a sudden thaw release more water than the river bed could hold. Tonight, man outdid nature. His weapons produced a force that rivaled a volcano's. But phosphorous was even deadlier than molten lava—it contaminated everything it touched and could not be extinguished. How could people hate each other so?

The ice on the river reflected the red glow of the fire. Its eerie beauty deepened his worry for Olga. Where was she? When had she fallen behind? He watched people run from the flames. Olga was not among them. Some of them had flames on the backs. They ran to the river, screaming. Desperate to extinguish the flames, they bent toward the water. Two of them slipped on the wet bank, were caught by the ice and carried away into the darkness. Their screams for help soon stopped. More people came, collapsed on the cold wet ground, and sobbed.

The bombers had left. A church bell rang out, battered in its tower by the powerful winds. Anyna slept in Gottfried's arms. Where was Olga? Should he risk his life searching for her? Return to the inferno? Their meeting in the shelter had left a deep bond, one that had evaded them all those years. Her adoration had flattered him. There had been others smitten by his voice. From the time he had fallen in love with Lucie she had been his life, or a good part of it. Passion, yes, but compassion? Now, in the midst of this disaster, so close to death, love had a different meaning. Olga was so much more than a pretty woman to lust after. Her despair, fear, and vulnerability moved him. A courageous young mother who would do anything to save her child, she had touched his innermost sentiments, that had nothing to do with the girl who had craved his attention. Olga needed his help. Only he could rescue her.

His days on earth were probably numbered. Facing the fire had shown him what lay ahead. That finality struck him—hard and merciless. He had enjoyed an exceptionally good life as an heir, a handsome and gifted musician with a tenor that sent women into ecstasy. He had taken all that for granted, rather than as special gift.

The fires consuming his adored Dresden would kill Olga. She deserved to live, and it was up to him to make it happen. He could not remember ever going out of his way for others. Now was his chance to show some gratitude for his good fortune.

Gottfried laid Anyna down on the bench he had been sitting on, and scanned the burning city. No sign of Olga. An unfamiliar tenderness welled up. "I must go and look for Mami," he told Anyna. "That may take some time. Promise that you will stay here, on this bench, no matter what. Don't wander off. I'll come back as soon as I can." He hugged her.

Sleepily, she put her arms around his neck and pressed her head against his cheek. "I want to go with you, Uncle Gottfried."

"Did you hear what I said, little Baroness?" he asked sternly.

She nodded. "Of course, Uncle Gottfried. You will go and look for Mami. I will stay here and wait for you."

"Good. You saw people die. I may not come back, nor Mami. If I'm not back when daylight comes up, go to Frau Kroll's on Gutenberg Street. Here is some money for the streetcar, though I doubt it will be running. Don't worry about her. She will not turn you away. Remember Gutenberg Street."

"I know, Uncle Gottfried. But I'd rather go to Frau Ehrhardt," she said in a clear voice, wide awake now.

He took off his coat, dipped it into the turbulent waters, and put it on again. The wet uniform dripped, chilling him like a cold compress. After a quick hug, he left Anyna and jogged into the burning city. "Olga, I'm coming."

Olga struggled to her feet, her hands burning from the hot stones. Cursing her ridiculous shoes, she picked her way around burning beams that had fallen across the street. The storm blew the flames off to the left now, leaving a tunnel-like opening over the charred wood. Running to get across before the wind shifted, she slipped on a mound of rubble, stumbled over to the other side, and fell into a gaping hole in the street. She landed on something soft.

"Sorry," she said to the woman under her. "You must get out. The fire is coming this way." No answer. Olga pulled at the shoulder. No response. Dead! Everybody in that hole was dead. Olga crawled out, and ran off.

A door in one of the damaged buildings opened. A women peeked out. "We're trapped."

"You must get to the river," Olga said, gasping, and followed the woman into a dark, smoke-filled hall. In the basements were people with their eyes closed. Were they asleep or dead? A bucket of water inspired her to wet her shawl and coat. Lightheaded, she looked around. The people made no effort to move, exhausted from lack of oxygen. She too felt the effect, and could barely move. But she must live.

In her wet coat, she braved the heat and hurried along the center of the street away from the howling flames. Screams erupted and died down. The immense heat had no equal. Olga breathed through her wet handkerchief, fighting the suction that pulled her toward the fire. Her head buzzed like a bee caught in an empty drum. She stumbled and fell to the hot stones. Father's light appeared. "Are you coming for me?"

Somebody lifted her, and carried her off. Father? Wet, coarse cloth rubbed against her cheek

"We'll make it, Olinka."

"Gottfried?" she whispered, folding her arms around his neck.

"Yes, Olinka. We're almost at the river."

He risked his life to save hers. "Gottfried!" She clung to his neck, and kissed his sweaty face. The heat and blazing fire no longer frightened her. He had come for her. Father had sent him.

"I can walk now," she said. "You're a true friend. You saved Anyna, and now me. How can I thank you?"

"You would have done the same for me."

Olga let him pull her toward the dark river. Soon, cool fresh air revived her. The scorching heat diminished. They slowed down. The pain in her feet and the blisters on her face could not dampen her joy, knowing that Gottfried had saved her. She took his hand and kissed it, overwhelmed with deep gratitude. "Thank you, my dear friend, from the bottom of my heart."

"There is Anyna," he said in a thick voice.

Olga saw her child curled up on a bench, watched over by other survivors. She ran and took Anyna into her arms. Sobbing, she looked up at him. "How can I thank you?"

Anyna awoke. "Mami! I knew you would come back."

"We're saved." He met her glance, tenderness and compassion in his eyes. Pain and suffering had mellowed his heart. She would give anything to save him, but destiny had other plans. Father would take him, and make his passing easy.

Leaning against each other, Olga, Gottfried, and Anyna dozed on the bench. Olga woke first and wiped the drizzle from her face.

"We must get going," Gottfried said, stretching his cold limbs. The fires were still raging. The Allies had done a thorough job. "Phosphorus acts like fuel that keeps the fires burning."

Olga shivered. The damp air rising from the turbulent river penetrated her wet coat.

"Neustadt was hit too," he said. "But not as badly. Probably stray bombs that did not find their target."

Survivors had gathered, and talked in low voices.

"We must get back to town," Olga said. "Look for my Mother. Tante Lore. Help the wounded."

Gottfried held her back. "There is nothing you can do for them, Olga. The fires are as deadly as ever. Whoever survived will have to find their way out. The fire consumed all the oxygen. Even if you could get past the fires, you would not get very far."

Father's warning came to mind—get across the bridge. A long walk, but she could do it now, after the rest. If necessary, they would carry Anyna and get to Ehrhardt's.

Gottfried agreed. He lifted Anyna up on his shoulders, and headed for the bridge.

"On the other side we might find a soup kitchen," Olga said.

Trucks, horse-drawn wagons, and fire engines passed in an endless procession, heading toward the stricken city. Rescue workers had been summoned from all over the county. Dazed people in tattered clothes and painful burns limped away, supporting each other. "Your beloved Dresden is no more," she said. "Ingo will be crushed when he finds out."

"He still has you. I'm sure that's more important now. During my student years my cousin and I used to walk along the banks of the river and have picnics in the meadows."

"Yesterday we had no idea that we would lose Dresden and our family," she said. "Anyna, remember the circus? How the children dressed up in costumes for Mardi Gras? Who would have thought."

"My outfit is ruined," Anyna said from her lofty seat on Gottfried's shoulders.

Among the flames, under a thick cloud of ashes, they could make out the *Kreutzkirche*, the tower of the Residence Castle and the round cupola of the Frauenkirche. A brigade of POW's passed in formation, detailed to fight the fires or do clean-up work.

At the end of the bridge, Gottfried put Anyna down. "There might be something in my pocket for a special young lady. Why don't you take a look, Anyna?"

Her face smudged with soot and ashes, her mittens torn, she reached into the large pocket of his greatcoat and pulled out a piece of candy in a pink wrapping. "Look, Mami! Candy! Thank you, Uncle Gottfried." She hugged him.

"That's for being such a good and brave little girl."

Approaching planes droned in the distance. Olga's heart jolted. She shot a frightened glance at Gottfried. "They wouldn't! Not again!"

He shrugged, his lips tense. "I guess they still have bombs to spare." The sarcasm in his remark hit Olga like a sledgehammer. She clenched her teeth, not to cry out and frighten Anyna.

"We may not get to a shelter in time," he said in a cold, calm voice. "And we can't stay here. They'll target the bridge again. With zero visibility they'll bomb at random."

Paralyzed with fear, Olga stared at the long bridge, where people and vehicles hurried off in both directions. Gottfried took her and Anyna's hands, and pulled them to the open space along the banks of the river. "Hurry. They'll be here in minutes." Olga could barely keep up with Gottfried, running along the wet and sandy path. No place to hide. Not a tree or shrub anywhere. She felt like a lightening rod, inviting the bombers to drop their explosives on her head. Once again the air vibrated from the deep roar of the planes bringing their lethal cargo.

"American Flying Fortresses," Gottfried said, panting. "Another armada." His presence kept her from throwing herself to the ground and surrendering to the inevitable. The thick cloud blanket, saturated with smoke and ashes, filtered out the daylight. Then the horrifying whistling of falling bombs broke out. In a few seconds they would strike. Olga dropped to the ground, Anyna beside her. Gottfried sheltered them with his body, as if he could save them from the blockbusters. Still, his arms gave her a sense of security and that vague comfort of not being alone. They held each other as the first cluster bombs exploded over the city. Some fell into the river. Olga heard the splash. With her eyes closed she awaited her death.

Anyna trembled. "Mami, Mami. I'm so scared."

"They can't see us," Gottfried assured her. "Stay low, and breathe deeply."

Minutes later Olga wriggled free, jumped up, and shouted at planes she could not see. So far, the bombs had fallen on the stricken city and exploded in the meadow, but had missed the bridge. Fresh fires broke out. Gottfried grabbed her arm, pulled her down, and pinned her to the ground. "That's enough. Now stay low," he ordered.

His command broke the spell. Back on the ground, she curled into fetal position and sobbed. "I can't take this anymore. Father, help us."

Gottfried and Anyna clung to Olga, trying to calm her down. She craved death now. Get it over with. Wave after wave of planes flew over Dresden, dropped their cargo, and turned around. After what seemed an eternity, the bombing stopped. The last planes left. Their roar diminished and faded away. Silence.

"Let's go," Gottfried said, and took Olga and Anyna in his arms. "Do you suppose the Ehrhardt's..."

"Yes, of course," Olga said, "they will take us in, if their home wasn't hit. Let's thank Father for saving our lives." Brushing the dead grass and mud from her wet coat, Olga watched the flames rise from the burning city. Several fires burned on their side of the river, but nothing big. The floating ice kept grinding downriver. Spring would come, no matter what men did to each other. The turf they stood on would once again be a meadow where children would play and lovers enjoy their romance.

"Look, Gottfried. The Frauenkirche Cathedral survived."

Holding each other Olga said, "The steeple of the Residence Castle and the Augustus Bridge survived. They might have missed the marshalling yards. But the hospital is probably gone. The wounded, doctors, and nurses found their final resting place." She wiped the tears from her eyes and kissed Anyna. "My brave little girl."

"They're gone, Mami," she said, as if she'd awoken from a nightmare. "Will they come back?"

"Let's hope not. Remember they always bomb twice."

"Yes, I know," Anyna said quickly. "But that was the third time."

"There are always exceptions," Gottfried said, fishing for another piece of candy.

Before they could reach the road, the sound of approaching planes appeared. This could not be, Olga thought.

"Finally our Luftwaffe," Gottfried said, leading the way along the narrow path that led back to the city. "No point in sacrificing them to those flying fortresses." The sound of the motors rose steadily. There they were. Fighter planes cut through the clouds. They had white stars. "Americans," he said, and pulled Olga and Anyna to the ground. The planes dove toward the bridge and machine-gunned the people hurrying away. They fired at people huddled along the banks, and the fire fighters who had come to rescue survivors. It seemed so unreal. Olga forgot to scream, numb from pain and horror, her nerves spent.

"Don't move," Gottfried ordered. "Those are Mustangs. They shoot at individuals."

Bullets sprayed the ground. Machine guns hammered them out like hail. The Americans wanted to make sure nobody got away. And why? So that the Russians would find an empty city in ruins? One of the fighters flew so low that his craft crashed into a wagon and exploded. People cheered. Other pilots avenged their buddy.

The Mustangs finally curved away, leaving Dresden a dead city. Olga thought of Sodom and Gomorrah—cities God destroyed for their sinful ways. What had the people of Dresden done to deserve this?

Anyna wailed inconsolably, her head buried in Olga's lap.

"I believe I am fresh out of candies," Gottfried said, and could not calm her. "Sorry, my little baroness. Come, let's find something to eat. There must be a soup kitchen somewhere."

"After this?" Olga said, following him to the street.

Neustadt, had also been scorched with incendiaries, obliging Olga and Gottfried to follow side streets to the Ehrhardt home. It had survived. The wooden shutters had protected the windows, which now let in the sparse light filtering through layers of ashes floating in the sky. Frau Ehrhardt and her daughter, Helga, received Olga and Gottfried with open arms. They mourned Ingrid's and Frau Kroll's death—her home had been hit. The bomb had killed Frau Kroll. Olga mourned her for Ingo's sake. She could not blame his mother for her attitude toward the woman he had chosen. Should they find each other, Olga would prove her wrong. Her heart overflowed with sorrow and went numb. First she would have to come to terms with her own mother's death. Gottfried's presence comforted her. He was like family now.

Hot goulash and bread settled Olga's composure. Anyna was too tired to complain, or did she understand that she had to do her part to make the situation bearable? Frau Ehrhardt heated the boiler so that Anyna could take a bath before bed, then Olga, and finally Gottfried would soak away the horror of the past hours. Helga found some clothes and shoes for Olga, while Frau Ehrhardt rummaged through the attic where she kept some of Helga's childhood favorites. Returning, she held up a pleated skirt in Scotch plaid and a red sweater that would be just right for Anyna. "Helga insisted I keep them. I am sure she will be glad for Anyna to have them. I could offer you some of my husband's clothes, Herr Hasselblatt," she said, "but I know that you must wear your uniform."

"Or be executed as a deserter."

The following morning, the radio announced that neither the marshalling yards nor the railroad tracks had been seriously damaged. Trains from Neustadt would be running again in a day or two, but the conflagration in Dresden could not be extinguished. The smoke blended with the clouds and seeded them with ashes, creating a thick blanket that kept out most of the light and spread for miles. Survivors somehow left the city. The remainder were considered dead. Emergency crews worked under great difficulties, coping with smoldering debris and duds searching for trapped people. The fire had burnt up the oxygen, killing most people through asphyxiation. They piled bodies on trucks and wagons, and hauled them to the square where they were laid out for identification.

As soon as the post office opened Olga sent a wire to Ingo. "Your mother and Ingrid perished. STOP. Deepest sympathy. Anyna and I are fine. STOP. We're heading for Aunt Gertie's. Olga."

On Thursday Olga and Gottfried crossed the bridge, heading toward the smoldering city. The ice kept streaming by, as if nothing had happened.

"Look!" Olga cried out, "the Frauenkirche held up as long as it could. Dresden's icon gave up and collapsed."

Gottfried took her hand, and swallowed hard as fresh flames appeared. Dresden's most treasured building had succumbed. "The heat must have eroded the mortar," he said in a thick voice. He had tears in his eyes. Her arm around his waist, she leaned her head against his shoulder. What could she do other than show him that he was not alone? Consoling him made her own pain bearable. For her, the worst was yet to come. In a way she hoped they could not find her mother, that she had not been incinerated with thousands of other victims, leaving Olga thinking she had survived somehow.

Friday the sickening yellow-brown smoke still billowed from the burning city. Charred fragments of buildings, trees, and vehicles that had been sucked up into the sky appeared miles away, coming down in the steady drizzle of wet ashes. Olga and Gottfried had gone to Old Town to identify her mother, Ingrid, and Tante Lore among those that had been lined up by the thousands. Despite her cologne-drenched handkerchief, Olga felt nauseated by the stench. Even those who had died of asphyxiation had deteriorated in the heat. The broken streets were covered with mud and ashes. How lucky she had been that Gottfried had saved her and Anyna.

"Here they are," Olga whispered forcing herself to look at the remains of her mother and Tante Lore's bodies, which only days ago had been alive and well. If Gottfried had not held her up, Olga would have collapsed. Summoning the last shreds of her will-power not to embarrass him, she stuffed the handkerchief into her mouth and muffled her screams. All she had was Anyna.

"It was a gentle death," he said, a consolation of sorts. No, she had to be fair. Knowing her mother had burnt to death, phosphorous on her body, would have been unbearable. She had to be grateful for that, and for him, and for having Anyna and Ingo. He was alive, she was certain of that. Father had promised.

Gottfried wanted to see whether his relatives had survived. The hotel had to be in ruins like all the buildings in the city, leaving hollow walls and random piles of rubble in a dismal world of total destruction. In this city, all life had been extinguished. The once unique Frauenkirche, built by fitting large stones to support each other until they formed the dome, had turned into a huge mound covering the whole square. Uncle Hermann and his family had perished. Gottfried stood in front of the fractured walls and said a silent prayer, then they returned to Frau Ehrhardt in Neustadt.

The news claimed that some 150,000 had died. Nobody knew how many refugees and wounded had been in the city, nor how many people had been at the station waiting for a train that never came. Hundreds of children evacuated from the war zone were among the victims. The heat had reached 1,000 degrees, and killed seventy percent of the victims through carbon monoxide poisoning.

By Saturday the railroad tracks were repaired. "We can leave from Cottbus," Gottfried said. They would travel to Berlin together. He would return to his unit in nearby Zossen, while Olga and Anyna would go to Tante Gertie's in Wunsdorf.

The station was packed with people eager to escape the Russians, now a mere seventy kilometers away. Their tanks could show up any day now, taking over what was left of Dresden. Frau Ehrhardt would stay. She saw no point in fleeing. Sooner or later, one of the Allies would capture her and do whatever victorious armies do. She had packed sandwiches and a bottle of tea for their trip. As a soldier, Gottfried was given preferential access to the train and could pull Olga and Anyna along.

Squeezed into an overcrowded compartment, they spent the nineteen hours reminiscing about their past rather than making plans for the future. Bombed-out stations obliged the train to make detours and hide in the country during the day to avoid being attacked from the air.

"If I were you, Olga, I would stay away from Berlin," Gottfried insisted.

Olga ignored his warning, and headed for Wunsdorf.

Chapter 27

Olga stood at the window of her room in Aunt Gertie's home, looking over the dormant vegetable garden. Passing clouds cast their shadows over bare fruit trees. The snow had melted. Two months had passed since she and Anyna had arrived at Tante Gertie's door, exhausted and hungry. Ingo's aunt had welcomed them with open arms and nursed them back to health while they grieved over the loss of their families in Dresden and awaited news from Ingo.

So far this small resort on the outskirts of Berlin had been spared by the bombs that dropped daily on the capitol. Olga's and Anyna's nerves had settled down. The constant rumbling of the ongoing bombardments had become familiar background noise. Nobody knew when and how the final act would manifest itself. Hitler directed the war from his bunker and believed in miracles. Could he hold out until the Americans reached the city rather than the Russians? Not that he would surrender. He fought for his life on the blood of those he commanded. Olga's intuition steered her west, like so many others, rather than live through the final showdown. She would not need a suitcase for the dress and coat Tante Gertie had made for her, and neither did Anyna. Was it already too late?

Today was Friday, the 20th of April—Hitler's birthday. The radio was dead. Just as well. No more talk about miracle weapons and the like. The thousand-year Reich was down to its capitol. While Hitler toasted his birthday—a curse on mankind—his men and those of his enemies fought on because nobody would let them stop.

Olga joined Tante Gertie in the kitchen and picked up the *Volkischer Beobachter*, the ink on the flimsy paper staining her fingers. While she scanned the headlines, Tante Gertie stirred farina into boiling milk for Anyna's breakfast. "Our Fuhrer," Olga read aloud, "accepted the congratulations of his people in his bunker where he will celebrate his special day. He assures the German people that final victory is at hand.

The miracle weapon will defeat our enemies and return the Reich to its full and deserved glory…" Olga dropped the paper on her lap, careful not to smudge the white apron of her nurse's uniform. "Aren't they ashamed to print this?"

Tante Gertie shrugged her broad shoulders. Unlike her sophisticated sister, Lore, she believed in homey comfort and did not bother with fashionable clothes. Being a widow, she felt no inclination to improve her appearance. She wore her gray hair in a bun, and rarely bothered putting on her good shoes. "Who wants to be executed?" she asked.

Olga felt that onslaught of fear again. "We must leave," she said, wiping the ink from her fingers. "The Russians…"

Anyna, wearing a blouse and skirt Tante Gertie had made for her, grabbed Olga's hand. "It's all right, Mami. Our teacher said that we'll be protected. You mustn't always get upset." Her cheeks had filled out, and had a rosy complexion. Tante Gertie's beautician had cut the hair into a page boy with bangs. She could not do enough for her little baroness.

The farina bubbled in the enamel saucepan. The kettle whistled. Anyna sat in her chair at the kitchen table and watched Tante Gertie pour warm milk into a mug with rabbits painted on it. It had belonged to Tante Gertie's son Rolf, who had been killed in action—shot down over the Channel. Her husband had lost his life in Italy.

"Why can't Hitler accept that it's over," Olga said. "What is he waiting for? The Russians to knock at his bunker?" She sipped her tea, despite its bitter taste.

"He can't face defeat and death, admit that he lied to us," Tante Gertie said. The picture of a handsome young man, his hand on the Messerschmitt fighter plane he had commanded was Rolf. It stood next to the radio in a silver frame.

"I'm so glad you came, Olga. You're my family now."

Olga hugged Tante Gertie, glad to be in Wunsdorf, a picturesque town where Berliners had their weekend homes. "I'd better go to work now," she said. As a nurse's aide, she was excused from digging trenches or setting up traps for Allied tanks. Hitler had declared Berlin a fortress with the usual consequences. It would be a battle to the last man. Her heart bled for all the people yet to be sacrificed. So far the Allies had not bombed the German High Command where Gottfried was stationed. If she could only get rid of that nagging feeling that she must leave. But travel was risky. During the day dive bombers attacked the trains, and at night they could attack the station. They fired at people walking in the streets, or working in their fields.

"You and Ingo were made for each other," she said. "He and Johanna had nothing in common." Tante Gertie gazed at the lacy curtains, as if she could see her family behind them, smiling at her from the blue sky. "Ingo used to visit me whenever he came to Berlin," she said, pushing up her metal-framed glasses. "I was obliged to marry a man I didn't love. I know what it means."

Olga stroked Tante Gertie's back, listening to the story of an unhappy marriage she could relate to. "Oskar was a decent man and a good husband. I fulfilled my duty. When Rolf was born, I pretended Siegfried was his father and devoted my love to him. He was the man I loved."

"I understand," Olga said, enjoying the fresh scent of Tante Gertie's cologne. "Before I met Ingo I devoted my life to Anyna." She did not mention Lothar. Perhaps Tante Gertie assumed that he had been killed too. Anyna only talked about Grandmaman. "I must go," Olga said. "The men keep coming. A tide of misery. You can't imagine the condition they're in. We don't have enough morphine. Why talk about it? When you see what they go through you forget your own problems."

The following Sunday, Gottfried came for a visit. His sergeant, a Baltic German, understood that there was no point in depriving his men of what little food and freedom they could find.

Olga received him gratefully. Tante Gertie, who had met him before, had bean soup for him. After lunch they took a walk along the lake. The sand crunched under their slow steps. Pensive, he watched the weeping willows bend toward the water. Olga could read his thoughts, his concern, his fear. Since Dresden they had bared their hearts and shared their pain.

"Remember how we fed fresh eggs to the hogs," he said, referring to the family estate he had grown up on, and later managed. "We had the finest pork in the county. I'd give anything for those boiled potatoes the workers cooked for them in a cauldron. Or work the soil for spring planting. Instead I must practice killing. It will come in handy any day now. We're coming to the bitter end." He gazed into her eyes. She wished she could comfort him, assure him that all would be well. That they would escape the Russians and he would join Lucie and his children in Austria. But he would know that she was lying, and consider it a cruel joke. He held her.

"They have your name and address as the person to be notified in addition to Lucie's. Amazing how she got on that train that took the children out of Dresden before the raid. In Austria they're safe. That's something to be grateful for." How would Lucie and her children manage without him?

"She saved my diplomas so that I can find a job after the war. She wants to go to America." He took Olga's hand and kissed it. "It's so good to have a friend like you, Olinka."

"America," she said. "Lothar is there now. He always gets away with things."

They walked hand in hand, watching three ducks paddle through the tall reeds searching for fish. The moist air had the heavy fragrance of spring. Their last spring of freedom. Gottfried did not believe in miracles, and accepted the inevitable like the man he was. They gazed at the calm water of the lake. He threw in a pebble. The water splashed and threw off circles.

"You are very precious to me, Olga. Thanks again for all the wonderful things you did for me. And I don't just mean musically—you taught me to be human and to cherish love, not just passion." He chuckled. "You must admit, I was a pretty arrogant bastard."

She loved this man in his crude uniform. "You mean the world to me, Gottfried," she said. "We need each other." What would she do when he was gone? "Come. Let's go home and have some of Tante Gertie's *streuselkuchen*."

His eyes lit up. "Did you say *streuselkuchen*? By all means."

Tante Gertie did not disappoint. She had set the table for tea with her fine Meissen dinnerware. The aroma of freshly baked cake aroused all the senses of life and its sweetness.

"I can't thank you enough, Tante Gertie," Gottfried said. "At the barracks we are starved for everything that connects us with life." He ate three pieces of cake, and drank several cups of tea before he rose to entertain his hostess. When he sang *Yours Is My Heart Alone*, she had tears in her eyes. "I've never heard it sung so moving. I'll never forget this day."

Olga applauded. "It's our favorite song, wouldn't you say, Gottfried?" They nodded at each other.

On their way to the station he said, "I'm no fool, Olga The Allies are coming in for the kill. We have run out of food, ammunition, and everything else one needs for a defense. Our Fuhrer sits in his bunker and issues contradictory orders. I doubt he has an inkling of what is really happening at the front. Probably doesn't want to know. The Russians could reach Berlin any day now."

Twilight lingered over the station when they arrived. "My little son will never know me. He has strength and determination. I'll keep an eye on him from up there." He pointed to the sky, where a last golden strip of light slowly faded. "Tell my sons not to bow their heads like slithering worms. The moment you lower your head you invite a kick. Lucie knows that. She's a powerful woman. Life will be very hard for her." He pulled Lucie's letter from the pocket of his greatcoat. "She wrote from Austria." He read it to Olga with the help of a flashlight. "We watch the bombers fly toward Germany by the thousands and think of all the people who will be killed. The magnificence of these mountains teach me how irrelevant our lives are. The local people are kind and friendly. They help whenever they can. I am waiting for you, my love. Perhaps you can escape somehow. We miss you, my beloved Gottfried. My heart and body long for you. Someday we'll be together again. Yours forever, Lucie.

"You would not expect Lucie to say that, would you? I wish I could be there with her now."

"You will be, Gottfried." At least in spirit, she thought.

That night, the news reported that General Busse's Ninth Army, Heinrici's Army Group Vistula, Manteuffel's Third Panzer Army, and General Wenck's Twelfth Army would defend Berlin and turn the tide. Was Ingo among them? Would he show up again? Olga did not dare hope. Someday he would come to her, and they would live in peace.

The following day, Olga heard tank chains rattle by. Their sonorous engines revved up and headed for the lake. Peeking through the lacy curtains, she saw the iron cross on their dull hulks. German tanks. The men rode with their hatches open, enjoying the spring air. A formation of

R.A.F. bombers passed overhead, but ignored the tanks. Their mission was Berlin. Not even a flash, a gesture of token anti-aircraft flak, interrupted their journey.

On her way to school, Anyna waved at the men in their tank. They waved back. "Aren't they nice, Mami? Karin's and Maria's family left. Christa's family will stay because her grandmother is ill. They cannot leave her behind. Will the Russians come soon? We should go to Bavaria and stay with Grandmaman."

Olga ignored the comment. She would rather face the Russians.

"Grandmaman wrote that Inning is beautiful. No bombs. There is a big lake like this one. It is called Ammersee. The mountains are so high that they touch the sky. The farmers give her milk and potatoes. We could find a room."

"We'll stay with Tante Gertie," Olga said, hugging Anyna before she entered the school.

Tante Gertie awaited Olga at home, a big grin on her wrinkled face. "Guess what I have here," she said. The twinkle in her eyes reminded Olga of the day when Ingrid had brought Ingo's letter to the hospital.

Olga reached for it. "A letter from Ingo! Is he all right? Where is he? Where?"

"I don't know, Olga."

Tante Gertie handed Olga the field post envelope.

April 23, 1945
My beloved Olychka,

My thoughts are constantly with you and Anyna. For the moment you are safe at Tante Gertie's, but that will change. You must leave Wunsdorf right away. Go to Bavaria or join Lucie in Austria. I know that trips are dangerous, but you cannot stay. You know what I mean. Think of your life, your freedom. Trust your visions. We'll find each other. I have the Countess's address. Your surviving the raids on Dresden shows that God is merciful. Some day we'll be in each other's arms again. For that you must take some steps. Do take my advice and leave. I love you, darling, love you with all my heart. When I close my eyes, I see you in the light of the pink room, hear your music and feel you so close. My favorite song is Miracle. *It's true. It will happen if you follow my advice.*

Yours forever, Ingo.

Olga swallowed. She had to be strong. She turned to Tante Gertie. "Ingo writes that we must leave and go west. He is right. The Russians are coming. I saw German tanks. We're getting into the war zone. Think about it, Tante Gertie." Olga handed her the letter.

"Let's not jump to conclusions," she said without reading it. "Ingo has no idea what it means to be a refugee. What makes you think the Americans will treat us better than the Russians?"

Olga pressed her palms against her temples. "They just will. The Countess always talked about them," she said impatiently. She was so tired of all this, of people who obliged her to follow their inclinations, and herself for doing it. Right now I must go to work."

Chapter 28

The following day Olga felt so tired that she wasn't sure she could make it to work. After spending the day traveling to Berlin to get medication for the hospital, she had once again experienced the horrors of the war. Uniformed men had been hanged for deserting. She couldn't understand how people still survived in that city, went to work, and supposedly visited the Berlin Philharmonic's daily concerts. The theater and movies had shows. With the constant bombardment, the scene was surreal. People ignored death, and the ever increasing number of ruins. *Goetterdaemmerung.* The final showdown would take the life of the last man, or something like that. She had no business exposing herself and Anyna to Armageddon.

Angrily, she tucked her curls under the stiff nurse's cap and pinned them down. A male voice came on in the kitchen. The radio? It had been dead for days. Tante Gertie must have turned it on. Perhaps things were not as bad as all that. Tying her crisp white apron over her gray dress, she headed for the kitchen, where a voice reported that the American President Roosevelt had died and would be replaced by the Vice President, Harry Truman. She stared at the brown wooden box, as the voice told his listeners that it would change the course of the war. Now the glorious and final victory was assured. The Fuhrer, directing the war from his bunker, had full confidence that the German people would not spare any effort in bringing about their deserved destiny.

"Did you hear that, Tante Gertie?" Olga said startled. "Roosevelt dead? What now?" She fished a frying potato slice from the pan and devoured it. She was always hungry. Their rations had diminished to whatever the stores had to offer.

Anyna looked up from her bowl of farina. "I'm so glad the radio is playing again," she said. "Now we'll have music." A zesty victory march celebrated Roosevelt's death. Why not Hitler's?

"With Roosevelt dead," Tante Gertie said, "we might get a conditional surrender."

"Hitler wants victory," Olga jeered, and slammed three plates on the table. "Our Fuhrer is determined to fight to the bitter end." The smell of burned potatoes fouled the air. The weather was still too cool to open the windows, though the day promised to be sunny. She had not slept well, always haunted by nightmares and tortured by hunger pangs. Emotionally drained, Olga forced a smile. It did not come easy. If she could only think of a plan that might stave off the encroaching disaster. Stroking Anyna's soft head, she wondered what would become of her.

General Schoerner would support the Battle of Berlin, the radio said.

"How long can they last? And then what?" Tante Gertie said. "Berlin is a dead city."

Would Ingo be part of the final bloodbath? If the Russians caught him, he could face a slow death in some Siberian prison camp. Father's support was her only hope, "After work I'll bicycle over to Gottfried," she said. "Who knows how long they'll keep him in reserve. Being the father of five has no bearing anymore."

Tante Gertie dished out the potatoes. Olga added a pickle to her plate. "Breakfast for a hangover without the night before," she said without even cracking a smile.

Anyna scraped out her farina, exaggerating her manners the way Grandmaman had taught her. "My teacher says that we must go to the community shelter. It's safe. Remember, Mami, when the man in Dresden told us to get off the street and go to the shelter? He was right, wasn't he? Else we would have burned to death like the other people. I'm not afraid. Still, I'd be scared to death if the basement collapsed. Martha said that her grandmother was buried alive and died. Imagine that."

Tante Gertie sat down at the table. "I'll check it out. But you'd better be off to school."

Olga left for the hospital. The nurses, doctors, and wounded appreciated her help and encouraging smile. A humorous remark eased pain, and relaxed the tense faces of the overworked staff. "What do you think of Roosevelt's death?" she asked Dr. Frankenfeld while he took a break, smoking a cigarette. They sat in the courtyard, surrounded by stretchers. A brisk breeze whirled up the dust and cleared the air of the acrid smell of smoke coming from the burning city.

"So Harry Truman will celebrate victory. Lucky man. He didn't fret over waging the war. Our problem is Hitler. He should surrender."

"Surrender? There isn't much to surrender," Olga said, noticing the bloodstained white coat. He looked so tired. How would it all end?

That evening, Olga left the hospital deeply troubled. Lately they had received wounded civilians who awaited their turn in the yard. If she only knew what to do. Bicycling along the road, Olga passed refugees pushing carts, prams, and wheelbarrows to who knows where. They walked in a daze, their eyes half-closed. Tired and hungry horses pulled creaking wagons. Nobody cared that dusk fell. Berlin was encircled. The sporadic, distant rumbling reminded them that the Wehrmacht defended the heart of the Reich.

Approaching Zossen, Olga walked her bicycle not to be run over by a convoy leaving the High Command of the Wehrmacht. Tanks rolled by. Their treads clinked and rattled. Barrels pointed forward. The exhaust fouled the cool spring air. Gottfried awaited her at the gate. She had grown accustomed to him in a soldier's uniform. "I am so glad you came," he said, "I had hoped you would…" He took her arm. "Let's find a quiet place." They passed the barracks, where soldiers climbed into trucks. Others attached huge guns to tractors, or loaded ammunition. Orders cracked through the noise of the engines starting up or shifting gears. The whole operation took placed under pines that hid the headquarters from enemy planes.

They sat down on a broken wall. "Did you contact Father?" he asked.

She shook her head. "I wished we had a piano now," she said, "We need music—food for the soul."

He kissed her hand. Was he grateful that she had changed the subject? Music was their bond. Holding her hand he sang in a soft, longing voice:

Alle Tage ist kein Sonntag, alle Tage gibt's keinen Wein,
Aber du sollst alle Tage recht lieb zu mir sein.
Und wenn ich einmal tod bin sollst Du denken an mich
Auch am Abend eh Du einschlaefst, aber weinen darfst Du nicht.

She loved that song, and reminisced over the last lines.

"And should I die, do think of me before you fall asleep, but you must not cry. It brings back so many memories of a life we once shared back in Latvia. Little did we know of the deeper meaning we must face now."

"Didn't I sing it for Ingo when you came to visit us in Litzmannstadt? Sometimes I wonder whether there has ever been such a place in my life. My darling Lucie. She was so courageous."

"Still is," Olga reminded him, knowing how worried he was about his family. She leaned against his chest. The proud and haughty man of her youth needed her support. "For five long years we watched the water rise over our heads, unable to prevent it or escape it. So we made music and pretended all would be well. We were wrong." She watched the golden rays of the setting sun cast its warm glow against the darkening sky. A last burst of light, and then darkness took over. A last moment of happiness. She squeezed Gottfried's hand. He hummed, "and should I die, think of me before you fall asleep, but you must not cry."

"Life," he whispered, as if he had given up on the word and saw no reason to say it. "How about love? I love you, Olga. I never realized how much you mean to me. Your dedication keeps me in awe. I don't deserve it."

Venus appeared above the silhouette of the pines. The din of motors, the rumbling explosions, and cracking commands dropped away, and did not disrupt the music of their souls.

"I believe you should stay in Wunsdorf," he said. "It's too late to escape. The old Countess knew what would happen. Our propaganda minister couldn't fool her. But why think about that now? Try to hide from the Russians when they come. You know their language. That could be suspect. Stalin not only murdered his people, he tried to kill their spirit."

Gottfried accompanied her to the station. The stars blinked in the black sky. Vehicles and motorcycles passed on their way to the front.

"Farewell, my beloved Gottfried. I'll always love you," she said. The train approached, puffing. They kissed. "The life we shared will help me get through the life to come," she whispered.

"Our music will accompany me on my last journey," he said and sang *Caro Mio Ben.*

Olga boarded the train to the sound of his song. She waved, humming the melody until the train departed.

Three days later, a messenger brought Olga the news that Gottfried had fallen for *Fuhrer, Volk, und Vaterland*. Her vision blurred. The note shook in her trembling hands.

"He was sent into action with his brigade," the messenger reported, twisting his cap. He stepped nervously from foot to foot. "Only one of the men returned, saying that the Russians ambushed them. Hasselblatt died instantly. A head wound." The young soldier pointed to his temple. "I'm very sorry." He avoided her glance, embarrassed by her tears. Olga could not help herself. Though she had known this would happen, she could not control her grief, and stared at the man without seeing him.

Tante Gertie took charge. "Thank you for letting us know."

"Hasselblatt and I were friends. He did not deserve to die like that. Then again, it was quick. Considering..." He broke off, glancing at the rain against the window. The gusty wind bent the trees to and fro as in a game.

"He was a great man," Tante Gertie said, wiping her eyes with the corner of her old apron. "Why don't I fix you a sandwich," she led the way to the kitchen. "I just happened to get our bread ration today."

The man's gaunt face lit up. "I would be much obliged."

As soon as they left, Olga tottered to her room, dropped on her bed and burrowed into the pillow. A bottomless abyss deepened her sense of nothingness. Alone. She would have to cope with her loss, carry her pain by herself. "Gottfried!" The name threw her into the pitiless reality of her life. She rolled into herself. "Ingo! Father!" Everybody was gone. She longed for encouragement, empathy, support. There was none. Abandoned. Olga sobbed and wailed, "Gottfried, you beautiful man with the golden voice. Even you left your blood on the battlefield. Why am I still here?" Overwhelmed by despair, she bit into her flesh and sucked at her skin. "Father! I'm lost. Speak to me, Father. Tell me that we'll be all right. Save me! Please, protect Ingo. I beg you." The rain pelted against the pane. The shutters rattled. "Can you hear me Father?" A tree branch knocked against the window—was that his answer? Or was the Evil One seeking her out again? The smell of mothballs reminded her of death and decay, the suffering men at the hospital. Her own broken life at the mercy of strangers; an uninvited guest awaiting her doom.

Through her tears she saw the photograph of a young Ingo in knickers and shirtsleeves, smiling at the camera. An unfamiliar man in a world she did not share. The pain slowly gave way to a numbness that removed her from herself. She shivered. Goose bumps ran over her arms. A light appeared and spiraled into the darkness. Relieved, she reached for Father's spirit and her salvation. "You came. You heard my call. Is Ingo with you?" There was no tremor in her arm. "Father!" she cried out. "Are you here? Is Ingo with you?"

The branch kept knocking at the window. The rain poured over the glass. "What happened to Ingo?" Olga insisted, staring at the fading light. Gone. The limb resembled a bony arm. Olga clutched the pillow, kneading it. Crumpling it in her hands. The Russians would come, and nobody would save her. Howling, she pounded the mattress until her fists burnt and her tears were spent.

Olga sat up and stared at the wet, desperate face in the mirror. No! She must not give up. Where was her strength, her courage and fortitude? She had become a whimpering victim. How disgusting. She must get hold of herself, and talk to the soldier who had come all the way from Zossen to bring her Gottfried's last message.

Anyna tiptoed into the room and wiped the tears from her mother's cheeks. "Uncle Gottfried is in Heaven. He can see us and always be with us. We can talk to him whenever we want, right? You said that when Omi died, and Tante Lore. You said that they're not really dead, and that we don't have to grieve over them because they're better off and don't have to die again. You said that they're happy in Heaven where they can fly about and never feel hungry, or cold, or pain." She held Olga, leaning her head against her mother's. "Don't cry, Mami. You have me. I'll always be good."

Olga kissed her little girl. "Yes, my darling, we have each other."

After a sleepless night, Olga dragged herself to the hospital, did her work, and smiled on cue. More wounded men arrived. The rumbling, flares, and fires went on. The mortally bleeding Wehrmacht fought the Russians and the fanatic Nazis who forced them to their deaths. The news promised final victory. Hitler lived in his bunker deep in the bowels of the earth, shielded from the death cries of the people he commanded. Perhaps he even believed in the miracle he promised. The Red Army, millions strong, rolled relentlessly toward him, killing everyone in their path. Their Katyushas fired avalanches of missiles at the German defense. Their aircraft buzzed over the German soldiers like hornets. When would they enter Wunsdorf?

Nurse Klara caught Olga in the hospital yard. "Did you hear the news?"

Olga shook her head. At this point there could only be bad news. "The radio is off again. What happened?"

"Hitler is dead."

"What?" Olga swallowed. "Dead? Assassinated?"

"No. Heart attack. Worked too hard. *Gross-Admiral* von Doenitz is taking over."

Olga scraped the sand under her feet. "What'll happen now?"

"I supposed, he'll sue for an armistice."

"Unconditional surrender," Olga whispered. "They'll come and kill us all." A cold shiver ran down her spine, despite the warm sun. The Russians could appear any moment now, drive through the open gate along with the tarp-covered trucks marked with a Red Cross. Enemy fighter planes flew overhead. Their target was still Berlin. The siren wailed. Soldiers ignored it, and unloaded their wounded comrades. Anyna was safe—school was held in the shelter. Tante Gertie bought groceries wherever she could find them, and stored them in their basement. She canvassed the stores for special allotments. Food was worth its weight in gold. Discipline prevailed. Anybody caught plundering was executed.

Dark clouds gathered. A cold wind came up. Typical April weather. Hitler was dead, she thought, unable to grasp the enormity of the news. Too late. The land was devastated, and the enemy at the doorstep of the capitol, thirty kilometers away. Gottfried and millions of others had died. Latvia had been taken over by the Soviets. Only Lothar was still alive and well in America.

"So much for final victory," Nurse Klara said. Her young face was fresh and untouched. Only her blue eyes expressed fear. Other than caring for the wounded, she had not yet experienced the cruelty of this war. What would the Russians do to her?

That evening, Tante Gertie awaited Olga with a letter from Ingo postmarked April 15th—two weeks ago. Father kept his promise, despite her disobeying him.

Too upset to feel her usual euphoria, she read: *...considering the circumstances, I am fine. Not even injured. A miracle. Father's help? I am glad you* *are with Tante Gertie. I think we've landed in a black hole. Have you consulted the cards lately? Too bad I can't sit at your table and cut the deck so that you can divine what is in store for me. For us?*

Wherever my fate takes me, you will always be with me, a permanent resident in my heart and thoughts. Nobody can take that away from me. In the meantime, we'll make the best of our circumstances and cherish our memories. I am so fortunate that I can look back on those unforgettable hours we spent together. Remember your commitment. You will always be my beloved wife. Some day we shall make it legal.

My beloved Olychka. The wings of our love hold me up, and carry me through the difficulties of this war. Some day they will bring us together again. We must believe in our future. Your music dwells in me. You are my salvation.

Was any of this real Olga wondered, and put the letter down, then reread it, kissed the paper, and handed it to Tante Gertie. If Ingo could keep his faith, so could she.

Later that day, Olga brought bloody bandages from the hospital. She would wrap them around her head when the Russians came. Anyna would hide under the bed. The brigade of men from the *Volkssturm* marching by with their bazookas, submachine guns, and ammunition boxes could not stop the Russians, who would mow them down along with the young boys who carried their cartridge belts across their thin chests like decorations. Soldiers pushed heavy artillery into strategic locations, reminding Olga of the village in Poland where she had found her mother, Anyna, and Ingo. Was that only three months ago? Nobody mentioned evacuation. There was no place left to go to. Berlin was encircled.

While *Gross-Admiral* von Doenitz negotiated an extension of the armistice with the Allies—so that the civilian populations of Silesia, East Prussia and Pomerania could escape the Russians—Olga took care of the wounded. General Eisenhower, the commander of the Allies, felt no pity for the plight of the Germans. The only good German was a dead German.

"We'll be at the community shelter," Tante Gertie said before Olga left for work. "The Russians could drop their bombs any moment now." Olga sensed fear in her friend's quivering voice. "We were bombed while I stood in line. A women and her two children were killed. The rest of us stayed…"

Dressed in her uniform, Olga hugged Anyna, her heart pounding.

"The shelter is fine, Mami," Anyna said. "You'll see. We set up a place where the bombs can't get us." She blushed with excitement. Perhaps she enjoyed being with other people, rather than at home with Tante Gertie.

"I'll bring the bedding," Olga said. "Perhaps I can trade one of your dresses, Tante Gertie, and a silk shawl for food. Frau Altmann might be willing to let me have some margarine and cheese for it. She's a young woman, and will enjoy something new to wear." Young, Olga thought. She was still in her twenties, but felt one hundred. The stress of the past months had taken its toll.

In the dim store, Frau Altmann not only agreed to trade food for the clothes as long as nobody found out about it, she told Olga that some people had pillaged the warehouse. "Just don't tell anybody I said so. Else...you know." She nudged Olga. "We don't know what's going to happen." She touched her lips, whispering, "Never hurts to be prepared."

Olga ran home, picked up two large totes and headed for the warehouse. On the way she passed slow moving vehicles and military trucks. The distant fires and explosions in Berlin gave her a sense of direction. German and Russian soldiers were engaged in street fighting, house by house.

Darkness had set in. Olga saw obscure shapes sneak in and out of the warehouse. Those leaving hauled heavy sacks, baskets, and totes. "What's going on?" she asked one of the women jerking a loaded crate. The smell of sauerkraut and alcohol wafted from the dark building.

"We're not going to leave our supplies to the Russians. You might as well help yourself while they last. Just make sure the Gestapo doesn't catch you."

Olga was not worried about the Gestapo. She wanted her share of the loot. Inside the warehouse, people bustled, stepped on each other, cursed, and grabbed whatever they could find in the dark. Olga found some cans and stuffed them into her tote, wishing she had bags for the open flour and sugar. Those who had them, took what they could carry, then stumbled out, bumping into the people entering. In a frenzy of discovery, she threw whatever she could find into her bags. Somebody stepped on her foot. She winced but ignored it. An arm pushed her aside. She fought back. "This is mine," she insisted, and kicked the body obstructing her path. There was a whole section of wine. Somebody broke a bottle. The wine spilled over the floor. Olga found an empty crate and filled it with bottles, then hauled it all into the street, where she hid it in a dark corner. With the black-out fully enforced, nobody dared show a light. She ran home and brought more bags, along with Tante Gertie's handcart. Now she could really go to work. On her third trip, the warehouse was abandoned.

Back in the street, she sidled along the walls to avoid the military motorcycles rattling past. Olga enjoyed pulling her treasures home. In the kitchen she treated herself to a glass of wine, sat down at the table, and gazed at the stars. "To you, Ingo," she whispered, humming *I Know Some Day A Miracle will Happen*. The wine raised her spirits. Chewing on a piece of bread with margarine, she felt new strength. As long as she was alive, there would always be an opportunity for survival. Did she not get through the firestorm in Dresden?

The prolonged echo from a heavy gun did not bother her, nor was she afraid of the barking and howling of Russian missiles. Pouring herself another glass of wine, she felt the satisfaction of accomplishment. The cans would come in handy. Salvos of *knackvoom knackvoom*, very fast, accompanied the Russian missiles. The battle had begun.

At the shelter Tante Gertie whispered, "Oh God, have mercy."

"At least the Russians don't believe in carpet bombing," Olga said, watching German tanks rattle through the street. How long could they hold their position? Soldiers ran by, rifles in hand. Open trucks took German troops to battle. Olga remembered the men who had given her a lift back in Poland, talking about joining the Americans to fight the Red Army. These men would rather go home. *Ingo, where are you? Dodging bullets while ordering your men into battle?*

Olga's arm trembled. Father! She pulled a pencil and pad from her purse and withdrew to a dark corner. *Father, I'm scared. What's going to happen? The Russians are coming. I know it's my own fault, but please, please, protect us.*

Soon the world around her vanished. Her hand wrote: "My dear daughter. Gottfried is with us, and sends you his love. It will take some time before he can communicate with you. But he is with you. His parting was merciful. We awaited him. We shall protect you and his family. We cannot spare you the pain you will endure. Evil is on the prowl, and preys on the souls of foolish people. Be brave and have faith.

Follow our guidance." There was a pause. Olga looked at her writing. Then her hand vibrated again and wrote: "When you are free of bondage you will find Ingo."

"Free of bondage?" she whispered.

Chapter 29

Here it comes, Olga thought, crouched in her corner at the shelter, and chewed on her hand. Her stomach contracted. The ground trembled from the impact of the explosions. She must stay calm. *No panic. Think of a song.* Where was music when she needed it? The *tacktacktack* of strafing planes and the ping, ping of antiaircraft guns announced the battle.

The women at the shelter had set up their bedding and emergency suitcases. Two refugee women and their elderly father wandered in. They paid no attention to the long kaboom, followed by a prolonged echo from the heavy guns that sent Olga into a dither. The Reich had thrown their last reserves into the country's defense. How many men were left?

Frau Bauerle, a neighbor, let out a muffled cry when quick explosions accompanied the insane howling and barking Olga had heard before. "They're here," she whispered, lips quivering. "The Stalin Organs." Tense faces stared at her and turned ashen, as if she caused all the trouble coming toward them.

Frau Henkel, who worked at the butcher's, came in, carrying four loaves of bread. "Shut the door," shouted the women. "You want to get us killed?"

"The baker is giving her bread away," said Frau Henkel, unperturbed, as if the Stalin Organs played music. "They're not even close. That noise is supposed to scare us. Not me! I'm going back and get more bread. Once the Russians get here... By the way, Frau Altmann is selling off her groceries. Why let the Russians get fat on them?" She put down the fresh, shining loaves and wiped the sweat from her face. She had been running and wanted to get back while the supply lasted.

The other women forgot their fear, grabbed their shopping bags, and stormed out. Olga dumped her toiletries from the tote and ran after them. Bread. Groceries. Food!

"Be careful," Tante Gertie shouted after her.

Anyna caught Olga's hand. "Mami, don't leave us."

Olga pushed her aside. "We must get what we can, while it lasts. We don't know what will happen when the Russians get here."

Out in the street, soldiers fired their artillery. Enemy shells exploded here and there. The hungry women ran on in a pack and barged into the grocery store. Frau Altmann insisted, "I'm not giving anything away. I need coupons. Do you want me to get arrested?"

"For heaven's sake, Frau Altmann," Olga said. "Do you want the Russians to have it? Coupons! Arrested! There's nobody left to arrest you. We'd be lucky if the Russians don't take us prisoner."

"Everything in due time," Frau Altmann said, and took her time measuring out flour, sugar, and salt. Olga had to wait her turn. "Come on, Frau Altmann. What's an extra gram or two? The Russians are at the outskirts of town. We don't have all day."

"Now hold your horses, young woman. No panic, yes? We'll show the Russians that we're civilized people." She watched the scale before pouring the farina into a bag.

"Civilized?" Olga mocked. "As if they care. We're their enemies!"

"Now you're going too far."

The other customers debated what to do when the Russians came. Olga said no more, not to interrupt Frau Altmann and slow things down. When her turn came she smiled sweetly, and watched the shopkeeper measure out her groceries, collect the coupons, and count the change down to the penny. Loaded down with her treasures, Olga ran to the bakery despite the shooting, skirting a woman and her child who lay prostrate in their blood. Hungry shoppers stood in line for bread, indifferent to the German soldiers running through the street. A tank passed with its hatch closed. Stalin Organs sent off their missiles. The women held their places, determined to get some bread.

Olga got three loaves, wishing she had more hands to carry it all home. Should the bread dry out, she could soak it in water and re-bake it. A salvo of gunfire erupted. Debris fell into the street. A house burst into flames. Windows shattered. Olga ran faster, breathing hard. After stowing away her treasures she ran back to the shelter. Anyna cried out, "You're back, Mami. We were so worried. Will the fire break out again?"

Holding the trembling little body, Olga kissed the tears from Anyna's cheeks. "No, there will be no fire. But look, the book seller's wife and her daughter are bringing a pot of soup." They watched two women haul a cauldron into the shelter.

"We made enough for all of us," the book seller's wife said. "Bean soup. The gas is still on, but the electricity is off. Nobody knows where the Russians are, or what we are supposed to do when they come. So let's eat."

Olga wished she had brought a loaf of bread to share. Women chatted. One of them shared her bread. "We might as well eat it while we can." Devouring their soup, the women became friends. Many of them were neighbors. Tante Gertie told them about Olga's experiences in Poland and the firestorm in Dresden. Asking questions, they forgot about the explosions outside, the motorcycles rattling by, and the buildings being hit. Better not to think about it. In the shelter the acrid stench of smoke was barely noticeable.

At nighttime the exhausted families bedded down. Olga curled up against Anyna and closed her eyes, listening to the snoring and whispering. What would it be like when the war was over? Would Ingo come home, tired, hungry, and happy? They could get married and live in Tante Gertie's house. Anyna would grow up into a lovely young lady. But more likely he would be taken prisoner, and kept for a long time.

Loud voices woke Olga. The silence outside frightened her more than the explosions had. The door stood open. Smoke wafted in with the cool air.

Frau Bauerle stumbled in crying, "They're here. I saw them climb through the window at the liquor store. How did they know?" She towered over the people curled up on the floor, staring at her dumbfounded from under their blankets.

"That's insane," Olga protested. "Didn't anybody think of distributing the liquor rather than leave it to the Russians? Now we'll have to deal with drunk Russians. They're bad enough sober."

"You know how it goes. We live by the rules. Good thing we got those groceries. Men have no more sense than a fly."

"We must hide," Frau Henkel said. "If they see us…" She broke up.

"Let's hide at home. Here we're too obvious. Our war is over," Tante Gertie said, and sighed. "There'll be no victory." She wiped her eyes with the back of her hand. It was not so much about victory as the hope that things might work out.

Olga peeked through the door. In the early morning light she saw a Russian battery turn the corner, its four barrels pointed at the sky. Two Russians stomped behind it—broad backs, leather jackets, high leather boots. Now jeeps pulled up. Fieldpieces rattled by. "I must go to the hospital," she said. "The wounded need help."

"The hospital?" Tante Gertie cried out. "Are you out of your mind? There's nothing you can do for them now. They're at the mercy of the Russians, like us. They're military. We must go home before they take over the town—get ready." She put on her coat. Olga and Anyna picked up their clothes. The women talked in low voices, as if the Russians could hear them. The turmoil in Olga's stomach felt as if she was about to be sick. What would the Russians do if they found out that she came from Latvia? An enemy of the people. Deport her to a gulag in Siberia?

Feeling the weight of her destiny, Olga blinked at the sun that had risen to illuminate the remnants of yesterday's bloody battle. Homes smoked, but no major fires had broken out. Olga, Tante Gertie and Anyna passed corpses in blood-stained uniforms. Flies feasted on dead men's eyes still staring at the blue sky. Tante Gertie and Anyna passed in silence.

Olga carried their bedding. The stench of burnt-out vehicles, tanks, and spilled fuel polluted the air. Germany was still at war, but Wunsdorf was no longer part of it. Tante Gertie's large shoes flopped on Olga's feet. Behind the shrubs lining a narrow path, she felt hidden from view. *Gottfried, are you watching us now? There will be no grave for you. The Russians dig up German graves and rip out the crosses.*

Silvery, diamond-shaped formations of American flying fortresses headed toward Berlin with the familiar deep droning. Canvas-covered trucks carried wounded from the nearby front. Their motors labored on inferior fuel. Had nobody told them that the Russians were here to finish Germany off?

Late that afternoon, a Russian supply train rolled into town. From the basement window, Olga watched stout mares stroll along the street, foals running between their legs. A cow mooed, asking to be milked. Some Russians set up a field kitchen. The men looked sturdy, with close-cropped hair and broad foreheads. They were at ease, well fed, and did not seem to fear anybody. Certainly not the trembling people sitting in their shelters. Russian soldiers bustled about cheerfully like children at play.

Frau Bauerle showed up, her face flushed, her hat askew. "What should we do?" she asked Olga.

"Your guess is as good as mine. We mustn't lock the doors that's for sure. Why don't we go to the attic and see what's going on down below?"

Anyna followed. Tante Gertie wanted to keep an eye on the house, in case somebody came in. Right now there was no sign of Russians interested in civilians.

From the attic window, Olga watched a young Russian polish his new German motorcycle. A Zundapp yet. Others wheeled stolen bicycles up and down the street, teaching each other how to ride them. One of them crashed into a tree. His buddies laughed. Horses were led through the street leaving their droppings. Though the front had to be nearby, there was no German flak or bombs of any kind. The Russians showed each other collections of wrist-watches lined up along their arms. Others fed hay to their livestock, or watered them from garden wells. Running water had been shut off.

At dusk, the Russians stumbled around, visibly drunk, tired of childish games. They wanted the real thing.

Somebody banged at the front door.

"I'll open before they break the door down," Olga said, waving Anyna toward the bedroom, and adjusting the blood-stained bandage around her head. Tante Gertie went to the kitchen.

A burly Russian, built like a bull, and his equally husky buddy marched in. The bull, dead-drunk, brandished a pistol and pointed it at Tante Gertie, who peered at him from the kitchen. He had her move aside, looked around, then returned to Olga. His eyes pierced her. The lecherous grin left no doubt as to his intention. Olga groaned. She had a sharp pain in her stomach, which twisted in fear. Whatever considerations he had did not stop him from grabbing her wrist. She squirmed and cried. His grip tightened. He was not about to be refused. In the living room he threw her onto the sofa.

Olga struggled.

Anyna came out screaming. "You leave my mother alone, you dirty Russian!"

Before the Russian could hit her, Tante Gertie pulled the child back to the bedroom and closed the door. Olga struggled again. Her bandage slipped. She blushed. He fumbled with his revolver, too drunk to hold it straight. It went off and hit the ceiling. Stunned he let her go. Olga escaped to the bathroom and locked the door. He came after her and kicked at it. Tante Gertie screamed. Olga bit into her fist. Should she jump out of the window? What good would that do? They would not rape Tante Gertie, she told herself. But why not? To those drunken monsters a woman was a woman. Tante Gertie was in her fifties. After a noisy scuffle the front door slammed shut. There were plenty of young women in town they could pick from.

In a quivering voice Tante Gertie announced, "They're gone."

Olga came from the bathroom. "We must hide. Or look for protection."

In the street, Russian women in quilted jackets and straight skirts cooked over open fires. The flattened corpses of German soldiers, and the flies feeding on their blood, did not bother them—they had seen worse. Nor did they scold their men for going on a rampage. That too was common practice. What else were defeated enemies for? Some soldiers kept pushing their stolen bicycles around like treasured toys. They sipped from bottles, laughing. What would happen to the wounded, Olga wondered, glad that Gottfried had met his fate.

Anyna watched the goings on through the window. She would crawl under the bed as soon as Russians came, and stay there until called. At least she would not witness whatever might happen to her mother and Tante Gertie. "Look, Mami," she cried out. "The Russians jump on their horses and ride off like the men in the circus, remember? Come see the goats and pigs. I wish I could go out and watch. Will the men come back?"

"They might. So be sure you stay under the bed, do you hear?" Olga did not mean to sound harsh, but this was no time for niceties.

Anyna knitted her brows. "What if they kill you?"

"They won't." She stroked Anyna's soft hair.

The street turned into a Gypsy camp. The women cooked while men sat around drinking vodka. Ingo had called them a flexible army— moving with their provisions, avoiding direct confrontations. Invisible to the traditional German forces, they encircled them like bloodhounds catching their prey. Centuries ago, Prince Alexander Nevsky had defeated the Teutonic Knights by luring them onto the frozen Lake Ladoga. The ice broke under the weight of their heavy armor and the knights sunk and drowned. Prussian tradition prevailed over common sense, at the expense of millions of lives. Ingo. A wave of joy washed over Olga. She would never forget his showing up at the Esplanade and asking for *Some Day A Miracle Will Happen*. That had been the happiest time of her life.

Two Russian soldiers showed up with a kerosene lantern. One of them pointed his bayonet at Tante Gertie. "*Soldati? waffen?*" he demanded, teetering.

"*Nix soldati. Nix waffen*," she told them. *No soldiers. No weapons.*

"*Davai uri*," the other ordered, and rolled up his sleeve, displaying a collection of wrist watches. He checked that they all ran on time, and repeated his request. Tante Gertie shook her head, pushed up the sleeve of her home-knit sweater to produce an empty arm. The soldier shrugged, his face red from alcohol. His body reeked of sweat.

Olga watched them leave from the dark living room, where the men could not see her.

"Children with a new toy," said Tante Gertie. "So far, so good. If I only knew what was going on in those square heads of theirs. Something cunning."

"They'll be back," Olga said, wishing she were wrong. Throughout the evening, Russians staggered along the empty streets, sipping vodka and singing their praises to Katyusha, their super-gun, rumbling in the distance. The screams of the women they raped were part of the ugly cacophony. The war was still on. The Wehrmacht was fighting to the last man.

Three soldiers approached her home. Olga ran into the pantry and pulled the bloody gauze over her forehead. Tante Gertie greeted them at the door, believing they would not violate her if she addressed them properly.

"*Uri! Uri!*" one of the men demanded. He was in his twenties.

"*Nix uri*," she said, showing her bare arm.

He grabbed it. "This old witch isn't bad," he said in Russian. Olga understood, and froze. After taking a long sip, he pulled Tante Gertie to the bedroom. "*Komm, Frau.*"

Olga gasped. She desperately wanted to do something. But what? Even if she offered herself, they would only take both of them. The man dragged Tante Gertie to the bedroom. "Let go of me, you drunken scum," she screamed. "Don't you have any respect?" Ignoring her, he told his buddy to keep Tante Gertie down.

Slipping into the bedroom, Olga felt torn, desperately trying to think of some rescue. These men were drunk, and would kill just for the fun of it. Who knew how many people they had killed already. What was one more German?

"Damn you all," Tante Gertie shrieked. Her muffled cry was followed by deep moans. Almost overwhelmed by empathy and helplessness, Olga clenched her fists and stuffed them into her mouth not to give herself away. The soldiers' cruel laughter echoed through the dark home. So the old hag wanted to fight. Let her struggle. This was fun.

Olga prayed for Anyna to stay in the bedroom, and that the soldiers would not find her. The first soldier returned to the living room, buttoned his trousers, and pulled his tunic into place, then went to the kitchen. In the pantry, he pulled off the burlap sacks that hid Tante Gertie's preserves, and stuffed a few into his pocket.

She felt helpless, embarrassed, furious. If she could only split those cropped skulls of theirs. At last they stumbled out, singing of glorious victory.

"You stay here," Olga told Anyna, "until I call you."

"But they're gone, Mami."

"I said, you stay here," Olga insisted.

Covering the room with her flashlight, she found Tante Gertie curled up on her crumpled bed, blood mixed with thick white semen running down her thin legs. Her stockings, old-fashioned garter belt, and underpants were torn. She held Olga's hand and whimpered. "The shame of it all," she sobbed. "An old woman like me. Those men have no decency. Animals wouldn't do that."

"They're sick with hatred," Olga said, handing Tante Gertie a wet towel, then picking up the torn garments. "Don't feel embarrassed, Tante Gertie dear. We should've left. Still, it's better than being shot. At least you're still alive." She helped Tante Gertie get out of bed, dressed her, and took her to her rocking chair in the living room.

"I can't believe they would do this to me," she repeated. In the scuffle she had lost her dentures. Olga found them in the bedroom, and brought them to her.

Instead of putting them in, Tante Gertie said with her toothless mouth, "Thank God, it was dark."

Cradling her friend, Olga smelled the stench of sweat, sex, and Russian tobacco.

"Why didn't they shoot me?" Tante Gertie whimpered.

"Because we need you. We will not let the enemy defeat us. Not now or ever. This is what war is all about. Let's have some peppermint schnapps, before the Russians find it and rape us in gratitude." Olga brought the bottle, filled two shot glasses, and had Anyna join them.

"We'll help you, Tante Gertie," Anyna said, leaning her head against Tante Gertie's trembling shoulder. "You can count on us. Mama can fix anything."

By midnight another horde had swarmed in, swinging kerosene lanterns. Their leader pointed his gun at Olga. His buddy shot at the painting above the sofa and laughed. Several of his teeth had been knocked out and a thick scar ran across his skull. Too had the blow had not finished him off. Olga cringed under his malicious grin. "Father protect us," she whispered.

"Do come in," she said in Russian. Tante Gertie sat in her rocking chair. Anyna had returned to her hiding place under the bed. The kerosene lamp landed on the dining table, leaving a pool of light in the dark room.

"Vodka," demanded the leader, a wiry fellow.

Olga shrugged, gesturing at the wrecked home. "*Bolshe nyet vodka.*"

"*Nyet vodka?*" his buddy said in disbelief, ogling her with glassy eyes. He towered over her like a gorilla, pushing his broad chest against her small frame, his paws on her shoulders. She petted his unshaven cheeks and stroked his chest. "You're a sweet Pushkin."

"Pushkin? I'm no Pushkin!" he protested.

"Don't you love poetry?"

The wiry one pointed his gun at her. "Shoot her, Sasha. Shoot the German bitch."

"But she's no German. She speaks Russian," the giant said. "But I'm no Pushkin. And I don't like people who make fun of me."

Olga giggled. "But I was only joking. Of course, you're a real man. Strong like a bull." She tested his biceps. "Hard as iron."

"She's crazy," one of the other men said. "I don't like this place."

The giant leered at Olga and licked his thick lips. One of the men went to the bedroom and returned with Anyna.

Olga stifled a scream. Anyna showed no fear. She even smiled. Her arms akimbo she said, "How do you do?"

The Russian pulled some candy from his pocket and offered it to her.

"Take it," Olga said in German, and say "*spocebo.*"

Anyna curtsied. "*Spocebo.*"

The men were beside themselves. The gorilla picked her up and threw her into the air. She squealed. When he put her down he placed more candy into her little hand.

"*Spocebo!*"

"Isn't she adorable? Just like my daughter, Natasha." The men walked out. The door slammed shut.

Thank you Father for protecting us.

Sitting on Tante Gertie's bed, they heard Russians come in again, talking and laughing. Outside, screams pierced the darkness.

"Get under the bed," Olga told Anyna. "And stay there, do you hear?"

"Mami, I'm scared."

"I know. Just do as you're told and everything will be fine."

Tante Gertie slipped into the garden through the back door.

"*Zdrastvuitse,*" Olga greeted the intruders politely.

A swarthy fellow grabbed her arm and pulled her to the floor. The stabbing pain obliged her to obey. Still, she managed to say, "Why do you hurt me?"

"Cut that shit out. Come on, Grisha, let's take her."

The man he addressed pointed his gun at her face, while the swarthy fellow pinned her down, his naked organ erect, a malicious smirk on his twisted lips. Vengeance shot from his lecherous eyes. This was for all the pain and injustice he had endured.

"*Tovarisht*, please," Olga pleaded. No mercy. This man was consumed with rage at the world that had destroyed his. He had become a sadist who took pleasure in torturing her.

"If she wiggles, shoot her. You're next." He ripped off her panties, despite her tight legs. She went limp, nauseated by the stench of his body and the sulfur rising around her. The Evil One had come. *Father. Father* ...

His massive organ was forced into her tight opening and tore the delicate tissue. She did not struggle. *Just endure and get it over with, the way you had with Lothar.* The man stuck his dirty finger into her mouth. She gagged. He grunted. Soon his warm semen squirted into her and ran over her thigh. All worked up he would not stop, punching her chest like a boxer. The young stud was insatiable. Her revulsion grew. Bile rose from her guts. Retching, she choked, trembling under his excruciating thrusts. He pumped harder and faster, seeking an outlet for his fury.

His buddy shoved him aside. "Enough, Dimka. My turn."

Dimka resisted the shove, his arms clamped around her so that he could push even deeper into her bleeding opening. He would use her until he was done.

Her body on fire, Olga retched and retched. Bile flowed from her mouth. *Father. Father.* The thundering rhythm of the *Mephisto Waltz* drummed in her head, while the panting and sweating man worked himself to another climax.

Tired of waiting and watching, his buddy shoved him aside like an obstacle, and ripped the bandage from her head. Olga cringed. Too busy satisfying his desire, he did not notice the mass of golden curls streaming from her head. He worked hard, thrusting his penis into her and moaning with pleasure, repeating "German pig," like a term of endearment. Annoyed by the vomit smeared on her face and neck he grumbled, "Disgusting German. Can't even give you a good fuck," pulled back, and left Olga on the floor like a dirty rag.

The door slammed shut. They were gone.

Anyna whispered, "Can I come out now, Mami?"

"No, no. Not yet." Did her voice sound normal? She picked up her bandage and wiped up the vomit on the floor, then staggered to the bathroom and knelt in front of the toilet to expel what was left in her stomach. Exhausted and bathed in cold sweat, she dipped a drinking glass into the fresh water bucket and rinsed her mouth, then washed her face and wiped off the filth from her body. How many more would she have to endure?

Men fought each other with bullets, women paid with their bodies.

Back in the dark living room, Olga licked the blood from her bruised lips, picked up her torn blouse and panties, and joined Anyna in the bedroom.

Several Russian women in quilted jackets and military boots came in. They had no weapons, but did not need any. Germany was finished and available to them. In the light of their kerosene lamps, they pulled linens and clothes from the drawers and dumped them on the floor. Silver and china followed. Half of Tante Gertie's crystal glasses broke on their way to their sacks. Like scavengers, the wide-hipped and round-faced women took whatever caught their fancy. This was their reward for serving as cannon fodder. The enemy must pay for their pain and their losses.

Olga and Anyna watched them from under the bed. "Let's hope they don't touch the piano," Olga whispered.

The women finally left. There were plenty of other homes to investigate.

Tante Gertie returned from the garden. "I feel so stupid. What made us think the Russians would leave civilians alone? Let's take whatever is left, and hide it in the garden."

Olga picked up the laundry basked and started filling it, hoping that nobody would notice her bruised face. The wounds inside were well hidden, and would fester for some time. She must not let this get to her. She must be strong and carry on. She had known it was coming, but had been too arrogant to admit that it could happen to her.

Anyna fell asleep on the living room sofa while Tante Gertie and Olga hauled whatever they could into the dark garden. Tomorrow they would find a better solution.

The door opened. Olga dropped the clothes in her arms when a giant Russian walked in. Was he not the one who had given Anyna the candy? He faced Olga in the light of her candle, then picked up the clothes for her. "Here. You want to hang them up?" he asked.

She could not restrain her trembling. "Um, yes," she stammered, and pointed to the mess on the floor. The man had kind eyes and an intoxicated grin. His tunic and shirt were unbuttoned, and his cap askew.

Anyna awoke and rubbed her eyes. Recognizing the man she said, "*Spocebo.*"

He gave her a handful of sweets. "I have a daughter like her," he told Olga. "Natasha." He placed his hand at chest level.

"My name is Anna Magdalena von Schenck," Anyna said, and extended her little hand. He shook it gracefully.

"Valentin Ivanovich. Vanya for short."

A brigade of women traipsed in, carrying half-loaded sacks. He clapped his hands and chased them away like chickens. "Get out of here," he thundered in a deep bass.

The women hesitated. Their greedy eyes reminded Olga of bitches protecting their meat-picked bones.

"Out!" he shouted, pointing his gun at the scavengers. Grumbling, the women backed up and left. He shut the door behind them. His dark whiskers gave him the rugged look of a man from the country. He scratched his head under the cap, enjoying the relief, then sat down on the sofa, pulled a bottle of vodka from his pocket and invited Olga to join him. More at ease now, she took the bottle and, encouraged by his urging, took a sip. After the strain of the past hours it quickly eased the tension and numbed her pain. Anyna watched them, sucking on her candy.

"Anna must go to bed," he said.

"Valentin Ivanovich is right," Olga said in German. "Go and tell Tante Gertie that we have protection now." She did not say anything about the price, glad she would only have to please one man, one who would not shoot or torture her. Had Father finally heard her prayers?

Olga would rather go through the ordeal without spectators, especially Anyna, and let Vanya carry her to the bedroom. The first light of dawn broke. *Ingo! You knew this would happen, but I refused to listen. When will I ever learn?*

Back at the sofa, Vanya pulled Olga down beside him. He handed her the bottle. "*Na zdorovie!* Let's drink to victory."

"Victory? Yes, of course. *Na zdorovie,*" she toasted, and took another long sip. It felt good. The vodka, lukewarm from his body, tasted better the more she drank, and eased her pain. Vanya chatted along. This was her tomorrow.

"You're a nice woman, Olga. You be my lady." He petted her cheek and held her hand. "Your girl is like mine. I haven't seen my Natasha for three years. She can write now. Smart little girl," he told her with the pride of a father. They kept drinking. Olga felt drunk, and grinned over the broken dishes on the floor and crumpled table cloths. He was from the Ukraine and on his way to take Berlin and the bunker, whether Hitler was alive or not. Russia would occupy Berlin before the Americans came, that was their order.

Vanya yawned, showing big, yellow teeth. His wide nose had pockmarks. He had been on the go for days.

"Why don't you go to sleep," she said.

He nodded. "With you."

Olga shook her head, and pointed at her bruised face.

"Russians are bad boys. You're a nice woman. I'll take a nap, then I must go." He stretched out, putting his worn boots on the upholstery.

"You're a good man, Vanya. God will reward you."

"God?" he asked, a blank stare in his sleepy eyes, then smiled sheepishly and fell asleep.

Tante Gertie had returned from the garden and barricaded herself into her room. She opened when Olga knocked.

"As long as Vanya sleeps here, we'll be fine," Olga said, noticing that Tante Gertie had been packing. "I'll go far, far away," she said in a sing-song, then cackled like a madwoman. "I'll go away. Don't tell anybody. Rolf came for me. He will take me with him to heaven. My Rolf did not forget his Mami." She sang. "Nobody can touch me, tra-la-la-la."

"You need rest. Rolf can wait."

Vanya's protection lasted three days, then he was off to capture what was left of Berlin. Olga was convinced he had saved her from the worst. The debauchery lasted another three weeks before the military stopped it. The women and supply train remained as rear support, using the streets and gardens for their livestock. The odor of horses and cow manure was everywhere, including the homes the soldiers visited with their dung caked boots. Like animals they peed wherever they had the urge—on the floor, in staircases, and in the street. They used toilets to wash their potatoes. The women wore pretty scarves and ribbons they had "found." The locals stayed out of sight.

Anatol, a fellow from Moscow, took a fancy to Olga and offered his "protection." That meant she only had to please him. After the first ordeal, she had learned to detach herself from her body and even the world around her, dwelling with Father, Ingo, and now Gottfried, though he could not respond to her. The scenes with Anatol took place as if in a movie. He treated her with bread, herring, and butter. Whenever he brought meat and potatoes Tante Gertie cooked a stew. He invited his buddies, and feasted with them into the night. They preferred the kitchen to the living room, and littered the floor with scraps, bones, and cigarette butts. Passing their bottle around, they sang to Olga's accompaniment on the piano.

Her speaking Russian allowed Olga to bargain and negotiate for the local people, though there was little she could do for them. Olga grew accustomed to her new way of life, though she knew that things would change as soon as Germany surrendered and the Soviets established their regime.

Two days after the Russians arrived, Olga had gone to the hospital, appalled by the bloodshed. The drugs she had risked her life to get had been smashed by the plundering hordes, and the food taken or dumped on the floor. The physicians and nurses, including sister Hildegard, had been taken prisoner. They would now treat the Russians. The young nurse's aides salvaged what they could, and fed the men who had not died or been shot.

"Who will bury them?" *Schwester* Klara wondered, her eyes searching restlessly for new assailants. "It's so embarrassing." She blushed. "I tried to hide, but they found me." Crimson-faced she stared at the ground. "They shot the men in their beds and those on the floor. Good thing you weren't here. They would've gotten you too."

Olga did not mention her own shame.

"I have no idea what we can do for our patients now," Klara said. "We have no food, no medication, nothing. But we can't just let them die." Moans echoed through the halls. Some would die that day or the next from lack of food and blood. Olga saw the wan faces of the dying who desperately prayed for help and salvation. The stench of their decaying bodies filled the wards.

"I'll try to find the Russian commander. Perhaps he has some humanity left in him. But I wouldn't count on it."

"Do you think we can still flee?" Klara asked innocently. "I have an uncle in America. He lives in Chicago. He'll help me. I'm no enemy. If only the Americans would come, so that I can contact him." Her wrinkled apron was covered with blood stains, ashes and dirt. Dark shadows had formed under her eyes.

Judging from the explosions and the fires that lit up the sky at night, the Battle for Berlin was still going on. The Americans dropped more and more bombs on the stricken city, but did not come. Ingo was out there, fighting. Or had he been captured? The radio was dead. Newspapers no longer reached Wunsdorf. Soon the Russians would take Berlin. Olga shuddered. There would be purges, deportations and executions.

The Russian commander—a young officer with sharp, narrow features and blond hair—sat behind a large desk, annoyed by Olga's visit. The quizzical look from his cold eyes did not undress her, only noticed her unkempt appearance. She should have prepared herself for the visit, rather than come straight from the hospital in her dirty nurse's uniform. At least her face and hands were clean, and her hair neatly tucked under the cap. She explained the plight of the suffering men at the hospital to the disinterested officer and officially requested his permission to care for them.

"You came to the wrong address, nurse," he said with unconcealed disdain. "Germany started this war. You let our men, your POW's, die of starvation." He shrugged. "Need I say more? We have more casualties every day because your people don't have enough sense to surrender. And now you want me to care for your soldiers?" He shook his head, his cold eyes cold spoke its own language. How dare she come and waste his time. "Consider yourself lucky," he broke off. She did not need his explanation as to why that should be so. "You obviously don't know what was going on out there, at the front."

She kept eye contact. *Let him have his say. What was one more insult?* Yet, she detected no malicious glint. Every human being had emotions, and he could not hide that he would like to help her, but that it was against his orders. "They're human beings," she said softly, focusing on his mouth and the tight lips that harbored more pain than he could bear. What had happened to this man? "Imagine being in their place."

"I'm not," he said curtly. "But I know what it's like. So don't expect me to do anything." His uniform was clean and pressed. She could not tell his rank, nor the meaning of his medals. Unlike the men who came to rape her, this man commanded respect, rather than taking it with his pistol. He pronounced his words distinctly, and used sophisticated vocabulary she was not familiar with. An educated man.

"It wouldn't cost you much," she insisted, "to let us care for the suffering men. A few words and your signature would ease their pain. The war is almost over."

He laughed, hard and sarcastic. "Almost! Save lives! Don't you know that war is about killing? The more the better. Yes, it's almost finished. Hitler is dead. Soon you'll be safe in the bosom of the Soviet brotherhood."

Brotherhood indeed, she thought. "Then why can't you start now? Show some compassion. It is in your power to make a difference. Those men did not fight because they wanted to. Anymore than you did."

"Oh, really?" He was listening. His twisted smile could not hide his feelings.

She was on the right track. "All it takes is your signature."

He did not offer her a chair. An orderly worked on a typewriter. The commander fidgeted with his new fountain pen, pretending she had left. Olga waited while he sifted through the documents on his desk. Finally the officer looked up. His cheek twitched. She held her ground. Could he sense her compassion for him, as well as for the men? His soul was in pain. He longed for home, his family, peace like everybody else.

"You don't want to have the lives of these men on your conscience," she persisted. "They will come to haunt you."

"What are you talking about," he said irritably, but she could tell that he did not mean it.

"Of course we'll care for the wounded," he said casually, and lit a cigarette, but the ice in his eyes had not melted. "What do you think? That we're monsters? We're not like you. We honor life."

Olga bowed her head. "Thank you, comrade."

The official cease fire would commence on May 8 at 2400 hours. According to the Soviet News, *Generalfeldmarschall* Wilhelm Keitel had signed Germany's unconditional surrender. From then on, the German people would be under the jurisdiction of the Soviet Union.

Tante Gertie poured vodka from the bottle Anatol had left into two glasses, and handed one to Olga. "This is not the kind of peace we hoped for," she said in a thick voice. "We must make the best of it. If only Ingo gets through. That would be a victory of kind."

Olga raised her glass, tears filling her eyes. "Ingo! May God protect you!"

"Will they stop shooting?" Anyna asked, raising her teacup. Tante Gertie had filled it with hot water, some chamomile leaves and saccharine. She wore a new apron Tante Gertie had embroidered with little rabbits. Her school had been closed. She now helped tend the garden, weeding and cultivating. Their livelihood depended on their crops.

"I would think so," Olga said, and took a long sip, wondering how she would manage under communism.

Chapter 30

A year had passed since the thousand year Reich had surrendered unconditionally. With Berlin in ruins, 1946 had not improved the lives of its citizens, except that they now lived in their basements because their homes were gone. A deep resignation had set in. People eked out a living from non-existent resources. Like Olga, the women waited for the return of their men, and stretched their meals with water and potatoes, if they were lucky to get some on special allotments. So far there had been no news of prisoners of war.

Olga raised her sweaty head from the debris she was clearing, and pressed her fist against her aching back. Her white headscarf and long-sleeved blouse barely protected her from the burning sun that stung right through the cotton. Her emaciated face had a deep tan. Dust and ashes irritated her nose and throat.

"Must be time for our break," she said to Frau Sauter, who worked to her right as part of a human chain, passing debris from hand to hand until it landed in an old truck. She took the bricks the woman to her left handed over, and swung them to her right. This sea of destruction would take years to clear. Since she did not expect to live that long, why think about it? Traffic had ceased to flow, other than occasional bicycles the Russians had missed. The bricks, stucco, rebar, and boards that had once been part of buildings were now scattered about in piles. Fractured walls marked the streets. The massive air raids had pretty much destroyed every building. Empty windows and door frames formed an abstract monument to war. The horrid smell of decaying corpses buried under the rubble was gone—they had been dug out and buried.

With Olga's help, some of the wounded from the Wunsdorf military hospital had survived and been released. Most had died from infection and diarrhea. Now she was obliged to work in this clean-up brigade.

"Let's hypnotize *Gernegross*," said Frau Sauter, a local, middle-aged woman. Over the past nine months the women had become friends, and entertained each other by poking fun at Herr Schmidt, who they had nicknamed *Gernegross*—show off.

Olga wiped the sweat from her face with her burlap mitt. The hours dragged. "I bet *Gernegross* gets his kicks from watching us slave away," she said for the umpteenth time, just to be saying something.

"Vengeance is sweet," said her neighbor. Over the months her duster had faded, torn and stained beyond repair. Her fallen husband's shirt covered her thin arms. There was no sun lotion or anything else people needed in now partitioned Germany, divided into four zones. Their borders could only be passed with special permits. The City of Berlin had also been divided into four zones. Wunsdorf was in the Russian Zone.

Gernegross, a heavy set man in his forties, had spent time in a concentration camp for being a communist, and was compensated with extra food and housing allowances, as were other people who had suffered under the Nazi regime. Sitting on a rickety chair, he watched his flock of women do their work. His signature on their time cards was a life or death sentence—no time cards, no ration coupons, no food. Olga was so thin and weak that she could barely stand up. The heat, hunger pangs, and exhaustion took their toll. If she could only get a piece of bread and a glass of milk. Like Gottfried, before his untimely death, she imagined dishes she had eaten back in the good old days in Latvia. Instead of food, she sucked in a lungful of air. The other women were just as hungry and tired as she, and would have to take over Olga's work if she passed out.

Three bricks held together by mortar came flying toward her. She received them and tossed the clump on, then turned to her left again, watching Frau Sauter throwing a partly burnt plank to her. They worked automatically, trading places from time to time. Other people were obliged to dismantle factories, pull up railroad tracks, or take down telephone poles to be shipped to the Soviet Union as war reparations.

A few managed to escaped the obligatory work and traded in the black market. They did not care that if caught they would be punished with heavy jail sentences, or deported to a Siberian labor camp. Herr Schund, who had offered to "protect" Olga from mandatory labor, served as go-between, selling stolen goods from American Army depots to his Russian contacts. Cigarettes, chocolate, fuel, falsified documents, and border passes were always in demand. This slick fellow from Bohemia had a motorcycle and a leather coat. Olga could not bear having anybody touch her. She'd rather go hungry.

Ingo. If only he were around, she'd do anything. Visualizing him coming toward her through the haze hovering over the ruins, the bricks slipped from her hands, and hit her foot. She stooped down and picked it up, her teeth clenched as the pain shot up from her injured toe.

"Can't you watch what you're doing!" bellowed *Gernegross*, wiping his face. He always wore a coat, tie, and felt hat, as if he worked in an office.

Tears welled up in Olga's burning eyes. She swallowed the lump in her throat, tasting the dust in her mouth that crunched between her teeth.

The women waited until she could pass the bricks on to Frau Arnold. A hot breeze stirred up the ashes and billowed her skirt. *Gernegross* perked up like a dog, raw lust on his feisty lips. What did he see in a body reduced to skin and bones?

"Get back to work," he ordered.

The women picked up their loads and resumed the routine. Olga noticed the carving in a stone that had been part of an ornate building that had once graced this street.

"It's heavy," Frau Sauter warned, swinging a large block of concrete over to her. The weight wrenched Olga down to her knees, and obliged her to carry it over to Frau Arnold, rather than swing it. "Why don't we work on lighter pieces?" she asked. "We'll never make a dent in this mess anyway." Her calloused hands hurt. The burlap mitts were torn.

"Should I need your advice," *Gernegross* said, "I'll ask for it." He always picked on her, because she spoke her mind.

"Let's cast a spell on him," Frau Arnold said. She was older than Olga and had four children. "Stare at him until he gets nervous and gives us a break."

The word passed along with the load. So did the snickers. *Gernegross* shifted on his chair, lit a cigarette, and adjusted his felt hat against the sun.

"It's working," Frau Sauter cheered. He could not hear her through the clanking of stones landing on the truck bed.

"You got yourself a terribly boring job, Herr Schmidt," she mocked. "Not much of a reward after standing up for the victorious Soviet Union..."

"That's none of your business, Frau Sauter. Stick to your work."

"Why do you treat us like enemies?" Olga asked. "We're all Germans."

Yesterday's villains were today's heroes. Her throat felt sore and scratchy. She craved for water. Sweat trickled into her eyes. Her wooden sandal slipped on the loose rocks. She teetered, regained her balance and swung a plank over to Frau Arnold.

"What's wrong with you, Frau von Schenck?" *Gernegross* shouted. "Can't you watch what you're doing!"

Olga rubbed her injured knee. "Why don't we work on solid ground?"

His big face flushed. He was always hot and sweaty. "I decide how we conduct our work, Frau von Schenck."

"Just a thought," Olga said innocently. "Besides, why don't you make yourself comfortable and sit in the shade, over by the broken wall. It's a lot cooler there. We could all work there. No need to suffer if you can help it, Herr Schmidt." Her solicitous smile had a beguiling appeal. Not that she had anything to smile about. What time was it anyway? With all the church bells melted into cannons, and the steeples holding them razed to the ground, the hours passed unmarked.

He finally blew his whistle. At the concentration camp he had been obliged to jump, now he could make others do it. "Take a break," he said.

As soon as the last fragment landed in the truck, the women stretched their aching backs and reached for their jars of water. They rinsed the dust from their mouths, then gulped it down. Most of them lived in rooms that had but two or three walls left, to which they climbed up on ladders. They cooked on open fires, and hauled water from the community pumps that had once served as fire hydrants. For those who had stoves, like Olga, the gas came on in the mornings and evenings. Everybody lived on potatoes and carrots, with 500 grams of bread per week. Tante Gertie had to share her house with a refugee family from Thuringia. Frau Kroeger and her four children had been quartered into the master bedroom.

Olga could only think of food now. The water had refreshed her, but could not still her hunger pangs. Her boiled potatoes were long gone. Anyna suffered from severe malnutrition, manifested by an ugly eczema that covered most of her face and body and scalp. Pus oozed from scabs that would not dry. In a week their garden vegetables should be ready to eat. The days dragged on forever, followed by sleepless nights and ongoing hunger pangs.

Stretched out on the rubble, Olga felt sweat pour from her skin and soak her cotton blouse. The air always had some residue of fire. How many people had died here, she wondered. The thought did not improve her overall fatigue. At least the Russian rapes had stopped, leaving the survivors to die of starvation. Now the KGB kept people on alert, especially those who had been members of the Nazi Party. Friends talked about loved ones who had been arrested, and probably deported to some Siberian gulag. Had Olga remained in Poland, she would be among them. The KGB could trace her background and arrest her here. People who had fled from what they considered Russian territory, including the Baltics, were convicted as traitors.

Some Day A Miracle Will Happen had become a thing of the past. Now Russian songs were *de rigueur*, reminding people of their lot. No more hope, no more illusions, nothing to wait for. People accepted reality and coped with the Russian occupation. Under present conditions, their lives would be short. Still, the time was precious. Once the German population was eliminated, the territory would be annexed to the Soviet Union. From the time Peter the Great had built St. Petersburg as window to the West, Russia had aspired to become part of Europe. Now their dream would come true. Russia did not need *Lebensraum*; they wanted Europe.

Did Ingo land in a Russian POW camp? Or had he been killed? Men taken prisoner by the Western Allies had sent postcards home.

Once again Olga fell into an emptiness she had suffered since her rape. If she could only see a tiny crack in that wall of hopelessness, something on which to attach a plan or solution, but nothing came to mind. She heaved herself up, and slowly rose to return to her work. Quitting time was hours away. Receiving and passing load after load, she watched the shadows grow until *Gernegross* blew his whistle again.

After a quick stretch, she picked up her tote and, joining her friends, she headed toward the streetcar stop, humming, *I know Some Day a Miracle Will Happen.*

"I've had all the miracles I care to see," Frau Sauter said. "Damn all those lies."

"They got us into a hell of a mess," added her friend.

In the tram, Olga found a place by an open window so that the flowing air could cool her hot face. The humidity begged for a thunderstorm. A passenger got up. Olga took his seat, and leaned back wondering what she could fix for supper. The commuter train took her to Zossen. If only Gottfried were still alive. Their music would lift her from the doldrums, from the sense of having brought all this pain upon herself.

She dozed off and saw Ingo running toward her. Faster and faster, yet the distance between them grew farther apart. He waved, beckoning her to come. But she could not move. *Olga, I'm coming.* Somebody blew cigarette smoke in her face. Would she ever see Ingo again?

In Wunsdorf, Olga passed Frau Bauerle working in her vegetable garden. Everybody had one now. They never talked about the shameful incidents with the Russians, as if nothing had occurred. The evening air carried the scent of blooming trees and the lake. Though no longer a summer resort, the beauty of the lake and the country-style homes and gardens of Wunsdorf soothed her strained nerves. The stores had opened again and sold goods on ration coupons. 1,000 calories a day did not go very far. Frau Hellmann's chickens scraped in the moist soil of her yard. Frau Warnecke raised geese for their Christmas dinner. Olga's chicks were only three months old, and would take at least another nine before she might get an egg. Anyna gathered weeds for them. They had no food scraps.

Olga gazed at the golden rays the setting sun cast over the lake. Anatol had been a romantic and a generous friend. His food had helped them through the worst. Was he still alive? The Soviet Union was sealed off from all contact with the rest of the world, which included the Russian Zone of Germany. He had not even left an address, knowing that any contact with German civilians would endanger his life.

Lothar had probably been released from his POW camp in America. The British and French kept their prisoners. Where was Ingo? She would never see Lothar again. Why did he even pop up in her mind?

Olga opened the squeaking gate to Tante Gertie's yard. Passing the lettuce bed, she selected a small, delicate head and tore off one of the tender leaves, stuffing it into her mouth and chewing hungrily until it dissolved.

Olga entered the dark and musty hallway like a thief. Anyna? Why did she not come to greet her mother? "Anyna?" Olga called out, leaving the front door open so that some fresh air would come in. No answer. In the bathroom she soaked her swollen and burning hands in cold water, washed her face, and brushed her dusty hair before looking for the child. Without soap she could not get her fingernails clean, nor wash the dust from her cuticles.

Anyna appeared in her nightshirt. "You're home, Mami."

Olga picked her up and swung her around. She was so light. "Why aren't you dressed? Are you sick, my sweet?"

Anyna shivered. Red blotches had formed on her infected, eczema-covered cheeks. "My head aches, Mami. And I don't feel well. Tante Gertie said I can stay in bed."

Olga carried Anyna to Tante Gertie's room.

Lying in bed, Gertie reached for Olga's hand. Her skin felt clammy. "I've been thinking, dear," she said in a low voice.

"About what?" Olga asked, sitting down at the edge of the bed.

"The future."

Olga closed her eyes. *As long as Ingo is away, there is no future for me.* She got up again and puffed Tante Gertie's pillow. The Russian ordeal had turned her into a frail old woman, or was it starvation? Her sallow skin sagged. The wrinkles around her mouth had deepened, and her braided gray hair had thinned. The once vibrant fifty-year-old was on the verge of death. Only her deep-set eyes still expressed warmth and life.

"How long do you think we can survive this kind of life?" she asked, slurring. She no longer bothered with her dentures.

"Until Ingo comes home," Olga said irritably. Why did she have to bother with this now, when she should be preparing supper?

Anyna climbed into Tante Gertie's rocking chair.

"What if he doesn't come home?" Tante Gertie asked softly.

"But he will," Olga said. "Father promised."

Tante Gertie's bony hand reached for Olga's. "Has it occurred to you that you might not be here when he comes?"

Olga bit her tongue. *What do you want me to do?* she wanted to shout. Fuck a man trading on the black market? "I'll make us some tea and prepare nettles. Did you collect some, Anyna?"

"I did this morning. And I got potatoes. Tante Gertie…"

"What?" Olga cried, picked up Anyna and swinging her around. "Why didn't you tell me right away? Potatoes! What a treat. Anyna, you're an incredible girl."

"They'll go well with the nettles," Anyna said quietly. She really was not well.

Olga danced around the room. "And I picked some lettuce. You see Tante Gertie, everything works out when you least expect it. Once the crops come in, we'll be on easy street."

Tante Gertie smiled, showing her gums. Loose strands framed her ashen face. After supper, Olga would give her a sponge bath and wash her hair with clay soap. It worked as long as you gave it a good rinse.

Using the firewood Anyna had brought stacked by the kitchen stove, Olga built a fire." You're a treasure, Anyna. What did you eat today?"

"I had a piece of bread and some jam. This is for you, Mami. I know how hard you work. You must be awfully hungry."

Famished, Olga thought. "We are all hungry. But you can have the bread now, since we'll have the potatoes later. That'll make waiting easier, right? And drink a glass of water. It fills the stomach. Did you have your milk?"

Anyna nodded, squeezing the pus from a pimple. Olga let it happen. All children suffered from malnutrition—rickets, eczema, swollen bellies. The child would die unless she got some help, both physically and emotionally. She was humiliated by her looks. How could Olga be so blind?

"Come, sweetie, you're such a big help. I don't know what I'd do without you." Olga quavered. What if she lost her child? If Anyna became an orphan, she would be one of the thousands of lost children roaming the ruins of Berlin, living off God only knew what.

Anyna sat at the kitchen table while Olga cut up the potatoes. "Tante Gertie is very sick, Mami. She can't get up anymore."

"I know, Anyna. Thank you for helping out, when you're not well yourself."

"It's nothing, Mami." She nibbled the bread, savoring every crumb. The radio went on about the Nuremberg Trials. Olga could not believe the accusations made against the leaders of the Reich. Admiral von Doenitz was a military man, and Speer an architect. Rudolf Hess had defected to England at the beginning of the war, supposedly seeking peace. The concentration camps? Killing Jews and others by the millions? Olga had not paid any attention to what was going on in the Jewish Ghetto. So that was why the Poles killed the Ingelheims. He had been in charge of the Ghetto, and knew what was happening to the Jews there. Why? How could all that happen? She had heard of the final solution, but had no idea that it meant killing millions of people.

Now the Russians took their turn in killing Germans, in retaliation for Germany killing their people. When would all this come to an end? Gas chambers? Genocide? Olga's grumbling stomach empathized with the victims of the camps. Must she die for that too? She remembered the patients at the insane asylum. Sweet Beate. No wonder the nurse was convinced that Olga was crazy. Why would anybody attempt suicide when people were murdering each other everywhere?

Admiral von Doenitz had implored General Eisenhower to give him another week before the unconditional surrender took effect so that he could save German women and children from the Russians. But the American general had no sympathy. Expecting no mercy, the *Kriegsmarine* had still rescued some 2.5 million doomed people. Millions more had perished. The work of the Devil was booming. Father had warned her. Where was he? Would he spare Ingo from torment? Four years of war at the front and now this! Did he land in one of those gulags, another cauldron of Hell?

Olga pricked the boiling potatoes. Almost done. The kettle steamed. She poured the gurgling water over dried tea leaves in the teapot, then checked the simmering nettles. Who would have thought of eating them?

"You must return to your husband," Tante Gertie said, taking the plate Olga brought to the bed.

"What?" she cried out. Anger flushed her face. Her heart pounded. "Never. I'd rather starve to death!" Why had she told Tante Gertie that she was married, and that Lothar refused to grant her a divorce? Lothar!

Disgust and loathing welled up. "You don't know what you are saying, Tante Gertie. He's a monster!"

Anyna rocked in Tante Gertie's chair. The mellow light of the evening hid the pimples covering her little face. "But he's my daddy," she said.

"So he is. But he has no use for us." Olga was so upset she could hardly contain herself. Lothar was all she needed.

Anyna came, put her thin arms around Olga's neck, and leaned her head against Olga's shoulders. "Grandmaman will be happy to see us. Daddy didn't do anything bad. He didn't really make me eat flies. And I only stayed in the closet for a little while. He always gave me candy."

Olga was furious. "Candy!" Had the world gone mad?

Anyna kissed Olga's cheek. "Don't be angry, Mami. What if Uncle Ingo never comes back? He could be dead like Omi and Ingrid and Uncle Gottfried."

"I happen to know that he will come back, and we will be here to receive him."

Go back to Lothar so that Anyna could play the little baroness! Honestly! She had enough of, *my son sacrificed his career for you and your child...* She'd rather sell her soul to the Devil. "Tomorrow I'll take Anyna to the doctor," Olga said. "Now let's eat. We're all starved." It had never occurred to her that Anyna could be lonely, that she missed her family. Lothar was her father, and Ingo her mother's friend. Anyna had seen him twice and had enjoyed his attention, but that was not the same as being with her father. Guilt washed over Olga, as if she'd been caught lying. Her obsessive love for Ingo had blinded her to Anyna's needs.

Noticing Tante Gertie's pleading glance, and Anyna's sad eyes, Olga said, "Fine. I'll write to the Countess," convinced that she would either never get an answer because mail to the West was censored, and possibly confiscated, or that the Countess would refuse to have them. Then both Anyna and Tante Gertie would have proof.

Anyna jumped up. "Please, Mami. Grandmaman will be so happy to hear from us. Then I'll be a baroness again."

Of course! A baroness. The little girl had ambitions. She was vain, and enjoyed the homage given to an aristocrat. Olga dished out the nettles—they looked like crude spinach—and put two potatoes on the plate, sprinkling some salt on top.

She and Anyna sat at the kitchen table and ate very slowly, savoring every bite. Even if they had three time that much, they would still be hungry. Anyna licked her plate clean. Olga scraped out the last drop. The empty bowls were perfectly clean, but remained on the table as if some fairy godmother might come and refill them. Olga felt rotten. Her child was starving to death, and yet had the dignity and self-discipline not to cry out and demand a right to live. What could, or would, Lothar do for her, provided he even wanted to see them again? The Countess would certainly do all she could to convince him that he had no obligation to take in a wife who had openly committed adultery and had asked for a divorce. He should consider himself lucky to be rid of the family he never wanted. Why couldn't Anyna see that? She was almost ten, and should know something about life.

Tante Gertie said from her bed, "This is a special day. Could we have some music for dessert? It's almost as good as food."

Hardly, Olga thought, raising her cracked and swollen hands. "Just look at them. How do you expect me to play with these fingers?"

"We're not at the Berlin Philharmonic. Do the best you can. It will do us good. Ulli and Rolf are here waiting for me. Can you see them?"

Olga shook her head. "I lost my touch. All I can see is the light in your eyes."

"We loved each other so much," she whispered. "The war took them from me. Then God in His mercy brought you and Anyna. It's been good to have you here with me."

Olga leaned her cheek against Tante Gertie's cool face. "Thank you for taking us in."

"You must go back to Lothar."

"I'd rather be a prostitute."

Tante Gertie chuckled. "That profession is overrun. Besides, if that was what you wanted, you could have taken Herr Schund. Lothar is Anyna's father. The Countess…"

"…is a bitch."

Tante Gertie grinned, showing her toothless gums.

"Have you two been plotting behind my back?" Olga demanded, amused by the game. Her anger had vanished.

"You and Anyna are too young to die. Ingo needs you. He'll be heartbroken when he comes home and learns you died waiting for him."

This was absurd, Olga thought, sitting down on the bed. Tante Gertie closed her eyes. The old clock ticked.

Olga relaxed. A divine spirit found her and carried her away. "Father?"

A familiar voice said, "You ignored my warning and were punished. You must leave. It will not be easy, but you can do it. Trust our guidance." The sweetness of dwelling in that other world held on a moment longer, then reality returned.

She saw Tante Gertie's radiant smile. Her suffering was over.

"Ulli and Rolf are here," she said cheerfully, as if the man she loved and her son were with her, the way Olga had just felt her father. "They await me. You must leave, Olga dear. Leave before it's too late. I wish I had taken your advice when you said that we should go west. I am truly sorry. This is your last chance."

A brilliant light expanded against the dark ceiling.

Tante Gertie stretched out her arms as if welcoming a dear friend. "They're here. Can you see them?"

That night Olga knew that she had to trust Father's guidance and find a way out of the Russian Zone. Though Tante Gertie was still alive, it would not be long before her loved ones would take her home. Lothar's hatred was no excuse, nor could she wait for Ingo. Should he come, Frau Kroeger would be here to give him the Countess's address in Bavaria.

Chapter 31

The following day Olga took Anyna to the doctor. Entering the waiting room, she nodded to the mothers and their children sitting on benches and chairs, staring at Anyna's pimpled and pus covered face. The sudden silence and curious look on their hollow-eyed faces said it all. Anyna braved their unconcealed shock, or was it empathy?

Olga squeezed Anyna's shoulder in support. They had to face facts, and do something about this eczema before it got even worse. If she could only sit down for a moment. Her feet burned from the hot sidewalk. The soles of her shoes were worn out, and offered little protection. This was a particularly hot and humid day. The room was stuffy, but not sweltering like the air on the rubble. *Gernegross* would give her an earful for not showing up to work. He still tried to intimidate her, upset that he had not succeeded.

Wiping the sweat from her face, she felt physically and emotionally exhausted. The struggle for survival was getting to her. She had spent the night wondering how to escape. For the moment she had no idea how to go about it, unless she walked across the border and risked getting caught by the guards and their dogs. Perhaps there was a way in which she could sneak into one of the refugee trains that brought expelled people from their homes in Silesia, Thuringia, and Bohemia, as well as other areas where the locals had forced ethnic Germans to leave. She would have to check it out.

"You're so kind. I'm very tired."

"Aren't we all?," the woman said, as Olga sat down and pulled Anyna on her lap. "Who would have thought."

The other people watched them. Complaining was not appreciated.

Anyna leaned her face against her mother's chest, embarrassed by the curious glances of the other children and their mothers. Olga felt sorry for her little baroness. They would leave, had to leave, before their health and strength gave them no choice. Her concern for Ingo and the fight for survival had sucked her dry. The prospect of facing the Countess and Lothar made her ill. What would they say when they saw the pus oozing from Anyna's scabs? *Was that soldier of yours worth sacrificing your child for? They come and go, you now.*

Yes, Olga thought. *Yes, A thousand times yes.* She rocked Anyna's frail body on her knees. *This isn't his fault. He did his duty for his fatherland, and now endures the consequences of a lost war.*

The waiting women whispered with each other. The children sat in silence, resigned to seeing a doctor who was bound to hurt them. Doctors and dentists always did. Olga picked up the flimsy newspaper. The cheap ink soiled her fingers. The headlines mentioned the Nuremberg Trials, and showed pictures of the accused leaders of the Nazi Reich.

The door opened. A woman carried her weeping child from the doctor's office. Sympathetic glances watched her leave.

"Next," the nurse called out.

Anyna dozed. Olga returned to the paper. The accused would be executed no matter what they said. If the Russians found out that she had not only come from Latvia, but had spent the war years in Poland, she would be deported.

Anyna's body smelled rotten. Hunger was a fatal disease. A warm breeze came in through the open window, blowing out the fetid smell of decaying bodies and gassy stomachs. A woman dragged her reluctant boy to the examination room. "Come on already. Dr. Forster doesn't have all day. See all these people?"

"I'm next," said the woman sitting next to Olga. "It won't take long. All I need is a disability certificate. It's my arm, see?" She pulled up the sleeve of her cotton blouse to show off a blood-soaked bandage. "You don't want to see what's underneath." She gestured at Anyna's face. "Nothing like that, though. Poor child. My arm will heal. I'm so fortunate."

The women exchanged quizzical glances. Fortunate? She was as thin as the rest of them. Her washed-out blouse and skirt hung loose over her skeletal frame.

"See?" she said triumphantly, holding up a foreign envelope. "It's from my husband. He's alive and well, a prisoner of the Belgians. Works in a coal mine. He says he might be released soon." Everyone envied her for her radiant smile. One of the women examined the envelope, the stamp of censor and the word *Belgique.* "That means Belgium," she said. "If I only knew what happened to Werner."

"By the time my husband comes home my arm will be fine," the lucky woman said. "He left two years, two months, and sixteen days ago."

Olga would give anything for a note from Ingo. Anyna heaved a sigh.

They were finally called in to see the doctor. Olga did not expect much from the thin, dark-haired woman behind the desk. She was writing. Since most of the physicians had been taken prisoner or, as former members of the Nazi party, suspended from practicing, Dr. Forster's workload was overwhelming.

"Undress her quickly," the nurse told Olga, and put Anyna up on the examination table. "That eczema looks pretty bad."

The doctor looked up. She had dark rings under her tired eyes. "Let's see what we can do," she said, rising. "As you know, our remedies are extremely limited." She lifted Anyna's chin, and took a close look at the skin. "I imagine it burns and itches, but you don't dare touch it."

Anyna nodded. She had tears in her eyes.

"I can tell that you're a brave girl. Nowadays, most children are," she told Olga. "Deprivation seems to make us humble. But let me take a look at the rest of the body." She talked with the easy manner of a trained physician, accustomed to dealing with suffering people. Her small hands were as white as her face. She had no time to get fresh air or take a stroll by the lake. Her white coat was buttoned up, and no other clothes showed, though Olga was certain that she wore a dress, or at least a blouse and skirt.

After examining Anyna's lungs, her mouth, and skinny body she said,. "Other than the usual malnutrition, her being extremely underweight and anemic, her main problem is the eczema. What she needs is vitamins. Lacking that, we must depend on the sun. It shines for everybody."

"The sun, Frau *Doktor?*" Olga wondered, feeling guilty and helpless.

Dr. Forster let the stethoscope drop to her flat chest. "Considering that she does not suffer from tuberculosis or any of the other diseases going around, you should count your blessings, young lady. We should soon be able to get legumes and possibly eggs. That should provide enough protein to build up some strength. Outdoor activity is essential. Get as much sun as you can, Anna. It not only produces vitamin D, it has all sorts of miraculous healing agents we can't put our finger on."

The doctor took Anyna's hand and checked the fingers. "What's that?" she asked Olga. "Didn't you see this boil? An infection like this is dangerous." She looked into Anyna's eyes. "It throbs, and hurts badly, doesn't it?"

Anyna nodded, biting her lower lip.

Olga felt dizzy. Her head buzzed. Boil? Why didn't Anyna tell her that she had a boil on her hand?

Dr. Forster said, "I'll lacerate it and clean it out so that it can heal. Your eczema will get better too."

Anyna hid her hand behind her back and would not let go when the nurse handed Dr. Foster a shining scalpel.

"It'll just sting. Like a bee. Isn't that better than having it hurt all the time? And it'll get worse. A lot worse." She frowned. Her arching brows drew toward each other. "If I don't treat it, you could lose your hand. You wouldn't want that to happen, would you? Now be a brave little girl."

"Will you cut up my hand?" Anyna asked timidly.

What if she cried, Olga thought, certain that she could not bear it. How could she neglect her child? The boil was on the verge of blood-poisoning. She felt sick to her stomach. That's all they needed, a squeamish mother to deal with while the patient endured the pain without a whimper.

"Of course not," Olga heard Dr. Forster say in the distance. Her head felt hollow and dizzy. "I'll just open the wound so that the pus can drain and the wound dry up. Why don't you watch the birds in the tree outside. It'll only take a moment."

Olga's ears buzzed. Her vision blurred and her senses waned. She held on to the edge of the examining table, feeling her body go limp.

She must not faint.

"I'll be fine, Mami."

The room swirled. The doctor, the nurse, and the instrument cabinet swam around in grotesque shapes and vanished in a fog. *Please, God, help me.* Darkness swallowed her.

"Mami, Mami! Ow, ow, ow…" reached Olga from far away, another world she no longer belonged to. Peace. *Father. Are you here?*

A light appeared, and with it the power that had carried her through so many dark hours. Tante Gertie? Ingo? Are you in the other world? The acid smell of ammonia forced her to gasp. Death was beautiful. Why did she have to come back?

"I'm fine, Mami. Look, it's all done. My hand will heal now."

"Keep your head down," the nurse told Olga. She was lying on the floor.

"We're done," Dr. Forster announced. "Anna is a brave little girl. This will make you feel much better. Come back in a week. I'm sure it'll all be healed by then. The eczema will take longer. Make sure it can dry. Stay in the sun."

The nurse helped Olga up.

"We all have our breaking point," Dr. Forster said. Her consideration and gentle touch broke Olga's restraint. Sobbing, she clung to Anyna like a life preserver.

"Anna will be fine," Dr. Forster reassured Olga, stroking her shoulder.

"We're waiting for Uncle Ingo," Anyna said. "He's in prison, and we must wait until he gets out."

"We all wait for somebody," Dr. Forster said. "I hope he will come soon. But this is not a good place to wait."

"I know." During the past months, Anyna had been dreaming of her father and grandmaman. "Let's go, Mami," she said. "Tante Gertie is waiting. Thank you, Dr. Forster."

The women in the waiting room gazed at Olga's tears and the cheerful child.

"I'm fine now," Anyna told them, raising her hand. "Dr. Forster lacerated it."

Back in the street, Anyna declined to climb into the handcart Olga had brought her in. "I can walk now," she said, and took the handle.

"I'm so sorry, darling," Olga said, walking beside her. "I neglected you. I…" A new outburst of despair welled up.

"But you didn't, Mami. We'll go to Bavaria. To Daddy and Grandmaman."

Gisela Zebroski

"Yes, love, we'll go to Bavaria," Olga said, feeling the hot sun burn her back. By now there was no doubt that her destiny would take her there. She would never be free until she got an official divorce from Lothar. That required courage.

Frau Kroeger awaited Olga at the front door, surrounded by her four children. Anyna pointed to her face and said cheerfully, "The sun will heal it. I'll be as good as new. That's what the doctor said."

"So glad to hear that," Frau Kroeger said, reaching for Olga's hand. "Sorry to be the bearer of bad news."

"Bad news? Now what?" Though they were both refugees and lived in Tante Gertie's home, Olga had not made friends with her housemate.

"Your aunt passed away. I am so sorry. Please accept my condolences. She was a kind woman."

Olga thought she had not heard right. "What? How do you know?"

"Tante Gertie is dead?" Anyna asked, a frown on her pimpled face.

Frau Kroeger, wearing an old apron over her cotton frock, had tears in her eyes. Had she and Tante Gertie formed a friendship Olga did not know about? The children stood around. Their clothes were too tight and too short, but they always looked tidy and their hair combed. Everybody was barefoot, saving their shoes for winter.

"While you're at work, I'd visit with your aunt in the kitchen. When she did not show up this morning, I got concerned. I knew how weak she was. She had talked about dying and worried about you, Frau von Schenk. So I knocked at her door. She didn't answer. I opened it. She was in bed. I thought she was asleep. But when I called out, she didn't move. I checked her pulse." Frau Kroeger put her arm around Olga's shoulder. "I'm terribly sorry. She must have suffered a heart attack. Just thought I'd prepare you for it."

Olga was at a loss. "Thank you."

"Let's go inside, Mami," Anyna said, pulling her mother's hand.

"We all need comfort at a time like this," Frau Kroeger went on. "I know how fond you were of each other. One could think you were mother and daughter. If there's anything I can do. I fixed some rosehip tea. Tastes quite good, even without sugar." She gestured to her oldest son. "Alfred, take Frau von Schenck's cart and put it away."

"Come, Mami," Anyna said, tugging at Olga's hand. "We must go inside."

"I'll be in the kitchen," Frau Kroeger said. She and her family had escaped the Russians in Thuringia. "I also have some potatoes. Would you join us for a bit of supper? It isn't much…"

Olga hesitated.

"Yes, thank you," Anyna said, and headed for Tante Gertie's room. Standing at the edge of the bed, Olga could not believe that her friend was dead. The face was serene, but her hand was cold and foreign to Olga's touch. "Good bye, my beloved friend. Your suffering is over. Ulli and Rolf are with you now." Gazing at the waxen face, she felt the presence of their spirits.

"Good bye, Tante Gertie," Anyna said quietly. She had grown accustomed to seeing people depart.

Olga pulled the sheet over Tante Gertie's face and joined Frau Kroeger and her children in the kitchen.

"After we bury Tante Gertie," Anyna told them, "we'll go to my Daddy's in Bavaria. He's a baron and I'm a baroness."

"A baroness?" Alfred mumbled, staring at Anyna as if he saw her for the first time. "You sure don't look like one."

"That's because we live here. In Bavaria my grandmother has a castle. She's a countess, you know."

"A countess? You don't say? Will you invite us to your grandmother's castle?"

"I might." Anyna said with a haughty smile.

"I'm good with horses," Alfred assured her. "We had a farm."

"You could be my coachman," Anyna said, with a regal gesture she had learned from her grandmother.

Later that evening, Olga played folk tunes on the piano. The children sang along. Anyna watched them from the sofa. She wore the dirndl Tante Gertie had made for her from a red swastika flag.

Olga played Schubert's *Ave Maria* and Bach's *Sheep May Safely Graze. I Know Some Day a Miracle Will Happen* brought Ingo into the room.

"Do you really believe that?" Frau Kroeger asked, wiping the tears from her eyes. "Do miracles happen? If only my Kurt would come back. But he is dead."

The children applauded.

Gisela Zebroski

Olga played *Rhapsody in Blue*—the music of her future.

Soon Olga's plan took shape. Over the following month she made four trips to West Berlin without encountering any difficulties. The western zones were islands surrounded by Soviet-held territory, making an escape to the city meaningless. Besides, West Berlin looked as dismal as the eastern part of the city. Getting to Western Germany was another matter. Not only did she need a permit to enter any of the Western Zones, she had to be a resident of West Berlin to get on the train. The autobahn served as corridor for the Western Forces, transporting supplies and personnel in and out of the city.

Five weeks had passed since Olga had mailed her letter to Lothar, asking him for help. His answer arrived in an envelope that had the countess' coat of arms embossed on it. She stared at the familiar handwriting, too nervous to open it, and took it to the lake. Moved by the beauty of the setting sun's golden light on the ripples, she sat down on her favorite bench. Last year she had sat here with Gottfried and reminisced, rather than talk of the dark days that lay ahead. Nothing had prepared her for what had happened. Now she must face the future. Take the big step into what could only be an unpleasant world, and hope for the best. Reluctantly she tore the flap open. Once again she would be at the mercy of her husband and her mother-in-law.

Inning, October 2ⁿᵈ, 1946

Olga!

Your letter caught me by surprise. I did not expect to hear from you, but Maman had assured me that you would get in touch with us sooner or later—in this case sooner.

Considering the circumstances of our relationship, I have to agree with Maman that it would be quite improper to have you come here to stay with us. (Housing of any kind is difficult to come by for official residents, and definitely not available to wayward refugees.) But as Anna Magdalena's legal father, it is my duty to look after her. I am very sorry to hear of her malaise and have contacted my cousin, Adelaide, in Switzerland, asking her to take the child into her care. She agreed to do so and will contact the Red Cross. They will help get a visa for Anna Magdalena.

As soon as you send her to us, we shall look after her. As I mentioned before, there is no space for you here. Maman and I share a room in which I have a piano. I work on my compositions. Presently I have a small jazz band and entertain American service men. I have always been interested in jazz, and have established a reputation as serious jazz musician.

You may give Anna Magdalena our regards, and tell her that we look forward to seeing her. Grandmaman is eager to continue her lessons in proper manners before we let her travel to Switzerland.

Let me know when we can expect her.

Lothar.

Staring at a brilliant sky which would soon darken, she dropped the letter on her lap. It was so typical of him. He could not have told her his mind more succinctly. He knew how painful it would be for Olga to give up her child. But to have Anyna travel by herself from Berlin to Bavaria could only come from a sick mind. Not only were the borders closed for Germans, the trains were packed with refugees and uprooted people from all over Europe.

The serene beauty of the lake, the trees abounding in fall colors, and reeds swaying softly in the gentle breeze could not ease the turmoil in her heart. Of course Anyna had to go to Switzerland. Adie and her husband Richard, a Swiss, would treat her well in a world that had not been touched by the war. They had the means, and no children of their own. There would be specialists, medications, and healthy food for her. Olga would make this sacrifice and let Anyna go, but the pain of living without her beloved child was unimaginable.

Soon darkness would set in, and with it the winter of her life. Her long struggle for independence would end, and her freedom once again be taken from her. Lothar would demand gratification for his generosity.

Chapter 32

On the 3rd of November Olga and Anyna were ready. During their tearful farewell, Frau Kroeger promised to inform Ingo of Olga's whereabouts. They would stay in touch. Over the past weeks Olga had befriended one of the guards at the Berlin station while pretending to help refugees with their children and luggage. He would be on duty tonight. Olga would talk with the guard, so that Anyna could take their suitcase to the train and then wait for Olga. In the faint light of the station lamps, she could slip among the regular passengers milling around or waiting for their trains.

"I'd better help those people again," Olga said to the guard, a former soldier who had walked home from the war and escaped being taken prisoner.

"Go ahead. As soon as I'm free, we'll go to *The Lame Duck* and have a beer."

"I can't wait," she said, and joined the women leaving the train that had brought them from the east for another that would take them further west. The guard watched her. She waved at him, then offered her services to a tired woman with two small children and a heavy piece of luggage.

The woman, wearing a wrinkled coat and scarf, looked up in surprise. Her eyes had the drawn look of a haunted being who could not escape the horror she had witnessed. "Very kind of you. We've been through hell. I didn't think I'd ever get out alive. You can't imagine what's going on in the Sudetenland. I must get on that train."

"Me too," Olga said. "I'm escaping from here."

"You are? The Russians. Is that it?"

"Worse—we're starving to death. My child is very ill. We must get to her father. Can you pretend I'm one of your people?"

The woman did not bother to understand, just said, "that's fine with me," and let Olga help her carry the basket, while she had one of her children on her arm. The older one, no more than five, teetered along, too tired to care where he was going. A cold wind blew through the broken walls of the station.

Winter was setting in. More cold and hunger, illness and despair. Olga shivered. Once again she would be homeless. Only this time she would be obliged to knock at the door of people she despised.

"You have no idea how brutal people can be," the woman whispered.

"I know," Olga said. Death came in many forms. She had survived a firestorm, rape and starvation, and somehow that seemed less painful than the carefully aimed insults of her husband.

The woman's basket was heavy. Why had she picked her?

The dark train pulled in, the locomotive puffing and hissing. There was Anyna. She left her suitcase and came running to Olga, landing in her mother's arms. Together again. With that, all doubt and pain vanished.

"Let's go, darling," Olga said, and climbed aboard the already overcrowded train. She had no pass, no ticket, no right to be here. That they would leave Berlin was all that mattered now. People bustled and shoved, setting up a place that would make the long journey bearable. Their breath and the warmth of their bodies would soon take the chill out.

Once the train was in motion, people settled down. Luckily they traveled in a regular passengers car. Many were transported in open cattle cars and froze to death. The elderly were in a stupor, depending on their daughters to fend for them.

Olga took out one of the sandwiches she had prepared from their bread rations. She had taken all the food allotted for the month and traded with Frau Kroeger, who shared her bread coupons for milk. They settled down on their suitcase and ate. The world immediately felt and looked better, despite the people squeezed into the dark train, the smell of their bodies, and the cold.

"When will we get to Bavaria?" Anyna asked again. Ever since she had been told that they would go there, she had revived and taken charge of the chores while Olga was at work. She was going home, not once more an uprooted refugee. "And then I'll go to Switzerland, right Mami?. Frau Kroeger said it's a beautiful country with high mountains, even higher than those in Bavaria."

"Yes, even higher than that," Olga said, a twinge in her heart. The train jumped switches. Occasionally they passed the lit window of a home that had been repaired. Olga could not imagine that Berlin would ever become a real city again. But that was not her problem. She listened to the women talking about the homes they had been obliged to leave, the farms that had belonged to their families for generations, and the animals they had loved.

"Try to sleep, my darling. Put your head against my shoulder."

Children talked to each other. They'd been on the go for days with little food, long waits, and grumpy mothers.

The woman Olga had helped introduced herself as Frau Hartmann. "The past year was a nightmare," she told Olga.

"We were always scared," said her five-year-old son.

Olga could not distinguish her face, and paid no attention to another tale of cruelty and humiliation. *Ingo. If I only knew where you were. That you're alive. My heart aches for you, now more than ever. I tried to stay away from Lothar, but you must understand. As mother I must look out for my child. You should see her now. Seems that she loved her father more than me. Figure that one out. If I had you, I could bear it.*

She visualized him, and imagined him standing beside her. Love washed over her heart. He would always be with her. She had to believe in it, and feel the magic that would shield her from what was yet to come. Love had the power to turn every moment into a beautiful experience. Some day they would find each other again.

The train lurched to a sudden stop. Startled, Olga looked around in the darkness. She couldn't see a thing. Had somebody pulled the emergency brake? Passengers rammed against each other and groped for a hold. Through the window, Olga recognized a small station. Floodlights lit up the train. Was this the border? Would the guards check papers? Where could she hide? The toilet? No, they would force it open. How would she get there without arousing suspicion? Male voices shouted orders. Somebody knocked at the wheels. Had her date reported her? The women whispered as if they were also hiding out. The engine puffed idly. Men in Russian uniforms and steel helmets passed along the platform. Doors were opened and thrown shut. Olga's heart raced. They pulled a man into the station. Had he also been a stowaway?

A whistle blew. The commotion stopped as the engine jerked into motion. The wheels accelerated. They were on their way. Olga held Anyna for a long time. They dozed off.

Daylight woke them. Nobody knew where the train was going, or how much longer they would have to stay in the packed car. Rain washed the dirty windows. Villages, barren fields, and knolls passed. A forest. Stations had unfamiliar names. Olga dozed off again.

Anyna's voice roused her, "We're coming to Hannover, Mami." Stiff and sleepy, Olga blinked through the window. They passed sinister looking ruins under gray skies. The train jumped switches. Her body ached from sleeping on the suitcase. Passengers rustled and spoke in loud voices. The city looked as dismal as Berlin, but it was in the west.

"We're in the British Zone," said Frau Hartmann. "Do you supposed they'll have some food and a bed for us?" She and her children were exhausted. Nobody had a watch, not that it mattered. They were hungry and tired. A baby wailed, hungry and wet. The women talked. During the long journey many of them had struck up a friendship. The children teased each other.

"When will we get to Bavaria?" Anyna asked. "Is it far from here?" Her large eyes stood out in her blemished face, framed by her white rabbit cap and new blue coat.

Leaving the train, a cold wind welcomed them. The station had lost its walls and glass roof, but the rubble had been cleared away and the platforms repaired. They had to wait their turn to descend the steep iron steps. The refugees congregated at the exit, where a representative of the refugee organization received them. Anyna stared longingly at the make-shift stands that offered sandwiches and beverages for coupons. The smell of fried sausages drew the hungry refugees toward food that was not available to them.

Without saying it, Anyna understood that they had no ration coupons and tugged at Olga's hand. "We must find a train to Bavaria. Daddy is waiting. What will Grandmaman say when she sees me? I must go to Switzerland right away." Her eyes on the sandwiches, she added. "I'm sure she has some food for us. Jadwiga always had a snack for me."

Olga shivered, wishing she could stay in this city. But Anyna would not settle for less than seeing her family and going to Switzerland.

Leaving the station, Olga noticed bleached-blonde women swaying their hips at the British soldiers standing guard. Their short coats, high heels, and red lipstick were an unfamiliar sight. The Russian Zone did not tolerate prostitution. The buildings around the station had been hollowed out by carpet bombing, but trams had resumed. Some people rode bicycles, others walked, carrying shopping bags or briefcases. A British convoy of military trucks passed. Soldiers in berets and greatcoats strolled along the sidewalk, smoking. Everybody had a place to go home to. The war was over. The jagged remnants of what used to be a hotel testified to the bloodshed.

A man in a fedora and a thick black mustache accosted Olga. "Looking for a place to stay, Fraulein? I've got a warm room. Chocolate for the poor child. American cigarettes." He spoke with a thick Hungarian accent. His feisty and lecherous lips invited her into his bed.

Here was her chance, Olga thought. Enter the trade and forget Lothar. But she said, "I'm not for sale."

He looked deep into her eyes. The man had a day's growth of what would be a black beard. "No?" he said with a sidelong glance at Anyna. "Your little girl looks hungry and sick. Here, take this. Uncle Janosz is good man." He smiled at Anyna, pulled a chocolate bar from his pocket, and petted Anyna's fur cap. He had large yellow teeth and a fleshy nose. If Olga took care of him, he would take care of her and Anyna. Why be a prude? As soon as she got to Inning, her body would be abused by Lothar. For all she knew, Janosz would be easier to get along with. He had no bone to pick.

"May I take it, Mami?" Anyna asked.

Olga examined the man's cunning eyes. "You are a cruel man. Using chocolate on a hungry child as bait for me. I'm a respectable woman." She had no idea why she was so upset. Things were getting to her. Just thinking of Lothar brought out the worst in her.

"Now, now, don't get angry with Uncle Janosz," the man said in a soothing voice, and stroked Olga's arm. She withdrew. He ignored the gesture. "You're a pretty woman. I like you. I take care of you. Hannover's a bad town."

"We're going to Bavaria. To my husband."

"Husband?" he said in disbelief. "You don't have a husband. You come with me. We can be happy."

"Yes, she does," Anyna insisted. "We go to Daddy and Grandmaman." She took the chocolate bar, and curtsied. "Thank you."

The man shrugged. His heart would not let him take his gift back. "You're a nice little girl."

"I am a baroness. My father is a baron. He will send me to Switzerland."

"Really? Switzerland? I come from Budapest. Glad to be of service, Baroness. You can keep the chocolate." He tipped his hat and left.

A sign fastened to a broken wall said, "*Bahnhofsmission*." Olga entered the warm hall. The sudden heat made her dizzy. Circles spun in her eyes. Leaning on Anyna's shoulder, she dragged herself toward the reception desk, where a nun in modern habit greeted Olga as her consciousness faded. She stumbled. The nun caught Olga in her arms, and led her to a chair.

"Mami is hungry," Anyna said. "We must go to Bavaria. That's where my Daddy is. But we don't have papers."

The nun's helper brought tea and bread. "Here. This will make you feel better. We'll have lunch in an hour. My name is Sister Maria."

Helpless and weak, Olga broke into sobs. "Thank you. Thank you so much." This haven had caught her off guard.

"We're all going through hard times," Sister Maria said softly, and helped Olga shed her coat and headscarf. "God knows why. He is testing our faith in His son, Jesus Christ, our redeemer, who will lead us back to our Father. You see, people replaced God with Hitler! Satan destroyed our world. Now we must do penance, and lead a God-fearing life to return to grace. Christ in his infinite love and mercy died for our sins. Those who believe in Him will find salvation."

"Thank you, Sister Maria, for your kind words," Olga said dutifully. She couldn't entirely agree. Yes, Satan had taken charge of a world that had denounced God, including her. But who was to know what was cause and effect, not that it mattered? She had to live through her trials, and not let anybody run her life again.

"God did not abandon us, we abandoned Him," Sister Maria said, a serene glow in her hazel eyes. Her pale skin had never been out in the sun, nor had her white hands ever washed dishes. "Tonight you can stay here on one of our cots. Tomorrow I'll direct you to the refugee office. They will give you a border crossing permit, so that can get into the

American Zone and reunite with your husband. But come, lunch is ready. Then I'll show you to your bed. Some rest will get you back on your feet. Thank the Lord that your husband survived the war. A miracle."

Women and children of all ages sat at long tables and ate the soup prepared from food donated by American churches. It had meat and vegetables, but tasted peculiar. "That's because it's made with dried vegetables," the women at the table explained. "The Americans even dry potatoes. Not bad, just, well, one has to get used to it. Hungry people eat everything."

Olga's stomach filled up right away with the unaccustomed food, but she still felt hungry.

Anyna braved the staring children. "That's what you get when you don't have vitamins," she explained. "We're going to Bavaria, and then I'll go to Switzerland for a cure," she told them.

"To Switzerland," one of the boys said, wiping his nose with his sleeve. "Where is that?"

"Don't tell me you never heard of Switzerland," Anyna said. "It's a beautiful country where they have no war and all the food you can eat, and clothes, and beautiful homes and people ride in cars." She not only told the children all she had heard about the famous country, but conjured all the wonders she could think of. The children listened wide-eyed, as if listening to a fairy tale. They forgot about Anyna's eczema, and admired her like a princess visiting them from her castle. They wanted to know more and more, inspiring Anyna to talk about Grandmaman who was a countess, and the real princes who had paid homage to her. She told them of her Daddy, who had been born in New York and was a famous musician. Even the adults were listening, fascinated by this extraordinary girl and her illustrious background—a fantastic prospect when they would be taken to a refugee camp.

Stuffed to capacity, Olga stretched out on her cot with Anyna at her side. She had fallen asleep. Somebody sobbed. An infant cried, then stopped.

The young woman on the cot next to Olga's nursed her baby. She had roughly snipped off hair, scars across her head, and a patch on her face. Her suckling infant rested his tiny fists against her breast. She held him with her arm. Her hand had been amputated.

"She introduced herself, "Anneliese Rotmann. I'm from Posen. We had no idea the Poles hated us so. Remember that Posen was declared a fortress. That meant our soldiers would fight to the last man." She cackled sarcastically. "The battle didn't last long—the Russians broke through in no time. The commanding officer surrendered, and came out carrying a white flag. The Russians mowed him down, and the men he had with him." She rocked the baby, agitated by the memory. The baby opened his eyes, looked at his mother, then suckled again.

"Now the men had no choice. They'd be killed no matter what they did, and fought until their ammunition ran out. I don't know how many the Russians killed. They took no prisoners. When they searched the cellars they found us. They didn't care whether we screamed or fought. They shot one. After that, the rest of us knew what to expect and let them rape us until we passed out. Then the Poles took their turn." Her lips quivered. Anneliese rocked her baby hard. The infant cried.

"Shh. It isn't you fault, *Ernstchen*. He's the result of all that. But he's mine. Only mine." She kissed the baby's head, and placed her nipple back into his tiny mouth. He suckled quickly as if somebody might take it away again. With the baby in her arms she regained her composure, wiping off her tears with her stump. "The Poles were worse. Turned people into living torches, smashed babies against walls, cut up women, did whatever they could think of to torture us. Nobody stopped them. When they found me…" Sobs broke off her story.

Olga stroked the young woman's arm and swallowed her own tears. The people on the cots around them had fallen asleep. Olga thought of Beate, who had saved her at the mental institution.

"My mother bled to death. We couldn't save her. They chased me down and pumped into me like wild dogs. Then they chopped off my hand because I fought back. You can't imagine what it's like. Thank God it was my left hand. I pretend it was a nightmare, and take care of my baby."

Olga thought of the Russians at Wunsdorf who had unloaded their hatred and frustration on helpless German women. She had learned to put it behind her, like Anneliese. Did Vanya survive, and return to his family in Russia to watch his daughter Natasha grow up? His fate had been as bad as hers.

Anneliese went on. "They left me bleeding and crying. Others came and dragged me to prison. The women took care of my wounds, wrapped the stump in their underwear and stopped the bleeding. When the Polish guards saw I was getting better they had me clear rubble with my stump and one hand. We lived on watery soup and a daily potato. Can you imagine? I was pregnant; the father was one of those maniacs." She kissed the baby's soft head. "The women in our work camp delivered him. One of the guards took pity on me, and brought us warm water. Later he let me escape. Amazing, isn't it? For all the bad ones, there's one who cares. I never knew anything about Jews being killed, or that calling Poles *Untermenschen* was bad. Now I've got half an *Untermensch*." She chuckled. The baby wrapped his little hand around her finger. Her hand was chafed, the nails broken to the quick. Ashes and dirt were lodged in the folds of skin on her stump. "I named my baby Ernst, after my father. He fell in Russia two years ago. Now I must live for my baby."

Olga smiled. "He'll grow into a fine boy. Like my little girl here. Children are born because their destiny wills it. We're only the vessel. In the end, they have a life of their own. You'll find a life, and a place for the two of you. I must return to my husband, the father of my little girl."

Anneliese looked dumbfounded. "Why do you say that? I'd think you'd be happy to reunite with your husband, and that he'd be happy to find his family."

Olga smiled ruefully, thinking of Ingo. "Yes, I know I should be. We all have a cross to bear."

The light was turned off. Silence fell over the hall. People went to sleep, or dwelled on their memories of the places they had called home. Olga tried not to think about the reception awaiting her in Bavaria, but that anxiety would not leave her.

With her eyes closed she saw the light she had been waiting for, and felt the joy of Father's presence. "Father, my beloved Father. You did not abandon me. Is Ingo with you? Please tell me. I can bear it as long as I know he is with you and you will not leave me."

Ingo is alive, she heard a voice say. *He will survive and come to you when he can.*

Her heart raced with joy. "When, Father, when?"

When he is free. You must return to Lothar and wait for him. Trust our guidance. Take pity on Lothar. The light faded, and was gone.

Two days later Olga and Anyna fought their way onto a train to Munich. Olga pushed Anyna inside, and fought her way against the stampede of passengers. Sister Maria had supplied them with sandwiches for the long journey to southern Germany. Every station was packed with desperate travelers trying to reunite with their families. Refugees stormed the trains as they had during the last days of the war. They clung to steps and bumpers. Transports from Eastern Europe brought expelled Jews from Russia, refugees, and released POW's.

Hours later the train pulled into Munich. Olga was weak, hungry, and discouraged. Anyna had eaten the sandwiches.

Stumbling down the steep steps, Olga lost her balance. Helping hands caught her before she hit the ground. Somebody took her over to a bench. Anyna sat down beside her. "Mami, we're in Munich. You said, it wouldn't be far now. We must find another train. Grandmaman is waiting for us."

Where had she failed? Olga wondered. How could Anyna be so eager to see her father and Grandmaman? Didn't her mother mean anything? Olga—neglected, unloved, superfluous. What was the use? Once she delivered Anyna to her family, she might as well disappear.

Passersby stared.

"Come on, Mami, we must go to Inning."

A woman dressed in a winter dirndl watched them.

Olga looked up, teeth chattering. "I'm a bit weak. It'll pass."

The woman left. Olga noticed a pair of polished shoes in front of her, and looked up. An elderly man in a Tyrolean hat and loden coat placed a wax paper package in Anyna's lap. "Nobody can blame you for this," he said in the Bavarian dialect.

Olga nodded. "Thank you. Things have been hard."

Anyna unwrapped the sandwich. "Look Mami, salami. May I taste it?"

"Of course, my sweet. You can eat it all. I'm not hungry."

Anyna took a couple of bites then handed the rest to her mother. "This will be good for you, Mami. You need food so that we can get a train to Inning."

Olga did not know what to say. She took the half-eaten sandwich and ate it quietly. Snowflakes fell on the platform, and soon formed a thin white cover over the cracked flagstones.

"Come, Mami," Anyna insisted. "Grandmaman is waiting."

Chapter 33

Muhlstrasse 2 was a normal, two-story stucco building a block from the church and the bus stop. Inning did not have a train station. Anyna rang the bell.

Olga expected to be chased away by the father of her child like an unwanted solicitor. Ridiculous. She had to get over this notion that Anyna was hers alone. Every child had two parents.

A heavy-set woman opened and faced her, broad-legged, arms akimbo. She blocked the way with her rotund body. A washed-out duster strained over a voluminous bosom. She looked Olga and Anyna up and down, a deep crease between her thick, unkempt brows, cold rejection in her eyes. "Don't tell me you're his wife."

"If you're talking about Herr von Schenck, I am. Is he at home?"

"What do you think?" she said in a raspy voice. "Can't you hear him? Plays the piano day and night. His mother, the so-called Countess, thinks I'm her servant. Acts like she's in some castle or something. So you're his wife. I guess this is his daughter."

"Yes, I am," Anyna said unperturbed. "My name is Anna Magdalena."

"Is that so?"

"Can we come in?" Olga asked.

"If you're his wife, what can I say? It's not something I condone." She stepped aside, and pulled the door open all the way. There was just enough light to see the hallway. Everything else was dark. "And let me tell you right now, don't think you'll stay here. I rented the place to the Countess. Then comes her son. An ex-POW. Wants to be with his mother. What can I say? Not that he doesn't have his own room." She closed the door again. "All that cold air. Don't you know that we got no wood? No. Don't say anything. You people come from some place nobody ever heard of. I don't care where it is. Just go down the hall. Follow the noise."

Olga and the woman went down the stuffy hallway, where clothes and shoes were scattered along the wall, and stopped at the end.

"Never asks whether it's convenient," the landlady said. "Aristocrats. I should have known better when that old lady first rented the apartment. Then they put another family in. More refugees. I'm telling you, this is getting to me. But I'm stuck. First Hitler, now the Americans. Act as if they own the world."

Behind the door Lothar practiced American jazz, just as he had mentioned in his letter.

Anyna opened the door and ran into the dim room. "Daddy! Grandmaman! We're here."

Olga followed, and saw Lothar look up from the keyboard of a baby grand that occupied a third of the small room.

Anyna threw her arms around his neck. "Daddy! Daddy!"

"Anna Magdalena, is that you?" the Countess asked from her bed.

"Yes, Grandmaman. We finally got here." Anyna ran over to the Countess, and took her hand. "I'll kiss it this time. But people don't kiss their grandmother's hand anymore."

"But you are not 'people,'" she said. "You are my little baroness."

"Yes, of course. We've been away so long. I'm so glad you can see that I'm still a baroness."

Lothar awoke from his shock. "Well, so you are here." He had probably hoped they would never make it. The small table lamp on the piano shone on his notes, leaving the rest of the room dark. Olga noticed two beds along the wall, an armchair, and a small table with stacks of sheet music strewn over it, the chair, and the floor. His face had matured but not changed. His even features—the straight nose, distinct jawbones and petulant mouth that always impressed people. His sky blue eyes looked past Olga, as if she did not warrant his attention. She remembered his dry chuckle, a sign of uncertainty. He still wore his favorite black turtleneck under a tweed jacket, and the corduroy trousers his mother had taken to Bavaria, anticipating his return. He gazed at Olga with a blank stare.

Olga nodded a greeting. "Good evening, Lothar. Countess," she said, as if she dropped by from next door. "Your landlady showed us in. She isn't exactly friendly."

"No, she isn't," Lothar said. "So you made it."

Anyna sat on the Countess's bed, and stroked the famous red fox throw that warmed her grandmother's feet. "We came by train," she said. "It took days. We had to escape from Berlin, and stopped in Hannover and in Munich."

"That's the only way you can get here, Anna Magdalena," Lothar said sarcastically. He looked healthy and virile. His thick dark hair had outgrown the military cut.

"I can't believe we finally got here," Olga said. "I didn't think we'd get out of Berlin, and then across the border into the British Zone." Nobody offered her a chair.

"Daddy, we're starved," Anyna said. "I missed you. But first we must have something to eat. Mami fell down at the station. A stranger gave us a sandwich."

"We're very hungry," Olga echoed, feeling faint again.

"That's what you get for taking off on your own," the Countess said in her icy, articulate voice. "You'll find some potatoes on the shelf above the hotplate. That's our kitchen now. With all the refugees flooding in, I had to give up my apartment. I am not about to share a kitchen with them. Until we get some civilized living quarters, I shall use a hotplate for tea and potatoes. Don't think we have food to spare. Our rations here are no better than those in the Russian Zone. Thank God, Lothar works for the Americans. They have plenty, and don't mind trading for his music. For that, he degrades his art and plays jazz." She glanced at him. "He is quite good at it."

Olga went to the shelf in the dark corner, and found a plate with boiled potatoes. She stuffed one into her mouth. The pleasure of having some food helped her cope with the rejection. The worst was over. She was here, and they could not send her away. Chewing, she opened a can of American sardines, cut three slices of bread, and gulped some milk straight from the bottle. It tasted heavenly. The food perked her up like a shot of vodka. Buttering a slice of bread for Anyna, she prepared herself for the attack that was bound to come from Lothar and his mother.

Anyna took her open sandwich and the cup with milk. "Thank you, Mami." Then she returned to Grandmaman and Daddy, who had remained at the keyboard. The prominent baby grand had the only light of the room. They did not bother with the ceiling lamp. All the light was concentrated on the music book.

Olga ladled water from a bucket into an aluminum tea kettle, and placed it on the hot plate. Once it boiled she would fry potatoes. In the meantime, she stuffed a buttered piece of bread into her mouth.

"Don't think we have extra food," the Countess reminded Olga again.

"I'll fix a snack for us," Olga said, and kept eating. On the shelf she found a hunk of Swiss cheese, a can that had *Spam* written on it, some jam, and a jar that said *peanut butter*. Olga had no idea what it was, opened it, and dipped her finger into the brown substance. She found that it was quite tasty, and probably meant to be spread on bread since it was called butter. Anyna would like it.

"Lothar entertains at the American NCO Club," the Countess said. "They occupy the garrison and a good part of Fuerstenfeldbruck. Lara made friends with Sergeant Aldrich, a nice fellow from Texas. He set things up for Lothar, and has good contacts in the black market. You get goods rather than worthless money. American cigarettes are worth their weight in gold. Tobacco addicts give anything for a pack." The Countess had Anyna fluff up her pillows, forgetting that she despised talking of money. "Lothar understands the black market better than anybody, don't you Lothar?"

Olga remembered Ottie's addiction to tobacco. She missed her feisty sister.

After dropping some loose tea leaves into the boiling water, she sliced the potatoes into the frying pan where butter sizzled. Those red hot coils provided an amazing amount of heat. While the potatoes fried, Anyna joined Olga at the kitchen shelf, picking a slice from the pan and taking the bread Olga had prepared for her. She bit into it, and chewed. "Hm, that's good, Mami. I'm so hungry."

Where would they sleep, Olga wondered, examining the crowded room. There was a screen behind which Olga noticed a bed pan— obviously in use—which cast its stench into the room. The Countess probably spent most of her time in or on the bed. The room had no space for her or Anyna, not even floor space for them to sleep.

She poured tea for everybody into English bone china cups. Sleeping with Lothar was unthinkable; so was asking the landlady for a place.

"After Tante Gertie died," Anyna said, munching on her sandwich, "we could not stay in Wunsdorf any longer. We had no food, and Mami had to work all day clearing rubble." She spotted the Countess' life-size portrait on the wall. "Look, Mami, Grandmaman brought my favorite picture."

"Grandmaman was, and still is a very beautiful lady, Anna," Lothar said, taking the lamp to the table. The room lit up.

The Countess gasped. "Your face, Anna Magdalena. What happened to your face? How could you let this happen, Olga? You've ruined your daughter."

"Why do you think I wrote to you? Anyna…"

The Countess interrupted, "Please, don't use that vulgar name. My granddaughter is no Latvian peasant."

"To me she is Anyna," Olga insisted, dishing out the potatoes. "Now you can see for yourself how ill she is. She needs immediate attention—food and vitamins." She handed Anyna a plate. "Come, darling, let's eat. Grandmaman cannot do these things anymore. She is too frail to take care of her guests. So we must help ourselves. And Daddy must work on his compositions. He cannot help us either. So let's eat. I'll put some sugar in your tea. You've been talking about Grandmaman and Daddy all the time. And here we are—you came home to your family."

"Is that true, Anna Magdalena?" the Countess asked.

Sitting at the small round table Olga had cleared, Anyna turned around. "Of course, Grandmaman. I missed you so much, and Daddy too. I haven't seen you for a long time. Will you teach me to be a baroness again? I'd like that very much."

"You must not talk with your mouth full. A baroness would never do that." The Countess took her tea cup. "Of course I shall teach you. We cannot send you to Switzerland acting like a street urchin. Tante Adie is very particular. She is your Daddy's cousin."

"I'm sorry."

"We are so happy that you came, my little one," Lothar said. "I wrote to Tante Adie. She will be glad to look after you. The Red Cross will get you over the border. I'll miss you, but that face of yours," he paused, "looks pretty awful. You wouldn't want to run around like that for the rest of your life. What will people think?"

Anyna stared at Lothar. Her lip quivered. "But Daddy, I can't help it. Dr. Forster said that food and vitamins will clear it up in no time. Only she didn't have any vitamins to give us. My hand healed up. She had to lacerate it. In summer I'd sit in the sun. But now there isn't any."

Olga could not believe Lothar's lack of tact. But then, he'd never concerned himself about the feelings of others. He took a closer look. His glance had a malicious gleam, and the twisted grin of a mischievous boy. No. Not tonight—or any night, if she could help it.

"I know my face looks terrible," Anyna said. "But when I tell people that I'm a baroness, they don't care what my face looks like."

"Of course," the Countess said. "And you're right to feel that way. Being of noble blood is an honor we must live up to. I told you about noblesse oblige. Do you remember?"

"Or course, Grandmaman. I missed you so. Now I can practice again."

Lothar smirked, nodding at his mother, who raised her head from her pillows. Her now-white hair was in a chignon, and her face made up with eyebrow pencil and lipstick. Olga detected a touch of rouge. Did she expect some gentleman caller?

"It's in your blood, Anna Magdalena. You are an aristocrat," she said.

Anyna finished her potatoes and picked up her plate. "Thank you, Grandmaman. I want to go to Switzerland. When I come back, my face will be as good as new, right Mami? But I'll miss Mami, and you too, Grandmaman," she added quickly when she saw Olga shake her head.

"I suppose we should consider the sleeping arrangements," Lothar said.

"I can sleep anywhere," Olga said quickly, though she had no idea where that would be. "Didn't the landlady say something about your having a room, Lothar? Why can't I sleep there?"

"Out of the question," the Countess said. "It's in an attic down the street. I keep my belongings there, since we don't have enough space here. Not with Lothar's piano and his music. Besides, it's cold."

"I'll manage," Olga said, "so long as I have a blanket and a pillow."

"The place even has a bed," Lothar said.

Olga's heart sunk. He was hungry, not necessarily for her, but she would do. Her mind raced, but there was no way out.

"I see no other solution," the Countess agreed. "The whole idea of your coming, Olga, is most inconvenient. Is that not what we wrote to you? Did we not mention that we have no space for you? This is quite embarrassing, considering the circumstances."

Olga swallowed her justifications. On second thought, there were none. She had to life with the consequences of her love for Ingo.

"You, my dear Anna Magdalena," Lothar said with a benevolent smile, "can sleep on the floor under the piano. Would that suit you?"

Olga gathered that her mother-in-law did not want Lothar to re-establish a relationship with his wife. Obviously he had his own plans. She could see the desire in his eyes and the lecherous expression on his sardonic lips.

Lothar pulled blankets and pillows from the armoire, and helped Anyna prepare her bed under the piano. "You'll have your own little nest here," he said.

Once the bed was made up, Lothar told his mother, "I'll see Olga to the attic. She has no idea how to find it." He was determined to have her tonight, and there was nothing she could do about it.

"Don't be long," the Countess said. "It's only a three-minute walk."

After bidding Anyna good night, Olga left, feeling alone and helpless at the mercy of the man who happened to be her husband. Her little girl was happy. She had come home to Grandmaman and Daddy, and did not care what her mother would have to go through for her child's pleasure. She owed Anyna so much. Let her enjoy this time of being with the people she loved.

The cold dark night pulled Olga deeper into her loneliness. Snowflakes fell in a soft gauze in the light of the street lamp, indifferent to her anxiety and pain. They melted on the wet ground, turning into slush. Her feet were wet and cold again. The light coming from the farmhouse they passed held the bucolic tranquility most people enjoyed in this part of the world. Even the barn looked more desirable than Lothar's attic. The dung heap had the homey smell of country life.

Olga fell behind, tempted to vanish into the darkness. Join the animals in their stable. Lothar's grip caught her arm and pulled her forward. "I don't have all day."

"I'm exhausted. We spent two days on the train."

"Don't give me that old song and dance," he said in crisp German, without a trace of their Baltic accent.

She pulled her hand from his hold. "Let me go."

"Not before you please me. It's been a long time. You're my wife. You got away with murder—almost. That's over now. People make mistakes. I made a few myself. Now we're a family again. It's about time you remember where you belong."

"Not by choice," she said defiantly. "And not that you invited me."

"Let's not get into that. Just come. If you're nice to me, I'll be nice to you. Fair enough?"

They passed the church and graveyard. Fresh snow covered the graves and the crosses that marked them. Rest. She needed rest. First Anyna had to go to Switzerland, then what? Right now she was a legal prostitute, and would have to do his bidding.

At one of the dark buildings, he pulled a key from his pocket and unlocked the door. Stumbling behind him up the squeaking stairs, Olga noticed the stench of dung and stuffy winter air of homes where they wouldn't open the windows. At the top of the stairs, he switched on the light to the attic. The smell of mothballs greeted her from a room where rolled rugs, furniture, and boxes had been stacked up. Linens were piled up on the gilded bed Olga knew so well. The bed the Countess lived in now was narrower.

Lothar cleared the bed by sweeping everything to the floor, and pulled back the blanket. "There, that should do. Somewhat mildewed, but you can change the sheets later. Now get those clothes off," he ordered, slipping out of his coat. The jacket followed. Then the shirt. His pants landed on the floor.

Shivering, Olga stared at him as if this weren't real.

"Come on, don't be a prude. We don't have all night, though I wouldn't mind spending it with you. But Maman is waiting. You heard her. She is not pleased with your coming, and suggested I get a divorce. But I'm inclined to let bygones be bygones. We have a daughter, and you appeal to me." He ripped off her coat.

She pulled away. "I can do it myself."

"Then do it! I bet your lover did not have to wait for you to get undressed," he added, and dropped her coat to the floor.

Olga shrugged. If only Ingo were here, she would kiss and caress him, joining him in bed delirious with anticipation. They would cuddle until they were warm again, and then explore the tenderness they shared. Instead she took off her dress and undershirt, and unhooked her garter belt. Leaving her bra and panties on, she slipped into the damp and icy bed. He pulled off his shorts, but left his undershirt and socks on. The stench of his feet and body odor brought back memories of his ruthless demands on her body. How she hated this man. The disgusting smelled of his breath was worse than that of the Russians, who had smelled of tobacco and vodka, but had at least been clean. Why think of that now? To all of them she was nothing but a body, obliged to satisfy their needs. She must detach herself, and dwell on a vision that would divert her from her suffering. Women did this all the time. Think of the night she had married Ingo.

Lothar clamped his arms around her, and penetrated her from the back. He pumped hard, grating at her tight opening. "Skinny little shrew," he grunted. "I bet the Russians gave you a good fix. I consider myself a gentleman. Not that you deserve it."

No matter how hard he pumped, he could not climax. His face was hidden. She had her eyes closed, and no desire to see his frustrated grimace. When he could not get anywhere, he withdrew and turned her around. "Let's try it this way," he said, and went at it again. He panted and groaned, his stinking breath in her face. Was it pleasure or frustration? He was such a pathetic bungler. It would be funny if it didn't hurt so much. By now she was raw, every thrust a stab, his breath nauseating. At least he didn't kiss her. How she hated these slimy intimacies. Suppressing her disgust, she participated in the act, pretending it gave her pleasure. A pained moan rather than joyous giggles, but he wouldn't know the difference. Perhaps it would speed things up.

Ingo, my love. I can't help it. Some day we'll be together. You know we will. Just a little while longer. I know what makes him tick. I hate him so. Despite how hard he pumped, Lothar's prick softened and fell out.

"Damn. You're truly good for nothing, Olga. Well, I must get back. We'll finish tomorrow."

Relieved, she said, "Certainly. You wouldn't want to upset Maman, would you?" Did her voice sound normal, or was the sarcasm coming through?

Minutes later the door closed behind him. Olga raised her clasped hands toward heaven. From now on she would take charge. She had a bed, and a door with a lock. Once Anyna left for Switzerland, she would lock it and wait for Ingo.

Chapter 34

Ingo Kroll stood at the train station and blinked into the blinding sun. Stuttgart! Erich Haberle's town. His liberation had finally come, though not the way he had envisioned it—coming home to Dresden with Olga waiting for him there.

Was she still in Wunsdorf, or had she left before the Russians came? He inhaled the warm summer air, free at last. Free! Thin and straggly, but free. As soon as he got to Erich's, he would dump the threadbare uniform that had taken him through the last year of war and two years as prisoner of war in a coal mine. The Brits had ripped off his insignias and medals, but had let him keep his personal belongings and Olga's last letters.

The Americans, his former enemies, now sauntered through the streets, probably as glad as he that the war was finally over. Now they could talk to each other, even become friends. The sun penetrated his body. As soon as he got something to eat, he would be a new man. A miracle. How many men had come home, alive and well? He had survived the war without major injuries.

Ingo watched the yellow streetcars drive up, let passenger off or on, and then take off again, turning at the corner. The square tower had a huge clock, and proudly carried the Daimler Benz sign on top. Gottfried Daimler and Carl Benz had been Swabians who had designed the first motor car in Germany right here. While hammering coal in the dark shaft of the mine he had wondered what it would be like to come here. He coughed. Coal dust lodged in his lungs. Soon, that would be gone too.

An American convoy passed. The exhaust had a pleasant smell—clean fuel. They still had plenty of everything, and could have kept on fighting for years. They had won.

At the tram stop, Ingo noticed two teen-age girls among the waiting people, whispering behind their hands. Watching him, they giggled. Did he look that bad?

He smiled at them. "I guess my uniform looks pretty worn," he teased.

They nodded. "You must be a returnee."

"Pretty obvious, is it?"

The girls wore flowery dresses and wooden sandals, their hair braided.

"I'm afraid so," the older girl said, blushing.

"I'm trying to get to Degerloch. Any idea how I can get there?"

"Sure," the younger girl said. "Take the number five all the way to the end. Degerloch is quite a ways from here. We live in Vaihingen."

"Thank you. I just arrived and don't know my way around."

"That's pretty obvious. Glad we could help," the older girl said, and nudged the other. They had rosy cheeks, and did not look undernourished at all. Perhaps civilian life had adapted to the new regime, or were the Americans helping out with food? They seemed to be helping everybody, perhaps even their former enemies.

Ingo felt so elated that he shook hands with the girls. "Ingo Kroll. You can't imagine how good I feel. Seems that you had some serious bombing here." He pointed to the ruins all around.

"We did, but not in Vaihingen. Our house is fine, except that we have a refugee family staying with us now. But we don't mind. Our neighbors have Americans quartered in their home. They're really nice people, and don't give them any trouble." Their streetcar came, and they left.

The five came a few minutes later. Ingo got on, and found a window seat. What would Erich's mother say when he showed up at her door? He had assured Ingo that she would be more than happy to take him in. They had a farm and plenty of food. The thought reminded him how hungry he was—he'd do anything for a bite to eat. He could make himself useful in the home and on the farm until he found a job. He was entitled to a monthly stipend that would see him through the first weeks, so long as he had a place to stay.

The streetcar soon left the ruins of the inner city, where trees eased the broken walls and empty windows, and climbed up one of the steep hills that surrounded it. Vineyards yet. Well tended too. Since he had not had the opportunity to appreciate wine, he was looking forward to the experience. Olga had eased their first meeting with a bottle of Bordeaux, or something like that. Where was she? As soon as he got settled, he would look for her.

If he weren't so hungry he'd have enjoyed the hills and solid homes basking in the sun. The architecture was not as spectacular as that of Dresden, but he could tell that people were well off and enjoyed a traditional life. The world was at peace again, and he was here to enjoy it. The thought filled him with joy.

Tears of happiness welled up. From now on, it was up to him to create a life that would suit Olga.

Degerloch had half-timbered buildings, a church, and grocery store like all the other German towns he had come across. Ingo asked one of the women standing in line at the bakery for directions.

"The Haberles? Of course I know them. Everybody knows everybody around here." She laughed. "Welcome home. You must be a returnee. Are you Erich's friend? He told me the other day that he expected you."

"Did he really?" Ingo wondered, so pleased that he was even expected. Erich was a chum. If his mother was only half as nice as he, Ingo could look forward to an enjoyable stay in their home.

"Oh yes. We welcome everybody who comes homes. Not enough of you are coming back. We lost two in our family. But life goes on, and we make the most of it." She was in her fifties and wore a kerchief around her head. "Congratulations for getting through. I'm sure we'll see each other again. Just go down the street and make a right. Their home is the third on your right. Tell Frau Haberle that you talked to Christa Leonhard."

The warm welcome gave Ingo wings. He almost skipped down the street. Erich would be home. First at Tubingen University, then in Russia, and finally in the Belgian coal mine they had been friends, avoiding their hunger pangs by talking about philosophy, giving each other tasks to think about, topics they would report on to each other in the evening, or memorizing poetry that one or the other knew. They had invented mind games which diverted their attention to lofty subjects. They had played with Latin grammar, and argued over Einstein's theory of relativity. Erich had talked about farming and animal husbandry so that Ingo would know about their farm and about wine-making. Now he would see the facilities first hand, meet the mother he had talked about so often, and his sister, Irmgard.

The gardens on both sides of the streets sported trees and shrubs. Instead of flowers, people grew vegetables. The tomatoes were almost ripe, and he noticed little cucumbers on the trailing vines.

A cuddly middle-aged woman in a light duster opened the door. Before Ingo could say anything, he was in her embrace, inhaling the fresh soap scent of her skin. "Ingo! You are Ingo! Welcome home. How wonderful that you made it. Erich has told me so much about you. I'm so glad you came." She kissed him on both cheeks, and pulled him into the hallway, leaving the door open so that the sun could shine in. "Come straight into the kitchen. You look starved. First, I'll get you something to eat, then you'll have a bath and put some fresh clothes on, and then," she winked, grinning, "you have choices. There is taking a tour of the home, taking a nap, or just keeping me company over a glass of wine."

Before Ingo could say anything, he was in the spacious kitchen, where she pushed him down into a chair and set a plate in front of him. "I know you're starved. Here's a welcome home drink while I get some food." She brought an earthenware pitcher from the larder, and poured what looked like dark apple juice into two glasses. "Our own hard cider. Good stuff. You'll see. We have a secret recipe. Just taste it and tell me what you think."

He laughed, wiping the sweat from his forehead. "I can't think at all. I'm overwhelmed." He took the glass, clinked it with hers, and drank— again and again.

"Fantastic. So refreshing. Slightly sweet. I haven't tasted alcohol in years. It makes my head spin. The world has never looked better. What a lucky day." His cheeks burnt.

She refilled his glass, then put two slices of fresh bread with butter and sausage on the plate.

"Fresh pickles and a tomato yet," he said, chewing and smiling. "You're an incredible mother. Erich is so lucky."

"So are you. It's wonderful to have you here." Her smile was as straightforward and wholesome as her face. He delighted in her warm blue eyes, rosy cheeks, and soft chin. Her mouth had the open appeal of an easy-going, caring woman—one in charge of her life and well-being. She was right. They would get along famously.

"I can't thank you enough for taking me in like this."

"It's my pleasure," she said, cutting cheese from a big hunk. "I know you're starved, but let me advise you to take your time eating so that your stomach gets a chance to digest. I wouldn't want you to suffer."

Ingo grinned, and took a long sip from his glass. He felt so light, so good, so cared for. His own mother would not have treated him like this. He took her hand and kissed it. "I'm so grateful. Thank you."

She ran her fingers over his hair, which desperately needed washing. He hadn't shaved in days. It didn't bother her. She put her arms around him, and said softly, "It's an honor to have you here. Erich told me what you two went through. Hell is too mild a word. Let me spoil you."

"That would indeed be a new page in the book of my life. Thank you, Frau Haberle." He touched the warm skin of her bare arms and leaned his head again them. The alcohol opened his heart and body, which now felt mellow and tired. His head was buzzing, and his stomach bursting.

"Well, my dear Ingo, since you're a member of the family, we might as well set formalities aside. I'm Renate." She raised her glass. "There. Let's drink to that."

"Yes, Renate," he said, somewhat embarrassed. He had never called a woman her age by her first name, unless she was a relative and then always added *Tante* to the name. But as long as she had offered, why refuse?

"In a couple of days you'll feel great. It took Erich about a week. You should see him now—a picture of health. He'll be so glad to see you. And so will my daughter, Irmgard. She's having a hard time coping with the loss of her fiancé. He'd survived the war fine. The Americans took him prisoner, and put him into one of the local POW camps they set up, right here in Heilbronn. His serving in the SS obliged him to go through the denazification process—interrogations and screening, what do I know. You can imagine how long it took checking out thousands of men. They were kept in open fields behind barbed wire. Not that anybody would have escaped. All they wanted was go home to their loved-ones. But that was not to be for Erwin. The Americans didn't care that the men were starved and ill from exposure. I believe he got dysentery, and probably died from dehydration. Irmgard visited him. Took sandwiches and water. But the American guard wouldn't let him have it. He threw it into the dirt and trampled on it. Erwin stared at her through the barbed wire. No matter how much she begged, cried and pleaded, the guard just chased her away. All she could do was wave to him.

"When she received notice of his death, it broke her heart. She hasn't been herself since. You'll see. Have pity on her. That's all we can do. She's at work right now, and should be coming home after six. Then we'll all have supper. We can eat on the terrace. We have a nice garden. But first, I'll draw you a bath, get you some fresh clothes, and let you take a nap. Have another glass of cider while I heat the water. Gas and electricity are rationed, and only come on in the morning and evening. But we have an old fashioned water heater that uses wood or coal. So just relax until I call you."

She refilled his glass. "You need a thorough washing. Get rid of all the dirt your body and soul accumulated during the war and in the POW camp." She left the sunny kitchen that reminded him of home. Everything was neat and clean, the white cabinets spotless, and the floor freshly mopped. Gingham curtains framed the open window. Birds chirped in the garden, much like at his home in Dresden. The city and his family were gone, but Olga had to be somewhere.

Half an hour later, he lay soaking in a tub of water that covered him all the way up to his chin. His thin body didn't take much space. With his eyes closed, he imagined Olga by his side, talking and laughing. Some day, Olychka. He lathered himself with good soap, not that ersatz stuff he had used for years. Where did Renate get all those treasures? A fresh towel awaited him on a stool. His clean body made him feel whole again, and the fresh clothes gave him a sense of being himself, vibrant and alive. Renate was anything but a mother. She was a woman looking for a lover. Being without a man for years could affect a woman that way. Her hug had been sensual, inviting though she hardly knew him and he was not much to desire, scrawny and exhausted. He chuckled into the mirror. *Ingo, you've also been alone too long, deprived of all human needs—including women.*

Wearing Erich's sport shirt and slacks, Ingo returned to the kitchen. Renate stood at the sink and turned around. "What a change. You look great! Still tired, but no longer starved. Would you like to keep me company here while I prepare supper, or would you rather take a nap?"

He watched her cut up a hunk of raw beef. A head of cabbage and potatoes waited on the side. "Where do you get all this food?" he asked.

She turned on the faucet and let the water splash into a dishpan. "The black market."

"Of course." People lived on food rationing, which provided something like 1,200 calories per day. What she had here was a week's ration for four, if that.

She winked confidentially. "Don't look so shocked. Everything worth doing is illegal. As farmers, we can hold back some food and trade it. To hungry people food is the most valuable trading item. Why starve and suffer just because we lost the war? Survivors adapt."

Ingo agreed, though it bothered him that people took advantage of those in need. During the war, he had used his ingenuity to save his life. Rules were made by those who have what they need obliging others to follow them. Renate had put on lipstick, and brushed her brown hair into soft waves. She was no beauty, but attractive, and had a wonderful personality. In her white blouse and bouncy skirt, she accented her femininity. She had even put on sandals that showed her polished toenails. He had never seen a woman wear nail polish on her toes, certainly not his mother or Ingrid.

"My parents left their farm to my brother and me. He takes care of it. Erich and I help out when he needs us. As soon as you feel up to it, you can come with me and enjoy the fresh country air. Last year we had an exceptionally good crop of grapes. Now we trade some of our wine with the other farmers for whatever they have in excess." She grinned. Her plump figure invited his touch. "You'll get to taste some at supper. The cider is more for daytime drinking."

"What if they catch you?" he wondered, reaching for a slice of cheese.

"We could go to jail. But don't you worry. The inspector loves our wine."

This was the new Germany, where people lived the best they could. He had a lot of catching up to do. Renate's unconcealed desire for a man, her voluptuous lips and bosom, waited for his touch. But he must not think of it.

"You have nothing to fear. You served our Vaterland." She took his hand and held it. "Did you notice the flowers blooming on the ruins?

The world belongs to those who can adapt. I never believed in miracles, weapons or otherwise. After my husband was drafted and killed by Polish partisans, I knew that life went on. That it was up to me to make it worth living. And that's what I do. See?"

Ingo remembered Stasya and her triumph in Olga's ransacked apartment. Her victory had come.

"We had a good marriage," Renate said. "Two fine children. Now I am alone. Do you know what it's like for a healthy woman not to have a man? I'm wasting my best years without any hope of finding one. They're all dead."

The fire in her eyes showed a burning desire, open and unabashed. He had never thought of a widow as a woman. Wasn't she supposed to grieve for her husband? Germany had millions of widows. Were they all like Renate? Offering themselves to needy men? Was he imagining all this, because he too... Her smile, the twinkle in her eyes, were not just the result of alcohol.

"I'm in a daze," he mumbled, "and feel lost."

"I can see how tired you are," she said. "Let me show you to your bed. Take a nap, and sleep off the past."

"The past," he murmured, and rose to lean on her shoulder. "I'm free, Renate," he said in a thick voice. "Imagine. Free."

"Yes, Ingo, you are free. From now on, you can do whatever you like. We have plenty of food. This your home." She took him to a bedroom, and drew the curtains. Through half-open lids he noticed a desk, bookshelves, and an armoire, then the door closing behind her.

Olga.

A week later Ingo sent a letter to Aunt Gertie in Wunsdorf. The Haberles had become like family. Over a glass of wine he and Erich spent their evenings telling Renate of their experiences at the front and in the mines. Irmgard, a thin and pale young woman who carried her grief on her sleeve, usually stayed in her room. Her only utterance was, "They would not let him have the food I brought. The guard threw it at my feet. He died like an animal," and broke into tears.

Ingo soon got used to the scene and paid no attention to her. Renate's unconcealed desire amused him. She did not talk about it anymore, though she had plenty of opportunities on their numerous trips to the country and the city, and in the hours they spent caring for the vegetables in her large garden. The more he got to know Renate, the more he came to appreciate her company. An educated woman, she was also a good listener, who enjoyed his philosophical digressions and poetry. Her wit and sense of humor made her an ideal companion.

Still, Ingo felt that he should contribute something to the family needs other than the amusement of Renate. His help in the house and garden, looking after her little pick-up, and occasionally delivering some produce did not compensate her for all the wonderful luxuries he enjoyed. He longed to go to work rebuilding Germany. But he had no trade, or special skills of any kind. Though the Americans did not dismantle German factories like their allies, they did not support production. Astronomical reparations imposed on the country left no capital for reconstruction. Germany's worthless currency had no buying or trading power. Some of the old companies, like Bosch, Leitz, and some textile companies worked on a minimal scale. Daimler Benz and all the others were in ruins. People either cleared rubble brick by brick, or dealt in the black market.

Nonetheless, Ingo followed Erich's advice and visited the Daimler-Benz Company in nearby Unterturkheim. Even if they had nothing to offer, he wanted to see what the future for the famous cars looked like. He was not surprised by the rubble, the open spaces where manufacturing facilities had been, the lack of activity of any kind. He walked on, and finally found the fragmented walls of the former administration building. It had scaffolding, so that bricklayers could repair the missing sections. Old railroad cars stood around on broken tracks. A guardhouse had been set up, where a man in knickers manually lifted the bar. A pre-war Daimler passenger car passed. All was not lost, Ingo thought, and noticed the soot-stained and fractured sign on a three-story building which said "Daimler-Ben." The "z" had been knocked out. The bottom floor had been repaired, and the window panes replaced.

A tired and hungry-looking receptionist suggested that Ingo see Herr Ensler, the project manager, and directed him to the office Ensler shared with four other men. File cabinets covered the raw brick of the wall. Ensler, an elderly engineer with sparse white hair and sallow skin, shook Ingo's hand. His gray eyes, behind metal-framed spectacles, welcomed him. He wore a clean but threadbare suit, and faded tie. "Employment?"

he said, pursing his thin lips. "Yes, we could use men like you. After negotiating for a year we've finally got permission to build a 170 V model car. We have plenty of orders, but, as you can see, we don't have the facility. We'll build the body in our Sindelfingen plant, where we hope to set up tools and machinery for the engines. For the moment, we're working on plans for an installation, and sources for equipment. Eventually, we'll need skilled tool and dye makers, machinists and mechanics. Once we get production going, we must transport the parts from Sindelfingen to Unterturkheim. Quite a challenge." He cleared his throat. "At Daimler-Benz we are used to challenges. That's how the company developed some of the finest cars in the world. Yes, we need manpower, and welcome every returnee with open arms. That includes you, young man." His eyes grew moist and his smile wistful. "In a year or two we'll have something going. Over the past two years all we could do was clear the rubble to rebuild. That's done, as you probably noticed." He took off his glasses, and polished them with a clean handkerchief. "I see a fine career for you, Herr Kroll."

Ensler explained that they were setting up an apprenticeship program for men like Ingo, so that they could acquire the necessary skills quickly, and receive a living wage for their work. "We hope to rebuild our workforce with highly trained craftsman, and deliver first class goods. Yes, yes, we'll get back on our feet."

Encouraged and inspired, Ingo shook Herr Ensler's hand, convinced that the Daimler-Benz Company was in good hands. "We need enthusiastic, optimistic men who are willing to learn new ways."

Renate was delighted when he told her that he would have to wait for a job, and would be glad to work with her and her brother for room and board.

The following day, Ingo put on overalls and drove Renate to the farm. Her brother Werner and his wife Frieda welcomed them, and loaded eggs, milk, cheese, and wine into the old three-wheel pick-up truck, covering it with burlap. Returning to Stuttgart, he whistled *Friends, Life Is Worth Living*. Renate sang along. They passed lush fields thriving under the sunny sky. A warm breeze carried the scent of the flower-dotted meadows through the open window. Green wheat fields undulated.

"I'm so glad you share my love for the country," Renate said. "My husband was an engineer, and had no inclination for farming." Over the past weeks they had learned a lot about each other, and never grew tired sharing anecdotes and experiences. He drove the rickety vehicle carefully, avoiding ruts and potholes. During the long war years, nobody had repaired the country roads.

"I'm a businesswoman, Ingo. I'll teach you how to make money, even in times like these."

Over the following weeks, Ingo watched and learned. He bartered and traded. People trusted him. Renate boosted his ego with never-ending praise. He was insatiable when it came to doing real work, and was getting good at it. Most of all, it appeased his pride and his need for independence. Ingo could not bear to be provided for by a woman, no matter how often Renate assured him that his help and presence made it worthwhile.

At the farm, Werner taught him how to feed the horse, harness him to the wagon, the plough, and the harrow. He swept the stable, forked hay from the loft, and cleaned out manure. The pungent animal smell, their curious glances and grunts during feeding time, were part of his new life. At supper time, the family relaxed over a glass of wine. Werner and his wife Frieda traded anecdotes of life in the country, their families and friends. Ingo was a partner and a member of the family.

Soon Renate's affectionate good mornings and good night kisses made him wonder. Should he respond to her holding his hand in the car? Were her frequent remarks that she was not cut out for widowhood an invitation? Was Olga real, or a fond memory of a life that no longer existed? There was still no word from Wunsdorf. More than two years had passed since he had held Olga in the burning village. A lifetime ago. Men courted younger women—what was wrong with a younger man enjoying the company of an older women? Olga would always be in his heart and soul, but there was more to life, like food and sleep and sex. Now that he was well-nourished and well-rested, his need for sex was susceptible to Renate's offer. Their friendship had grown into an intimacy that throbbed. Ingo longed for affection, and Renate offered it. Whenever she served strawberry tarts, crisp potato pancakes, or his favorite apple cake she left with a hug—an open invitation. Her low-cut blouses and the way she swung her generous hips teased. Now she pulled up her skirt during their picnics in the meadow. Not just to get a tan. The hot summer weather, the tasty snacks, and the hard cider they enjoyed among the rolling hills of the Swabian countryside lulled him. His restraint softened. There was nothing wrong with joining her and her family, the home she offered, and the comfort he had found.

So he traded forbidden goods—forbidden by whom? The Allies? They had all they wanted and needed. There was no need to feel guilty. Renate and Werner looked after their interests, rather than letting others exploit what was rightfully theirs. Still it bothered him, either because of his upbringing, or because he saw the suffering people in their threadbare clothes gleaning harvested fields, picking up half rotten fruit from under trees and gathering beechnuts in the forest on their hands and knees. But depriving himself of what Renate offered would not aid the starving refugees who had fled to western Germany. To them the war was on-going, more vicious than during the fighting years.

"All we need is love," Renate said, picking up the dishes from the ground.

"Ah yes, love," he said lightly, and lifted the basket into the back of their pick-up. *Olga, are you still alive?*

In the car Renate said, "I know what it's like longing for somebody. I know it only too well—I feel it all the time." She leaned over and kissed his cheek. "You can't imagine how much I enjoy our outings." Her hair smelled fresh, and her perfume enticing. Her world was like a tropical island in the eye of a hurricane. He had grown accustomed to the calm, and rarely thought of the men and women tossed around in the storm.

"You are such a dear, Ingo," she said, while he maneuvered the ruts on the country road. "Such a wonderful friend. Ever since you came I've felt young and alive." She ran her warm hand over his hair, which had grown back to its normal length. "I never knew a man like you."

"I owe you so much, Renate."

She stroked his arm. "On the contrary."

That evening, they found Erich sitting in the garden with a glass of wine reading the *Stuttgarter Nachrichten*. The warm breeze rustled the leaves of the apple tree. "Imagine that," he said, looking up. "Konrad Adenauer is setting up a government. As head of the Christian Democratic Party, he's negotiating a constitution for Western Germany.

We're going to be a republic. The Russians don't want any part of it. They'll veto any suggestion to reuniting Germany. Which doesn't surprise anybody. They want world communism. The Western Allies don't seem to have much to say about it, or don't care to argue with Stalin. Whoever can, escapes to the west. The Soviets fortify the border. Olga should try to get out while she can."

"I still didn't get an answer to my letter," Ingo said, sitting down at the table, set with a table cloth and a basket with apples and pears from the garden.

Irmgard had joined them with her knitting. "Perhaps it got lost," she said. "The world is crazy."

Like most Germans, Ingo admired Konrad Adenauer, the elderly politician who had not been a member of the Nazi Party, and enjoyed the trust of the Allies. They were ready to grant Germany a government and give her some autonomy. The country was now a safe haven for millions of people uprooted from Soviet-controlled countries. The UN Refugee Relief housed many of them in former Wehrmacht barracks, or accommodated them in German homes where they were fed and housed. Renate traded with a fellow from Romania who had served in the German military, but qualified as Displaced Person. Every non-German refugee did.

"Once we have a valid government we'll become a nation again," Ingo said. A breeze fanned his hot face. "Perhaps I should check with Daimler-Benz again, and see whether their apprenticeship program started."

"No rush for that," Renate said. She had joined them with a bottle of wine. "First we must take care of the harvest. For Thursday I bought tickets for *The Flying Dutchman* at the Stuttgart Opera. Or I should say I traded some eggs for them. They're hard to come by. People love their opera and the theater. Art helps them forget their hunger."

For the opera, Renate wore a dress that had been altered with a scooped neckline and bouncy skirt. She nudged his arm. "Do you think I could pass for thirty? All right, how about thirty-five?" she teased, giggling.

Ingo gazed into her impish eyes. Even a blind man could see her desire, and he was not blind, but felt touched, confused, and guilty. They walked through the Schlossgarten Park under chestnut trees. The leaves rustled, showing the first signs of autumn. Though 1945 had been the coldest winter anybody could remember, 1947 was an unusually hot summer with little rain. Farmers worried about their crops. American potatoes had brought potato bugs which devoured whole fields, while June bugs swarmed around like locusts. Germany was banned from producing chemicals, including fertilizers and pesticides. To make sure that her economy remained dormant, the victors had dismantled factories and hauled the machinery home. The Russians even ripped up railroad tracks and shipped them to the Soviet Union.

During the second act, Renate held Ingo's hand. He pressed hers in gratitude. At intermission they strolled through the lavish opera house, which had miraculously escaped the carpet bombing. Stopping at a balcony overlooking the park, where the warm air buzzed with chirping crickets and the low voices of the theatergoers, Renate rubbed her shoulder against his. "You're a man and I'm woman," she said tenderly. The sun was still up, and spread its light over the pond.

"That's pretty obvious," he teased, surprised at her sultry voice. Her dress had polka-dots on a navy blue background. A double strand of pearls draped around her neck. Her tan and shining lipstick perked up her face. The scent of her perfume struck him as robust, rather than sensual.

"You know that I care for you very much," she said in a seductive purr.

"You're my best friend, Renate," he said, and pressed her arm.

"You know what I mean," she said, staring into the park. "If this offends you, please forgive me. But I must say it or go mad."

He put his arm around her. "Go right ahead. We have no secrets."

"I know how much you love Olga. I respect your love for her. But, you see…" She struggled for words. "What I am trying to say is…" She blushed. Her breath quickened. The large chest heaved.

"Say it, Renate. Don't be shy. We are friends, aren't we?" People walked by. What was she getting at? He turned toward her, surprised to see her crimson, all the way down to her cleavage. She looked lost and vulnerable, like a young girl on her first date.

"I feel very awkward saying this, Ingo. This is a special night." She twisted her handkerchief. "It's about my being a woman, though somewhat older than you. But still a woman…" She gazed into his eyes. He knew what was coming, glad that she would say it. "…who is in love with you."

Gently putting his arm around her shoulder, he gave her a comforting squeeze. The twinkle in her eyes invited him. No woman had ever offered herself to him. Certainly not Olga. Ingo was pleased and tempted. Was he not a young man hungry for sex? Men took prostitutes when they needed it, and here was this loving and caring women who suffered for him. With all that had happened in the past, there was no right or wrong, only life and death. She lowered her lids shyly, afraid to be rejected. He owed her so much. But it was not about that now. Why should he not accommodate a woman's needs as strong as his? A powerful desire turned to lust. Yes, why not?

He kissed her hand. "You are wonderful, Renate." As desirable as fresh bread, still warm from the oven, he thought. "I knew you cared for me, and now that you've come out with it, I feel so good. There is no greater gift than being loved. I appreciate your openness. Why shouldn't we share what nature gives us so generously?"

She looked deep into his eyes. Her shining red lips waited for his kiss. But he would not kiss her in public, though he wanted to very much. Yes, Renate would be his. Not only did he owe it to her, he owed it to himself.

"Ingo," she whispered, as if her deepest desire had been fulfilled. She wanted to be loved, and so did he. They would enjoy each other—not in passionate love, but in fulfilling their lust.

Renate on his arm, they returned to their seats. Later, in the streetcar, she told him how she had longed for this moment from the time he had come. That she had hoped he would catch her hints. Her thoughts bubbled forth. "I understand that you're waiting for Olga. I will not be in your way, should you find her. But I can't tell you how happy I am that in the meantime you'll let me love you." Renate's eagerness aroused Ingo even more. Her face aglow, she sat across from him in the almost empty streetcar. A demure jacket hid her tempting dress. He felt the fire coming. His blood throbbed. He was ready.

When he joined her in her double bed, he could barely restrain himself. The night was too short to satisfy their hunger. Her ways of manipulating him had no equal. Collapsed, sweaty and exhausted, he knew she had still more to offer. He was hot, throbbing with desire. So it wasn't Olga. This insatiable, voluptuous body belonged to Renate—here.

From that night on he shared her bed, enveloped in comfort and warmth, stirred by her desire, and aroused by her eagerness to please. She responded to his touch in a way he had never experienced before. A mature woman without inhibition; she was in control of her sensuality and comfortable with all aspects of their love-making. Within days he felt the benefits, and relaxed. How did he not feel guilty? Was it natural that a man did what he was created to do—fulfill a woman's needs?

Renate thrived too. Her effervescence affected everybody. Now, that she no longer needed to signal him, they conversed freely. Her caresses helped him heal. He came to love Renate. Not the way he loved Olga of course. He loved the woman in Renate, and the friend who made no demands, always willing to adapt to his needs and desires. During the day, she dressed in bright colors, and looked young and appealing. At night, she wore a silky black gown. Everything about her was fresh and clean and available. In her company he felt like a very young man, eager to oblige in any way.

In October, the long awaited letter from Wunsdorf arrived. Ingo examined the censor's stamps before he slipped a kitchen knife under the flap. Some of the words had been blocked out with black ink.

Sehr geehrter Herr Kroll!
I wish to inform you that Frau von Schenck left for Inning, in Bavaria, a year ago. Her daughter, Anna, was very ill. They were both on the verge of death.
The sentence that followed was crossed out, and probably describing how she got out, or what had happened to them. From what he had heard about life in the Soviet Zone, he was surprised the letter had come through.
Your aunt, a very dear and kind woman, passed away. The house is yours, should you care to live here. Otherwise you can take whatever she left.
My children and I now live here, and expect to stay. There is no indication that we might ever go home again. Our homeland is now Polish territory. I would enjoy meeting you and seeing Olga again, but that is not very likely.
No, surely not, he thought. Nobody in his right mind would go to the Russian Zone, unless he was a communist or the regime was gone.

Frau von Schenck and I became close friends. She told me how much she loved you, but could not wait any longer. She returned to her husband to save their child. I understand that you have her address in Bavaria. She hopes that you will contact her there.
Sincerely,
Emma Kroeger.

"Olga is alive!" Ingo cried out, holding up the letter. "She's in Bavaria. Imagine, Renate. She returned to her husband. What a sacrifice. Amazing what mothers will do to save their children. I must leave immediately." Letter in hand, he rushed toward the kitchen door.

Renate held him back, her eyes filled with compassion, or was it anxiety? Could she appreciate what he was experiencing? Olga was alive; she was waiting for him. He had to go to her, deliver her from that husband of hers. Things must have been very bad. Olga, my darling.

Renate pulled him to the kitchen table. "Come, Ingo dear. Let's sit down and think this over," she said, and took a bottle of wine and two glasses from the cupboard. "I'm your friend, remember? I share your feelings, your joy, your..." She blushed, as if she'd been caught telling a lie.

The radio played *Liebestraum. Olga. This is your message.* He felt so guilty he could cry. What had he done? Then again, she had returned to her husband, while he had found a woman who loved him.

"Her husband might not appreciate your barging in on him," Renate said, as if she read his mind. "Men don't take their wife's affairs lightly, especially while they're fighting a war."

He gulped down the wine, not even tasting it. The liquor could not ease his frustration. He held his glass out for a refill. Even if he rescued Olga from Lothar, where could they go? Surely not to Renate. Even her generosity had limits. He took long sips, until his heart beat slowed and the butterflies in his stomach stopped twinging.

Renate held his hand. Her wistful smile touched him. "If I were you," she said softly, "I would write to the countess. She'll tell you what is going on with Olga without your compromising her. If you write to Olga directly, I doubt she would get the letter, certainly not without having the countess read it first. That's how it goes when you live with your mother-in-law. I never had to go through that, but I know women who have to put up with it." Renate poured more wine, and sliced a hunk of Swiss cheese. "Marriage isn't all that great when you have to put up with a family that hates you. From what you've told me, her in-laws obviously hate her. I wouldn't advise showing up on their doorstep and having him chase you away." She sipped, leaning her elbows against the table. "I know how you feel, dear. How much it hurts. You can't take her away from him. Without his consent, she can't go anywhere."

Blood rushed to his face. His anger flared up into fury. He poured the wine down his throat. Damn. Renate was right. They were not at liberty to live their lives as they pleased, but obliged to abide by the laws that controlled them. His showing up would only cause more trouble for Olga.

The third glass of wine left him drowsy and helpless. Tears crept into his eyes. No, he must not weep. Once again destiny had delivered a heavy blow. The cruel reality of his impotence hit him like an enemy encirclement. Now Lothar was his enemy, his sneers and sarcasm the attack. The worst of it was that Ingo had nothing for his defense. Why was life so unfair? What had he done to deserve this punishment? The letter had wiped out his hope. "You're right, Renate," he whispered in a thick voice, his head buried in his arms. How could she return to Lothar? How could she? Didn't she know that it cut off Ingo once and for all? Frau Kroeger wrote that they were near death. A mother would make the ultimate sacrifice for her child. Olga had made that sacrifice, and he had to accept it.

Renate leaned over his shoulder to comfort him, letting him feel the warmth of her body and smell the scent of her perfume. She was there for him, and would be there for as long as he needed and wanted her. He was not sure he wanted her now.

"It'll all work out, you'll see. Let's consider the options, make a plan, see where we can go from here." She said "we," emphasizing how closely her life was linked to the outcome. Her soothing voice eased his frustration. The ache in his heart would remain, but he'd have to come to terms with that. Renate understood. She would be there for him when he needed her. She was a truly wonderful woman, and he was fortunate to have her now.

Wiping his tears, he swallowed his pain, then took her hand and kissed it. "You mean the world to me, Renate. Your love and generosity have no limits." He smiled, putting his arm around her ample waist.

"I'll always be here for you. You haven't seen her in years, and then only under trying conditions. Frau Kroeger will surely write to Olga and mention your address. Why don't you write to Frau Kroeger and the Countess? Let's see what they say before you make your plans. You may be jumping to unwarranted conclusions." Her Swabian dialect soothed his anxiety like gentle music. Olga was lost, and he had to come to terms with it.

What about Father? If Olga had not proved to him he had a guardian angel, Ingo would still question it. Olga, with Father's help, would find a way to bring them together.

He rose on wobbly legs. Renate held him. "You're so good to me, dear heart. How can I ever thank you for all your love and care? You're right. I'll write, and wait for the answer. It's a difficult decision, but I see no reasonable alternative. I know that you can appreciate my need to be alone for awhile. I certainly don't want to hurt you in any way."

"You never will, Ingo. I know a lot about love and desire, that powerful urge that drives us to the beloved. I'll get you some paper. Write your letters. Tomorrow we'll drive out to the farm to get those eggs for the Romanian, and see what he has to offer for them. We should start harvesting."

From then on, Ingo slept alone in his cold and empty bed. He missed Renate's warm and cuddly body, and her tenderness. Their affection remained, and he considered returning to her when he received a letter from the Countess or Frau Kroeger. If Olga wasn't available, there was no point in depriving himself and Renate of each other.

When told what had happened, Erich commented on the absurdities of the war. Irmgard shook her head, shed some tears, and cursed the injustices of the world. Lately she had spent the evening hours in the living room where the family gathered, and participated in their conversation. Ingo had noticed her blushing whenever he talked to her, but ignored it. Unlike Renate, she had a long, oval face and flat body. She always wore the same unattractive tailored blouse and straight skirt, her hair pulled back and the braids wrapped around her head. An occasional smile would make her human, but she had taken on the role of a suffering widow, sulking and pouting because she had forgotten what a smile was like. Nobody encouraged her, or even criticized her for being a pill. Ingo was certainly not going to court such a self-centered young woman.

Ingo continued his chores at home, drove the pick-up, and cared for the farm animals whenever they were in the country. He related to the cows, the horse, and the pigs as if they were his pets. They recognized him, and greeted him with their big eyes. After the work was done, he and Renate would take a break with Werner and share stories. Frieda would treat them to sandwiches and beer—coffee was not worth the exorbitant price the Romanian asked. Werner had fought in Italy, and witnessed the Allied invasion in Sicily. After a slow retreat, he had escaped surrender by hiding out in the Alps. With the help of local farmers, he had walked home.

While awaiting an answer from the countess or Frau Kroeger, Ingo received a letter from Herr Ensler; Daimler Benz had started their apprenticeship program for veterans.

I am writing to you personally, as I was impressed by your eagerness to work. The Personnel Office will send you an official offer. As soon as you sign the contract, I'd be glad to get you started here in our department. You will have to take classes in trade and business practices, as well as in various aspects of automobile manufacturing. With your background, I think that you'll do well in marketing. Come and see me so that we can talk about it. I am also glad to report that the Allied High Command has given us permission to start production on the 170V model. A fine car that is already sold out.

Ingo was touched by Herr Ensler's interest and went to see him.

The Countess' reply arrived two weeks later. Renate handed him the envelope at the door. "Sit down and have a glass of wine before you open it. Something tells me that whatever she has to say will be unpleasant. Her kind must hurt others to prove their superiority."

Ingo kissed Renate's warm cheek before following her into the kitchen. The countess' tirade when she had discovered his coat and cap in Olga's apartment sprung up in his mind.

In the warm kitchen, where the cold weather left sweaty window panes, Ingo prepared himself. The fact that the Countess had written, rather than Olga, was a bad omen. The watermarked enveloped was embossed with a golden coat of arms and had "Friederike Grafin von Herzogfels" printed underneath in gothic letters.

Inning, November 18, 1947
Herr Kroll!

Your thoughtlessness caused me considerable chagrin. You must admit that it is most impudent of you to write to me after you broke up, or tried to break up, a perfectly happy marriage, while my son suffered in a prisoner of war camp. I appreciate that the war brought us many hardships, and understand the feelings of impetuous young hearts when left alone too long. Alas, that is no reason for individuals to disrespect ethics and morality—in this case it does not justify taking what does not belong to you. You do not seem to understand that you are addressing Olga's mother-in-law, who expended considerable effort taking care of Olga and her child. My son is her husband, and will remain so though she is no longer with us.

Ingo stared at the last sentence. "No longer with us?" he wondered aloud. The letter dropped from his hands. The room was spinning. He closed his eyes. "Why don't you say something, Renate? You don't believe it, do you? Olga can't be dead!"

"Well," she said gently. "I'm very sorry, but it is possible. There were plenty of people who died from malnutrition. If she left Wunsdorf in bad health, she may not have recovered. Why would she lie?"

"Because she wants to keep me away. Revenge. That's the kind of a bitch she is. She wants to control Olga, can't you see?"

Renate shrugged, took the letter, and read on.

When Olga arrived from Berlin, she was so weak that she fell seriously ill. Since, as you know, we had no one to turn to for her treatment, she passed away despite our self-sacrificing care. Anna Magdalena survived. She is now in Switzerland, in the care of a relative.

I am writing all this to spare you the effort of searching for Olga. As a good Christian, one must forgive. Olga had fallen into the hands of the Russians. She would not take my advice. Those who cannot hear must suffer. The ordeal caused the infection that contributed to her death. God has His ways in dealing with those who do not respect His commandments. May that be a lesson to all of us.

Friederike Grafin von Herzogfels.

Ingo's lips quivered. "Fallen into the hands of the Russians! Good God. What a disaster." He shuddered, unable to imagine what Olga must have suffered. No wonder she was... No! She was alive—she had to be. If she had survived the ordeal long enough to get to Inning, she had to be alive now. He stared at the window. The wind whipped the bare limbs of the apple tree back and forth. His temples throbbed. He took the wineglass from Renate, tears running down his cheeks, and poured it into his mouth. The thick lump remained. Crumpling the stiff paper of the letter he cried, "Damn, damn, damn." His trembling hand almost dropped the glass. Renate took it from him. He jumped up, and stomped on the stone floor. The knot in his gut tightened. "Olga is not dead," he shouted. "The bitch is lying. This is her victory. But she can't intimidate me." He sat down, then jumped up again as if the seat were hot.

Renate retrieved the letter. "I don't believe all that highbrow nonsense either."

"She's evil, Renate. Olga told me all about her. If she died, it wasn't from natural causes. Those people are capable of anything."

Renate held him. "We'll get to the bottom of this."

Ingo stared at the rain pelting against the pane. "I must go to Inning and find out for myself."

The bus arrived in the middle of a downpour. The rain drummed on his umbrella, and splashed on the cobblestones. It gurgled from the gutters of the Bavarian farm houses, and ran in rivulets past the *gasthaus* across the street. This was all he needed now, Ingo thought, picking his way between puddles toward the inn. Perhaps he could get some information about the von Schencks.

The place was empty. The waitress, wearing a dirndl, stood behind the counter and polished beer glasses. As soon as he sat down, she took her notebook and walked up to him. Unlike the hollow-eyed people he had encountered at the railway station, she looked healthy, well-fed, and appealing, like a young horse. Her people probably had a farm like Renate's.

"I'll have a beer. Do you happen to know Frau von Schenck?" He watched her search her memory for a person with that name, then shake her head. "I know about everybody. I mean, all the local people. The refugees don't talk much when they come in, or stick to themselves. Women don't usually come in by themselves."

"What about Herr von Schenck, her husband? They're refugees. She's small, has blonde curly hair and a dreamy look in her eyes."

The waitress shook her head again. "No, can't say that I recall such a woman, nor a man by that name." She returned to the counter and slowly drew a beer for him, still thinking about the people Ingo had asked about. When she brought the foaming brew with a "*Zum Wohl*," she said, "They must be refugees. We've got some in town. You might want to ask them."

"Can you direct me to Muhlstrasse?" he asked.

"Sure. Pass the church, then make a quick left. The second street on your right is Muhlstrasse. What number are you looking for?"

"Two."

"That's Frau Meier's house. Yes, she has some refugees living there. A countess of all things. I've never seen her, but I'm told she's quite something. Doesn't leave the house much, but has Americans come to visit her. Imagine that. From the Base in Furstenfeldbruck. They took over the garrison. You should see the cars. Just like the ones in American movies." Her brown eyes widened in awe. "Refugees will do things like that. They don't care what anybody thinks. Their name could be von Schenck, though I think the Countess' name is different. She's been here since 44. Came from Poland, Frau Meier said."

"Thanks for the information." Ingo drank up, left money on the table, and left. The rain had stopped when he stepped outside. Following the waitress's directions, he passed the church and found Muhlstrasse. Now that he was here, he felt like an intruder. What should he say when he met Frau Meier or Lothar? This was worse than facing the Russians. That was part of war, impersonal. Men in uniform had no face or name, just a rank and serial number. Now he felt guilty. The house was a non-descript stucco building with small windows, and a front door that did not invite visitors. If Frau Meier opened, he could ask for Olga. If it was Lothar, he could pretend, but what? That he had come to the wrong house, among the few in this village? His accent would give him away. What if Olga opened and fell into his arms?

Dark rain clouds hung over the village, dimming the empty street. The dung heaps in front of the stables steamed, and smoke curled from the chimneys of the Bavarian-style farms with their decorated shutters and carved trims along the eaves and windows. Some had Alpine flowers painted on their facades. A fairy-tale world, where an evil witch hid in one of those gingerbread homes. Ingo wondered what to do, then sat down on a bench, waiting for a sign. If Father meant for them to be together, he would have Olga come out and greet him, or let something happen that would further his quest without jeopardizing her life. The scene around him remained a still-life, a painting that could not change. The longer he waited, the harder it was to make a move. Instead, the obstacles and reasons why he shouldn't intrude on this peaceful world mounted. Renate was right, he had no business being here. Still, he couldn't just leave—he should at least knock.

The resolve brought him to his feet. He approached the door again, and knocked. After a long wait, the door opened. He faced a hard-nosed woman in a duster he was sure never left her body.

"What do you want," she demanded.

"I'm looking for Frau von Schenck."

"Who? No she isn't here. Do you want to talk to Herr von Schenck?"

"No. Where is she," he insisted, braving the frown on her face.

"How am I supposed to know? She's gone."

"What about the little girl, Anna?"

"The one with all that pus on her face? She's gone too. Well, since there's nothing I can do for you, unless you want to see the so-called countess, I must close the door. It's getting cold. Mind you, we're not heating the great outdoors. We got enough problems without people coming by asking all sorts of questions." She closed the door, and that was that.

Ingo stared at the weathered door and backed up. What did all that mean? Was Father telling him that he had no business being here? Olga was gone, and so was Anyna. That much he could see. The Countess had written that Anyna was in Switzerland. But Olga? What had happened to Olga?

Puzzled and heart-broken he returned to the bench across the street where he could observe the house. Not that there was any reason for it. Olga couldn't appear, because she wasn't there. That was a fact he had to live with.

The door behind him opened. The high-pitched voice of an old woman asked, "Can I help you?"

Ingo turned around, and met the withered face and frail body of a very old woman. She leaned on a gnarled cane. The toothless mouth and angular chin, jutting out like that of a skeleton, emphasized her age. Her black dirndl, made of home-spun cloth, had faded. A black wrap over her head and shoulders sheltered her against the moist wind that swept across the wet street.

"Do you know the Countess von Herzogfels?" he asked.

She tilted her small head. "If you mean the lady living across the street, I know who she is. But I don't know her. She wouldn't talk to people like me." She spoke in a thick Bavarian dialect, slurring her words. "Why do you ask?"

He rose. "I'm looking for her daughter-in-law, Olga. Is she there?"

"How would I know if those people don't talk to me? There is a young woman living there. She's with the Americans."

"What Americans?"

"The ones at Furstenfeldbruck. She's with them. You know how refugees are. No pride. No respect."

"Does she have blonde curly hair?"

The old woman sat down on the bench beside him and shook her wizened head. Deep wrinkles criss-crossed her face from a life out in the fields. "I wouldn't know. Where do you come from?"

"Stuttgart," Ingo said. "Before that I lived in Dresden."

"I know Stuttgart, used to work at the Marienspital. During the other war. Are those people friends of yours?" she probed.

"No. Else I wouldn't sit here. But I must go and catch the bus back to Munich."

"I wish I could be of help. But nobody talks to those people. Talk to Frau Meier. You can't stop her when she gets going about them. The woman is going with that American who visits them. What does that tell you?"

Ingo shook his head. Olga would not do that, not if she had returned to Lothar. "I should go."

The rain clouds darkened. A wet breeze carried the smell of dung from the yard, where a hen scraped, clucking. Ingo wanted to leave the whole distasteful scene. Renate was right—it had been wrong to come. How could he think that just being here, where she lived, would bring her back? But she wasn't here. What right did he have to upset her life when he had nothing to offer? The world was topsy turvy. The chance of living together was zero.

"What's your name?" the old woman asked. "I'm Frau Moser."

"Ingo Kroll. Glad to make your acquaintance."

They parted when the rain set in. The cold shower brought him back to his senses. Still, his heart clung to the vague hope of catching a glimpse of her, or finding some evidence of her existence.

As soon as Frau Moser returned to her home he crossed the street. Nothing had changed, except that somebody played the piano. Dissonant sounds that were painful to his ears. Olga would never play anything like that. She would play *Rhapsody in Blue* or *Liebestraum*, remembering the happy hours they had spent together in her apartment in Poland. Tears formed in his eyes. A deep longing for her washed over him, along with the hopelessness of their situation. Once again, he had to live in that void he had hoped to fill. Renate was a dear, dear person who spoiled him with everything she had, but she could not replace Olga. Nobody could.

Peeking through the window, he saw a man in a black turtleneck at the keyboard. He recognized the countess, sitting in one of the two armchairs, a mohair wrap around her shoulders. Notes, books, and papers were scattered all over the long, narrow room and two single beds stood along the wall. On the small round table were two teacups. No sign that a third person might live there. The woman going with the Americans was probably Lothar's half-sister, Lara. Like her father, the count, she probably did not care who provided for her. The Americans had the means. But what could have happened to Olga? Did she go to Switzerland with Anyna? How? Nobody was allowed to leave Germany.

By the time the bus arrived, thick raindrops were coming down, splashing in the street. He found a window seat, and soon was watching the sleepy farm homes go by. Lights came on. "Father," he whispered. "You protected me during the war and promised Olga that we would be together. Where can I find her to at least tell her how much I love her? Please, lead me to her. I don't believe she is dead."

Munich's dimly lit station was still in ruins and would remain so for years to come, but all the platforms had been cleared and the trains ran on schedule. The night train would leave at 23:34, getting him to Stuttgart by early morning. Renate would be there to welcome him back. She would respect his tears, even console him, glad that he would be staying with her. Wandering about, he waved off the hungry prostitutes. Their painted faces looked so pathetic. They were desperate, and swarmed around him like insects looking for blood, assuming that a man in a quality trenchcoat and felt hat could afford their services, and even trade some food. They were right. He traded in the black market, and could certainly be a generous client. But not even pity would move him to take on one of them. Germany had become a nation of destitute people. The nation hibernated in a long winter. When would Germany's spring return?

Four years had passed since he had met Olga at the Esplanade. "Father," he murmured, looking up at the blackness. The clouds hid the stars, as if to say that his destiny was unforeseeable. "Please, Father, don't leave us now. We need your help, more than ever. Give me a sign. I'm lost." He did not expect an answer. It was up to him.

The eyes in the painted face of a hungry woman pleaded.

Ingo handed her a ten mark note and walked on. He wanted to go home and bury his head in his pillow.

Chapter 35

Olga's arm trembled as she pulled one dish after another from the hot sudsy water, and placed them on the drying rack. The pleasant smell of detergent made her task easy. Her hands had grown accustomed to the hot water, which had lifted the ingrained dirt from her fingernails and the creases of her palms.

Ingo was nearby. She felt it so strongly as if she could see him. She must tell Sgt. Johnson, her boss at the NCO Club kitchen, to let her leave right away. An emergency. Only what could she tell him? He knew that Anyna was in Switzerland. Perhaps the Countess? Olga certainly could not tell him that her long lost love was waiting for her, not when he knew that she was married to Lothar. A dish slipped from her hand, and fell to the floor. The clatter had everybody staring at her. Her friend, Liesl, came over from the stove and helped pick up the shards.

"So sorry, Sgt. Johnson," Olga said. She was studying English and could already make herself understood.

"You got to watch out, young lady. But it's all right." He grinned, showing a mouth full of big white teeth. "I won't make you pay for it." The Americans had taken over the former German Luftwaffe garrison and remodeled the kitchen, bringing in a new stove and oven, stainless steel pots and pans, and setting up a serving area where Liesl plated food. The women working in the kitchen were refugees like Olga.

Should she tell him that she had a stomach ache, or just run off, grab her bicycle and peddle back to Inning? The rain came down in sheets. Please, Father, don't let him talk to Lothar or the Countess. They would spoil everything. He did not need their sneers and cynicism.

Ingo! Wait for me—I'm coming. He was in Inning, she was sure of it. The women chatted. Sgt. Johnson was an easy taskmaster, and enjoyed the cheerful kitchen help, though he couldn't understand a word they said. As long as they did their job, he left them alone. Olga appreciated that.

Overall, the Americans were easy to get along with, so unlike *Gernegross*. Sgt. Johnson even let them take leftovers home to their families, though it was against regulations. Now that Olga supplied Lothar and the Countess with food, they no longer picked on her.

She worked faster. One more stack and she was done. The flatware soaked in a pan, and just had to be pulled out and rinsed. Her arm trembled again. She must leave right away. Father had not contacted her since she had come to Bavaria, and now wanted to tell her that Ingo was looking for her. *Ingo! Ingo! Please wait. I'm coming.*

Sgt. Aldrich's round head appeared in the doorway. He was Lara's provider, and a friend of the family. He beckoned Olga. "Come here. I must talk to you."

"Not now. I very busy," she said, pulling the knives and forks from the hot water.

"I need you." He turned to Sgt. Johnson. "Can I borrow her for a moment, Ernie?"

"Sure thing, Sarge." Everybody jumped to attention when Aldrich, the sergeant major, called. Johnson waved at Olga. "You can go. Liesl will finish."

"I, I must…" Olga stammered, resisting Aldrich's pull on her arm.

"This won't take long. You owe me a favor."

"What is favor?" she asked, following him reluctantly through the hall. What did he want from her? From the dining room came the voices of the NCO's.

"Never mind. Just come along."

Why did he have to come now? "What is it, Sergeant Aldrich? Why you want me?" She liked the burly sergeant, who always had a warm grin on his broad Irish face. The gleam in his blue eyes puzzled her. Those men were like children when it came to games. Only she had no time for games now.

She followed him through the lounge, where men sat smoking. Their steps pattered against the wooden floor. Aldrich held her wrist in a tight grip. He always got his way. Her blue sweater and narrow skirt, as well as the flat shoes they called moccasins, were hand-me-downs from Lara, who shamelessly exploited his generosity by playing the aristocrat. Like her father, she had never done a useful thing in her life, nor did she care where the money she spent so lavishly came from.

Opening the door to a dark room behind the stage, Aldrich confided, "I made a bet."

"Bet? What is bet?" Olga asked, still hoping to escape.

"You'll see in a minute. I'm counting on you. Don't let me down."

The room was crammed with props and musical instruments. An upright piano stood against the wall. She was starved for music, her kind of music, not Lothar's ridiculous compositions.

"I told my friend Irv that you're a pianist. That's what Lara told me. Are you?"

"No, no, not now. I must go."

He held her back. "Of course, now. I have to win the bet, Olga. It's a big one, and I don't like to lose." He sat her down on the piano stool and opened the dusty lid. "After you play, you can go."

A smaller, well-built, soldier joined them. "This is my friend, Sergeant O'Malley," Aldrich said.

Olga nodded a greeting, then faced the keyboard. She might as well get it over with.

"Do you need music?" Aldrich asked, pointing to a stack of music books.

She shook her head. "I got music."

"Good. Then let's hear it. You play something fancy, okay?"

Olga caressed the ivory and black keys. As soon as she touched them, *Autumn Leaves* came to mind. She threw in some arpeggios to simulate falling leaves, and drummed out a couple of chords for emphasis. Melancholy underscored the melody. She imagined Ingo standing at the house, waiting for her in the rain.

Aldrich applauded. "Good show, Olga."

"I can't believe this," Sergeant O'Malley said, surprised and disappointed. "Where did this girl come from? How come you let her work in the kitchen?"

"She's Lothar von Schenck's wife, the guy who entertains on Saturdays with his combo. He's a baron, which makes Olga a baroness. An aristocrat and a pianist. Do you see what I'm getting at? We could promote her to entertain on the other days." Aldrich stroked his clean-shaven round chin, all business now. Olga saw the twinkle in his eyes. "Do I win my bet?"

"Can I go now?" she urged.

"Just a minute, young lady," O'Malley said, caught up in Aldrich's excitement. He didn't seem to mind that he'd lost his bet. "You're terrific. Hank here is right."

While the men patted each other on the back, Olga clenched her fists to keep from crying out. "I must go," she insisted, unable to keep her tears in check. Men were so selfish. Aldrich had promised that she could go, and now he had forgotten she was here. "Please, Sergeant Aldrich. Can I go now?"

"Not yet. We're not finished," he said. "One more piece, then you can go." To O'Malley he said, "That's fifty bucks for you, buddy."

Olga played *Happy Days Are Here Again*. The applause from the dining room had her regretting the choice. She should have played a classical piece. Now she was doomed. Every minute counted. How long would Ingo wait? She played the piece fast and unembellished. Still, the men in the dining room stomped their feet and sang along.

"What did I tell you, Irv?"

Hitting the last chord, Olga jumped up and ran off.

Aldrich caught her wrist. "Thanks. You're quite an artist, honeybunch. For that, I'll take you home in my car."

She whirled around, staring at him in disbelief. "Yes? Thank you so much, Sergeant Aldrich. I got important..." Olga stopped herself. Why should he care what took her home in such a hurry, or that the villagers would call her an Ami whore when they saw her ride in an American car? Lothar had called her worse. Ingo would understand. He was here, looking for her.

Aldrich steered the car over the narrow country road. "I'll never know how you and Lothar..." He cleared his throat. "Arrogant bastard, if you ask me. But that's none of my business, is it? Your music is grand. I'm gonna make use of it. Forget that dishwasher bit. Just let me think this over—I'll make you a star."

They reached Inning at dusk. The cobblestones glistened in the rain. Thick dark clouds hung over the onion-shaped cupola. Aldrich stopped the car and escorted her to the house. Olga charged into the stuffy room, where the Countess rested against her pillows. "Did somebody ask for me?"

"Not that I know of. Are you expecting somebody?" And then, conjuring her mellifluous English, she turned to Aldrich. "How nice of you to stop by."

Olga ran outside and looked at Frau Moser's house. The bench was empty. Had he left with the last bus? Ignoring the muddy water, she ran to the inn.

The waitress said, "Yes, we had a guest. He asked for Muhlstrasse. Had a beer and looked very sad. Came twice. First in the afternoon, then returned to wait for the bus."

"Blondish hair?" Olga asked. "Blue eyes? What did he wear?"

"A trench coat." The waitress ran the change in her pocket through her fingers. "Good looking man. He didn't say much; asked for a blonde woman." She took a closer look at Olga. "Somebody like you. I told him that I'd never seen you before. He took the 4:45 to Munich."

Olga stared at the waitress, so distressed that the words stuck in her throat.

"Too bad I didn't know you, else I would've told him."

"Thanks anyway. He's a dear friend I haven't seen since the war. Now I don't know where to find him. That's how it goes, I guess." Olga left quickly. *Why did you do this to me, Father? You knew I couldn't let Aldrich down.* She didn't care that the rain came down in buckets, or that she had stepped right into a puddle. Weeping, she stumbled down the street. *Ingo! My beloved Ingo!* He must have written to the Countess. The rain drummed on her umbrella and diffused the light coming from the small windows of the homes along the street. Passing the cemetery, she resisted the urge to lie down on a grave and wail into the wet soil. The church reminded her of the days in Poland when an evil entity had pretended to be Ingo. He was alive, and had come for her. They would find each other again. When the time was right, Father would bring them together. Was he telling her not to give up, reminding her that she must be free? She must work on that, must find a way to untangle her life.

Today Father had given her two wonderful gifts—proof that Ingo was alive, and a piano she could play. "Ingo," she cried into the dark and empty street. "I love you so. Please come back."

Olga went to the church, where saints looked down on her from gilded frames. Christ hung on his cross. No, she must stay away from the spirits. Never again would she play into their hands. Never. Ingo would return on his own.

Over the following days, Olga did her chores, studied English, and tried to contact Father. Nothing happened. Instead, she heard Lothar's steps clamber up the squeaky stairs to her attic room.

"I'm not in the mood," she said when he came in and took off his coat.

"You are my wife."

"True, but not your property, Lothar von Schenck. I am nobody's property."

"Who said you were?" The attic was cold and musty, and smelled of mothballs. She had stacked up the boxes, and set up the Countess' dainty secretary along with a brocaded chair. The bed had fresh, crisp sheets and Sergeant Aldrich's woolen army blanket. Up until now, Olga had obliged Lothar's demands. He had not been around lately. Why tonight?

In proprietary fashion, he unbuttoned his pants.

"I told you, not tonight," she said, facing him with her arms crossed over her chest. She had kept her coat on. The room had no heat. Fall had set in with its rain and cold winds. "Liesl is coming to pick me up for the movies. An American film with German subtitles. Helps me with my English."

"I can't see any improvement," he sneered. "You better stick to German, rather than insult English speaking people." He dropped his pants, and stood in his wrinkled underwear. She hated his hairy legs and ridiculous erection. Why should she care that he needed a woman? He could get any one of the millions of widows who'd be glad to oblige. Everything about him disgusted her. She swallowed, rather than spit in his cold and arrogant face. That would only excite him, the sadist. She would no longer serve him. Her doormat days were over.

"I do what I can," Olga said, ignoring the shirt-tails hanging over his shorts. His socks had holes in the toe and heel. She overlooked that too.

"Your cockiness is rather irritating," he said, frowning. "Maman is right. I'm too lenient." Reaching for her, he flaunted his erection.

Olga stepped back. Anyna was safe. Adie loved the child, and would keep her no matter what Lothar said or did. Olga pursed her lips. "What makes her think I'm at your disposal? I pay for my upkeep, and even bring food for you and her, clean the room, and empty her stinking chamber pot. I expect Liesl any moment now, and suggest that you pull up your pants, unless you want her to get a kick out of this." She turned to the mirror and brushed her curls.

He stared at her as if he hadn't heard right. "Have you gone mad?" His erection had fallen limp. Soon it would shrivel up. "What's gotten into you? Just because Aldrich drove you home and wants you to perform for them doesn't make you anybody special." He stumbled forward, hampered by his trousers, which had slipped to his ankles. "So your dishwasher friend is more important than your husband?" he said, spewing a sarcasm that could not touch her.

"Assistant cook!" Olga fired back. "I don't care to have sex with you. Is that clear? So, please excuse me. I must fix my hair."

He made another step, not quite ready to pull his pants up. She read surprise, anger, and exasperation in his eyes, and fought back her guilt. She must liberate herself—for Ingo.

"How dare you talk to me like that," he said, obviously at a loss, and pulled up his pants. "Women are dying to get a man."

"Lucky you. Why don't you go and amuse them, Lothar? I'd be glad to resign from my obligation," she heard herself say.

"You've gone mad. I'll let it pass this time, but you'll be sorry. There are ways to enforce a husband's rights!" He grabbed his coat and hat. "It's Saturday, and I have to play at the NCO club. Just remember that I will not stand for this kind of behavior. You're my wife!" he shouted, slamming the door behind him.

Stunned, she stared at the closed door. What could he do? She better keep that door locked and the key in the keyhole. Her heart pounded. Liberty would not come easy, but she had a goal and must be strong. Ingo had come for her. They would be reunited. Let Lothar sulk and retaliate and the Countess toss her poison darts. They could no longer touch Olga. Her love for Ingo would shield her.

The following afternoon Sergeant Aldrich came to the NCO Club kitchen. "I'll take you home, Olga, and then pick up Lara. Are you ready to leave?"

Riding in the big, luxurious Buick, Olga felt transported into a world where people took comfort for granted. The radio played a piece by some American big band. The windshield wipers swished back and forth. Relaxing in the soft white leather seats, she watched him steer. What difference did it make what people thought of her? He was Lara's lover and treated her like a royal concubine. Aldrich chewed on his wet cigar instead of smoking it. Empty fields passed, a knoll, then the lake. The trees lining the road formed a golden canopy. The rain stopped, and the clouds opened up. The setting sun came out and cast its flaming light against the dark sky. Louis Armstrong sang *Blueberry Hill* in his peculiar raspy voice. Over the past year Olga had come to like American pop tunes, but Lothar would not let her touch the piano, though he knew that music was her life.

"Now, listen to me, honeybunch," Aldrich said, overtaking a wagon pulled by an ox. "The other day you brought me luck."

"You win bet?"

Grinning exultantly, he took off his cap and scratched his large head. "I only make bets I'll win. You should know that. Now listen to me." He took the cigar from his mouth and flipped it out of the window.

"Yes, Sergeant Aldrich."

"I talked to our entertainment committee. You probably don't know what that is. Never mind. They want you to play for us Friday and Sunday nights at happy hour. On Saturdays, we have Lothar and his combo. I know our ladies will appreciate your playing the piano for them."

How would Lothar take this? His entertaining at the NCO Club had opened the door for Lara meeting Aldrich, and the whole American connection they profited from. Olga had no intention of rejecting Aldrich's offer. If she could play the piano, she could cope with everything else.

"Your *Autumn Leaves* and *Happy Times*, are swell," he said, slipping his hand along her thigh. Olga did not react, hoping he would get the message. "I'll try to get that piano for you to practice on."

"Really!" she said, glad that a sharp turn obliged him to use both hands. She smoothed out her skirt where he had pulled it up a bit.

"We'll pay you twenty marks a night and a carton of cigarettes," he said, his eyes on the road, maneuvering around potholes and cow turds. "I bet you know how much you can sell those cigarettes for. You'll make a killing." His smile was not about cigarettes. He desired her.

"Carton of cigarettes?" Of course she knew what they were worth—they were the ultimate currency on the black market. What had Lara told him about her sister-in-law other than that she could play the piano? Did she mention Ingo? That would give Aldrich the idea that Olga was available.

"That's right, honeybunch. I know you don't smoke. You can trade them for pretty clothes. Nylons."

"Shoes maybe?"

"That too. Coffee, tea, chocolate and perfume. Anything you like."

"And what I must do?" she asked suspiciously. Men always wanted sex.

"I told you. Play the piano for us." He smiled mysteriously, took her hand, and squeezed it. "I'll make you a star," he said simply. "No more work in the kitchen for you. We got to keep those pretty hands smooth and limber."

She only understood half of what he said, and let him hold her hand. For all he did for her, she could at least give him that pleasure. Not that she wanted to become a star, but his thoughtfulness touched her. Other than Ingo, she couldn't think of anybody who had taken an unselfish interest in her life. No, that wasn't true. Ingo's aunts had been so good to her and Gottfried. Now it was Aldrich, the big man who always smelled of Old Spice. She liked him a lot, and trusted him. In his company, she felt safe and appreciated.

He drove down a dirt road and stopped. What should she do if...?

Turning toward her, he cradled her face in his warm hands and gazed into her eyes. She smiled shyly, and did not resist when he pressed his lips to hers. It felt good. She returned his kiss with an innocence that surprised her. "You're so good to me, Sergeant Aldrich," she said softly. "I love you too." She felt drawn to him. In her loneliness, having somebody who cared was so gratifying. She leaned her head against his broad chest, asking for his protection. She longed for a friend.

Abruptly, he let her go and turned toward the wheel. Starting the car, he said, "I'd better move on before we get carried away. Practice some American songs like *Moonlight Serenade, In the Mood, That Old Black Magic.*" The car hit a pothole. "I sure am in the mood right now. Hell, this takes a choir boy. Anyway, you'll go places, I'll see to that. You got rhythm. Hey, that's another good song. And you are a beauty, honeybunch. I'd trade you for Lara any day. Get some cute clothes and the men will drool over you." He chuckled as if he could see the scene. "And the women will imitate you—as if that's possible. You're unique, my lovely Olga. Irresistible."

At home, Lothar explained Aldrich's terms to Olga. "I'll never know why they want you to play," he said after Aldrich had left. "He could have asked me. I could play on Fridays as well. But you?"

"You should see her flirting with him, when she knows he is Lara's beau," the Countess said, propped up against her pillow. "You don't know what's going on behind your back. That innocent look of hers doesn't fool me. You should have seen her come out of her bedroom when that German soldier visited her back in Poland. The one she picked him up at the café. Now it's Aldrich, an American. Our little martyr loves uniforms. Not uncommon for women of her station. Just remember, Aldrich is Lara's beau, Lothar."

"That's enough silly talk, Maman. I must get back to work. My composition is taking shape. *Catacombs* will be a sensation. A new approach to music." He turned to Olga. "Don't count on using this piano to practice on."

Rather than strike back with "I wouldn't dream of it," she prepared tea. "Aldrich will let me play on the piano in the storeroom."

"Storeroom?" the Countess jeered. "How convenient. Does it have a sofa?" Neither the frown on her white forehead nor the drawn lips of her painted mouth impressed Olga. She filled the kettle with water from the bucket and placed it on the hot plate, then sat down and waited. "From now on I won't have to disturb you."

"Well," the Countess said in a huff. "That's a blessing. At least you won't come in at all hours. We'll have a set time for cleaning up."

"That depends on when I'll be available. I intend to spend most of my time practicing to make up for lost time," Olga said, pouring the boiling water into the teapot.

"Listen to her, Lothar. Lost time? We put her up and now she calls it 'lost time.' Why don't you say something, Lothar? The whole idea is absurd. Aldrich doesn't know what he's getting himself into." The Countess dabbed her nose as if Olga had passed gas. "And your riding in his car is an affront. What will people think?"

"You don't seem to mind Lara riding in his car," Olga said, unperturbed. For once, she had the upper hand. The Countess' desperation amused her.

"Enough of this jabber," Lothar said, and played a passage from his composition. "Can't you see that I'm working?"

"I insist on getting the respect due a mother, Lothar. Can't you see that she'll make a fool of herself? Olga should let you take the job and keep working in the kitchen. That's what she's good for. This whole affair is *degoutant*. First she arrives uninvited, then she takes over my attic, and now she steals your job. If you don't take a stand, Lothar, we'll soon be living in the attic, while she resides in this room. You must stop her, dear, before it's too late!" She threw up her slender, manicured hands in despair, and screwed her eyes, sighing.

"Your tea, Countess," Olga said, setting the cup before her. "And some of Ernie's cookies. I must be on my way."

"I would not want to put you out, Olga. My son can look after me," she said, while Olga set up the tray for her. The aromatic tea eased the stench of urine. The Countess insisted on using a chamber pot Olga emptied twice a day, convinced the fresh air would kill her.

Lothar handed Olga some sheet music. "These will get you started."

"Thank you," she said. "I'm rusty and unfamiliar with American music. I'm so glad you understand. Once we have enough money, we can bring Anyna back. I miss her so." Olga slipped into her coat, took the music, and left before the Countess could launch into a fresh tirade. Behind the door she heard Lothar say, "Why don't you stop picking on Olga, Maman? You're acting like a yipping dog."

"Lothar!" the old lady screeched, forgetting her nobility. "How dare you talk to your mother like that? This is all her doing. She wiggles her fanny and you jump. And now Aldrich. Honestly. If you don't stop this, you'll be sorry. Mark my word."

"I've heard enough stupidities for one day, Maman."

Clutching the music, Olga tiptoed down the musty hall. Lothar had some backbone after all.

Back at the base, Olga was stirring thick brown gravy when Aldrich came into the kitchen. "Your sergeant caller," Liesl teased.

Olga waved at him. "Hallo, Sergeant Aldrich. I got music now."

"And I have a piano, honeybunch. Does that make you happy? I see it in your eyes. So blue. So German. Now you can practice as long as you like. I figured that Countess Dracula wouldn't let you play at home. She's jealous, the old hag. Her show isn't working too well," he mused, putting his hand on her shoulder. "Come, try out the piano." Winking at Ernie, he pulled Olga toward the door. "She'll be right back."

"You make trouble for me, Sergeant Aldrich," Olga teased.

"I wouldn't mind making real trouble for you. But for now, this will do." His excitement rubbed off on Olga. As his protégé, she enjoyed a special position at the Club.

At the storage room, they cleared away the chairs, a mirror, dresser, and wardrobe until the piano stood unencumbered and the stool was in place. Olga opened the lid, admired the keyboard, then ran her fingers over all the black and white keys, striking a couple of chords and arpeggios, and finishing with scales. Her cheeks warm and her eyes shining, she looked up at her benefactor. "This is *wunderbar*, Sergeant Aldrich. So *wunderbar*." She threw her arms around his neck and kissed his cheek. Next to this big and burly man, Olga felt like a little girl, and leaned her head against his broad chest.

He held her. "So, we're in business."

"You make me so happy."

"So I see. Does it play well?"

She nodded. "Maybe...how you call it?" She returned to the keyboard, and hit the keys that needed tuning. "You hear?"

"Yes. We need a tuner."

Olga was all business. "You call it tuner, yes? I am so happy." She smiled, showing her dimples. "Now I can play," she said, and did, *I know Some Day A Miracle Will Happen*. Her miracle was happening. Aldrich's Old Spice reminded her that she was in a new world now, and everything would work out. She was no longer at anybody's mercy.

"Nice piece," Aldrich said. "Can you start tomorrow?"

"Tomorrow? But, but," she stammered. "I must practice first." She turned toward him, and read victory in his eyes. He obviously could not wait to show his discovery off to his buddies.

"You can practice all you want now," he said. "We can have a short program. Half an hour. Surely you can do half an hour? Play anything you like. People will enjoy it. Just wait until Irv sees you. He's crazy about

417

you. But don't worry about that. He can get some other German *fraulein*. When you're hungry, go to the kitchen. Ernie will take care of you. I'll come by this evening to take you home, okay?"

Of course she could do it. The music Lothar had given her would not take long to read and learn. Then she could do some of the classics everybody loved. Aldrich would not be disappointed. Irv would be pleased. Perhaps even Sgt. Johnson would come to hear her. "Okay," she said.

"Then it's settled."

As he made his way to the door, she ran after him, almost stumbling over some costumes on the floor. "Wait." She threw her arms around him, hugged and kissed him. "Thank you, dear Sergeant Aldrich. You so good to me. Nobody like you. I thank you so much." She had tears in her eyes when he kissed her forehead. "And you're my sweet honeybunch, who'll be our star."

Olga had no idea what time it was when Aldrich returned, chewing on his cigar. "Time to quit," he said, pulling a sandwich from his pocket. "I figured you'd be hungry. You can eat it on your way home. We'll surprise people tomorrow with your performance, okay?" He turned off the light, and took her through the darkened club. "You sound very good. I got more music for you too. Here's your pass. You can enter and leave the base whenever you like. Nobody will bother you in there—I had two soldiers pull the big doors shut so that people in the dining room can't hear you."

After leaving the building, they crossed the courtyard. The lights in the barracks were still on. The guards saluted when Aldrich drove by. Everybody knew him. Soon, they would know Olga too.

"I talked to Ernie. He has plenty of help, and can manage without you. He'll come to the performance tomorrow and bring his friends. He can't believe you're a pianist. But you'll show him." The lights of his Buick flooded the dark and empty streets of town.

"I feel like an archeologist who's discovered a rare find. I'm so glad Lara told me about you."

Olga did not bother asking what she had told him. Her English was not good enough to understand.

That night, Olga barely slept, imagining herself on stage at the NCO Club. At daybreak, she pulled off the sheets from the Countess's wardrobe and went through it. Perhaps she could wear one of the tailored dresses, or a blouse and a suit. Would it look too extravagant, considering the NCO wives usually wore twinsets, matching woolen skirts, and flat shoes? Some wore blouses and sweaters, and once in a while a suit. Would that salmon satin blouse with long sleeves and a ruffled collar go with her black skirt and a patent-leather belt? She could wear pumps. Olga felt like a little girl trying on her mother's clothes, except that those of the Countess fit quite well. Since she would probably never come up here again, or in any case not know that Olga had worn her clothes, this should work out well. The transformation amazed her. Soon she would be able to get her own clothes from the PX, which was only open to members of the American forces.

Rummaging some more, she found two glittering combs for her hair and a rose-colored lipstick. She would touch up her brows and wear earrings. As a final touch, she draped a silver fox boa around her neck. Smiling into the mirror, Olga liked what she saw. No wonder Aldrich was excited. She was no beauty like Lara, but he was obviously taken by her innocent charm. He was such a dear man. It was impossible not to love him for his kindness.

The following morning, Olga was working on her program when Sergeant Aldrich stepped in to listen. "Not bad. What am I saying—it's great, honeybunch. You'll have those fellows going gaga when they hear you."

"Thank you. I got nice clothes too."

"I forgot all about that," he said, leaning against the upright the way Ingo had, way back in Litzmannstadt.

"You want to see?"

"You never cease to surprise me. You better go see Ernie and eat something. I can't have you fainting during your performance. I bet you didn't even have breakfast."

"No time."

"Or lunch?"

She shook her head. "No time."

"That's what I figured."

When Sergeant Aldrich came to the storeroom to get her, she was ready. He was so stunned that he forgot to close his mouth. "Is this the Olga who used to work in the kitchen?" he said, gallantly taking her hand, as if she were a grand lady. Not even Lara received such reverence.

"You like?" she asked impishly, her large eyes proud and pleased. The shy young woman who did Lothar's and the Countess's bidding was transformed into a *femme fatale*, or at least Olga hoped she was. "We can go. I'm ready."

"I'm flabbergasted," he said gazing at her in awe. "Swell. Simply, what can I say, *magnifique*." A father escorting his daughter to the altar could not have shown more pride than Sergeant Aldrich did now, escorting Olga on stage. A rousing applause erupted. The dining room was not full, but the people who happened to be there, sipping their highballs, gave it their all, applauding until their palms burned.

"All right. All right," he kept saying, trying to get their attention, and cleared his throat. "Ladies and gentlemen. I bet you don't even recognize this young lady who's been working in the kitchen preparing your food. Well, in real life she is Baroness Olga von Schenck. Yes, a baroness, by marriage to none other than Lothar, whom you know well. Thanks to Lara, I learned just the other day that Olga is a pianist who performed during the war." He pointed at his mistress, who sat at a front table and waved. "This is Olga's debut at our club. Just wait 'til you hear her play. Beauty and talent are a good combination, don't you think? Please welcome our new star, Olga von Schenck."

The sergeants and their wives chuckled. They clapped, stomped, and whistled in support of their sergeant major.

Olga bowed, all smiles, cheeks burning. She had not expected this, and was glad that it all came about in such a lighthearted fashion, so unlike the night when she had met Ingo in far-away Poland. The cigarette smoke had a pleasant smell. The women wore sweaters, silk scarves and brooches. The uniforms of the men were well made, and always clean. Olga remembered the German soldiers on their way to their deaths at the Russian Front. Ingo had survived. That was all that mattered. If he could only see her now. But he was not among the complacent faces of the American men.

The applause ebbed, and even the whispers stopped. Olga sat down at the keyboard and placed her music on the stand, then turned to her audience with a slight nod. All eyes were on her. "Thank you for inviting me to play. I'm sure you know the pieces Sergeant Aldrich suggested I do for you." After the first measures of *Happy Days Are Here Again*, she had the audience singing and humming along.

Sergeant Aldrich and Lara sat at the front table. Olga was too engrossed in her music to see them. Reading from the notes, she played *In the Mood, Stardust*, and *The White Cliffs of Dover.* After a couple of weeks of practice she would do better, but the audience didn't seem to care. They knew the melody and the beat. Their applause came from the heart. Olga's German waltz, sensuous tango, and dreamy slow-fox were equally well received. The music she had carried in her heart for so long now poured from her, like giving birth to a new life through art.

Aldrich came on stage, walking like a sailor on high sea. Those scotches he loved had gone to his head. "There you have it, guys. Our own Olga. If you want her to play Fridays and Sundays, let's hear it."

The applause, whistles, and shouts went on and on. Olga bowed, holding Aldrich's hand. "Thank you very much. I love piano and music. So glad you enjoy it too. *Rhapsody in Blue* is my favorite. It introduce me to America years ago, when I couldn't play American music. You are a great audience."

Aldrich took her to his table, where the raven-haired Lara awaited them. "Not bad, Olga. But these fellows don't know a thing about music. Still, I must admit, good show." She smoked through a long silver cigarette holder. "Lothar is the artist. He should play..." She interrupted herself. "I know he's busy with his composition. Serious work, you know." Her face didn't flinch when she added sarcastically, "And these men here like female flesh."

Olga smiled at Aldrich, as if Lara had made a compliment. "This is a good piano," she said, referring to the baby grand she had played on.

"Whatever you say, Olga." He didn't call her honeybunch in front of Lara. "You did a great job. People liked it. Now you're our official entertainer. The personnel office will take care of your papers. Everything's grand," he said in a thick voice. His eyes looked tired. He was drunk, but not like a Russian.

"You such a nice man, Sergeant Aldrich," she said. "I cannot thank you enough."

"You don't have to," Lara said. Her smile was artificial, and the look in her eyes frosty. But she couldn't touch Olga now, not as long as she had Aldrich's support. Enjoying her hamburger with lettuce and tomato, Olga took long sips of her screwdriver. Lightheaded from the unaccustomed alcohol, she giggled every time somebody came by to compliment her. "Don't mention it," she said.

"It's thank you," Lara admonished curtly. As usual, she was made up as if on stage, favoring dark red lipsticks on her alabaster white face and thick mascara for her lashes. Her eyes stood out like those of a cat watching her prey. The pencil-thin brows had a Marlene Dietrich affect. No, she was not one of them, those army wives who came from regular families and lived regular lives. She was Larissa von Schenck, sister of Baron von Schenck, and happened to enjoy Sergeant Aldrich's company. With her dyed black hair swept back for that classic look, and the elegant clothes he provided for her slender body, she had every woman's admiration. He lit her cigarette. The long, silver-tipped holder rested between her gloved fingers. Lara played the game to perfection. The Countess had trained her daughter well, passing on centuries of breeding.

Chapter 36

Another May put its magic touch on the world. Nature flourished with sensuous abandon. Olga feasted on the blooming chestnut tree across the street and inhaled the fragrant air. Outside the Countess' rancid room the world was so beautiful. She noticed Frau Moser waving at her. "Olga! Would you like some strawberries?"

"Oh yes, thank you very much. The first of the season?" Olga danced over the cobblestones as if let out from a cage where she had been at the mercy of her cruel masters.

After a warm handshake Frau Moser went into the house. Olga sat down on the bench behind the table, her face and bare legs toward the sun. Its warmth penetrated her body. This had become her home. How she missed Ingo. Perhaps he had written to the Countess' address and the old witch had intercepted his letter, the way Ingo's mother had in Dresden. Everybody condemned her "illicit" love. She pulled up the sleeves of her blouse. No, that was not true. Ingo's aunts and Ingrid had accepted her into their family. Only the Countess insisted on waging phychological warfare. Had she shown Ingo's letter to Lothar to rub in his wife's infidelity? Olga doubted that he was jealous, but it justified his tormenting her.

A painful longing tore at her heart, igniting the loneliness she felt whenever she thought of Ingo. She knew that he had been here last year, looking for her. Why didn't he leave her some clues as to where she could find him? Leaning back against the wall, she swallowed the lump in her throat. All her misfortunes were her own fault, because she had not followed Father's guidance. When would she learn to do what was right for her, instead of obliging others? Ingo. That ache in her heart, her desire and love for him refused to pass. Whenever music, nature's magnificence, or feeling alive and well her love for him flourished and filled her with bitter-sweet happiness. She cherished those feelings, and let them transport her into that world where she was whole. Without it she would suffocate under Lothar's cruelty, and die from his mother's venom. Pleasure required pain. For her, pain outweighed pleasure, still, she must not give up hope – that sprung eternal. Father had promised that they would be together when they were free. Hah! As if that were possible. Lothar would never grant her a divorce. Mental cruelty was only acceptable in America. The people over there understood that it was as painful as physical abuse. America was the place for her – she might as well wish to go straight to Heaven.

If Lothar claimed adultery, they could get a legal separation. But he had to punish her rather than reach out for a desperate widow longing to satisfy anybody who would have her. The sadist wanted Olga because she hated him.

Frau Moser put two wooden bowls with shining red strawberries in milk and sprinkles of sugar on the table. From time to time Ernie let Olga take home sugar and oil. Over the past three years, since Germany's surrender, nothing much had changed. The cities were still in ruins and food rationed. The allotments were too little to live on and too much to die. Non-fraternization required no enforcement as long as both sides frowned on those relationships. Once a girl was seen with an American soldier her reputation was ruined and with it any chance of marrying a local boy. Only the border crossing between the western occupation zones had been lifted, but the Russian Zone was shut off for good. West Berlin had turned into an island.

"It's all politics," Frau Moser said through her toothless mouth. New dentures were not available – not that she was eager to get any. She mashed the berries between her gums. Drops of red juice appeared on her thin, sunken lips.

"What is, Frau Moser?" Olga wondered, savoring the sweet berries Frau Moser had gathered in the forest.

She looked up. Thick folds of skin drooped over her angry eyes. "You should see what's happening to our potato plants. Their leaves remind you of Swiss cheese when we still had some. Yet the Allies refuse to let us manufacture pesticides. Before they came, we hadn't even heard of potato bugs. Now we get them like locusts."

Olga usually defended Americans, but now she was hard pressed to justify their strict rules that punished their enemy.

"It's a crying shame," Frau Moser went on, eager to get that grudge off her chest.

"I wish I could help," Olga said. "Sgt. Aldrich can get almost anything for cigarettes, but I doubt he could get enough pesticides to cover a whole field. Besides, they're all over West Germany." She spooned up the rich milk of Mosers's cows. A gentle breeze blew bits of straw across the farmyard where brown hens scratched for insects. On this beautiful spring day her heart cried out for Ingo. How she would love to admire the snow-covered Alps with him. He had to be here somewhere.

Frau Moser licked her lips. "Last year we had schoolchildren assigned to pick off the bugs only to watch them trample down the plants." Her arthritic hand held her soupspoon like a dagger. The black vest of her ancient dirndle had been tied another notch to accommodate her flat chest. "You like the Americans, don't you, Olga?" she said disdainfully, dropping the corners of her pinched mouth. "I guess they pay you well."

"They do. And they treat me like an equal, not like that show-off, Gernegross in Berlin. You should have seen him push his weight around. He wanted us to pay for the crimes committed during the war, including his time in a concentration camp. Now he plays the martyr who is rewarded by the Soviets for his heroic opposition. Got a cushy job supervising a brigade of helpless and starved women. He didn't care whether it rained or the sun beat down on us, as long as we kept the chain going, picking up the rubble in Berlin, clump bu clump. I'm sure the poor women are still at it, provided they're still alive. I wouldn't have lasted another month. My sweet, patient Anyna was dying of starvation. Her body rotted away. Those were horrible times. How I miss my baby. My only consolation is that she's well taken care of in Switzerland. Proper food and vitamins got her back to health. She attends a private school where she studies French and English instead of Russian! I miss her so. You're a mother and know what it's like when you can't be with your child." Olga blinked the tears from her eyes. If she could be with Anyna, her longing for Ingo would be easier to take.

"My Peter was killed," Frau Moser said,"but I still have Maria and her two children and feel blessed."

Olga drained the last drops of milk from the bowl. "Hm. That was so good. Thanks again, Frau Moser. What a treat." She stacked up the empty bowls.

Lost in thought Frau Moser watched Olga pick up the spoons from the weathered table. "Say, did I ever mention that a man came by last year asking whether Herr von Schenck had a wife? I didn't know whether he did or not. The Countess never talked to anybody and I don't get along with Frau Meier. I hate people who complain all the time. You know what I mean. Never has a good word to say about anybody."

Olga's heart thumped. "Was he blonde and blue eyed? A dimple in his chin? Did he talk with a Saxon accent? Polite and charming?"

Frau Moser scratched her head under the scarf. "My memory isn't the best. I felt sorry for him. He looked so sad when I told him that I didn't know anything about you or a little girl. Said that he met you in Poland."

"Yes, yes. That's true. Go on. What else did he say?"

"That he was trying to find you."

"I felt that he was nearby, but couldn't get away from my job." Olga remembered her trying to leave when Sgt. Aldrich had shown up insisting that she play for his buddy. That took forever. To make up for lost time he had taken her home in his car. It had been raining. But Ingo had left.

"He talked about the war. I think you helped him recover."

"In a way. Would you believe that he asked me to play the Mephisto Waltz. To my surprise I did. As surprised as he was. That's how we became friends. Did he say where he lives?" Olga asked, holding her breath.

"Somewhere in Stuttgart. I used to work there. That's how we got talking."

"Stuttgart? That isn't very far, is it?"

"No. From Munich about three hours by train."

"This is earth-shattering news, Frau Mother. Ingo was looking for me. Do you know what that means to me?" Olga jumped up. "I must find him right away. It's been over three years. We saw each other last in a Polish village. We were fleeing from the Russians. I got separated from my mother and from Anyna. The front was all around us when I found them. Then Ingo showed up, walking up to me like a vision. Grenades exploded all around, but we were protected as if we stood inside an invisible shield. For a few minutes we were already in heaven, but my mother and Anyna had to be saved. He stopped a truck and forced the driver to take us on. At gunpoint, mind you. My mother perished later, in Dresden and I lost track of my sister. He had asked me to go to his aunt's in Berlin and wait for him there. I did. Only he couldn't come and I had to get out. And now I found him. Frau Moser, I can't thank you enough." She hugged Frau Moser's thin shoulders. "What time does the bus leave in the morning? In Munich I'll catch a train to Stuttgart, go to the Registration Office and get his address."

Frau Moser leaned over the table. "Sounds very exciting, but what will your husband say when he finds out?"

Olga pulled back as if she had been struck. "My husband?" She had never considered Lothar her husband, nor did she care what he said.

Lothar was at the keyboard when Olga entered the room, working on "Rhapsody." The Countess sat on her bed, listening. Olga stayed in the dark corner that still served as their kitchen facility and picked up the dirty dishes, stacked them into the pan and ladled water over them from the bucket. She would leave soon for the Club. Get away from the evil smell – and not just from the chamberpot the Countess still used regularly to avoid contact with Frau Meier.

"How do you like my arrangement, Olga?" Lothar asked, without looking up from the keyboard. He could not see her, but had heard her come in. "I emphasized Gershwin's jazzy style. Too bad I can't perform it in a concert hall. How does it sound? Good rhythm, don't you think?" He played a few measures with the natural ease of an accomplished musician, running his tapered fingers effortlessly over the keys.

"Intriguing," she said, joining him at the piano, "but that isn't Gershwin."

"Is that all you can say," the Countess retorted. "I'll never know why Lothar puts up with you. Do you realize how lucky you are to play with a genius?"

"I am," Olga teased, "and envious that he can use the piano all day."

"Huh! What do you expect? All you can do is tinker around. I couldn't bear it."

"Sorry. I won't bother you anymore," Olga said, watching Lothar scribble some notes on his score. "By the way, I'll be off for Stuttgart first thing in the morning."

"What?" the Countess asked, visibly taken aback. "What do you mean you're off to Stuttgart? No doubt, meeting your lover."

"Why else would I go there? – Besides, how do you know he lives in Stuttgart?"

The Countess ignored the question. "Did you hear that, Lothar? How can you let her talk to me like that? The least I can ask for is some respect. You can't just let her do whatever she wants, Lothar." She touched her forehead with the back of her dainty hand.

He shrugged. "And why shouldn't she go to Stuttgart, if that's what she wants to do?"

"And meet her lover? This is too much for me. What is happening to you, Lothar? How can you tolerate the insult. Any other man would have slapped her and thrown her out, but not you. Decent to the core. Your concept of honor is going too far. You can't have this woman step all over you."

Amused, Olga watched the scene between mother and son. He enjoyed teasing his mother and she fell for it. Olga had finally learned not to take his insults to heart. It did not come easy.

In her desperation the Countess said, "Don't you remember the letter I showed you? That fellow, who had an affair with your wife, had the nerve to address it to me, your mother, asking for his mistress' whereabouts."

"So he did. You should have done him the favor. No need to get all worked up."

"Lothar! You are going too far. I am still your mother."

"What letter?" Olga asked, fuming. The witch had interjected Ingo's letter and shown it to Lothar. How she hated them. They would pay for it.

"The one your lover wrote. What an imposition to ask me, your mother-in-law. Naturally, I told him that you were dead – at least for him – and not to bother me anymore."

"How could you do that? What right do you have?" Olga cried out. Fortunately, Ingo knew better than to believe her and had come looking for Olga.

"The right of protecting my son, and you. Save you the grief of pining for a man you have no business having an affair with. You are married, which you conveniently forget, to a man who takes his marriage serious. How often do we have to tell you that we don't believe in divorces."

"That's not what Lothar said in Riga when we were married. It was to be a formality so that the baby would have a proper name. Then you interfered and turned our world topsy-turvy. Is that not so, Lothar?"

"He is way too lenient with you," the Countess said. "Instead of appreciating his generosity you openly announce that you are going to see your lover."

"Oh, that would suit me just fine, and finally get us on the right track," Olga said, heading for the door.

"Did you hear that, Lothar? Now you know what this woman is really like." Turning to Olga she added, "don't you think you owe us an apology?"

The Countess was right, Olga thought, but she would not bend her head to people who see her as a necessary evil they had to put up with. Hypocrites. She was so sick of this game and her dependence on them. If she could only run away. "I'm through having others tell me what to do."

"Well, well," Lothar said. "So my little kitten turned into an alley cat. I rather like it."

"Lothar!" the Countess cried out. "I can't take this anymore. My heart!" She pressed against her chest, dramatically gasping for air. "Did you forget what Olga did to you, to us? Your reputation, your career? Show her who is master in this house."

"Now don't get all worked up, Maman. It's bad for your heart, remember? As far as I recall, your past wasn't all that immaculate. When I think of that imposter, the Count, I could go on for hours. But enough theatrics, I must get back to my work."

The Countess breathed heavily, her white face a mask of controlled fury. Leaning into her pillows she showed no sign of the turmoil brewing in her chest. *Noblesse oblige*, Olga thought and admired her mother-in-law for her discipline, then left.

Tomorrow she would see Ingo and fall into his arms pretending that none of this existed. Once again they would be the happiest people on earth.

The overcrowded train reached Stuttgart at 14:02. Refugees and expelled people still sought safety or searched for their lost families. Daily broadcasts read off the names of people looking for each other. Olga jumped down the steep iron steps of the train car and hurried toward the exit. Unlike her trip to Munich two years ago, where she dreaded seeing Lothar again, she now had wings that carried her through the ruined station. She sidled through the mass of people streaming toward the exit. The moment she had pined for was at hand.

A cab took her to the Inhabitants's Registration Office where a hollow cheeked woman behind an ancient counter thumbed through file cards. "There it is," she said. "Kroll, Ingo. Born March 12, 1921 in Dresden. Address: Gartenstrasse 10, Degerloch. Employed by Daimler Benz in Unterturkheim. Married to Irmgard Haberle. They have a son named Fritz."

"What?" Olga said. "Are you sure it says 'married?'"

"Why would I lie to you?" the woman said, pouting.

"Sorry, I didn't mean to imply that. It's just that I didn't know he was married," Olga said in a low voice. "I was—"why should the woman care that Into Kroll was married and Olga shocked? People watched her. Ignoring their curious glances, Olga stepped out of the crowded office.

Back in the street she leaned against the rough stucco wall unable to cope with her pain that had taken over like a sudden illness. Ingo was married. With that the beautiful world of her imagination had been crushed and dumped into a thick fog. A father yet. That sealed their destiny. Neither he nor she would ever be free for each other. Why had Father done that to her? He had promised that they would get together, but not for a long time. How long would she have to wait and what would happen then?

Drained, emotionally devastated, she could not even think of her next move. The hot sun drove the perspiration from her body. She felt alone and abandoned, deceived and robbed of everything that was dear to her. What now? Should she go back to Inning and leave well enough alone, except it was not well enough. The pain in her heart robbed her of her senses. It made her ill, helpless, lost. Her knees felt weak and her heart crushed. Death would be a welcome solution. Join Father and be done with all this misery on earth. Her love could not pass. It would remain a festering wound that had no cure.

Wandering off Olga sorted out her turmoil. At least Ingo had tried to find her and had been very sad when he was told that Olga had perished. Then one thing led to another. In his disappointment he had found solace in the arms of an equally unhappy woman. She could not blame him for that. Had he not suffered the loss of his family, his home, his land? Who was to know what had happened to him toward the end of the war and in the prisoner of war camp. She had heard that some prisoners were obliged to sleep in the ovens where bodies of the murdered Jews had been cremated.

A huge white cloud rose toward the sun. Like her dream it would soon dissipate and vanish. So much for taking charge of her life. She felt stranded in the ruins of this strange city that harbored the ashes of her love. Perhaps she should go to Unterturkheim after all and see him for the last time. Say good-bye. She owed him that. He had a valid explanation and might enjoy seeing her. There was nothing wrong with that. They could talk things over and stay friends. The sun burnt on her back. People passed casting sympathetic glances. They all mourned over something or other.

The mutilated trees had fresh foliage, but lacked the full crowns they used to have before the explosives cut them apart. Olga would revive as well. She would work things out and go on living the best she could, devote her life to her music and to her child. It was time that she brought Anyna home. Then the image of the night, when they had exchanged their vows and returned to the sweetness of their love, came to mind. His tenderness and the ecstasy of their union. It had been a sacred act. Father had sanctified it and blessed them. He could not just drop them. He had some plan in mind she could not see now, but had to believe in. Her love had given her the strength to carry on through the bloodshed of the war. Without closing her eyes Olga could see Ingo stand in front of her celebrating their wedding.

Accelerating her steps she headed for the tram stop. The windows she passed were still covered with plywood and could not reflect her appearance. Olga had taken great care when she had picked out the linen suit and silk blouse with its cooped neck imagining that he would enjoy seeing her cleavage when she removed her jacket. Her hair had been freshly washed with American shampoo and she wore nylons and pretty pumps. Other than having her own place, she had a good life. The noncoms enjoyed her performances and Sgt. Aldrich saw to it that she was well treated.

Ingo. They had so much to talk about – the last days in Berlin, her escape to the West, Anyna's life in Switzerland and her own life at the American Base in Furstenfeldbruck.

Riding through Koenigsstrasse she noticed that make-shift stores had opened behind plywood facades. What had taken Ingo to this city? How would he react when he saw her?

The tram climbed up a steep hill that would take her to Unterturkheim where she hoped to meet Ingo at his workplace rather than show up at his home and find his wife opening the door. In the outskirts of Stuttgart the world had not changed. Well-tended vegetable gardens, solid homes with balconies and shining windows and children running around reflected an undisturbed consistency of life for those who had been spared the pain of the war. Did Ingo live in a place like that? Irmgard Haberle had to be a local woman who had offered him her home.

Why was the tram so slow? She must get to the plant before quitting time.

Unterturkheim had been the home of Gottfried Daimler and Karl Benz when they built their first motorized vehicle. How did Ingo fit into that picture? Nervously Olga pulled some loose tendrils into her moist face. Should she take off her hat and meet him the way he remembered her, though her hair had been cut in the latest style? Her bag had plenty of space, not only for the packs of cigarettes she had taken along, but even her little hat. Leaving the tram she thought about the river that separated their lives. Could they build a bridge? Ilona Huzak, her soothsayer, had foreseen Olga's future across the ocean. America? Without Ingo it did not matter where she lived – with him she would be happy anywhere.

The Daimler Benz property was not far, but there was no plant. The huge, empty lot resembled a playing field that had no purpose and was way too big for any particular sport. A damaged building was under construction, surrounded by a fence and had a guardhouse. Bricklayers worked from scaffolding building a wall, brick by brick. The Allies had leveled the area to the ground.

Olga went to the guardhouse. A one-armed guard greeted her in regular work clothes.

"I am looking for Ingo Kroll," she said. "I understand that he works here."

"He certainly does," the guard said with a Swabian accent. "A nice young man. Usually stops by for a little chat. I'd be glad to give him a note when he comes out. It's almost quitting time. Why don't you wait at the café across the street. He can meet you there."

The man's easy banter put Olga at ease. She wrote: *I'm at the café and would be glad to see you. Olga.* "Thanks for your help," she said. "We haven't seen each other since the war."

"The war tore the world apart. I lost my wife and part of my body. But I'm alive, that's a lot to be thankful for."

On her way across the dusty yard Olga passed a rambling rose clinging to a piece of broken fence. She picked a flower and stuck it into her cleavage. Would he notice? She had not bothered with make-up, relying on her healthy complexion and natural red lips.

The café had tables set up in the shade of a linden tree. Olga sat down at one of the rickety folding tables covered by an oil cloth. Though she had not eaten all day she did not feel hungry nor had she brought ration coupons for a sandwich or some pastry. A buxom waitress in black and white came out crunching over the gravel and took Olga's order for mineral water. How different all this was from her envisioning their reunion, Olga thought, keeping an eye on the guard house. There would be no falling into his arms and staying there forever. He was married. What should she say?

The waitress soon poured the bubbly water into a glass.

"Thanks. I'm waiting for my friend who works at the Daimler plant. Will they quit soon?" She pulled a cigarette from a pack of Pall Malls and offered it to the waitress. "Please, be my guest."

The young woman's eyes lit up. "Are you serious? That's an extraordinary gift. I don't know what to say."

Olga laughed. "Thank you will do."

The waitress blushed and looked delightful in her joy. "Well, thank you very much. I could get you some wine. It'll make the time go faster.

Der Chef owns a vineyard nearby and makes some very good wine." She placed the cigarette on her tray. "Nobody hands out presents like this, or any for that matter."

"This is a special day for me and I would like to share it with somebody. I'm going to meet a very dear friend of mine whom I haven't seen since the war."

"You're very lucky indeed. I wished I would hear from my friend. He was probably taken prisoner by the Russians. They don't bother telling us whether he's still alive or not. That's the worst." Biting her lips she turned around and walked away, dragging her steps under the load of her sorrow.

When she returned with a glass of wine Olga said, "Never give up hope. I didn't expect to find my friend either. And here he is. Unfortunately he thought I was dead and got married." She sipped the wine. "You're right. It is excellent. Please thank your chef." The unaccustomed alcohol sent its soothing effect into her bloodstream.

"I gave him the cigarette. He's crazy about American cigarettes. Spent some time in an American POW camp and loved it."

"Do you suppose," Olga asked, "he would trade a snack and a bottle of wine for a whole pack?"

The waitress perked up. "I'm sure he would. He has some homemade pickles too. Very good."

Handing her the pack Olga said, "But please wait until my friend shows up."

Her glass was almost empty when Ingo came out. She recognized him immediately by his determined gait, the posture and the friendly gesture toward the guard. He took the note and waved running toward her. "Olga!"

She jumped up and almost tipped her chair over, then ran until they collided in a stormy embrace. He lifted her up and swirled her around like a child. Laughing they kissed each other, over and over again. Her Ingo was here, alive and well. He still loved her. What more could she want?

Hand in hand they returned to her table accompanied by the smiles of his colleagues.

"I can't believe you're here," he said, "alive and well and more beautiful than ever. My darling, I can't tell you how much I missed you. I was crushed when the Countess wrote me that you had died. I didn't believe her, but the evidence. You would never leave Anyna. Peeking into the window I saw Lothar, heard him play, and saw the Countess. No sign of you or Anyna. Then I talked to Frau Moser. She hadn't seen a child or you. What was I to think? I couldn't ask Lothar or his mother. Not after what she wrote. She was right, of course. From her point of view we committed a sin. How silly it all is. But you're here now. Let's sit down and order something, then you can tell me all about it. Where you live? What you're doing? How is my little baroness?" He held her hand and kissed it when the waitress came with a tray of cold cuts, a basket of rolls and a bottle of wine.

"Where is all this coming from?" he teased.

Olga winked to the waitress who said, "a little gift from my chef."

"Do you want me to believe in Santa Claus? Please thank him for me. I do have some coupons, but probably not enough meat coupons for all this."

"It's on the house," Olga said quickly. The waitress left. Olga lifted her glass. "To our love and to Father who brought us together again."

"Father," he whispered. "He's been giving us a hard time, wouldn't you say?"

Olga did not know what to think, all she knew was that she was immensely happy. A new beginning. – What about the rest?

"I love you, Olychka. Had I known you're alive, I would've never married Irmgard. We'll figure out what to do, except that I can't leave my son. Fritzle needs me the way Anyna needs you. But let's not think of that now. Irmgard knows that I only love you. She was very lonely, and her family was so good to me."

"I understand," Olga said dryly. She must not let her disappointment spoil this evening. He was here and still loved her. He had not been wounded again nor suffered any illness. On the contrary, he looked even younger and more dapper than she remembered. Well fed his face had softer lines and the eyes a happy glow – a young man in love. They could start a new life, if... They would somehow. She had to believe in it and make it happen. "I wouldn't have returned to Lothar if Anyna had not been at the verge of death. As long as we love each other, Ingo, we can work things out. I'm yours, only yours, and always will be."

Somewhat later, Ingo left the table. Olga summoned the waitress. "Der Chef wouldn't happen to have a room for another pack of cigarettes?"

The waitress smiled secretively. "That's a big secret, of course. We're not allowed to keep private rooms. But I think he might have one for you. He gets so excited when people find each other again."

When Ingo returned she raised her glass. "To our miracle."

Talking about their lives Olga noticed that his jacket and shirt were of good quality and fit well. The Haberles were doing well, he explained, mentioning their farm and the black market he had participated in. "It's like your working for the Americans. There is an underground economy where people live well. Eventually we'll have a government and an economy that will give everybody an opportunity to acquire some wealth."

Over food and wine, their hearts and loins heated up, the world looked better and better. Olga wished the evening would go on forever.

"We were a misguided and misled people at the mercy of ruthless fanatics," he said, his cheeks warm and eyes glowing. "When you reward evil and spread terror that is what you get. Unrestrained madmen taking pleasure in their superiority over those they can exude power. Human nature must be tamed over and over again. A never ending process against greed and destruction." That concept had obviously nothing to do with what he felt. "Working at a regular job, with regular people, doing meaningful things, rather than killing others, is such a blessing. I'm an ordinary man and the father of a little boy. "

Olga cringed at the *little boy* part, bit her lip and let it pass. The waitress waved at her. The room was available. "Do you suppose you could stay for the night?" she asked Ingo. "Der Chef managed to make one available to us."

Ingo looked at her incredulously. "He did? How's that possible?"

"He wants to see us happy."

"No joke? Is there something going on I should know about?"

Olga grinned. The wine made her giddy. "No. Just accept and enjoy. Another miracle, that's all. Can you stay?"

Ingo took her into his arms. "You are a magician. Of course I can. Just let me call home. We even have a telephone!" he added, laughing. "I'll be right back. I would not want to miss this for anything in the world. It'll be the happiest night of my life – no, perhaps the second, or the third happiest. I don't know. I lost count. Let's say, it'll be the first happiest night after our reunion. How do you like that?"

During his absence Olga asked the waitress: "Does your piano work?"

"It should. We have a blind man come and tune it every so often. It's pretty good."

When Ingo returned he found Olga at the keyboard playing "I Know Some Day A Miracle Will Happen," and joined her, leaning against the upright as if they were back in Poland at the Esplanade. The guests sang along. The rotund proprietor came in with his wife. Everybody celebrated a miracle along with the lovers performing for them.

Olga thanked "Der Chef" with a spontaneous kiss on his cheek. "Thanks a million. You can't imagine how much this means to us. Our years of suffering are over."

"I know all about it," his wife said, leaning her head against his burly chest.

On the stairs Ingo and Olga stopped at every other step, held each other and kissed. At the threshold to their room he picked her up and carried her to the freshly made bed. "My beloved Olychka. You are not only alive, but the most wonderful being God created." With every piece of clothing he removed he exclaimed expressions of surprise and joy, kissing her unfolding body until she was exposed in all her loveliness. His rising desire gave her the greatest joy until she could no longer restrain and let go of her passion for him.

Though the night was too short, they not only found the very essence of each other, they knew that there would be a time when they would join their hands forever.

"Father will tell us when the time is right," Olga said in parting.

Chapter 37

At home life resumed its customary rhythm. Ingo was no longer a dream, he was her goal. It was up to her to bring them together. Since Irmgard loved her deceased fiancé and Ingo loved Olga, Fritzle would not be enough to hold their marriage together. Something was bound to happen that would bring their differences to a head, and Olga would be there for him when that happened. In the meantime she had to liberate herself and create her independence, not only making a living but establish a home for Anyna where they could live together. For the moment she had no idea how to bring that about, but had faith that she could do it.

Even Germany's second Dark Ages had possibilities. Father was helping her, how else could she have become a piano player at the NCO Club? For the moment Anyna was happy with Adie and Richard in Switzerland. Lothar and his mother would stay in their dark and stinking room, dwelling on memories of past grandeur while Olga pursued her music with Aldrich's help. He had extended his stay in Germany; this was too good a place to leave for a boring life in Texas. He had sent for sheet music from the States so that Olga and Lothar could work on the pieces Mr. Whitney, the agent from New York, would want to hear.

Practicing the piano, Olga wondered how Aldrich had lured this Al Whitney to Germany. He had assured her that there was indeed a Mr. Whitney who would come to audition them. Why should Olga question it, other than ask herself what was in it for him? Aldrich never did anything for nothing. His confidence in Lothar's and her artistry flattered her. Now that she had a keyboard at her disposal, she spent whole days at the piano. When she worked with Lothar, she ignored his sneers and adapted to his rhythm, beat and those improvisations he loved. "People want to hear the music they know," she would say. Overall they worked rather well together, considering their differences in style and approach.

They slowly became a true duo, playing as if their four hands belonged to the same person. He knew his craft and could enhance any melody or sharpen any beat. By the time Mr. Whitney arrived on July 15th, Olga would know the pieces by heart and could easily adapt should Lothar take off with one of his improvisations. She was confident that the man from New York would be pleased with their performance.

On June 20th, the Allied High Command announced that they would implement a currency reform the following day, exchanging Reichsmark for Deutschmark. Since Olga had no bank account or extra cash, she lost very little. Admiring the crisp notes, she wondered what would happen to others whose millions—savings, bank accounts, money stashed away under mattresses—were now nothing but worn out, worthless paper. Her next paycheck would be in Deutschmarks. Overnight goods she had forgotten existed appeared in stores. The new currency had real value, and people now had to face its scarcity. She was so excited that she bought rolls, eggs, butter, cheese, and a liter of milk. At the butcher's she got ground beef for patties, and at the grocer's fresh fruits and vegetables that had appeared as if out of nowhere. With carefree steps she sauntered home, swinging her shopping net. Was Germany finally turning into a regular economy? Konrad Adenauer, the Mayor of Cologne, had the confidence of the Allied High Command. Together they must have worked out this amazing feat, secretly printing banknotes and distributing them to the exchange offices. Once the Marshal Plan went into effect, life could resume a healthy rhythm. The credit the Plan offered would be like a blood transfusion to a dying patient. Rather than strip Germany of her factories, the United States would let West Germany buy much needed seed, fertilizer, livestock, and raw materials, as well as the necessary machinery to replace what had been taken. On that basis Germany, could become self-sufficient again. Better yet, with a solid currency, they could re-open international trade and exchange German goods for those produced in other countries. The borders were still closed, but this was a start. For the moment, Germany needed everything it could get its hands on, providing an insatiable market for American goods.

Chewing on a crunchy roll Olga felt a sense of renewal. Things would work out, with or without Ingo. She certainly could not spend the rest of her life waiting for him.

Once Germany set up political parties and the people could elect representatives and Konrad Adenauer as Chancellor, the country would recover. People could not wait to do real work for real pay. The American Army recruited German men for guard duty. Young men who had returned from POW camps, or had fled from Eastern Europe, now wore navy blue uniforms and did the tasks American soldiers most despised. The pay was good and they had comfortable housing in former German barracks.

Lothar was sitting at the keyboard when she entered the gloomy, stale room. The Countess looked up.

"See what I bought for my new money! The shopkeepers hoarded all this and waited until they could sell it for good money rather than trade it for cigarettes." She laughed. "From now on cigarettes will be for smoking." She buttered a roll and put a thick slice of cheese on top. "Here, try this. It's delicious. And have an apple. Perhaps we'll even get bananas and oranges again."

He took it, while she prepared another roll for the Countess. I'm not sure this is good news," she said. "What will Nicky do? You can't expect him to go to an office?"

"About time he learns a trade," Lothar said. "How long do you intend to spoil that boy, Maman? He's twenty-eight—old enough to do something useful, don't you think?

Olga smirked at Lothar's jealousy toward his step-brother. He resented him as much as he had hated his step-father, the count. "We'll keep on performing at the NCO Club," she said, proving that she was no parasite but could hold her own. "And earn real money. We could work out a new deal with them. I wonder what this Mr. Whitney will be like?"

"He's an agent who wants to make money. If he represents us he'll make sure it's worth his while. That's what agents do. So don't think he's doing us a favor. He should be glad if we accept his offer."

"What do you mean *if*? I'd be delighted to go to New York." She knew that neither Lothar nor his mother appreciated her enthusiasm and dropped her voice. Inflated with their counterfeit superiority, they could not bear her enjoying anything and always had to put her into her place. But that would not stop her. She had discovered ways of taking charge of her life while still playing their game.

Mr. Whitney and Sgt. Aldrich awaited Olga in the dining room—beefy men with wide chests and big heads. Other than that they had nothing in common. Whitney wore a light suit and an outrageous red, yellow, and green tie. She had never seen an American in civilian clothes. On the Base everybody was in uniform. A thick, walrus mustache covered the man's mouth. His curious, perhaps even hostile, eyes convinced her that she would have to win him over. Whitney, like most other Americans, believed that nothing good could come out of Germany. Complacent, he chewed on a fat cigar and measured her up like a head of cattle. Rather than let him intimidate her, Olga produced her most seductive smile, showing off those dimples people loved. Her curls had been tamed into soft waves which framed her face. With her new Deutchmarks, she had bought a silk georgette blouse to complement her narrow skirt and the glossy white belt that cinched her tiny waist.

"I'm so happy to meet you, Mr. Whitney."

He showed no inclination to shake her hand nor did he get up.

"I didn't expect you to be so young," he said.

"She not only has those looks," Aldrich said, offering her a chair. "You should hear her play. She brings the house down." Olga saw the pride of a father in his eyes. He certainly gave her all the support she could ask for and more. "Thank you, Sgt. Aldrich. He always looks out for me," she said.

"I'm her mentor," he said, rubbing his big chin.

Olga sat down, holding herself upright, her feet set tidily so that Whitney could admire her new black pumps.

"Yes, my mentor," she repeated, trusting him though she had no idea what the word meant. "I play American jazz and Big Band swing. You see, my husband and I like playing together. He is artist. But I'm okay too. I can play when you like."

"Sgt. Aldrich praised you to the heavens," Whitney said. "Now I can see why." He winked and shook a Chesterfield cigarette from an open pack.

"Thank you, but I don't smoke. I like Coca Cola."

"Let's see how you do on your own, the way you usually entertain the folks here. Then we can watch the two of you. Lothar, is it? You people have strange names, but that's the least of our problems."

Her fans had gathered in the lounge and applauded when Olga and Lothar entered. Everybody knew what was going on and who Mr. Whitney was. They wanted Olga to succeed and to witness that moment in her life; the least they could do was show Mr. Whitney how popular she was.

From the corner of her eye, Olga saw Aldrich cross his fingers as she opened with "Happy Days Are Here Again." The playful rhythm immediately energized her audience. They tapped to the beat and sang along. "Jealousy" and "Chatanooga Choo Choo" were always popular, but Whitney showed no interest. The usual stuff—Olga agreed and wished she could play the Mephisto Waltz for him. But he had not come to hear classical pieces. He wanted the kind of music he could sell to bandleaders. Lothar, in his usual open neck sport shirt and slacks, joined Olga at the keyboard. The women applauded; they adored this cool, debonair aristocrat. Lothar was a true baron—not some regular Joe like the rest of the men here. His thick dark hair had an insouciant flair, unlike the sober military cuts on their husbands. The sharp features of his oval face, the mocking light blue eyes, and the slight twist on his handsome lips all fascinated the NCOs's wives, who adored him as they would a celebrity.

Olga and Lothar played "In the Mood" and "Stardust" while their audience hummed along. Lothar's regal demeanor earned him the spotlight while Olga played along demurely at his side, secretly inventing many of the fascinating variations.

Whitney nodded a "not bad."

"Let's do 'Blue Moon,'" Olga suggested.

"Whitney's a pompous ass who doesn't know a thing about music," Lothar said. "He wants a show; let's give him a show."

Ingo, she thought. This is for you—for us.

"Blue Moon" was not much of a show piece, but it expressed her longing for him. Lothar would probably reprimand her later for making it sound so sentimental while he hammered out a pronounced, jaunty beat. The audience was spellbound; perhaps they just wanted to impress that poker-faced Whitney.

"*Rhapsody* in *Blue* is obviously not a dance piece," Lothar announced, "but I thought you might like to hear what we've been working on. We'll do the first movement."

Great idea, Olga thought. Whitney wanted something spectacular, and this would be it. She loved the piece, which transported her back to the days in Poland and her dream of Ingo. A dream that was over. Reality had hit hard. He was alive and within reach and yet farther away than ever before. With the crescendo she renounced their hopeless bond, liberating herself from a desire that had consumed her for years. Her fingers touched the keys in arpeggios and runs up and down the keyboard as if she were darting through a dense forest in search of a clearing. She overwhelmed the entire keyboard, releasing all the hope she had cherished for so long. Swaying to the music she lifted her hands with the ease of a virtuoso who could find her place with her eyes closed.

Lothar remained constrained, but did not let her down. When they pounded out the finishing chords, their ecstatic audience screamed and whistled, stomped and clapped. The women, beside themselves, nudged their men to join in the applause, watching Mr. Whitney's reaction.

He clapped and smiled, the cigar clamped between his teeth.

Olga and Lothar bowed. Whitney looked pleased. This was the sensation he had come for.

Overjoyed, as if the accomplishment was his own, Aldrich ordered a round of scotch and a Coca Cola for Olga, celebrating another victory in good old Germany.

"Not bad," Whitney said, raising his glass. "I like the idea of a couple playing duets. Has a romantic appeal. Show biz is all about make-believe. A German baron and baroness should make good publicity, considering our political reconciliation. A white tux for the young man and a glittering gown for the young lady along with the usual trimmings will do the trick. You'll be a hit." He swirled his ice cubes around. Overweight and badly dressed, he looked as if his dearest wish had been fulfilled. "I'm glad you invited me, Sgt. Aldrich," he said. "Now I know what you meant when you said there was real life among the German ruins. This is novelty all right. As good as it gets. When you leave the Army, come and see me. You'll make a hell of a good agent."

Aldrich laughed. "Thanks. But I think I'll re-up. The ruins of Germany have been good to me. No, don't give me that look. Nobody back home has any idea what's going on here. I know more guys who went home with pockets full of dough."

Whitney turned to Olga, wiping the sweat from his forehead. "What will it be, kiddo? You can't just drink Coca Cola. Let's put some rum into it." He ignored her protests and ordered rum. "We got to celebrate. Imagine yourself at the Waldorf, the Coconut Grove. You'll be the toast of the town. I hope you're a real baron," he said to Lothar. "If not, you're an excellent fake."

"I beg your pardon, Mr. Whitney?" Lothar said.

"That's real enough. You don't give a damn about Hollywood or the Diamond Club, right? Right," he answered himself. "That's okay. Neither do I. Anyway, I'll get the contracts, you do the music. Your English is great. It should work."

"You mean that, Mr. Whitney?" Olga said, flushed with excitement. Could it be?

"You bet, kiddo. You got the looks and the talent, and I got the connections. Let's give it a trial run. Six months. New York, Los Angeles. People got money to burn; the war's been good to us. I'll get you a visa. A real problem these days. But don't you worry."

Olga sipped her sweet drink feeling the alcohol racing through her bloodstream. The pleasant ease reminded her of the days when she had drunk vodka with the Russians. What was his name? Vanya, Dimitry, Sasha? Something like that. It had happened in a stupor she had blocked from her memory. America. Playing in prestigious clubs. Olga felt so elated that she did not care where she went, so long as it was far from the Russians.

Liesl refilled Aldrich's glass. She had an American boyfriend who loved her and talked about taking her to America.

"How soon do you expect an answer?" Lothar asked.

Olga gasped. An answer? As if there was anything to consider. They had to go, move into a new life far from all the pain, as far away from this place, and from Ingo, as possible.

The Countess sat in her arm chair, a blanket wrapped around her legs despite the heat. Summer had arrived in all its glory. With the heavy drapes drawn, the room was dark, unbearably stuffy, and hot. "Now, listen Lothar, you can't just take off and leave me here after I waited for you all these years," she said. "No. Don't even think about it. I will not stand for it." She sipped the tea Olga had prepared for her, holding the cup with her pinkie extended. A weekly appointment with the hairdresser returned her to an attractive aristocrat.

Same old game, Olga thought. Why did the Countess pretend to be an invalid instead of going to Munich to attend an opera, a concert, or enjoy the Grosse Pinakothek Museum that had recently opened?

"It's just for six months," she said. "We'll wire you some money for a housekeeper."

"You cannot pay me off, Olga," the countess said. "I know your tricks. I was not born yesterday. Your naiveté cannot fool me. My poor son is so gullible. I maybe getting old, but I still have my faculties."

Olga ignored her mother-in-law and ladled water from the bucket into a dishpan. She barely heard the Countess lament: "I am only trying to save my son from a horrible embarrassment. Olga at the Diamond Club." She cackled sarcastically. "Honestly. What else will you think of? A pig among thoroughbreds? A fiasco I wouldn't want to witness. She'll embarrass you, Lothar. Think of it. The Diamond Club. A place where Rockefellers meet. How can you think of taking this little tramp there? She doesn't have the faintest idea of how to act in polite society. I cringe thinking about it." She talked as if Olga did not exist. "She'll be stumbling all over the place and curtsy in awe like a servant. What else can you expect from a mongrel?" The twist on her still handsome painted lips missed its target. Her words made no impact.

"Lothar is the star," Olga said. "I'm his accompanist. Mr. Whitney wants us as a duo."

"I wish I could meet that Mr. Whitney of yours and tell him a thing or two. I know New York City; I've stayed at the Park Plaza and dined at the Waldorf. I've been to the Diamond Club and know the people who frequent it." Lothar went on playing. "You are asking for trouble, my dear," the Countess went on. "You can't introduce Olga as Baroness von Schenck. That's an insult to your father."

Olga straightened the bed and put the kettle on the hot plate. She had to bring the Countess around, she thought, watching her mother-in-law rise from her wicker chair, tall and serene. She played her role to perfection. No wonder that Texan Mr. McCormick and the Russian prince had been fascinated.

"You should have visited the Count's estate in East Prussia," the countess said.

"He had no estates," Lothar said. "He was an imposter who milked you dry."

"Lothar!" she screeched. "I forbid such talk. We will not drop to the level of your so-called wife. Why don't you ask her what she did in Stuttgart?"

"I did. Besides, that's our affair."

"You don't say. Well, in that case, my husband is my affair."

"Not when he takes off with my inheritance. My money," Lothar said, rising.

"I beg your pardon? What inheritance?" She faced Lothar. "It was my money and still is. Now the currency reform has taken whatever I had left in the bank. We are penniless."

"That is why we must accept the offer to go to America," Olga said quickly.

"Do you know what you are saying?" the Countess warned.

"I think so," Olga said softly, pretending submission.

"She is right," Lothar said, annoying his mother. He had to provoke someone.

"You see!" Olga triumphed. "The game is over. We must think of our future. We have a daughter who should come home and live with us. For that we need money. You need money as well. Talking about it is only vulgar when you have plenty. Well, we don't have any and must earn it. We can't live in this stinking hole forever."

"That's enough, Olga. How dare you tell us what to do?" She dabbed her nose with her handkerchief. "Your pretty face does not compensate for poor breeding."

"We're going to New York to work," Olga said, lifting the lid off the kettle. Steam rose; the water was near the boiling point. "Has it ever occurred to you that nobody cares whether you're a countess or not? It's of no consequence whether..."

"Now wait a minute ..."

"It is impolite to interrupt others," Olga went on unperturbed. "You are not ill. Your vanity deprives you of a beautiful life. Think about that!"

"Stop her right now, Lothar."

"I am not finished," Olga continued, when Lothar did not interfere. She faced the Countess. "Your selfishness deprives your beloved son of his own life and the chance to make his mark on the world. Instead of supporting him, you reduce him to a servant." A new, cool strength opened up and let her speak. She had to win this battle.

"You know, Olga," Lothar said calmly as if they talked about the weather, "you're right. Playing with the big bands will give me a chance to introduce my compositions. Besides, if we don't like it, we can always come back."

Olga smiled, glad that the Countess could not see her. "So true, Lothar. Your mother will be proud of you. You're a great artist." Why not lie like everybody else? "You deserve recognition for all the work you've put into your compositions."

"Jazz is not what I call music," the Countess objected, not about to let Olga get her way.

"To Americans it is," Olga said. "Let's go and sign the contract while Mr. Whitney still is here." She poured boiling water into the teapot and served the Countess a fresh cup while Lothar read the typed document, scribbled his signature down and returned to the keyboard. Olga added her signature, writing in precise letters, then folded the paper.

"Lothar, how can you be so blind," she heard the Countess say. "You're a hopeless naïf."

He was still playing when Olga left.

The following day Lothar and Olga met Whitney in Aldrich's office. Aldrich leaned back in his chair, but refrained from putting his feet up on the desk. "So the deal is sealed," he said. "Congratulations." Over the past year he had developed a paunch his uniform could not hide. His cheeks had filled out and Olga noticed some gray in the dark brush of his hair. "I know you can do it. You've got class. That's what New Yorkers like." He lit one of those huge cigars he loved. "Those who can afford the Diamond Club that is. I wouldn't mind seeing you there, all dolled up, the German Baron and Baroness. It'll be a good number, right Al? Let's drink to that."

After a short discussion of the terms Lothar excused himself. Olga stayed on and joined the men on their way to the bar. Crossing the yard she asked, "You think I look like a baroness?"

"You will when this guy gets through fixing you up, honeybunch. You'll do fine."

"Thank you. You've done so much for me." In Aldrich's company she always felt appreciated and admired. Right now he was a close friend who shared her good fortune.

"We're in this together, honeybunch. How did it go with Mr. Right?"

Olga shrugged not to show the pain in her heart. "He's married."

"You don't say. How could he do that?"

"Imagine, the Countess told him I'd died."

"She didn't, did she? Well, I'm sorry. She's a bitch. Wants a handmaiden who provides for her." He put his arm over Olga's shoulder and followed Whitney over the hard sand. Army trucks passed and reminded her of Zossen, except these belonged to the former enemy, now friend. The war was over.

Olga leaned her cheek against his warm hand. "You're so good to me, Sgt. Aldrich. Ingo was so happy to see me. He still loves me. Some day he'll come for me."

One week later she and Lothar traveled to the American Embassy in Frankfurt to apply for their visa. The train stopped in Stuttgart. She got out and walked along the platform remembering how she had come here a month ago so sure she would find Ingo and join him. Instead she was with Lothar, soon on their way to America. A vendor offered papers. She bought the Stuttgarter Nachrichten. Reading it would take her mind off Irmgard and Fritzle.

Trains arrived and left with their usual clamor, steam and smoke. Two years ago she had come through here a refugee—starved, cold, without a place to go to except to Lothar. That was past. She had survived the pain, and now had to bury her hope.

Back on the train she found him working on his composition, using the empty seat next to his for his work. Olga sat down across from him and opened the paper. The train was in motion. Goodbye Stuttgart. The bombed-out city passed in the warm light of the sun. Ingo.

Blinking the tears from her eyes she read, "Berlin Airlift Aggravates Soviet Union." The Russians had not expected that the Americans and Brits would defend their sector, considering they had no means of getting the needed supplies across Russian territory. But the Americans were a determined people, and found a way. Still, the world held its breath wondering whether the two super-powers would clash over this. How long could the Allies keep this up? The Soviet Union wanted to control Europe, and then rule the world.

Anyna was safe in Switzerland. Adie made frequent calls to the Post Office so that Olga could talk to Anyna. Her heart ached for her little daughter. Why was everything dear to her taken away?

On New Year's Eve, Lothar and his band entertained at the NCO Club for the last time and introduced 1949 with "Auld Lang Syne." The dining room was packed. From the time of the airlift on July 1, the Base had been manned to capacity. The Americans were not about to let the Soviets bully them around. Instead, they perfected their mission and transported whatever Berlin needed by air. Perhaps they regretted that they not stopped Stalin from overrunning Eastern Europe.

Over the past six months, two hundred fifty American, and over one hundred fifty British, aircraft flew some 5,000 tons of supplies to the besieged city every day. The media hailed their heroic efforts and showed photos of ten-ton capacity C-54 Skymasters being harassed by Soviet Yaks. On other occasions, "Chocolate Bombers" dropped sweets through their signal chutes for the children of Berlin. A plane landed every 45 seconds. The operation ran like clockwork and the German people marveled at their former enemy. How could Hitler have been so naïve to believe he could defeat them, no matter what kind of miracle weapon he might have thought of?

In her new black gown, a white satin sash around her midriff, Olga felt re-born. Two sparkling rhinestone combs keep her mound of curls back, leaving her features open. NCO's and their wives came over to her table, wished her a Happy New Year or blew on their paper horns. The wives applauded Lothar, who played some solo pieces on the piano. In his white tux he looked the part of the aristocrat.

Their duets, "Happy Days Are Here Again," and "I'm in the Mood for Love", had everybody clapping and shouting. If Ingo could see her now, would he admire her? Was he celebrating with his new family? Did he think of her? "This is to you, my love," Olga whispered raising her glass of Henkel Sekt, a fine German sparkling wine. "Remember your last night in Poland? You knew how painful your parting would be and turned it into one of the happiest nights in my life." She drank in quick gulps, but could not quench her tears.

"Tears of joy?" Sgt. Browning asked. He came from the new school of airmen—younger, sophisticated, and friendly.

"Yes. We'll be in America soon."

"You'll love New York," he said. "Though I prefer Louisiana. You should see those alligators lie motionless in the water like logs. You can hardly tell they're there until something comes by and then zap! they catapult up and catch it."

People talked about their homes and the families they had left behind. Olga shared their longing. Like them, she had to wait until she might be reunited with Anyna…with Ingo?

Tipsy, her head spinning, Olga stumbled through the dark hall to the room where the Countess lived in her imaginary splendor. Why couldn't they just throw open the windows and let the cold fresh air blow out this stinking life? Nevermind. In a few days she would be gone, gone, gone. Far away, to America! Leaving all this behind. A life she would rather not remember. She straightened Lothar's bed, struck by the horrible thought that she would have to share it in the hotels they would live in. The thought wiped all others away, like a snowplough clearing the street of the clean, white fluff that had fallen overnight.

The Countess, arrayed in a black velvet gown and ermine capelet as if awaiting a gentleman caller, watched Olga. Her diamond earrings sparkled in the dim light of the table lamp, the only brightness in this squalid place. A reminder of a past when they had a home and a country they belonged to. Now Olga had to find a place she could make into a home, a country that would accept her, where she could grow and put down her roots again. She pushed the chamber pot under the bed rather than take it out.

"That dress does nothing for your figure," the Countess said in a dry, distant voice as if talking to a servant. "Before we know it, you'll show up in pants like a street sweeper."

"Katherine Hepburn looks great in pants," Olga said.

"Oh please, have you lost your mind completely? How can you compare yourself with Katherine Hepburn?" The Countess screwed up her large dark eyes under hooded lids.

Olga giggled. "I am playing Cinderella escaping from my nasty, ugly, mother-in-law."

"Lothar!" the Countess cried out, as if she had been slapped. "Get this creature out of my home. How can you just sit there and let that woman insult me? I am your mother!"

"So I see," he said unperturbed.

Olga laughed and laughed, then raised her arms in the pose of a grand diva. "How do you like that? You should hear the people applaud. Standing ovations are what I get. That's right, Chère Madame la Comtesse, adored by Russian princes and Texas cowboys."

"Stop her. Get her out of here. She'll be my death."

"A grand lady does not lose her temper," Olga mocked.

Lothar leaned against the grand piano and laughed. "Fine performance, Maman. A classic scene between mother- and daughter-in-law. I didn't think you had it in you, Olga. Not bad at all."

Olga had not intended to amuse him, but his comment gave her an idea: from now on she would be as ridiculous as they. "Well, dear Countess," she teased, "you'll be my model for playing the proper baroness. We'll both have fun."

The Countess wrung her hands. "Lothar, your wife is mad. Get her out of here before I scream."

Lothar grinned.

"Did you say wife, Countess?" Olga mocked. "What an honor! I never expected you to admit to that." With her manicured thumb and forefinger she lifted a piece of Swiss cheese from under the glass bell and held it up against the low-hanging lamp to inspect its quality. "Actually I prefer being an unwanted appendage to your household. Olga Bergmann from Riga—no title, no history, no fame—just myself. People like me that way. I don't need your title." She chuckled.

Lothar, as tipsy as she, gesticulated dramatically, not inclined to take anybody seriously.

Olga slipped the cheese into her mouth. "Rather tasty. Quite passable, wouldn't you say, Lothar? I wouldn't mind having a high ball for a nightcap. You should take one too, Countess. It eases the tension and improves one's mood. It'll mellow your strained nerves."

"Lothar. If you don't get her out of here, I'll have to go." The Countess rose from her bed, her sharp voice grating. "I told you what you'll be up against. And you want to take this creature to America? Wake up, Lothar, before it's too late. She cast a spell on you. I told you she communicates with the Devil, but you wouldn't believe me. Thank God Anna Magdalena is growing up in an appropriate home." She paused. "Say something, Lothar!"

"You are quite amusing, Maman," he said, picked up a bottle of whiskey and one of 7-Up.

Lothar was getting tired of his mother's meaningless tirades. Perhaps he was also glad to get away from it all. America. The land of the free. She giggled.

"You'll be the death of me," the Countess breathed, pressing the back of her hand against her forehead. When no one came to her assistance, she bent back as if about to faint—a trick the troubled actress had used in silent movies. "How can you be so cruel, Lothar? My heart. It's… it's…" She stumbled to her bed.

Olga darted forward and helped her mother-in-law stretch out, putting a cold compress on her forehead. "There, that should make you feel better. I'm sorry if I upset you. We had a lot to drink."

With her eyes closed, the Countess breathed heavily. Was she truly suffering, or was this another one of her performances? Olga sensed the pathetic panic of a mother about to lose her son. Lothar had always been her baby, and always would be. Perhaps their being in America, occupied with the kind of work they enjoyed, he might find his own place. For the moment all that mattered was that they left.

"Don't bother, Olga. You've robbed me of my son.."

Olga saw no reason to stay on. She took her highball and headed for the door before she said something she might regret. America. They had to get to America.

Lothar followed her. "Sorry, Maman," he said. "I happen to like her, and she is my wife."

Their visas arrived the first week of February. Olga held her passport like a treasure; she would get a fresh start. Not with friends, true, or a situation she could easily adapt to. On the contrary, she was nervous, insecure, and afraid. She would be stuck with Lothar, at his mercy, but once again she had no choice but to humble herself to his whims.

Though the attic was cold, it now felt like a sanctuary. The Countess' boxes stood in neat piles, her clothes hung up and covered with sheets. The smell of mothballs was almost gone. Olga's white pillows rested on a burgundy bedspread, and gilded chairs stood around the carved table.

Figurines, vases, and artifacts decorated the room. Leather-bound books lined the shelves she had set up. The milky light of the cloudy day came in through clean windows. This had become her home. It would all be left behind to go to an unknown country.

Later that day Olga found Lothar at the keyboard working on a particularly dissonant passage of his composition. The Countess sat on her bed listening. She had calmed down, and seemed to understand that her beloved son had his limits when it came to tantrums. No matter how awful his composition sounded, she always complimented him—a sure way to win his love.

"You got a letter from Ottie," he said, pointing at the table where he kept his notes, then returned his attention to the notes.

The envelope carried all sorts of stamps and was written in Ottie's hand. She was alive! Olga ran a knife under the flap and pulled out a lined sheet of paper torn from a notebook.

Bautzen, December 5, 1948

My dear Olga,

I wish you a Merry Christmas and a Happy New Year. I thought I would write to Bavaria in case you landed there, else the Countess would know where you are and forward the letter to you. You probably wondered what had happened to us. Bertie and I are alive. The Poles had captured me and put me to work. Most of the others died of starvation, but I managed to survive. Pays to have some extra fat, I guess.

Olga imagined her sister's grin and smiled. Ottie was alive. Her family was alive!

I should have continued walking with you rather than take the ride on that truck. It broke down. Poles came and took us prisoner. I'll spare you the details. It's too painful to put on paper. You always talked about miracles—this was one. Did one happen for you too? All through my pain I remembered your saying that there was a purpose to whatever happens. When the Poles finally released us they expelled us to the Russian Zone of Germany. That's how I wound up in Bautzen.

The conditions here under the Russians are unspeakable. The rations barely keep us alive. Bertie is suffering from severe malnutrition. The Russians want to get rid of us through starvation. I hope you got away. I feel so alone. No homeland, no family, no friends. At camp I had some. Now I'll have to start all over again. I don't believe Gerd made it through the war. I did not hear from him while the world was still whole.

I am working on a farm so that Bertie can get some food and milk. Food is all we can think of. But I have a warm room and get along with the people. Nobody knows how long they'll be able to keep their land.

How is Mutter? I imagine she is still with you, wherever you are. I hope your life was easier than mine and that Ingo returned. Do write soon. I am desperate for news.

Your sister, Ottie with Bertie."

Olga wiped the tears from her eyes. "Ottie and Bertie are alive," she said. "The Poles imprisoned them and kept them all this time."

"What did I tell you?" the Countess said. "Those who can't listen must bear the consequences."

"So we did," Olga said. "Please excuse me."

She returned to her room, sat down at the secretary and dipped her pen into the inkwell. There was so much to tell. Mutter's death in Dresden. How she and Anyna had survived with Gottfried's help. The Countess telling Ingo that Olga was dead. That she and Lothar would soon go on a concert tour in America.

...sounds unbelievable, I know. One of the miracles. Ingo lives in Stuttgart. He is married and has a son. Some day the Countess will pay for all the misery she caused. I'll send you a food package before I leave. I am so glad you're alive. I know what life in the Russian Zone is like. Anyna and I almost starved to death. We managed to escape....

On their way to the airport in Frankfurt, the train stopped in Stuttgart again. The station had been rebuilt and the twisted beams removed, though the glass roof was still missing. Snow had been cleared from the platforms, and the crowds of tired refugees were gone. Trains ran on schedule. Kiosks and stands offered reading material and snacks. The phone tempted Olga to call Ingo. But why aggravate a wound that was still so raw. He had not contacted her, though that was hardly possible without going through the Countess.

The first German made cars—Mercedes, BMWs and Volkswagens— cruised along the boulevard in front of the station. By now, Ingo would be delivering some of the cars people had ordered a year ago. His future had come. Hers would start in New York as Baroness von Schenck.

Goodbye my sweet love. Goodbye Germany. Only my memories will remain.

Later that day, settling back into the comfortable seat of the Pan American Strato Clipper, Olga watched the plane take off. It cut through the clouds and suddenly reached a blue, blue sky. *Somewhere over the rainbow, skies are blue.* Now she knew what it meant, saw it with her own eyes.

America! They would land in New York. A deep joy, gratitude, and feeling of freedom rose in her soul. *Somewhere over the rainbow way up high, there's a land that I heard of once in a lullaby...* That's where I'll find you, my beloved Ingo.

Lothar read the New York Times, acting as if he had spent his life on airplanes. An American stewardess dressed in a light blue uniform offered Olga magazines. "Vogue, Ladies Home Journal, Life?" Another, pushed a narrow cart down the aisle, offering drinks. Everything was neat, clean, elegant and available. No wonder the people at the NCO Club longed to return to this.

"Do you recognize New York, Lothar?" Olga asked as they descended toward Idyllwild Airport. "There, look! The Statue of Liberty."

They had slept, had been served breakfast, and were now ready to land. The sound of the engines changed as the plane dipped to the side toward the runway. There were the skyscrapers of New York City. The real thing still looked like a postcard. The water of the Atlantic Ocean was a thick, steel gray. Boats of different sizes cruised around. This would be her new home.

Whitney met them at the gate, his hat pushed back, the cigar between his teeth. After evaluating their appearance he shook hands. "Adequate. Welcome to New York. Or should I say, to America? I couldn't get as many press agents lined up as I had hoped. People aren't hot on Germans. But we'll change that." He took the tickets for their luggage and led the way to the baggage claim. "The Berlin blockade and airlift is godsend. Now that we're protecting Germans we've become friends. That's politics for you. We should've wiped out the Soviets while the going was good."

They walked along a hallway with shining floors and bright walls. Everything was as immaculate as if the airport had just been built. People in expensive clothes carried their luggage toward the exits, or stood around waiting for their plane or arriving passengers.

"We must make sure that we say the right things to the press," Whitney said.

"You can tell them that I fought under Rommel in Africa. Spent two years as POW in Oklahoma," Lothar suggested while they waited for their luggage.

"That won't do. Just say you fought in the underground."

Olga sensed Whitney's irritation. "Adam von Trott solicited Allied support for the 20th of July uprising," she remembered.

"Now we're getting somewhere. Just say you were involved in that, Olga, okay? The press loves to ask questions. After all, they need something to write about. If you're not sure what to say, tell them that you're tired. Better yet, burst into tears. You're so moved to be in America. Been waiting for this all your life. Got it? Now, let's go." He took one of their suitcases and whisked them through the large door. Lights flashed out. Cameras clicked. Men in suits and hats crowded around them the way she had seen them do on newsreels.

"How do you like America? What's Germany like now? Did you see the airlift? How are our boys doing?"

"Fine. I'm so happy to be in America. Waited for it all my life. We'll give a concert soon. With Buddy Jones band. Yes. We play duets." Olga repeated it all over and over again and smiled like a movie star. Her new fur-trimmed coat and hat had been chosen for the occasion.

Lothar gave them a haughty look that would appear in the paper the following day. "We have an excellent program. I will add some of my compositions."

The men from the press followed them out to the street, where Whitney had a black limousine waiting. The chauffeur opened the door and helped Olga inside. During the ride from the airport, Olga admired the brownstones and the approaching skyscrapers of Manhattan that reached beyond her line of vision. But the people were poorly dressed and the streets littered with trash. How could that be? Blinking advertisements in garish colors praised the virtues of Lucky Strike, Coca Cola, Ford, Chevrolet, and Wrigley's chewing gum. On Fifth Avenue, she couldn't look away from the eye-catching window displays. The soft purring of the limousine motor reminded her of Sgt. Aldrich's Buick.

A uniformed doorman at the Waldorf Astoria opened the door and helped Olga out. A bellhop took their luggage. Olga and Lothar followed Whitney up a red carpet that had been laid out on the sidewalk under a burgundy canopy that kept people from getting wet. Another doorman held the door open and waited until they had stepped inside the famous hotel. The décor was so different from the elegance of Berlin's Avalon Hotel. Gilded moldings and trims gave the bright green, red, pink, and yellow carpet a dramatic setting. America! The new world had left the old one long ago.

Delightful fragrances and the smell of expensive cigarettes filled the air. She admired the beautifully made-up faces of the ladies and their fancy hats, and envied them their nonchalance, the way they relaxed into the plush armchairs. Olga would have to get a new lipstick and learn how to use make-up.

Whitney took care of the formalities at the reception desk, where uniformed men took care of arriving and departing guests. "Your first concert is scheduled for the 7th," he said. "That will give you two days to rest and look around. And remember, your new boss, Buddy Jones hates people who argue with him. We need good reviews. I'll invite the press for opening night."

"We'll do okay," Olga said, convinced that she could please this Buddy Jones. "Thank you for the clothes. We don't have things like this in Germany."

"That's why I got them for you. I'll deduct it from your pay of course. We can't have impoverished aristocrats. You got to play the role all the way, young lady. People don't just come for the music. You got to put on an act."

Olga's face dropped. Who needed expensive clothes when she had come here to earn money? If they flopped, she would have nothing but debts. Knowing Lothar that might just happen.

"Tomorrow you go to the hairdresser," Whitney went on. "Get yourself a fabulous hairdo. And I do mean fabulous. You got the looks. Now let a pro put it all together. And don't you dare tell them what to do. The beautiful women of Hollywood look like hell when they take off their make-up. Show biz is about make-believe—remember that."

One of the clerks handed Lothar the room key.

"Well kids," Whitney said. "I'll pick you up for rehearsal tomorrow at ten. Have a good rest. Don't go overboard with your dinner. This place is expensive." Then he was gone.

After what she had seen so far, Olga expected a luxurious room, but nothing had prepared her for the suite they found. It not only had a bath as big as their room in Inning, it was decorated for royalty. She fell into one of the two beds, content that she would have some privacy. The rest would fall into place.

The bellhop turned a knob on a large wooden box. Olga watched flickering lines on its black glass eventually form a picture, showing a film the way a radio played music. Though she was dying to watch, she couldn't resist taking a bath. "I haven't had one since I left Dresden." Noticing Lothar's frown, she regretted mentioning Dresden. They had never talked about her experiences there, and decided not to mention it again. That life had nothing to do with him. He did not comment now. Olga was so tired of him. But she must keep Lothar in a good mood until their tour was over and they could return to Germany with pockets full of money.

The following morning, after a scrumptious breakfast of bacon and eggs, toast and coffee, Whitney showed up in a gray flannel suit and another one of his outrageous ties. Olga had noticed that New Yorkers preferred loud colors to the subdued hues worn in Germany. Everything about this country was big and wild and unfathomable. She greeted him with a cheerful smile, posing in her new outfit—a dark green twinset and brown skirt that went well with her comfortable flat shoes.

"Not bad." With her curls pulled back from her forehead, her attractive features, arched brows, and small mouth that broadened whenever she smiled, were shown off to their best advantage.

After the long bath she had felt at home in this palace-like suite. Lothar had not bothered her in the least. Perhaps having her so easily available had diminished his desire for her. Being in America was more than a dream come true. She wished she could share it with Ingo. Despite the war the country was as well off as ever. The thousands of planes and bombs, ships and tanks, they had manufactured and sent abroad had not emptied the treasury. They probably could have gone fighting for years to come. Now those planes took food and fuel to the desperate people in Berlin.

On their way to the studio Whitney sat next to the cab driver. "Now remember, this is your audition. Buddy Jones is the boss. Leads one of the most popular bands in the country. He knows his stuff—as good as Tommy Dorsey, Jack Teagarten, and Glenn Miller. He draws the crowds. People pay big bucks to hear him."

The windshield wipers cleared the falling snow. Buddy Jones. What could she say that would please him, or make up for any of Lothar's potentially offensive comments?

"Jones made two movies and gets top billing for his records," Whitney explained. "That's where you make the real money. His band is as smooth as butter. You better thank me for making this possible. The idea of a German duo intrigued him."

"Now, wait a minute," Lothar said, irritated. He was probably dwelling on his composition. "I don't have to prove anything to anybody—I'm doing him a favor by coming here."

"Hold your horses, Baron," Whitney said, puffing on his cigar.

Please, Father, don't let him spoil this for me. Please. You got us here. Help me succeed.

"You came here to fulfill a contract," Whitney snapped. "You signed a contract."

Lost in thought, Lothar gazed at the snowflakes shrouding the street. The windshield wipers clicked rhythmically.

This Buddy Jones was probably no different than the men at the NCO Club, Olga reasoned. It would all work out. He surely would see beyond Lothar's irascible behavior and appreciate his gifts as a musician.

The Diamond Club resembled an Arabian palace straight out of "A Thousand and One Nights." The plush carpet was as soft as moss. In the lobby, a giant bouquet of fresh flowers greeted them; beyond that was the dining room, where the band had assembled on stage. Columns, palm trees, and gold and purple trim added to the exotic splendor, and an opulent chandelier caught the light coming in through doors. Each table had a fresh rose in a silver bud vase.

Buddy Jones, a medium sized, slender man in a V-neck sweater, walked in and greeted his musicians. In his thirties, he had the build of a sportsman and exuded energy, authority, and certainly respect. She had been wrong: he was far more sophisticated than the NCO's, and would not tolerate any nonsense from Lothar. She suppressed her anxiety. Had she not eased tensions before?

Curious, Jones turned to the dimmed dining room, and waved to his visitors to join him at the brightly lit stage.

Olga smiled. Musically, she was up to the task, glad that her hands had recovered, and that she had spent her years in Litzmannstadt practicing.

Lothar and Jones shook hands.

Flushed, Olga greeted Jones with a timid smile. This man was no slouch, but a musician who expected perfection and would settle for nothing less. His blue eyes showed no hesitation, and his smile was no more than a polite gesture. The musicians watched the scene, their shining brass instruments in hand, evaluating the newcomers.

"So you are the famous German Baron and Baroness von Schenck," Jones said. "Leftovers of the Great German Reich. Sieg Heil."

Lothar ignored the insult and introduced himself, "Lothar von Schenck. Pleased to meet you Mr. Jones."

"And I am Olga von Schenck, or just Olga. We are honored to play with your famous band."

"Glad to see that your blue blood isn't frozen."

Olga would not let him intimidate her and gazed straight into her future boss' eyes, certain that they would deliver for him.

"Well, Al," Jones said, addressing Whitney, "just hope for once you were telling me the truth. Personally I couldn't care less who these people are as long as they can play the piano. The idea is novel. If you two play half as well as this guy promised, you have a deal."

"Then consider it a deal," Lothar said.

"I don't think you'll be disappointed," Olga added.

"Okay. So let's see. Sit down and listen to us while they haul in the piano for you." Jones turned to his band and raised his baton. "A one, a two, a three —"The musicians showed off like schoolboys in a contest. America versus a defeated Germany. Olga knew what she was up against—Aldrich had explained American opinion to her. They had won the war.

The men played in perfect harmony. The music soared from their instruments. The percussionist involved his whole body in hammering the song out with the precision of a Swiss watch until sweat dripped from his hot face. Olga's legs twitched. She could barely keep herself from stepping out on the dance floor to swing along to the beat. Tapping her foot against the carpet, she felt the tempo and caught on to their style. Blend. They had to blend! After their tour in America, they could take this kind of music back to Germany and perform in Munich. They could be a sensation, if only Lothar would play along.

Olga followed him to the stage where he adjusted the piano bench to fit his height. She sat down beside him at the white Steinway. "Bless us, Father," she whispered, listening to the band perform a piece she did not know. With her eyes closed she felt the rhythm, absorbed the harmony, and analyzed the instrumentation Jones had created. The orchestra sounded like a single voice. The subtle shading, the easy crescendo ebbing away so that the melody could flow undisturbed to a rousing climax. She massaged her fingers until they felt warm and limber. The keyboard was her home and this one was a castle.

Jones stopped the band and had them repeat the last passage. The performance concluded with a percussion solo. The exhausted drummer pulled tissues from a box and wiped the sweat from his red face.

Jones turned to Lothar and Olga. "Well. How do you like it? Now let's see the master race perform."

Unperturbed Lothar said, "My compliments, Mr. Jones. A fine performance. But I would suggest more crescendo in the second movement where the trumpets use their mutes. You need a climax there. Could be subdued, but it needs a punch line."

Olga held her breath. Jones frowned, but did not answer. He raised his baton. "You have a point, Baron. Let's try it. A one, a two ..."

Whitney, sitting at the front table in the dining room, gave them a thumbs up.

After conducting the piece according to Lothar's suggestion, Jones stopped. "You were right. Now let's hear you play."

Olga stroked the keys affectionately, imagining herself back in Poland playing the Mephisto Waltz Ingo had demanded.

"I composed this arrangement of 'Tea for Two'," Lothar said. "Tell me what you think." A nod at Olga and they took off. Her loathing for Lothar vanished. When it came to music, he knew his stuff. While he embellished the piece with trills and arpeggios, she moved the melody to the bass in the minor key: dreamy, melancholic. "Tea for Two" turned into a tango, by way of Chopin, found its way to a march and finished as a boogie-woogie the sergeants had always appreciated. Olga hit a succession of quick chords for the grand finale.

"There," she said, lifting her hands and looking up, aware that she had been carried away again, gone beyond Lothar's clever variations. Her music had revealed her desires and aspirations. Buddy Jones and his men had heard her message.

Their silence prevailed.

"'Rhapsody in Blue' is our favorite," she said. "We can play the first part, if you like. George Gershwin is very popular in West Germany," she added, smiling.

From his chair Jones nodded a "go ahead."

Lothar tapped out the beat. Olga thought Gershwin would have appreciated his arrangement of the duet. The jazzy number represented America, but combined European harmonies with American style. It was a dance—different, foreign, but easy to understand. The piece put America's energy and bustle into the throbbing rhythm with its ever-changing style. Even the difficult passages came off. Her cheeks flushed. This was what she had been waiting for—recognition from an outsider, a professional musician, who could appreciate her artistry.

While Lothar showed off his technique, Olga turned into an actress, performing with subtle twists of her body and the changing expressions on her small face. Absorbed by the sounds she created, she did not see Jones get up, raise his baton, and lead the band in accompanying the piano.

When it was over, the musicians congratulated each other and applauded.

"Thank you, Father," Olga whispered. Jones shook her hand and held it in a warm grip. His smile said that they understood each other.

"Welcome to the band," he said. "What else do you have that we can play together?"

"How about 'In the Mood?'" Lothar suggested.

"Sure enough."

They sealed their contract over a bottle of champagne.

"We start rehearsing at eleven," Jones said, returning the fountain pen and paperwork to Whitney. "Tomorrow night you'll be my guests." Jones lay his hand on Olga's shoulder. His aftershave smelled so fresh. No doubt, they would become friends, or had that happened already? "I want you to get a feel of the place and its guests. Saturday will be your opening night. We'll take it from there. The pieces you played are fine, but don't forget, people want to dance. I'll figure out the program."

On their way home Whitney was so solicitous that Olga could not wait to get rid of him. Had the door to her independence finally opened? The Countess had been a good teacher when it came to selfishness. Her unbending nature obliged people to do her bidding. Olga did not have it in her to act like that, but she could try to prepare herself for the day when Lothar would get moody and homesick. By then she must have gained Jones's friendship and trust. Lothar would not ruin her life again.

Chapter 39

Olga entered the Diamond Club ready to do whatever it took to make their tour a success. Her long black gown with its plunging neckline and almost bare back, had been Whitney's choice. She did not mind. All around her, couples decked out in ostentatious evening wear and dripping with jewelry pretended not to see her, but Olga could feel their hidden glances as if they were open stares. Of course they recognized the "German Baroness" from the poster at the door. Besides, Lothar never failed to impress people with his striking bearing and almost rude disregard for social form. At his side she felt like a fragile maiden obediently following her dark master. The double strand of pearls, tear drop earrings, long black gloves, and silver fox boa draped over her arm all came from the Countess. Whitney's stylists had transformed her face and hair into that of a Hollywood diva, insisting that they had been instructed to created that image.

"What an incredible place," Olga whispered in German. "Should I speak English?"

"Don't be silly," Lothar said. "This is a free country. We can talk anyway we like."

Olga remembered Jones's greeting and was not so sure about that. Perhaps people really did not care about Germans, including aristocrats. British Royalty or French nobility would probably be admired, but German?

The maitre d' ushered them to their table. "Mr. Jones asked me to start you off with a bottle of Veuve Clicquot champagne. He'll join you at intermission. The filet mignon is excellent, as is our chicken Kiev. I recommend the Waldorf salad to start." He handed them leather bound menus and unfolded the crisp white napkin over Olga's lap.

"Thank you," she said with confidence, as if dining at a first class club was a daily occurrence. Olga had never seen such decadence, not even at the Berlin opera, where she had sold cigarettes and chocolates from a box hanging from her neck. America. The chandelier showered the dining room in intimate light, where people talked in low voices. The dance floor had been polished to a slick sheen. Perhaps Fred Astaire would come out dancing with Ginger Rogers. What would her script be, Olga wondered, peeking at the magnificent ladies in close-fitting silk gowns, elaborate hairstyles, and glittering jewelry.

The musicians assembled on stage. Olga smiled at her new colleagues. "Isn't this splendid?" she said.

"Nothing but a bunch of clowns," Lothar said, watching the waiter wiggle the cork from a champagne bottle to fill their delicate, bowl-glasses.

She laughed. "Don't you ever have something nice to say?"

He raised his glass. "You're such a child, Olga. Will you ever grow up?"

The waiter praised the quality of the meat, the freshness of the fish, and the crab bisque that was the chef's masterpiece.

"We'll have the bisque," Lothar interrupted. "Hot. I hate lukewarm soup." He spoke English with a crisp accent. Nobody would believe he was German, Baltic yet, where people rolled their 'r's. The attractive woman at the next table smiled at him. Her dark hair had been built up into a impresive roll and her lips painted dark red.

Had Lothar acquired his gourmet taste in France? Olga wondered. Had he kept a mistress there as well? She really did not know much about the man who happened to be her husband, and cared less to find out.

Buddy Jones, wearing a white tux and sky-blue bow tie, appeared on stage and turned to his applauding audience. The members of the band awaited his signal. He tapped out the beat. "A one, a two, a —" The band played the opening measures of "Moonlight Serenade" while couples flocked to the dance floor. Olga was immediately drawn to this song that had taken the world by storm. Too bad Ingo was not here to dance with her. She imagined them gliding across the shining floor to the precise beat of a master. The piping hot bisque arrived in gold-rimmed bowls.

"Thanks," Olga said. "Buddy Jones makes great music. We'll perform with him on Saturday."

"So you are the German Baron and Baroness?"

"What if we are?" Lothar asked in a nasal tone.

Olga smiled, apologizing for his rudeness.

The waiter's eyes lit up. "Welcome to the Diamond Club. I can't wait to hear you play." Then he was gone.

"You didn't have to tell him that, Olga!" Lothar said. "It's none of his business!"

She ignored the reprimand and smiled as if he had complimented her. People were watching. "Why are you so grumpy? We're in New York. The Diamond Club."

He waved her off. The dim light softened the tension on his taut face. "You don't know a thing about this country. This is not Furstenfeldbruck. The people in this club rule their country and possibly the world. They made fortunes manufacturing bombs or are gangsters who extort money from the masses who earn it. Their wives or mistresses are decorations, trophies. To them we are exotic birds, just something to talk about. Americans adore aristocrats but hate Germans. How will they react to us?"

Olga stared at him. "What do you mean, react?"

"Nothing." The irritattion in his voice was uncalled for, as was his bad mood. Olga lowered her head, her cheeks burning as if he had slapped her.

He tasted his soup. "Just don't give the papers food for a scandal. That's what they want. We would make good cannon fodder for the media. Krauts, remember? They want us to come crawling on our knees and beg their forgiveness. Be humiliated and punished for the Jews we killed. Playing Gershwin does not make us American."

The band played "Begin the Beguine" in a way Olga had not heard before.

"Nice," Lothar said. "Could use some zest."

Olga ate her soup, keeping her eyes focused on the bowl. If she slapped Lothar's disgusting face right now, the newpapers would have plenty to write about tomorrow. What a triumph—and the end of her career in America. Taking a long sip of champagne she watched the couples dance to Buddy's irresistible rhythm. The tiny bubbles eased her anger. "Why is it so hard for you to say something pleasant?" she asked, finishing her soup.

"No need for drama, Olga. Just eat and smile. People are watching you."

"So they are. I can put on a show just like your mother," she said impishly, and emptied her glass.

Lothar's eyes darkened. "Leave my mother alone. And remember that duets are played by four hands, not two people."

"Sorry," she said, her anger rising again. Buddy Jones appreciated her playing. That was good enough. He was in tune with her style, valued her originality. The musicians had felt it too. "Don't tell me you're homesick for that stinking little room in Inning," she said, watching the waiter pick up their plates.

"Your manners are atrocious. Just keep your mouth shut and do as you're told."

Olga sipped her champagne. The gentleman at the next table gazed flirtatiously at her. She winked back. Could he see that her husband was a pill?

"Jones is getting syrupy again," Lothar said. "He needs some spice in his cake."

"Now look, Lothar, you were not hired to tell him what to do!" Blood rushed into her face. Lothar and his stupid arrogance.

"Please keep your opinions to yourself," Lothar said icily.

"Remember what Whitney said."

"Whitney doesn't know a thing about music. Just wants to make money."

"What's wrong with that? We need money too."

"Olga, you're intolerable. Neither Whitney nor Buddy Jones runs my life."

She giggled. "Your mother does."

He crushed his napkin, then caught himself, his eyes cold and hard, his face white. "One more silly remark and we are going home."

She gasped. "Going home?" she whispered."We just got here."

Judging from the fury in his eyes, Lothar was indeed ready to break their contract and go home. She nibbled on her roll. "I'm sorry. Just wait until Jones hears your compositions. You'll be the talk of the town." She gave him that innocent, obedient smile he loved.

His mouth relaxed. The frown disapapeared. "I have an exciting idea for 'Jealousy,'" he said. "With a punch line. Great tune. I bet

Buddy will go along with my idea." He was still talking about his music when their steaks arrived. The storm had blown over. From now on Olga would keep her mouth shut.

At intermission Jones came to their table. "How do you like it, Lothar?" he asked, blotting the perspiration from his forehead. "Those lights are like a furnace."

"You're fantastic. We just talked about that," Olga said, her face burning. She hated to lie. "Did you study at the conservatory?"

He laughed, showing two rows of pearly white teeth. "Why, natch. They don't teach you orchestration on Bourbon Street, that's for sure." He offered Lothar a cigarette before lighting his own. "This is serious music. I studied Bach and Chopin, but I love jazz. Lets me improvise. Mozart never ran out of ideas, or minded embellishing as he went along."

"True," Lothar agreed. "That's how I came to appreciate jazz. You see, Mr. Jones."

"Call me Buddy, like everyone else." He looked around and greeted acquaintances. "Seems that people have discovered who you are. The German aristocrats have their adrenaline pumping. Especially the ladies. Tomorrow you'll have a receptive audience."

"You don't have to tell them we're German," Lothar suggested. "We were born in Latvia."

The waiter brought Jones a highball.

"Who cares about Latvia? German is fine. I was born in Hamburg; my German name is Jonas. My mother is Jewish. We left before Hitler went on his rampage."

"Do you speak German?" Olga asked.

"Of course," he said, but went on speaking English. "But this is not a good place to reveal one's background. We came here in 1938. My uncle Hugo helped us get started. My father did well, and wanted me to get into real estate, but thanks to Mutter I was free to study music. Though she doesn't like jazz."

"I bet she got over it," Olga teased, "now that she knows how great you are."

"You'll get to meet her one of these days. She's a lovely lady. You're quite an artist yourself, Olga."

"You've got to keep her in line," Lothar said, "else she'll take off like a galloping colt. I'm having a hell of a time."

"We'll see how it goes," Buddy said, nodding at Olga. "You're a classy musician, Lothar. Different. Methodical but innovative. We'll rehearse in the morning. You both look stunning. People watch while they listen. Glamour sells."

Olga thrilled to the compliment. "Thank you, Buddy. We'll do our best."

Buddy gulped down his drink, the ice tinkling. Putting down his glass he said, "I'd better get back to work. People want to dance. Order whatever you want; it's on me."

Olga watched him cross the empty dance floor. He was a great man, one who might take her side when Lothar became obnoxious. "Isn't it wonderful that he likes your music?" she said in a gentle voice. "You're a genius, Lothar von Schenck."

"That goes without saying."

Later that night, after Lothar turned off the light, Olga curled up in her bed, pressing her face into the pillow. Tears welled up in her eyes. Two years ago she would have given anything for a bite to eat and a warm room. Now she slept at the Waldorf Astoria, the finest hotel in Manhattan, her stomach bursting, her head dizzy from champagne, a fabulous career ahead of her, and yet she felt devastated. *Please, Father. I'm so miserable.*

Lothar snored. At least he would not bother her tonight. A light appeared and formed white circles that turned golden and then purple.

"Father, my beloved Father. You came! Why can't I be with Ingo? What more do you want me to do? Have I not suffered enough? How can I free myself?"

"He is a troubled soul," a voice said. "Be kind to him. He needs your love."

"My love? How can I love him when he hates me so?"

"He can't help himself. The time will come when you will find a way to part. The Evil One is on the prowl."

"Lothar?"

"No, my child. His mother. He will return to her. Bless him and let him go."

"What about Anyna? I miss her so."

"You will find a way to be with her when you are free."

The word echoed as the light faded and darkness returned.

"Thank you, Father. Thank you for coming to me."

The following evening Olga prepared herself for her grand entrance into American show business. After rehearsing and a stroll along Fifth Avenue, she took a long bath in a tub big enough to wallow in. The sensual fragrance of the soap awakened her desire. Luxury felt so good. Physically, mentally, and emotionally refreshed she felt beautiful and clean. If she could only find a friend to talk to. She slipped into a soft white robe and turned on the radio. Listening to Beethoven's Fifth, she applied her make-up and arranged her hair the way she had been taught: swept up in glittering combs that allowed her curls to cascade down her neck.

Whitney came in. "Is this the same Olga I met in Germany not so long ago? The transformation is remarkable. Hey, kids, this is terrific."

Lothar frowned.

"Sorry, Baron von Schenck. Is that better?"

"Much. I often wonder why I put up with you, Whitney." Lothar headed for the door. Olga followed him. What could she say? Any comment on her part would only make matters worse.

The Diamond Club was sold out. Curious glances followed Lothar and Olga to the stage where Buddy and his band waited. Polite applause acknowledged their bow. Guests kept on talking and laughing. Olga sensed Lothar's irritation and felt her anxiety rise. How would they get through this? Buddy seemed relaxed and raised his baton; his job was to entertain the guests with background music and dance tunes, not give a concert.

"A one, a two, a …," and the band played the opening measures of *Begin the Beguine*. Lothar and Olga joined in, the rippling piano a soulful accompaniment to the reed instruments. The percussionist set the pace and added drama. Some couples danced, others listened. The conversation had dropped to a whisper. People watched the shining saxes, trumpets, and clarinets rising and falling as they entered or left playing. Muted trombones interacted with the piano in unexpected harmonies.

Olga was all music now; the notes came on their own. Father was guiding her. Lothar resisted, playing the pieces as written to guide the musicians back to order. They ignored him until, drawn into their rendition, he finally acquiesced.

This was the kind of music people paid a fortune to hear. Their applause would not end. Dazed, Olga bowed and smiled. The magic had happened without the Evil One. Lothar gave a quick nod convinced that his part had made a significant difference.

Buddy took Olga's hand and kissed it, then shook hands with Lothar as if they were on a concert stage. People settled down again. Olga felt the heartbeat of the audience. When you give love, you reap love. They did not object to "Baron and Baroness von Schenck would like to treat them to 'Rhapsody in Blue,'" and voiced their approval with a rousing applause.

Olga and Lothar's intricate rendition of George Gershwin's masterpiece caught the spirit of people in restless pursuit of life, eager to improve their lot. Accompanied by the saxophones and trumpets, they held their audience suspended in another world until the music found its glorious end.

Buddy escorted Olga off the stage to applause and cheers. "How did you do it?"

"I didn't play it."

"No? Who did?"

She did not dare say, Father. "My soul."

He understood. "Stick around. We'll talk later."

Picking her way between the tables with Lothar, Olga greeted the people congratulating them. "I think we made a good impression."

"Sure," he grumbled, "like an orgasm. Whatever happened to art? Gershwin would turn over in his grave. But I am through preaching; have it your way. I just wish I were not a part of this. Pearls to the swine."

A waiter brought a bottle of champagne and filled their glasses.

Olga silently thanked Father, then grinned to Lothar, "Swine are fine animals who feed us with their flesh. And I don't think they care for pearls." The cool bubbles fizzed in her mouth and complemented the sweetness of the chocolate soufflé Lothar had ordered.

The corners of his mouth drawn, Lothar wished he could feel some of the joy Olga flaunted so shamelessly. This silly music student he had taken a fancy to years ago had once again ruined his reputation. All he had wanted was to prove that he was as much of a man as, if not more than, that rich and handsome Gottfried. That cool supremacy had been disgusting, especially coming from an upstart whose father had made his fortune in real estate. New money. Bourgeois. Olga should have been flattered that he, Lothar von Schenck, had taken an interest in her. But no. She fought him off like a feral cat. He pursed his lips, sipped his champagne, and cast a glance at her. She was pretty, but her natural charm infectuous. No wonder the men here ogled her with unconcealed desire. Those cuties they had in their company were no match for Olga, despite all their glamour and glitz. Everything here was artificial and overdone. Diamonds and furs, tight gowns on carefully cultivated bodies, and smiles as plastered as the paint on their lips.

He had never understood why women adored Gottfried. So he was taller and had a flair for dressing—Lothar made a point of not competing on such superficial ground. Who needed them when you had a name as old as von Schenck and a talent for the keyboard that was second to none? But women didn't understand. They languished for some Romeo who flattered them with music he had not composed.

That afternoon, after playing duets with Olga, he had to have her. In retrospect, it wasn't worth the effort, especially considering the result. What a ridiculous aberration that was. Was her insisting on keeping the baby a trick to make him marry her? To this day she could not see things his way and kept on fighting. He was so sick and tired of the game.

Lothar emptied his glass, noticing her flushed face. Those dimples and big, innocent blue eyes gave everyone the wrong impresion. Whitney's people had completely changed Olga's appearance. Her purple gown and his mother's fox boa made her look like one of those million dollar babes. But clothes couldn't fool him. He saw the music student, Olga Bergman, who lived with her mother and step-father in Riga. Their home had had three apartments and a rather nice garden, where the Bergman sisters entertained their friends in summer. He had enjoyed the young crowd of fun-loving students and had played the piano for them, happy to show off his talents and win their admiration.

He put his glass down. The lady in black at the next table gave him the eye, flirting shamelessly as if her escort, a short, bald, and pot-bellied man, did not exist. Honestly. Lothar was not blind, nor was he interested in women who played up to him. Still, he felt aroused, something he had not enjoyed lately. Now that he shared a room with Olga, there was no conquest to excite him. She was just a bore, indifferent to his advances. This woman's interest pitted him against the man who had paid a fortune to bring her here. A sugar-daddy. How pathetic. He deliberately avoided her glance and watched the waiter refill his glass. He was nobody's trophy.

A young man approached their table, his dark hair slicked to his skull, a thin mustache on his upper lip. "May I ask your wife for a dance?"

"My wife –?" Lothar paused. Olga watched impassively. "Be my guest," he said. "She isn't much of a dancer, but go ahead."

From then on, Olga danced every dance, whirling around from arm to arm until Buddy joined them for champagne. Raising his glass, he toasted, "To the German Baron and Baroness, who understand American music better than most natives. Prost!" He drank and then settled down. "I like your arrangement of "Beguine." Let me take a look at your compositions. You've got me intrigued."

Lothar felt a jolt of joy flash through his heart, of a kind he had not felt in ages. Buddy was a pro who understood music. Once his compositions were published in America, Lothar would be famous throughout the world. His music would make history. "America loves innovation. Germany is steeped in tradition. Neither Schoenberg, Alban Berg nor Stravinsky got the credit they deserve," Buddy said.

Olga returned from the dance floor. Seeing the two men in deep conversation she quietly raised her glass, "To music," drank, and then added, "Thank you Buddy, for letting us play with you."

"You got that magic, Olga. Tomorrow my wife and our daughter Trish will come to hear you. We live out on Long Island. A long commute. No school on Saturday. Trish is ten."

"So is our daughter, Anna. She is in Switzerland."

Buddy raised his glass again. "To those we love."

Lothar shrugged.

Chapter 40

Three weeks later Olga doubted they would last their contract. The novelty had worn off. Weary of their nightly engagement, Lothar's performance had slacked off. He pounded at the piano to demonstrate his disgust at music that was supposed to entertain. "I'm so sick and tired of all this. I'm no vaudeville entertainer. Aristocracy is not for sale." The fact that Buddy had rejected Lothar's compositions had turned his pleasure to disgust.

"Who said it was?" Olga said, more harshly than she intended. "And what difference does it make?"

He was obviously working on an excuse not to perform tonight, claiming a migraine he did not have. Buddy's earlier suggestion that Lothar could be a great composer had him obsessed with working on his own music rather than performing for money.

Olga coaxed him into getting dressed. She was getting sick of this game, but had to keep it up in order to fulfill their contract. They had left the Waldorf and moved to an apartment Whitney had found for them uptown. Now they had a piano Lothar could play all hours of the day and night, but he wanted out completely.

Lothar's pounding insulted her musical ear - nothing but aggravating noise. The kitchen door could not keep the racket out. Even if he found a publisher, who would care to perform his work and be booed out of the concert hall? Lothar's gloom had everybody keeping their distance. Whitney did all he could to accommodate Lothar's needs, but got no gratitude. They had not only a piano but comfortable furniture, utensils in the kitchen, and linens for the beds, yet Lothar complained about the bread, the coffee, and the traffic in the street, whining like a spoiled child.

If only Anyna were here. Together they could explore Manhattan, shopping at markets where people helped themselves to the merchandise, letting Mr. Goldstein explain to her what Jell-O and spam were all about.

Olga knew that Anyna longed for her mother as much as she longed for her child. Neither Richard's and Adie's affection, nor their generosity, could replace her. But Lothar did not care. His mother's letters left him even grumpier. No matter how much money he sent, it was never enough.

They were in their fourth week with another eight to go. Olga could see that Buddy would not put up with Lothar's cutting remarks and constant criticism much longer. Nothing she could say or do, neither flattery nor raving about the progress he was making on his composition eased the tension. He was convinced that his mother could not do without him and that money could not compensate her for his absence. Finally she gave up, especially after Whitney reminded them that they had another engagement coming up with Ben Hanley in Los Angeles.

They were in their fourth week with another eight to go. Olga could see that Buddy would not put up with Lothar's cutting remarks and constant criticism much longer. Nothing she could say or do, neither flattery nor raving about the progress he was making on his composition eased the tension. He was convinced that his mother could not do without him and that money could not compensate her for his absence. Finally she gave up, especially after Whitney reminded them that they had another engagement coming up with Ben Hanley in Los Angeles.

Olga was not surprised when Whitney showed up after their rehearsal and invited them for coffee.

"Well, there you finally did it, Baron!" he said as soon as they sat down.

"Buddy had it and released you from the contract."

"That's good news," Lothar said, leaning back and untying his shawl. "I'm ready to go home."

Olga was crushed, feeling ashamed, guilty and sad that they were letting Buddy down. She would have to return to the stinking hole where the countess held court. She blew her nose to hide her tears.

"Not so fast, Baron," Whitney said. "You're under contract with me! This will cost you a stiff penalty and I'm not about to forfeit your obligation with Ben Hanley. So I suggest you pack your things and get ready to leave for Los Angeles." He had never been a man who bothered with niceties, but this time he was downright rude. Olga's face burnt with guilt. Biting her lip she watched the waitress put down the coffee mugs. No more gold-rimmed cups. She had seen it coming but could not avoid the shock effect. If only Lothar did not insist on calling it quits and going home, she would be grateful and do whatever Whitney suggested.

When Lothar realized that he did not even have enough money to pay the penalty he grudgingly agreed to fly to Los Angeles and play with the Ben Hanley band.

They left New York the following morning. Thick snowflakes fell over the skyscrapers and partly his them from view. She remembered her flight through Poland, the cold and fear. Now she was heading for a place that enjoyed year-round sunshine and warm weather. Ilona Huzak had been right when she predicted that Olga's future lay across the ocean. Now she only had to find a way of bringing Anyna and staying here. One step at a time.

Ben Hanley met them at the Los Angeles airport. Olga guessed him to be about forty. His lively brown eyes and broad smile showed no reservations toward her and Lothar. He treated them with the ease of a host who enjoyed easy conversation and the acquaintance of strangers. "Glad you came. I know, it's a hell of a long flight from New York. Just did it once, and that was plenty for me. You can have New York, but I wouldn't mind finding out what Germany is all about. I was born and raised in Pasadena." When he noticed their blank looks he added, "It's a nice town nearby. I'll take you out there some time. Home of the Rose Bowl, the Rose Parade and Caltech."

When neither Lothar nor Olga reacted, he added. "Oh well, we'll talk about that some other time. Let's go and have some breakfast first. You don't want to make deals on an empty stomach." Judging from his girth, Hanley's stomach was rarely empty. His tan reflected the local climate. Olga felt as if she had known Hanley for years. Working with him should not be as strenuous as working with Buddy.

"Germany is a very nice country, Mr. Hanley," she said. "People are rebuilding it."

On their way to the coffee shop, Lothar talked with ease, even mentioned that he liked California. "Or should I say Los Angeles, since I have not seen much?"

Olga had obliged him last night, leaving him in a good mood. As long as he did not force her, it wasn't so bad. Everything was relative, and she had even felt a need.

At the coffee shop, the dark green walls made a distinct background for the paintings of summer landscapes. Some people sat at the counter and conversed over a cup of coffee. The lighting was subdued, giving it an atmosphere of timelessness.

"I imagine you know my style of music," Hanley said after placing their orders with a pretty waitress in a pink and white uniform.

"I'm afraid not," Lothar admitted, "but we can adapt to almost anything."

"Good," Hanley said, watching the waitress pour their coffee into mugs. "Buddy told me that you're both accomplished musicians. Out here in Los Angeles, we tend toward the avant-garde. Artistic freedom. I understand that you like to improvise. That's fine with me, as long as it doesn't disrupt the band. People don't mind exotic ideas—to a point. But they do want to dance rather than listen. If you can stick to that, we'll do swell." He poured sugar into the steaming black coffee and stirred.

Lothar had no objections. "I'm also a composer. Primarily a composer. Perhaps you can take a look at my compositions. When you have a spare moment, that is. They're not dance tunes."

Hanley showed no interest in Lothar's composition. "We'll rehearse in the afternoon. At the Avalon we strictly play dance music. The crowd wants to dance. You should see some of the acrobatics they do. In case you didn't know, it's one of the largest halls in the world. Now, the Coconut Grove is a different story." He sipped his coffee and watched the waitress put down their plates of food. "Thanks, Kathy. That'll do for now."

"Sure thing, Ben." She left, swinging her full hips.

"Where were we?" he asked, spreading butter on his toast.

"The Coconut Grove."

"Ah yes. A discriminating audience. The place where movie people meet. We get celebrities. But that won't bother you, Olga, will it? You're a down-to-earth girl who has her head screwed on right."

She laughed, feeling her head. "I think so."

"Now at the Grove we could stick in a concert piece. 'Rhapsody in Blue' seems to be your show-stopper." He dug into his scrambled eggs and stuffed them into his mouth. "Let's see how it goes. You're quite a dish, young lady and you, Lothar, are the perfect baron."

"Glad to hear it," Lothar mocked, but did not object to being called by his first name. He really was in a good mood. If sex was the answer, she could take care of that, Olga thought, flattered by Ben's positive assessment of her.

"In show biz you've got to do what people like. I understand you studied in Berlin. The airlift is still going on. Pretty amazing stuff, wouldn't you say? During the war, I entertained our troops in the Pacific. Me and my band traveled all over the islands."

The waitress refilled their cups and left.

"I guess Buddy told you," Lothar said, "that I like to play my own arrangements. Olga can follow along."

Hanley nodded.

"We're a team," she said between sips of orange juice.

"No doubt. Did you bring your notes?"

Lothar's eyes lit up. "Yes. Right here. They're not in print yet. But you can see what I mean. Take a look at the variations for the piano and the saxes. The trumpet solo is too heavy here. If you move it to the next part, you'll get people to swell into 'In the Mood.' Just wait until you hear it."

As soon as Hanley had finished his breakfast he studied the music. "A clever idea."

"The audience at the Diamond Club gave us an ovation," Olga said, her cheeks burning.

"So I heard. Let's see how our fans react. I'll certainly give it a try." He returned the sheet music to Lothar, finished his coffee, and rose. "See you at rehearsal."

The studio was on Sunset Boulevard. The musicians, dressed in patterned sport shirts and slacks, watched Lothar and Olga walk in. They had played with soloists before, but aristocrats from Germany? What was going on? They had had drummers and singers, trumpet soloists, and occasionally violonists. But pianists?

"Olga and Lothar von Schenck," Hanley introduced them. "They're the German Baron and Baroness." He waved Lothar down. "We don't stand on formalities." After introducing each member of the band, he tapped his baton on the podium and opened with "Night and Day".

The soothing melody and dreamy rhythm went straight to Olga's heart. Great stuff. She could not wait to learn it. Ben Hanley and his band acted more relaxed than Buddy Jones. She appreciated being here, and thanked Buddy for his recommendation.

Two hours later every member of the band felt at home with the newcomers, and even enjoyed their fresh approach. They had swing in their blood, and played everything from memory, improvising whenever the feeling overcame them, like true jazz musicians. The drummer, an exhibitionist, took off with solos, drumming away at the speed of light. Sweat poured from his black face.

The following Friday was their opening night. Olga's royal blue gown had a salmon train draped down her back. Rhinestones sparkled with her every move. Her lipstick glistened in the light of the chandelier. The Coconut Grove was sold out.

Olga and Lothar sat backstage while the band performed and watched the guests dance. Was that tall, slender man Gary Cooper? She touched Lothar's arm. "Look. Isn't the man at the second table on the right Darryl Zanuck?"

"So what? A man like any other who happens to have some talent and a lot of luck. If you take off his fancy white coat and tie all you have is a flabby old man who happens to be rich." Not that Zanuck was old, but Lothar always had to criticize people she admired.

"Think positive," she said, noticing that Lothar's white face had assumed a cruel mask. "Relax. Everything will be fine."

"Of course it will be. My arrangement of 'Beguine' will make them jump out of there complacent seats. Just play what we practiced. Don't get carried away, else I'll walk out."

The voices of the guests rose with the music. The dancers stepped to the beat. Lothar's presence had her on edge. *Father, please. I know I must not call on you all the time. Please, Father...* She wished she had Lothar's confidence, his trust. But all she had was his disdain.

The band played "Temptation." Then a lovely singer named Ginger Joy came on. She was good and earned a warm applause.

Lothar rose, his face tight and strained. Olga led the way. *Father, my life is in your hands.*

They bowed to a lukewarm applause. People kept on talking. The glittering Hollywood crowd was not interested in entertainers it didn't know. Lothar watched Olga take her seat at the keyboard, then sat down beside her. Ben Hanley, dressed in a pale blue dinner jacket, raised his baton, winked at Olga, and gave the signal. Listening to the opening measures, she imagined Ingo in the front row and felt the warm anticipation of being with him swell in her heart. "Blue Moon" would be for him. She played her part with passion, reliving their reunion. Love had come to her again. Lothar caught her lead; he too longed for someone. Ben and his band adapted to her style. People fell silent. The dancers lingered in each others arms, giving in to the romance of the moment.

Her fingers fell on all the right notes, driven by the deep love she felt. If it was the Evil One leading her on, so be it. The last reverberations of the music lingered on in silence, before the audience erupted with applause. Olga, awakened from the spell, turned toward them and bowed her head. Ben reached for her hand. The band had been with her; the magic of her music had once again spread its wings over the souls of those sharing it. With tears in her eyes and a bewildered smile, she stood at Lothar's side, bowing.

From then on they could do no wrong. "Stardust", "Begin the Beguine", "In the Mood", and finally, "Happy Days Are Here Again". The evening was an unforgettable experience. Darryl Zanuck sent her his card, "Not bad for a German baroness."

During intermission, Ben came to their table. "Nice going. Buddy was right—there is a fire in you. Stick around, kids. We'll celebrate after the show."

Lothar did not stick around. "I have work to do."

Riding back to the hotel, Olga knew that she was fighting a losing battle.

The Los Angeles Times gave raving reviews, the musicians enjoyed playing Lothar's arrangements, Ben went along. Word got around and people flocked to their performances. Still, despite all the praise, Lothar became grumpy and morose. Olga knew she was dancing on quicksand. No matter how hard she tried to please him, he was tormented by homesickness and longed for Maman. Not even her efforts in bed could ease his morbid disposition. He knew Olga would never be his, and made no effort to court her. For all her efforts to cheer him up, she was desperate for a kind word, a gesture of approval, some friendship. If he hated her so, would he not grant her a divorce?

"We are part of some set here," he said over breakfast, "except I have no idea what roles we play." Every table at the coffee shop was taken. Businessmen read their paper or had meetings. Lothar had bacon and eggs. He scooped up the egg yolk with his fork and slipped it into his mouth. "Money is God. Preachers sell God to gullible people after convincing them that they have the keys to Heaven."

Olga had no idea what he was getting at, and sipped her coffee. The waitress put down a bowl of cornflakes and a pitcher of milk. Something was up. The way his mouth twisted and his cheeks twitched spelled trouble. Her stomach contracted. Once again the tension was driving them to a crisis—she had to find the dynamite before it blew up.

"Everybody has to make a living," Olga said, wondering whether that was the answer he wanted. His arrogance and pride grated on her nerves. What was so special about his title? He had not earned it. This black knight had no shining armor. He was an unbending, demanding, and selfish son of a bitch. Everybody saw through his ridiculous act. He couldn't even impress his mother who used his yearning for her approval against him. The old trick of bemoaning his absence made him feel guilty. When she had caused enough pain he would relieve it by going home.

That evening Lothar's gloom was deeper than ever. "I'm through," he said, leaving The Grove.

"Ben is so good to us," she said at his heels. "He's doing all he can to make you happy. He even invited us to a party."

"I need my time for my work," he said. "At home I can work without interruption."

"What home?" Olga cried out. "Not that stinking little room in Inning? You must be out of your mind. What will we live off? Why can't you think of your family for once!" Overcome with emotions she swallowed hard but couldn't get rid of the lump in her throat. "Admit that it's your mother who drives you crazy. I'm so sick of it all. She's even more selfish than you." Curious people leaving the club stopped to peer at their quarrel.

"Those heart attacks are fake," Olga went on, too upset to hold her tongue. "She knows how to get under your skin. She'll outlive both of us."

Lothar grabbed her shoulders and shook her. "Who took you in and fed you when you arrived in Inning with your child, you ungrateful creature? Maman was right when she said you always get your way without ever thinking of others."

She wriggled from his grip. "Let go of me."

"Have it your way." He headed for the taxi stand.

Olga stayed behind. He did not seem to care. She would walk for awhile and calm down.

The following morning he did not mention their argument and called Whitney. "Sorry, Al, but I am through. Yes, I know. Hollywood is every artist's dream. Not mine. My creativity has come to a standstill. I must go home."

No matter what Whitney said, Lothar was adamant. Neither the penalty he would have to pay if he broke his contract, nor the appeal to Lothar's honor made any difference.

Too upset to argue, Olga went to the lobby and called Ben. Her hands trembled. Lothar was insane. Where was his sense of noblesse oblige, the egotistical maniac?

"I felt it all along," Ben said. "Still, I thought things were going well."

"They were," Olga assured him. "I'm so sorry. Please forgive us, Ben. He'll regret it."

"I understand. We can't detain him. It's a free country."

"You're so good to us, Ben. How can I ever thank you for all your kindness?"

"By coming back."

Olga thought she had not heard right and gasped, "Coming back? He won't come back, you know that."

Ben chuckled over the phone. "I know, and that's fine with me. I'll be glad to have you without him. You're a lovely young woman and an incredible musician."

She could tell that it was not just her music he was interested in. He wanted her. "Thank you, Ben. I'll consider it. I have no idea what's going on in Germany."

"I doubt anything's changed. Just remember what I said, and let me know. I'd be glad to sign whatever papers you'd need to immigrate."

"Immigrate?"

"What else? You must come to stay. I need you, Olga."

Olga swallowed. "Dear me, Ben. I'm speechless."

"Good. Just remember what I said and come."

"I can't tell you how good that makes me feel. All these weeks. I didn't know what to do. Only the music kept me alive. Your band is fantastic. I love playing with you." Her heart swelled in gratitude. "Thank you, Ben. You are such a wonderful man and musician."

She would be back, and she would bring Anyna.

Chapter 41

Lothar and Olga landed in Frankfurt on the 5th of April 1949, a Tuesday. The sun had come out to greet them. From the air, she had seen the ruins of the city. Coming from sunny California, the ruins of Germany looked grimmer than before. What did she expect? This was not Hollywood; this was reality.

Stepping onto the ramp of the Pan Am Clipper, Olga inhaled the mellow spring air and stretched. It had been a long flight. She had chatted with her fellow passengers as if she belonged among them—people who flew across the ocean for business, journalists went to cover the news. Germany would never be her home again. When could she return to America? Unlike the Countess, who had spent her life reminiscing about America, Olga would move there.

"We'll surprise, Maman," Lothar said in a happy voice she had not heard from the time they had left Inning. He did not complain about the wooden benches in the train, or the people staring at his foreign finery as they unwrapped their sandwiches and poured hot tea from thermoses. People like Lothar and Olga did not ride in third-class cars. Foreigners enjoyed superior status, and had taken over the first-class world. Americans lived in Germany's villas and the fine hotels. They were the masters of the country.

Lothar was going home, glad to return to the world he adored. His mother's stinking room was a paradise no Beverly Hills Hotel could compete with.

The train stopped in Stuttgart. If she could only see Ingo, tell him about her adventures in a world he could not imagine—one that would be their home once he had the courage to break from his wife and the child he had not asked for. But he was a man of principle who honored his obligations. How could Father promise they would be together some day? Some day could be a hundred years from now. Yet, destiny had its ways. Doors had opened when she least expected it. The dozing people in patched clothes on the bench across from her had nothing in common with her life. She had moved on, and would return to live in Los Angeles, a warm city where people wore deodorant and aired out homes where flowers bloomed all year.

Two women munched on sandwiches. Olga was hungry and remembered the days when all she could think of was food. Now she could buy whatever she wanted. Why not go to the dining car and get something to eat? Though Al Whitney had deducted their expenses and a penalty for breaking their contract, Olga still had some money left. Her American tour had been an unforgettable experience that had opened the door to her future. She cuddled into her soft wool coat. Her feet were warm in leather boots. She had leather gloves and a matching purse.

In the dining car, she ordered a *wienerschnitzel* and potato salad, then leafed through the "Frankfurter Allgemeine." The Marshal Plan had granted Germany credit to buy goods from the United States. Now Germany could replace the raw materials and machinery she'd lost. Seeds and fertilizers would boost Germany's agriculture. The want ads had plenty of job offers. Though displaced persons were provided for by the International Refugee Organization, they too would soon become part of the German economy. Many of them had emigrated, others still waited for their visas. Men returning from POW camps were offered short apprenticeships like Ingo, so that they could enter the workforce with decent skills.

A picture of West Germany's new Chancellor, Konrad Adenauer, showed him with members of his cabinet. The United States, Britain, and France promoted the concept of a federal republic. The stout Bavarian, Ludwig Ehrhardt, had taken charge of Germany's finances, as approved by the Allied Occupation Forces.

The Berlin blockade was still on and going strong. The Allied Supreme Command outwitted Soviet harassment. Stalin made no bones about his plans—he wanted the Americans out of Europe. Should anybody still doubt the communists' true intentions, they only had to look at how the Soviets had manipulated the Eastern Bloc into a network of puppet regimes. The iron curtain had fallen, trapping everyone east of it in Stalin's clutches.

Gazing through the soot-stained window, Olga watched dark clouds move in over bare fields. The dormant trees left no shadows. Three years ago, she had escaped from Berlin and had survived the Countess' intrigues. Her next move would be - get back to the blue skies of Los Angeles.

The train left Stuttgart while Olga enjoyed her crisp schnitzel. "My beloved Ingo, some day we'll be together. That's a promise."

Back in Inning, Olga dragged behind Lothar's eager gait, bracing herself for the stench of urine and poverty awaiting her. The small windows of Frau Moser's home were lit. Pulling the door open, Lothar hastened down the musty, dim hallway she knew only too well. At the end was the door leading to the Countess' world. Olga watched him run up to his mother, bending over the bed to embrace her. It was the same old disarray of clothes and books, only Lothar's sheet music had been stacked up on the piano.

"We're home, Maman."

Rather than return the embrace of her long lost son, she remained stiff and disdainful. "Lothar! What on earth? What are you doing here?" she said when he kissed her cheek. "Don't tell me you broke your contract?"

"I did. I did. You told me how much you need me, Maman. Aren't you glad?"

His disappointment hurt. Couldn't she at least pretend to be glad?

"You mean you left the tour?" she asked in her icy, articulate voice. "You still had a month to go. Or was it two? How could you? We need the money, dear. Think of Lara. She is pregnant."

"She is what?" Lothar asked, drawing back.

"Well, yes. And Jimmy Chu is no Aldrich. Even if he marries her, how would they live?"

His smile froze. "But Maman, you said you could not get along without us. That you needed my help. That you were lonely for me."

"True, true," she said quickly and took his hand. "I did miss you. But I managed. As I did before, looking after your daughter while you served in the war. I'm not helpless. You must have misunderstood. The money you sent me." She pointed to the chair next to her bed, ignoring Olga who had closed the door and now unbuttoned her coat. "Burgl did my shopping and cleaned the room. But fine, you are back. I guess I should be glad. I am," she added.

Olga saw Lothar's ill-concealed embarrassment. How could he not see that his mother used him shamelessly and would continue to lie to get him to cater to her? The Countess noticed Olga taking off her coat, and raised her thin, penciled brows. Her painted lips in the powdered face tightened. "Don't you look all dolled up, Olga," she said. "America is an amazing place, isn't it? I can't imagine where you will wear that coat around here. Not bad, Olga. A hat yet. The modern baroness. But so out of place here and pointless. The NCO Club is no Coconut Grove."

"Al Whitney insisted that I buy decent clothes. We had to pay for our wardrobe and pay a big penalty because Lothar broke the contract. I tried to convince him that you could manage without him for a couple of weeks. But why should he listen to me?"

"How touching. The caring wife. I appreciate his thoughtfulness. He isn't a person who cares about money. Unfortunately, there are times when we need it. What were you thinking of, Lothar? I really must scold you for this. Olga can work at the NCO kitchen. But what about you?"

"I will finish my composition, 'A Night in the Catacombs,'" he said. "I didn't have time for it in Los Angeles. Rehearsals, performances, working on fresh arrangements. We had a busy schedule. The music came to me while we stayed in New York. Something like Gershwin's 'An American in Paris'. I want to do a piece about Manhattan. All that traffic. You can't imagine the endless stream of cars. People running here and there. They never walk. In and out of subways. Constant motion. Lights blinking from advertisements. Something for a Charlie Chaplin flick." He sat down on the bed.

"Sounds pretty interesting," she said, without any indication that she wanted to hear more.

"Would you like to see the presents we brought you? Did you have something to eat, Maman? We brought chocolate. Olga would be happy to fix you tea."

The Countess leaned back into her pillows, and closed her eyes to recover from her shock. "Thank you, dear. I just told you that I have learned to get along on my own. So don't patronize me. I may be old, but I am not senile. I had no idea you would show up out of nowhere. It's getting to be my bed time, Lothar. I need my sleep. We had better think about where you will stay tonight. And do put another piece of wood into the stove. Spring is slow in coming. I don't have anything to offer you. I guess Olga will sleep in the attic. I haven't been there in ages. Some day I'll go up and look at the souvenirs of my incredible life."

Lothar helped her get up, and handed her the white chenille robe Olga had sent.

"I will not keep you up, Countess," Olga said. "We've been on the go for many hours. Los Angeles is on the other side of the globe. Lothar slept on the plane. Considering the time difference…"

"I know," the Countess retorted. "You may recall that I've been to America before."

"How could I forget," Olga said. "Sorry we disturbed you, Countess. Tomorrow we'll see where to go from here. Good night."

She took her suitcase and slipped out the door before they could object. Outside, she inhaled the cold, clean air and let the wind cool her face. The smell of dung from Frau Moser's yard was like a greeting from a friend. The light in her kitchen was still on. Olga needed somebody to talk to and Frau Moser would understand. A glass of hard cider would be so good.

Frau Moser opened the door and almost choked on her dentures. "Olga? Where did you come from?"

"From America, of course."

"You say that as if it was next door! I'm so glad you're back. Come right in. Have a glass of cider; it's very good. Tell me about America— what's it like?" Her eyes in the wrinkled face were all love. "To think you went there and came back all in one piece and looking more beautiful than ever. If that young man could see you now, he would worship you on his knees." She pulled the black scarf from her head and uncovered the thin white braids she had wrapped around her head.

Olga hugged her frail friend. "It's so good to be here, Frau Moser. I just had to see you. Cider would be great. Perhaps you even have a slice of bread and a piece of smoked goat meat? America is glorious. Everything went well." She sat down on the bench and leaned over the freshly scrubbed table that had served generations of Mosers.

"The people must have gone wild when you came on stage. The prettiest thing that ever came to America. Look at that coat and hat! Did you wear real evening gowns, like the ones in movies?" She wore her usual black dirndl and an apron.

Olga laughed. "Of course. People come to see glamour. "

"Glamour! Yes. And that's what they got. How did you make out with your husband?" She talked through her thin lips. Her mouth had caved in forming a multitude of wrinkles. The skin on her face resembled cracked old leather.

"What do you think?" Olga said, watching Frau Moser pour cider into two jars. "Ill-tempered and bossy. He finally broke the contract, and insisted we come home to Maman. So, here we are. But America is a dream. Honestly. I loved Los Angeles." Olga noticed Frau Moser's puzzled look. "Not like Bavaria, of course. The Alps are magnificent."

"That they are. But go ahead and drink up. Prost. I'm so glad you're back."

Olga drank with tears in her eyes. "You did not happen to hear from Ingo, did you?"

"No. Why would he write to me?" Thoughtfully she sipped her cider. "Years ago, when I was young, I used to love a man. But his parents did not think I was suitable. They made him marry somebody else. So I took Jakob. Not a bad man, you know, but it wasn't love. So it goes." Her dentures kept slipping as she talked. "Times were different then. We did as we were told. I tried to be a good wife to Jakob, but my heart was with Paul. He once told me that he missed me too. He was killed in the war. Volunteered, you know."

Olga nodded, surprised that the shriveled and wrinkled Frau Moser had once been a passionate young woman in love with a young man. And she still was. Love! Lothar had never experienced it. Olga closed her eyes and thought of Ingo. What was he waiting for?

The smoke-stained farm kitchen held the scent of the ages. The stove had a fire going. "To the ones we love and loved," she said. "To Ingo and Paul." How she wished she had a piano now, to pour her emotions into music. "Some Day A Miracle Will Happen." It would take that, she thought.

"I never thought I would like Americans," Frau Moser said. "Then that big sergeant came along in his car. Everybody in Inning knew him. He always said hello and smiled. People liked that. I certainly did. He has a good heart."

"Seems that we fought those wars for nothing," Olga said. "Millions of people killed, and we are friends again. Figure that one out. People in America are kind. Once they got to know me, they liked me. I made all kinds of friends. Ben Hanley, the band leader, wants me to come back. A very nice man. If I didn't have Ingo, I'd take him up on it."

Olga ate the fragrant bread with butter and smoked goat meat. "It's so good. You probably never heard of filet mignon, shrimp, or hamburgers. They are wonderful, but there is nothing like your smoked meat. I'm so glad you were still awake, Frau Moser. I had to talk to somebody before I went to my moth balls. If I could only be with Ingo. I miss him so."

"Then you had better go and find him before it's too late," Frau Moser said, refilling the jars from her earthenware jug.

The following morning, Olga found Lothar preparing tea for his mother. They exchanged silent greetings.

"You should not have quit your job, Lothar," the Countess said. "Why can't you think of others for a change? Nicky and Lara are in dire straights. When the currency reform dried up the black market your bother and sister had no income. You could not expect them to work in a factory. Chu is no Aldrich; his pay barely covers the necessities. With the black market gone, an American sergeant is just that. Lara did not know that Aldrich was a rich man, else she would have gone with him to America."

"Lara was not interested in marrying a sergeant," Lothar said, irritably.

"Is that not what I just said?" the Countess retorted. She wore a gray dress under her black cardigan. Her gray hair was twisted into a chignon.

Olga smiled to herself. Aldrich had no intention of marrying his aristocratic whore and taking her to America. Here she had been Aldrich's pet, in America he had no use for her.

The Countess sat down at the little round table, while Olga poured the boiling water over the tea. "Lara did not intend to get pregnant. She probably thought Chu's family would help out. But nothing. American Chinese have different ways."

"What did you say about American Chinese?" Lothar asked, as if the truth had only just struck him. "A Chinese baby? I thought Lara had more sense than that. But then, I should've known. She's never done a useful thing in her life."

"The baby will become a charming, exotic count from the Land of Smiles," the Countess informed him. "Look what you produced. If it were not for Adie, I don't know what would have become of Anna Magdalena."

"A fine young lady, Countess," Olga said, putting the tea pot on the silver tray. "She is bright and would do well anywhere."

"That's neither here nor there. Of course, Lara will get some support from the government. But that will hardly suffice."

"Generally called welfare," Olga said, watching Lothar squirm under the shocking news. He did not care for his half-sister. Her beauty, breeding, and shady dealings had never produced money. "Mr. Whitney might take us back if Lothar guarantees to fulfill his contract," Olga said, watching the Countess count the potential income.

"Out of the question," he said. "I came home so that I can work on my composition. 'Catacombs' is a revolutionary piece. A new concept." He forgot the Chinese baby, went to the piano, and played some measures from the piece.

The Countess' did not let on what she thought. Olga hated the piece, which lacked any sense of harmony, melody, or even a distinct rhythm. A revolting conglomeration of meaningless sounds—a portrait of Lothar's troubled psyche.

"What do you think, Maman?" he asked, his eyes wide with expectation.

"You said it yourself, Lothar. You've captured the cacophony of Manhattan. I don't particularly like Gershwin, and I can't say that I'm fond of this piece. In that respect, I am old fashioned. I like music that has a melody and such. You know, the kind that touches the heart. I have no patience for Stockhausen, Schoenberg, or Hindemith. Why don't we have our breakfast now?"

Pouring the tea, Olga sensed Lothar's despair. He was convinced of his genius, but if he could not please his mother, his work was meaningless.

Olga went to the piano and played "Happy Days Are Here Again".

"What is that supposed to mean?" the Countess quipped. "Have you gone mad?"

491

"I thought you might enjoy hearing the kind of music we played in America. As far as my working in the NCO kitchen is concerned, let me tell you that my Cinderella days are over. At least the ones before the prince showed up. I've had my share of the wicked stepmother."

"How dare you talk that way!" the Countess screeched.

Olga chuckled, and left the piano. "Unless Lothar needs me as an accompanist in America, I've decided to take charge of my life and take care of my daughter. First, I'll go to Furstenfeldbruck and see what is happening there." She picked up her cup. "Tomorrow, or the day after, I'll go to Stuttgart and visit my friend Lucie before committing myself to a job. For the time being, I'll keep the attic. If you want my company for breakfast or supper, I'd be glad to join you and help with the dishes, but I am no longer part of this household. I'll soon know where I go from here."

"Seems you have quite a plan," the Countess said coldly, her dark eyes intent on Olga's. "So much for gratitude. The cuckoo is taking over the nest."

"On the contrary. The fledgling is leaving the nest." Olga drained her cup.

"Your comments are inappropriate," Lothar said. "Anna Magdalena is part of our family."

"Really," Olga mused. "Since when? Family means people who love and care for each other. I haven't sensed that from you as far as Anyna is concerned. Nor do I see how you could care for her in addition to all your other obligations. But, why not leave that decision up to her? For the moment she's in Switzerland and will want to stay there until the end of the school year. Then we'll see. But as far as taking on another contract with Whitney is concerned, I'd be more than glad to return to America. I love that country and all it stands for, as you do, Countess. There are plenty of Mr. McCormicks around—generous, caring people. It's up to you, Lothar."

"I see," he said, indifferent to whatever she did with her life.

The Countess shrugged. She would attack later. Like a prowling cat, she would strike when her victim was unaware.

Furstenfeldbruck had changed. On her way from the station, Olga had noticed new shops, a restaurant, café, and bars. Liesl and her friends wanted to hear about America. John, who now watched over the kitchen, wanted to know all about Olga's success in America and Lothar's homesickness.

"Of course, you won't return to the kitchen, but we'd be honored to have you entertain us on weekends. You speak such good English now. You could work in the office."

"No, thanks. I'd rather entertain," Olga said.

"Then let me talk to Sgt. Goldsmith. Our members would be thrilled to have such a famous pianist entertain us. In the meantime, come and look around. You might find a job at one of the cafes. This is getting to be quite a town. Our G.I.'s love the German frauleins and Bavarian beer. You should see how many re-enlist if they can stay. We get a lot of deutschmarks for our dollar. Why don't you move here?" he asked.

Olga touched his hand. "You're such a great guy, John. But there's no housing for Germans. As long as I'm married to Lothar, I must live with him. And I can't get a divorce unless he agrees to it or sues for adultery. I'm stuck. It'll be another couple of years before new construction will accommodate the neediest families. But thanks for mentioning it."

He gazed into her face. "You turned into a real beauty, Olga. Your hair, those clothes. America did wonders for you, young lady. A Hollywood star in our midst. I'll be damned." He held her hand in a warm grip and gazed into her eyes longer than necessary. John was a good looking man of about thirty-five, tall and somewhat heavy-set. His uniform was always clean and his face freshly shaved. "You'd do great in America," he said.

"That's what I'd love. Let's see how things will work out. For the moment I need a job so that I can feed myself ..."

"Of course you can come and eat with us in the kitchen," he said. His smile told her that he would not mind having her around all the time.

John was right about the developments in Furstenfeldbruck. Among the bars, Olga found one that had class. She imagined officers frequenting it. She would talk to the owners as soon as she knew what her schedule at the NCO Club would be. Her new wardrobe would be too elaborate for a small town club. Perhaps she could move to Munich, and entertain with a sexy singer—American music, the swing and the lindy.

Move? Without accommodations? Not a chance.

The following day Olga took a train to Stuttgart.

Chapter 42

The train from Stuttgart took her to Ditzingen in twenty-five minutes. Olga found the church, half- timbered farm houses, and corner store Lucie had described. There was a grocers and bakery and dairy shops where women bought milk ladled into their milk cans. An ox, harnessed to a crude wagon, dragged his clumsy body on thick stubby legs, pulling a load of dung like a martyr. The farmer walked alongside, reins in hand, dreaming of a tractor. He would soon turn the gems he had acquired during the black market days into fulfilling his dreams.

"How do I get to the barracks?" Olga asked.

He scratched his head under the tattered cap, took the pipe from his yellow stained teeth and examined her curiously. "What would you be doing there?"

"Visiting a friend of mine. Am I going in the right direction?"

"You are." His large bulbous nose and big belly were signs of a drinker. "I'm going that way myself. Taking the dung to the field. Time for planting. We can walk together."

Olga had no time to keep him company. He walked at a snail's pace. "I'm in a hurry."

"What's your big rush?" he asked. The iron-shod wheels of the wagon ground against the asphalt and reminded Olga of her refugee days. A breeze blew the stench from the steaming dung toward them and whirled up some dead leaves. New ones had not come out yet.

"Ever heard of time is money?"

"I have. But I'm no American. Nature can't be rushed. Besides, patience is a virtue." He drew on his pipe and puffed out the smoke.

"I suppose," Olga said, ready to ask the woman crossing the street with a shopping tote and milk can for directions. She could not wait to see Lucie. "I must go."

"Young people are always in a hurry. Old Wilhelm will not keep you." He pointed down the farm-lined street. "Just keep going until you come to a bridge. You cross it, pass the mill and then the barn. There you'll see the barracks. Nothing to look at, that's for sure. Russian prisoners of war built them and lived there. Now they're used for refugees."

"I wished I had a place like that," Olga said. "I live in an attic."

"You don't say. "

She could tell that he admired her American coat and stylish hat. But her fine leather pumps were out of place in this village that didn't even have a sidewalk. People walked on the cobblestones. Olga was dressed for Ingo. Her heart throbbed. She just had to see him, tell him about America, and lure him away from Irmgard. Make him know what he was missing.

A creek turned the huge wheel of the mill—free power. The road beyond the old barn was not even paved at all, just dirt marked by ruts filled with water. The two story wooden barracks looked even grimmer under the low hanging clouds.

This was the home Lucie raved about because it afforded her some privacy. A far cry from the elegant villa in Poland where Olga had introduced Ingo to her friends. She blushed remembering the childish game she had played pretending Ingo had lost his way. That afternoon was still fresh in her memory. Gottfried was dead and Lucie left a widow living with her children in one of those disgraceful buildings. She had known that things would be bad, but how could she envision what would really happen to them? Better yet, that they had survived and adapted to a new world order. Olga more so than Lucie.

Climbing up the dirt steps, Olga watched a girl lift a heavy wet sheet from a bucket and pin it to a clothes line. Another flapped in the moist wind like a sail. Should it rain they would get wet again. The girl noticed Olga and watched her climb the long flight that led to the upper level. Suddenly she darted off. "Auntie Olga, auntie Olga," she cried, waving her arms as she raced down the steps.

"Nora?"

They hugged. "I can't believe you came. That you found us. Mama will be so happy to see you." She kissed Olga's cheek and clung to her as to a life saver. "You look like a movie star. Is that what people in

America look like? Your food packages saved our lives. Thank you, Auntie Olga. If only Papa… I miss him so. But come. I have no tears left." She pulled Olga's hand toward the building. "Is Anyna still in Switzerland? She's so lucky. Going to a fine school. I had to quit; Mama needs my help. I keep house for her and help with the children." Nora was as tall as Olga. The excitement had flushed her cheeks and her shining blue eyes expressed the joy of a young girl. She wore her hair in braids wrapped around her head. Both the washed-out cardigan and cotton skirt looked American made. They probably came from donations sent over by generous people.

"You have not changed much, Nora, except that you've grown up a bit. Some day you'll be a lovely young lady," Olga said, stroking her shoulder.

"You think so? I wish I were grown up. Then I could go to work and pay off our debts. It's so embarrassing going into the village hoping the merchants won't see you. But they usually do, and remind you that your mother owes them money." She took Olga's hand and pulled her up the rest of the stairs. "Let's not talk about that. I'd be glad if the boys would stop wetting their beds. It's a mess. But let's not talk about that either. Mami will be so happy to see you, and then you can talk about Litzmannstadt and how it all used to be when we lived on Skagerrack Street and Papa was still alive."

They reached the building, where young children played in the stairwell. The raw, squeaky stairs had been scrubbed and stood out against the dark stained walls. "Did you see Uncle Ingo?" Nora asked. "Mama said that he lives in Stuttgart. Remember how he let me ride on his knees? I liked him a lot."

At that time they had still believed in miracles. Faith was supposed to move mountains. It had not worked then, and Olga knew it would not work now, else she would be with Ingo.

"Sorry about the smell," Nora said on their way to the second story. "You get used to it. Our toilets go straight into the cesspool. In summer it gets pretty bad. Maggots come up and we have flies all over the place. But we have our own apartment. You can't imagine what it's like having two rooms in somebody else's home."

Oh yes she could, Olga thought as Nora opened the door to their apartment. Lucie's voice came through. Olga wished she had brought some food. But she had been so eager to come. How could she forget the pain of hunger?

"Look, Mami, who came to see us," Nora called out from the tiny ante-room, cluttered with coats and shoes.

"Olga!" Lucie cried out and ran toward her friend. "Can it be true? Olinka, my dear, dear friend. You came!" They held each other for a long time and wept.

"Auntie Olga, Auntie Olga," ten-year old Hans said. Four-year-old Dieter and six-year-old Heidi looked on, wondering what this was all about. Walter was still at school.

"I can't believe you came," Lucie said over and over again. "My old friends shun me as if I have the plague. Poverty is a curse that embarrasses people. They can't see that I'm dying for a kind word, a chance to talk about the past. I'm still the same person I was four years ago when Gottfried was still alive. Two years ago my mother passed away." She pulled a heavy, carved oak chair out for Olga. The long dining table occupied most of the room, with Lucie's blue sofa squeezed into one corner and a make-shift bed in the other. The hand-loomed rug covering the dark stained wall reminded Olga of Poland and she remembered the mahogany credenza.

"Frau Wittgenstein, who owns the castle, let me take the table and chairs," Lucie explained. "I smuggled the other pieces out of Saxony. That was quite an adventure, as you can imagine."

Olga was glad they would have time to share stories of the time since they had seen each other last. "They're too big for this place, but better than nothing and the only pieces left from my past. All our luggage was destroyed in an air raid on Vienna—it almost wiped us out too. But you know that. Your ordeal in Dresden must have been horrendous. Those carpet bombings take you straight to hell. Am I ever glad the war is over. We expected a somewhat better outcome, but at least it's over. If only Gottfried had survived." Tears welled up in Lucie eyes.

"I'll start a fire," Nora said quickly. "Make some tea. I'll ask Frau Hirt for milk and sugar." Hans cleared away his copybook and the children's clothes.

"Poverty is a curse, Olga," Lucie said. "But we're alive. I'll never take anything for granted again. I should have followed the Countess' advice and moved to Bavaria instead of Saxony. Who would have thought the Russians would get as far as Saxony and keep on going? How could we have been so naïve and think they would not take Germany? When I think of all those lies and our blind belief in them..."

"We believed what we wanted to believe," Olga said.

Lucie looked as attractive as ever. Slimmed down, her cheekbones were more pronounced. Her complexion had not suffered. Some crowsfeet had formed. She wore her gray sweater and dark skirt gracefully that distracted from their ill fit and signs of wear. Her vivacity and impulsive manners pulled Olga into her spell as they always had. "Tell me about America. About Ingo. Let's not waste time on Lothar. He's the same old creep, I'm sure. How is Anyna? I bet the Countess is still pulling her old tricks."

While Olga and Lucie traded stories, Nora shaved slivers off a piece of wood, carefully lit them with a match, and placed the burning kindling in the hearth, stacking twigs around it.

"Look, dear," Olga said. "Take this money and run to the store. I'm sure we could use some food for supper. Buy whatever you think we need for tonight and tomorrow. Sausages, noodles, vegetables, bread, butter, and two liters of milk for the children. We could probably use some tea, right Lucie?" She pulled thirty marks from her purse. "Will that cover it?"

"I'll go with Nora," Hans offered, and slipped into his tight jacket. He had grown so much since Olga had seen him last." He picked up a shopping tote, a net and the milk can. Olga noticed Gottfried's features in the boy's oval face.

"Olga, you're such a dear for helping us out. I'm embarrassed that I can't receive you properly. But I see that you understand," Lucie said, blushing.

"You helped me out and now it's my turn to reciprocate. Hurry, children. We'll look after the fire."

After the children left, Lucie told Olga how she had smuggled her furniture out of the Russian Zone with the help of her brother-in-law. "To think that I had furniture for several rooms, beds, mattresses and linens. I didn't dare mention anything. At least I have this. Living off alms is so humiliating." She blew her nose. "How are things with Ingo?"

Olga shrugged. "The same. I haven't seen him for almost a year. Do you suppose you and I." She gazed in Lucie's deep blue eyes. "That we could get in touch with him."

Lucie jumped up. "Of course we can." The prospect of adventure brought her back to the days when she had played games, flirted and teased. "Why not visit him at the plant? Or call him and make a date? Meet him at the Hindenburgbau, a lovely café right across from the station. I bet he can't wait to see you. He loves you, for life. He's that kind of a man. Most of them have short memories. All they want is sex. I'm a widow, I know. You should hear some of the propositions I get. With the shortage of men, they can take their pick. My being penniless and living in the slums, nor being the mother of five seems to cool their desire." She chuckled. Olga admired her friend who had not lost her spark. Her charm and sex appeal had not diminished. No wonder Gottfried fell for her. Lucie was irresistible. Her smile was genuine and exuberant, like that of a child. Her sadness was forgotten. Olga caught the spark and could not wait to lure Ingo to a meeting place. Irmgard was no obstacle.

Lucie's young daughter Heidi leaned against her mother's lap. Little Dieter watched Olga tend the fire, stoking it carefully before putting a piece of wood on top. Once the flames flared up again, she put the kettle on.

"You can find some crumbs of tea on the top shelf in that tin box," Lucie said, pointing at two shelves that housed their dishes and mugs. "It's the end of the month and I'm out of everything. My widow's pension and my job don't cover the essentials. Somehow there's always something good coming my way, like your visit now." The answer to a prayer I hadn't bothered saying." Lucie was her old self.

As soon as Nora and Hans returned with bags of food they spread their treasures out on the table for everybody to admire. While she prepared the supper, the others nibbled on cheese and bread Olga cut from the hunk. She remember her hunger pangs.

The meal turned into a feast with laughter and anecdotes of life in the slums. "That was so good," Hans said, looking around for more.

Lucie said, "That's it for today. Thank Tante Olga for the treat."

While the children did the dishes in a pan Olga felt the joy of a benefactress, excited by the prospect of seeing Ingo tomorrow.

"I'll call him," Lucie said, leaning back into the chair. "They don't like personal calls, but we can tell them that an important visitor came from America."

Olga laughed. "But we have no visitors from America."

"What about you? No one in her right mind would stay with a creep like Lothar and share a room with the Countess when you have other choices. Just promise me that when you return, you'll remember me and find me a sponsor. I signed up for the refugee program—something is bound to come through. I'll take the children and go at the bat of an eye. Walter is almost seventeen, practically an adult. Nora will do fine no matter what, and the younger ones will go to school. I know there'll be a man for me. My friends will help, but I need a sponsor."

That night, Olga felt like a teenager at a sleepover. She and Lucie shared their experiences from the war, going back to memories of their childhood in Riga, and making plans for their future.

"I don't know what I'll do once I'm back in Los Angeles. Ben Hanley is a kind man, he promised to help."

"We all need a springboard. Ben Hanley is yours. Do find one for me. Widowhood is a lonely place. Sometimes I'm so lonely I could die. I don't belong to the expelled. They're coming by the millions and now organize themselves politically. They even formed the Refugee Party. The locals look at me as an intruder. How can I teach my children some manners when all they see is uncouth behavior and hear swear words I can't even repeat. Still, I'm grateful to have my own place rather than share an apartment with a woman who hates my presence."

Thinking of Frau Maier Olga could not agree more.

"1946 was my lowest point," Lucie continued. "Homeless in the midst of winter among the Stuttgart ruins. If it had not been for a nun who found me at the edge of a bridge, I guess, I wouldn't be here now. She took us to their mission, found foster homes for the children and admitted me to a hospital."

Olga had tears in her eyes. What were her problems compared to Lucie's? Anyna had been sick and starved, but they had always had a roof over their heads.

"Little Dieter was taken to an orphanage." Lucie choked with tears in her eyes. She could not go on.

"What happened at the orphanage?" Olga asked, sipping her tea. The children sat around the table, listening.

"He was dying," Nora said. "After Mama told me where he was I went there. I was staying with three sisters in a lovely house. They let me visit Mom and the baby. They gave me the streetcar fare." Lucie covered her face with her cracked hands.

"Dieter was two," Lucie said.

"When I saw him in that big cold hall he didn't recognize me," Nora said. "He just stared at me. His face was as white as the plate here. I didn't know what to say except, 'I'll come for you soon.' Finally he'd let me hold him." She put the little boy on her lap and rocked him. "But I couldn't take him anywhere. Mom was in the hospital. I told her that Dieter would die if she did not take him. The way he clung to the nurse when I left and she'd kick him away. That was so bad." Olga stroked the girl's shoulder. She had lived through the pain of watching her child suffer from starvation, but Ingo had provided for them. It had never occurred to her how much she owed him. If he could not be with her now, it was because he felt that same sense of obligation to the mother of his child.

"When Nora visited me again," Lucie continued in a thick voice, leaning against the table as if she could not hold up under the burden of her pain, "she was so upset she couldn't talk.

"I told Mom that we had to get Dieter out before he died."

Lucie nodded. "I was still too sick to be released from the hospital. Nora got my clothes so that I could dress in the washroom. The woman at the reception desk was busy and didn't see us sneak out. Nora knew the way. We took the tram to the orphanage, and got there before visiting hours were up."

Olga was afraid to hear the rest, then remembered that Dieter was right there, playing with his spoon. He had recovered and did not even remember the ordeal.

"A hard and tired nurse brought him to what used to be a bunker. When I saw my baby, I thought my heart would break. His white face was a deathmask. He had given up. I held him like a ragdoll. There was no time to waste. I ran off."

"I told Mom that we could go to the Weber's," Nora butted in. "The family that took in Heidi. The man was a doctor."

"Imagine the relief when they let us stay," Lucie recalled. "Better yet. They helped the best they could, insisting that Dieter must feel me at all times in order to get over the trauma. We fed and diapered him for three days until I noticed him stir. His 'Mami' was like a blessing from heaven. He was saved." Tears glistened in Lucie's eyes, tears of joy and gratitude. "The Housing Authority found us a room in a castle. That's how I came to Ditzingen. Eventually I got this place and could bring the other children home."

Olga and Lucie embraced. They had each other again. The children talked about the families they had stayed with until they were ordered to bed.

The following morning, Olga and Lucie walked to the Post Office, where an operator connected them with the Daimler Benz plant in Unterturkheim. Once they got through to Ingo, he agreed to meet them at the Hindenburgbau. Olga was beside herself with joy. The day took forever despite Lucie's lively company. They admired the displays in the recently opened shops, and ate liver-dumpling soup for lunch. The hands on the clocktower simply did not move. Some people rode motorized bicycles or the new Italian Vespa motor-scooters. The sun came out and softening the jagged ruins of Stuttgart.

While strolling through a new department store, Lucie told Olga how she had convinced the commanding officer of a train for wounded to take her and the children along, and Olga shared her recollections of the firestorm in Dresden, how she had met Gottfried in the bunker, and how he had saved her from burning to death.

"Are you sure he died right away?" Lucie kept asking. "That he did not fall into the hands of the Russians? I miss him so. My heart breaks every time I see a returnee. Why couldn't he be among them, safe in the hands of Americans or Brits? Destiny dealt me a bloody hand." She admired a negligee, as if she wanted Gottfried to see her in it.

They stopped at the café in the basement and ordered coffee with whipped cream.

Olga sprinkled sugar on top of hers. "After I met Ingo, I pretended that I played for him. With him in my heart, I feel strong and talented, ready to take on anything. It's amazing how much he influences me. When Lothar was in one of his moods, I thought of Ingo, how it would be if he were with me. From that moment on the music would take off." She licked the sweet cream from her spoon.

"We'll see him quite soon," Lucie reminded Olga, as if she needed reminding. Whenever she checked her watch it was as if time stood still.

"Gottfried was so worried that you would not make it with all those children," Olga said, sipping her coffee. "He asked me to help you, as if I could. Instead you are helping me."

Back in the street, Olga saw a yellow streetcar pass. It had Degerloch written in the little box indicating its destination.

Lucie headed for the station, wearing Olga's lipstick and her silk shawl. She talked about the recent developments in Germany while glancing at the window displays they passed. The new government under Chancellor Adenauer had received its first loan under the Marshall Plan. Factories were refurbished and slowly resuming production. The Federal Republic of Germany, as West Germany was now called, had more jobs than men to fill them.

The big station clock across the street of the Hindenburgbau finally showed six o'clock. Olga appreciated the warm and cozy dining room of the restaurant, which had been set up like a Hungarian village inn. Braids of garlic, onions, and dried paprika hung over red, white, and green rugs. The waitresses wore Hungarian costumes and head-dresses.

"Just the place we need for a romantic reunion," Lucie said, choosing a table in the far corner. "Don't you love the smell of Hungarian goulash? Thank you, Olinka, for including me in your tryst. Look, I think the Gypsy violins are about to play."

Olga ordered wine and cheese. "We are waiting for a friend," she told the waitress.

After finishing her *viertele* of wine, Olga relaxed, glad that Lucie was doing all the talking. The minutes dragged on. When would he come, and what should she say? How should she receive him—fall into his arms or play it cool? She ordered another *viertele*. "That'll get us warmed up for the great event," she explained, watching the door.

"Ingo!" she whispered when she saw him enter, searching for her. She was so excited, her cheeks burning, that she was afraid she would faint. His trench coat was open and he carried his hat and a briefcase.

Lucie waved. Waving back, he sidled toward their table. Olga jumped up and fell into his arms. "Ingo!" she whispered. "I can't believe you're here."

"I wouldn't miss seeing you for anything. I had hoped you might show up." The Gypsy trio played a czardas. Olga sank into his embrace. Her body vibrated with love and desire. His touch still had the magic she remembered. Now it was real, only they were not alone to cherish this moment. "Ingo," she whispered, "Ingo." They were one again.

"Olychka!"

"I dream of this meeting every day."

With one arm around Olga, he greeted Lucie. "How good of you to bring Olga to me. Who would have thought that we would meet here in Stuttgart of all places? A long ways and a lifetime away from Poland."

The waitress took his coat and his order for a viertele.

"When I got your message I thought I was dreaming," he said. "Did you come all the way from Bavaria?" Their superficial banter hid their desire. *Your soul and mine never parted*, Olga read between the lines. *You are always with me.*

I cannot live without you, Ingo, Olga's eyes told him. Her smile and laughter tempted. Together, at last. She had not felt so alive and happy since they had parted last summer.

Lucie suggested zigeuner schnitzel with potato salad.

"I am now on a full salary," he said. "Finished my apprenticeship with flying colors. I'm working in the export department. Orders keep coming in from all over the world. We finally have real production going. My boss, Herr Pfeiffer, has been with the company for forty years and tells us 'greenhorns' what an honor it is to work for Daimler Benz. People can't wait to get new this and that. I'm fortunate that the Haberles didn't lose anything in the war. Some people were lucky. The rest of us concentrate on the future. What do you say, Olga?" He squeezed her hand and kissed it while the waitress placed sizzling schnitzels on the table.

"Why don't you bring us a bottle of Unterturkheimer red?" he told the waitress, then turned to Olga. I met some of our local vintners who understand the art of winemaking. I've learned so much since I came here."

Olga could tell that he was well cared for, and wondered what she should say about her plans for the future. Should she hint that she hoped he would be part of them? "I'll emigrate to America," she said, cutting off a piece of juicy meat to avoid his eyes. There was no hiding anything from him. He knew her like nobody else. "I want to be free. Allow Anyna to chose her own life and profession. Father will guide us."

Ingo nodded. Would he miss her and join her some day? "Daimler Benz might open a sales office in Hollywood," she tempted.

"I wouldn't be surprised. We have more orders from America than we can fill."

"You'd love Los Angeles."

"Fritzle," he said, before Olga could dwell on her dreams. "-is a sweet boy. Very shy. Irmgard is too strict with him, like my mother used to be. Ingrid knew how to get her way. I am glad Renate is keeping an eye on things. She's Irmgard's mother. You couldn't imagine a nicer, more understanding woman. We are very good friends." He seemed to like his mother-in-law more than his wife. How could that be?

"How is Anyna, our artist? She is so talented."

"And very fond of you, Ingo."

"Likewise," he said, cutting off some meat. His slender hands handled the knife and fork as skillfully as if he were performing a ritual. Everything was right, if not for the question: where do we go from here? At least they could exchange letters and see each other from time to time until she left for America.

Lucie was thrilled to be away from the barracks and the stench of poverty. She sparkled with anecdotes. Sipping the mellow Unterturkheimer wine, Olga and Ingo laughed and laughed, not so much over Lucie's splendidly reenacted tales, but their own happiness. The pain of waiting rewarded them with a deep sense of knowing the answer. Ingo kissed Olga's cheek and rubbed his knee against hers. The power of their love was more evident than ever. Ingo was her life. He captivated her every thought, every wish, every dream.

Lucie excused herself and left.

"Did you feel me playing for you, Ingo?" Olga asked. "My success in America was because of you. My music is filled with my love for you. Remember that night when you first asked for the Mephisto Waltz? My fingers took off and played. That's what happened in America. Even

Lothar and the band were affected by it. When it didn't come off, we were in a bind." She gazed into his eyes and saw his desire for her. "With music in my heart, I can feel you inside of me. My senses rise above the notes and guide my fingers. When it happened, people went wild. At first Lothar got upset, but then he went along." She leaned her cheek against his warm hand. "You are all I have, all I care for, all I need and want. Without you I wander about in darkness. I know I shouldn't have come, but I just had to see you and remind myself that you exist. Irmgard must understand."

"She tries. It's not a good situation. We have Fritzle. He needs me."

"But you will consider it, right?"

He put his finger on her lips. "Say no more, my love. There is nothing I would rather do. It was stupid of me to say that we must not meet. I can't live without you. I'll look forward to your letters. Anticipating them will lift my days."

Tears crept into Olga's eyes. She took a long sip of wine. He was here, holding her hand. They would be together. Some day they would find a safe harbor and set anchor.

"I feel Father's blessing," he said.

She received his kiss with the innocence of first love. "We must be free of the obstacles that keep us away from each other. Father can't do that for us."

He raised his glass. "We'll make it happen."

Olga's heart swelled with a happiness she had not felt for a long, long time. Hope had returned. Yes. He had said yes. They would find a way.

Lucie returned. "Let's drink to love. I would go to the end of the world to find Gottfried. But he is gone forever. This is such a special evening. Seeing you together brings back so many memories of the days when I was as happy as you. I married the man I loved, and bore his children. He lives on in them." She emptied her glass. "I must go to America, get away from my memories and my life as a war widow. I want to start fresh."

Olga couldn't agree more. Returning to Inning, she was determined to make her dream come true.

Chapter 44

Spring had finally returned, spreading its lush green over the countryside. The meadow behind the farm was dotted with bright yellow buttercups and white daisies. Olga wanted to see Frau Moser before going to Furstenfeldbruck and practice. The NCOs felt honored that she entertained them. Little did they know how much she depended on their pay, most of which she saved to bring Anyna home.

Her friend must have seen Olga coming. "I got a letter from him," she shouted from the open window, waving an envelope. Her last tooth had fallen out. She hated her dentures.

Olga darted across the cobblestones, hugged the bony old woman and took the letter. "Thank you so much, my dear, dear Frau Moser."

"Easy, easy. I'm an old lady, Olga. You mustn't forget that."

"Old? Nonsense." Olga tugged playfully at Frau Moser's sleeve "You're so good to me. I don't know what I would've done without you, just died of loneliness, I guess."

Embarrassed, Frau Moser withdrew from Olga's embrace. "I never knew a woman like you, Olga. You take charge of your life and don't care what anybody thinks."

"I wish it were true. I always feel guilty, but that doesn't get me anywhere. So I ignore it, and do what I know I must. You've got to fight for your freedom."

"I wouldn't bother. But then, I'm old and this is my home."

"You are very fortunate, Frau Moser. I must find one, and that isn't easy." Olga kissed the envelope before running her finger under the flap.

"I should have stayed in Stuttgart," Frau Moser said while Olga pulled out the letter. "I already told you that I loved a man from the city." She chewed on a cracked fingernail. "No point crying over what can't be changed."

Olga sat down on the sun-warmed bench.

"While you read your letter, I'll get some cider and streuselkuchen," Frau Moser said. "Still warm. Jakob finally fixed the draft. The streusel turned out nice and crisp."

Olga's glance caressed the familiar handwriting. Back in Poland every letter had meant that he was still alive. Now it was a message of love.

> *Olychka, my one and only love,*
>
> *I am yours, despite the distance that separates us. For the moment I see no compromise. Fritzle is my little son. I can't make him another victim of this war. He needs his father. You should see him run toward me when I come home. He is such a sweet child. You would love him too, except that he is the reason for our separation. Please understand that for the moment I cannot leave him, though Irmgard would not miss me. Unfortunately, in a divorce the law would not let me have the child. I have inquired.*
>
> *We must believe in the future. Have you read the cards lately? I'm dying to hear what's in store for us. Wouldn't it be nice to know that we could count on another miracle? In the meantime I must fulfill my obligation. Please write. Your letters are a blessing from Heaven.*

Olga choked down the lump in her throat, watching a dark cloud roll in from the Alps, quickly blocking out the sun and blue sky. A cold wind came up, and whirled loose bits of straw over the cobblestones. Spring was fickle, like the promise of love. Only the steaming dung heap stood its ground, winter and summer.

He was doing the right thing, of course. If it only didn't hurt so. Another blow. Another disappointment. She was too vulnerable, too prone to feel sorry for herself. Father had promised, but the time was not right. Anyna was still in Switzerland and Olga's life had not changed.

A cold chill ran through her body and raised gooseflesh on her bare arms. Her summer had not yet come. Father would not change the conditions to make things easier for her. "Be merciful, Father. I am doing the best I can. Give me a sign of hope. Lift me from the darkness of my disappointment."

A flock of swallows circled the farmyard. Fat brown hens clucked, scraping for worms and stray grains. Some day Ingo would come to her, and until then, Olga would live for that moment. Frau Moser was right:

there was no point in crying over what cannot be changed. The miracle she had prayed for had come true—Ingo was alive and loved her.

Frau Moser brought the old earthenware pitcher and two pieces of freshly baked cake out. "I guess Ingo can't leave his son," she said, as if she had read the letter. "Imagine somebody taking Anyna away from you." She had lost two sons in the war. Her daughter Ellie was a war widow with two daughters. Frau Moser accepted her loss. Nobody knew about her tears.

The alcohol, warm cake with its crunchy cinnamon streusel, and Frau Moser's empathy eased Olga's pain. She no longer felt cold, though her California-style summer dress was not warm enough for the cloudy day. As soon as she got back to the keyboard, she would forget her pain and concentrate on the pieces she would play in America. Ben Hanley had assured her that he would take them back. She would send a telegram to Whitney and get him to arrange a tour.

Nearby, Jakob sawed a log into foot-long pieces he would split later for firewood. Olga watched the rhythmic back and forth of the saw biting into the log. The dust falling to the ground had formed a mound underneath. She loved the fresh smell. The cat curled up on the straw ignored the black dog sniffing at her. After surviving Armageddon, Olga was grateful to be living in peace.

The fast moving clouds changed their patterns. One resembled Ingo's face. It had a big plume shooting from his head, then it drifted apart. He was here, looking over the snow-capped peaks of the Alps, the farm houses, and the passing women on bicycles.

"I am in your hands, Father."

Frau Moser sat down on the bench, her head wrapped in a black shawl that framed her wizened face. Olga touched the gnarled hand. "It's so good to be here with you, Frau Moser. You are my home. Thank you for the cake. You're right about Ingo's son. Children need their parents. I need Anyna. My life is empty without her." She put the mug on the empty plate. "If I had to chose between Ingo and Anyna, I suppose I also would chose Anyna. It's a choice I don't want to think about. She'll come home next month. I can't wait to see her." She hugged Frau Moser impulsively and got up.

"I'm sure it will all work out," Frau Moser said, crossing her arms against the cold wind. She would never understand why anybody would want to leave this beautiful place, with its majestic mountains, picturesque knolls, and lush meadows.

A week later, Whitney's contract arrived. He had booked them for a four-week engagement with Buddy Jones and for six weeks with Ben Hanley. Secretly, Hanley had sent her an affidavit for an emigration visa. Lothar would get a regular business visa, based on his contract.

At the American Consulate in Munich, Olga testified that she didn't have tuberculosis or any other communicable disease. She had not been affiliated with the Nazi or the Communist parties, nor had she ever worked as a prostitute. She was not pregnant, nor did she have a criminal record. Her blood test was negative and the doctor couldn't find anything wrong with her. She received her visa.

Lothar's "Catacomb" composition hadn't found a publisher. The heavy-handed and dissonant score of "Life in an Ice Age," was unbearable. "What do those idiots know about true art?" he said, looking up from the keyboard. "I bet American editors will appreciate the novelty of my work." He had written the piece for piano and violin. Olga had had no part in his composition and vanished whenever he pounded out the notes in an expression of his deep-seated anger and frustration.

Olga practiced Gershwin and Cole Porter, along with the tunes Ben Hanley had asked them to work on. As part of her morning routine, she took long walks. Lake Ammersee reminded her of the lake in Wunsdorf, and the hours she had spent with Gottfried. The wounded men at the hospital popped up in her mind, but the pain was gone. Instead, she admired the peaceful body of water reflecting the sky in shimmering silver. A ferry docked at the pier. People got off, others on.

Ingo enjoyed selling shining new Mercedes cars to happy buyers.

Olga hummed "Fernando's Hideaway", which Ben Hanley had asked her to study. The Cuban Xavier Cugat was all the rage in America and Hanley wanted to get on the bandwagon. At the base, Sgt. Ford had his records, and let her listen to them to get a feel for the rhythm of the catchy melodies.

"Did you hear from your sister Ottie?" Frau Moser asked when Olga stopped by the garden where she was planting tomatoes and cucumber seedlings. "She'd better get away from the Russians before they close the borders for good."

Olga nodded. "I keep telling her that. Actually, the borders are closed. She's still waiting for her husband. They didn't have much of a relationship, but she's lonely. The Russians are still holding their prisoners. Adenauer negotiates their release. I'm worried—the Russians are building up their forces. It's not a good sign. If they invade us, will the Americans stop them? Their air lift defended Berlin…"

Frau Moser had no sense of the threat. Inning had survived two major wars without a scratch, other than the loss of some men. "The Russians take whatever they can get their hands on, especially foodstuffs," Olga said. "I'm surprised anybody in their zone is still alive. Ottie survives on my packages. She trades some things for fresh milk and eggs. Nobody can survive that way forever. I know what it's like." She pulled a photo from her purse and showed it to Frau Moser; her emaciated sister was almost unrecognizable.

"Doesn't look like you at all," Frau Moser said, returning it.

"We're very different. Never got along."

Frau Moser pulled a thistle from the ground.

"Anyna will come home in a week," Olga said. "I miss her so much."

The third of July was a Thursday. Olga stood on the platform of the Munich station, watching other people crane their necks in the direction the train from Switzerland would come from. There it was. The huge black engine hissed and puffed, releasing steam as it came to a stop. Anyna jumped from the first class car and ran toward Olga. They landed in each other's arms and danced around in a stormy embrace. "You're back, you're back!"

"Yes, Mami. Yes. And I'll stay with you." The words Olga had longed for were like music to her ears, ending long months of loneliness. Passengers passed with a smile. Family reunions always touched people, reminding them of loved ones they longed for. Every family had members missing or killed in the war.

Olga greeted Adie, the slender, elegant woman she had come to admire. She had the von Schenck flair without their arrogance. Yet, when Olga saw the tenderness Adie shared with Anyna, she felt jealous. How unfair it all was.

"Thank you for looking after my child," she said in a somewhat frosty tone.

"She was the joy of our lives. I am so grateful to you for letting us have her. You would do us a great favor if you would let her come and stay with us whenever possible. We became a family."

Jealousy crept through Olga. "We are going ..." She caught herself before she mentioned America. "I mean, we should be going. It's quite a ways to Inning, as you may know. I've reserved a room for you at the local guesthouse."

"How kind of you, Olga. I'm so fond of you, and can't wait to see Lothar and my dear Aunt Friederike. Is she still so high and mighty?" Adie signaled a baggage handler to take their luggage. "Take us to the taxi stand."

"Taxi stand? You can't take a taxi all the way to Inning."

"And why not?" Adie asked, as if it were perfectly natural.

Olga understood. Not only did Adie get a bundle of Deutschmarks for her Swiss franks, she had plenty of the latter. There were people who had kept their fortune, even profited from the war others had fought, like the Swiss and the Swedes. Richard and Adie had it all. How would Anyna adapt to Olga's less than adequate circumstances? Sleeping surrounded by rubbish in an attic that smelled of moth balls and dust? Her little princess wore a white linen coat and matching bonnet. She had narrow straps on her shoes and carried a pink purse. Her face had all the sweetness of her character, as well as the sophistication of the von Schencks. Those dark eyes, the broad mouth, and fine nose were not classic, but unique in their pronounced self-assurance. It was Adie's work, and that of the private school she had attended. How would this young lady fare in America?

Adie did not care that the taxi driver insisted on charging her for the return trip, amazed by the long ride he was about to undertake. "And I must get some gas. I don't think there are any stations out in the country. As far as I know, people there still use their horses or ride bicycles." He was a young refugee, and spoke in an unfamiliar dialect.

"Naturally," Adie said. "Just load up our baggage and let's go. Ammersee is not at the end of the world."

"Pretty near," the driver said, and bowed before he opened the doors for them.

Talking about their lives in Switzerland Adie barely noticed the ruined capitol of Bavaria. Anyna talked about her art classes and that she studied music and knew how to fish. "Onkel Richard loves math like Papa, but he doesn't play music. Tante Adie does."

"It's in our blood," she said. They reached the outskirts of the city, which had not been bombed. The open countryside with blooming meadows and undulating wheat, rye, and oat fields darkened with the setting sun. They passed gentle hills and quaint Bavarian villages, grazing cattle and the occasional horse-drawn wagon. Tall pines cast long shadows across the empty road.

"With Anyna around," Adie reported, "we discovered the world we live in. She got us in touch with the education system. We had meetings with her teachers, and learned of the problems in our schools. Anyna had more questions than either I or Richard could answer. You wouldn't believe how often we pulled out our encyclopedia and discovered new facts. We visited museums, climbed mountains, and attended concerts. Theater and movies became part of our lives. Anyna was like a fresh breeze in our musty winter air." Adie sighed behind the veil of her white hat. "We'll miss you, Anyna."

The child, sitting in the front seat, turned around and smiled. "I'll miss you too, Tante Adie."

Anyna did not mean it, Olga was sure of that. She was merely being polite.

Adie had no idea what deprivation or pain meant, what it was like being separated from her child while living with a husband who tortured and despised her.

"Why don't you adopt one of the many orphans left by the war? A child who deserves a home and parents? Anyna and I were fortunate. We survived, and thanks to your help, Anyna was healed and is now educated. Without your care she would have died. You are the perfect mother and Richard needs a child."

They passed Lake Starnberg shimmering in the mellow light of the setting sun.

"Did you hear from Uncle Ingo?" Anyna asked.

Olga did not know how much to reveal it in Adie's presence. "He lives in Stuttgart now. He is married and has a son. Fritzle." What a stupid name, she thought.

"Fritzle," Anyna said. "How sweet. I'd love to meet him. He's like a brother to me."

Adie did not react, and Olga quickly changed the subject. "We could visit Tante Lucie and her children. She also lives in Stuttgart now." Olga told Adie of her friendship with Gottfried and Lucie, going back to their youth in Riga. Sometimes she wondered whether there had ever been a Riga in her life, or a Litzmannstadt.

Anyna said no more, as if she sensed that it was not a subject her mother cared to talk about. With Uncle Ingo married, she could probably see that things were not the way she had expected them to be. Only when they were finally alone, after politely greeting her father and grandmother, did she say, "Uncle Ingo said I'm his special girl."

"Of course you are."

"Then why did he get married to somebody else?"

"Because I am not free to marry him."

Anyna did not like that answer. "He promised he would come home to us."

"You have a daddy, Anyna. Uncle Ingo is our friend."

Adie stayed two days, and then ordered a taxi to take her back to Munich.

"I've been thinking about your suggestion, Olga. You're right; we would enjoy a child. I will get in touch with Caritas and see whether they can help me. I'll let you know."

The driver held the door open.

Adie embraced Olga, then Lothar, and finally Anyna. The Countess did not come out. "Be sure to stay in touch while you're in America. I'll be grateful for a visit, my little love."

As soon as the taxi left, Lothar returned to the house.

Frau Moser waved Olga over and Anyna ran ahead.

"I've got something for you," Frau Moser said. "Look!" She pulled an envelope from the pocket of her wide, heavy woolen skirt. And here is something for my favorite little girl." She had a dish of chocolate pudding waiting for Anyna. "I'm so glad you're back, and prettier than ever."

Anyna enjoyed her pudding while Olga read Ingo's letter.

...I am quite concerned about Fritzle. He is a sensitive, lovable boy who needs affection and care. Irmgard scolds and punishes him constantly. Watching her destroy

my sweet boy makes me sick. She insists on mindless obedience and punishes the child for my objections. She acts as if he is not hers, but an unwanted intruder in her life. I wouldn't mention this to you if I were not so upset. She is his mother. What can I do? The company has more orders than they can fill, which means long hours at the office. I barely see Fritzle. She has him in bed when I come home, and will not let me kiss him good-night. What does she want?

My darling Olychka, I need your love more than ever.

Anyna finished her pudding and licked the spoon clean. "What does he say?"

"That he loves us very much and wishes he could be with us."

Frau Moser put her hand on Olga's bare arm. "The news is not too good, is it?"

"He is finding out what it is like to live with a partner one doesn't love."

"Make the best of it, is all I can say."

Olga shrugged. "Easier said than done."

At the room, Olga fried potatoes and onion with bacon while the Countess complained to Anyna about the cold draft that came in every time Olga opened the door.

Lara stopped by with her baby. Jimmy Chu had not married her, but was obliged to send child support after Lara had filed a demand with his commanding officer. Aldrich sent an occasional gift. Lara didn't mention what he wrote in his infrequent letters.

Olga now had two burners, so she could prepare tea and fry potatoes. Their income, along with the Countess' pension and Olga's free lunches, allowed them to live modestly. The housing situation had not improved. New housing was under construction, but would go to the most needy families. Refugees still kept coming in from the Russian Zone. The crossing was exceedingly dangerous; the Russian terror machine kept on grinding up its victims, a category that had expanded to include anybody they suspected of disloyalty.

Lucie had been paid ten percent of Gottfried's life insurance, and had settled her debts. Now the money was gone. She had found a job in an American snack bar, where she washed dishes and cleared tables. Whenever she wrote, she asked about America. She desperately wanted to leave, and hoped to be accepted to a program that took ethnic German refugees.

Olga wondered whether Ingo's supporting her plans to emigrate to America meant he might join her some day, or if he was glad she would no longer interfere in his life.

Lothar sat at the piano, repeating a phrase over and over again, then marking it in his notebook.

Lara sipped tea. "I need a nanny, Maman. Little James is a handful. I can't spend my life changing his diapers. Think about my face, my figure. You can't expect me to stay home and miss my chance of meeting somebody with substance."

"You should have thought of that before," Lothar remarked icily. "Who'll take you with a Chinese bastard?"

"Why don't you shut up, Lothar?" Lara blurted out. "I'm so sick and tired of your stupid comments. You act as if the world should bow to you. I'll never know how Olga puts up with it."

Olga's ears perked up. Nobody in that family had ever come to her support.

"You know, Lara," he said, playing one of his painfully dissonant measures, "you don't deserve a title. You act like a high class whore."

"I said, shut up, Lothar," she screeched. "Did you hear that, Maman? And you always protect him, the high and mighty good-for-nothing baron." Frightened by the scene, the baby cried.

"With fresh troops arriving, there should be plenty of opportunities for you, Lara. There will be other Chinese who'd be flattered to take over ..."

Lara jumped up, grabbed Little Jimmy, and headed for the door. "Lothar, you make me sick." Her beauty turned monstrous. Olga empathized with Lara. She was in a worse mess than Olga had been years ago when she found herself pregnant with Anyna. Her bastard was of mixed race.

Lara slammed the door.

Olga turned to the sizzling potatoes as though she had not witnessed the scene.

Anyna looked up from her drawing. "Mme. Bretin hung my pictures on the wall for everybody to see," she said in a Swiss accent. "She said, I should become an artist."

"Did she really?" Lothar teased. "That isn't much of a profession. You should become a teacher or find yourself a nobleman. Just don't pay any attention to Aunt Lara. She is the misfit in the family!"

"Lothar!" the Countess fumed. "That is enough! Don't you dare tell Anna Magdalena such things about her aunt. She is doing her best under trying circumstances. We don't get to go to America and break up contracts because we don't feel like finishing a job. I still can't believe you did it. Terribly childish, you know."

Lothar chuckled sarcastically, but made no comment.

Three days later Olga's visa for the Unites States arrived in the mail.

Chapter 43

The weeks in New York City were more pleasant than Olga could have hoped. Lothar behaved like a gentleman and did not insist that Buddy play his "Ice Age" or "Catacomb" compositions. From the time the Countess had told him that she needed his income more than his presence, he valued his job. Buddy and his musicians enjoyed Olga's arrangements of pop tunes, especially her "I Got You under my Skin", which she performed as a solo. The audience loved her flair, and adored the petite blonde woman running her fingers up and down the keyboard. Her passionate performances created the romantic mood they came for. Lovers, would be lovers, couples, and even those celebrating their fiftieth anniversaries danced to her music. Merriweather, the man who had danced with her whenever he had an opportunity during Olga's previous engagement, showed up frequently with his mother and danced with Olga between performances. By now she was a natural in the role of the sophisticated baroness who lived in a Bavarian castle. What difference did it make whether he believed it or not as long as he enjoyed her and and her music? Her being married seemed to add to the attraction.

Though the German Baron and Baroness were no longer a novelty, they had name-recognition and a reputation as serious musicians. Fashions had changed along with the music. Mid-calf skirts had been replaced by knee-length ones, and ruffled blouses were de rigueur. Olga could wear anything, but preferred slinky gowns with low-cut backs. Glittering rhinestones and ostrich feathers in her hair, as well as a tempting slit showing off her slender legs, were show-stoppers. The audience watched her leg peeking from the slit as much as they watched her fingers bounce over the keyboard. She suffered from the hot and humid summer weather, the airthick with cigarette smoke, but pretended she was fine.

Olga was glad when they left New York, and hoped they'd find fresh air in California. Their farewell concert brought a standing ovation. Buddy and his daughter Trish accompanied Anyna and her parents to the airport. The two girls had become friends. Anyna had spent most of her time on Long Island at Buddy's beach home. "I'll write," they promised.

"Do come and visit us in Los Angeles," Anyna said in parting.

During the long flight, Lothar talked about Buddy Jones. He's quite an artist," he said, while they enjoyed a filet mignon. "Buddy is a good musician who knows that the big band era is coming to an end. I bet Maman would enjoy living in the Hamptons."

The thought did not sit well with Olga. All she needed now was her mother-in-law, when she had worked so hard to get away from her. "I don't think she's up to such a long trip. Without a Mr. McCormick courting her, she'd be rather lonely, wouldn't you say? The world she remembers no longer exists for her."

Lothar did not hear the insincerity in her laughter. Over a glass of burgundy, they admired the sun-baked desert below. Some day, Olga thought, she and Ingo would drive across this vast country and explore it. Ingo.

My sweet Ingo, I was so naïve to believe that some miracle weapon could save Germany.

With her eyes closed, she imagined the rickety table under the blooming chestnut tree, their passionate greeting, the unforgettable night. For once she had been in charge, had had the means to make things happen. From now on she would not be afraid. Never again would she let others dictate her life. Father would guide her to Ingo as soon as she was free.

"Ingo," she whispered. A sudden turbulence caught the plane and shook it with a mighty force. Father was with her again.

Ben Hanley awaited them in his white and green Buick. The shining chrome gleamed in the bright sunlight. He looked dapper in his colorful sport shirt and tan slacks. Olga returned his warm embrace. "It's so good to be back," she said, enjoying the fresh scent of his after-shave.

"Finally," he whispered into her ear, while Lothar loaded their luggage into the trunk. "So glad you came back."

Olga smiled, touched by his affection. She longed for acceptance and friendship. His admiration could open the door to her future.

Helping her into the back seat, he held her hand, then lifted her legs inside as if she could not do it herself. He shot her a last glance before he pushed the door shut. Was that desire she read in his gray eyes?

"I am so happy to meet you, Mr. Hanley," Anyna said in Swiss-accented English. "Mami talked so much about you."

Hanley helped her into the car. "I bet you have music in your blood."

"I hear music all the time, Mr. Hanley, but it's not in my blood. I'm no good at it. In Switzerland I had drawing lessons." Anyna sat in the hot car, and watched him drive off. Fresh air blew in through the open windows.

"Just wait until you hear 'Catacombs,'" Lothar said as Hanley left the parking lot. "It's a masterpiece. The most original piece of music written since Stravinsky came out with his 'Firebird,' and Arnold Schoenberg invented his twelve-tone concept. Too dissonant for my taste. 'Catacombs' is not like that at all. You'll see." Lothar spoke with more animation than Olga had heard from him in years. Perhaps his being away from his mother had something to do with it, or that he valued Hanley's expertise. Like Buddy Jones, Hanley had formal training in classical music. Anyna chattered about their flight while they drove through Inglewood. No longer sleepy, Olga wondered how she could bring off her plan of staying here after Lothar returned to Germany. He would leave, she was certain of that.

Hanley would help. His affectionate greeting assured her that he cared for her. Physically, he lacked distinguishing marks—Hanley was neither tall nor striking—but his personality and showmanship drew in the crowds as did his unfailing sense of rhythm and catchy beats. Olga could not wait to work with him again. As a conductor, he took her to another level. Whereas Buddy Jones was a relentless taskmaster, Hanley inspired. Before they knew it, the members of the band became a single organism, part of the music they created. Masculine, poised, and self-assured—he now steered the car as he conducted his band. Nothing seemed to bother him, nor did he ever question his approach. Olga admired that. Lothar demanded the impossible from himself and others.

Hanley made it happen without a second thought. He enjoyed the music and accepted the business side as part of the job that had to be done.

Watching his relaxed head and shoulders from the back seat of the hot car, the warm air coming in through the open windows, she knew that she had come home. Here, far away from Germany, her problems would find resolution. Under the blue and sunny skies, in a world that did not struggle through cold winter months, nor did it know hunger and deprivation, she would recover and bring her troubled soul to rest. Like Hanley, who did not seem to suffer over his divorce, Olga would accept her separation from Ingo and come out of a long, dark winter like a plant under the spring sun. She would flourish and grow and bloom, until Ingo joined her to carry on together till the end of their days.

She watched the quaint homes and lovely gardens go by. Space, space, and more space for wide streets that could accommodate those huge cars, buses, and streetcars. Nobody seemed in a hurry. People had all they needed. Life was so simple when basic human needs were met.

Anyna could not get enough of what she saw. "I really like Los Angeles, Mr. Hanley," she kept saying. "Look at that fountain. I never saw houses decorated like those. Nothing here looks like Switzerland."

"Because you're not in Switzerland," Hanley said good-naturedly. "You're in California now. We have the ocean and mountains; we have deserts and orchards. Just wait 'til I take you to an orange grove and you can smell all those blossoms. They're so sweet you'd never go for perfume. I'll show you those big waves and teach you how to body surf. You'll love it. You can even go skiing."

"Really? You should see me ski, Mr. Hanley. I can zoom down the slope—schuss, you know. Uncle Richard taught me. We raced each other. I'm getting so good that he has a hard time winning. Do you ski, Mr. Hanley?"

He did not, but said all the right things about how much he admired her skills and that she would enjoy living in Los Angeles. Lothar had been trying to explain the structure he had used for "Catacombs." Olga could tell that Hanley preferred Anyna's happy chatter to Lothar's intense explanation, and was glad that Lothar didn't throw a fit.

"Why aren't there people in the street?" Lothar asked. Had he noticed that his lecture was uncalled for? "Is everybody out at the beach?"

Hanley chuckled. They had turned onto Century Boulevard and admired the tall, slender palms lining the street. "Hardly. People are at work. You probably didn't know this, but Los Angeles has a major defense industry. It's what provides the jobs that support our pleasant life-style. During the war, we built the liberty ships that took our men to the Pacific. I was drafted into Special Services and entertained the men on the islands. I was fortunate. The Japs were tough. They had to fight to the death."

"I know all about that," Olga said. "Hitler did not accept retreat either."

"But that's because the Allies insisted on unconditional surrender," Lothar threw in. "When you have only death to look forward to..." He stopped. "I was also lucky. I spent a good part of the war in a POW camp in Oklahoma. Nobody talked of escape." He chuckled. "Where would we go? We had plenty of food and decent quarters. Since I knew English, I became the spokesman for the camp. The guards got me books and even a piano. They shared their records with me. That's when I learned American jazz. I couldn't complain about a thing, considering the circumstances. It was when I got my idea for 'Catacombs.' So you see, it's almost an American piece. And hear this: on Saturday nights we had young women drive up with their daddy's cars and take us to town. Nice girls. Naïve, of course, but nice." Olga had no idea what "nice" meant to him. They were probably impressed by the haughty baron, like the women at the NCO Club. Lothar had a way of coming across like an English Lord.

Olga felt they had to get back on track and silently thanked Aldridge for launching this career for her. They exchanged letters. He was proud over his winning his bet. "I knew you had it in you, Olga" he wrote. "I'll try to come out to California and see whether Hollywood knows what's good for them." *Dear Sergeant Aldridge. You were god-sent. Perhaps, Father sent you to me?* "How much time to do we have for rehearsals, Ben?" she asked.

"Whatever it takes to deliver a first-class performance."

"In that case, it will not take long," Lothar said condescendingly. "Olga needs to rehearse. She is not that good. That'll give me time to work on 'Catacombs.'"

"Suits me fine," Ben said, obviously eager to have her alone.

"I can keep an eye on Anna Magdalena while Olga rehearses," Lothar offered, "isn't that so, Anna Magdalena? You can draw or read or play with the neighborhood children."

"Of course, Daddy. I can study English." Anyna pointed at a white bungalow where two girls played with a puppy on the front lawn. "I'd love to have a puppy like that. I'd call her Princess and take her for walks. Isn't she cute? Do you have a dog, Mr. Hanley?" she asked.

"I did when my family still lived with me. My daughter, Kimberley, loves animals. She has a dog and a cat. She's your age; you might want to meet her. She's a sweet girl, like you."

Olga heard his regret. Lothar had a family, but rejected it. He pontificated about the Soviet threat while Hanley pushed the lighter into its socket, shook out a cigarette from the pack in his shirt pocket, and placed it between his lips. "As long as they get away with their mass murders and their expansionist policies the world is in great danger. France and Italy already have a strong communist party. Good thing Senator McCarthy keeps it from spreading in this country." Hanley drew on his cigarette and blew out the smoke. It trailed out the open window. He handled the steering wheel with his long, tapered fingers. Everything was easy and convenient. "Coming back to music, Lothar," he said. "Television is the new medium. Have you considered composing for the movies? It's a great market. Your macabre pieces might work with Count Dracula movies. Hollywood is always looking for new talent."

Lothar perked up. "Movies are not exactly my field, but who knows? My 'Catacombs' is a concert piece." He pursed his lips in thought. "It could lend itself to a music score as well. One doesn't preclude the other."

They were talking about the latest movies when Hanley drove up to the Beverly Hills Hotel. Olga recognized the familiar pink and white building, so very Hollywood. She still wore her New York suit, and couldn't wait to change into a light summer dress.

"Are we staying here?" Anyna asked, duly impressed by the luxury.

"Nothing but the best for our little baroness," Hanley teased on their way to the lobby. "Famous people come here from all over the world to talk about movie productions."

The receptionist remembered the German Baron and Baroness and was now introduced to Anna Magdalena. No, she had never heard of a composer by the name of Bach. "What movie was he in?"

"He was not in movies," Anyna told her. "He lived in the 16th century and wrote church music."

The receptionist shrugged. "I'm not much of a church-goer," she confessed.

Anyna explained that movies did not exist in Bach's time, which didn't bother the receptionist. Foreigners didn't know a thing about Hollywood, but she had to treat them with respect, even the children. This one had some manners and looked rather sweet in her blue coat and bonnet.

After checking in, Olga and her family followed Hanley to the coffee shop where he ordered a milkshake for Anyna and coffee for the rest. Nobody was hungry after all that delicious food on the plane.

"Will you be ready to join us for rehearsal in the morning?" he asked Olga. "We're ready to add some new pieces to our repertoire. As you said, Lothar, swing and jitterbug is fading out. We need a fresh beat. Cuban music is in now. Xavier Cugat and his band is the thing."

"I did some work on 'I'm in the Mood' and 'Jealousy,'" Lothar said.

Olga felt Hanley's glances on her. What was on his mind, a romance? Should she play along just to keep the close relationship she desperately needed? Or play the role of a dutiful wife who would not consider a fling?

"My sister looks after my mother," Lothar said suddenly, blotting his lips with his napkin. "My mother is seventy-two and could have an emergency."

Hanley nodded. "Just remember, Lothar. A breech of contract will cost you."

"You have to set your priorities straight, Ben," Lothar said.

After three days of rehearsals and two performances, the reporters had done their interviews and written their reviews, all of which flattered Olga. They gave Lothar most of the credit for their virtuosity. Fair enough, Olga concluded. The less visibility, the easier it would be for her to evaporate when the time came. Once they found an apartment, Anyna would have to go to school, which was not something she appreciated. "You'll get used to it," Olga kept saying.

Hanley understood Olga's plan of staying in California and seemed eager to help. Now that Lothar no longer came to the rehearsals, they had time to get to know each other and develop a friendship. There was so much she had to find out before she could make her move.

During a break, Hanley faced Olga across the table stirring his coffee. He always used double sugar and lots of cream and loved donuts. "My Aunt Josie has a house she rents out. I told her about you. Though she normally likes long-term tenants, she'd be willing to take you on. I'd be glad to show you the place. It's not far from here. She'll put in some furniture. It'll be adequate."

Olga thanked him. Of course she would like to have a place of her own, a piano and a kitchen so that she could prepare the meals they were accustomed to. She reached for his hand. "You're so good to us, Ben."

He returned her smile. "I'm very fond of you, Olga," he said, as if this were a revelation. By now they felt comfortable saying whatever came to mind. She trusted him, and believed that he would seek a closer relationship once Lothar left. For the moment, Lothar seemed satisfied with his work and living in California. The Countess had not asked him to come home, preferring the money they sent. As long as Lothar remained normal, she was glad to have him here.

"You said that Lothar might leave. What then? Would you consider being friends with me?" His humble request touched her. Who was to know how things would turn out? "Let's wait and see," was all she could think of.

"You will stay after Lothar leaves," he confirmed, gazing into her eyes to elicit a promise she wished she would not have to make. He held her hand.

"I would like to. For the moment I have no idea how I can swing it," she said honestly.

"Don't you worry about that, Olga. As your sponsor, I'm obliged to help you," he assured her, grinning confidentially. "Not that I wouldn't do it anyway."

"In that case, let's look at your aunt's house. Do you have time after rehearsal?"

"For you, I have all the time in the world," he said, rising. With his hand on her shoulder, they returned to the band.

Later that afternoon, Hanley drove her through residential streets of Los Angeles, passing whimsically decorated homes with turrets, porches, and balconies nestled among flowering hibiscus, gardenias, and roses. Some people grew banana trees and huge cacti. By bringing water to the desert, people had created a tropical paradise. Here, at the end of the western world, people lived in a blooming outpost surrounded by citrus plantations and palm trees. Benefiting from the steady light of the sunny days, they had set up movie studios that became the envy of the world. Olga could not wait to settle down in this lovely city, far away from all the pain of her past.

"Some day you'll own a place like that, Olga," Hanley said, parking his car in front of a neat lawn that looked like a welcome mat for the one-story home. Its unassuming charm, with a front porch under an overhang, large windows facing the street, and a rustic front door, appealed to Olga. She was tired of the lavish extravagance of the Beverly Hills Hotel and playing the part of a baroness. Here she could feel at home and live in peace listening to the birds and enjoying the fragrance of the flowers. This would be her home, something she had not even dreamed of before coming to America. Just having a room of her own would have been wonderful. Now, in this land of unlimited opportunities, she might even own a house.

"But I have no money," she said.

"Nobody pays cash. You'll take out a mortgage and live like everybody else."

Olga pondered Hanley's suggestion. Everybody else? Join the world of regular people who lived ordinary lives? Now, that would be a true miracle; it would mean so much more than the nightly ovations. She would have her own piano, cook meals in her own kitchen, and have her own bedroom that did not smell of mothballs and was free of the Countess' boxes and belongings.

Hanley opened the door and let her pass. As soon as he closed it, he took her into his arms and pressed his warm lips against hers.

Startled, she withdrew. "Ben!"

He breathed heavily. "You're so beautiful, Olga. I've admired you from the moment I first saw you. I've been waiting a long time for this." He held her. Not to disappoint him she remained in his embrace feeling his hot breath on her face. The ugly faces of the Russian soldiers appeared. No, Ben was kind and caring. He would not take what she did not give him freely. Perhaps he even loved her. Olga felt comforted and protected, though she did not want to encourage him.

When he kissed her again, she withdrew and looked around the cool living room. "This is lovely," she said quickly. "More than I need."

"Just a regular home," he assured her. "And a lot cheaper than the Beverly Hills."

"No doubt." She sat down in one of the arm chairs rather than the sofa, to not invite further intimacy, and looked around. Though it was sunny outside, the room appeared dark, with oak floors and pine green walls. Heavy floral drapes framed the large window. She bent over toward the coffee table and admired the bouquet of fresh roses he must have placed there. "How beautiful. Thank you, Ben. You are so kind. It's so good to feel welcomed."

"We'll get you a baby grand as soon as you decide that you like the place," he said. "Come. Let me show you the kitchen, the bedrooms, and the bathroom."

"I'm so touched," Olga said, opening the kitchen drawers to find cutlery, cooking utensils, and even trivets. With tears in her eyes she whispered, "I can't tell you how much this means to me. My first home. I've never had a place of my own. Even the apartment in Poland belonged to somebody else. How can I ever thank you?" As soon as the last sentence slipped from her tongue, she wished she had not said it. Following a sudden impulse she hugged him and kissed his cheek. He smelled so fresh and appealing, but this was all wrong.

He held her. "I hope you'll stay for a long time."

The following day Lothar, Olga and Anyna moved in. As soon as the piano was delivered, Lothar took possession of it. Olga would have to wait until he left before she could make use of it. Anyna roamed through the house and garden finding new things to admire. "It's so good to be here, Mami. To have our own home." Olga knew how much her little girl had missed her family. All the luxury in the world could not compensate a child for her mother. Ben had stocked the refrigerator with milk, eggs, cheese, and cold cuts. There was butter, bread and sugar, coffee and tea. Everything was good. The war was finally over for her.

During the week, Olga discovered the joys of shopping in the local grocery store, where she could get everything she wanted. For Monday, their day off, she invited Hanley for dinner and served a typical German meal: wienerschnitzel, potato salad, and green beans. He brought a bottle of Gallo wine and an apple pie. While they enjoyed their coffee and pie, Olga mentioned that a neighbor, Hazel, was looking after Anyna. "She came over and introduced herself. We struck up a friendship. Everything here is so unbelievably wonderful. In Germany it would take years before you got to know somebody."

"That's as it should be," Lothar said. "People have no business meddling in their neighbor's affairs."

"I disagree," Olga said. "Frau Meier is a pain. I prefer to live with people who are kind to each other."

Lothar shook his head in disgust. He had put on a jacket for the occasion. and had traded his turtleneck for an open sport shirt. "You see, Ben, why it's so difficult to live with a wife like Olga. She always has to have it her way."

"We call that being adaptable," Ben said, and leaned back. "People who come to California want to get to know each other."

"That's what makes living here so special," Olga said.

"See what I mean?" Lothar said, his tone as condescending as if talking to a naughty child. "She doesn't care who she talks to. No sense of *comme il faut*. I suppose this is the right place for her. Not for me, I can tell you that. No. I believe in proper etiquette and prefer not to talk to uneducated and uncouth people. I owe that to my mother's upbringing."

"That's the problem," Olga said, smiling apologetically at Hanley. She hoped he would not consider this an affront. "I truly feel at home here. That's more than I can say about Germany. You see, Ben, my in-laws never accepted me."

Ben lit a cigarette. "I haven't heard a word out of Anyna. Is it not proper for children to talk at the table?"

Anyna, wearing the new floral cotton dress Olga had bought for her, glanced at her father. He shrugged. "It's not a strict rule," he said. "But we prefer that children do not interfere in adult conversation. But it's all right, Anna Magdalena, since Mr. Hanley would like to hear you say something."

"I would indeed," he confirmed. The whole scene was so ridiculous, Olga thought. So typical of Lothar, who couldn't even see how absurd he must appear in Ben's eyes. "How do you like your school? I bet it's different than the one you went to in Switzerland."

"Oh, yes, very different," Anyna said, blushing. At eleven she was losing her innocent little girl look. She had inherited Olga's dimple and her father's frown. "I told the children that I'm from Switzerland because they don't like Germans. I know a lot more about Switzerland and about Poland than about Germany. I like school. The teacher helps me when I don't understand her and lets me ask questions. Everybody can ask questions. The children don't have to stand when the teacher comes into class. I'm learning better English now; the teacher doesn't care that I can't write it very well. She says that I'll learn it in time. She isn't angry at all. Miss McEwan is the nicest and prettiest teacher you ever saw."

"You'd better not get too attached to Miss McEwan and her ways of teaching," Lothar said. "We must get back to Germany before she does irreparable damage. What will Grandmaman say when you return acting like a street urchin?" Lothar pinched Anyna's cheek.

She blushed. "But Daddy, you said that I must go to school and that I better get along with the other children. You know that I can behave properly when we go home."

Hanley touched Olga's foot under the table. "Anna is doing the right thing," he said. "When in Rome…"

"But we're neither in Rome nor Romans, Ben. I don't want my daughter to act like yours. She doesn't even shake hands."

"True," Ben said. The corners of his mouth dropped. Olga sensed that Lothar had gone too far. What business was it of his to tell Ben how to raise his daughter? "But let me remind you, Baron, that breaking your contract will cost you. I will not take it kindly. I think I'd better be on my way."

Olga saw him to the door. "I'm sorry, Ben."

"I'm not, as long as I know that you're staying."

"I am."

"Are you available tonight?"

Olga's cheeks flushed. Nobody had ever approached her so directly. She was shocked, and felt guilty. He had done so much for her, had rescued her from the Countess, but obliging him would be all wrong. No need to give him false hopes. "Would you let me play solo with your band?"

"Goes without saying."

"Thank you, Ben."

He certainly expected gratitude, and would get it. But she could not see herself sleeping with him for the favor of sponsoring her to come here. She was not for sale. How could men be so ignorant of women's feelings and needs? Ingo knew and understood. His tactful reserve had sparked her desire for him. She had come to him on her own because she loved him.

Olga looked at the star-studded sky. From now on she would manage on her own, dig into her savings until she had a job. There was no point in even considering playing with Hanley's band. Something would come up. Father had opened doors for her in the past, had wanted her to be free and independent. *"...That's when you will find each other,"*

Before making any plans Olga visited Sam Goldstein, a known agent. Sitting in his office, the bald, heavy-set man had little to offer. "Sure I've heard of the German Baron and Baroness. Good act. Hanley is a well-known band leader. He does well. But if he won't keep you on, there's no work for you here. Pianists are a dime a dozen, young lady. You got the looks. Can you sing?"

Her voice had nothing special to offer. She would have to find her own way.

On their last night, Hanley allowed the Baron and Baroness to open with the beginning of "Rhapsody in Blue." It would be Lothar's farewell. He had stayed on for another six weeks and finally set the date for his return and did not insisted that she and Anyna return with him. He just wanted to go home, and did not care what anybody else did. Relieved, yet anxious, Olga played her part. Gershwin's clever arrangement for saxes, muted trumpets, and oboes, and his brilliant piano passages, found an appreciative audience. Her fingers took the lead and played the complex phrases in quick succession. Lothar pounded out a dark accompaniment to her seductive rendition of the upper voice. In his heart he was already on his way home, playing for Maman. Olga picked up the ponderous mood, then took off with syncopated trills that echoed through the melodies. The saxes did their fling. Olga saw her life open up for her. The boisterous show proclaimed her liberation. From now on she would be on her own.

The grand finale turned into a show stopper. The audience gave them a standing ovation.

Chapter 45

Their parting was not nearly as painful or dramatic as Olga had anticipated. "Good luck, Olga," Lothar said sarcastically, driving his cold eyes into her. She would remember him as the sardonic character he had played in her life—his face the handsome mask of a devil. Why did he hate her so? "You're taking on a big responsibility," he said with a twisted smile. "You're in for a surprise, young lady. How do you expect to feed the two of you? Remember Berlin. Some people take a very long time to catch on. It's your decision. You can always return to Inning. Your actions never did make any sense." Dressed for Germany in a trench-coat and felt hat, he put his arm around Anyna's shoulder. She leaned her head against him. "You come from old nobility, Anna Magdalena. Tante Adie and Grandmaman taught you what a baroness knows instinctively: *Noblesse oblige.* Don't ever forget that. Your mother is a commoner, but you are a von Schenck. Something to be proud of. I expect you to uphold your heritage."

"I will, Daddy. Please give Grandmaman my love. Tell her that she should take walks. It's so beautiful outside where the air is fresh. We'll come for a visit as soon as we can. Will you come and do another tour with Mami? Do you think I can become an artist? Paint landscapes and things? Or a decorator? What do you think about my becoming an architect? I could design homes for movie stars." Not waiting for an answer, she kissed his cheek and stepped back so that Olga could shake his hand. The mere gesture was repulsive.

He picked up his suitcase, and walked off to passport control. Then he was gone. Olga took Anyna's arm and headed for the exit and the beginning of a new life.

Anyna pattered alongside talking about Grandmaman. "She'll be so happy seeing Daddy come home. I'm glad we're staying here. I hate that stinking room. I love Switzerland, but I'd much rather be here with you,

Mami. I missed you so. Now we can always be together and talk any way we like."

They embraced. From now on, nothing and nobody would separate them. No more sacrifices, deprivations, or humiliations. Millions of immigrants had found a home in this hospitable country. Olga could not imagine anybody who yearned for freedom more than she. She was on the swell of a big wave carrying her ashore.

Her marriage was finished. The divorce they had agreed on before Anyna was born would be no more than a formality. From now on, Anyna was her child. Olga hummed "Free at Last," the old Negro spiritual. Like them, she had broken her shackles and taken charge of her life.

"Well, Anyna, where would you like to go?" Olga asked. Some passengers and those seeing them off laughed and talked. Unlike the old railroad stations, the airport was new, spacious, and immaculate, built for those who could afford air travel. A loudspeaker announced the upcoming flight to New York. Lothar would be on. Deliverance washed over her.

From now on nobody would wait for her. She could sleep all night undisturbed by uninvited visits. She was free, yet guilt still twisted in the pit of her stomach.

"Why are you running, Mami?" Anyna asked when they reached the parking lot. "Where are we going?"

"Looking for a job," Olga said, as if she had something specific in mind. "From now on we're in charge of our future, my little baroness, or are you still my princess?"

"Just call me Annie, like the kids at school. I like Annie. Now that Daddy has gone, I don't have to pretend to be a baroness. I can wear regular sweaters and skirts, and flats and a pony tail and bangs. I know you'll let me, Mom. Now we can laugh and dance when we feel like it. Nobody will come to my room at night to see whether I'm asleep."

Olga fished for her car keys. "What do you think about having an ice cream at Dairy Queen? Or would you rather have a milkshake?" The heat from the car gushed out at her. She opened all the doors to wait until the car cooled off.

"Hazel said I can come over and watch TV with her whenever I want," Anyna said. "She loves 'Life with Father.' Do you mind, Mom?"

"I'm so glad you like Hazel. She's a wonderful friend."

"I want to become an artist," Anyna said, slipping into the hot seat. "Uncle Ingo said I have talent. Remember when I sent him my drawings at the front?"

"Uncle Ingo," Olga murmured, starting the engine of her blue 1949 Chevrolet. Ben Hanley had helped her buy it before Lothar sent their money to the Countess. He had taught her to drive, and kissed her every time she'd made a mistake. Olga had enjoyed the attention. She would miss him. Ingo would not be available for years, but still, she could not have an intimate relationship with anybody else.

The traffic on Century Boulevard rolled along at an easy pace. Early afternoon was not a busy time. The radio played, "How Much Is That Doggie in the Window." Anyna talked about her friends at school, her teachers, and her dance classes. She had spent her afternoons with Hazel while Olga rehearsed with the band. That was over now. For the moment she had no job. Hanley would let her play occasionally on weekends, but that would not cover her expenses.

To Anyna, Hazel had replaced Tante Lore and Tante Gertie. She never talked about them, or their flight from Poland. Surviving the Russians, almost starving to death, and escaping to the West had all vanished into a state of amnesia.

The sun slipped behind dark clouds coming in from the Hollywood Hills. A gusty wind whirled dust and the scraps of paper that always littered the streets of Los Angeles. Stopping at a traffic light, Olga noticed the red hibiscus blossoms in front of a home, and pink roses that bloomed in winter—no more cold, hunger, or the smell of moss balls.

On Fairfax Avenue, Olga passed the Old Heidelberg restaurant. She had eaten there a couple of times, though the cuisine and service left a lot to be desired. Sepp Sailer, the owner, tended bar while his wife did the cooking. The waitress, a grumpy matron who hated her job, did not cheer up a place that needed a complete overhaul that the Sailers were not inclined to undertake.

The parking lot held only one car—an old, banged-up Ford that probably belonged to the owners. The building was covered with wooden planks and fake shutters that were a far cry from an Alpine chalet. The Old Heidelberg was dying of neglect. Its pre-war diners had integrated into the mainstream of Angelenos. During the war, many had anglicized their names to escape discrimination.

"What are you going to do here, Mom?" Anyna asked. "The place is closed."

"I'll ask for a job," Olga said.

Anyna let go of the door handle she was about to open. "A job? Doing what?"

"I don't know yet. But something tells me that I should inquire."

"Oh Mom, not one of those ..."

"Yes. Intuition. So come on; let's find out. Something tells me that the Sailers need me."

Anyna left the car reluctantly, and slammed the door shut. She couldn't see what Olga could possible do for the Sailers. "You're not going to wash dishes, for heaven's sake," she protested.

"If that's what it takes. I need a job." Olga smiled. She too was curious about what would become of her visit.

Drops of rain fell on the dusty and cracked asphalt.

Anyna ran across the parking lot, and then waited for Olga at the door.

The dining room was dark. The smell of stale cigarette smoke and beer lingered over the empty tables. In the deserted bar, the only thing visible was the prominent beer tap, which Sailer had polished to a high shine. The open beams reminded Olga of the Old St. Petersburg Inn in Dresden before the bombs had turned it to cinders. Water splashed in the kitchen. Somebody was washing dishes.

"The place is closed, Mom. They just didn't hang up a sign."

"So it is. That means Mr. Sailer is not too busy to talk to me." Anyna might as well learn that closed doors could be opened.

"What are you going to tell him? What if he throws us out, like the people in Germany?"

"I don't think he will," Olga said, surprised by her confidence. She stopped at the door that had "office" written on it. In her blue gabardine suit, white hat, and gloves, she felt like the owner of the place, rather than somebody asking for a job. Anyna wore her favorite yellow sweater and argyle skirt, white socks and saddle shoes.

Olga knocked.

"Come in!" said a male voice.

She opened the door. Sepp Sailer sat behind a battered desk cluttered with papers, bills, ads, and promotional flyers. Empty boxes, dusty plastic vines, and left-over Christmas ornaments had been strewn over the two chairs, the file cabinet, and the floor.

He looked up over his half glasses and raised his bushy brows. "What can I do for you?"

Olga had met him before, but doubted that he remembered her. Sailer had not changed since she last saw him: paunchy, with sparse hair combed back, jowls and a fleshy nose. She noticed a sign of recognition he preferred not to acknowledge, as if avoiding a solicitor. His suspicious gray eyes, imbedded in folds of loose skin, shifted from her to Anyna, evaluating them. Pen in hand, he leaned over the stack of receipts on his desk.

"You my not remember me," Olga said. "My name is Olga von Schenck, and this is my daughter, Annie." She spoke German. "My husband and I ate here several times. He liked your beer. And I enjoyed your Schnitzel. A bit thick, but otherwise tasty. Do you have a minute?"

"What can I do for you?" he said again, obviously curious about what a well-dressed, pretty young woman and her daughter could want from him.

Anyna cleared the chairs while the adults shook hands. Olga mentioned Bavaria and that she had immigrated to Los Angeles. "I am performing with the Ben Hanley Band."

Sailer's tired eyes perked up, like those of a dog alerted by some mysterious sound. "Ben Hanley? Our favorite band. What brings you here?"

"It's a long story. In essence, I would like to offer my services."

Sailer's mouth dropped open. "Your services? Doing what, may I ask?"

"That depends. I need a job." She explained her circumstances, then said, "I believe in destiny. I know your business is not exactly booming. But something tells me that it could be turned around. I don't quite know how yet, but it will come to me. I am a woman with a sixth sense. When I drove by I knew I had to stop. And here I am."

He threw up his swarthy hands in protest.

She stopped him. "No, don't say anything, Just hear me out. I am not only a pianist, I have worked in a restaurant."

Sailer looked at her as if he wanted to believe her, but knew better.

"Don't worry about paying me. For starters I'll be glad to work for tips only."

"Not in the kitchen. A lady like you belongs on stage or at least at the reception desk of the Beverly Hills Hotel. Let's face it. This is a dump. Ilse-Marie and I decided to call it a day and close the place. Liquidate it since there are no buyers. The German market is as dead as dead can be. The Old Heidelberg will be put into moth balls," he chuckled. "It will probably be torn down and replaced by a hamburger joint or a third-rate bar." He watched her reaction. "You're one of the few customers who knows what a wienerschnitzel is. People want hamburgers and fries, fried chicken, or Salisbury steak. Ilse-Marie can tell you all about it. She is the cook."

"I know. I've lived here long enough to know what people eat when they don't dine in Beverly Hills." Olga smiled seductively, and noticed his reserve relax. Of course he would want to have her here, but felt insecure and probably saw himself as the man he was, rather than what he used to be, or wanted to be. "Germany lost the war and we must pay for it," she said, as if he did not know that. "That doesn't mean we must stick our heads in the sand and play the victim. No, my dear Herr Sailer. We must pick up the pieces and rebuild. That's what they're doing in Germany. We can do the same here. We live in the most beautiful city of this great country. You have the place, and I'll bring in the customers."

Sailer leaned back, resting his double chin on the heel of his hand. "I've had my share of America. We came here in 1936. German Americans enjoyed coming to the Old Heidelberg. Then the war broke out. We were sure Hitler would win as long as America stayed neutral. Not that they did. Before we knew it our world was turned upside down. We Germans became the enemy. Some of the hot-heads got so excited, I expected them to torch this building. You have no idea what was going on." He lit a cigarette and puffed the smoke at Olga. His stubby fingers trembled. "You don't know what it's like being an enemy of the people, living in fear."

Anyna signaled that they should leave.

Olga ignored it. "I know. But that's past. We must look forward. I know the Old Heidelberg could be a gold mine."

Sailer chuckled. Hid double chin waddled. "A gold mine yet. My dear young lady…"

"Olga."

"All right, Olga. You've seen too many Hollywood movies. Film producers can put anything on celluloid to come up with a happy ending. Real life is nothing but a big disappointment."

"It doesn't have to be. Just keep on trying until something works." Visions of her past flashed through Olga's mind, followed by glimpses of her future. She saw the place redone in light colors, with outdoor tables, good food, and music. The romantic Germany of the past.

"Really?" he said. His lips stretched to a smirk.

"You've got to offer what people want. Like beer imported from Munich. People love German products. They're good and they're cheap. The dollar is so high, everything you import costs a fraction of what you would pay for it here. We'll have music and sing-alongs. Show me a German who doesn't like to sing. Is there a German club in town?"

He shook his head. "We still have a German paper. "Kalifornische Staatszeitung". There are plenty of Germans living here, but they're not noticeable. You can see why. Some had been taken to internment camps like the Japanese."

"I see. Well, I bet they'll come back as soon as they know the Old Heidelberg is in business. I mean, really in business. That there are things going on that make it worth their while. Once the place is ready, we'll advertise in the German paper. The Reich is dead. We must resurrect Old Germany with its music, food, and *gemutlichkeit.* You did not commit any war crimes, kill Jews, or bomb London, did you, Herr Sailer? You were not even in Germany when all that happened."

"Of course not. We came here because Ilse-Marie hoped to get into movies. I loved her and went along. Kind of stupid, when I think of it now. After the war broke out, we couldn't get back to Germany and kept our heads down. We were lucky not to get locked up in an internment camp."

"The whole war was a mess. Everybody knows that," Olga said, getting all worked up by the prospect of going into business. It would be her business, no doubt about that. Sailer had no idea what he was doing. "No one could have imagined how bad things would be. Now we must think of the future. I know we can do it, Herr Sailer." She stressed the "we." "You heard me right."

"I did indeed. You would do great as a stand up comic." His laughter had no mirth.

"My mother is a pianist," Anyna said, tired of the long discussion that was going nowhere.

"A pianist at Old Heidelberg?" Sailer said, screwing his eyes as if he was talking to a mad woman, while his brain calculated how much all that would cost him. He was a tightwad, else he would not have let this place run down like that.

Olga would bring him around. "You don't seem to get it," Olga insisted. "There is nothing wrong with steak and French fries. I like them too. I have a plan."

Sailer settled back in defeat. "We had a good season over Christmas," he said. "People liked our hot mulled wine and gingerbread cookies. Now they are staying at home watching television."

"You didn't hear my mother's plan, Herr Sailer," Anyna said. "This is not about Christmas."

He shook his big head. "Now I have children telling me what to do."

"You could put up a television," Anyna said.

"A television? I suppose. But then, this is a German restaurant, not a Howard Johnson's. To tell you the truth, I am flattered by your taking an interest in our business. My wife insists that I must get rid of the clutter. That takes time."

"She's right. Here is my offer." Olga raised her hand before he could protest. "Hear me out. I can play any song, Schunkelmusik, you name it. 'Ich weiss es wird einmal ein Wunder geschehn,' is my favorite. Remember Zarah Leander? She is so good."

"You forgot that I was here during the war. My luck, I guess." Sailer warmed up to Olga's enthusiasm. "Cigarette?" he asked, offering her an open pack of Pall Malls.

"Thanks, but I don't smoke. However, I love beer."

Anyna rolled her eyes; had her mother gone mad? "We must go," she said.

Olga winked. This was not about a happy life at Aunt Adie's. This was about getting along in the world.

He flipped his lighter and lit his cigarette. "So let's hear what you have to say. I am extremely busy, as you can see." He blew out the smoke.

Olga sensed he was dying for a drink. "I would love to have a beer. It's on me, since I'm stealing your time."

"I wouldn't go that far, but a cool beer would do us both good. Let me get a Coke for the young lady here."

Anyna's eyes lit up. Now they were getting somewhere.

Olga followed him to the bar where he drew a beer from the tap. "Are you actually from Heidelberg?" she asked.

"Absolutely. Crossed the Neckar twice a day on my way to school."

"In a way we are both refugees. Let's celebrate the discovery of a gold mine that will make both of us rich." Leaning over the bar she took a long sip. Beer had never tasted better.

His coarse features softened to a friendly smile that showed big, yellow teeth. "If you say so." He took another swig then ran his large hand across his full lips.

"Let me entertain your guests on Friday and Saturday nights," Olga said. "During the week I'll help serve, wear a dirndl, and amuse the guests. They'll love it. My sing-along will get them in the spirit. They'll drink and eat and tell their friends about the good time they had. The first month will be my trial period. After that, we'll see how things work out. My daughter and I have great plans. Old Heidelberg will make them come true. We'll turn this place around."

Anyna sipped her Coke through a straw directly from the bottle. "Don't you think you should put that old Santa Claus away?" she said, picking up the cardboard figure.

Sailer nodded. "How can I refuse your offer, Olga?" he said and drew himself another beer. "We worked ourselves to death here, Ilse-Marie and I. She's sick and tired of doing the kitchen. Who can blame her? We've been here too long."

Olga drank the cold brew. "You see, my intuition was right. I knew I was needed here.

"Together we can get this place back on its feet. Just you wait. This will become the in place with live entertainment. '*La Vie en rose*.' People know me."

Sepp Sailer did not question that. "Let me call my wife. Ilse-Marie is not an easy woman to please. If she goes along, you've got a deal." He left.

"Mami, have you gone crazy?" Anyna said. "You don't want to work here."

"I do, Anyna. Something tells me that my future is here. Yours too. So relax. There are many things we can't see right away—that's why we must trust our guidance." Before Anyna could object, a sweaty, heavy-set matron came in, her apron wet from the dishwater. Her frizzy hair had not seen a beauty shop for some time, nor did she care about her clothes. Olga rose and shook Frau Sailer's hot, moist hand. "I came to make a proposition," she said after the usual preliminaries.

"Actually a very good one," Sepp agreed, watching his wife.

Olga got up and offered her the chair. "You must be exhausted."

"Now wait a minute. You act as if you own the place already." Her big face and angry eyes rejected the uninvited guest. "We don't need anything. Got our hands full as is."

"Sit down, Ilse-Marie, and listen," Sailer said, while Olga cleared another chair.

"I am Olga von Schenck. A piano player who would like to work for you."

Ilse-Marie plopped down on the old creaking chair, shaking her head and wiped the sweat from her tired face. "As if we don't have enough problems already."

"I know. That's why I came," Olga insisted. "I can play any German song, old or new, run sing-alongs, amuse beer drinkers, and get your guests to enjoy themselves. Word will get around. In no time, this restaurant will be booming. For the first month I'll get along on tips. After that we shall negotiate. How do you like that? While you cook, I'll be waiting tables. I've done it before. How can you run a place like this without help?" Olga gave Ilse-Marie a sympathetic smile. "A good waitress brings in business, you know that."

"We manage," Ilse-Marie said reluctantly, unwilling to be bowled over. "What did Sepp tell you? He doesn't understand a thing about this business."

"I have eaten here, Frau Sailer. I know what is going on. If you close down, you'll lose everything you worked for. What a shame. Besides, what's wrong with my proposition?"

Olga watched Frau Sailer struggle with her decision. Deep lines crossed her forehead. Her lips tightened. Perhaps she had been pretty once. What had happened? Had years of hard work in the kitchen thrown her into such despair that she gave up on being a woman? Now her pride was at stake, but she was too exhausted to argue. No doubt she had been frustrated, not only with never ending demands of the restaurant, but also the thought that it had all been for naught. Her stern face relaxed.

Sepp Sailer got up and brought his wife a glass of beer. She took a long draught, as if to wash down all the pain and disappointments of the past years, and put down the half empty glass. Letting out a deep sigh, she untied her wet apron. "What you are saying just kills me," she said. "To think that I slaved all these years for nothing. We have never been to Hawaii. We have a lovely cabin at Lake Arrowhead, only we never get to visit. I am sick, so sick, of sauerkraut and wienerschnitzel that I could scream. If I never saw red cabbage and Koenigsberger Klopse again, I'd be a happy woman. How I hate these dishes and glasses." She broke into tears that rolled down her puffy cheeks. "Most of all, I am sick of a man called Sepp Sailer who can't see how pointless it all is. Yes, young woman. Do come and save me from purgatory. Start tomorrow, so that I can take a couple of hours off. Once you know the business, perhaps I can take a couple of days off. I am so frustrated that I could jump into the lake." Long, drawn-out sobs rose from her big chest. "All this is so ridiculous. I came to Hollywood to becme a star and wound up as a kitchen maid."

Olga put her arm around Ilse-Marie's thick shoulders and smelled the sour sweat. "I believe in destiny," she said softly. "When I passed the Old Heidelberg, I felt that I must come here and look for a job, and that's what I did. Now I know why. The three of us need each other. Can you think of a better reason for people to work together?" She sat down again. "Today is Wednesday. Yes, I will start tomorrow. I'll come in the morning and help you get ready for lunch, then take it from there. We'll tell guests that I'll entertain them on Friday and Saturday nights, and advertise in the Kalifornische Staatszeitung."

"I can't believe this is happening to me," Ilse-Marie said, her eyes aglow, a big smile on her rather attractive lips. "We'll start you at ninety cents an hour plus tips. How's that? Unfortunately, that's all we can afford."

"That's more than I hoped for."

"Then we have a deal. Why didn't you think of that, Sepp Sailer? When will you ever think of something that makes sense? When will you realize that your wife is a human being, not a work horse?"

Anyna got up. "My name is Anna Magdalena and I am a baroness."

Ilse-Marie stared at Anyna as if she had not seen her before. "You are what? A baroness? I never met one before." She bowed her head. "It's my pleasure making your acquaintance. Don't let me wake up now. I don't want to find myself back in the kitchen."

At ten the following morning, Olga reported for work. Before going to the kitchen, she tested the old upright piano. It was no longer a musical instrument, just a noise maker, with sounds so flat that they hurt; the cheap instrument was beyond repair.

"We must get a better piano," she told Sepp, admiring his clean shirt and coat. "This one is a disgrace."

"Since you're our celebrity, I guess we must take care of the problem. But we have no money for things like that. You do understand that, don't you?"

"If my plan is to work, I need a decent instrument," she said with that honest, endearing, irresistible smile people took notice of. Sepp was no exception. "This will be a swanky place. People will come to hear me play. But not on this clunker. It was never meant to be a professional instrument."

"I agree," Sepp said, and lit a cigarette. "I'm not tone-deaf, you know. But we can't afford a decent piano."

"I know," Olga said, dumping potatoes into the sink. "We can rent one. Even professionals rent their instruments. We did it in New York and out here in Los Angeles. Let me talk to the man we are renting from now. He'll give me a good deal."

Sepp patted her shoulder. "You amaze me, Olga. You know something," he confided, "I have a feeling you will actually turn this place into a gold mine."

She kissed his cheek. "We will. Thanks, Sepp, for letting me work with you."

The work at Old Heidelberg taxed Olga's energy to the limits. She got up early and worked out a sing-along program. At ten, she joined Ilse-Marie in the kitchen, then set the tables for lunch, lined up clean glasses for Sepp, and sliced the bread. When the first guests arrived shortly before noon, she received them in a clean dirndl and with a bright smile. She introduced herself and learned the names of the guests so that she could address them personally. Her easy conversation did not slow down her service. With most of the food ready, she could serve it quickly. Lunch guests were in a hurry and appreciated returning to their offices on time.

Within a week, the number of their customers had doubled. Some brought colleagues or came in with friends. Ilse-Marie did not mind doing her red cabbage and dumplings now that she knew they were getting ahead. Sepp investigated importing beer from Munich, and found that Loewenbrau had a general distributor in New York who could arrange for some to be sent to Los Angeles.

Olga organized a celebration when the first keg arrived, and Sepp tapped it ceremonially. The foaming brew spilled out to the cries of enthusiastic beer drinkers. Singing "*Trink, trink, Bruderlein trink*," they clinked their mugs.

In May, an unexpected heat wave turned the Los Angeles basin into a furnace. Exhaust fumes gathered into a thick layer of smog. In a week, it was so thick that it began to irritate people's eyes and hamper their breathing. They wheezed, wiped the tears from their eyes, and moaned. Paradise had turned into a fume-belching inferno. Smog alerts warned people to stay indoors and refrain from incinerating their garbage in their back yards. The air in the kitchen was so stuffy and hot that Olga felt ill. Sweat ran down her back and dripped from her face. She sneezed constantly as if suffering from a cold.

"It didn't used to be like this," Ilse Marie assured Olga, as if responsible for the heat, her face as red as a radish. "As soon as the wind comes up from the ocean it will all clear up. You should see our place at Lake Arrowhead, as cool and fresh as if we were in the Bavarian Alps. But, as you can see, we never get to go there." In her loose floral duster she stood at the stove and fried meat *rouladen*. "The kitchen is about the worst place to be right now."

Olga's blouse fell over her skirt, but there was no air to cool her body. She wore sandals on her bare feet. Even if she had been naked, she would have been too hot. Who would order hot *rouladen* in this weather anyway? For days like these they needed a light, cold supper on their menu. She had iced tea available, as well as sodas. Perhaps they should settle for chicken and tuna salad sandwiches instead of sausages and sauerkraut, but Ilse-Marie insisted that they could only compete with other lunch places by serving German food. What would they do in summer when it got really hot? Olga had not experienced a California summer. "Can't we at least get a fan?" she asked.

"Sure we can," Ilse Marie agreed. "Not that it will change anything. It's the air that is bad. A fan…"

"… will give us the illusion of coolness," Olga said.

"Illusion? That's all it is," Ilse Marie said, turning the meat in the sizzling grease. Her hair dripped with perspiration.

Olga's sweat-soaked curls looked as if she had just stepped out of the shower. How could she entertain their guests looking like that? "Why don't we get an air conditioner? I understand they work quite well. Hazel, my neighbor, told me all about them."

"For a small room, yes," Ilse Marie argued. "Not for a restaurant like this."

Olga said no more. People accommodated to familiar, unpleasant conditions rather than look for better ways.

"Sepp can't understand what it means for me standing at the hot stove."

"How much is an air conditioner?" Olga asked. "We could get one for the kitchen."

Ilse-Marie wiped the sweat from her big face. "Not that much, really."

"Then why don't we get one? That will make both of us feel and look better. I can't wait on guests looking like this." She wiped her face with a wet towel and fluffed up her moist curls.

"By evening it will cool off," Ilse-Marie promised. "Sepp did get a fan. So far we have a reservation for a group of twelve. With the windows open and the fan going it should cool off pretty fast. Erna Bauer and members of the German choir are having a party."

"I could accompany them," Olga suggested. "Perhaps that'll inspire them to come back."

"Great idea, Olga. They could be steady guests." Ilse-Marie sliced potatoes for the salad.

Just before the Bauer party arrived, Olga took a quick sponge bath, then slipped into a fresh dirndl, laced the bodice over her white blouse, and fastened a gold chain around her neck. With lipstick, a touch of eyebrow pencil, and her hair pinned up in a wreath of curls, she looked as fresh as if this were a normal day. She greeted Frau Bauer with a warm handshake. "Welcome. We set your table up by the window. The air is cooling off," she said, adjusting the fan. What a difference. Sepp was finally getting it.

The seven women and five men settled down and appreciated the air. By late afternoon, the westerly coming in from the ocean had blown the smog further inland. The party ordered hasenpfeffer, dumplings, and red cabbage. They probably would have been happier with cold fare. With only two other couples in the dining room, Olga took time off to play the piano. Everybody sang along when she did "In Munchen steht ein Hofbrauhaus." With "Du, Du, liegst mir im Herzen," and "Trink, trink, Bruderlein trink," she had them going.

The choir sang louder and louder, ordered more beer, and wiped their sweaty faces. Soon they had locked arms, singing and swaying back and forth, quenching their thirst with cold beer. Sepp stood behind the bar and poured. This was the best evening he had had in years. In celebration he kept his glass filled, laughed at the jokes of the party, and toasted the giggling women.

"Olga, you're just the musician we are looking for," Erna Bauer said. She wore a pink and red sleeveless dress. "You have great talent. Can we hire you?"

Olga distributed another round of beer steins. "To tell you the truth, I'm committed to working here six days a week, including weekends. But, if you use our banquet room for your rehearsal on Tuesdays or Wednesdays, I could do both."

"What do you think, friends?" Erna Bauer shouted. "Can we meet here on Wednesdays?"

There were some objections, which Frau Bauer quickly overruled. The energetic little woman who had devoted her life to German music, her choir, and culture in general, enjoyed Olga's company and asked many questions about Germany. "I am sure you can all adapt your schedules so that we can meet on Wednesdays," she told her friends. "Sepp will keep us from dying of thirst and Ilse-Marie will feed us *knodel* and *kassler rippchen*. And Sepp, you'll get us an air conditioner, *nicht wahr?*" she added.

Olga nudged him. "What do you say, Sepp?"

"That you women will lead me into the poorhouse."

"It's still a long ways from *Oktober*," Olga said, "What do you think about having an Oktoberfest? Brass band, choir, dancing? Let's show the people what Germany is really all about it. We need a lot of good will around here."

Erna Bauer raised her glass with iced-tea. "You're so right, Olga. You can count on us." Her lipstick had worn off. Her full lips and cheeks had the healthy complexion of a gardener. She wore her thick gray hair in a twist. Narrow eyes, rather straight brows, and a wide nose had no beauty, but her energy and good spirits were magnetic.

Olga played, "I Know Some Day a Miracle Will Happen" for Ingo. Some day…

"I know that song," Frau Bauer said and sang "…when all the fairy tales will come true," imitating Zarah Leander's sultry voice. "My favorite," she said, to the applause of her friends. "People here don't know the song. They are doing fine without miracles—living here is a miracle. What other German tunes do you know, Olga? Enough to fill an evening? We'll bring our families and friends, let them hear and see what Germany is all about. All they know is war propaganda. We've had enough of that."

"If that isn't the truth," Ilse-Marie said. She had joined the party, and looked quite attractive in her green two-piece outfit and heels. She had pinned her hair back with combs.

The air had cooled off. Once they had an air conditioner, people would come to escape from their hot offices.

"Let's hear some more songs," Frau Bauer said. "How I miss German music. I was seventeen when we came to California and grew up on songs from the thirties. So did all my friends here. I love the way you play, Olga. Aren't we fortunate to have you?"

Olga remembered the Esplanade. Now she had no one to wait for.

Frau Bauer introduced her friends. There was Erna and Fritz, Willy, Anneliese, Renate, Helga and Hannelore. She had an Ute, Maria and Waltraud, Manfred, Helmut, Peter, Horst and Oskar. Olga shook hands with every one of them. "Amazing," she said. "I can't believe I'm in California. If not for the heat, I'd believe I'm back in Germany."

She counted the beer and food being consumed. On her suggestion, Ilse-Marie had stocked up on German-style rye bread, cold cuts, and cheese, which they now served to the choir. With a wink at Olga, Ilse-Marie too added up the revenue that would buy her time off for a visit to Lake Arrowhead and the long overdue vacation in Hawaii.

By the time the happy crowd left the restaurant, Olga was exhausted. Her feet ached. Sepp poured himself a last beer before dropping into a chair as if he would never get up again.

Ilse-Marie headed reluctantly for the kitchen. "If we keep this up we can hire a dishwasher."

Saturday's party convinced Olga that she had found her gold mine. Two weeks later, they hired a young Russian woman who cleared tables and washed the dishes so that Ilse-Marie could concentrate on food preparation and Olga could entertain. The new air conditioner kept the temperature down, though the heat wave had passed. Olga's music inspired people to sing and dance. The more they sang the more they drank. The guests remembered the songs from their youth, and talked about Old Germany. Usually, the last guests left somewhere around one in the morning. With the dishes washed, Ilse- Marie and Olga would sit down and have a snack and a beer while complimenting each other.

Tonight Sepp joined them, on somewhat wobbly legs. "People kept buying me beer," he said, puffed up with pride. "Now that's what I call a good turn-out." He had rolled up his sleeves, and wore his lederhosen with traditional suspenders. Olga put up her feet on a chair. It had been a long day, yet she was not tired at all. This was more than she had ever hoped for. If only Ingo could see her now. She had written to him, but did not expect him to understand how fortunate she was to be here.

"Not bad, Ilse-Marie," Sepp said, patting his wife's thick shoulder.

"Don't you dare take credit for any of this, Sepp Sailer," she said. "It was Olga's idea and her music that brought people here and kept them eating and drinking."

He took her reproach with good humor and washed it down with a long swig of beer. Ilse-Marie munched on a *landjaeger* sausage and fished a pickle from a large glass jar. "How about giving Olga some credit, Sepp? A true lady and a pianist. At first, I was convinced she was a flake. And look at her now. Olga, you've got that intuition all right. Perhaps you can teach me something about it."

Olga chortled. She enjoyed the bickering between her two friends. Would she be like that with Ingo after years of marriage? "When I first walked in here, I imagined Old Heidelberg in its glory. I'm so grateful that you gave me a chance to make my vision come true."

"As if we had a choice," Ilse-Marie said. "You were our destiny. So there you have it. Annie said that you're also a fortune teller." She gazed into Olga's eyes, as if she could reveal some secret in her life. With her shoes kicked off she wiggled her toes. "These shoes are killing me. I should stick to sandals."

"I used to read cards," Olga said. "But I haven't done it for some time. Not since I got in trouble with an evil spirit."

Ilse-Marie jerked up. "You don't say. What did he do?"

Olga saw the alarm in Ilse-Marie's eyes, and said softly, "Nothing much. Just tried to spook me. There are evil entities, you know. But I haven't seen any for years." She laughed as if joking. "Fortune telling is a craft. Anybody can learn it. When we have some time, I can teach you. In the meantime, we'll make the Old Heidelberg the place to be in L.A. We should have a marketing plan. Perhaps hire a professional who will set us up. Mistakes are costly; we don't want that. If you let me share the profits, I'd be glad to invest my money for improvements." She drained her glass. "It's getting late. We're on the right track. The word will spread. There are lots of restaurants in L.A., but nothing like the Old Heidelberg. I think we have a good formula." She thought of Dresden, and saw flames engulfing the world. That was passed. She was in America now. That was a miracle.

Ilse-Marie said, "You're right."

"We need fresh paint, curtains, table cloths. Lighter colors," Olga recited with her eyes closed. "All kinds of people will come here." The old world charm would attract curious visitors. "We need some American dishes, and a pie or two. I can pretty much play any popular piece, American or German. People from my former audience will come. Even Ben Hanley himself might show up. They remember me as the German Baroness."

"You don't have to convince me, Olga," Ilse-Marie said with adoring eyes. "You're too good to be true. I'm afraid I'll wake up and find things the way they were when you came."

"Don't you worry. Tomorrow we'll make an appointment with a marketing man and an interior designer and take it from there. Los Angeles is no longer a western outpost. It's industries will grow. Hollywood studios are only a small part of it."

Sepp stretched out his hairy legs. "I'm not sure whether this woman is a curse or a blessing."

Ilse-Marie sighed, rolling her eyes. "Oh, Sepp. Sometimes you say the dumbest things. No wonder we landed in a rut. Olga's proposition is fine with me. See you tomorrow, Olga. I'll lock up and take this fellow home."

When Olga returned to her house, she found Anyna sound asleep. Kissing the warm forehead, she smelled her child's warm skin. Deep gratitude for Anyna overcame her. Tears filled her eyes. All this was too wonderful. They had a home. She would have the money for Anyna's education, who would become a smart and beautiful young woman who could support herself. The slumbering child was still innocent. Soon her lovely hands would create great art, and nobody would take advantage of her. Olga would see to that. She smoothed the sheet over Anyna's shoulder.

"You're home, Mami," Anyna mumbled sleepily. "I don't need the sheet. It's too hot. How did it go? Did the choir come?"

Olga sat at Anyna's bed and smoothed the hair from her warm face. How lovely she was, and so wise for her age.

"I can help you after school and on weekends. My schoolwork isn't hard at all. Not like Switzerland, where I had to study French and English too. I'm way ahead in math. So you see, I can help while you play the piano."

"Let's see how it goes. Good night, my sweet."

Anyna flung her arms around Olga's neck and pulled her down. "Stay a little while. We haven't been together like that for a long time. I miss you, Mom. Let's just cuddle and talk about Uncle Ingo. I do miss him. Imagine how much fun we will have when he comes."

"When he comes," Olga whispered, taking off her dirndl, then slipping into bed. "You are my home."

Anyna soon fell asleep against Olga's shoulder. Olga cherished the love they shared, aware that her child's need for her would soon diminish. Ruminating over her own childhood, she could not remember having spent intimate moments with her mother. Mathilde had never shown real affection toward her girls. They respected each other. Olga and Anyna had always been close, despite Anyna's being away in Switzerland and the Countess' slander toward Olga. Anyna understood her mother's love for Ingo.

The night air was cool. The sky glowed with city lights. Crickets chirped outside the open windows. A dog barked. The sweet scent of gardenias wafted in with the ocean breeze. Olga gazed at the starry sky, where the crescent moon was making its first appearance, starting a new cycle. *Thank you, Father, for your love and guidance. You took me to Old Heidelberg, and opened the door to a new future for us. You gave me the talent that attracts people to my music. When will you take me to Ingo? I miss him so.*

A light appeared on the ceiling, and grew into circles that soon illuminated the whole room. *You came to me, Father. I feel your love and your blessing. Under your care Anyna and I can thrive again.*

Weeks later, Erna Bauer and her singers filed into the Old Heidelberg. "What's all this?" she asked admiring the fresh tablecloths, flowers, and cool air. "Come in quickly and close the door," she shouted. "The place looks terrific. Hello Sepp." She said this every week, admiring the progress taking place. "Olga. When will you quit? The new floor looks great." They had put in new carpeting—the consultant Olga had hired had suggested they take out a loan for the improvements. The interest rate was so low that it was almost like free money.

"Now look, Erna," Sepp said, "I don't mind giving credit where it's due. But the Old Heidelberg still belongs to Sepp and Ilse-Marie Sailer."

"Fair enough," Erna said, watching him draw beer for the men in her choir. Several of the women had one too. It was another dry, hot summer day.

When Ilse-Marie, in a fresh blue and white dirndl, came in with platters of cold cuts, cheeses, butter, and fresh rolls, the "aahs" and "oohs" would not stop. Anyna brought potato salad and a tray with sliced tomatoes, cucumbers, pickles, radishes, and green onions. They even had a bowl with cottage cheese.

After greeting the guests, Olga played the "Radetzky March". Everybody tapped and clapped to the fiery beat, then sang along to the familiar tune. Ilse-Marie's cold buffet was all you can eat for three dollars. Anyna danced with whoever asked her, and took orders for beer and side dishes. With Nadia helping out in the kitchen, Ilse-Marie could join the festivities. To everybody's amazement, she had a real talent for telling German jokes she remembered from her days in Berlin. With every stein he poured, Sepp's smile broadened. There was no doubt he had never enjoyed his bar as much as today.

The German choir not only had their rehearsals here, they celebrated their birthdays and anniversaries at the Old Heidelberg as well. Sepp poured himself another beer, to celebrate. The gold caps on his teeth sparkled under his walrus mustache.

Olga pounded three loud chords on the keyboard. "All I can say, Erna, is that you made this the best of all possible worlds. From now on, we'll enjoy the best of Germany while living in the best part of the world. How can you beat that? I know Oktober is still two months away, but planning and preparations take time. We'll have a real *Muenchner Oktoberfest* out in the garden. I understand that we can count on the weather. The first *Muenchner Oktoberfest* in Los Angeles with lots of Loewenbrau, *bratwurst* and *sauerkraut*. I even found an *Oom Pa Pa* band at the Swiss Club.

They drank to that, and many other toasts until they noticed that it was past midnight again. As soon as the last guest had departed, the helpers collapsed around the table Nadia had cleared for them. Next week they would have Heidi, a young German immigrant, come on board. She would contribute to the high spirits. Trained in Germany, she had charm and wit, as well as a delectable young body that would keep the men drooling. Olga liked her infectious smile, and the girl's natural charm.

"What's this about an Oktoberfest?" Sepp asked. "Just where will you find a garden?"

"Right here, in the back yard," Olga said, stretching. Carrying all those beer steins and plates had been hard work. If only Ingo could be here and experience this. She yawned. He wrote occasionally, and had suggested she get more experienced help. *You can't just count on your luck and hard work*, he wrote. *Running a business, especially a restaurant, is tricky. With proper guidance and planning, you can avoid major mistakes. I'm grateful that Daimler Benz taught me the basics during my apprenticeship. How I wish I could be there with you. But Fritzle needs me. I can't abandon him.* Then he went on to say how much he loved and missed her, and all the other sweet nothings she thrived on.

Erna Bauer had suggested James Hill, who not only gave them good advice, he took over the bookkeeping and put Sepp's helter-skelter numbers in neat rows in formal ledgers that recorded the financial life of Old Heidelberg. "You'll need these when you fill out your tax return," he advised. "So far Sepp hasn't made a profit, but that's changing, isn't it? You don't want to get into a hassle with the IRS. They're serious when it comes to submitting evidence of your income and expenses."

Olga had never dealt with taxes before, as she'd never had much income, and she doubted that Lothar ever bothered filing a tax return. From now on, she would live a regular life and fulfill her duties as a citizen. A sense of pride and accomplishment washed over her and drew the blood into her face, as if the others could read her resolve.

Sepp had his doubts. "You can't just clear out the yard," he protested. "So far you've always gotten your way, Olga. But there are limits."

Olga laughed. The evening had been an unbelievable high for her. Father had returned and guided her to success. "Didn't I tell you that I helped clear away an ocean of rubble and debris in Berlin? Your backyard is a cinch. We'll plant vines and string up Chinese lanterns. Turn the yard into a beer garden with long tables where people can meet each other. I've got it all figured out."

"So I see," he grumbled and poured himself another beer.

"We'll rent a dance floor. It'll be authentic."

Sepp reached for Ilse-Marie's hand and implored, "I think we've fallen under the spell of a demon."

Ilse-Marie chuckled, then laughed and laughed until tears rolled down her red cheeks. "Sepp Sailer, you don't understand a thing. But I do, and we'll do exactly what Olga envisions."

"Anyna will paint Heidelberg Castle, Neuschwanstein, and snow-covered mountains on the walls. She is very good at that, right, darling?" Olga said.

"That's right, Frau Sailer," Anyna assured her patron. "I can show you my portfolio."

"Portfolio yet? But you're only thirteen."

"Don't you worry about that," Anyna said in the von Schenck fashion, never doubting her genius.

"This might be a good time to talk about a partnership," Olga reminded them.

"I am not sure," Sepp said, "that we are up to your grand ideas for Old Heidelberg."

"Of course you are. Just remember how good you both feel tonight. Just take me on as your daughter. I'll never act without your approval. That's a promise." She looked deep into Sepp's eyes, then turned to Ilse-Marie, knowing that she would have the last word.

She did. "It's about time we enjoyed the fruits of our labor, Sepp," she teased, and poured herself a shot of brandy. "Here's to you, Olga, partner and daughter, and to you, Baroness Anna Magdalena. You'll make a wonderful grandchild. And to you, Nadia, should you care to become a permanent employee of the Old Heidelberg. We'll have a lawyer draw up the papers tomorrow. It's about time that we get to live the American dream. Been slaving away long enough."

Chapter 46

The Oktoberfest surpassed everyone's expectations. People had flocked in like long-lost relatives from as far away as Pasadena, Long Beach, and Covina. Olga was putting the last plastic grapevines into a box to use again next year, when Al Whitney showed up, puffing on a cigar. Had he lost weight, or did the light suit, open shirt, and loafers make him look thinner and younger? Or was it his tan? "Al!" she cried out, running toward him as to an old friend she had missed for ages. "How good to see you. What brings you to Los Angeles?"

"Business," he said, holding her in a warm embrace. "Ann, as your daughter calls herself now, directed me to you. Looks like an all-American girl, and talks like one too." He winked. He had the same brown eyes under heavy brows that had impressed her back in Bavaria ages ago. "Said she doesn't miss Germany."

"We didn't leave anything worth missing," Olga said, steering him toward the bar where Sepp was watching suspiciously.

"The impressario," Sepp teased. "How about a beer? Genuine Loewenbrau. Can you tell the difference?" He drew some from a shining spigot, watching the foam build up.

"I got your whereabouts from Ben Hanley," Al told Olga. "He's doing okay, though Big Bands are giving way to Cuban rhythms and whatever else. He's adapting." Glancing around the dining room, he added, "Don't tell me you gave up music?"

"No, of course not. That would be like giving up breathing. I entertain here. We're doing very well."

"So I see," he said, admiring the freshly decorated dining room. The tables had red and white table cloths which matched the curtains on the small, rustic windows.

Sepp handed Al the foaming mug of golden brew, and watched him taste it. "When it comes to German beer, people forget about the war. I came here before it started, and couldn't get back. So I opened this restaurant. German immigrants used to gather here. I'm from Heidelberg. Had no idea that years would pass before I might see it again. I haven't been back and don't intend to go.

"Since Olga joined us, we've had other newcomers show up as well. Young people, tired of the war, eager to make some dream come true. They have good training and lots of energy. Just look at this young lady here," he said, pointing at Olga. "In a couple of months, she took over the place as if she'd been in the business all her life. Tells me what to do. What's worse, she's right. Figure that one out?" He grinned, massaging his double chin. Though it was November, there was no sign of fall. The vines Olga had planted in whiskey barrels still had green leaves, and the oleander blossoms were a fresh pink. The heat had subsided, leaving the air warm and mellow.

"Anyna painted the Heidelberg Castle," Olga said, touching Al's arm. "How do you like it? She did it from an old postcard." She took his hand. "I can't thank you enough for giving us the chance to leave Germany. To think that I played at the Diamond Club. Merriweather still keeps in touch, so does Buddy Jones. Amazing, isn't it?"

"I knew you had it in you when I first saw you at the NCO Club," Al said. "Aldrich was right when he told me about you. Buddy Jones is German. He trusted my judgment. He didn't have much to lose, since I took the risk. The reputation of his band doesn't depend on his guest soloists. Mine depends on the clients I sign up. You have to earn that trust."

"Thanks, Al. You gave me the break I'd never had. I couldn't believe that you meant it. I'm glad you took your due when Lothar broke the contract. The Countess didn't even appreciate his coming home. She preferred the money to her son's presence." She crossed her legs, and her skirt slipped up. Olga didn't bother with hose, and wore open-toe pumps on her bare feet. "To tell the truth, I don't miss Germany. Surely not the Countess and her stinking room. All that nonsense about aristocracy." She smirked, curling her nose. "She never respected me for going to work and keeping things going. Talk about delusions of grandeur. But she's getting away with it."

Al raised his glass and drank, leaving traces of foam on his dark mustache. "You're right, Mr. Sailer. A fine brew."

"Do call me Sepp. Thought you'd like it. Germany may have many faults, but we know how to make a good brew. I hear the country is on the mend." He chuckled. "This beer will conquer the world without shedding a drop of blood."

"The Marshal Plan works," Al said, "A genius idea."

"More than that," Olga said, checking her watch. It was almost time to start the dinner service. "The grand gesture of a true humanitarian. The war is over and life must go on."

Al took a closer look at Anyna's painting. "That kid has talent. Must be going on twelve?"

"Thirteen," Olga said, "and loves her school. She doesn't care that kids make fun of her accent, which she is losing in a hurry. The teacher enjoys her quick mind. Anyna helps out here on weekends. She talks to the guests like an adult. Amazing girl."

"You certainly adapted to L.A., Olga," Al said, helping himself to a tiny pretzel from the bowl on the counter. He did not comment on her dirndl, or the tight bodice revealing a deep cleavage. Quite a change from her role as a baroness. Once Ilse-Marie retired, Olga would wear elegant clothes. Sepp was not eager to keep working much longer either, and agreed that they could use more help.

Tucking the unruly curls behind her ears, Olga noticed that Al had changed. He no longer looked like a stuffy New York business man in a weird tie. In his sport shirt, his hair longer with a stylish cut, she felt drawn to him as to an old friend, rather than her agent.

"I love this city," she said. "People care about each other. My neighbor Hazel has a heart of gold. She looks after Anyna and checks her homework. And the Russians will never come here. I'll never know what those drills for a nuclear attack are all about. They just frighten the children. Another war is unthinkable, don't you agree, Al?"

"I don't know about unthinkable, let's hope unlikely." He took a handful of pretzels and stuffed them into his mouth.

Olga got up and took a Coke from the refrigerator, then poured the fizzing contents into a glass over ice. Heidi was setting up the tables for dinner. The place was booked solid. People didn't mind waiting as long as Sepp quenched their thirst with his now famous Loewenbrau beer. "I'm so glad I found you, Olga. You look lovelier than ever. Healthy, content, at ease. You always gave the impression of somebody who had to hide. No more—you're your own boss now." He took a long sip. "Doesn't work for me." He leaned toward her. "Myrtle left, you know. Coming home to an empty house is no fun. I didn't think she'd do it. Warming up a can of Chef Boyardee or frying Spam while I whip up powdered mashed potatoes and boil frozen peas isn't much of a life. We had our differences, but I never thought she'd leave me. Took the kid and was gone. Now I'm not only alone, I have to pay alimony and child support." He lit a fresh cigar. "How are Lothar's 'Catacombs' coming along?" he said to change the subject.

"We don't correspond much. I help out with money, so I get an occasional thank you note. He's desperately trying to launch his compositions. People like music that appeals to their heart."

"He's so full of himself," Al said.

"Runs in the family. They despise my vulgar pursuit of money without an inkling of how to provide for their own needs. I'm so glad you came, Al. You're the only person who knew me back then."

"I admired you then, and I admire you now," he said, taking her hand and holding it. She did not withdraw. She too was lonely. Independence had its price.

"The reason I came," he said, "is that Buddy Jones wants you to play with his band."

Olga perked up. "Are you serious? Where? Solo?"

He nodded. "Solo. He has an engagement at the Palladium. Opens New Year's Eve."

Olga held her glass and raised it like a chalice. *Father, you did this for me?* Buddy Jones wanted her. "What does he have in mind?" she asked, trying to hide her excitement.

Ilse-Marie brought out a giant sandwich. "Any friend of Olga's deserves a treat. Come on, Sepp, refill his glass. Can't you see it's empty? Olga is part of our family now. The only family we have." She spread a white napkin out in front of him. "I'm Ilse-Marie, and you are?"

"Al." They shook hands, then admired the fare. "No wonder your restaurant is thriving," he said. "I bet these cold cuts come from a German butcher." He carefully lifted the upper slice of bread. "Pickles, lettuce, tomatoes, and red onion rings—just the way I like it. You can't even get them in New York. And those fries – still sizzling."

Ilse-Marie's eyes beamed. "I do my best, Al."

Olga picked up a French fry with her finger tips and placed it into her mouth. "She makes them from scratch, none of that frozen stuff."

Ilse-Marie wore her faded apron. Her frizzy brown hair showed threads of white. "Genuine *jagdwurst*, *Thuringer*, and Swiss cheese," she said. "The real thing. I bet you haven't tasted anything like this since you visited Germany." She joined them at the bar, leaning her thick arms against the counter.

"Smoked salami; it's my weakness. Ilse-Marie, you are a gem of a cook. If I lived here, I'd eat here every day. I'll certainly be your guest for as long as I'm in L.A."

She watched him bite into the sandwich. "I hope you're not allergic to mustard."

"On the contrary. I guess it's German too."

She nodded. "Ever since Olga came to us, we do things right. She brought us more guests than we ever dreamed of having. You should hear her play the piano. Now that's talent. She plays anything people ask for, accompanies the choir, sometimes she even plays serious stuff. You know, like Chopin and Brahms and things. They wrote some pretty good music. Come on Friday, then you can hear her play."

Al swallowed. "She's a pianist. That's why I'm here. I'm her agent. I brought her and her husband over from Germany to play with Buddy Jones and Ben Hanley."

Ilse-Marie stared at him in disbelief. "You mean, THE Buddy Jones? Olga is good, but she's not that good."

Al stopped the sandwich in mid-bite. "You'd be surprised. She is that good, and then some. This young lady is a first-class pianist, wasting her God-given talents on this ridiculous piano."

"Now wait a minute," Ilse-Marie protested. "You haven't even heard it. Besides, we got it for her. You should've seen what we had before, then you'd have something to complain about." She wiped the sweat from her face. "I don't know that much about music. You're probably right about Olga being a good pianist. But I do know something about Buddy Jones and Ben Hanley. That's my kind of music." She got up and did some dance steps to "You Ain't Got a Thing if You Ain't Got that Swing." They laughed. "How do you like that? I came to Hollywood to be another Mary Pickford or something. And this is where I wound up. A mess, is all I can say."

"I wouldn't say that. I can see that you have talent. A bit out of shape, but what the heck."

"Did you hear that Sepp Sailer?" she proclaimed in the pose of a star, her arms stretched out.

He busied himself polishing a beer stein and said nothing.

"He has no idea what's going on. But he'll find out when Olga doesn't show up for work. Who'll entertain the people coming to hear her, accompany the choir, and greet the guests as if they were her friends?"

"They are," Olga said, amused by the spectacle. One never knew what dwelled in the heart of man until it was called for. Ilse-Marie had a pleasant enough voice. She had probably been attractive and charming. But running a losing restaurant had pulled her down. Now, overweight and desperate, she had given up on her dream. Olga must never give up. Her dream was as solid as anything in life could be. Which wasn't saying much. But she would pursue it to her last breath.

"You must understand, Al," Ilse-Marie said, "our guests don't just come to drink beer."

Al chewed on his monumental sandwich and washed it down with fresh beer. "Surely you can find a piano player who can accompany the choir and entertain your diners? I'll even pay the wages, how's that? A small token to give people a chance to hear Olga's performance. You just wait and see. She's phenomenal. One of a kind. People hold their breath when she does 'Rhapsody in Blue.' Imagine her in an evening gown, a fur draped over her shoulders, her hair done up and decorated with jewels. Sensational. You helped Olga in need, and her dirndl looks charming. No, it's the truth. We all must work for a living. But Olga is an artist, a performing artist, and the most beautiful woman I met."

Now he had everybody's attention. Sepp and Ilse-Marie stared at Olga as if they had never seen her before, and felt guilty for having her wear that dirndl.

"That's enough, Al," Olga said, rising. "You're overdoing it. I love the dirndl. It looks perfectly good on me. Sepp and Ilse-Marie share this restaurant with me. We're a team, and I'm not about to abandon them for a short engagement. I'm part of Old Heidelberg. We created it together and we're doing well. Very well, right Sepp? Our plan works. We could sell it tomorrow for a good price, but we enjoy our work and have plans for the future. Right Ilse-Marie?" Her friend was not as inclined to jump in as expected. At least not right away.

Sepp agreed. "Olga has many talents, I guess."

"What are you saying, Sepp?" Ilse Marie retorted. "Olga has German discipline. She does what she sets her mind to. She believes in what she does, unlike you, Sepp. Now that she's with us, so do I. But I tell you what, Al, I'm not about to stand in her way. She's a great woman and an artist. I know we can work this out."

Olga jumped up and hugged her friend impulsively. "Thank you, Ilse-Marie." She blew Sepp a kiss. "Thank you, Sepp. I'll make it worth your while."

He grunted. "We don't need money. We're doing good."

Ilse-Marie held her stein up to Sepp. "Let's drink to Olga's success. Heidi can run the floor while you're away, and I'll do the kitchen, though I had planned on retiring."

Olga hugged her friend again. "I could do the early shift; my performances usually start around nine. Then it's settled. And you'll get a special table at the Palladium and meet Buddy Jones. How's that?"

Ilse-Marie stared at Olga as if she had seen an apparition. "You mean that?"

"I never say things I don't mean," Olga said.

Al had finished his sandwich and offered his hand. "Then it's a deal."

"It's a deal," Ilse-Marie said. She had tears in her eyes. Nothing worthwhile had ever happened in her life, and now all this. "Hollywood," she whispered dreamily. "Our Olga a Hollywood star?"

Al took Ilse-Marie's hand, and kissed it. "You're a swell woman. And you, Sepp, a fine restaurateur. Olga's engagement will last a month. Show business goes from contract to contract. As soon as the contract is over, she'll be back in her dirndl. But you'll get to see the glamour part. She's terrific," he said, an adoring look in his eyes.

"Olga deserves it," Sepp said. "The Oktoberfest was a financial feast. We made more money than I could have imagined. We almost ran out of beer! Thanks to this young lady, we ordered twice as much as I intended. She has that sixth sense."

Olga patted his shoulder. "Thank you, Sepp. It's because we invested heavily in advertising. In America, you've got to do it the

American way. I'm learning, Al, as you can see. You didn't think I would catch on when you met me in Bavaria, did you?"

"Oh, I wouldn't say that. Then, Lothar was the big shot, and you played second fiddle. But not for long. When you took off, musically that is, nobody and nothing could stop you. That's when I knew I'd found a treasure. The two of you were dynamite. People felt the tension—the cool knight who can't keep his passionate and beautiful wife under control. The guys were drooling. You were great."

"Lothar didn't like it one bit," Olga recalled. "But he's decided to enjoy California sunshine and come for a visit in January."

After a moment's silence, Al said, "Would he be willing to sign up for a short tour with Hanley, or somebody like that? Palm Springs, Las Vegas, even the Palladium might have a spot for the German Baron and Baroness. Seems to go well, despite his obnoxious attitude."

Olga saw dollar signs in Al's eyes.

"It's worth a try," she agreed. If Lothar earned his keep, she wouldn't have to support him. This time, her part would be deposited in a separate account rather than wind up in his. "I'll write to him, Al. I bet the Countess will urge him to go."

"What's all this about?" Sepp asked, rubbing his chin. "What countess? German Baron and Baroness? What are you talking about?"

Al laughed so hard that he choked on his beer. "Sounds like a farce, doesn't it? You should see the Countess. She is really something. So is Lothar."

Olga took her Coke. Having Lothar here would test her patience beyond endurance. Why did Father do this to her? Was it another test? Did he tempt her with the Holy Grail? Was this the way to Ingo? She thought she was rid of Lothar, but without a divorce it was not legal.

"I'll give Buddy a call," Al said, and rose. "He'll be delighted to hear that Lothar might be part of the act, though he'd probably prefer to live without him. But business is business, and there's no business like show business." He put his glass down. "I guess it's moments like this that keep me doing it."

The sun shone through the small windows, catching raindrops clinging to the panes. The first rain of the season. Olga longed to go outside and inhale the fresh moist air. The prospect of seeing Lothar put a damper on the prospect of being out in the limelight again. Why was she always living for others? She and Anyna were doing fine. But Lothar was her father. It was a fact that could not be eradicated. Every child was entitled to two parents. Without the Countess' influence he might... Olga ran her hand across her forehead, as if she could rub her thoughts from her mind. This would be her opportunity to make a final break between them. "By playing with Buddy I'll earn enough money to put some modern equipment in the kitchen and fix up the patio," she told Sepp, as if he needed convincing.

"Well, Olga, you never cease to amaze me," Al said. "Didn't you tell me once that your motto is 'with patience, audacity, and tact everything is possible'? Sure works for you. I'll never know where you get that patience from. Can't think of a single woman who wouldn't have thrown a fit when her husband broke that contract and gave up all the money you'd worked for. You accepted his crazy plan and went home with him to a mother-in-law you can't stand. I bet in a couple of years, I'll find you in one of those Bel Air homes. More power to you."

She laughed. "Glad you feel that way, Al. Things just worked out for me. Destiny, you know. Remember the story of seven good years and seven bad years? It seems that I'm coming to the seven good years part. Right time, right place, so to speak. When you can't go home, you move on. There isn't a place I'd rather be than right here, in Los Angeles."

"She has the power of a Sherman tank," Sepp said. "You can't resist her."

Al took her hand and held it. "I better say goodbye, Olga. You're getting to me."

She sensed his desire. It excited her. She should loosen up, and start living. It'd been too long since she had last been with a man other than Lothar.

"I'll get off a telegram right away," she promised, remembering the one Ingo had sent back in Litzmannstadt.

Al hesitated, as if he had something on his mind. "You certainly speak good English. Almost like a native. Did you know that Sgt. Aldrich had a thing for you? The way he promoted you wasn't just altruism. He wanted you. Did he name his price?"

Olga stared at Al. "Price? For what?"

"Well, you know. Everything carries a price tag."

"What price tag? Sgt. Aldrich is my friend."

"I'm sorry, Olga. I'll never know how you get away with your innocence. But I believe it's genuine."

"I don't know why you talk like that, Al?"

"Neither do I. You obviously weren't part of the gold mine Americans found in Germany. Aldrich, and a lot of men like him, turned into millionaires. Imagine Sepp, those guys traded cigarettes for gold. Cigarettes! You should've seen the stuff they sent home. People were so hungry they'd give anything for cigarettes and food. Not that the G.I.'s had anything to stop them. They just took. I should've gone there earlier. Aldrich set himself up in real estate. He's doing great. Money would have kept my wife at home, instead of betraying me. Never thought I'd get sentimental. In a way I'm a refugee too."

"I'm sorry, Al," Olga said, her warm hand on his arm. "You must try to not think about it. You did the best you could. Women get lonely." She thought of Ingo, and her longing for him.

Chapter 47

On the second day of Lothar's visit, Olga was already wondering how much longer she could put up with him. Even worse, why had she allowed him to come at all. Of course, he objected to her sleeping in Anyna's room. "In case you've forgotten, let me remind you that you are my wife,"

"On paper only," she said curtly.

"How can you say that after all I've done for you?" he implored in a nasal, superior tone. "Why do you think I came here? The sun? Buddy Jones? You still don't know me, do you? Your indifference toward me is uncalled for, not to mention that a husband has certain rights. Did you ever ask yourself why people get married?"

The question caught her by surprise. Had he forgotten what had brought them together? Love was the last reason that came to mind. "To legitimize the birth of a child."

He sipped his tea at the kitchen table, and ate Hazel's apple pie with ice cream.

"I thought you'd enjoy performing with the Buddy Jones band and make some money to take home to your mother."

His eye caught hers. "Aha. So that's it. You think everyone is as greedy as you. Money! That's all you can think of!" He dropped his fork, and wiped his mouth as if he'd endured a slimy kiss. "The word makes me sick. Instead of being proud to be married to a genius, sharing his gifts with the world, all you think of is money. Did I ever ask for any? Did you not have a roof over your head and food to eat?"

She held her cheeks as if slapped. "Not because you offered it." All this was so pointless, demeaning, ridiculous.

"I didn't ask you to come. Didn't I tell you that we had limited means and no space?"

He pushed the plate away like a spoiled child. "But you came anyway, barged into our lives without an ounce of gratitude. And that after you openly entertained a lover."

Olga stared at her plate. So that was it. He was her benefactor, to whom she owed gratitude. It had never occurred to her that to him she had always been an unwanted appendage. That she was destitute, and Anyna on the verge of starvation, when they arrived from Berlin held no meaning for him. Her efforts to provide some comfort to the Countess and hold her own meant nothing. She meant nothing to him, other than as a physical convenience he was entitled to.

She rose and took her plate to the sink. Why was she so shocked?

"Why did you come here?" she asked, unable to keep her emotions in check. He dipped his spoon into the melting ice cream. "To see my daughter. I like Los Angeles, and thought it would do me good to spend some time here. Besides, you asked me to come."

Holding the dishes under hot running water, she said, "I thought you would enjoy playing with Ben Hanley. Your mother always needs money..."

"Get money out of your mind. We manage," he said, cutting off a piece of pie with his knife and then pushing it onto his fork. He sat erect, as if attending a banquet. "I don't want to be ungrateful—extra cash comes in handy at times, but is not essential. However, considering that you earn it as a bar maid is rather degrading. On the other hand, you seem to enjoy that sort of thing, and have no appreciation of my efforts to create something that will enlighten the world. I'm advancing the progress of mankind. There is a price to pay, but it's worth it. I am devoting my life to this." He blotted his lips with his napkin, and leaned back in the chair, his hands folded on the edge of the table. "You don't understand any of this. Not that it makes any difference."

Olga admired his conviction; Lothar could not see that his work was meaningless.

"Any idiot can work at a mindless job and make money," he said, "but how many creative people do you know who produce unknown elements, create new theorems, compose music, and devise new ways of thinking? If not for this war, I would be honored for my work with a chair at a university. As soon as I publish my work, the public will see its importance. Important conductors will beg me to perform with their orchestras. And here you talk about the pittance you send us, instead of paying attention to my work. You don't even listen to my compositions. You close the door and turn on the radio to annoy me."

Olga didn't know whether she should laugh or cry, play the fool, or give him a piece of her mind. How could he be so wrong? Or was she wrong? Wiping the table, she avoided his eyes. If he felt that calling, it was only natural that he would devote his life to it. Who was she to say that his music was unbearable? So far nobody had responded to it, but if he felt that it was important enough to devote his life to, she had to accept that. All she knew was that they had nothing in common except the child they shared. She would do whatever it took to fulfill the contract with Buddy Jones. Once Lothar returned to Germany, she would file for divorce and make a clear break.

He went to the piano, a grim look in his eyes. What did he expect her to say? The whole matter was hopeless. What she considered a sacrifice was looked upon as an intrusion. So be it. But she could not help feeling guilty, that she had failed. Once upon a time, during their early years of their marriage, she had truly tried to create a family life. He couldn't blame her for not trying. After she met Ingo, she saw what life could and should be like, with a man who loved and respected her and supported her endeavors. Then again, where was he now? They were both in the same boat, having children with partners they had not chosen.

The tea kettle whistled. She poured the boiling water into the tea pot. While it steeped, she took out one of the green glass mugs Lothar hated. With him here, her home felt hostile and foreign. She took her tea to the living room. "We should go over the music Buddy wants us to play," she said. "I must leave in a hour."

"Of course, the guests have to be served," he sneered. "Sepp Sailer expects your services. For that, you left the refined atmosphere Maman and I provided for you and the girl. Do you know how many beautiful and talented women would cherish my company? And you, my wife, prefer to live here, at the end of the world so that you can work in a beer joint that serves food no decent German would eat. The disgust in your eyes is uncalled for, my dear," he said cynically, his handsome mouth twisted. "A touch of gratitude would go a long way. What did I do to make myself so despicable in your eyes? My serving in the Wehrmacht provided you with a palatial apartment, a maid and a comfortable income, but you chose to entertain soldiers at a café."

Olga leafed through the stack of notes Buddy had sent her. "We've played most of the pieces before. I enjoy Buddy's easy swing, especially when he does 'Tea for Two.' It shouldn't take much practice."

"Just as well, since you're so busy. Playing for Buddy will pay a lot more money than you're getting now. I suppose you want to pay off your car and put a down payment on a house. Credit is the American way of life."

She ignored his sarcasm. "Your mother will appreciate it."

"You leave Maman out of this. Let's look at the music. It's hardly worthy of our talent. But all right. Now that I'm here, let's see what we can do." He played "Hernando's Hideaway." His improvisations turned the simple tune into a concert piece. Lothar had talent and skill. He lived for his music and the keyboard was his home. Dressed in his usual black turtleneck and tweed coat, his hair falling carelessly over his forehead in thick brown waves, he was his own man. His long, slender fingers ran over the keys with ease. Did he ever play the "Mephisto Waltz"? Ingo had asked for it in his despair, Lothar would embody it. Sunlight caught his pale face. Last night's rain had washed away the smog and dust, leaving the air fresh and clean. The deep blue sky beyond the window made a perfect backdrop for the orange tree covered with blossoms and fruits. Their scent wafted into the living room. If only Ingo were here instead of Lothar.

Anyna came in through the kitchen door and took the milk bottle from the refrigerator to pour herself a glass. The door closed with a thud. Glass in hand, she came into the living room and watched her parents play a duet.

Olga turned the page. "Don't you like Buddy's arrangement? You can add your improvisations to the second refrain."

"Good idea." He tried a variation. "By the way, did it ever occur to you that I admire you as a woman and a musician? But all I ever got from you is resentment. Do you know what that does to a man who puts himself out to please his wife?"

Please his wife? By torturing and humiliating her? Just don't say anything. Don't let him trick you into speaking your mind. Not now.

He looked at her, an uncanny innocence in his blue eyes. Mephisto himself.

Father, please protect me.

"This score is extremely sentimental and stupid," he said, playing the simple tune. "How do you like that?" He took off with clever arpeggios and chords held together by his complex phrasing to end the song in a torrent of sound. Bang! His hands landed on the keys like a burst of anger.

"Buddy will be pleased," Olga said, as if nothing had happened. "He wants show pieces and you know how to create them. Just tell me where I come in. Or do you want me to play my own variations, a sort of a his and hers solo?"

"Do whatever you like," he said in a gruff voice, and then proceeded to play as if she did not exist.

Olga went to the kitchen. "Anyna, you and Daddy have your dinner without me. I'm very busy getting things ready so that Erika and Heidi can get on without me."

Erika had caught on quickly. She and Heidi had become friends, and worked well together. Sepp and Ilse-Marie enjoyed the girls and shared their easy chatter. So did the guests, who brought their friends and colleagues. This is what we mean by German *Gemuetlichkeit*, they would say. Weekends were always fully booked. Olga tried to convince Sepp and Ilse-Marie that they could expand, tear down the wall to the storage room and use the basement for their supplies. Sure they would have to run up and down the stairs a lot, but Erika and Heidi were young and Olga did not mind. The evenings in winter were too cool to sit outside in the garden.

Driving home along Wilshire Boulevard, Olga admired the glittering Christmas decorations and lights. Buddy would arrive tomorrow; they would meet him at the airport. Olga felt relaxed. A thrill of expectation washed over her—she would be glamorous in a shimmering midnight blue gown, a white fox stole draped over her bare shoulders. She had matching satin pumps, and would wear a white orchid in her hair. Al would approve. People would listen to their music and applaud the Baroness. Life was grand, why couldn't she be happy?

Ingo. She must find a resolution, rather than spend her life waiting for him.

Tell me, Father, what shall I do?

Before going inside, where Lothar was still at the keyboard, she gazed at the stars. Venus stood out in all her brilliance. Others blinked. There was Father, beckoning.

Please, Father, show me the way.

Anyna sat at the kitchen table doing her homework while Lothar worked on one of his bizarre compositions.

"Are we back at the Catacombs?" Olga teased.

"It will make history like Igor Stravinsky's 'Firebird'," he said. "Think of Carmina Burana. People thought Orff was crazy. Now it's a classic. You have a closed mind, Olga. No wonder you like Old Heidelberg. That world is gone and should be buried. Perhaps it never even existed. You must move forward. You're as nostalgic as a grandmother."

Was he right? But she was not alone; people came to Old Heidelberg because they longed for tradition. Who could survive on "Catacombs" and "Ice Age?" She threw her jacket onto the armchair and kicked off her shoes. She was tired. Not from her work at the Old Heidelberg, but because of the enemy in her home. The threat of another outburst created constant tension. Why had she let him come? He was right about her need for money. Was it worth the pain she had to endure? Even Anyna felt it. Ever since Lothar had come, she was quiet and withdrawn. Was he tormenting her while Olga was at work?

"Would anybody like some goulash and potato salad?" she asked and opened the plastic containers she had brought from Ilse-Marie's kitchen. Anyna had not prepared dinner. They should be hungry by now.

Lothar kept on playing, resenting her interruption. He'd rather she listen to him and applaud. She had to put on an act, if she wanted some peace at home.

Should she lie to him and pretend all was well?

Anyna gave Olga a warm hug. "We waited for you, Mom. Dad and I had a long conversation. Did you know that Grandmaman misses us? I miss her too. It's not like we think. She's been trying to teach me how to be a baroness. I really am one, Mom. It's not just pretending." She poured the goulash into a pan and placed it on the stove, then lit the gas with a match. "I really don't care that much about being a baroness. But Daddy says that it's an obligation and we must preserve our heritage. Being of noble blood is a great privilege. Did you know that?"

Olga held her daughter and kissed her clean, smooth skin. The eczema had healed without leaving a single scar, but the horrors of the war still festered in her soul. Olga had noticed that Anyna's paintings had little flames. Though she never mentioned the war years, the Russians, or Tante Gertie and Tante Lore, they were in her memory. She had accepted the loss, but not without pain. Now she wanted to be a baroness again. Why?

The smell of goulash soon wafted through the kitchen. Anyna set the table. Olga had new dishes and cups Ilse-Marie had given her, and brown and white sofa pillows.

Why was Lothar telling Anyna that she was a baroness as if she didn't know it all along? What was he trying to accomplish? He could not seriously convince their child that she would be better off in Germany, living in that stinking room, rather than enjoying life in this beautiful city where she shared a home with her mother. Those comments about Olga's demeaning work at Old Heidelberg, the beer joint bit, was that to show Anyna that Olga was an inferior woman, unfit to be her mother? Would Anyna fall for it?

Lothar hammered out his maddening music. "Messengers from Hell," would be a good title. He stuck to his wife just to annoy her. It gave him pleasure to impose his will and power on her, the egomaniac.

"I don't particularly like that piece, Daddy," Anyna said. "It sounds angry. People here don't like that kind of music. They like tunes you can sing to."

"You don't understand a thing, Anna Magdalena."

"My name is Ann, Daddy. And I understand a lot more than you think." Her fresh young face had the knowing expression of a woman, with the innocent smile of a child.

What did she know? What made her think that Anyna hated her father and wanted for Ingo to join them? Olga dished out the bubbling goulash. Of course Lothar had told Anyna that Ingo was Olga's lover and could never be her father. That was a fact. What did she really know about her daughter? Lothar's dissonant noise grated on her already tense nerves.

Lothar said from the living room, "It's all about money, isn't it?"

Had she missed something?

Anyna blushed. "In a way, Daddy. I know what it's like when you don't have any and are cold and hungry. Tante Adie has lots of money and is always happy. I like pretty clothes and living in a nice home. Don't you? For that we need money."

He joined them in the kitchen. "Oh, so that's it. Grandmaman's world is not good enough?"

"No," Anyna said, facing her father. "Mom is working very hard so that we can have a nice home. It's good to have money. I like being a baroness, and for that I need money. You can't be a baroness and have nothing nice to wear, can you? You didn't care whether we had money or a place to stay. You didn't even want us to come to Inning. I know that. You didn't care that we had no food and that I was very sick. That Mom worked so hard just to keep us alive."

"That's enough, young lady!" he said. "How dare you talk to your father like that?"

"I'm just telling the truth, Daddy. If you don't want to hear it, then we won't talk about it anymore. Still, I like living in this home and going shopping in a car—then we don't have to haul all those groceries around. You don't go shopping, so you don't know what I mean."

Anyna's innocence was precious.

"I don't really like my school. It's not like my school in Switzerland where kids didn't call me Kraut."

"You see," Lothar triumphed, whistling as if he had heard what he wanted. "You like this home, but you have to live here, with people who don't respect anybody. Now you can see why I want you to be my little baroness who tactfully avoids unpleasant conversation. It's an art, Anna Magdalena, one you still have to learn, like so many other things." He sat down at the table.

"When we have money, I can go to a private school."

Olga secretly waved to Anyna to be quiet.

Anyna ignored the signal. "Mom could play with Buddy Jones solo. But she wanted to help you and Grandmaman out so that you would have some money to get an apartment. That old stinking room is so disgusting. That's why grandmaman is always sick..."

"I forbid you to talk to me like that, Anna Magdalena. You ought to be ashamed of yourself. Grandmaman's room does not stink, and she is quite content. Wouldn't want it any other way. We have lots of space now that you are gone."

"I'm glad. We are happy here, where I have my own room."

He stretched his long legs under the table, his gaze fixed on Anyna. "Can we talk about something else now?"

"Yes." She spread her napkin over her lap. "I was so looking forward to your visit, Daddy. But not when you are always angry. You told me that I'm a baroness, and that I don't have to put up with things. That includes you, Daddy."

"Is that so?" He drew his eyes to narrow slits, casting a sharp glance at Olga, "So this is how you raise our daughter. Grandmaman will be horrified when she hears what happened to her beautiful little baroness."

"But Daddy, I'm only telling you so you'll know."

"Well, thanks. I'd rather be treated with respect." He dished out some goulash. The thick brown gravy spread over the plate and flowed into the potato salad.

Olga sprinkled some fresh green onions on top. She was not about to interfere, delighted that Lothar had no control over Anyna.

"In America kids speak up. So you can't blame Mom."

"Do you think it is right for kids to insult their parents?"

Anyna stared at him. Her lower lip quivered and tears filled her eyes. "I'm sorry, Daddy. I don't want you to leave us again."

"As you should be. You'll never be a baroness unless you learn the refinement of tact. You musn't ever voice your opinion in a way that hurts other people's feelings, as you have hurt mine."

"I am really sorry, Daddy." Anyna wiped her tears. She had worn her favorite blue dress with the white collar and belt for Daddy, and her black patent leather shoes.

Olga said nothing.

He took Anyna's small hand. "It's all right, my little one. You'll learn. Grandmaman will teach you. Being an aristocrat isn't easy. It takes practice. I know you'll take my teachings to heart, Anna Magdalena. Let me watch you act like a baroness, so that I can tell Grandmaman how lovely you are, and that she can be proud of you. By the way, there are still no apartments in Germany. I am sure Grandmaman will be pleased to know how much you care for her."

"Oh, Daddy." Anyna flung her arms around his neck and kissed his cheek. "I am so glad you forgive me. I'll show you that I can be a baroness—just watch me."

She took her seat at the table and sat perfectly straight, her hands poised at the edge. "I do hope you'll stay for a long time, Daddy. Then you can teach me. I want you to be proud of me."

"That's my girl," Lothar said, content with his victory. "From now on, we will treat each other with respect. People will admire you for it and tell their kids that they should follow your example. You will be a model for all to follow. Everybody loves a gracious, well-brought up girl. When kids call you a Kraut, just smile and say, 'wouldn't you like to be one too?' Never show defeat, or sulk, or, worse, show that you're hurt. A baroness is like a fortress, strong and proud, that nobody can touch."

"Yes, Daddy," she said quietly, restraining her enthusiasm.

Shocked, Olga wondered, Was the Evil One luring her child away from her again?

The following day The Beverly Hills Hotel with its sensuous mauve and cream décor brought back so many memories that Olga fell into Buddy's arms as if she had longed for him from the time they had parted. In her pale blue suit with white lapels, a pill-box hat fastened to her curls, she relaxed into his warm embrace and appealing after-shave. His navy blazer felt soft to her touch. This was the world that knew her as a musician. After a year struggling on her own, she appreciated the comfort and luxury money could buy. She would get there too, but it would take time. Too bad Ingo couldn't see her now.

"Buddy," she said. "I can't thank you enough for inviting us to play with your band again. You gave us our start, taking us in when everybody despised Germans. America is my home now. You wouldn't recognize Anyna." Olga laughed. "An all-American teenager. She hopes to see Trish again."

"Trish sends her love. Her school starts in three days, that's why she didn't come. I understand she and Anyna have quite a correspondence going." Taking her arm, he said confidentially, "We missed you and your music. The men enjoyed working with you."

Lothar paid no attention to their conversation. After a stiff handshake, he stood aside.

"I like your selections, Buddy. They're different," she said.

"Popular dance tunes. The Palladium is a dance hall, not a nightclub. How does it feel being back in the Golden West?"

"Nothing golden about that smog," Lothar said. "But then, I don't intend to live here. Wait until you hear my improvisations, Buddy. Show-stoppers, to say the least."

Buddy's brows shot up. "I'll certainly take a look." He led the way to the bar, passing orchids and palms. A soft, red carpet cushioned their steps. "I just did a tour in Miami. Great city. A winter playground for the rich. You should see those beaches—the ocean is as blue as the sky. We had sold out performances."

A Christmas tree blinked in the bar among the chrysanthemums and orchids. Buddy helped Olga into her chair, then ordered a Manhattan for her, a scotch on the rocks for Lothar, and a martini for himself.

"I've been hooked on beer every since Sepp introduced me to Loewenbrau, Olga. We don't make anything that's even close to it." He passed a box of cigars around.

Pulling off her white gloves, Olga watched the men cut off the ends of their cigars and light up, blowing out puffs of smoke. Lothar paid no attention to her. To him she did not exist. She would file for divorce—mental cruelty required no further explanation. He could not stop her. Enjoying the sweet cocktail, she listened to Lothar answer questions about Germany. "People are on an eating binge," he said. "The results are already visible; all those skinny girls are filling out like yeast dumplings. They don't mind long hours, overtime, what have you, anything to earn money and make up for lost time. Bars, restaurants, and cafes are crowded. Now that they've gotten some decent clothes, they're looking for motorcycles, saving up for a car, and eventually a place of their own. Housing still is not available, though cities are starting to build apartments for refugee families. Things are looking up. Still a lot of debris around. Little by little." He seemed proud over Germany's recovery, though he had probably nothing to do with it. "Some communities provide lots for refugees to build on. You should see them go to work. They dig out their foundations by hand, and organize joint ownership with friends and family."

"What do you think of Adenauer?" Buddy asked, finishing his drink.

"So far so good," Lothar said. "You know politicians—once they get some power anything can happen. Right now he's the man of the hour. A genius in arbitration, diplomacy, and organization. A true statesman who's pulled Germany from the grave."

Olga had never heard Lothar use poetic language, or even say something complimentary about anybody. His biting sarcasm usually offended people.

"Then we have Ludwig Erhardt, the Minister of Finance. Another genius. None of the members of our new government were in the Nazi party. With those talents, it's surprising they stayed out. The Allies have lifted most of the restrictions on the manufacture of steel and large equipment. With the factories back in business, and an insatiable market for quality goods...what can I tell you?" He had the man's attention. "Krupp is now manufacturing household equipment, rather than tanks. Entrepreneurs are popping up everywhere. Refugees are rebuilding their lives and starting new companies, like Telefunken, which is building radios. Everybody wants one, of course. In a couple of years, West Germany will once again enjoy a normal life."

Olga did not bother ask what was happening in the Russian Zone, glad that she had escaped before it was too late. Getting out now was a lot more dangerous, not that it had been easy when she slipped through the border patrol in East Berlin. That belonged to another lifetime now. She rarely thought about it. Los Angeles had become her home, and the Old Heidelberg her place. With Buddy at her side, and the prospect of once again playing her favorite kind of music, she had arrived. The cocktail affected her like a happy pill. Buddy noticed her smile and nodded. He knew what she thought, only she doubted that he had any idea what it was like as a musician to not be able to play.

Olga remembered his reception when they had first arrived in New York. What had he been trying to prove? Perhaps his sarcasm was unintentional, meant as a joke.

"With the Soviet Union as mutual enemy," Lothar said, "Germany is a valuable ally and a buffer against a surprise attack. Stalin is not about to bury his expansionist politics; with Central Europe in his pocket, he's ready to take the next step. He wants all of Germany. Imagine him fuming during the Air Lift."

Olga shuddered as the horrors of the war came to mind. The communists had taken China, and were now fighting in Korea, a much larger chunk of humanity than Germany. For some unexplainable reason, the French and Italians voted for the communist party in large numbers. Didn't they know they were playing into the hands of the Soviet Union? Wars went on, despite the millions of casualties. Among them, her dear friend Gottfried.

The men puffed on their cigars like suckling babes and turned to music. The ice in their glasses had melted, and the dew dried up. Buddy fished out an olive, and popped it into his mouth. He was not only a gifted musician, but a capable band leader and business man who adapted to the taste of his public. Olga knew she would please the crowds who came to hear her. She felt the beats on which the pieces anchored. Her artistry was as solid as ever. Even the "Mephisto Waltz" would not throw her, should somebody very special show up and ask for it.

Al, in a open sport shirt and light coat, drained his beer. He winked at Olga, with a questioning glance at Lothar. She shrugged. The dating game did not appeal to her. Invariably, she would surrender to some intimacy she would come to regret. Not that she felt she had to be faithful to Ingo—that relationship had moved out of reach and might not ever be available to her again. She was slowly coming to terms with it, though she was not ready to bury the dream altogether.

"Let's drive over to the Palladium," Buddy suggested. "Get a feel for the place. The young swing crowd loves it. They'll be coming in droves. Didn't you say, Al, that most of the tickets are sold already? As we said before, Lothar, dancers want a strong beat that prickles in their blood, not a concert, no matter how great."

"I know," Lothar agreed. "My combo in Germany entertains dancers. We do mainly tangos and waltzes, rumbas and sambas. They also love swing and enjoy a zippy foxtrot." He talked with authority. His crisp white shirt and striped tie changed his appearance, and he always wore the family seal ring.

Buddy nudged Olga, as if to say, Lothar can be a regular guy.

Her smile said, Don't bet your life on it, but enjoy it while it lasts.

"Here's the contract," Whitney said, pulling several sheets of paper from his briefcase, eager to collect it signed. His efforts would earn him enough to cover several alimony and child support checks. After explaining each item, the conditions, and the amount due, he took out his fountain pen, unscrewed the cap, and handed it to Buddy. He signed with a quick scribble and dated it - December 29, 1950. Lothar and Olga signed the carbon copies, and Whitney the acknowledgement. As soon as the ink was dry, he handed a copy to each participant and kept one for himself. A handshake sealed the transaction.

On their way out, Lothar talked about the new banking system that allowed Germans to trade deutschmarks against any foreign currency. "As you know, our constitution is based on the American model. Now we hope to follow the American way of doing business as well. Things are looking up."

Stepping outside Olga blinked into the bright sunlight. Unlike the Beverly Hills Hotel, Old Heidelberg was a friendly place where daylight prevailed. It had open windows with bright curtains like a European inn. A warm, spring-like breeze fanned her burning cheeks. Life was so good, she thought as she settled into the front seat of Whitney's Buick. Driving leisurely along Wilshire Boulevard, she admired the old hotels, department stores, and new car dealerships offering luxury. Jaguar, Cadillac, Rolls Royce and Bentley—the sleek bodies were polished to a high sheen. One of these days, the latest model Mercedes Benz cars would be among them, proudly displaying its tri-star emblem.

There it was, that premonition that Ingo would be running the dealership. He stood at the front of the showroom in a light suit, waving to her. Why not? In this land of infinite possibilities, it could happen. She leaned into the softly cushioned seat. The car rolled over the smooth street, absorbing whatever bumps there were. Behind her, Buddy and Lothar talked over the contract. Once again she would be a star, right here in Hollywood. Perhaps even appear in a movie. Everything was possible, she just had to believe. Stranger things had happened.

Aluminum fringes wrapped around plastic garlands swung across the avenue and rustled. American Christmas decorations were as colorful and uninhibited as the people. A fresh breeze from the ocean had cleared the air.

"I suggest you get a white gown, Olga," Buddy said. "Something low-cut, with gold trim and glitter for New Year's. The band will wear white rather than light blue. Since I can't expect you to wear a showy brocade tux, Lothar, black will have to do. People in Tinsel Town expect a musical and visual show. You wouldn't want to compare yourself with Liberace." He chuckled.

"Definitely not Liberace," Olga agreed, and explained to Lothar that Liberace's TV show brought classical music to a broader audience. His trademark were elaborate ruffled outfits that matched the romantic décor people enjoyed.

"The two of you in black and white would make a stunning duo. You'll perform from ten until midnight. About eleven thirty you'll do your show piece. Nothing too long. As you heard, we're sold out, right Al? Your performance is the icing on the cake."

New Year's Eve was a Friday. Berenson & Smith had decorated the hall with hundreds of colorful balloons ready to drop from the ceiling at midnight. Garlands wound around white columns and every table had a candle flickering under the thick layer of cigarette smoke. Olga remembered the Esplanade, where soldiers talked in loud voices, pretending they were on their way to a vacation resort, rather than the front. Most of them had been killed in action, or died in some Russian POW camp.

Behind the curtain, she could watch the band perform "Perfidia." The finely tuned instruments played in silky smooth harmony. "Old Man River" followed. Dancers sang along. There would be no "Lily Marleen," or "Miracle." The people here lived a miracle, and did not even know it. Every day was a treat; Mephisto stayed away from this bit of paradise.

These people glorified the Mississippi, rather than the Blue Danube or the Rhine. The trombones wailed to the muted trumpets and romantic clarinets. The bass players plucked along to the intense beat of the drummer, while the saxophones slipped into a bluesy mode. The white Steinway concert grand had been pushed to center stage. They would open with "Happy Days Are Here Again." Ingo had come to her, and breathed his love into her heart.

Young women in their party finery turned in the arms of their partners. They danced in sensual abandon to Buddy's irresistible rhythm. To them, the war was no more than a distant memory; their men had returned years ago. Pearl Harbor had been rebuilt and the Great Depression, D-Day, and the dropping of the atomic bomb were history. Life moved on, like a river washing away the mud. Former friends, like the Soviet Union, had become enemies, and Germany, the enemy, an ally. The men in that truck in Poland had visualized it, but did not live to join the Americans in their fight against communism.

Buddy Jones tapped his baton and faced the audience. "Ladies and gentlemen, for your dancing pleasure, let me introduce our soloists, the Baron and Baroness von Schenck. They came all the way from Germany for a short engagement in your city. Please welcome these fine artists."

Olga and Lothar walked out on stage, bowed to rousing applause, and took their seats at the grand piano. "Happy Days Are Here," did it again.

Half-drunk, the people applauded noisily, whistling and stomping enthusiastically to voice their approval. Olga, small and graceful, bowed her head. Her skin-tight white satin gown clung to her gentle curves. The modest neckline did not prepare the audience for the plunge in back that went as deep as decency allowed. Rhinestones glittered with her every movement, like frost sparkling in the rising sun. Ginny, the make-up artist, had applied mascara and eye-shadow, framing her blue eyes like lustrous gems. The matte foundation and silvery lipstick emphasized the softness of her features. Two white orchids had been fastened in her curls as if they'd grown there. Lothar's proud demeanor and cool appearance reminded women of Cary Grant. Yes, that was nobility.

People sang along as they danced, some loud and off-key, too tipsy to notice. Shrill laughter rang out. Lothar tensed up. Olga smiled flirtatiously. People had come to amuse themselves rather than listen to a grand performance. Lothar stayed, and performed all the numbers on the program. Olga braced herself for his reproaches, his outburst of temper, and wished they could play for the rest of the night.

Buddy and his band continued playing after Lothar and Olga left the stage. Lothar did not complain. "I did my duty. That's what we're paid for. But I can't say that I enjoy working like a hired hand."

Olga could take that. Lothar's improvisation of "Begin the Beguine" was their grand finale. As much as she disliked Lothar, playing with him was a treat. His arrangement captured the essence of the haunting tune everybody loved. Dancing to it gave the music another dimension. Her feet longed to glide over the parquet in Ingo's arms.

The ovation did not stop until Buddy announced that midnight was approaching. "Make your resolutions and wishes. 1951 will be great year."

Olga and Lothar sat at one of the tables, champagne glass in hand, watching the huge clock above the stage strike twelve. Champagne corks popped. People blew their paper horns. Screams of "Happy New Year" erupted as the balloons descended. The band played "Auld Lang Syne" and everybody sang along. The dancers in silly hats hugged and kissed. Everybody drank. More and more couples flocked to the dance floor. Balloons popped. Paper snakes trailed across the hall. Laughter, shouts, and Buddy's stirring beat had everybody going.

"Happy new Year, Lothar," Olga said, extending her hand. Knowing that people were watching, he took it gallantly and kissed it. They really did not have anything to say to each other. Her wishes for the new year had nothing to do with him, other than wishing him far away from here. The very thought of intimacy with him made her shudder. She was through sacrificing herself for his pleasure. If things had been more amiable before she had met Ingo, Olga would have considered his sadistic impulses retribution for her love for Ingo. But he had never considered her feelings, so why should she oblige him now or feel guilty? Did he know that his mother had told Ingo Olga was dead? That her lie had ruined Olga's life? Was he part of that plot?

"I see no reason to stick around here," he said. "Let's drive over to the Coconut Grove."

Olga did not feel like going anywhere with him, surprised that he even suggested it. Everything about their relationship was so wrong.

"Why don't we go home and see whether Anyna is still awake? Perhaps she would like to celebrate the New Year. I have a bottle of Mumm in the refrigerator." She did not mention that it came from Al Whitney, who may have hoped that it would lure her to his bed. Al wasn't a bad fellow, but any intimacy with him was out of the question, even an embrace, not to mention those slimy kisses she hated.

Anyna was watching TV when they came home and jumped up. "Daddy, Daddy, how did it go? Next time, can I come with you?" Her pink robe fluttered and her fuzzy slippers flopped. She had brushed her dark hair to a sleek shine as if expecting a date. Olga would welcome a decent boy who kept her company. For the moment Hazel and her two children served that purpose.

Lothar picked up Anyna and swung her around. "Absolutely lovely, my little baroness. A lady to be reckoned with. You'll set Hollywood on fire."

"Really, Daddy? Do you think, no, of course not... You're so silly," she said flirtatiously, playing the bashful damsel. Only there was nothing bashful about her little girl, Olga thought. Anyna knew how to play up to men. She had done it to Ingo years ago, and now flirted with her father. It worked.

Olga left them alone. In her bedroom she smiled into the mirror, imagining she was talking to Ingo. "Still beautiful," she said. "But for how long? You better come home soon, darling." She unzipped her rhinestone studded gown and watched it fall to the ground. Whisper thin panties covered her flat belly and round bottom. Her slender legs and small feet would still delight him. He had loved her little breasts. They had not grown since he had caressed them, had teased her nipples with his tongue, and sent waves of delight through her body. It was coming up now. With her arms stretched out, she danced to "In the Mood." The silver pumps sparkled in the low light of the lamp. Good thing Lothar was busy with Anyna else she could not stop his taking possession of what he believed belonged to him.

After removing the orchids from her hair, she loosened her blonde curls and let them fall over her shoulders. Like Narcissus in love with his image, Olga wrapped it all up into her new green chenille robe. With her make-up removed, the magic was gone. "Back to the kitchen," she said and left the room. She took two glasses from the old cabinet. Anyna would get a sip in her juice glass. Lothar and Anyna watched a variety show on TV. She sat poised on the kitchen chair, her back straight, her hands folded on the yellow formica table, a demure young lady eager to impress her aristocratic father. He had taken off his tux and bow tie, and now relaxed in his shirt sleeves. Olga twisted the cork from the champagne bottle until it popped, and then filled the glasses.

Taking them, Lothar said, "Here comes our bar-maid." He bowed to Anyna, and handed her the juice glass as if she were royalty. "Next time around I'll make sure that my lovely little baroness gets a real champagne glass. Why don't we shop for one tomorrow?"

"We could go to Saks, Daddy. They have such beautiful things."

"That's a deal. We'll go."

She hugged him. "I'm so glad you came, Daddy. It gets so lonely here when nobody is around. Hazel is okay, but she doesn't know things like you do. Nobody does."

"Uh oh," he laughed, holding her. "You're my little temptress." Then he took one of the glasses from the tray. Robert Taylor could not play the part better. Only what role did Lothar play? "The prettiest little baroness in Christendom."

"Do you mean it, Daddy? Then you're my knight in shining armor."

"Flattery will get you everything, Ann. Why don't you tell Mom what we did on this beautiful day? What impressed you most at the museum?"

"Oh, it was marvelous, Mom. Next time you must come with us. They have the most extraordinary paintings. I hadn't been to a museum since I left Tante Adie. I loved it, Mom." She opened her arms enthusiastically. "We looked at paintings of the Last Judgment by Hieronymus Bosch. You can see the people drop straight into hell. And there was a painting by Gainsborough of lovely ladies in gorgeous hats and gossamer gowns. I would love to be a portraitist and do Hollywood stars like Myrna Loy and Katharine Hepburn. I bet I could do it if I study art. Paint them with their pets and mansions. They're every bit as beautiful as the aristocratic ladies in England."

"But they're not aristocrats," Lothar said. "They're just playing a role, whereas you are the real thing."

"I'm so glad you said that, Daddy. Did you notice how I sit up straight and don't jump around like a silly little girl?"

"I did indeed, which makes me very proud."

"Mom used to call me princess. But that wouldn't be real, since I'm a baroness."

Anyna's reasoning amused Olga. Raising her glass she smiled. "To our lovely baroness."

Anyna tasted the bubbly wine and wrinkled her nose. "Not bad, but not that good either." After the second sip she giggled. "I like it, Daddy. I wish I could have been at the Palladium."

What was this game all about? Anyna barely knew her father, had never spent time with him, and now, all of a sudden, all this affection? With Olga gone most of the day they were alone. What was happening?

Knowing Lothar, he probably spent most of his time at the piano or exploring his math theorems, unless he had something in mind. Olga could not help feel guilty and jealous. Lothar, who had not wanted the child in the first place, now played the loving father he was not. In four weeks all this would be over. He would be gone, and Anyna would come to her mother again.

Sipping champagne, they watched Jack Benny tell his jokes and play his violin. He was still on when Lothar and Olga took turns tucking Anyna into bed. Once again, Ingo's telling Anyna Grimm's fairy tale of the Bremen City Musicians came up. Lothar told no tale, he kissed Anyna's forehead, only she was no longer a child, but a budding young woman.

Since Olga slept in Anyna's room while Lothar was there, she asked him to please turn off the lights. "Good night and happy New Year."

Disappointed, he lingered at the door trying to make her feel guilty. But it did not work. Not that the potential danger had passed. He would be on the prowl until he caught her off guard. Playing the loving daddy to Anyna was part of some scheme. He took her into his arms. During the kiss, his tongue came searching for hers. No, no and no, Olga thought clenching her teeth. Those tricks did not work anymore. She unwound herself from his embrace, pushed him out, and closed the door.

"Good night Daddy," Anyna called out.

Stretched out on the bed, Olga wondered whether he would embarrass her in front of Buddy, or whether his pride and reputation would prevail. His vengeance would come in subtler forms. She must be prepared for it.

Over the following week, Anyna played up to Lothar as her long lost father. He reciprocated, giving her rides on his knees, taking her shopping, to the movies, and the beach. He amused Anyna with math games and puzzles. They played duets on the piano and laughed at "I Love Lucy." Olga doubted that Lothar had had a change of heart; it was not in him. She grew more suspicious. Surely he would not take Anyna back to Germany. The Countess would not have Anyna back, nor would Anyna care to live in that dark and stinking room catering to the self-centered old lady. Then what was he after? Would he seduce her? No, he was neither a pedophile nor sexually deprived, and had women begging him to do whatever he desired.

Standing at the kitchen stove, Olga watched the water heat up for a soothing cup of tea. Anyna giggled in the living room. "Not now, Daddy. That tickles."

"It's supposed to make you feel good, but a baroness doesn't giggle like a silly goose. Are you a silly goose?"

"Of course not, Daddy. You know I'm not. It's just –"

"Then why do you carry on like that?" he said in a stern voice.

"I thought we were playing. I'm not sure I like this game."

Olga could not see his face, but imagined his knitted brows. Peeking into the living room she saw Anyna smooth out her skirt. What was going on? They had returned from their concert early while Anyna was still watching TV. Pouring the boiling water into the tea pot, Olga sensed that something was wrong. What was going on between them?

Before she could look and see, Lothar and Anyna came into the kitchen. They sat down at the table while Olga dipped a teabag into the boiling water. Nobody spoke.

"We went to the movies this afternoon," Anyna said finally. "I don't like Bette Davis. She has funny eyes. Tomorrow we'll see 'The Wizard of Oz', right Daddy?" She dug her teaspoon into the sugar bowl as if it were sand.

"I must work on my composition," he said. How could he resist that sweet, imploring smile? Olga reproached herself for being so sensitive and protective. Lothar's good behavior could be well intended. Only vulnerable people were prone to pain and suspicion.

"Too bad you can't come with us, Mom," Anyna said. She blushed when she noticed Lothar watching her. The first signs of womanhood had appeared. Her breasts had started to form, as had her pubic hair. The way she looked at Lothar now was not the look of a child. Was she hiding something?

"You're getting to look like a silly teenager," Lothar teased. "Just don't carry it too far. Noble women always look dignified. They are as smooth and impenetrable as a marble pillar. Did you ever see Grandmaman cry, though she had plenty to cry about?"

Anyna thought. Her forehead wrinkled as she shook her head. "But you can't help it sometimes, Daddy. Not when people tease you. Or when you long for your Mom." She looked straight into his eyes as if he understood her pain. Lothar had never felt pain, Olga thought, only anger and vengeance. In his maddening righteousness, he had to punish those who did not live up to his expectations. He had no idea that a child like Anyna longed and suffered because her life was not like that of the other children. Her parents did not get along. She had been farmed out, and now spent her days alone because Olga had to work. His being here made her feel important. Now that he had proclaimed her to be a full-blown baroness, she had something to be proud of. Though she was still a foreigner and a refugee, she had an identity nobody could trump. Her Daddy was a handsome baron who performed with the famous Buddy Jones Band. That was even better than being a Hollywood star.

"Why should you let people offend you? Nobody can touch a baroness. Whatever others say is of no consequence to you. Remember, you don't have to prove a thing to anybody, or ask for forgiveness, or humble yourself into pleasing others. Didn't you learn that from Grandmaman? People respect her. Just think of Sgt. Aldrich. He adored Grandmaman. Even Al Whitney."

Anyna cheered up as she picked up her teacup, holding it daintily as Grandmaman had taught her. "Yes, Daddy. I'll learn to be like Grandmaman."

Olga watched Lothar's amused smile. The child was nothing but a toy to him. He didn't care that every one of his words left a mark that would last a lifetime in the receptive soul of his little girl. Anyna might as well learn what her father was all about. She didn't understand it now, but would be useful later when she was older, faced with men and job options. Would she want to play the role of a pretty but idle baroness, like her Grandmaman, or would she rather go out and create a world for herself like her mother? That remained to be seen. Olga desperately wanted to protect her little girl from disappointments and hurt, wanted to hug and hold her and tell her that everything would be fine. But that would be unreasonable. Lothar was her father, and Anyna was a part of him too.

Olga passed a dish of lemon wedges to Lothar. The evil streak in his eyes had returned, and the twist on his lips. His sardonic laughter, while she had vomited in disgust, echoed in her memory. Nobody would ever touch her uninvited again. In this country her rights were protected. He no longer owned her. Nobody did. She was a free person, her backbone as strong and smooth as a marble pillar for everybody to admire, no more.

Lothar was back, prowling around like a predator. Why couldn't he see that she was no longer at his mercy. What if he molested their daughter to hurt Olga's? Would he stoop that low?

Glorifying her as a baroness drew Anyna into his camp. But he would not succeed. Anyna had witnessed too much to become his victim. Then again, she was lonely, had no family, and no real friends other than Hazel. Olga would keep careful watch. Her role at the Old Heidelberg had taught her to make decisions and persuade others to follow her lead. Surely Lothar knew that he faced a stiff prison sentence should he molest a child.

Goosebumps crawled over Olga's skin. She took the warmed sweet rolls from the oven, but their appetizing aroma could not appease the horror in her heart. Rather than vanilla and cinnamon, she smelled sulfur. Her hand trembled.

"What's gotten into you, Olga?" Lothar said, through tight and angry lips. "Are you getting one of those spells again? You look as if you've seen a ghost."

She hid her face behind the warm cup she cradled in her hands. "The ghost of years past."

"Another one of those riddles."

Anyna put her arms around Olga's shoulders, and leaned her head against Olga's. "I love you, Mom. Daddy and I are only playing games, right Daddy? He didn't mean to tickle me where he did. I'm so glad Daddy came to visit us."

Olga held Anyna, glaring at Lothar like a lioness. "Don't you dare touch her."

"Why would I? Anyway, it's time for bed, Ann," he said. "Tomorrow is a school day. You wouldn't want to miss out on America's famous education," he added sarcastically. "It's not like Switzerland, is it?"

Anyna got up to get ready for bed. "It's different, but I like it. The teacher wants us to speak up and tell her what we think. We can ask questions and talk about how we feel about things. It's really very nice. She makes us study on our own, rather than tell us what to memorize. "

"Is that so? And you call that an education? Not in my book."

"You don't understand, Daddy. America is different," Anyna told him from the bathroom through the half-open door.

"I understand better than you think. It's not the kind of place where they teach you how to act like a baroness, is it?"

"I guess not. They don't have any baronesses around here. They don't believe in titles. Everybody is as good as he likes to be. That's called democracy. "

"You don't say. In that case, you would be better off coming home to Germany."

Anyna left the bathroom in her white robe with butterflies on it. Olga watched her from the kitchen.

"No, Daddy. I like California. You could come and live here."

"I'm sorry, my little one. I prefer the ruins of Germany and its culture to the wild west."

Olga made a note of that. Would he kidnap Anyna? Surely he knew better.

Ilse-Marie and Sepp could not believe that they would be seated at a front table of the Palladium facing the stage. The glamorous lady at the piano was none other than their little Olga. Who would have thought? They had watched her walk up on stage with Lothar in a rose-colored gown made of gossamer silk like a cloud kissed by the setting sun. Ilse-Marie mentioned it to Sepp, pleased by her poetic imagery. "Doesn't she look like a star coming out on Oscar night?" Lothar wore a white tux. His blue bow-tie matched the suits of the musicians. Only Buddy wore a deep blue blazer and white trousers.

He introduced the pianists. "The Baron and Baroness von Schenck."

The musicians raised their shining brass instruments. Ilse-Marie clutched Sepp's arm. In his dark suit, white shirt, and tie she could hardly recognize him. He was not bad looking. With Olga's help, she had found a two-piece outfit in navy blue that hid her bulging middle. The silver piping gave it a touch of class. Her rhinestone pin glittered like the real thing. How long had it been since she and Sepp had danced together? That music went right into her blood. It was never too late to catch up on life.

Couples flocked to the dance floor, stepping and turning to Buddy Jones' famous beat. "Isn't that wonderful, Sepp?" Ilse-Marie said after ordering a martini. She was sick and tired of beer.

Sepp ordered a scotch on the rocks. "That's a man's drink."

Ilse-Marie felt as if she had spent her life in prison, and was finally released to enjoy what was left of it. Though her high heeled pumps felt awkward, she would not change them for anything. Sepp took her hand and asked, "How about it, Ilse?"

"It would be my pleasure. It's been so long, Seppel."

Mingling with the other dancers, she followed his lead. "You're a good dancer, Sepp. We should do this more often. Olga certainly changed our lives, didn't she? Who would have thought? A baroness, working in the kitchen."

"Not anymore," he said, turning her around.

"What good is all that money if you can't enjoy it?" she said, breathing heavily. "Get in shape. Go to a movie. Have some fun. Dancing is good for you."

He did not argue. Sepp had warmed up to the dance, and was doing very well.

"Back in Germany we used to dance a lot." Sweat formed on her brow. She glanced up at the stage, where Olga and Lothar performed on a huge white grand piano. "I can't get over it. Look at her, Sepp. That pianist is our Olga."

At the end of the piece, Ilse-Marie applauded so hard that her hands burnt. "Remember that afternoon when Olga walked in? We almost threw her out. But the little girl. And then she was no solicitor, not really. Just wanted a job without pay. How could we refuse? I can't imagine where we'd be without her. Before we know it, we'll have a fancy restaurant. She knows what she's doing, better than you and me. It's time we retired to Lake Arrowhead—the woods, the grass, snow in winter, and year-round fresh air." She took Sepp's hot hand and held it. "Starting tomorrow, we'll let Olga take the evening off, rather than have her run back and forth. This is more important than serving customers beer and bratwurst. No, Sepp Sailer, let's count our blessing and sell the place to her and just become investors. We'll make plenty of money and won't have to worry about a thing."

During the final applause, Olga waved at them.

"Did you see that, Sepp? She thinks the world of us. We can manage without her for two weeks. We did before. After that, I'll take a long vacation to Mexico."

He chuckled. "You don't say. Never thought you'd go anywhere without me."

"It's about time that I grew up, don't you think?"

The following day, Ilse-Marie told Olga, "No point in knocking yourself out in the evening. We can manage; we've got plenty of help."

Olga hugged her friend. Father had once again come to protect her and Anyna. From now on she could spend her days at home.

"You don't have to give up your job on my account," Lothar said when she told him.

"I'm not losing any money," she assured him.

He ignored her comment. "I came here to spend time with my daughter, now that she is starting to make some sense."

"We can do it together. There is so much to see in Los Angeles. And we'll have more time to practice. I really don't feel all that comfortable with 'Rhapsody,'" she lied. "I won't bother you. You can take her out and show her the world. I'll get some things for Lucie for you to take back to her. She's having a hard time with all those children."

If she could refrain from bringing up something that would annoy him, he would leave on January 30th. Once the plane took him away, she would finally be free!

Only he was not about to comply with her wishes. The following Monday, after Anyna left for school, he showed up in his bathrobe as usual. Neither one of them got dressed until they left the house. Lothar had his breakfast that Olga prepared for him: rolls, butter, and jam. Freshly percolated coffee with lots of sugar and cream. Olga had been practicing all morning while he slept. At first he had complained, but Olga would not relent. "This is my home. My practicing is as essential as yours." She bought him earplugs he didn't really need. It was just one of those ploys he used to make her feel guilty. The anxiety still stirred in the pit of her stomach.

The sun had warmed the air, and dried the dew that always fell overnight. Warming up his rolls in the oven, she set up the percolator with his coffee. Soon the appetizing aroma wafted through the small kitchen and over into the living room. She busied herself with beating the eggs and throwing a piece of butter into the pan, then watched it sizzle and dissolve.

"In a week you'll be on your way again," she said. A mistake. He resisted everything she said and did so now.

His brows shot up. His eyes darkened. There was that cruelty again. "Leaving? Who said I'm leaving? Stop counting the days. I've come to like it here. Hanley said he would have us play with him as soon as Buddy's contract is done."

"Al didn't say anything to me," she said, smiling innocently.

"Because he doesn't know about it. We don't need him anymore. Why give him a commission when we can collect the money ourselves? After all, it's our performance." He buttered his roll.

"But Al is a good friend. He's done so much…"

"And he got paid for it. What is it between you and Al? First that soldier. Now the agent. Who'll be next? The busboy?" His sarcasm provoked an argument. He sat with his bathrobe open, his legs spread apart.

Olga ignored him, and poured the coffee. Of course, he would not lower himself to make it look as if he wanted her. What he meant was, if he really wanted her, he would take her. They were alone in the house. And here she had been so concerned about protecting their daughter. What made her think he would let her get away with ignoring his needs? He had all the music he wanted in Germany, but it irked him to see her enjoy her life, be satisfied, ignore him. He wanted her to crawl, begging for his favor, as she had done when she arrived from Berlin. That must have been the height of his pleasure, to make her suffer for his generosity. Should she run off? In Los Angeles women went to the store in a bathing suit and curlers. Why not in a robe and slippers? But she would have to come back unless she wanted to leave Anyna at his mercy. He would be here waiting for her. His penis thrust out like a dagger. Without looking she knew it was there to entice her.

Standing in back of him she put the coffee mugs with steaming coffee on the table ready to escape should he reach for her. He didn't, pretending this was a morning like every other. The salacious expression on his cruel lips reminded her of all the insults and humiliations she had endured over the years. Where was her freedom now? Her liberation? If she did not play this right, there would be none. "Would you like some fresh orange juice?" she asked, cutting up the oranges on the kitchen counter. Why didn't she get dressed before he got up?

"You know what I want and what you will give me," he said, like a master speaking to his valet.

"If you don't care for orange juice, there is nothing I have to give. No, no, don't get all puffed up," Olga added quickly before he reached for her.

His knitted brows drew a triangle and his lips tightened, but she was not afraid. She was in America where laws protected women and children from maniacs, including spouses. The air had never felt better, the sun never looked brighter, nor had the sky been ever as blue. But the last dice had not fallen yet. It was her own fault. Buddy had been quite willing to have Olga perform solo. Nor had it anything to do with Anyna. She would be fine without Daddy.

"You don't seem to understand that you're my wife."

"What's there to understand? A formality, Lothar, as you said yourself. Excuse me, I must get dressed." She knew her feeble escape would not work. There really was none, not if she wanted Anyna to remember him as her loving Dad, rather than the monster he was.

"The formality served you well, Olga. You never served anybody. Least of all me. When did I ever ask anything of you?" His cold voice was as calm as a frozen river. "I never got a thank you for taking you in despite the shameful way you behaved while I was fighting."

"Spare me the rest. I know it, have heard it, and am done with it."

"How convenient."

She thought for a moment, putting the milk containers into the refrigerator. Anyna loved her milk. "I appreciate all you did for me and our daughter. There is no future for us. I will no longer be a burden to you and your mother."

He rose, and his robe opened all the way. She would not look. How she hated his dick, that throbbing invasive thing that turned him into an animal. "Burden? We did what was expected."

She smiled. "Of course. Then let me thank you for it. We can now manage our lives. You'll always be Anyna's father. She loves you," Olga said quickly before he could jump on her. "No, no, let me finish. From now on I'll take charge of her needs. No need for you to worry. You can go home and take care of Maman."

He grabbed her arm and pulled her toward him. His hot breath hit her face like a slap. "You can't just do what you want, young lady. You have obligations."

She did not fight him. That would only arouse his sadism. "You can count on my monthly contributions."

"But I want you," he said hoarsely, grabbing her by the shoulders and pressing his mouth against hers. Even if he meant it, his presence repulsed her as much as if she had been thrown into a cesspool. His slimy tongue fought for entry. Just get it over with, Olga thought and let him enter. He immediately filled her mouth with disgust. It would be her last sacrifice. His pride and manhood were at stake. He would come quickly, and leave her alone. Let him have his victory, and go home celebrating his conquest. It would be the last.

The thought eased the pain, the disgust and revulsion. Women had no choice. It could be worse. Letting him bend her pelvis toward his stiff penis she pretended to go along. An automatic action she had performed in the past. Stimulating him would accelerate the process. Now that he was consumed by the act he no longer noticed her. With her body on automatic, the melody of "Some Day a Miracle Will Happen" on her mind, she let it happen as if she was under a doctor's knife. It was the lesser of evils. The beloved tune took her to another place and time when the act had been heavenly.

He spread her legs apart, and forced his big hard organ into her tight, dry cavity. He squeezed her nipples expecting her to wince. She didn't. She ground her teeth suppressing the pain as he struggled for entry. As if her body sensed her revulsion, it fought his intrusion. He grew impatient, and then violent. His forceful thrusts set her on fire. This too would pass. Everything passed. The Russians in Berlin. Ingo. Their last night together. They would see each other again; they would. Father had promised. Lothar's wet mouth fumbled with hers. He panted. His body slid against hers. Sweat dripped from his face.

With her teeth clenched, her fingers dug into her palms. How much longer for heaven's sake? She bounced her hips. Her suppressed moans fooled him into thinking she was in ecstasy. Anything to make him come and quit. One more, two more, faster and faster, a last jerk. There! She silently breathed a sigh of relief when his hot semen spilled over her thigh. His organ shrunk, collapsed and slipped out. It was done. Her vagina would burn for a few days. He would not be back.

By the time Anyna came home, Olga had showered and put on a green jumpsuit, a black cardigan thrown over her shoulders. Her passionately hug had Anyna wondering.

"Are you all right, Mom?"

"Yes, my sweet, completely so," Olga said, nuzzling her child's warm cheek. How she loved the smell of fresh air and clean sweat. Stroking the silky, tousled hair, she saw Lothar go through his music. They were done. "Everything is wonderful," she told Anyna. "So wonderful."

Chapter 48

Lothar left according to his schedule. Olga and Anyna saw him off. They did not talk of a visit. Whether his final sex act had showed him how ignoble he'd acted, or whether it meant final victory was not relevant. He was gone. They had parted amiably. Now the question remained – how would she get a divorce. Consulting a lawyer Olga explained her circumstances. When she mentioned that Lothar and she had no common property he suggested she get an annulment, plain and simple. That would dissolve the legality of a marriage that had never existed as such. A perfect solution.

Two months later, Lothar received a copy of the decree by registered mail. He sent no comment. Considering how Olga had fretted over it all these years, the simplicity of it all was almost disappointing. Only in America, the land of unlimited opportunities, was such a thing possible. Legally she had never been married, yet Anyna was a legitimate child.

Sepp and Ilse-Marie reviewed the papers. "Perfectly legal," Sepp said.

"But why did you do it?" Ilse-Marie asked. "Lothar is an incredible man. The way he plays the piano. And a baron yet." They stood in Sepp's former office. Olga occupied it now, and had furnished it with matching chairs and fresh curtains—no clutter, stacks of bills, or boxes anywhere. Instead, she had neat file cabinets. A bookkeeper came once a week and took care of the accounts. Olga was amazed at her knack for organization. She had never imagined herself as a businesswoman. Gazing through the window, she saw her guests sitting on the patio under large umbrellas, drinking a glass of beer or a cup of coffee.

"All that glitters is not gold," she told her friends. "Now I can pursue my life without worrying about him. If you recall, Ilse-Marie, I love Ingo more than anything. He is my true husband."

Ilse-Marie and Sepp exchanged glances.

Olga laughed. "I know it sounds weird. We knew that some day we would be together. While the war was on that seemed an unlikely fantasy. Somebody up there kept an eye on us. Now that I am free at last, I intend to look for him. Perhaps he can liberate himself too."

"I see," Ilse-Marie said, her eyes wide open. "It's all about love. Well, I have you, Sepp, and that is good enough for me. Too bad we couldn't have a child. Old Heidelberg was our headache. Now, thanks to Olga, we can reap the fruits of our labor."

"Nicely put," Olga said. "When I first came here, I told you that a good business deal should serve both parties. Ours was the best deal I ever made."

"Listen to her," Ilse-Marie said, blotting the sweat from her big face. Lately she had suffered from hot flashes.

Olga had the kitchen renovated and invested in new appliances. Ilse-Marie supervised the new cook, Martin Krantzberg, who made the best potato dumplings and light and crispy breaded pork chops. He even baked his own bread, a country rye people loved.

Anyna accepted the annulment without fuss. "Daddy will always be your Daddy," Olga told her. "You will always be his little baroness. Mine too."

"It's okay, Mom. Just call me Ann. Someday we'll go to Germany and visit Daddy and Grandmaman, and then to Switzerland to see Tante Adie and Onkel Richard." In the meantime, she kept a regular correspondence with her relatives and sent them drawings and explained that *Mom now owns the Old Heidelberg. She is looking for a place in Newport Beach. She loves the ocean and so do I. You should see it at sunset. My palette does not have enough colors to paint it, so I'm not even trying. I took some pictures, but even they can't show you how beautiful it is. The water is alive with colors you can't even imagine.*

Olga admired Anyna's paintings and had her take private lessons.

The following year, Olga organized a special New Year's Eve celebration at Old Heidelberg to ring in 1952 and invited all the people she had met over the past four years. By now, she knew most of her guests—their background, family, and personal interests—and greeted them with a warm handshake, like old friends. Sepp tended bar. Unlike Ilse-Marie he loved the job, and didn't want to have it any other way.

"You don't expect me to sit around all day looking at the lake?" he said. Instead, he drew fresh Loewenbrau from the tap whenever he felt thirsty, filled the glasses of his guests, and enjoyed their easy conversation. Ilse-Marie came for the occasion, and inspected the new kitchen. Martin and his sous-chef, Sebastian Schneider, had already established a considerable reputation among their countrymen, as well as former G.I.'s who had enjoyed their stay in Germany. Their *wienerschnitzel, sauerbraten*, pork chops and red cabbage were all favorites.

Olga's piano stood on a small stage where she performed on weekends. During the week, she had an accordionist play German favorites. Members of the German choir showed up regularly, not just for their practice sessions. On the last Sunday of every month, Martin prepared *salzburger nockerl* for their Austrian guests. For that treat, people came from as far away as San Diego and Santa Barbara. The trio, Black Forest Boys, would play Viennese songs.

New dinnerware from Bavaria carried the Old Heidelberg logo, designed by Anyna. The exchange rate of dollars for Deutschmark made German products a steal. No wonder German cars sold so well. Ingo toyed with the idea of getting Daimler Benz to open a dealership in Beverly Hills. So far he was reluctant to break up his marriage and leave Germany. Perhaps things for him were not as bad as Olga hoped so that he would break up his marriage and come to her. He answered her question evasively, "I must wait and see. Fritzle attends school now, and Irmgard works on the family farm. Help is hard to find, and it does her good."

With her earnings from her tour with Buddy Jones, Olga had bought out the Sailers. Sepp kept twenty percent of the bar revenue, rather than work for a salary. He had decorated the bar with Bavarian beer steins and Munich Hofbrau posters. The dimensions of his large round face and body kept growing. "People expect me to drink with them," he said whenever Ilse-Marie and Olga mentioned his weight as a health problem. He was now on his third pair of *lederhosen*. Lately, he talked about opening a liquor store next door, selling German beer, wine, and schnapps, as well as popular German newspapers and magazines.

His buddy, Max Feldmann, a young man from Berlin and a trained butcher, talked about starting a German delicatessen as soon as he found an empty store nearby. "There are plenty of customers asking for

German-cut meat and sausages. They want German bread, fresh sauerkraut and herring. American cotton bread is a joke. I'll have German chocolates and marzipan on hand. *Summa sumarum* was his favorite expression "I see a gold mine right here. With the German movie house only three blocks away, we'll have a bit of Germany right here in Los Angeles."

Sepp and Olga offered to invest in Max's Wursthaus. She had learned the basics of the trade.

Raising her glass to a "super 1952" something told her that her dearest wish would finally be fulfilled. Should she go to Germany and visit Ingo again?

She greeted a couple being seated in the dining room Anyna had decorated for New Year's Eve with garlands and balloons. Every table had a bowl with fresh pink and red camellias from Ilse-Marie's garden that matched the red and white table cloths. They had placed the tables in a checkerboard pattern, a colorful effect against the dark wood paneling. Party favors, hats, and confetti were included in the price. Posters of dancing couples hung on the walls. The aroma from Martin's famous kitchen wafted out every time the door opened. Heidi and her two helpers, dressed in blue and white dirndls, ran back and forth carrying three, and sometimes four, plates at a time. Their enthusiastic faces, big smiles, and warm greetings were part of Old Heidelberg's success. It was a true *gasthaus*, the kind they had in German villages where people had their *Stammtisch*. As new immigrants arrived, they invariably found their way to Old Heidelberg.

Olga returned to the reception desk, where she greeted arriving guests in a midnight blue knit dress that clung to her small body and then flared out below the hips. The dining room resounded with laughter and the shouts of people greeting each other. The girls sidled between the tables carrying five beer steins in each hand, just like their colleagues in Munich. They had hired a college student, who picked up plates and cleared tables. The ambiance was rising. People raised their steins and toasted each other. Behind the bar, Sepp had his hands full pouring. The evening progressed well.

Later, Olga would perform some of the old favorites. Her happy smile and intimate jokes gave no hint of the loneliness she felt. It was on days like this that she knew how isolated she really was. When the party was over, and Anyna had gone to bed, she would be staring into the night longing for Ingo. Would she ever get over it? Without him, all her success was meaningless.

The Black Forest Boys had the crowd going. They knew how to create German *Stimmung* and *Gemutlichkeit*. People locked arms, swayed, and sang along. The men ordered more beer and schnapps. Those from the Rhineland and Swabia ordered wine. Some women drank highballs like their American friends. Waltzes, foxtrots, and sambas had everybody going.

Olga's Steinway had been pushed aside to make room for more tables. One of her guests had sold it to her for a token price. "I would feel honored if you take it," she'd said. "Hearing you play is one of the few pleasures left to me since my husband passed away. He played quite well." She loved the instrument that now stood abandoned in the corner.

The Old Heidelberg was sold out.

The room was warm. Aromatic smoke hovered over tables covered with large platters of sausages, *schnitzel*, roast beef, and *koenigsberger klopse*. The city that gave the dumplings their name had been erased from the map of Germany and renamed Kaliningrad. Litzmannstadt was now Lodz again, and Breslau had become Wroclaw.

Olga felt alone and forgotten, like her piano. The smiling hostess had nothing to do with Olga von Schenck. Someone had stepped into her body and was performing an admirable act. The old Olga, who had struggled with the Evil One, who had loved and cried, fought and lost, was gone, like those cities whose inhabitatants would never reclaim their homes. Now mistress of the Old Heidelberg, free at last from hunger and pain, insults and humiliations, why wasn't she exultant? What was wrong with her? Ilse-Marie waved from one of the front tables. She was sitting with friends while Sepp tended bar. Anyna, in a blue and white dirndl, brought plates loaded with food from the kitchen. She would quit soon and go home. At fourteen, she was a tall, lanky girl with bright eyes, her hair braided like that of a Bavarian villager.

"Olga, you've outdone yourself," said a heavy set woman with a big smile Olga had seen before. "These are my dear friends, Hans and Lieselotte, and this is Gunther and his Maria. I've told them so much about you. They couldn't wait to come here and celebrate New Years at Old Heidelberg." She turned to her friends. "What did I tell you? Isn't this marvelous? You'll never go anywhere else. Just wait until Olga plays the piano. Now that's a treat. She's phenomenal."

Olga shook hands. "You're too kind." The name still did not come to her. Then she turned to the next guests.

Her cheeks flushed from wine, she felt tears in her eyes and blinked them away. What was wrong with her? This was a glorious night. Had she not triumphed over all adversity to get here? She certainly didn't miss Inning and the stinking room, or the NCO Club. Perhaps Sgt. Aldrige who had launched her into this. Litzmannstadt? No, of course not. She missed the world she came from, Gottfried and Lucie, and the music they had played together.

Why beat around the bush, Olga? You miss Ingo more than anything. He isn't about to show up, so get over it.

Her moist eyes glistened. Nobody noticed her deep pain, her loneliness, the emptiness inside that refused to be ignored.

The guests sang and danced. Los Angeles had become their home. So why couldn't she adapt? But the heart had its reasons, and refused to oblige to the dictates of her mind. She was homesick for a world that no longer existed.

She looked up at Sepp. He noticed her, and waved while filling a stein. His big face was all smiles. He had grown a Kaiser Wilhelm handlebar mustache, and looked quite funny since his head was practically bald. A checkered shirt covered his broad chest, crossed with Bavarian leather suspenders. The man was happy. This was his world. He never grew tired of pouring beer and keeping his glass filled. People on the dance floor did a polka, jumping around to the beat. Alfred, the band leader, announced, "All you happy dancers, come to the floor and form two circles. The women inside, the men outside. You know the routine. When the music stops, take the partner facing you. No cheating!" The game allowed everybody to participate and mingle. Most of the diners left their food and joined the fun.

Forming a circle, the men and women held the shoulder of the person in front, forming a chain. They laughed, teased, mocked, and flirted as the two circles passed each other. The music stopped and started a waltz. Men and women took whoever happened to face them and waltzed away. People loved it. Those who could not find a partner waited for the next round.

Anyna had joined the women's circle, and flirted with the passing men. Olga watched her enjoy the dance. She didn't care who got her when the march stopped—young or old, it didn't matter. She swung around laughing, and then rejoined the circle as soon as the march set in. Seeing her happy helped Olga overcome her own doldrums. Anyna was young enough to fit in. She would not suffer from homesickness, since there wasn't much for her to remember. Sometimes she talked about Switzerland, but she was mainly interested in her friends and her art. Aaron, one of her buddies, appreciated her art and amused her in many different ways. He was a year older than she. His parents came from Budapest, and were refined, educated people who enjoyed Anyna's company.

The music stopped. Three men rushed toward her. She paused, looked them over, and picked Tom Kramer, a young engineer and fine dancer. They waltzed away in happy abandon until the music changed to a march, and the couples broke up and formed a circle again.

Lately new immigrants had arrived in Los Angeles, many via Canada. They loved the California sun and stayed. With the Korean war and the Russian threat building up, the defense industry needed engineers and recruited them from European universities.

Olga could not stop herself from searching for Ingo among the happy crowd, asking for the "Mephisto Waltz." For him, morning had dawned. Had he been toasting a new year? What had he asked for? He no longer sent her love letters. Either he did not love her anymore, or thought he would not give her false hope. She answered in kind, pretending to be fulfilled. What were they waiting for? Another miracle? Those happened once in a lifetime, at best. They had missed theirs.

She stepped up to the bar. "How about a glass of burgundy," she told Sepp.

"Cheer up, girl," he said, as if he had read her mind. "It's not as bad as all that. Did it every occur to you that you can make things happen? Remember, you turned this place around. Prosit!" He clinked glasses with her.

"Thanks, Sepp. I'll think about that," Olga said, and walked away.

Lucie, who met Ingo occasionally, reported that his marriage was a disaster.

Irma is still obsessed with her lost fiancé. She feels that she betrayed him by marrying Ingo and having his child. To her, Fritzle and Ingo are a sin or something like that. She hates them, and can't get over that trauma of seeing him die because she could not get food to him. Normal people get over things and make the most of what is left. Not she. Ingo has to put up with it. Fritzle is shy. God knows what she does to him while Ingo is at work. Renate, her mother, knows the problem, but can't get through to her daughter. She is very fond of Ingo. Too fond, if you ask me. The whole picture is obscure. Why don't you come and see for yourself? I would love to see you, Olga. I found a darling friend. His name is Nikolas. We love each other. He is nothing special, but such a dear. Life is so lonely when you have no one to hold and care for.

Ingo is a lonely, tormented man. He doesn't say it in so many words, and doesn't need to. It's quite obviously from what he doesn't say.

Where are you, Ingo? Olga wondered, handing out menus. "Yes, the mock turtle soup is great. Our *wiener schnitzel* is as good as any you'll get in Germany. Mashed potatoes, made from scratch of course. None of that powdered stuff."

Tonight she would write to him. Not just the usual, she thought, taking the order to the kitchen. Ilse-Marie stopped Olga. "I can't get over Martin," she said. "Just watch him work. That man is priceless. I wish I could have trained under him. Considering I had no training at all, I did pretty good," she added, her big cheeks aglow.

"You certainly did," Olga assured Ilse-Marie, and headed for the kitchen. Why was she making everything so difficult for herself? All that fretting over her divorce, and then she had an annulment. Now a free woman, she could say whatever she wanted. There was nothing wrong with telling Ingo how much she loved him.

The guests talked about the German economic miracle. "I miss Germany," Ingrid, a young woman from Dusseldorf, said. "Still, I could never do the kind of work there that I do here. I hate that stuffy bureaucracy. You would not believe how much money we've saved. Furniture, two cars. Imagine, *two* cars. One for me and one for Kurt. In a year, we'll have our own home. And the climate? Year-round summer. How can you beat that? But on holidays like this, I miss my family."

Ingo was manager of the Export Department at Daimler Benz. Philosophy, literature, and his experience in a bloody war had taught him managerial skills he applied in marketing. His flair and easy conversation appealed to elegant and savvy customers. No wonder he did so well and had already enjoyed several promotions. Only what good did it do her? All she could think of now was packing up and going to Germany.

Al Whitney sat at one of the tables and waved to her. Olga had introduced him to a charming woman from Silesia. A war widow, Elsbeth had fallen in love with the lonely Al, and now laughed her happy, throaty laughter.

"Come and celebrate with us," he said. "There must be a vacant chair here somewhere." They had remained friends, and enjoyed chatting with each other whenever he stopped in for a beer and one of the special sandwiches she made for him. He had moved to Los Angeles, where he enjoyed a lucrative business as an agent for celebrities. From time to time he had urged Olga to take on another tour with Buddy or Ben Hanley, but finally gave up. She didn't feel she could take the time off to practice and perform. Old Heidelberg had become her life.

Olga hugged him and Elsbeth. "What are we celebrating?" she asked.

Al beamed. Elsbeth smiled. She wore a crimson two-piece and had never looked lovelier.

"Can't you tell?" Al asked.

"Isn't it obvious?" Elsbeth wondered. "Look!" She held up her hand and showed the sparkling diamond on her finger. "Al asked me to marry him. And what do you supposed I said?" She giggled. They had consumed quite a bit of champagne already and New Year's had not come yet. But it would shortly.

"That he's a preposterous, unreliable, but lovable, and a son of a gun," Olga said.

"That's what I should have said." She winked at Al, who took her hand and kissed it.

"It's true," he admitted.

"Never mind all that. I love this guy with all his faults."

"In that case, you certainly have my blessing." Olga went to the next table. Al's ex had married the man she had fallen in love with, relieving Al of his alimony payments.

Hazel and her husband Jake had joined the German crowd. "It's so much fun being here," they told Olga, their faces moist from the drink and dance.

The choir sat around the long table they used after their rehearsals and sang, "*Du, du liegst mir im Herzen.*"

Next summer, Anyna would go to Germany to visit Daddy and Grandmaman, and spend time in Switzerland. Adie and Richard wanted Anyna to stay with them while attending the university. Fortunately, that was still a few years away. The girl sidled between the tables like a bullfighter, delivering her plates to the customers with the flair of the von Schencks.

She also had Olga's sensitivity, without making it a crutch. America taught her to act as a responsible individual, rather than a self-centered and arrogant aristocrat. Now in high school, she wanted to study art. The little flames in the corner of her drawings had disappeared. She painted with precision and originality and received considerable recognition.

Sepp wiped his lips, watching the beer stream into a fresh glass. "Never thought I'd see Old Heidelberg in full swing like this. One could think we're at the Hofbrauhaus in Munich." He raised his glass. "Let's drink to that."

"The Hofbrauhaus of the West, Sepp," Olga said, and went over to the piano.

People applauded. After sitting down at the keyboard, she bowed her head. "Since this is a night for celebration, good wishes, and resolutions for the coming year, let me add my touch of inspiration for the future."

Olga warmed up with some familiar melodies, and then played, "I know Some Day A Miracle Will Happen," and sang to her accompaniment, reliving her passionate encounters with Ingo. Scenes from her past followed in succession. Litzmannstadt, Dresden, Berlin, Munich, Inning, Stuttgart, and finally Los Angeles. Gottfried and Lucie, her mother and Ottie, the Countess, the Ghetto, and Russian soldiers taking out their anger on German women passed in review. Gernegross and Liesl, Aldrich and Ernie, Buddy Jones and Ben Hanley. Anyna covered with pus. Their escape from Berlin. The stinking room where the Countess and Lothar lived. His cold demand for sex. Lara and her Chinese baby being raised in a home for illegitimate children of means. What would become of Lawrence Vincent von Schenck while his mother enjoyed the lavish lifestyle her new suitor provided? The guests sang along, absorbed in their own memories of the war years. She concluded with the refrain "And all the fairy tales will come true.." Once in the swing of things, Olga could have played all night. One song followed the next, except that Anyna came up, touching Olga's shoulder. "Mom. It's almost midnight."

Dazed, Olga looked up. "Really?" A roaring applause accompanied her bow. As if in a trance, she left the stage. Ingo had come to her. Father had brought him.

You marched to Stalingrad and back, yet we can't overcome the invisible barrier that separates us. Don't we have any right to live our own lives?

Firecrackers went off. People shouted "Happy New Year" and Olga watched them as if she were in a theater watching a play—the eternal outsider.

"I'm going home," she told Anyna after a warm embrace. "It's been a long day."

Unlike the blackout in Poland, Los Angeles was illuminated by a multitude of lights so bright that she could not discern the stars in the black sky. The Old Heidelberg sign invited guests to enjoy a glass of "genuine Loewenbrau beer."

The chilly air cut right through her coat. Walking quickly to her car, she thought of Litzmannstadt and those old streetcars squeaking around corners. Here, an endless stream of shining cars drove along Wilshire. The city of lights, she thought, though nobody thought that this was anything special. She inhaled the cold air, smelling wood smoke from fireplaces. Music formed in her mind and with it Ingo appeared. Stuttgart. He came running toward her. They had loved each other. They would always love each other. What was the matter with them? Why should everybody be unhappy? Irmgard was unhappy whether he stayed with her or not, so why bother? Couldn't he see that he was unwanted? They had a right to their happiness. "Happy New Year, my love. I shall always wait for you," she said into the night.

Ingo celebrated New Year's with Renate and her family at their favorite *gasthaus,* Zur Krone, in nearby Echterdingen. Nothing she, Ingo, Erich, or his young wife Katie said could liven Irmgard's morose mood. With every year her depression got worse. She refused to see a therapist. Her pathological guilt pulled her into a dark hole she could not escape, convinced she betrayed her fallen fiancé. Had she not promised to love him forever? That meant beyond death.

Renate did all she could to cheer her daughter up, but to no avail.

"Another year of misery," Irmgard whined when they toasted to the New Year.

"You know, Irmgard," her brother Erich said in a gruff voice, "I've really had it up to here. I'll never know how Ingo puts up with this nonsense. You have everything a woman could ask for, a fine husband and lovely child. Yet all you do is complain. If you weren't my sister, I wouldn't even talk to you."

"That's enough children," Renate said, waving them off with her manicured hands. She still looked delectable, despite being in her mid-fifties. She wore a fashionable brocade suit, her hair styled in soft waves, the face discreetly made up. Ingo would gladly return to her, but, considering she was his mother-in-law now, that was out of the question.

"But you have to admit, Mutterle," Erich said, "Irmgard is like bad breath."

"If you can't stand me, just leave me alone," she snapped, her cold eyes bulging angrily. She looked emaciated. Her face reminded Ingo of people after the war. Her once pretty dark blonde hair had lost its luster. The permanent frown and tight lips told people to stay away. Her plain black dress looked as if she were in mourning. She was, Ingo thought, permanently. Renate refilled the wine glasses. Irmgard covered hers. "Alcohol brings out the worst in people," she said, glancing at Ingo.

He shrugged. His cheeks felt hot from the alcohol. He wore a new suit, white shirt, and tie. He had gained weight. So far he did not use alcohol to ease his pain. "Just keep pouring," he told Renate. "It's the only thing that cheers me up these days."

"What did I just say? Doesn't do a thing for our relationship."

"What relationship?" Ingo asked, and turned to Renate. "I'm sorry this came up. Let's dance, Renate. No point asking Irmgard. You know what she'll say."

Dancing to "I Know Some Day a Miracle Will Happen," Renate said. "I'm so sorry things turned out this way. I thought it would be good to have you around, Ingo. You know that I will always love you, I wouldn't blame you if ..." she bent back, offering him her freshly made up lips, her cheeks warm and inviting. The cuddly body vibrated in his arms responding to his hug. She followed his lead with her eyes closed, her lips open, waiting to be kissed. He felt his desire stir in rushing waves. Had it been years since they had made love? Both he and Renate were hungry. He imagined her voluptuous body and her desire. Was that an invitation to her bed? If they had not been on the dance floor, he would have led her off to the bedroom right then and there.

She sang the refrain, sweet and tempting, "because I know that we shall see each other again." Olga! Why have you abandoned me? Moved so far away that I cannot come to you. Was that a message from Father? He turned faster and faster, his arm secure around Renate's waist. His fuzzy brain churned—what was he waiting for?

"It's been very lonely upstairs, Renate," he said. The melody took him back to Poland, where he had first reproached Olga for playing it. She had accepted his angry outburst and fulfilled his wish. "The Mephisto Waltz!"

Did she still play the Mephisto Waltz? The Evil One was playing his tricks again. America. He felt darkness descend on him. The voices around him buzzed.

Olga! I hear your message.

She was waiting for him. He sensed it so strong that he could hear her voice.

He swung Renate around in a final whirl. "You are right, sweet Mutterle," he said when the music stopped. "It's up to me to make a move. Irmgard is killing me and Fritzle. She hates us both." On their way to their table they greeted friends.

Irmgard had left. Erich grinned. "Said she didn't want to spread her stench around. Now we can have some real fun and celebrate." He checked his watch. "Twelve minutes to go. Come, Katie, let's have a last whirl until 1952 comes around. If only half of what I plan comes true, we'll be doing very well."

Ingo took Renate's hand, and gazed into her shining blue eyes. "You've been such a dear friend to me, the best I've ever had. Without your help, I probably would have fallen into a long depression like Irmgard. I can't blame her, but I must live my life. My very presence annoys her. Perhaps we should leave each other alone."

He paused before he said, "I will leave Irmgard. Can I count on you to keep an eye on Fritzle until we get things settled? The court will award him to her, of course."

Renate's eyes were an open invitation. "I still have Erich's room. You're welcome to take it."

Ingo shook his head, and pressed her hand, "that would be a temptation I'd better not invite, my dear friend. My morality leaves a lot to be desired, but I do have some principles. I am married to your daughter. I know you understand."

On their way home, Ingo held Renate's arm as they negotiated the icy sidewalk.

The door to his bedroom was closed. Irmgard had left no light on. Ingo took a blanket, and stretched out on the sofa.

The following morning his head felt heavy and his tongue dry. Though he did not hear or see Irmgard or Fritzle, he felt the tension in the home. Should he venture into the kitchen and fall under the bombardment of a deranged woman bursting with frustration over who knew what, or walk up to Renate? The big clock ticked away on the bookshelf.

He picked up the phone. Whom should she call? Renate? No. He placed a call to Los Angeles. It was past midnight there, but this was New Year's Eve. Olga might still be at the Old Heidelberg, or had just come home and was still awake.

Anyna answered.

"Happy New Year, little baroness," he said, his heart beating violently.

"Uncle Ingo!" she cried out. "*Mein Gott*, is it really you? Happy New Year. How is Stuttgart?"

"Cold. Snowflakes are dancing in front of my window." Hearing her voice was like coming home after a long absence. What would it be like talking to Olga? The anticipation threw him into a dither.

She must have heard Anyna call out his name, and butted in. "Ingo?" she whispered. "Is it really you? Happy New Year. I," she stammered, "I'm overwhelmed. I don't know what to say. Ingo? Did something happen?"

"Yes," he said in a clear voice. "I got Father's message. They played, 'I Know Some Day a Miracle Will Happen,' and guess what? Suddenly I knew what I had to do. Remember my telling you that miracles don't happen on demand? Well? I was right. You have to make them happen. And I'm doing it right now."

"Is that what Father said?" she asked in a halting voice, as if the words stuck in her mouth.

"That's right. When things are right, everything falls into place, isn't that what you told me? Are things falling into place?" he probed.

She paused.

He waited. "Well, are they?"

"Seems that they have."

"What I am saying is, would you consider making me part of your life again?"

"Ingo!" she cried into the phone, her voice carrying all the way from the other end of the world. "Ingo. Are you serious?"

"Have I ever lied to you?" he teased, too happy to make sense.

"No, no, of course not. It's too wonderful. I also heard Father's voice when he asked me to play, 'Some Day a Miracle Will Happen' and all the other songs we loved. I felt so close to you, and yet so far, that I had to walk out of Old Heidelberg. It wasn't dark, like Poland. Los Angeles has lights all over. Blinking, shining lights in white and all the colors of the rainbow. I stood and watched them, alone, lost and abandoned. And here you are. The miracle just happened. Ingo, I love you so, my darling."

"I've never loved you more, my Olychka."

They talked and talked, their thoughts and feelings bubbling through the telephone wire. "Getting a visa to visit you will take some time. Why don't you come and visit me? I will file for divorce and move out as soon as I find a room. There is still a long waiting list for apartments that always go to families with children. The company has places for visiting customers, and might put me up while they consider my application for a job in Los Angeles. They will be setting up a dealership down your way. You wouldn't believe how many customers we have there. Seems that the 300 SL is a very popular model with Hollywood stars. We'll have a dealership on Wilshire Boulevard. Do you know where that is?"

"Of course. It's quite close to where we live. I'll buy a home in the hills. Old Heidelberg is doing so well. Funny, not long ago I had a vision of you standing in front of a Mercedes showroom, a prominent tri-star on top. Ingo, I'm beside myself with joy. I'll come as soon as I can take off. In a couple of days. How's that? I'm a citizen now, and can sponsor you. Ingo. Hearing your voice is better than music. My love, my darling. I wish I could be a spirit and zip over to you through the ether. Just imagine that I can. That I'm with you, have been with you, and will always be with you."

Epilogue

The war is but a distant memory for those who had lived through it. Their tears had dried up. Blame, shame, guilt and retaliation had run their course. The sting over the loss of our homeland and all that it stood for is gone. Germany still pays compensation for survivors. Their numbers are dwindling. Perpetrators met their ultimate judge. New wars sprung up and were concluded.

Mephisto's Waltz came to an end. Love, life, and the pursuit of happiness do not require a declaration – it is the human endeavor, granted or not.

Ingo and Olga found their way to each other. America became their home as it did and does for so many stranded people – victims of political dictates. Dresden, Berlin, and Stuttgart were rebuilt. The rubble turned into landscaped hills. Mercedes Benz cars enjoy international popularity. Irmgard never got over her loss and was glad that Ingo and Olga took her son, Fritzle, to America where he pursued a fine education and landed a prosperous career.

The Old Heidelberg is gone. Ilse-Marie and Sepp never moved to Lake Arrowhead. After spending a couple of weeks in the mountains they got bored and returned to their home in Los Angeles.

Anyna designs movie sets. She married a fellow designer and has three children. She and Fritzle are close friends. He married a professor of literature from UCLA and has two children.

After Arnold Schwarzenegger was elected Governor of California, Olga ran for city council, was elected and serves her chosen hometown. She performs at charity events with Happy Days Are Here Again.

The Countess spent her last twenty years in bed not to impose her aging face on the public. Lothar kept her company composing his avant-guard music. Like many eccentrics they withdrew from society finding nobody worthy their attention.

After several decades of exploring, wondering and writing down personal accounts of the war I got it off my chest. Writing exorcised me from my disrupted childhood in the maelstrom of Europe's hotbed of hatred. The European Union diminished ancient feuds. The Soviet Union became a democratic Russia and joined the free world. My homeland, Latvia, welcomes us back, but our home is in America.

Breinigsville, PA USA
24 September 2010
245875BV00003B/2/P